तत्त्वबिन्दुः

TATTVABINDU

तत्त्वबिन्दुः

TATTVABINDU

BY

VĀCASPATIMIŚRA

WITH

TATTVAVIBHĀVANĀ

BY

ṚṢIPUTRA PARAMEŚVARA

EDITED BY

V.A. RAMASWAMI SASTRI

BKP

BHARATIYA KALA PRAKASHAN
DELHI (INDIA)

First Edition : 1935
Revised Edition : 2009

Published by **c.P. Gautam**
BHARATIYA KALA PRAKASHAN
3421-A, IInd Floor, Narang Colony, Tri Nagar,
Delhi-110035. Phone : 011-32967505, Telefax : 011-27393083
E-mail : bkp3421@yahoo.co.in
Website : www.bkpbooks.com

ISBN : 978-81-8090-216-1

Printed by :
Laxmi Offset Process, Delhi

DEDICATED

to

the Right Hon'ble D.S. Srinivas Sastri

Ex-Vice-Chancellor,

Annamalai University

CONTENTS

PREFACE

This edition of Vācaspatimiśra's *Tattvabindu* and of its commentary *Tattvavibhāvanā* by Parameśvara II is based on (1) a transcript of a manuscript *Tattvavibhāvanā* preserved in the Madras Government Oriental Manuscripts Library, and (2) the Benares Edition of the *Tattvabindu*. Since the commentator has made it a rule to quote the full text by parts before commenting on it, his text has been accepted for this edition. But the many *lacunae* in the text have been filled up with the help of the printed book. The readings both in the text and the commentary are however found defective in some instances, and suggestions of better readings are given in brackets.

The commentary is indispensable for a correct appreciation of the intricacies of Vācaspatimiśra's thought and style. Parameśvara II who lived more than half a millennium after Vācaspatimiśra, considers occasionally the interpretations of the earlier commentators on the *Tattvabindu* and the various readings of the text. In its *Sphoṭakhaṇḍana* section he cites kārikās and prose passages from the *Sphoṭasiddhi* of Maṇḍanamiśra and advances the important and interesting view that the first part of the *Tattvabindu* contains a direct refutation of the views of Maṇḍanamiśra on the theory of *Sphoṭa*. Parameśvara II was no doubt thoroughly familiar with all the works of Kumārila, probably including the *Bṛhaṭṭīkā,* and of Prabhākara with Śālīkanātha's commentaries thereon. He was equally familiar with other authoritative works like the *Nayaviveka* and the *Vivekatattva,* and he has displayed in his work a critical estimate of both the Bhāṭṭa and Prābhākara schools of Mīmāṁsā. Consequently he offers to students of Mīmāṁsā Śāstra solutions for many knotty problems concerning the historical and the doctrinal sides of this Śāstra.

It now remains for me to acknowledge the help I have received in editing this work. I owe a deep debt of gratitude to my friend and colleague Brahmaśrī K.A. Sivaramakrishna Sastrigal Avl., Vedānta and Vyākaraṇa Śiromaṇi, Pandit in Sanskrit, and to my friend and teacher Brahmaśrī S.K. Ramanatha Sastrigal Avl., Lecturer in Sanskrit, Madras University, for their valuable suggestions in the fixing up of the text and to my friend M.R.Ry. R. Satyanatha Ayyar Avl., M.A., L.T., Lecturer in History, for his valuable suggestions in the preparation of the historical portions of the Introduction. I am profoundly grateful to Professor K. Rama Pisharoti, M.A., L.T., Professor of Sanskrit, for his kindness in revising the manuscript of my Introduction. It is difficult for me to adequately thank my revered Professor Mahāmahopādhyāya Darśana-kalānidhi Vidyāvācaspati Kulapati S. Kuppuswami Sastrigal Avl., M.A., I.E.S., Retired Professor of Sanskrit and Comparative Philology, Presidency College, Madras, for the kindness and readiness with which he has enriched this work with his FOREWORD. I sincerely thank Pandit Lakshmana Sastri Tailang for having allowed me to incorporate in this edition the Tippaṇī of his late brother, MM. Manavalli Gangadhara Sastri. I cannot forget the great help that my friend Brahmārī Vedāntālaṅkāra Vedānta Siromaṇi T.V. Rama-chandra Dikshitar Avl., Professor of Vedānta, Sanskrit College, Mylapore, Madras, has rendered me in suggesting almost all the improvements to the printed text incorporated in Appendix V. I have to record my thanks to the Curators of the Madras Govt. Oriental Mss. Library and the Adyar Library for the facilities they have given me to consult many valuable manuscripts.

Lastly, I have to express my sincere thanks to the Superintendent, St. Joseph's Industrial School Press, Trichinopoly, for the neat printing and get-up of the work.

V.A. Ramaswami Sastri
Editor

FOREWORD

In compliance with the request of my friend and former pupil Mr. V.A. Ramaswami Sastri, M.A., Mīmāṁsā Śiromaṇi, Lecturer in Sanskrit of the Annamalai University, Annamalai Nagar, Chidambaram, I gladly write this short Foreword.

Mr. V.A. Ramaswami Sastri has rendered a highly valuable service to Sanskrit scholars who are interested in the study of advanced Śāstraic texts in the original, by bringing out a very reliable edition of Vācaspatimiśra's *Tattvabindu,* together with the commentary called *Tattvavibhāvanā* by Parameśvara II, of the Kerala country. Vācaspatimiśra belongs to the middle of the ninth century A.D. and Parameśvara II flourished in the Porkulam village of Kunnankulam, near Guruvāyūr, in the Cochin State, in the former half of the fifteenth century A.D.

Vācaspatimiśra's *Tattvabindu* is a short and highly difficult text. In his characteristically rhythmic and stately diction, Vācaspatimiśra reviews in the *Tattvabindu,* the Vaiyākaraṇa doctrine of *Sphoṭa,* mainly as expounded by Bhartṛhari and Maṇḍanamiśra, and amplifies and reaffirms Kumārila's criticism of *Sphoṭa* doctrine. Bhartṛhari and Maṇḍana in their exposition of the *sphoṭa* doctrine worked out fully the onto-logical implication involved in what may be described, in terms of modern psychology, as a *Gestalt view* of the experience relating to the complete and self-contained significative unit, called sentence (*vākya*), by establishing the doctrine of *abdādvaita* and reconciling it with the Upaniṣadic doctrine of *Brahmādvaita.* The *substantival pluralism* of the Mīmāṁsakas, both of the schools of Kumārila and Prabhākara, set its face against all kinds of Advaitism and was opposed to Bhartṛhari's *Śabdādvaita*. Though Vācaspatimiśra was one of the greatest Advaitins and was dominated, in a large measure, by the spirit of philosophical accommodation which characterised Maṇḍana's great Advaitic classic—*Brahmasiddhi,* he chose to maintain, in his *Tattvabindu,* the attitude which Kumārila adopted towards the doctrine of *Sphoṭa* in his *Ślokavārttika.*

The Commentary—*Tattvavibhāvanā*—which is incorporated in this edition, is lucid and very helpful in understanding the text of Vācaspatimiśra. Though this commentary is generally reliable, it must be said that the learned commentator *nods* in some places. For instance, the commentator has adopted a defective reading—पट्वभ्यासाहिता हि भावना प्रबोधवती स्मृतिः संगीयते"; and he has entirely missed the meaning of the technical terms used in this text. By the way it may be observed that the correct reading of this text is :—"पट्वभ्यासादरप्रत्ययाहिता हि भावना प्रबोधवती स्मृतिहेतुः" as given in the footnote; and that this text refers to the three types of cognitions which are capable of being reproduced in memory—*viz.,* पटुप्रत्यय, अभ्यासप्रत्यय and आदरप्रत्यय and which *Praśastapāda* describes in his *Padārthadharmasaṅgraha* in the *Saṁskāra section* of the *guṇagrantha.*

The elaborate and scholarly introduction, giving a historical sketch of the *Mīmāṁsā literature,* and the thoroughgoing analysis of the *Tattvabindu*, in English, which the learned editor has prefixed to his edition of the work, greatly enhance the value of this edition as an important book of reference. I heartily congratulate Mr. Ramaswami Sastri on this substantial and scholarly contribution, which he has made, in his edition of the *Tattvabindu,* to the printed Śāstra literature in Samskrit and to the study of *Indian Philosophy* in general.

—S. Kuppuswami Sastri

INTRODUCTORY NOTE

The *Tattvabindu* of Vācaspatimiśra with the commentary called *Tattvavibhāvanā* of Parameśvara II of Payyūr Bhaṭṭamana, rightly styled *Mīmāṁsācakravartin,* is here issued for the first time as Annamalai University and I have great pleasure to commend it to the public. The first of the series was Kulaśekhara's *Mukundamālā,* a hymn of praise to Mukunda, and the second, *Sabhāpativilāsanāṭaka,* a glorification of Naṭ arāja and this inquiry into Truth embodied in the *Tattvabindu* comes fittingly as the third.

The *Tattvabindu* of Vācaspatimiśra is the most authoritative treatise on the source of verbal cognition from the epistemological standpoint of the *Mīmāṁsakas* and it occupies an important place in the dialectic literature of this school of Indian thought. The abstruse problem discussed herein in the lofty and pregnant language of Vācaspati has always made the work a hard nut to crack even for the best of *Mīmāṁsā* scholars. A commentary giving an authoritative exposition of the text was a long-felt desideratum, and this is now supplied by the publication of the *Tattvavibhāvanā,* of *Mīmāṁsācakravarti* Parameśvarabhaṭṭa than whom a better exponent Vācaspatimiśra could not have had. The present publication will, therefore, be welcomed by all students of *Mīmāṁsāśāstra.* The work has been edited by my friend and colleague, Veda-Mīmāṁsā Śiromaṇi V.A. Ramaswami Sastri, M.A., Lecturer in Sanskrit. He has brought to bear on this publication the rare combination of the intensive learning of a *Śiromaṇi* and the critical scholarship of a Master of Arts. As the publication itself will bear out, the work has taxed all the critical ingenuity and scholarship of the editor and better justice, I believe, could not in the circumstances have been done to the text and particularly to the commentary.

The introduction is fairly long, but the length was obviously unavoidable, for so far we have no systematic history of *Mīmāṁsāśāstra* presented to us. It stands as a striking evidence of the patience and industry of the editor; for he has critically noticed with biographical details, as far as available, nearly seventy authors, more or less in chronological sequence, besides setting forth in Appendices I and II a list of fifty authors and works, partially or imperfectly known. This is a matter of no small credit to the editor, particularly when it is remembered that he has had to attend to his usual lecture work in the University and has had no direct and immediate access to any manuscript library. It is possible that all his conclusions may not be acceptable and some of them may even prove wrong in the light of fresh evidence that may be forthcoming, but that does not take away from the value of this piece of pioneer work. In any case he has certainly opened up a pathway in the tangled forest of the history of *Mīmāṁsāśāstra* and to that extent, at least, he has earned the thanks of all students of this branch of Sanskrit literature. Appendix III giving an alphabetical index of the *Kārikās* of the text, Appendix IV setting forth the quotations occurring in the text and commentary with their sources identified, as far as possible, Appendix V suggesting improved readings both in the text and commentary and filling up to the extent possible *lacunae* in the latter and the three Indexes—these, it needs scarcely be said, add greatly to the value of the publication to the critical student.

It is a matter of great gratification to me, as it must be to every lover of Sanskrit, that the Department of Sanskrit of the Annamalai University has been enabled to contribute its own humble share in the further elucidation of Sanskrit literature by the publication of unpublished works and for this the thanks of the Department are due to the authorities of the University.

—K. Rama Pisharoti

INTRODUCTION

PART I

A SHORT HISTORY OF THE PŪRVA MĪMĀṀSĀ ŚĀSTRA

The History of the *Pūrva* Mīmāṁsā Śāstra may be divided into—

(1) Pre-Kumārila period, from the earliest times to A.D. 600;

(2) Kumārila period, from A.D. 600 to 900; and

(3) Post-Kumārila period, from A.D. 900 to the present day.

Truth was passionately pursued in Ancient India. Her quest after truth gradually led to the development of the intuitionistic and the rationalistic tendencies and ultimately to the realisation of *dharma* and *mokṣa,* thanks to the emergence of upaniṣads in the philosophy of *ātman.* These two tendencies culminated on the one side in the *Vedānta Sūtras* of Bādarāyaṇa and on the other in Jaimini's *Pūrvamimāṁsā Sūtras.* The latter mark the development and culmination of the influence of the rationalistic tendency on the ritualistic aspect, both exegetical and doctrinal*. It is probable that the *Ācāryas* referred to by Jaimini might have composed their own *Sātras* of vedic interpretation. In all probability, Jaimini, like Pāṇini in the history of Sanskrit grammar, summed up all the labours of his predecessors and improved on their work to such an extent that he became the only *Sūtrakāra* in this realm of Indian Thought.

Mimāṁsā : References in the Vedic Texts

The term '*Mīmāṁsā*' is derived from the √*mān*—to know—with the desiderative suffix '*san*'; and it means the *desire for knowledge*[1]. In most recensions of the *Vedas* the *Sannanta* root '*Mīmāṁsā*' is found used either as a noun or a verb in the combined sense of desire for knowledge and of discussion. The *Taittirīyasaṁhitā* of the Kṛṣṇa Yajurveda understands the term *ṁimāṁsante* in this sense : thus VII—5-7-1 says "*utsṛjyāṁ notsṛjyāmiti mīmāṁsante brahmavādinaḥ taddhāhuḥ utsṛjyām eveti*"[2] VI—2-6-4 "*vyāvṛtkāmaṁ yaṁ pātre vā talpe vā mimāṁseran*" has the word '*Mīmāṁseran*' used in the sense of discussion; II—5-3-7 introduces a doubtful point with the words '*Brahmavādinaḥ vadanti*' without using the verb '*mīmāṁsante*'. The *Tāṇḍyabrāhmaṇa* of the Sāma Veda also supports the same view : thus VI—5-9 has a passage with the word *mīmāṁseta*—'*brāhmaṇam pātre na mīmāṁseta*'[3] and in XXIII—4-2 the form '*mīmāṁseran*' is employed: "*yaḥ talpe vā, udake vā vivāhe vā mīmāṁseran ta etā upeyuḥ*". In the *Kauṣītakibrāhmaṇa* of the Ṛg-Veda the verb '*mīmāṁsante*' and the noun '*mīmāṁsā*' are found used: II—9 states that "*udite hotavyam anaditam iti mīmāṁsante*—they investigate (the question) whether oblation should be offered to Fire when the Sun rises or before the Sun rises"; and after some remarks on each of the two alternatives, the conclusion is arrived at that "*tasmāt anudite hotavyam*—the oblation should be offered before Sunrise"; XXVI—2 and 3 use the words '*mimāṁsā*' and '*mimāiṁsante*': *athāto goāyuṣ oḥ mīmāṁsā*[4].........'*atha kaścit śastre vā anuvacane vā pramattaḥ upahanyāt vicikitsā vā syāt upahatam abuddham atikrāntam manyamāno manasā vṛttāntam īkṣamāṇo vinivṛtya upahatam anupahatam kṛtvā ānantaryāt prayogaḥ syāt vṛttāntāt iti mīmāṁsante*'[5]. In XVIII—4 of the same Brāhmaṇa the word '*Mīmāṁsā*' is found used in the sense of discussion, '*athātaḥ pari-dhānasyaiva mīmāṁsā*'[6]. In the *Kaṇva* recension of the *Śatapathabrāhmṇa* of the White Yajur-veda the word *mīmāṁsā* is used—'*saiṣā mmīmāṁsaiva*'[7].

In the Upaniṣads we frequently meet with this word. In the *Chāndogyopaniṣad* of the Sāma Veda V—11-1 it is said that "*Prācīnaśāla aupamanyavaḥ .... mahāśrotriyāḥ sametya mīmāṁsāñcakruḥ—Ko nu ātmā kiṁ brahmaiti*"[8]. In the *Taittirīyopaniṣad* of the Black Yajurveda II—8-1 occurs the word *Mīmāṁsā*—"*saiṣā ānandasya mīmāṁsā bhavati*"[9]. In the *Kenopaniṣad* of the Talavakāra recension of the Sāma Veda the noun form '*mīmāṁsya*' with the suffix '*yat*' is found employed: "*yadi manyase suvedeti daharam evāpi nūnaṁ tvaṁ vetha brahmaṇo rūpaṁ yadasya tvaṁ yadasya deveṣu atha nu mīmāṁsyam eva te manye viditam*"[10].

References in the Smṛtis

Similarly the words '*mīmāṁseta*' and '*mimāṁsā*' are found in some of the ancient *Dharmasūtras:* for example, the *Bodhāyana* and *Vāsiṣtha Dharmasūtras,* I—4-10 and XII—2 use the word '*mīmāṁsante*' in the sense of *discussion :* "*Astamite āditye udakaṁ grhṇīyāt na gṛhṇīyāt iti mīmāṁsante brahmavādinaḥ*".[11] "*Tatra (mithyāvyākṛtau) prāyaścittam kuryāt na kuryāditi Mmīmāṁsante*"[12]. The references from the Brāhmaṇas and Smṛtis, given above, show clearly that the later Vedic period witnessed discussion of many topics of a doubtful nature, and analysis of their *pros* and *cons* leading to final conclusions.

Mīmāṁsā : Rules of Interpretation—References in Smṛtis and later Literature

Such discussions regarding not only the Vedic subjects but also the interpretation of the Vedic texts came into vogue towards the close of the Vedic period. The *Gautamadharma-sūtra* 1-5 says—'*tulyabalavirodhe vikalpaḥ*'[13]. Jaimini also in his *Pūrvamīmāṁsāsūtras* XII—3-10 says—*ekārthāstu vikalperan samuccaye hi āvṛttiḥ syād pradhānasya*'[14]. The *Āpastamba-dharmasūtra* 1-1-4-8 says—'*Śrutirhi balīyasī ānumānikā-dācārāt*'[15]. Jaimini also holds the same in I—3. 3 : '*virodhe tvanapekṣaṁ syāt asati hyanumānam*' [16]. In 1.4. 12. 1. Āpastamba says '*yatra tu prītyupalabdhi-taḥ pravṛttiḥ na tatra*

Śāstramasti'[17]. This well resembles Jaimini's *Sātra* IV—1. 2[18]. Similarly Āpastamba's *Sātra* II—6. 13. I[19] bears a close resemblance to Jaimini's VI—1-15[20]. These parallel references, though they may not throw any light on the dates of those *Sūtras,* show that early enough, rules for the interpretation of Vedic texts must have been formulated and generally accepted.

Jaimini refers in his *sūtras* to many Acāryas[21]— Atreya, Kārṣṇājini, Bādari, Āśmarathya, Aiti-śāyana, Kāmukāyana, Lābukāyana and Ālekhana.

From the *Mahābhāṣya* of Patañjali (150 B.C.)[22] it is clear that the Mīmāṁsā doctrines were well developed and embodied in aphoristic literature. The references to *Nyāyavitsamaya* (II—4-8-13)[23] and *Nyāyavid* (II—6-14-13)[24] indicate that Mīmāṁsā as a system must have been elaborated before the time of Āpastamba. And since Jaimini refers to over half a dozen *ācāryas*—presumably *Mimāṁsācāryas*—one may legitimately conclude that this science must have been systematised long before his time.

Jaimini's Pūrva Mīmāṁsā Sūtras

Nothing definite can be said about the age of Jaimini; his *Sātras* may, however, be assigned to about 300 B.C.[25] They have no direct reference to the Buddhistic doctrine or philosophy, though according to the commentators, they refer to the *Mlecchaprasiddhi* in śabdas.[26] They refer to the *Smṛtis*[27] *ācāras* (customs), *Kalpasūtras*[28] and *Vyākaraṇa*[29] and establish their *prāmāṇya* so far as *dharma* is concerned; and these raise the presumption that Jaimini is post-Pāṇiniyan.

The relation of Jaimini's *Mīmāṁsā Sūtras* to Bādarāyaṇa's *Vedānta Sūtras* can be traced very easily. The authors of both the *sūtras* refer to each other as authorities on their systems[30], but Bādarāyaṇa objects to most of Jaimini's metaphysical views. Are we to understand from this that Jaimini is to be regarded as one among the Vedāntasūtrakāras whom Bādarāyaṇa quotes? On the authority of Sureśvarācārya's *Naiṣkarmyasiddhi*[31], it can be held that Jaimini has composed his own *Vedānta Sūtras,* the first two *sūtras* of which are the same as those of the extant *Sātras* of Bādarāyaṇa[32]. Jaimini and Bādarāyaṇa, however, agree in their doctrines regarding the ritualistic interpretation of the *Karma-kāṇḍa,* and Bādarāyaṇa quotes, according to the commentators, Jaimini's *Sātras* as *'taduktam'* in many instances; while in *Sūtras* like *'dharmam jaiminirata eva'* and *'ata eva ca nityatvam'* he recognises the doctrine of *apūrva* and that of eternity of the Vedas as established by Jaimini in the *Sātras 'Codanā punarārambhaḥ'* and *'uktam tu śabda-pīrvatvam'*.

About the personal history of Jaimini, we know next to nothing. The *Pañcatantra* tells us that an elephant crushed to death Jaimini, the author of the *Pūrvamīmāṁsāsūtras*[33]. While giving the Vidyāvaṁśa, the *Sāmavidhāna-brāhmaṇa* mentions Jaimini as the disciple of Pārāśarya Vyāsa.[34] In another place we find the divine origin of the Mīmāṁsā Śāstra mentioned and its popularisation by many ācāryas, the last of whom was Jaimini.[35] The *Bhāgavata-purāṇa* says that Vyāsa, the son of Parāśara by Satyavatī, divided the Vedas into four and gave instructions in the *Sāmavedasaṁhitā* to Jaimini, one of his four disciples[36]. In XII—6. 75 of the same Purāṇa, Jaimini is said to be the teacher of Sumantu and a promulgator of the Sāma Veda. In the *āśvalāyanagṛhyasūtra* the name of Jaimini occurs along-with Sumantu, Vaiśampāyana and others as one of the Dhar-mācāryas.[37]

The Contents of the Pūrva Mimāṁsā Sūtras

Jaimini's *Pūrva Mīmāṁsā Sūtras* contain 16 chapters, the last four of which are generally known as the *Saṅkarśakāṇḍa.* The first 12 chapters are more popular than the last four and most of the great writers like Kumāriḷabhaṭṭa on the *Pūrva* Mīmāṁsā Śāstra have written commentaries or nibandhanas on the Dvādaśalakṣaṇī. The arrangement of the Dvādaśalakṣaṇī is as follows: The first chapter deals with all *pramāṇas* on *Dharma*; the second, the *bheda,* the difference, between one Dharma and the other; the third, the *ahgatva*; the fourth, the *prayojya-prayojakabhāva;* the fifth, the *krama,* i.e., sequence between *karman* and *karman;* the sixth, the *adhikāra*—the qualifications of a sacrificer, etc.; the seventh and eighth, the *atideśa,* (the application and assimilation of one *karman* on the similarity of the other); the ninth, *ūha;* the tenth, *bādha;* the eleventh and twelfth, *tantra* and *prasaṅga* respectively. These constitute the most important part of the system.

The *Saṅkarṣakāṇḍa* constituting the last four chapters of the *Pūrva Mīmāṁsā Sūtras*, also known as the *Devatādhyāya* as a major portion of it deals with the devatās in vedic sacrifices, some modern scholars hold, is not a genuine part of the system. But it can be maintained that it is genuine and it completes the *Dvādasa-lakṣaṇī*[38], because just like the *Tantrādhyāya* and *Prasaṅgādhyāya,* it helps the interpretation of *dharma* such vVedic passages as are scattered and ambiguous. Further its genuineness is clear from the reference made by Bādarāyaṇā in his *sūtra—'pradānavadeva taduktam'* which refers to the Saṅkarṣakāṇḍa-sūtra— *'nanā vā devatā pṛthagjñānāt.'* And lastly, Upavarṣa, Bhavadāsa, Devasvāmin, Rājacūḍāmaṇi Dīkṣita and Bhāskarārya (makhin) have commented on those *sūtras.*[39] For these and other reasons we hold that the *Saṅkarṣakāṇḍa* is genuine. The full *sūtra* text is yet unfortunately not available and we cannot with exactitude speak of its contents.

Jaimini is also credited with another work— *Chāndogyā-nuvāda*—probably a ritualistic work of the Kalpasūtra character.[40] To him are also ascribed a *Śrauta Sūtra* and a *Gṛhya Sūtra.*[41]

UPAVARṢA

The earliest commentator on the *Sātras* is the famous Vṛttikāra Upavarṣa, the reputed author of the *Vṛtti* on the twenty chapters of the *Pūrva* and *Uttara Mīmāṁsā Sūtras.* He is held in great reverence as is clear from the association with his name of the honorific title 'bhagavān'. Śabarasvāmin refers to him as *Bhagavān Upavarṣaḥ* in his *Bhāṣya* on 1-1-5 : *'atha gaurityatra kaśśabdaḥ? gakāraukāravisarjanīyū iti bhagavān upavarṣaḥ.'*

Śaṅkārācārya in his *Devatādhikaraṇabhāṣya* says '*varṇā eva tu śabdā iti Bhagavān upavarṣaḥ* .'

Upavarṣa's Personality

Who this famous Vṛttikāra is has been a subject of controversy. MM. S. Kuppuswami Sastrigal holds that Upavarṣa is identical with Bodhāyana.[142] Dr. S. Kisnaswami Iyengar does not accept this identity[43]; for, the *Prapañcahṛdaya* mentions both Bodhāyana and Upavarṣa as authors of the commentaries on the 20 chapters of the *Pūrva* and *Uttara Mīmāṁsā Sūtras*[44]; and the *Maṇimekhalai* refers to one Kṛtakoṭi (along with Jaimini and Vyāsa) as an *ācārya* who has formulated *eight pramāṇas.*[45] Dr. Iyengar therefore tries to identify this Kṛtakoṭi with Bodhāyana,[46] the author of the *Kṛtakoṭi Vṛtti,* as the *Prapañcahṛdaya* holds, assuming that the name Kṛtakoṭi might be easily applied to both the author and the work. The identity of these authors—Upavarṣa and Bodhāyana—and—Bodhāyana and Kṛtakoṭi—is thus an open question. Still it may be reconsidered in the light of the following.

(1) Upavarṣa, it is contended has established the *Vibhutva* of *Ātman* in his *Vṛtti* on III-3.53 of the *Brahma Sūtras,* a *résumé* of which is available in the *Ātmavāda* of the *Śābarabhāṣya* on I. 1. 5 of the *Pūrva Mīmāṁsā Sūtras*. Bodhāyana, on the other hand, may be held to have enunciated the doctrine of *Jīvāṇutva* in his *Vṛtti* on the *Brahma Sūtras,* for Rāmānuja, in the opening words of the *Śrībhāṣya,* says that he closely follows Bodhāyana's *Vṛtti* and proceeds to establish the doctrine of *Jīvāṇutva* in his *Bhāṣya.* This would suggest the difficulty of the identity sought to be established between Upavarṣa and Bodhāyana.

(2) The Kṛtakoṭi of the Maṇimekhalai accepts eight *pramāṇas*. Bodhāyana, the famous Vṛttikāra of the *Pūrva* and *Uttara Mīmāṁsā Sūtras*, cannot have accepted the eight *pramāṇas* but only six, or less than six, according to commentators. So the authority of the *Maṇimekhalai* on this matter is questionable. It will be well to remember here that the *Maṇimekhalai* is only

a *romance*[47] and need not be taken seriously. We are not unaware of the contention that the question of the *pramāṇas* is one of classification and we would say that such a contention cannot stand in view of the fact that the *pramāṇas* constitute the fundamentals of every system of Indian Philosophy, particularly because the *Maṇimekhalai* is basing a classification of the systems on the number of *pramāṇas* accepted. Thus "six are the systems that are founded on the basis of those instruments of knowledge: (1) Lokāyata, (2) Bauddha, (3) Sāṅkhya, (4) Naiyāyika, (5) Vaiśeṣika, and (6) Mīmāṁsā."[48] The Laukāyatikas accept one *pramāṇa—pratyakṣa,* the Bauddhas and Vaiśeṣikas, two—*pratyakṣa* and *anumāna,* the Sāṅkhyas, three—*pratyakṣa, anumāna* and *śabda,* the Naiyāyikas, four—*pratyakṣa, anumāna, upamāna* and *śabda,* and the Mīmāṁsakas (Bhāṭṭas) as well as the Advaiti Vedāntins, six, *pratyakṣa. anumāna, upamāna, śabda, arthāpatti* and *anupalabdhi.* We may, therefore, conclude that Upavarṣa is distinct from Bodhāyana and Kṛtakoṭi.

Upavarṣa's Date (*c.* 100 B. *c.*-A.D. 200)

The date of Upavarṣa is as unsettled a question as that of his personality. We can here lay down only the limits within which he must have lived. Śabarasvāmin who lived about A.D. 200 quotes Upavarṣa and this gives us the latest limit. If the view that the *Vṛttigrantha* in Śabara's *Bhāṣya* on I-1.5 extends to the end of the *Bhāṣya* thereon is accepted, Upavarṣa must be taken as mentioning and refuting the doctrine of the *Samudāyaśabda* of the Grammarians; and in the history of Sanskrit Grammar it is Patañjali who first enunciated the doctrine that the *Sphoṭaśabda* is both *vācakatvāśraya* and (while manifest) *arthapratyāyaka,*[49] though Pāṇini, Vyāḍi, Kātyāyana and other ācāryas before Patañjali have spoken of the *śabdanityatva.* This would prove that Vṛttikāra Upavarṣa must be subsequent to Patañjali. Hence, the Vṛttikāra Upavarṣa may be assigned to the period from *c.* 100 B.C. to A.D. 200.

It is suggested that Upavarṣa might be placed between Patañjali and Kātyāyana about 200 B.C.[50] on the ground that Upavarṣa allows the *Caturthīsamāsa* in the compound '*Brahma-jijñāsā*' in the *Sātra* '*athāto brahmajijñāsā*' and that this *caturthī-samāsa* is sanctioned by Kātyāyana by the Vārttika '*aśvaghoṣā-dīnāmupasaṅkhyānam,*' but overruled by Patañjali who says '*aśvaghosādayastu ṣaṣṭhīsamāsā eva*'. *This is not convincing.*[51] Here we see only Upavarṣa's partiality for Kātyāyana which is justifiable because he himself is a great grammarian. A parallel instance of this *Caturthīsamāsa* can be cited here from Śabarasvāmin's *Bhāṣya* on I-1.1 '*dharmāya jijñāsā dharma-jijñāsā, sā hi tasya jñātumicchā.*' No doubt, Kumārilabhaṭṭa, a later exponent of the *Mīmāṁsā Sūtras* like Śaṅkara of the *Vedānta Sūtras*, has felt the unsoundness of this *Caturthīsamāsa* and tried to get over the difficulty by explaining that the passage in question in the *Bhāṣya* does not constitute the exact *vigrahavākya* but only indicates by *Caturthī* that the *dharma* is the final fruit or goal of the discussion and that the *ṣaṣthīsamāsa* is suggested also in the *Vivaraṇabhāṣya* '*sā hi tasya jñātumicchā*' by the genitive in '*tasya*'. This is not the only instance where a later commentator is driven to ingenious devices in his anxiety to justify his author.[52] In such cases the commentator makes clear not so much the meaning of the passage as his own desire for grammatical correctness. If the *Caturthīsamāsa* were an accepted factor in Sanskrit even in instances where there is no *prakṛtivikṛtibhāva,* then Kumārila would not have ventured to say that the first passage in the *Bhāṣya* does not give the *vigraha.* Nowhere is such a thing seen or accepted as the *vigrahavākya* without the *vigraha* and the *vivaraṇavākya* with it.[53] Most probably, Śabarasvāmin might have taken the *Caturthīsamāsa*—'*dharmāya jijñāsā*'—from Upavarsa's *Vṛtti* (which, no doubt, requires further proof), and as such, he might have in this instance only followed Vṛttikāra Upavarṣa and not Patañjali.[54]

Bhavadāsa (*c.* A.D. 100-200)

Next to Upavarṣa comes Bhavadāsa in chronological

order. No tangible evidence has been yet found for fixing up the date of this Vṛttikāra; but if the *Prapañcahṛdaya* is trusted, Bhavadāsa is to be placed subsequent to Upavarṣa and before Śabarasvāmin. That Bhavadāsa flourished before Śabarasvāmin is well proved by literary evidence. The very opening *Bhāṣya* of the *Jijñāsādhikaraṇa 'loke yeṣvartheṣu prasiddhāni padāni'*, etc. is, according to Kumārila's *Ślokavārttika*, open to *six* interpretations;[55] of these, the second is the *upālambhapakṣa* —negation or condemnation of some of the old interpretations of the *Sātras* by Vṛttikāra Bhavadāsa.[56] Kumārila himself mentions Bhavadāsa (the name of the Vṛttikāra) in explaining the *stutipakṣa*—

> *'pradarśanārthamityeke kecinnānārthavācinaḥ* |
> *samudāyādavacchidya Bhavadāsena kalpitāt'* | |[57]

This evidence proves that Śabarasvāmin was subsequent to Bhavadāsa.

Devasvāmin in his *Bhāṣya* on the *Saṅkarṣakāṇḍa* XV. 11.1 says *'asmin pāde 'apūrvāt tathā somaḥ' ityārabhya āpādaparisamāpteḥ bhāvadāsameva bhāṣyam iti';* and this indicates that Devasvāmin, an author of the post-Kumārila period, had great regard for Bhavadāsa. As the *Prapañcahṛdaya* states, Bhavadāsa, just like Upavarṣa, wrote a *Vṛtti* on the 16 chapters of the *Pūrva Mīmāṁsā Sūtras*. His *Vṛtti,*—only a summary of Upavarṣa's *Vṛtti* on the *Pūrva Mīmāṁsā Sūtras* —though criticised by Śabarasvāmin and his followers, was considered by Devasvāmin as a *Bhāṣya* and it was a guidance for him.

As Bhavadāsa's *Vṛtti* is not available, nothing can be said in regard to his views on *pramāṇas* and other topics. But from a study of Kumārila's *Vārttika* and its commentaries it can be understood that he considered the two words *'atha'* and *'ataḥ'* in the *Sātra 'athāto dharmajijñāsā'* as one word in the sense of *ānantarya;* similarly, he divided the fourth *Sūtra* into two, taking the former as laying down the definition of *pratyakṣa* and the latter emphasizing its unauthoritativeness *(aprāmāṇya)* on matters of super-normal *dharma.*[58] These views were, however, refuted by Śabarasvāmin, Kumārila and their followers.

Śabarasvāmin (c. A.D. 200)

The next great authority known to us is Śabarasvāmin. His *Bhāṣya* is the earliest extant commentary on Jaimini's *Sūtras* in the *bhāṣya style.* It is lucid and clear in expression and simple and mellifluous in diction. Both in matter and manner it resembles Patañjali's *Mahābhāṣya* and Śaṅkarācārya's *Brahma Sūtra Bhāṣya.* The simple conversational style which appears in its perfection in the *Mahābhāṣya,* is here again seen in its finished form after a lapse of over three hundred years, only to be seen once again five hundred years later in Śaṅkara's *Brahma Sūtra Bhāṣya.*

Regarding his date and personal history, he is certainly later than Upavarṣa and prior to Bhartṛmitra, as we shall show later. He has not, however, mentioned Patañjali by name as he has done Pāṇini and Kātyāyana.[59] Among the chief authors he has quoted Yāska as the *Śāstrakāra* and Piṅgala as the author of the *Chandaśāstra,* and among works, the *Bodhāyana* and *Āpastamba Dharmasūtras,* the *Manusmṛti,* the *Mahābhārata* and the *Purāṇas* as well as the *nirālambana and śūnyavādas of Buddhism.*[60] The place of his birth is not definitely known. Most probably he might be a Northerner. In II-3.2 of his *Bhāṣya* he makes mention of the *Āndhras* as against the *Āryāvartanivāsins,* as using the word '*rājan*' in the sense of a Kṣatriya who does not even protect a country or a kingdom. One verse, the authenticity of which is questionable, states that Śabarasvāmin had four wives belonging to the four castes and six sons by them[61]— Varāhamihira by the Brahmin wife, Bhartṛhari and Vikrama by the Kṣatriya wife, Hariścandra and Śaṅku by the Vaiśya wife and Amara (siṁha) by the Śūdra wife. Tradition says that his real name was Āditya-deva and that he got the name *Śabara* for his having disguised himself as a forester fearing Jain persecution. According to the *Dattaka-mīmāṁsā,* one Śabara has commented on the *Satyāṣāḍha Śrautasūtras.* It is also said that a Śabarasvāmin, son of Dīptasvāmin, wrote a commentary called *Sarvārthalakṣaṇi* on the *Liṅgānuśāsana*. It is very doubtful whether these are identical with the author of the *Mīmāṁsā Bhāṣya*.

It has been already said that Śabarasvāmin's *Bhāṣya* is the earliest extant commentary on the 12 *adhyāyas* of the *Pūrva Mīmāṁsā Sūtras*. In XII-2.11 he refers to the Saṅkarṣa,[62] but it is not known whether he wrote a *Bhāṣyā*[63] on it also. Many *Vṛttis* and *Bhāṣyas* existed before his time; the more important of the views of his predecessors are preserved in the *Bhāṣya*, as is proved by Kumārila. His work is, therefore, an important source-book for the reconstruction of the earlier aspects of this system of philosophy.[64] He refers in his *Bhāṣya* to some Vṛttikāras chiefly to Upavarṣa[65] as we have already mentioned, and it is from the *Bhāṣya* that we get any idea of the Vṛttikāras' contribution to this *Śāstra*. His remark that in grammatical operations Pāṇini is a greater authority than Kātyāyana is really interesting. He says that Pāṇini is the truth-speaker and Kātyāyana is a liar.[66] This indirectly supports the non-validity of the dictum of the grammarians—'*yathottaraṁ munīnāṁ prāmāṇyaṁ*'—so that the *caturthīsamāsa* in the compound '*dharmāya jijñāsā*' which is an instance not satisfying the condition of *prakṛti-vikṛtibhāva*, can be justified on the authority of the Vārttikakāra who does not impose this condition for *caturthisamāsa* as noticed below.

Bhartṛmitra (*c.* A.D. 300-600)

Just as there was an interval between Upavarṣa and Śabarasvāmin, so also between Śabara-svāmin and Kumārila-bhaṭṭa, the famous Vārttikakāra on Śabara's *Bhāṣya*, there was a long gap of time when many a commentator both on the *Sūtras* and on the *Bhāṣya* nourished. Among them Bhartṛmitra was one whose name was associated with the title *Ācārya*.

According to Pārthasārathimiśra's *Nyāya-ratnākara*[67], Bhartṛmitra is referred to by Kumārila in his *Ślokavārttika*.

'*Prāyeṇa sarvā Mīmāṁsā hanta lokāyatikṛtā.*' He was,

according to Kumārila, an Ācārya who had introduced many *apasiddhāntas* into the system of the *Pūrvamīmāṁsā* and thus made it *laukāyatika—an atheistic system.* On the authority of the *Nyāyaratnākara* which enumerates some of these *apasiddhāntas* such as '*nityaniṣiddhakarmaṇāṁ phalarāhityam,*' (There is no fruit for (the performance of) the *nitya* and prohibited *karmans*. MM. S. Kuppuswami Sastrigal in his paper on '*the Prābhākara School of Karma Mīmāṁsā*'[68] puts forth the suggestion that 'Prabhākara was not (perhaps) the founder of the Prābhākara School of Karma Mīmāṁsā which (according to P. Miśra's *Nyāyaratnākara)* must have been represented in the ante-Kumārila period by writers like Bhartṛmitra'. But MM. N.S. Anantakrishna Sastrigal, in the English Introduction to his edition of the *Prabhākaravijaya,*[69] contends that if Bhartṛmitra were ever the founder of the Prābhākara school, Prabhākara would not have commented on the *Śābarabhāṣya,* and that Bhartṛmitra could not therefore have been the original propounder of the Prābhākara doctrines. *In either case, it is not yet definitely known whether Bhartṛmitra has written a Vṛtti on Jaimini's Sūtras or a commentary on Śabara's Bhāṣya.*

On the authority of Yāmunācārya's *Siddhitraya,*[70] many scholars opine that Bhartṛmitra has commented on the *Vedānta Sūtras* of Bādarāyaṇa. But there is no further evidence to substantiate that view.

That the Vārttikakāra who is quoted by Sālīkanātha in his *Prakaraṇapañcikā* is Kumārila and none other is now accepted by all scholars,[71] since the majority of the Kārikās cited by Śālīkanātha may be traced to Kumārila's *Ślokavārttika and Bṛhaṭṭikā.*

Bhartṛmitra is referred to by Kumārila in 1-1.6[72] and by Jayantabhaṭṭa in two places in his *Nyāyamañjarī*[73] and to him is ascribed the view that the sensory organ—ear—is nothing but the *saṁskāra* (impression) produced by *dhvani.* Mukulabhaṭṭa in his *Abhidhāvṛttimātṛkā* mentions him with the title *Ācārya* and attributes to him the oft-quoted verse—[74]

abhidheyena sāmīpyāt sārūpyāt samavāyataḥ,
vaiparītyāt kriyāyogāt lakṣaṇā pañcadhā matā.

Bhartṛmitra may be placed between Śabarasvāmin and Kumārilabhaṭṭa *i.e., C.* A.D. 300-600. From the reference of Kumārila cited above, it is clear that his *Vārttika* on the *śabarabhāṣya* was intended to make the Mīmāṁsā system an *āstikadarśana* as against the heterodox views and *apasiddhāntas* propounded by Bhartmitra. Had Bhartṛmitra flourished before Śabarasvāmin, Kumārila would have given this compliment to the Bhāṣyakāra as an *āstikaśiromaṇi,* as he did in the *Ātmavāda* on 1-1. 5.

ityāha nāstikyanirākariṣṇuḥ ,
ātmāstitāṁ bhāṣyakṛdatra yuktyā.[1]

Kumārilabhaṭṭa is the most outstanding figure of the period under survey. It is a matter of great interest for a student of Sanskrit literature to learn that the period from A.D. 600 to 900, which we have named the *Kumārila Period,* produced many dominent *Śāstrakāras* in almost all branches of Sanskrit learning. In the field of Mīmāṁsā, Kumārilabhaṭṭa, Prabhākarabhaṭṭa, Maṇḍanamiśra, Śālīkanāthamiśra and Vācaspatimiśra are the great luminaries whose epoch-making contributions enriched the *Pūrva* Mīmāṁsā Śāstra and led to its branching off into two schools, popularly known as the *Bhāṭṭa* and the *Prābhākara.*

Kumārilabhaṭṭa (*c.* A.D. 620-700)

Kumārilabhaṭṭa, the most outstanding figure of the period, is the well-known author of the *Mimāṁsā Vārttika.*[76] In the Vyākaraṇādhikaraṇa of his *Tantravārttika,* he refers to Bhartṛhari's *Vākyapadīya* and as such he must have flourished after Bhartṛhari who, according to It-sing, died about A.D. 650. He is believed to be the *guru* of Maṇḍanamiśra *(c.* A.D. 670-740). So, he may be assigned to the 7th century.

Many scholars believe that Kumārila was a Southerner in view of the fact that he has used in his *Tantravārttika* many Dravidian words whose semantic relationship to Sanskrit words has been emphasised.[77] But Śālīkanātha's references to him in his works as Vārttikakāra *Miśra* probably indicate his Northern origin.

Kumārila the Vārttikakāra

Kumārila is the father of the *Bhāṭṭa* school of the *Pūrva* Mīmāṁsā System. As the Vārttikakāra of this *Śāstra* his position is unique, unlike that of the Vārttikakāras in other *Śāstras*; for, whereas these have been superseded in their authoritativeness by the Bhāṣyakāras, Kumārila is accepted as more authoritative than the Bhāṣyakāra (Śabarasvāmin) himself.

In many places, Kumārila's interpretation of the *Sūtras* differs considerably from that of the Bhāṣyakāra, not on account of personal bias but of stricter logical discipline. Thus, for instance, in I-3. 2 '*virodhe tvanapekṣam syāt asati hyanumānam*' we have got one striking instance where the Bhāṣyakāra and the Vārttikakāra give different interpretations. Śabarasvāmin says that if any *Smṛti* which is always an *anumāna* is in conflict with a *Śruti* which is accepted (as a *pratyakṣa),* the former becomes invalid as an authority on *dharma.* He illustrates this with the *Śruti—'audumbarīṁ spṛṣṭvā udgāyet'*—'the *udgātṛ* priest should chant by touching the sacrificial post,' which is in conflict with the *Smṛti 'audumbarī sarvā veṣṭayitavyā'*—'the sacrificial post must be completely tied' (with a cloth). Here the conflict is evident in that the touching of the post by *udgātṛ* is impossible in case it is covered with cloth. In this instance the Bhāṣyakāra has expressed the *siddhānta* that the *Smṛti* is unauthoritative since it is in conflict with the *Śruti* on the ground that *Śruti* is *pratyakṣa,* in independent authority, while *Smṛti* is *anumāna,* dependent on a *Śruti,* the existence of which is to be inferred from that *Smṛti.* Kumārila is not satisfied with this explanation. He asks: how can anybody assert that there was no *pratyakṣa-śruti* in the by-gone ages, a reproduction of which this *Smṛti* gives us? And where shall we hide our faces when the future reveals to us that *Śruti* which is now supposed to be lost?[78] He suggests that there are two aspects of *prāmāṇya*—the *bodhakatva* aspect and the *anuṣṭhā-pakatva* aspect. Of these the former is common to both *Śruti* and *Smṛti;* and the latter—the *anuṣṭhāpakatva* aspect—may not be accepted for the *Smṛti* if it conflicts with *Śruti,* till such time as the basis of the *Smṛti* is not revealed. If the future reveals to us the basic *Śruti* for the *Smṛti,* the *anuṣṭhāna* may be in either way.[79]

Kumārila's great work constitutes an extensive commentary on the *Śābarabhāṣya.* The various parts of this Commentary are known by (i) the *Ślokavārttika,* (ii) the *Tantravārttika,* and (iii) the *Ṭupṭīkā.*[80]

The *Ślokavārttika* is in verse mostly in the *anuṣṭup* metre and forms as much a critical commentary on the *tarkapāda* of the *Śābarabhāṣya* as it is an original work in the Mīmāṁsā System, where the author has displayed sound judgment in all matters of controversy coupled with poignant humour. His interpretation of the opening *Bhāṣya* in the *jijñāsādhikaraṇa* in six different ways—not to speak of his ten other interpretations mentioned in Śālīkanātha's *Ṛjuvimalā* and other Prābhākara works—is no doubt, a masterstroke of his versatile genius. While discussing in I-1.2 the authoritativeness of *codanā* on the super-normal *Dharma,* he has established the doctrine of *svataḥ prāmāṇya* of *pramāṇas,* i.e., the validity of a cognition is contributed by the causes of the cognition itself. This is one of the most important doctrines in the epistemology of the *Pūrva* and Uttara Mīmāṁsā Systems of Philosophy. Again, his critique of Upavarṣa's definitions of the six *pramāṇas,* as given by Śabarasvāmin in his *Bhāṣya,* is as complete as it is brilliant. His criticisms of the Buddhistic views of *nirālambanatva* and *Śūnyatva* ascribed to the cognitions and his refutation of Bhartṛhari's doctrine of *sphoṭa* are certainly models of exposition. In connection with the first of these he has established the *anumeyatva of cognition* from the *prākaṭya* or *jñātatā,* in contrast with the *svaprakāśatva* of cognitions as accepted by the Advaitins and others. He has further elaborated the view of the eternality of *śabda* and *artha* and their *sambandha* (relation) as explained by the *Sūtrakāra*, the Vṛttikāra and the *Bhāṣyakāra.*

In the Ātmavāda he has not denied the existence of Īśvara, for he has laid down that one should acquire the knowledge of the Supreme Self—Īśvara—by the proper study of the Upaniṣads. In the *Vākyārthādhikaraṇa* I-1.7 he has well elucidated the *abhihitānvayavāda* in *Śābdabodha* as explained by the Bhāṣyakāra. This is one of the important tenets of the Bhāṭṭa School, in contrast with the *anvitābhidhānavāda* as held by the *Prābhākaras* who represent a rival school in the Mīmāṁsā System of Philosophy.

The Vārttika on the *Bhāṣya* from 1-2. 1 to the end of the third Adhyāya is known as the *Tantravārttika.* It is mainly in prose but is interspersed with a good number of verses. Besides being a good commentary on the *Bhāṣya,* it is, like the *Ślokavārttika,* an original treatise on the *Pūrva* Mīmāṁsā System. In many instances he has given his own interpretations of the *nyāyas,* sometimes superseding and sometimes supplementing those of the *Bhāṣyakāra.* In the *Smṛtipāda* he has advisedly appeared as a great debator and controversialist and given his own interpretation of *Nyāyas,* and has thus been able to suggest new solutions for problems connected with the *prāmāṇya* of *ācāra.* Probably for the first time in a text-book of *Dharmamīmāṁsā Ātmatuṣṭi* as a *pramāṇa* on *Dharma* has been illustrated by a quotation of the words of King Duṣyanta from the *magnum opus* of the greatest poet-dramatist of India, Kālidāsa:

> *"Evañca vidvadvacanāt vinirgatam*
> *prasiddharūpamṁ kavibhiḥ nirūpitam* |
> *'satāṁ hi sandehapadeṣu vastuṣu*
> *pramāṇamantaḥkaraṇapravṛttayaḥ'"* ||

He has also elaborately discussed and tried to uphold the authoritativeness of some *ācāras* of doubtful moral value of some great and important personages—Kṛṣṇa, Vyāsa, Paraśurāma, Bhīṣma and the Pāṇḍavas. Each and every point of the *Pūrvapakṣin* he has answered from the commonsense point of view, and a successful attempt has been made to establish the

Prāmāṇya of the deeds of those great seers who are supposed to be *Śiṣṭas*.

The commentary (from the fourth Adhyāya to the end of the twelfth Adhyāya) is known as the *Ṭupṭīkā*. It is a short *Ṭīkā* or gloss, and his brevity of expression and his power of condensation of topics are particularly noteworthy in this part of the Commentary, as his power of exposition and elaboration is in the *Ślokavārttika* and *Tantravārttika*.

The Bṛhaṭṭīkā and the Madhyamaṭīkā

To Kumārila has also been ascribed the authorship of two more works—the *Bṛhaṭṭīkā* and the *Madhyamaṭīkā*—[81] the former probably an elaborate treatise and the latter presumably a summary of the former. For, authors like Someśvarabhaṭṭa and Nārāyaṇabhaṭṭa mention the *Bṛhaṭṭīkā* and quote from it verses which are not found in the *Ślokavārttika* and the *Tantravārttika*[82].

Prabhākaramiśra (*c.* A.D. 650-720)

Kumārila had the unique fortune to have a band of distinguished disciples some of whom produced epoch-making works. Amongst them are Prabhākara Bhaṭṭa, familiarly known as *Guru,* Maṇḍanamiśra and Umveka Bhaṭṭa *alias* Bhavabhūti.

MM. Dr. Ganganatha Jha holds that Prabhākara (miśra) belonged to the ante-Kumārila period and that he was not, unlike Kumārila, an innovator or reformer[83]. He has tried to prove that by showing that Prabhākara's style is very simple, natural and graceful while Kumārila's is elaborate, majestic and forceful. But MM. S. Kuppuswami Sastrigal has tried to prove that Prabhākara is a younger contemporary of Kumārila[84]. Tradition says that the former has studied under the latter. The title '*quray*' of Prabhākara is explained by a curious incident. Once when Kumāriḷa had to explain an ambiguous passage '*atrāpi noktam tatra tu noktam iti dviruktam*', to his own students, he could not make out the puzzle and went away to his house. But after some time, one of his disciples, Prabhākara, solved the puzzle '*atra apinā uktam, tatra tunā uktam iti dviḥ uktam*' and gave the solution in writing to the wife of their teacher when he was not in his house. On return, the teacher saw it and was immensely pleased with it and commended Prabhākara for his ingenius explanation by conferring on him the title '*guru*'. From that time Prabhākara is known as '*guru*' and his school as '*gurumata*'.

Prabhākara Works

Prabhākara has written two commentaries on the *Śābarabhāṣya*; the *Laghvī*, otherwise known as the *Vivaraṇa,* and the *Bṛhatī* also called the *Nibandhana.* It was presumed till very recently that the *Laghvī* was identical with the *Nibandhana*, and the *Bṛhatī*, with the *Vivaraṇa.* The mist is now cleared off[85]; for, Bhavanātha's *Nayaviveka* and Varadarāja's *Nayavivekadīpikā* show that '*Nibandhana*' is another name for the *Bṛhatī* and '*Vivarana*' for the *Laghvī*, though these two terms are apparently contradictory. It is also believed on the evidence of Śālīkanātha's commentaries[86] on these two works that Prabhākara in all probability wrote his *Laghvī* first wherein he has elucidated his doctrines, and that after Kumārila had written his *Vārttika*, he might have composed his *Bṛhatī* criticising now and then the Vārttikakāra's views.

Prabhākara and Kumārila Compared

That Prabhākara seems to be a greater genius than Kumārila is shown by the fact that he had his immediate follower in his disciple Śālīkanātha who has written first-rate commentaries on his master's works; but Kumārila had three great disciples, none of whom was so devoted to him as Śālīkanātha was to Prabhākara. Umveka, the earliest commentator on the *Ślokavārttika*, was no doubt a follower of Kumārila's school; yet he, as his opening verse '*Ye nāma kecidiha naḥ prathayantyavajñām,*' etc., and his other remarks indicate, had in many instances to deviate from his teacher's path. Maṇḍanamiśra, another famous disciple of Kumārila, has rooted out, in his *Sphoṭasiddhi,* the theory of *Varṇanityatva* as held by Kumārila in the *sphoṭakhaṇḍana* section of his *Ślokavārttika*. But later *the tables were turned against Prabhākara, and no work of his or of his followers has been studied.* On the other hand, Kumārila's works are widely read both by the Mīmāṁsakas and the Vedāntins, and his school has become known as the "Bhāṭṭa School". Vācaspatimiśra of the 9th century and Appayya Dīkṣita of the 16th century, two great makers of the history of the Advaita Vedānta, are pioneers in popularising the study of the Mīmāṁsā rules in other Śāstras. Pārthasārathimiśra, Someśvarabhaṭṭa, Mādhavācārya and Khaṇḍadevamiśra are some of the chief authors in the realm. of the *Pūrva* Mīmāṁsā Śāstra who have both synthetically and analytically explained the rules of interpretation of the vedic and Smṛti texts in the most successful manner.

A passing reference to some of the important differences in the doctrines propounded by Kumārila and Prabhākara may be quite interesting. As Commentators on the *Śābarabhāṣya* on the *Pūrva Mīmāṁsā Sūtras*, both have accepted the *Veda-prāmāṅya* as the fundamental doctrine of the *Pūrva* Mīmāṁsā Śāstra. Both have thus recognised the *āgama* or *śabda* as an authority on the *alaukika dharma*.

(i) Prabhākara holds that *śabda,* both *laukika* and *alaukika,* conveys a complete idea if it is related to a *kriyā* or *kārya,* i.e., if anything already known in our worldly experience is conveyed by the words in a sentence, that sentence cannot be called *pramāṇa*. Only that is *Pramāṇa* which conveys a new idea of a valid character. So to the Prābhākaras who are in a sense supposed to be the idealists among the *mimāṁsakas,* the Vedic injunctions alone are *pramāṇas* among *śabdas*. The words and sentences used in our everyday conversation are not necessarily conveying new, unknown or original ideas; hence *they are not pramāṇas*. But the Bhāṭṭas, *i.e.,* Kumārila and his followers, hold the contrary view and say that there is not much difference between *laukika* and *vaidika-śabdas;* all words alike convey their ideas, whether they are already known to the hearer or not.

How a verbal cognition arises from a sentence is a question which has been answered by Prabhākara and Kumārila in different ways. Prabhākara holds that *sentence is the unit of language* and that each word in a sentence conveys both the object and its *anvaya* (relation). Kumārila, on the other hand, observes that words convey their ideas—*padārthas*—and that those ideas are capable of conveying their relation which is considered to be the *Vākyārtha: 'padaiḥ abhihitāḥ padārthā eva vākyārthaṁ bodhayeyuḥ'.* This is known as the '*abhihitānvayavāda*' of the Bhāṭṭas, which has already been explained in the *Śābarabhāṣya* (I-1.7) and in Bhartṛhari's *Vākyapadīya* (Kāṇḍa II). Prabhākara's view is known as the '*anvitābhidhānavāda.*' Hence, it is one of the fundamental doctrinal differences between Kumārila and Prabhākara. Vācaspatimiśra in his *Tattvabindu,* Pārthasārathimiśra in his *Nyāyaratnamālā* and Brahmānanda Sarasvatī in his *Laghucandrikā* and *Siddhāntabinduṭīkā* have given a critical exposition of these doctrines and shown a partiality for the *Abhihitānvayavāda* of Kumārilabhaṭṭa.

(ii) Another important doctrinal difference lies in their explanation of *abhāva*. Kumārilabhaṭṭa and his followers have, like the Naiyāyikas, recognised *abhāva* as a *separate category.* But Prabhākara has explained it as the *adhikaraṇasvarūpa.*

As a corollary to this the Prābhākaras have not accepted the sixth *pramāṇa—anupa-labdhi.* On the other hand, the Bhāṭṭas who have accepted *abhāva* as a separate category, have been forced to recognise *anupalabdhi* as a separate *pramāṇa* for experiencing *abhāva,* and they define *anupalabdhi* as—'*abhāvopi pramāṇā-bhāvaḥ nāstītyasyārthasya asannikṛṣṭasya'.* Hence the general remark that the Prābhākaras are the *pañcapramāṇavādins* and the Bhāṭṭas, the *ṣatpramāṇavādins.*

(iii) The third important doctrinal difference between the

Prābhākaras and the Bhāṭṭas lies in their treatment of *bhrama-jñāna*. The non-recognition of a separate cognition, called non-valid cognition, by the Prābhākaras, is known, in the Śāstra-kāras' pharaseology, as *akhyāti,* which literally means 'absence of cognition.' The Prābhākaras say that the cognition'this is silver' is a combination of two cognitions: '*this*' is a perception *(pratyakṣa)* of the nacre which the man perceives and '*silver*' is the remembrance of some silver which the perceiver has already seen at a jeweller's. And then, why does the perceiver run to the spot where he sees only the nacre? The answer is simple. The man does not at that time realise that there are two cognitions presenting two objects, and this non-experience of the difference between these two cognitions is responsible for his instantaneous and insensate action. This is what is termed *Akhyāti* and it stands for the non-recognition of a separate non-valid cognition. The Bhāṭṭas, on the other hand, describe it as the *Viparītakhyāti*. This *Viparītakhyāti* is the same as the *anyathākhyāti* of the Naiyāyikas with the difference that the Bhāṭṭas call the *sannikarṣa* (relation) *asat* (non-being), while the Naiyāyikas accept it as *alaukikasannikarṣa—Jñānalakṣaṇā-pratyāsatti.*[87]

Some other important doctrinal differences between the two schools relate to the import of the potential mood—*liṅ*—and the exact subject-matter *(Viṣaya)* for discussion in most of the *adhikaraṇas* in the *Dvādaśalakṣaṇī*. In spite of these differences both Kumārila and Prabhākara are very great names in the field of Mīmāṁsā.

Maṇḍanamiśra (*c.* A.D. 680-750) : His Identification

According to Ānandagiri's *Śaṅkaradigvijaya* Maṇḍana-miśra was the husband of Kumārila's sister. Further he is traditionally known as a disciple of Kumārila. So, he should be a contemporary of Kumārila and may therefore be placed between A.D. 670 and 740.

Vidyāraṇya's *Śaṅkaradigvijaya* records the identity of Maṇḍana with Sureśvarācārya, one of the four disciples of Śrī

Śaṅkarācārya. *Many literary evidences, however, prove that Maṇḍana and Sureśvara are different.* Maṇḍana has written an Advaita work—*Brahmasiddhi*—and his advaita views as embodied in this work, are considerably different from those of Sureśvarācārya which are found elucidated in his *Naiṣkarmyasiddhi* and *Vārttika on the Bṛhadāraṇyaka and Taittirīya Upaniṣad Bhaṣyas* of Śaṅkarācārya. Those who hold the identity argue that Maṇḍana's views are completely changed after he became a disciple of Śaṅkara. This hardly convinces the other school of critics and they do not therefore accept the identity. But since the *Śaṅkara-digvijaya* of Vidyāraṇya identifies Maṇḍana with Sureśvarācārya and with Viśvarūpācārya and since Maṇḍana's identity with the former is out of place, they identify him with Viśvarūpācārya.

Here, there are three problems in identity: Maṇḍana-Sureśvara, Maṇḍana-Viśvarūpa and Sureśvara-Viśvarūpa. Of these identities, the identity of Sureśvarācārya with Viśvarūpācārya is more probable than that of Maṇḍana with Sureāvara or that of Maṇḍana with Viśvarūpa. For in the first place, Mādhava in his *commentary on the Parāśarasmṛti* quotes from Sureśvara's *Bṛhadāraṇyakopaniṣadbhāṣyavārttika* with the prefatory note—'*Vārttike viśvarūpācārya udājahāra—*

'āmre phalārthe ityādi hyāpastambasmṛteḥ vacaḥ;
phalabhāktvaṁ samācaṣṭe nityānāmapi karmaṇam.'

Secondly, in his *Vivaraṇaprameyasaṅgraha,* he quotes a verse from the same Vārttika ascribing it to Viśvarūpa. In his *Puruṣārtha-prabodha,* Brahmānandabhāratī speaks of Sureśvara's *Naiṣkarmyasiddhi* as a work of Viśvarūpācārya—

"ityevaṁ naiṣkarmyasiddhau
brahmāṁśaiḥ brahmavittamaiḥ |
śrīmadbhiḥ v iśvarūpākhyaiḥ
ācāryaiḥ karuṇārṇaraiḥ || "

Similarly many works like Rāmatīrtha's *Mānasollāsa,* the *Vṛttāntavilāsa* and the *Guru-vaṁśakāvya* support the identity of Sureśvarācārya with Viśvarūpācārya. On the basis of these literary evidences Mr. P.V. Kane concludes 'that Maṇḍana's literary activity lies between (A.D.) 690-710; that of Umveka between (A.D.) 700-730 and Sureśvara's between A.D. 800-840 and that Umveka and Bhavabhūti are identical, but that Maṇḍana and Sureśvara are separated by 100 years.'[88] So, Maṇḍana and Sureśvara are different authors.

Maṇḍanamiśra's Works

Maṇḍanamiśra is known to have written six works. The *Vidhiviveka*[89] is chiefly an exposition of the *Vidhyartha*. It refutes the views of the Bhāṭṭas and the Prābhākaras regarding *vidhyartha* (the import of the *vidhi-liṅ)* and accepts *iṣṭa-sādhanatva* as the chief import of *Vidhi* and elucidates it. Incidentally he discusses many an important topic such as the existence of *Sarvajñā* or *Iśvara,* and the conception of *apārva.* The *Bhāvanāvivekad*[90] is another important work of his, which primarily deals with the nature and scope of the *arthabhāvanā.* Here the author establishes well '*bhāvanā'* as the import of the *ākhyāta-pratyaya* which is considered to be separate from the *dhātvartha* (the import of the *dhātu)* in combinations like *pacati* and *yajate,* and also elucidates the differences between the two *bhāvānās—arthabhāvanā* and *śabdabhāvanā—*which constitute one of the fundamental views common to all schools of the Mīmāṁsakas, though they differ much in the explanation of the nature and scope of these two *bhāvanās*. Both these works contain *Kārikās* with *Vivaraṇa.* They would have become very good prakaraṇa works in Mīmāṁsā but for the terseness and obscurity of their language. Another very important work in verse is his *Vibhramaviveka,*[91] which elucidates the *five khyāti-vādas*. These works are generally not intelligible without a commentary. The *Mīmāṁsāsūtrānukramaṇī*[92] is a descriptive Index in verse of the *adhikaraṇas* of the 12 chapters of the *Pūrva Mīmāṁsā Sūtras*. It is a good introductory work for the student of Mīmāṁsā Śāstra in the *adhikaraṇaprasthāna.* Maṇḍanamiśra, in the *Sphoṭasiddhi,*[93] appears as a staunch advocate of the doctrine of *sphoṭa;* and as a close follower of Bhartṛhari he vehemently criticises even his teacher Kumārila-

Bhaṭṭa's refutations of the *sphoṭa* doctrine as set forth in his *Ślokavārttika*. Though the *Sphoṭasiddhi* is not an original treatise, it is a strong defence of *sphoṭavāda* against the attacks of the *Varṇavādins*. In his *Brahmasiddhi*[94] he elucidates his Advaita views which differ considerably from those of Śaṅkarācārya;' and so, like Gauḍapāda, he is a notable figure in the *pre-Saṅkara Advaita School.*

Umvekabhaṭṭa (*c.* A.D. 670-750)

Umvekabhaṭṭa is traditionally known as a young disciple of Kumārilabhaṭṭa and hence may be assigned to A.D. 670-750. MM. S. Kuppuswami Sastrigal suggests the identity of Umveka with the famous dramatist Bhavabhūti.[95] In support of this identification, some literary evidences may be cited. The first and foremost is that the Commentator on the *Tattvapradīpikā* of Citsukhācārya identifies Bhavabhūti with Umveka— '*Bhavabhūtiḥ Umvekaḥ*'[96] One of the early manuscripts of the *Mālatīmādhava* contains colophons attributing the drama to Umvekācārya, the disciple of Kumārilabhaṭṭa.[97] And lastly the commentary on the *Ślokavārttika* begins with the verse—

'Ye nāma kecidiha naḥ prathayantyavajñām' etc., which is found in the prologue to the *Mālatīmādhava* with full reference to its author— Bhavabhūti.

Some objections are however raised against this identity. In the prologues to the three dramas of Bhavabhūti, one Jñānanidhi—and not Kumārilabhaṭṭa—has been referred to as the author's teacher; and we have no evidence to identify Kumārilabhaṭṭa with Jñānanidhi. Again in the prologue to the *Mālati-Mādhava,* Bhavabhūti has spoken of his proficiency in various branches of learning—Vedas, Upaniṣads (Vedānta) Sāhkhya and Yoga systems of philosophy[98]; but he has not made any reference to Mīmāṁsā. Had Umveka and Bhavabhūti been one and the same, it is legitimately contended, he ought to have naturally mentioned Mīmāṁsā in which Umveka is a reputed author.

The second objection is not so serious as the first. Though

the dramatist has not included Mīmāṁsā on the list of Śāstras on which he is said to have acquired proficiency, one can well discern the dramatist's unrivalled Vedic scholarship, allusions to which are abundant in the *Mahāvīracarita* and the *Uttararāmacarita*. Moreover, the reference in the verse—'*yadvedādhyayanam*'—implies the study of the *Pūrva*mīmāṁsā system, without which the study of the Vedas is not complete: *c.f.* '*Svādhyāyosdhyetavyaḥ*' and '*Athāto dharmajijñāsā*'. But the first objection appears more serious since it is necessary, according to dramatic conventions, to mention all the *gurus* of the dramatist when a reference is made to them in the prologue. So if Kumārila were ever Bhavabhūti's teacher, his name also should have been mentioned.

Umveka's Works

Umveka is credited with the authorship of two commentaries, one on the *Ślokavārttika* of Kumārilabhaṭṭa[99] and the other on the *Bhāvanāviveka* of Maṇḍanamiśra.[100] Umveka is also known as a *Nibandhanakāra*.[101] Whether he has written any *nibandhana* (independent work) other than those commentaries is not known.

It is believed that the commentary on the *Ślokavārttika* is a joint production of Umveka and Jayamiśra (the son of Kumārilabhaṭṭa) and as such, it is the earliest commentary on the *Ślokavārttika*. From the opening verse of this commentary, it can be presumed that he was not appreciated in his days, but he was confident that posterity would recognise him. His adaptation of the epic verse in the *Codanāsūtra*—

"*Gurorapyavaliptasya kāryākāryamajānataḥ,*
Utpatham pratipannasya parityāgo vidhīyate | | "

well speaks of his independent outlook and love of truth on account of which he had the boldness to challenge even his *Guru*.[102] In this respect, Umveka has done the right thing as a critic and as such commands our admiration.

It is unfortunate that Kumārila had not even one disciple

to follow him. His disciple Prabhākara, we have seen, founded a new school called after his own name, which grew up as an *anti-Kumārila* school. Maṇḍanamiśra and Umveka were both uncharitable in their criticism of their teacher though they continued in the Kumārila school. So, the three disciples of Kumārila, each independent in his own way, instituted in a sense an *anti-Kumārila* clique.

Śālīkanātha (*c.* A.D. 690-760)

Mahāmahopādhyāya Śālīkanātha is traditionally known as the direct disciple of Prabhākarabhaṭṭa. He quotes verses from Maṇḍanamiśra's *Vidhiviveka.*[103] Vācaspatimiśra, the reputed author of the ninth century, quotes from Śālīkanātha's *Ṛjuvimalā.*[104] So. he might well be placed between A.D. 690 and 760, or even earlier.

As a devoted disciple of Prabhākara, Śālīkanātha has popularised his teacher's views by writing two valuable commentaries—the *Dīpaśikhā* on the *Laghvī* and the *ṛjuvimalā*[105] on the *Bṛhatī.* Besides these two commentaries, he has also composed the well-known *prakaraṇa* work, called *Prakaraṇapañcikā.*[106]

The topics discussed in the *Prakaraṇapañcikā* are varied and very important for the popularisation of the Prābhākara school. The work begins with the discussion of the *adhyayanavidhi*—whether the study of the vedas by the *Traivarṇikas* is enjoined by the *Vidhi* 'svā*dhyāyosdhyetavyaḥ*' or whether it is to be enjoined by the *ācāryakaraṇavidhi.* This is a subject which as an introductory topic of the Mīmāṁsāśāstra is discussed in most of the Mīmāṁsā works, both elementary and advanced; and while the Bhāṭṭas establish that the injunction '*svādhyāyossdhyetavyaḥ*' enjoins the *adhyayana* of the Vedas for the sake of *arthajñāna,* the Prābhākaras criticise this view mainly on the ground that the *svādhyāyavidhi* has no reference to *adhikārin,* which they find in the *ācāryakaraṇavākya.* In the beginning of his work

"Svādhyāyavidhivākyārthavicāre p rayatāmahe |
Prabhākaragurordṛṣṭyā mīmāṁsārambhasiddhaye ||"

Śālīkanātha promises to discuss (first) the true import of the *Svādhyāyavidhi,* as his teacher, Prabhākara, has expounded it. The first topic discussed is known as the '*śāstramukha*' i.e., introducing the student to the Śāstra. This is what Śālīkanātha has said in the compound—*Mīmāṁsārambhasiddhaye.* The other important topics discussed are—*Jātinirṇaya;* (the conception of *jāti*—generality); the conception of non-valid cognition (in the *Nayavīthī);* the conception of five *pramāṇas* (omitting *Anupalabdhi);* the *Vedaprāmāṇya* (in the *Nirmalāñjana* section); the conception of *ātman* (in the *Tattvaloka* section); and the exposition of *Vākyārthāvagama* (in the *Vākyārtha-mātṛka)* and other minor topics (such as found in sections like the *Atideśapārāyaṇā).*

'There is another work written by Śālīkanātha, known as *Mīmāṁsābhāṣyapariśiṣṭa*[107] which seems to be, as the title shows, a supplement to the *Śābarabhāṣya.*

Mahodadhi and Mahāvrata (*c.* A.D. 700-770)

Next to Śālīkanātha come Mahodadhi and Mahāvrata in chronological order. The commentary *Candrikā* on verse 3 of Act II of the allegorical drama—the *Prabodhacandrodaya*—

"Naivāśrāvi gurormataṁ
na viditam kaumārilam darśanam
Tattvajñanamaho na śālīkagirāṁ
vācaspateḥ kā kathā |
Sūktam nāpi mahodadhe-
radhigatam Māhāvratī nekṣitā
Sūkṣmā vastuvicāraṇā nṛpaśubhiḥ
svasthaiḥ katham sthīyate ||"

makes clear that Mahodadhi is a contemporary of Śālīkanātha and a representative of the Prābhākara school.[108] Mahodadhi is credited with the authorship of a *Nibandhana* work. Mahāvrata, a contemporary of Mahodadhi, belonged to the Kumārila school;

he is said to have refuted in his work the views of his rival Mahodadhi. The *Nayaviveka* of Bhavanāthabhaṭṭa of about 11th century refers to these two authors[109]; and so they may be well assigned to the period A.D. 700-770. About their works nothing is known except an extract cited by Bhavanātha in his *Nayaviveka*.

Vācaspatimisra (*c.* A.D. 800-900)

Next comes Vācaspatimiśra whose date is fixed by scholars from his references in his works. In his *Nyāyasūcinibandha* he has given the date of completion of that work 898 *Vikrama era* which is equivalent to A.D. 841-42.[110] He is certainly earlier than Udayanācārya, the reputed author of a commentary—*Pariśuddhi*—on Vācaspati's *Nyāyavārttikatātparyaṭīkā*. Udayanācārya's date can be fixed as the middle of the 10th century from the *Lakṣaṇāvalī* wherein he has given in the verse '*Tarkāmbarāṅkapramiteṣvatīteṣu śakāntataḥ*' the date of composition of that work, which is calculated by scholars as A.D. 984.[111] Therefore, the earliest date to which Vācaspati Miśra may be assigned is between A.D. 800 and 900, since he is later than Śrī Śaṅkarācārya.

Scholars are of opinion that Vācaspatimiśra belonged to a place in Behar or Bengal in view of the fact that he has repeatedly referred to mustard oil in his works. It has also been conjectured that in what corresponds to Ancient *Mithilā*, there were a city called *Bhāmā (Bhāmatī)* and a tank of the same name.

About his person and ancestry, nothing is known except the tradition that he is the incarnation of Śaṅkara himself in order to popularise the Advaita system through his '*Bhāmatī*'. That he was always devoted to study and was engaged in composing standard works like the *Bhāmatī* in all Śāstras is noteworthy. In this connection a curious story is narrated. It is said that during his marriage he heard some learned discussions of great pandits which was a custom prevalent in ancient India on such occasions. He was much attracted by the discussion and consequently cultivated that art all his life-time. The result was that he devoted his life to the task of writing authoritative treatises on all *darśanas*. Though he was a *Gṛhastha,* his enthusiasm and zeal for study was so great that he lived as a practical *Brahmacārin*. He was, however, not slow to realise his neglect of his duty towards his wife and as a compensation he called his *magnum opus,* after her name—*Bhāmatī*—in the pious hope of handing down her name to posterity.

About his teachers, one Trivikrama has been mentioned as his Nyāya teacher.[112] In his Bhāmatī one king '*Nṛga*' is mentioned.[113] Scholars have not yet been successful in identifying this king, though an attempt has been made by some to identify him with a king of *Mithilā,* a predecessor of Nānyadeva who is known to have ruled his kingdom about 1019 *Vikrama era, i.e.,* A.D. 962. This predecessor is also said to have been named in some inscriptions *Kirātādhipati* (the king of *Kirātas* who are believed to have possessed human vehicles). MM. Dr. Ganganatha Jha in the Sanskrit Introduction to his edition of the *Sāṅkhyatattvakaumudī* says that '*nṛga*' can be interpreted as 'one who has a human vehicle'. He also holds that Vācaspatimiśra was born in *Mithilā*.

Vācaspatimiśra a Literary Genius

Vācaspatimiśra is considered to be one of the greatest literary geniuses that India has ever produced. His name is ever associated with the honorific title '*sarvatantrasvatantra*' which is a rare honour conferred only upon literary prodigies. His literary productions bear ample testimony to the honour and dignity that are always associated with that title.

He is said to be one of these rare scholars who have written authoritative commentaries on the standard works in all the six Āstikadarśanas— Orthodox Systems of Indian philosophy. To his genius the grouping of Nyāya and Vaiśeṣika under separate heads did not probably appeal because he has not written any work on the Vaiśeṣika system; he has however composed a very authoritative commentary—*Nyāyavāarttika*-

tātparyaṭikā on Udyotakara's *Nyāyavārttika,* which would have sunk into oblivion but for Vācaspatimiśra's commentary on it. The great service that Vācaspati rendered to the *Nyāya* system is the establishment of the original *nyāya* doctrines as embodied in the *Nyāyasūtras* as explained by the Nyāyabhāṣyakāra and the Nyāyavārtikākara, but adversely criticised by eminent Buddhist Ācāryas like Diṅnāga and Dharmakīrti. In the *Nyā|ya* literature he is generally known as the *Tātparyaṭīkācārya.* His other work in Nyāya philosophy is the *Nyāyasūcīnibandhana,* which is regarded as an appendix to his *Tātparyaṭīkā.*

His contributions to the Sāṅkhya and Yoga systems of philosophy consist in the two commentaries—(i) the *Sāṅkhya-tattvakaumudī*[114] on Īśvarakṛṣṇa's *Sāṅkhyakāriās,* and (ii) the *Yogabhāṣyaviśāradī* on Vyāsa's *Yogasūtrabhāṣya.*[115] Next to Gauḍapāda's *Bhāṣya* on the *Sāṅkhyakārikās,* his *Sāṅkhya-tattvakaumudī* in the standard commentary; it even rivals the former in offering clearer and more exhaustive explanations of the Sāṅkhya tenets, which are much divergent from those of other systems.

His works in the Mīmāṁsā system of philosophy are : (1) the *Nyāyakaṇikā*—a commentary on Maṇḍanamiśra's *Vidhi-viveka*[116] and (2) the *Tattvabindu.*[117] Besides being a good commentary, the *Nyāyakaṇikā* is an authoritative treatise discussing many philosophical doctrines such as the *satkāryavāda,* the *asatkāryavāda,* the *khyātis* and the *kṣaṇabhaṅgavāda.* His *Tattvabindu* is a short treatise wherein the author in powerful language elucidates three main and two subordinate views, which were current among the scholars in philosophy on the important question—what actually constitutes the *karaṇa,* the efficient cause, in verbal cognition—*Śābdabodha.* First, he takes up the Vaiyākaraṇa conception of *sphoṭa* which as one ultimate *śabda—the sonant substratum,* accounts for all differences in the *śabda* perception and as such is the *karaṇa* of the *Śābdabodha.* This he refutes on the lines already enunciated by Kumārila in his *Sphoṭavāda* section of the *Ślokavārttika.* Then he considers the view that the last *varna* or the *varṇāvali* in combination with the *saṁskāras* produced by the experiences of the previous sounds in a word, is the cause of the *śābdabodha*. Even this view is discarded by him. Then he discusses at length Ṭīkākāra's view of the *anvitābhidhānavāda* from all points of view in its favour as put forth by the Ṭīkākāra (Prabhākara) and his great disciple, Śālīkanātha, and refutes them. Finally he elaborates his own solution 'the *abhihitānvayavāda*', according to which words while uttered convey the *padārthas,* which in their turn, convey the *vākyārtha,* the cognition of which is the *vākyārthajñāna,* otherwise known as the *śabdabodha*. In other words, the words or the cognitions of the words are not the efficient cause of the *śābdabodha,* but the *padārthas,* which conveyed by the *padas* do become the *karaṇa* of the *śābdabodha.*

His Vedānta works are—(1) the *Brahmatattvasamīkṣā*[118] a commentary on the *Brahmasiddhi* of Maṇḍanamiśra and (2) the *Bhāmatī*[119] an authoritative commentary on Śaṅkarācārya's *Brahmasūtrabhāṣya*. The former like his *Nyāya-kaṇikā* is considered to be an authoritative commentary on the *Brahmasiddhi*.

It is conceded now by some scholars that Vācaspatimiśra has drawn inspiration from Maṇḍana'ṣ *Brahmasiddhi* for his Vedānta views, which as embodied in his Bhāmatī, are afterwards known as the *Bhāmatīprasthāna,* just as the views of Padmapādācārya (one of the four disciples of Śrī Śaṅkarācārya and the author of the famous commentary *Pañcapādikā,* on the *Brahmasūtrabhāṣya* of Śaṅkarācārya) and of Prakāśātmayati, the author of the *Vivaraṇa,* came to be known as the views of the Vivaraṇakāra or the *Vivaraṇa-prasthāna*. On the indebtedness of Vācaspatimiśra to Maṇḍanamiśra, the editors of the '*Bhāmatī—Catussūtrī*' at the end of their Introduction observe :—

"The thoughtful student of Vācaspati, may, perhaps, find little that is original in him. For the distinctive aspects of his teaching, he owes much to Maṇḍana; where he differs from

Maṇḍana he elects to follow Śaṅkara, *not perhaps always wisely.* But there have been very few to excel or rival Vācaspati in the versatility and the extent of his scholarship, his vigour of style and clarity of presentation. The thoughts that so far we have been able to trace to Maṇḍana, would have remained little known and barren but for Vācaspati's linking them up with Śaṅkara's teaching. About Maṇḍana's own Advaita doctrines there has been as much uncertainty and speculation as about his personality in spite of scraps of information vouchsafed here and there in the course of commentaries on other works."

Between Vācaspatimiśra and Vedāntadeśika, *i.e.,* A.D. 900-1300, a group of authors appear to have flourished and written many important works in both the schools of Mīmāṁsā Śāstra. Their dates cannot be definitely fixed in the absence of sufficient literary or other evidences.

Devasvāmin (*c.* A.D. 1000)

Devasvāmin, according to the *Prapañcahṛdaya,*[120] has written a *Bhāṣya* on the 16 chapters of the *Pūrva Mīmāṁsā Sūtras*, which is only a *résumé* of Upavarṣa's *Vṛtti* thereon. He says in his *Saṅkarṣakāṇḍabhāṣya* that he has reproduced Bhavadāsa's *Bhāṣya*[121] in XIV. 11. 1. His *Bhāṣya* on the *Dvādaśalakṣaṇī* has not yet seen the light of day. His *Saṅkarṣa-kāṇḍabhāṣya*[122] is probably the only *extant* standard work which forms the most important source for reconstructing the lost *Sūtras* of the *Saṅkarṣakāṇḍa.*

In the history of the *Kalpasūtras* one Devasvāmin is known as the author of the commentaries on the *Āśvalāyana Śrauta* and *Gṛhya Sūtras* and it is on these that later commentators have based their works. That Devasvāmin seems to have also written a *digest* of *Smṛtis* where he has discussed all topics relating to *Dharma,* such as *ācāra, vyavahāra, āśauca* and *prāyaścitta* is evident from the references made by the Smṛti-Candrikākāra and other subsequent authors in the field. Mr. P.V. Kane concludes that sufficient data are not available to establish the identity of the two Devasvāmins;[123] but we may identify them on the ground that the *Dharmaśāstra* is only supplementary to the Mīmāṁsā Śāstra. If this identity is accepted, his period may be fairly fixed towards the close of the 10th century or the first half of the llth century; in any case he cannot be later than A.D. 1050, since he is mentioned in the *Prapañcahṛdaya*, a work which can well be assigned to the 11th century, if not earlier.

Sucarita Miśra (*c.* A.D. 1000-1100)

Sucaritamiśra, the famous commentator on the *Śloka-vārttika* of Kumārila, is another important figure in this group. Somanātha Dīkṣita, the famous commentator on the *Śāstra-dīpikā* of Pārthasārathimiśra, makes us believe[124] that he was earlier than Pārthasārathimiśra, another famous commentator on the *Ślokavārttika.* His work, Kāśikā, is referred to by Veṅkaṭ anātha *alias* Vedānta Deśikācārya[125] who flourished during the last quarter of the 13th century and the first half of the 14th century. Cidānanda, the reputed author of the Nītitattvāvirbhāva, refers to Sucaritamiśra's Kāślkā (as Parameaśvara II states);[126] and this Cidānanda may also be assigned to the close of the 13th century. So, Sucaritamiśra can be fairly placed between A.D. 1000 and 1100.

His commentary on the *Ślokavārttika* called *Kāśikā,*[127] is very lucid and authoritative. In certain places, it is more elaborate and polemic than even Pārthasārathimiśra's Nyāyaratnākara.

About his personal history, no information is so far available. From his name, it may be conjectured that he is a Northerner since all '*Miśras'* as a group, are believed to be northerners, probably belonging to Mithilā.

Pārthasārathi Miśra (*c.* A.D. 1050-1120)

To this period also belonged Pārthasārathi Miśra. His father is named Yajñātman,[128] who was also his teacher. The earliest direct reference to this author is found in the *Nyāyamālā-vistara*[129] and the *Vivaraṇaprameyasaṅgraha* of Mādhavācārya of the 14th century.[130] Parameśvara II makes us understand[131] that Cidānanda of the 13th century has referred in his *Nīti-tattvāvirbhāva* to Pārthasārāthimiśra and his works.

Pārthasārathi Miśra is the author of a number of standard works. His two commentaries, the Tantraratna on Kumārila's Ṭupṭīkā and the Nyāyaratnākara on the *Ślokavārttika*; his *Śāstradīpikā*, an independent commentary on the twelve chapters of Jaimini's *Pūrvamīmāṁsā-sūtras*; his *Nyāyaratna-mālā*, an independent treatise discussing important topics in the Mīmāṁsā Śāstra,—these bespeak the versatility of Pārtha-sārathimiśra's genius; and from these it will be seen that in the field of Indian Darśanas, he deserves to be well ranked with authors like Vācaspatimiśra and Udayanācārya.

His Tantraratna,[132] unlike the Nyāyaratnākara, is not only a very elaborate commentary on the Ṭupṭīkā but also an exhaustive treatise on Mīmāṁsā Śāstra which discusses many topics connected with the *adhikaraṇa* and *pramāṇa prasthānas*. From the references in his own works,[133] this can be said to be the earliest production of the author.

His next important work is the *Śāstradīpikā.*[134] It is a *nibandhana* work in the *adhikaraṇa-prasthāna* based on the Vārttika of Kumārila. It is the first among the standard works of the Bhāṭṭa school which do not at all explain the meaning of the *Sātras* constituting the various *adhikaraṇas,* but elucidate fully the six important constituents of the *adhikaraṇa—Viṣaya* (subject or proposition under discussion), *visaya* (doubtful point), *pūrvapakṣa (prima facie* argument), *siddhānta* (conclu-sion), *prayojana* (the result or fruit of the discussion) and *saṅgati* (relation between one *adhikaraṇa* and another, etc.)[135] In the treatment of the subject-matter this work has attained a unique place and become a model to later writers like Mādhavā-cārya, Khaṇḍadevamiśra. The *Tarkapāda* of this work I-1. 1-8 is a succinct summary of Kumārila's *Ślokavārttika* and forms a valuable guide for understanding the *siddhāntas* of Kumārila which are obscure in many places. His manner of presentation especially in dragging the opponent into his net is not void of humour and it is sometimes even satirical. The whole work is characterised by simplicity of language and vigour of style. Generally, he writes one or two verses to summarise the *prima facie* and *siddhānta* views of the *adhikaraṇa*, which he explains and supplements in easy prose. Next to Śabara's Bhāṣya and Kumārila's Vārttika, the *Śāstradīpikā* is the most authoritative work in the *adhikaraṇa-prasthāna* representing the *prācīna* views on the Mīmāṁsā rules of interpretation. It contains refutations of the Prābhākara views which have engendered many impediments in the development of the Bhāṭṭa school.

c.f. *'Nyāyabhāsatamacchanna-*
sāstratattvārthadarśikām |
Kumārilamatenāhaṁ
kariṣye śāstradīpikām' | |

Moreover, this work has led to a neglect of the study of the *Mīmāṁsā Sūtras* together with that of the *Bhāṣya*, the *Vārttika* and other commentaries thereon. The Nibandhana works like the *Śāstradīpikā,* the *Nyāyamālāvistara* and the *Bhāṭṭadīpikā* are however fully studied by students of Mīmāṁsā. In this respect this Śāstra stands different from the *Vedānta Śāstra.*

His *Nyāyaratnamālā*[136] is another important work which deals with some of the fundamental doctrines of the Bhāṭṭa school. It is written on the model of Śālīkanātha's *Prakaraṇa-pañcikā* and as such, is an advanced *prakaraṇa* work in the Mīmāṁsā Śāstra. Its importance lies in the fact that in many *prakaraṇas* it answers the views of Prabhākara as elaborated by Śālīkanātha in his *Prakaranapañcikā*, and maintains the views of Kumārila. In the *prayuktitilaka* section of his work he offers a criticism of the *Śāstramukha* of the *Prakaraṇapañcikā* and reestablishes the *Svādhyāyavidhi—"Svādhyāyosdhye-tavyaḥ"* as enjoining the *vedādhyayana* for the *arthajñāna—knowledge of the contents of the Vedas.* The *Vākyārthanirṇaya* section is partly a refutation of the doctrine of the *anvitābhi-dhānavāda* of the Prābhākaras as elucidated by Śālīkanātha in the Vākyārthamātṛkā of his Prakaraṇapañcikā and partly a statement of the doctrine of *abhihitānvayavāda* as elucidated by Kumārila in his *Vākyādhikaraṇavārttika* and by Vācaspatimiśra in his *Tattvabindu*. In the *Vidhinirṇaya* section he gives us a complete exposition of the import of the Vidhipratyaya as accepted by the Bhāṭṭas after a refutation of the Prābhākara view. The *svataḥprāmāṇyavāda,* the *vyāptivāda* and the *nityakāmyaviveka* are other important chapters elucidating the Bhāṭṭa views. The last section—the *aṅganirṇaya*—chiefly deals with the *aṅgāṅgibhāva* between two *kriyās, dravyas,* etc. as evidenced by *Śruti* and five other *pramāṇas,* and gives a summary of the later chapters of the *Pūrva*mīmāṁsāśāstra. The whole work is in his usual simple and vigorous style not divorced from humour.

The last but not the least of his works is the *Nyāyaratnākara,*[137] a commentary on the *Ślokavārttika* of Kumārilabhaṭṭa. It gives in many places a lucid summary of the contents of the Vārttika and refers to various Ācāryas— Bhavadāsa, Diṅnāga, Dharmakīrti, Bhikṣu and Bhartṛmitra— whose views are said to have been refuted by the Vārttikakāra. This work is very brief and clear and as such, renders great help in the elucidation of the obscure verses of the *Ślokavārttika.*

Śrīkara and Prakāśa (*c.* A.D. 1100)

Śrīkara and Prakāśa are known only from references in Bhavanāthabhaṭṭa's *Nayaviveka.*[138] Both are the followers of Prabhākara. Bhavanātha mentions Śrīkara by name, while he refers to Prakāśa by the words '*anye*', '*kecit*' etc., which according to Varadarāja refer to Prakāśa.[139] Though they are the exponents of the Prābhākara tenets, Bhavanātha severely criticises their views.

In the history of the Dharmaśāstra one Śrīkara is known[140] as a *Smṛtinibandhanakāra*, who is held to be anterior to Devaṇabhaṭṭa, the author of the *Smṛticandrikā* and to Vijñāneśvara, the author of the *Mitākṣarā*, the famous commentary on the Yājñavalkyasmṛti. He is placed by Mr. P.V. Kane between A.D. 800 and 1050. Whether the Mīmāṁsaka Śrīkara is identical with the Smṛtikāra Śrīkara is not known. Since our Śrīkara is known to Bhavanāthabhaṭṭa, he may well be assigned to a period not later than A.D. 1100. Prakāśa presupposed by Bhavanātha may have belonged to the period, A.D. 1000-1100. (See below). But P.V. Kane assigns a Smṛti work *Prakāśa*[141] mentioned by many *Smṛtinibandhanakāras* to the same period, without mentioning the author's name. Since the author and the work may be known by the same name, *it is not unlikely that the Mimāṁsaka Prakāśa was identical with the author of the work, Prakāśa.*

Bhavanāthabhaṭṭa (*c.* A.D. 1050-1150)

Bhavanāthabhaṭṭa, the author of the *Nayaviveka*, is the great champion of the Prābhākara school in the period under survey. He occupies a high place, next only to that of Śālīkanātha. His work called the *Nayaviveka*, is, as he says, a running commentary on the 12 chapters of the *Pūrva*mīmāṁsāśāstra, following the *Pañcikā* of Śālīkanātha,[142] *(i.e.)* the two commentaries, *Ṛjuvimalā* and *Dīpaśikhā* and the *Prakaraṇapañcikā*. He says in the introductory verses[143] that his aim is neither to indulge in literary flourishes nor to answer adverse criticism, but only to expound the subject fully and clearly.

The *Nayaviveka*, the only extant work of his, can be considered as a standard commentary on the *Pūrvamīmāṁsāsūtras* in the Prābhākara school and occupies the same position that Pārthasārathimiśra's *Śāstradīpikā* does in the Kumārila school. It elucidates the *adhikaraṇas* in detail and the more important of the doctrines regarding *pramāṇaṣ* and *prameyas*, and generally refutes the doctrines of the Bhāṭṭa school. It refers to the *Śābarabhāṣya*, Kumārila and Prabhākara and their works, Umveka,[144] Śālīkanātha and his works, Mahodadhi, Mahāvrata, Vācaspatimiśra,[145] Śrīkara and Prakāśa. The latest limit of his date may be the latter part of the 12th century. Possibly he is earlier than Cidānanda Paṇḍita also, for he is made by his commentator Parameśvara II to presuppose Bhavanātha's *Nayaviveka*. In any case he is earlier than *Vedānta Deśika* who in his Seśvaramīmāṁsā quotes Bhavanātha and refutes his views.

Bhavadevabhaṭṭa (*c.* A.D. 1100)

To the period A.D. 1100-1250 may be assigned the three great commentators on Kumārila's *Tantravārttika*, Bhavadevabhaṭṭa, Paritoṣamiśra and bhaṭṭa Someśvara. Of these, the earliest is Bhavadevabhaṭṭa. His date is given by Mr. P.V. Kane as A.D. 1100. His work on Mīmāṁsā is known as the *Tautātitamatatilaka*[146]— a commentary on the *Tantravārttika* of Kumārila. The colophon[147] of this work gives him another name 'Bālavalabhībhujaṅga'.

As Mr. P. V. Kane says in his '*History of Dharma-śāstra*'[148], the earliest reference to Bhavadevabhaṭṭa in a literary work is found in Hemādri's *Caturvargacintāmaṇi* (of the 14th century). He also refers to an inscription found in the temple of Anantavāsudeva at Bhuvaneśvara in the Puri District of Orissa, eulogising Bhavadevabhaṭṭa with the epithet '*Bāla-valabhiīhūbhujaṅga*'.[149] From that inscription (according to Mr. P.V. Kane), Bhavadeva is known to have belonged to the *Sāvarṇagotra* of Kauthumī school of Sāmaveda. His family originally belonged to a village—*Siddhala grāma* in Rāḍhā (west of the Hugli and south of the Ganges). Bhavadeva, one of the remote ancestors of our Bhavadeva, got the gift of an agrahara of Hastinībhaṭṭa from the Gauḍa King. The genealogy of our author is given thus:

Bhavadeva
(Sāvarṇagotra)
↓
Rathaṅga
(son)
↓
Atyaṅga

↓

Budh
(alias Spurita)
↓
Ādideva
(minister of peace and war of the king of Vaṅga)
↓
Govardhana-m. Sāṅgokā
(daughter of a vandhyaghaṭīya brahmin)
↓
Bhavadeva
(the author of the *Tautātitamatatilaka).*

Our Bhavadeva was a *protégé* and adviser of King Harivarmadeva who reigned long in prosperity. Besides being an author of works on astrology, *smṛti* and *mīmāṁsā*, he is described as the builder of a reservoir in Rāḍhā, and of temples of Nārāyaṇa, Ananta and Nṛsiṁha. The title Bālavalabhībhujaṅga is explained by Mr. P.V. Kane with reference to the fact that Bhavadeva probably made some innovation in the structure of the roofs or balconies of the temples he built and he was therefore styled 'a lover of little valabhīs.'

Dr. Keilhorn conjectures from its character that this inscription belongs to the 12th century. Mr. P.V. Kane[150] supports this date of Bhavadeva (i.e.) *c.* A.D. 1100, by internal evidences. He cites a passage from the Vīramitrodaya which makes the Pradīpa anticipate Bhavadeva. The Pradīpa was composed before A.D. 1150. So, Bhavadeva should have belonged to the closing decade of the 11th century and the first decade of the 12th century.

Bhavadeva's other works are the *Vyavahāratilaka,* the *Vyavahāratantra,* the *Karmānuṣṭhāna-paddhati* and the *Prāyaścittanirūpaṇa.*

Paritoṣamiśra (*c.* A.D. 1200)

Paritoṣamiśra, probably a native of Bengal, has composed the commentary on the *Tantravārttika*, named *Ajitā.*[152] It is brief and more helpful than *Nyāyasudhā* in understanding the *Vārttika* with its involved style. The earliest reference to the work and its commentary *Vijayā* by Anantanārāyaṇa, is found in Parameśvara III's Sūtrārthasaṅgraha.[152] The *Ajitā* is otherwise known as *Tantraṭikānibandhana.*

Bhaṭṭa Someśvara (*c.* A.D. 1200)

Bhaṭṭa Someśvara is the author of the *Nyāyasudhā* or *Rāṇaka*, the only printed commentary on the *Tantravārttika*. The earliest reference to him and to his work is probably made, according to Parameśvara II, the commentator on the *Nītitattvāvirbhāva*, by Cidānanda[153] in his work. Later authors like Somanātha Dīkṣita and Khaṇḍadevamiśra profusely quote him in their works.

Some[154] seem to have opined that he is the son of Vidyāraṇya Mādhava of the 14th century on the ground that he has mentioned in a colophon one Mādhavārya as his father. Evidently he is a different person. The only thing that suggests a later date for him is his style which is very coarse and resembles that of a much later writer. But the reference by Cidānanda suggests the period to which we have assigned him.[155]

His chief work is the *Nyāyasudhā:*[156] Besides being an elaborate commentary, it is a critical *Nibandhana* work in the Mīmāṁsā Śāstra which later authors like Khaṇḍadevamiśra, Somanātha Dīkṣita and Śaṁbhubhaṭṭa, have quoted now and then and sometimes adversely criticised. Another work of his, the *Tantrasāra,* is mentioned by himself in the *Nyāyasudhā*[157] and Khaṇḍadeva and Vāsudeva Dīkṣita in their works,[158] but is not yet available.

Murārimiśra (*c.* A.D. 1150-1220)

To the close of the 12th century and to the beginning of the 13th century belonged Murāri Miśra, who is supposed to have founded a new school in the Mīmāṁsā Śāstra *cf. 'Murāreḥ tṛtīyaḥ panthāḥ.'* His *Tripādīnītinayana*[159] is an exposition of his views on the basis of the *adhikaraṇas*, probably in the second, third and fourth *pādsa* of the first *adhyāya* of the *Mīmāṁsā Sūtras*. It is not exactly known whether he has commented on the whole of the *Dvādaśa-lakṣaṇī*. Most probably he might have done so; and his commentary on the *adhikaraṇa* XI-1.1,[160] lends support to this view; or it is quite possible that he chose to comment on certain *adhikaraṇas* only which he deemed necessary and important.

From a comparative study of the *Nītinayana* and the *Nayaviveka* of Bhavanāthabhaṭṭa, it can be observed[161] that Murārimiśra has in his work, *Nītinayana*, refuted Bhavanātha's views as embodied in his *Nayaviveka*. Gaṅgeśopādhyāya, the author of the *Tattvacintāmaṇi*, has, according to his commentators, presupposed Murārimiśra (who is generally known among them as '*Miśra*') '*Guru*' and '*Bhaṭṭa*' (Prabhākara and Kumārila), who represent the three schools of Mīmāṁsā Śāstra. Gaṅgeśopādhyāya is assigned by scholars to the first half of the 13th century;[162] and Murārimiśra might have therefore flourished after Bhavanātha Bhaṭṭa and before Gaṅgeśo-pādhyāya, *i.e.*, towards the close of the twelfth century.

It is only after the discovery of the *Tripādī-nītinayana* that scholars have been able to understand the truth of the observation, '*Murāreḥ tṛtīyaḥ panthāḥ*', that Murārimiśra is the founder of a third school of the Mīmāṁsā Śāstra. Till then they held that the above observation applied to the author of the *Anargharāghava* who differed considerably from the two well-known dramatists, Kālidāsa and Bhavabhūti in dramatic technique.

The identity between Murārimiśra (the Mīmāṁsaka) and Murāri (the dramatist) cannot be made, since the dramatist belonged to an earlier period, *i.e.*, the early part of the 9th century.[163]

Nandīśvara (*c.* A.D. 1220-1300)

After Bhavanātha comes Nandīśvara who has written a very good Prakaraṇa work, called Prabhākaravijaya, in the Prābhākara school. He says in one of the introductory verses—

'Nāthadvayāttasāresmin śāstre mama pariśramaḥ |
Śuktiśramāyate sindhau hariṇoddhṛtakaustubhe || '

that the essential doctrines of Prabhākara have already been fully elucidated by two Nāthas— Śālīkanātha and Bhavanātha and that his further attempt has not much of originality in it. The upper limit of his period is about A.D. 1200. He is said to have been criticised by Sudarśanācārya,[164] the famous commentator on the Śrībhāṣya of Rāmānujācārya and a contemporary of *Vedānta Deśika*. So, Nandīśvara may fairly be placed between A.D. 1200 and 1300. He has referred to and criticised Pārthasārathimiśra's Nyāyaratnamālā. His work, *Prabhākaravijaya,* deals with 21 or more topics[165] most of which bear on epistemology.

Cidānanda Paṇḍita (*c.* A.D. 1200-1300)

Cidānanda Paṇḍita is certainly later than Pārthasārathimiśra, Bhaṭṭa Someśvara and Bhavanātha Bhaṭṭa; and so he probably flourished in the 13th century. He might be a *Keralīya*. His only work so far known is the *Nītitattvāvirbhāva,*[166] which has been commented on by a host of writers of whom the earliest might be the celebrated commentator, ṛṣiputra Parameśvara II. The very fact that Parameśvara II who has commented on the standard works of two earlier eminent authors—Maṇḍanamiśra and Vācaspatimiśra—has commented on Cidānanda's bespeaks the greatness of both Cidānanda and his Nītitattvāvirbhāva. As he says at the beginning of his work—

'Acāryakṛtiprakṛteḥ āvirbhāvāya nītitattvānām |
Ayamiha yatnaḥ kriyate santaḥ puṣyantu santoṣam || '

he has completely based his composition on Ācārya Kumārla's *Ślokavārttika*. His work can be well said to be a *unique* production in that it contains on the whole 44 *vādas*,[167] topics for discussion. Although these have been already elucidated in the *Ślokavārttika*, this work throws much clearer light on those obscure and difficult doctrines.

Gaṅgādharamiśra (*c.* A.D. 1230-1300)

To the middle of the 13th century belonged Mahāmahopādhyāya Gaṅgādharamiśra. As the introductory verse in his commentary on the *Tantravārttika* shows, he belonged to the *Śālmaligrāma* and was the son of Bhaṭṭa Someśvara of the same grāma :

> c.f. *'Śālmalīgrāmsambhūta-*
> *Bhaṭṭasomeśvarātmajaḥ* |
> *Gaṅgādharostigambhīraṁ*
> *vyavṛṇot tantravārttikam'* ||

The name of the commentary is *Nyāyapārāyaṇa*[168], otherwise known as the *Tantravarttikavivaraṇa.*

Vedānta Deśika (*c.* A.D. 1269-1369)

Between the latter half of the 13th century and the former half of the 14th century flourished *Vedānta Deśika*[169] *alias* Veṅkaṭanātha, the great apostle of Viśiṣṭādvaita philosophy after Rāmānujācārya. He is the author of more than 120 works in the System of Viśiṣṭādvaita philosophy and in the epic, devotional and other branches of literature and won the title *'Kavitārkika-siṁha'.* He has produced two works—the *Mīmāṁsāpādukā* in verse on the *Tarkapāda* and the *Seśvara Mīmāṁsā* in prose on the rest of the *Pūrva*mīmāṁsāśāstra.[170] A critic of very violent temper, he has elucidated in these works the *siddhāntas* of the Bhāṭṭas and the Prābhākaras in many *adhikaraṇas*, now and then criticising both. Naturally, therefore, his explanations of the *sūtras* are not in many instances acceptable to an orthodox student of Mīmāṁsā, in view of the fact that they are deviations from the *siddhāntas* of the two great Ācāryas of the Mīmāṁsā Śāstra. His aim seems to be not to explain the *siddhāntas* of the Mīmāṁsā Śāstra but to attempt a *synthesis* as far as possible, of the doctrines of the two systems of Mīmāṁsā, *Pūrva* and Uttara. His work is rich in references to many Ācāryas and works, such as Vṛttikāra Upavarṣa, Bodhāyana, Śabarasvāmin, Kumārila, Prabhākara, Dramiḍācārya, Yāmunācārya, Śrī Rāmānuja, Bhavanāthabhaṭṭa, the *Kāsikā,* the *Dīpa* and the *Tattvaratnākara.*

His Personality and Date

Born at Ṭūppil, a village near Conjeevaram in 1269 A.D., Deśika was the son of Anantasūri Somayājin, an orthodox Vaiṣṇavite and a descendant of one of the seventy four *siṁhāsanādhipatis*. His mother was Toṭārāmbā, the sister of Ātreya Rāmānuja, otherwise known as Rāmānuja Appuḷḷār, the successor of Varadācārya as the *Ubhayasiṁha-āsanādhipati*. Tradition says that his parents had no children for years, and while they were at Tirupati on a pilgrimage, they saw God Veṅkaṭeśara in a dream and got a bell of the temple from Him to be swallowed by Toṭārāmbā, which resulted in the birth of an illustrious son to them. This story attributes some divine origin to *Vedānta Deśika*. As Prof. V. Rangachari, M.A., has observed,[171] "he (*Vedānta Deśika*) was throughout his life a man of great penance and prayer and an extraordinarily precocious genius. He was a Hindu in his crusades against the Mahomedan, a Vaiṣṇava as against Śaivite (or Advaitin) and a Sanskrit-Tamilist as against practically exclusive Tamilist in the holy studies....... More than 120 works, he has left; most of these are now extant, and prove how thorough his teachings were, how fertile his intellect was and how exalted his views of life and conduct were. Humble and modest in his deportment, profoundly learned, saintly in his habits, he was the embodiment of all that was good and great, of the divinity in man and man's devotion to the divinity." His great contempt for riches or temporal supremacy is evident in his blunt refusal of Vidyāraṇya's many invitations to the Court of the then King of Vijayanagar including an invitation to a discussion with the chief Madhva scholar—Akṣobhyamuni, though he complied with Vidyāraṇya's latter request by sending him his judgment in writing in very ambiguous language. As a staunch Vaiṣṇava propagandist, he has considered it even sinful to speak the advaita view of identifying man—individual soul—with God—the Supreme soul. In most of his writings he has expressed his faith that the relation between God and man is that between a master and a servant and thus he has inculcated his religious fervour and devotion to god and prayers to Him by man, besides imparting his religious fervour to his readers.

Mādhavācārya (*c.* A.D. 1297-1386)

After *Vedānta Deśika* comes his younger contemporary Mādhavācārya. His time has been fixed by scholars to be A.D. 1297-1386, and this is in agreement with the tradition that he lived for 90 years. From his own works, like the *Parāsaramādhavīya* and from an inscription of the Aruḷāla-perumāl temple at Conjeevaram,[172] it is known that Mādhava was a brahmin of *Bhāradvājagotra,* of Bodhāyana *sūtra* and a student of Yajuśśākhā, that Māyaṇa was his father and Śrīmatī, his mother and that he had two brothers —Sayaṇa and Bhoganātha.

c.f.—

śrīmati jananī yasya sukīrtiḥ māyaṇaḥ pitā |
Sāyaṇo bhoganāthaśca manobuddhisahodarau | |

Yasya Bhaudhāyanam sūtraṁ
śākhā yasya ca Yājuṣī |
Bhāradvājakulaṁ yasya
sarvajñaḥ sa hi mādhavaḥ | |

It is also known that he had a sister Siṅgale whose son Lakṣmaṇa or Lakṣmīdhara was a minister of the Vijayanagar king, Devarāja I.[173] Mādhavācārya is said to have had three *gurus*—Vidyātīrtha, Bhāratītīrtha and Śrīkaṇṭha of whom Vidyātīrtha was considered by Mādhava (and Sāyaṇa) as an incarnation of Maheśvara. Inscriptional evidences also show that Vidyātīrtha *alias* Vidyāśaṅkara was highly esteemed both as the temporal and spiritual guide not only of Mādhava but also of Bukka I, the famous king of Vijayanagar, whom Mādhava eulogises in his *Nyāyamālāvistara* and other works.[174]

Mādhava-Vidyāraṇya Identity

It is still a matter of controversy[174] whether Mādhavācārya is identical with Vidyāraṇya. Tradition holds that Mādhavācārya in his fourth *āśrama* is known as Vidyāraṇya. MM. R.

Narasimhachariar in his paper on '*Mādhavācārya and his Two Brothers*' maintains the traditional view with the support of the inscriptional and literary evidences. From the introductory verses of his *Nyāyamālāvistara*,[176] Mādhavācārya *(alias* Vidyāraṇya) is also known as a minister of Bukkaṇa or Bukka I.

Mādhavamantrin different from Mādhavācārya

There is another Mādhava otherwise known as Mādhavamantrin. He belonged to Āṅgīrasagotra. He was the son of Cauṇḍa or Cauṇḍi-bhaṭṭa by Māchāmbikā and was a disciple of the Śaiva teacher Kāśivilāsa Kriyāśakti and a governor of Banavase under Bukka I and Harihara II. As this Mādhavamantrin belonged to a different gotra and was of a different parentage he is distinguished from Vidyāraṇya Mādhava.[177] This Mādhavamantrin was a great warrior, '*bhuvanaikavīra*' and is surnamed '*Upaniṣaṇmārgapratiṣṭhāguru*'. He is known also as the author of many works like the commentary on the *Sūtasaṁhitā*.

Mādhavācārya's Works

Mādhavācārya *(alias* Vidyāraṇya) is credited with the authorship of many works in Sanskrit literature. He has written the *Nyāyamālāvistara,*[178] a commentary on the Dvādaśalakṣaṇī of the *Pūrva Mīmāṁsā Sūtras*. The style of this work is very simple and flowing and as such forms an easy text-book for a beginner in Mīmāṁsā. As a rule, he first gives the *Saṁśaya* in a particular vedic passage, then the main *pūrvapakṣa* and last the *siddhānta* of each *adhikaraṇa* in one, two or more verses; and in most *adhikaraṇas*, he supplements these verses with explanation in easy prose. He says in one of thc introductory verses that in view of the fact that Pārthasārathimiśra's *Śāstradīpikā* has not in all *adhikaraṇas* given the *pūrvapakṣa* and *siddhānta* views in verse, he proposes to do that uniformly in the *Nyāyamālāvistara*. In this work, he has further given in the important *adhikaraṇas*, the interpretations of Guru *alias* Prabhākara. For this reason the work occupies a unique place.

Among his other works, the *Parāśaramādhavīya,* a standard commentary on the *Parāśara Smṛti*, is treated even as a *nibandhana* work. In the introductory portion of this work the author justifies his attempt to write a commentary on the *Parāśara Smṛti* because that smṛti is a better and more reliable authority on dharma in this Kaliyuga. *cf. 'Kalau pārāśarāḥ smṛtāḥ'*; and he pleads for the adoption of *Kṛṣi*—agriculture, *Vāṇijyā*—trade, etc. as the *āpaddharma* for brahmins in this Kaliyuga, though such professions are condemned in other smṛtis. Similarly, he explains in this work the *sāpiṇḍya* in such a way as would permit one to marry one's maternal uncle's daughter as *asapiṇḍā*. The *Vyavahāra-Mādhava* is another work of his, supplementing the *Parāśaramādhavīya.*

His works on Advaita philosophy are :—the *Vaiyāśikanyāyamālā,* a commentary in verse on the four chapters of the Uttaramīmāṁsā Śāstra, with easy explanatory prose; the *Pañcadaśī* in verse dealing with all important topics of Advaita Philosophy, both of which he has composed along with his teacher Bhāratītīrtha; the *Vivaraṇaprameyasaṅgraha* which, as the title goes, is a succinct summary of the *Pañcapādikāvivaraṇa*; and his *Anubhūtiprakāśa* which expounds the Advaita tenets in a very forcible manner. His *Jīvanmuktiviveka* is another great work belonging to the Uttaramīmāṁsā Śāstra.

His *Kālanirṇaya* is a work on Hindu astrology. His unhistorical but yet a very popular literary Kāvya, the *Śaṅkaradigvijaya,* written in a very lucid style describes the life and career of Śrī Śaṅkara; the descriptions of Maṇḍanamiśra's house and of the hot discussions of Maṇḍanamiśra and Śaṅkarācārya on many a topic which finally ended in the former's defeat are, indeed, highly picturesque and poetic.

Mādhavācārya is also held to be the author of the *Sarvadarśanasaṅgraha.* But MM. R. Narasimhacariar in his paper on 'Mādhava and his brothers' has tried to prove on the basis of internal and other evidences that Mādhava (the author of the *Sarvadarśanasaṅgraha*) who has called himself *Sāyaṇamādhava,* was the son of Sāyaṇācārya, the brother of Vidyāraṇya Mādhava. Moreover, he has not dealt with the *Śāṅkaradarśana,* and he says at the end of the Pātañjaladarśana—'*itaḥ paraṁ sarva-darśanaśiromaṇibhūtam, Śāṅkaradarśanam anyatra nirūpita-miti atropekṣitam.*'—that he does not deal with the most important system of Śaṅkara, since it is already dealt with *elsewhere';* and at the end of the *Śāṅkaradarśana* (now available in the printed work) a colophon '*iti Śrī Sāyaṇācāryaviracite sakala-darśanaśirolaṅkāraratnam Śrīmacchāṅkaradarśanaṁ samāptam*' attributes its authorship to Sāyaṇācārya. These facts make clear that Sāyaṇa's *thesis* on the Śāṅkaradarśana was appended to the body of the *Sarvadarśanasaṅgraha* by his son, Mādhava. The references to some verses of Veṅkaṭanātha's *Tattvamuktā-kalāpa* in the *Sarvadarśanasaṅgraha* would be more justifiable if one thinks that the author of the *Sarvadarśanasaṅgraha* is the son of Sāyaṇācārya and not Vidyāraṇya Mādhavācārya on the ground that usually authors quote their predecessors removed from them by one or two generations rather than their contemporaries.

Bhaṭṭa Viṣṇu (*c.* A.D. 1400)

To the close of the fourteenth century might have belonged Bhaṭṭa Viṣṇu, the celebrated author of the *Nayatattvasaṅgraha.* The earliest reference to this work is found in the Nītitattvā-virbhāvavyākhyā of Parameśvara II; so Bhaṭṭa Viṣṇu is earlier than Parameśvara II. In an introductory verse[179] of the former he has referred to Bhavanātha, the author of the Naya-viveka; so he is later than Bhavanātha. Parameśvara's reference[180] to the Nayatattvasaṅgraha in his commentary on Cidānanda's work makes us even suppose that Bhaṭṭaviṣṇu might be subsequent to Cidānanda.

His work, *Nayatattvasaṅgraha*[181], contains a succinct and lucid account of the important tenets of the *Tarkapāda,* according to the Prābhākara school and so, though brief, it resembles Cidānanda's work. It is a commentary on the *Sūtras* of the *Tarkapāda* as well as an independent treatise discussing important topics like *pratyakṣapramāṇa, pratyayanirālambanatva*, (as held by Buddhists) anumāna, *arthāpatti*, *abhāva*, Īśvara, śabdanityatva, the karaṇa of vākyārthajñāna, prapañcamithyātva, etc. It ends with the vedaprāmāṇyā-dhikaraṇa—the last adhi-karaṇa of the *Tarkapāda* (I-1.8).

Anantanārāyaṇa (*c.* A.D. 1400)

To this period also might have belonged Anantanārāyaṇa or Nārāyaṇa who has written the *Vijaya,*[182] a commentary on the Ajitā of Paritoṣamiśra, already referred to as one of the earliest commentaries on the *Tantravārttika*. He was well known as the *Ajitācārya*. From the introductory verse and colophon,[183] it is known that this work is not only a commentary on the Ajitā but also a *nibandhana* work which is intended for the learned. His father's name is *Sūryaviṣṇumiśra.*[184] His full name is Anantanārāyaṇārya or Anantanārāyaṇamiśra after his father's surname '*Miśra*'.

The earliest reference to this work is found in the *Sūtrārthasaṅgraha* of Parameśvara III, where the vijayakāra is eulogised as one of the great authors on the Mīmāṁsāśāstra. *cf.*—

> "*Jaimini-Śabara - Kumārila -*
> *Sucarita-Paritoṣa - Pārthasārathayaḥ* |
> *Umveka- Vijayakārau*
> *Maṇḍana-Vācaspati ca vijayantām* | | "

Ravideva (*c.* A.D. 1400)

Ravideva, or Ravi is a commentator on the *Nayaviveka*. Nothing about his personality and date is so far known. His commentary known as the *Vivekatattva* (which also deals with the *Tarkapāda*)[185] is quoted at length by Parameśvara II in his *Tattvavibhāvanā.*[186] So, he may be placed between the 14th and the 15th centuries. His commentary is helpful in clearing up the obscurities of Bhavadeva's style which is characterised by careless syntax.

The three Parameśvaras of Kerala *(c.* A.D. 1300-1550)

Probably between A.D. 1300 and 1550 just before Śrī Appayya Dīkṣita, the great literary luminary of South India in the 16th century, flourished the three famous Parameśvaras and one Vāsudeva of the Payoor Bhaṭṭatiri family in the Porkulam village of Kunnankulam near Guruvayur in the Cochin State. In the Payyur family of Bhaṭṭatiris (Malabar brahmins) flourished one Ṛṣi (Ṛṣi I)—who had a son Parameśvara (Parameśvara I) by his wife Gaurī. This Parameśvara has written two commentaries on the Nyāyakaṇikā of Vācaspatimiśra—the *Juṣadhvaṅkaraṇī* and the *Svaditaṅkaraṇī*[187]—the former being his first production. He had two paternal uncles, Bhavadāsa and Śaṅkarapūjyapāda, the latter being his *guru.* He had five sons—Ṛṣi II, Bhavadāsa, Vāsudeva, Subrahmaṇya and Śaṅkara. Ṛṣi II had a son Parameśvara II by his wife Gopālikā. Parameśvara II is the reputed author of the commentaries on the Nītitattvāvirbhāva, the Tattvabindu, the Vibhramaviveka and the Sphoṭasiddhi. He says[188] in his Nītitattvāvirbhāvavyākhyā, that he was the disciple of his uncle, Bhavadāsa, and that his uncle, Subrahmaṇya, helped him to write the commentary on the section, Kāryavāda[189] (in the Nītitattvāvirbhāva) and that he commented on the Svataḥ-pramāṇavāda as his uncle, Vāsudeva, explained it to him.[190] From these statements it is clear that these three uncles of Parameśvara II were great scholars. It may be surmised that they were authors of some works on the *Pūrva-mīmāṁsā-śāstra.* It can also be conjectured from Parameśvara's references that Bhavadāsa and Vāsudeva were more well-versed in the Bhāṭṭa school, while Subrahmaṇya was in the Prābhākara school. And it is doubtful whether this Vāsudeva, son of Parameśvara I, is the author of the *Kumārilayuktimālā,*[191] since in a colophon of that work, he calls himself a son of Maharṣi and Gopālikā. Most probably, therefore, Vāsudeva, the author of the *Kumārilayuktimālā*, might be a brother of Parameśvara II, whose father was ṛṣi and mother, Gopālikā.

Parameśvara II, as has just been observed, is the son of ṛṣi II by Gopālikā, the grandson of Parameśvara I (the commentator on Vācaspatimiśra's *Nyāyakaṇikā*) and the reputed commentator on Maṇḍanamiśra's *Sphoṭasiddhi* and *Vibhramaviveka*, and on Vācaspatimiśra's *Tattvabindu* and on Cidānanda's *Nītitattvāvirbhāva*. To the credit of this author it must be said that all his commentaries are not only supplementary to the text but are helpful in understanding the difficult language of Maṇḍanamiśra and Vācaspatimiśra. Just like a good and reliable commentator on a Kāvya, our author, in many instances, dissolves the compounds and explains the misleading parts of the text, which would not be otherwise clear. In the commentary, *Tattvavibhāvanā*, on the *Tattvabindu*, he gives mostly at the end of each section a succinct summary of the discussions in verse which is of immense use for readers.

Of his four commentaries, the one on the *Vibhramaviveka* is the earliest, since it is mentioned by him in the other three commentaries.[192] Next comes the *Tattvavibhāvanā*—the commentary on the *Tattvabindu*,[193] which is found mentioned in the *Nītitattvāvirbhāvavyākhyā* and the *Sphoṭasiddhiv-yākhyā*;[194] the third is the *Nītitattvāvirbhāvavyākhyā*[195] and the last is the Sphoṭasiddhivyākhyā, otherwise known as the Gopālikā, after the name of the Goddess Gopālikā in the temple of Vedāraṇya.

The *Tattvavibhāvanā* refers to the *Nyāyasamuccaya*[196] which has not been traced out.

Parameśvara II had a son named Ṛṣi III who had in his turn a son called *Parameśvara* III. Parameśvara III is the reputed author of the *Mīmāṁsāsūtrārthasaṅgraha*[197] and of a commentary on the Kāśikā of Sucaritamiśra. The *Sūtrārtha-saṅgraha* is a commentary on the *Sūtras* following the lines of the *Śābarabhāṣya*. Its *Tarkapāda* is explanatory of the contents of the Bhāṣya according to Kumārilabhaṭṭa's *Ślokavārttika* and as such, is a guide to the Bhāṣyagrantha. It begins with a eulogy of the important Ācāryas of the P.M. Śāstra[198]—Jaimini, Śabarasvāmin, Kumārilabhaṭṭa, Maṇḍanamiśra, Vācaspatimiśra, Sucaritamiśra, Paritoṣamiśra, Pārthasārathimiśra, Umvekabhaṭṭa and Vijayakāra (Ananta-nārāyaṇa). He also pays a tribute to his teacher Vāsudeva,[199] probably his own paternal uncle. He refers to his grandfather Parameśvara II as having written commentaries on four Mīmāṁsā works (already mentioned) and states that he was considered an authority on the Bhāṭṭa school of the P.M. System, though he was equally well-versed in all the six Āstikadarśanas.

The dates of these Parameśvaras (and Ṛṣis) may cover nearly a period of about 250 years between A.D. 1300-1550. Parameśvara II has referred to the work of Bhaṭṭaviṣṇu but not to any work of Appayya Dīkṣita; so we may conclude that he must have lived between Bhaṭṭa Viṣṇu and Appayya Dīkṣita. Uddaṇḍakavi[200] in his *Kokilasandeśa* has highly spoken of one Ṛṣi and his family in the Porkalam village. In his *Mallikā-māruta* he says that he has received the approbation of a Parameśvara, son of Ṛṣi, the '*Mīmāṁsā-Cakravartin.*; Uddaṇḍa is described as a contemporary of Nārāyaṇa, the author of the *Tantra-samuccaya,* which was completed in the Kollam year 602 or A.D. 1426. He is again said to be a contemporary of one Bālakavi who flourished at the court of the King Rāma Varma of Cochin and composed the dramas of *Ratna-ketūdaya* and *Rāmavarmavilāsa.*[201] So, the period of the Parameśvaras may fall between A.D. 1300 and 1550.

Varadarāja (*c.* A.D. 1500-1570)

Just before Appayya Dīkṣita we may consider Varadarāja, the famous commentator on the *Nayaviveka* of Bhavanāthabhaṭṭa. The earliest reference to him is made by Somanātha Dīkṣita,[202] the commentator on the *Śāstradīpikā* (who is to be assigned to the beginning of the 17th century). His commentary begins with the second *pāda* of the first *adhyāya.* In the introductory verses and colophons[203] he pays his respects to his *guru, Sudarśana,* and to his parents; then refers to Sātrakāra Jaimini, the Bhāṣyakāra, Prabhākara (the famous Ṭīkākāra), Bhava-nātha and the Nibandhanakāras like Candra. Then he gives his genealogy and the place of his birth. On the bank of the *Śukāpagā* in the family of *Kiḍāmbi* was born one

Praṇatārtihara belonging to the *Ātreya* gotra; his son was *Devarāja* whose son was the erudite *Raṅganāthādhvarin*; and the latter's son was *Varadarāja*.

Varadarāja's *Dīpikā*[204] is a very lucid commentary on the *Nayaviveka*, which is very obscure in exposition. It is very helpful for tracing out the views of both Śrīkara and Prakāśa, the two authors in the Prābhākara school before Bhavanāthabhaṭṭa. This Varadarāja should not be identified with Varadarāja, the author of the *Tārkikarakṣā* and of a commentary on Udayana's *Kusumāñjali*. The latter has not however given his genealogy and the place of his birth, though he calls himself in his Tārkikarakṣā a great Mīmāṁsaka—'*Mīmāṁsāpāradṛśvā*. 'In view of the fact that the Tārkikarakṣā is quoted by the author of the *Sarvadarśanasaṅgraha,*[205] and by Parameśvara II in his *Gropālikā*[206] and has been commented on by Mallinātha (the famous commentator on the five Mahākāvyas), Varadarāja (the author of the Tārkikarakṣā) must be assigned to about A.D. 1100,[207] much earlier than the date of the author of the *Nayavivekadīpikā*.

Appayya Dikṣita (*c.* A.D. 1520-1593)

To the 16th century belonged the great literary genius Appayya Dīkṣita who is known to have written works on the Mīmāṁsā Śāstra—the *Vidhirasāyana* in verse with explanations in prose; the *Upakramaparākrama*; the *Vādanakṣatramālā*; the *Mayūkhāvalī*; and the *Citrapaṭa*. His contributions to the system of Mīmāṁsā philosophy as embodied in these works are not so great and important as in the Advaita and Śaiva works. In his *Kalpataru-parimala* and *Nyāyarakṣamaṇi* and in his *Śivārkamaṇidīpikā* and *Śivādvaitanirṇaya* and in such other works, he has in a most inimitable and unassailable manner explained and systematised many important mīmāṁsā rules of interpretation as understood and elucidated by the Bhāṭṭas. In some of his dialectical dissertations he has revealed certain truths which no author on the Mīmāṁsā Śāstra, probably except Kumārila, has so assiduously cared to investigate. For example, in the

Vedhādhikaraṇa[208] of the Uttaramīmāṁsā system, he has taken up the question for discussion—how *prakaraṇāntara* is a *pramāṇa* of the *karmabheda* in the Vedic proposition—'*māsamagnihotram juhoti*'. All Mīmāṁsakas have accepted that this proposition under the prakaraṇa of the Satra sacrifice known as *Kauṇḍapāyināmayana,* enjoins a new sacrifice called *agnihotra* which is accepted as different from the *nityāgnihotra* on the basis of the *prakaraṇāntara* which consists in the existence of an (1) *anupādeyaguṇa,* viz., *kāla* in the proposition referred to and (2) the *anupasthiti*—non-recognition (by want of means) of the sacrifice enjoined by the proposition in question, as its namesake—the '*naiyamikāgnihotra.*' But our author argues that the *prakaraṇāntara* suggests only the *prayogabheda* and *not the karmabheda.* This is a bitter pill for all Mīmāṁsakas to swallow. So as a Mīmāṁsaka, he is on his best in his Advaita and other works.

Appayya Dīkṣita[209] hailed from the village Adaiyapālam near the historic city of Conjeeveram, once a great centre of learning under the Pallavas. His paternal grandfather is known as Ācārya Dīkṣita of *Bhāradvāja gotra* who performed many Vedic sacrifices. He was much patronised by the famous king of Vijayanagar, *Kṛṣṇadevarāya.* When the king, during his visit to Conjeeveram, worshipped God Varadarāja in company with his wife and retinues, Ācārya Dīkṣita composed the verse—

"*Kāñcit kāñcanagaurāṅgīm*
vīkṣya sākṣādiva śriyam |
Varadaḥ saṁśayāpannaḥ
vakṣasthalamavaikṣata || "

"Beholding a woman glittering like gold and looking like Lakṣmī, Varada fell into a doubt and looked at His bosom (to see if Laksmī were there)". The God mistook the Queen for Lakṣmī, suspected that His consort had quitted her permanent place in His bosom and looked at His bosom to ascertain whether she was there. The King was very much pleased with Ācārya Dīkṣita's poetic description which is both original and suggestive of his (the king's) greatness and consequently honoured him with the title '*Vakṣasthalācārya Dīkṣita*'. Nīlakaṇṭha Dīkṣita in his drama—Nalacarita—has referred to Ācārya Dīkṣita as Āccān Dīkṣita, (*Āccān* in Tamil meaning *Ācārya)* who was much honoured by Kṛṣṇadevarāya. Ācārya Dīkṣita had two wives—the first belonging to an orthodox Śaiva family and the second, to an orthodox Vaiṣṇava family of repute known as *Śrī Vaikuṇṭhācāryavaṁśa*. In the days of Ācārya Dīkṣ ita, more than three centuries ago, inter-marriages between orthodox *smārtas* and *vaiṣṇavas* were not unknown in South India. He had by his second wife Toṭarāmbā four sons of whom the eldest was Appayya Dīkṣita's father, Raṅgarājādhvarin who, like his father, performed many vedic sacrifices. He is known to have written many works on Advaita Vedānta—the *Advaita Vidyāmukura,* the *Vivaraṇadarpaṇa,* etc. He had two sons, the elder being Appayya Dīkṣita, the younger Āccān Dīkṣita, the paternal grandfather of Nīlakaṇṭha Dīkṣita. Appādīkṣita was the original name of our author and the honorific 'ayya' was afterwards added to it in recognition of his greatness as a literary prodigy.

As regards his date, some controversy has recently arisen. On the basis of Śivānandayatīndra's *Dīkṣitavaṁśāvali* and of Nīlakaṇṭha Dīkṣita's works, Mr. A.V. Gopalachariar[210] has assigned him to the period A.D. 1552-1626. This date has been accepted by most writers on Appayya Dīkṣita. But Mr. Y. Mahaliṅga Śāstri, in his two papers on 'the Age of Appayya Dīkṣita'[211] has recently endeavoured to overthrow it and place him between A.D. 1520 and 1593, on *literary* and *epigraphical* evidences. Like his grandfather Ācārya Dīkṣita, Appayya Dīkṣita is also known to have come into contact with the Vijayanagar kings. In the beginning of his commentary on *Vedānta Deśika*'s Yādavābhyudaya, he has referred to three kings[212]—Rāmarāya, Timmarāja and Cinna Timma. Rāmarāya had a son, called Timmarāya, who had many sons of whom the most chivalrous and celebrated was Cinna Timma. His adventurous military exploits in the Cola, Kerala and Pāṇḍya Kingdoms and on the

Coromandel coast, are graphically described by Appayya Dīkṣita in his commentary on the Yādavābhyudaya. This Cinna Timma was a General and the Viceroy of the South from A.D. 1542-1550; and probably by A.D. 1550 Appayya Dīkṣita had been instructed by him to write this commentary. So *Cinna Timma* must be considered as his *first patron* among the Vijayanagar kings; and to write a very learned commentary on the Yādavābhyudaya, he, it is contended, must have been at least 25 or 30 years old, though he is known to have acquired proficiency in all branches of knowledge by his twentieth year.

Appayya Dīkṣita's *next patron* was *Cinna Bomma Nāyaka* of Vellore who is well-known in inscriptions dating from A.D. 1549 to 1578. The Aḍaiyapālam inscription dated in A.D. 1582 has referred to him in the past tense; so he must have breathed his last before 1582. Appayya Dīkṣita's chief literary activities especially in the renaissance of Śaivaism must have been well encouraged by Cinna Bomma, as he himself has expressly stated in his great Śaiva work—the *Śivārkamaṇidīpikā,*[213] the great commentary on Śrīkaṇṭhācārya's Bhāṣya on the Vedāntasūtras. On the completion of this work, the king, himself a great Śaivite, bathed Appayya Dīkṣita in gold. Nīlakaṇṭha Dīkṣita says in the prologue to his Nalacarita[214] that this event has been described by Samarapuṅgava Dīkṣita in his *Yātrāprabandha* —*'śivārkamaṇidīpikāvasānalabdha-kanakasnānaḥ praśaṁsitaḥ samarapuṅgavayajvanā yathā—*

'Hemābhiṣekasamaye parito niṣaṇṇa-
sauvarṇasaṁhatimiṣāt cina bommabhūpaḥ |
Appayyadikṣitamaṇeranavadyavidyā-
kalpadrumasya kurute kanakālavālam | |'

The Aḍaiyapālam inscription of A.D. 1582 says '*Yena Śrī Cinna Bomma kṣitipabalabhidaḥ Kīrtiravyāhatāsīt.*'

Most probably the bathing in gold might have been performed in A.D. 1582 and Appayya Dīkṣita, a staunch Śaivite, built a Śiva temple—the temple of *Kālakaṇṭheśvara*— with that gold in his birth-place.

His *third patron* is *Veṅkaṭadevarāja* or *Veṅkaṭa I,* who came to the throne in about A.D. 1585.[215] Appayya Dīkṣita wrote his *Kuvalayānanda*[216] and the *Vidhirasāyana*[217] (with its commentary) under the royal command and patronage of Veṅkaṭapati, who was described by him as 'an embodiment of boundless sympathy and charity'. This king had a Vaiṣṇavite *guru* Tātācārya[218] under whose influence he became a staunch Vaiṣṇavite; yet Appayya Dīkṣita was an influential *protégé* of his court and he defeated Tātācārya in religious and Śāstraic discussions.

It is also presumed that Appayya Dīkṣita had two more patrons in his earlier days—Narasiṁha and Candraśekhara. This Narasiṁha otherwise called Vīranarasiṁha, or Cellappa or Salva Nāyaka, is identified with Vīranarasiṁha who was raised by Kṛṣṇadevarāya to governorship in the Coḷa country. He was a powerful ruler and a thorough administrator, and so he revolted against Acyutarāya, the successor of Kṛṣṇadevarāya, who defeated Narasiṁha and kept him in prison in A.D. 1535. It is not exactly known whether he was afterwards brought back to the position which he had enjoyed under Kṛṣṇadevarāya. It is believed that he lived till A.D. 1545; and it is said that during this period he visited Cidambaram on the last day (*avabhṛtha*) of the *yāga* performed there by Appayya Dīkṣita, on hearing the miracle that the *paśus* had visibly ascended to heaven.

Candraśekhara was a Pāṇḍya king at Madura during the time of Acyutadevarāya of Vijayanagar. When he was attacked by Vīraśekhara Coḷa of Tanjore, he got help from Acyutarāya. Nāgama Nāyaka, Acyutarāya's nominee, subdued the Coḷa king in a battle and the Pāṇḍya King was restored to his old position. In A.D. 1542 or so, the Pāṇḍya King died without an heir to the throne. The dying king willingly nominated Viśvanātha Naik, son of Nāgama Naik, as his successor. But till A.D. 1558 Viśvanātha was only a nominal ruler of Madura, since Viṭṭhal and Cinna Timma were powerful Viceroys in the South.

From Śivānandayatīndra's Biography of Appayya Dīkṣita and his family it is known that Candraśekhara Pāṇḍya, on hearing the rising reputation of Appayya Dīkṣita as a great scholar, asked his Court-pandits to meet him in disputation; that Ratnakheṭa Śrīnivāsa Dīkṣita, one of the *protégés* of that court, accepted the challenge but eventually found no other means of making Appayya Dīkṣita bow to him than by offering himself as his father-in-law. It is thus believed that Appayya Dīkṣita, probably in his 20th year or earlier even, married Maṅgalanāyakī, Ratnakheṭa Śrīnivāsa Dīkṣita's daughter.

That Appayya Dīkṣita was a contemporary of Tātācārya and Vijayīndratīrtha and that all these three used to go to the Court of Sevappa at Tanjore[219] for discussion in the three systems of Vedānta—the Śaivādvaita, Viśiṣṭādvaita and Dvaita, are well borne out by the two inscriptions of Sevappa of A.D. 1580.

Thus, from the foregoing account, it is clear that Appayya Dīkṣita lived in the 16th century between A.D. 1520-1592, thus living for 72 years. It is also known that he spent many years of his youth in northern India, probably at Benares, and reached Chidambaram for worshipping God Naṭarāja in his last days. His last prayer to Lord Naṭarāja is thus known to posterity.

"*Cidambaramidam puram*
prathitameva puṇyasthalam
Sutāśca vinayojjvalāḥ
sukṛtayśca kāścit kṛtāḥ |
Vayāṁsi mama saptate-
rupari naiva bhoge spṛhā
Na kiñcidahamarthaye
śivapadam didṛkṣe param ||
Ābhāti haṭakasabhānatapādapadma-
Jyotirmayo manasi me taruṇāruṇoyam |"

So saying he expired embracing and kissing the lotus-feet of his Lord—God Naṭarāja.

Like Śrī Śaṅkarācārya, Appayya Dīkṣita is credited with the authorship of 108 works in Sanskrit covering many fields of literature. Five[220] works of his in the field of the Mīmāṁsā are so far known to us. The *Vidhirasāyana*[221] is a dissertation on the nature and scope of the three-fold vidhis—injunctions in Vedic texts—giving suitable definitions of each of them without any overlapping. Though his exposition is highly scholarly, he has overdone it, so that his definitions of the three vidhis are not generally accepted by his younger contemporary, Khaṇḍadevamiśra,[222] though the latter paid his respects to him by calling him '*Mīmāṁsakamūrdhanya*'. His *Upakramaparākrama*[223] as the title indicates, contains an elaborate and lucid exposition of the *Upakramanyāya* in the interpretation of propositions. His *Vādanakṣatramalā*[224] contains independent expositions of the *prima facie* and *siddhānta* views on some important *adhikaraṇas* in the *Pūrva* and Uttara Mīmāṁsā Sāstras. It is useful for an advanced student of Mīmāṁsā for giving a *vākyārtha* discourse in the *navyanyāya* terminology. His *Mayūkhāvalī*[225] is a running commentary on the *Śāstradīpikā*. It is, however, presumed that one descendant of Appayya Dīkṣita of the same name might have written this work; but this is also found included in the list of 108 works of Appayya Dīkṣ ita. His *Citrapaṭa*[226] is a summary in verse of the contents of the Adhikaraṇas of the 12 Adhyāyas of the *Pūrva* Mīmāṁsā Śāstra, like Maṇḍanamiśra's Mīmāṁsāśāstrānukramaṇī. It is called by its commentator '*Laghuvārttika*' as its commentary is known as *Laghunyāyasudhā*.

Vijayīndrabhikṣu (*c.* A.D. 1539-1597)

Viṭṭhalācārya, in his fourth *āśrama* known as Vijayīndrabhikṣu or Tīrtha, is a contemporary of Appayya Dīkṣita. He frequented the Court of Sevappa,[227] then the king of Tanjore and held Śāstraic discussions along with Appayya Dīkṣita and Tātācārya. Under the instructions of Sevappa in 1574 Raṅgarāya II of Vijayanagar granted[228] in (Śaka 1499) A.D. 767 the village of Ariviḷimaṅgalam *alias* Acyutappa-samudra (in Tanjore district) to our author. He is known as the author of 104 works, most of which contain learned disquisitions on various difficult topics in philosophy. His *Paratattvaprakāśikā* contains a refutation of the *Śivatattvaviveka* of Appayya Dīkṣita. His *Madhvamatakaṇṭakoddhāra* is another work which answers the refutations of the views set forth against the dualistic philosophy. That he is also a good poet is well attested by his *Subhadrādhanañjaya*.

His Mīmāṁsā works, so far known, are three—(1) the *Nyāyādhvadīpikā,* (2) *Mīmāṁsā-nayakaumudi,* both being running commentaries on the *Sātras*, and as the author claims, the first of these is an easier work than the Śāstradipikā for the beginners of Mīmāṁsā. His third work in Mīmāṁsā is *Upasaṁhāravijaya,*[229] which is an attempt to establish the *upasaṁhāra-prābalya* and as such, is a refutation of Appayya Dīkṣita's *Upakramaparākrama.* In his Nyāyādhvadīpikā he refers and pays his respects to Pūrṇabodha (Ānandatīrtha), Jayayogīndra, Vyāsadeśika (the disciple of Brahmaṇyaguru) and Surendra-tīrtha, the last being Vijayīndra's teacher. Even Vyāsadeśika, otherwise known as Vyāsarāya, was his spiritual teacher.[230] He is known to posterity by various honorific titles—*Sarvatantra-svatantra, catuṣṣastikalāvallabha,* etc.

Veṅkateśvara Dikṣita (c. A.D. 1600)

After Appayya Dikṣita comes Veṅkateśvara Dīkṣita. He was the son of Govinda Dīkṣita, the last of the series of the great Pandit-ministers beginning with Kauṭilya. Govinda Dīkṣita[231] was a *Karṇāṭaka* brahmin of *Bodhāyana gotra* and flourished in the 16th century as a contemporary of Appayya Dīkṣita. He was the minister of the three Nāyaka kings of Tanjore—Sevappa, Acyutappa and Raghunātha, and Veṅ-kateśvara Dīkṣita, his son, might have been a *protégé* in the courts of Acyutappa and Raghunātha. His brother, Yajña-nārāyaṇa Dīkṣita, has referred to these kings in his famous Kāvya, the *Sāhityaratnākara,* an encomiastic work dealing with the life and achievements of Raghunātha Nāyaka.

Veṅkaṭeśvara Dīkṣita was the teacher of Rājacūdāmaṇi Dīkṣita and Nīlakaṇṭha Dīkṣita— two great writers of the 17th century—who have referred to him in eulogistic terms in their works. Rājacūḍāmaṇi Dīkṣita's reference in his *Tantraśikhāmaṇi* (a commentary on the P.M. Sātras) gives some details about our author. 'Veṅkaṭeśvara Dīkṣita[232] was the son of Govinda Dīkṣita by Nāgamāmbā. He was well-versed in all branches of learning. He performed the Agni-cayana, Vājapeya and other sacrifices. He has composed (1) an excellent Kāvya called *Sāhitya-sāmrājya*; (2) the *Śeulbamīmāṁsā*; (3) the *Karmāntavārttika*; and (4) the *Vārttikābharaṇa*, a commentary on the Ṭupṭīkā.'

His great work on Mīmāṁsā is the *Vārttikābharaṇa*. It is a very lucid commentary on Kumārila's Ṭupṭīkā like the Tantraratna of Pārthasārathimiśra. Among his other works, the *Śulbamīmāṁsā* deals with the measurement and other mathematical details regarding the sacrificial *vedi*. It is based on those portions of Bodhāyana Kalpasūtras. His *Karmāntavārttika*[233] is a commentary on *Karmānta Sūtras* (a portion of the Bodhāyana Kalpa Sātras). In this work he refers to his father Govinda Dīkṣita with great reverence.[234] In the colophon of this work[235] it is stated that his father—Govinda Dīkṣita—was an *advaitavidyācārya*—a teacher of the Advaita System of philosophy and also one who has performed many Vedic sacrifices—*Agniciti, Sarvatomukha, Aptoryāma, Vājapeya,* etc.

To him is ascribed the *Caturdaṇḍaprakāśikā* —a standard work on *time (tāḷa)* in music. His contracted and little modified name Veṅkaṭamakhin is popularly known to students and lovers of music as an authority in the technique on the South Indian music. He flourished in the latter half of the 16th century.

Narāyaṇabhaṭṭa (*c.* A.D. 1560-1656).

After Appayya Dīkṣita and Veṅkateśvara Dīkṣita and before Āpadeva (the author of the *Mimāṁsānyāyaprakāśa)* flourished the celebrated Nārāyaṇabhaṭṭa of Kerala.[236] His full name is Meppattūr Nārāyaṇa Bhaṭṭatiri, a Nambūdiri Brahmin of Kerala belonging to the Meppattūr Illam or family, which is known in Sanskritised form as '*Uparinavagrāma*'. His father was Mātṛdatta, a great scholar in Mīmāṁsā and his mother belonged to the family of the Bhaṭṭatiris of Payyoor to which the three famous Parameśvaras and Vāsudeva belonged. So, both from the paternal and maternal sides he inherited highly scholarly *mīmāṁsāsaṁpradāya,* and he has written a very good *prakaraṇa* work—*Mānameyodaya*—and a standard commentary on the *Tantravārttika* called *Nibandhana.*

According to the Kerala tradition, Nārāyaṇabhaṭṭa grew an irresponsible youth after his traditional education in Vedas and in Sanskrit literature. It is said that he married a woman belonging to the Pisharoti Caste, the niece of the then well-known astronomer-astrologer Tṛkkaṇḍiyūr Acyuta Pisharoti; and he became thereafter very careless in the observance of his daily duties. One day he happened to get up late and he accidentally crossed the sacred plank on which Acyuta Pisharoti was doing his daily duties in connection with his studies on astrology. This infuriated the Pisharoti who consequently rebuked him, though the latter, as a brahmin, was of a higher social position and status. The Bhaṭṭatiri coolly received the rebuke and calmly requested him to teach him higher books in Sanskrit. The Pisharoti gladly acceded to his request and the Bhaṭṭatiri was able to acquire *Kāvya-vyutpatti* very soon and became a recognised scholar in Alaṅkāra and Vyākaraṇa Śāstras. As a descendant of an orthodox brahmin family, he had the desire to attain proficiency in the Śrauta literature; so he requested the Pisharoti to teach that branch of literature. But the latter had to refuse it on the ground that he, a *non-dvija,* was not allowed to study and teach that branch of literature. The Bhaṭṭatiri, on the other hand, was firm that he should not have more than one teacher, and so he insisted upon the Pisharoti's teaching him the Śrauta texts, though both were afraid of divine punishment for doing the prohibited thing. The Pisharoti being a first-rate scholar in more than one branch of knowledge, managed easily to master the Śrauta literature and taught it to him, and the Bhaṭṭatiri became a full-blown scholar. But ere long the Pisharoti had an attack of leprosy or rheumatism owing to the divine curse and he fell a victim to hard suffering. The Bhaṭṭatiri, out of sympathy and regard for his *guru,* prayed to God to free his *guru* from the virulent and fatal disease by transferring it from the body of his guru to his own body. Consequently his teacher was cured and he became a leper (or a rheumatic patient). He spent thereafter all his time in prayer to Lord Kṛṣṇa in the sacred shrine at Guruvāyūr (in South Malabar); he sang his great devotional lyric—the *Nārāyaṇīya*—in 1000 verses—which contains the devotional fervour and essence of the Mahābhāgavatapurāṇa and which, as tradition goes, took him 100 days to compose; and at the end of that period he was completely and miraculously cured.

Thus, tradition records that Nārāyaṇabhaṭṭa was a great devotee of Lord Kṛṣṇa and an ideal devoted student of his only teacher—Acyuta Pisharoti. But according to his *Prakriyā-sarvasva*—a running commentary on Pāṇini's *Aṣṭādhyāyī* —he had three *gurus*—Mātṛdatta, his father under whom he studied Mīmāṁsā, Mādhavārya from whom he learnt Tarkaśāstra, and the Pisharoti who taught him Vyākaraṇa (and Alaṅkāra).

Besides being a versatile scholar and writer of a good number of Prabandhas on Purāṇic themes in *campū* style which have been highly popular among all classes of people, especially the professional actors—Cākyars in Malabar,—Nārāyaṇabhaṭṭa has written two works on Mīmāṁsā—the *Mānameyodaya* and the *Tantravārttikanibandhana*. The *Mānameyodaya,* as the title indicates, was originally intended to elaborate both *māna* and *meya*; for reasons not exactly known he has left the work unfinished at the end of the *māna* section, which contains an exposition of the six *mānas* or *pramāṇas* as accepted by the Bhāṭṭas—*pratyakṣa, anumāna, śabda, upamāna, arthāpatti* and *anupalabdhi*. As the introductory verse goes, it is an elucidation of the six pramāṇas as explained in the *Ślokavārttika* by

Kumārilabhaṭṭa.[237] It may be assumed from a verse cited by him that he had free access to Kumārila's Bṛhaṭṭīkā,[238] which is unfortunately lost. He also cites Cidānanda'[239] as an authority. He also refers to one Nyāyanirṇayakāra.[240]

The importance of the *Mānameyodaya*[241] lies in the fact that it is written in a clear and flowing style in verse with explanations in prose on *nyāya terminology*; and that in many places it explains clearly the *gurumata* and refutes it. Though the *Tarkapāda* of the *Śāstradīpikā* and Cidānanda's Nītitattvāvirbhāva deal with the same subject more elaborately than in this work, the exposition in this work has the unique charm of simplicity and clearness, which characterise all the Sāstraic works of Nārāyaṇabhaṭṭa.

His *Nibandhana*[242] is a very readable commentary on the *Tantravārttika*. Like the Ajitā and unlike the Nyāyasudhā it explains the text directly without unnecessary discussions and digressions.

Among his other works, his *Prakriyāsarvasva*[243] is worth mentioning. It is a good commentary on Pāṇini's *Aṣṭādhyāyī* following the examples of Rāmacandra, (the author of the *Prakriyākaumudi)* and his other predecessors. Tradition says that Nārāyaṇabhaṭṭa had occasion to show his *Prakriyāsarvasva* to his contemporary Bhaṭṭoji Dīkṣita (the reputed author of the Siddhānta Kaumudī, the Prauḍhamanoramā, the Kaustubha, etc.), who, on a perusal of it, is said to have remarked that his commentary on *dhātus* is very meagre; and that it was to make up this defect that he wrote the *Dhātukāvya* which deals with nearly 3000 roots.

As regards his date, a few *Kali chronograms* are available in his works. The *Nārayaṇīya* was finished in A.D. 1587, as seen from the Kali-vākya—'*āyurārogyasaukhyam*', when he might be supposed to have attained the age of thirty years. His Prakriyāsarvasva also gives two chronograms '*yatnaḥ phalaprasūḥ syād*' and '*Kṛtarāgarasodya*' which are equivalent to February-March A.D. 1617. One astrological treatise of his says that he lived for 106 years. From the available data it may be said that he must have completed his education before A.D. 1587 when he finished his great devotional lyric, the Nārāyaṇīya, and that he must have lived as a great recognised scholar between A.D. 1587 and 1656, when he breathed his last.[244] He must have therefore flourished in the latter half of the 16th century and in the former half of the 17th century as a younger contemporary of Appayya Dīkṣita.

Laugākṣibhāskara (*c.* A.D. 1600)

Just before Āpadeva might have flourished Laugāksibhāskara, the author of the *Arthasaṅgraha.*[245] There is difference of opinion among scholars[246] whether Āpadeva's Nyāyaprakāsa has preceded the Arthasaṅgraha or it is only an elaboration of the latter. In fairness to both the texts it may be observed that though the Arthasaṅgraha has preceded the Nyāyaprakāsa, the latter has successfully elaborated many obscure topics of the P. M. System. Whether the Arthasaṅgraha is the chief source-book of the Nyāyaprakāṣa is extremely doubtful. On the other hand, Āpadeva, in the Nyāyaprakaśā, has unmistakably followed the *siddhāntas* of Pārthasārathimira as embodied in his Nyāyaratnamālā, Tantraratna and *Śāstradīpikā*.

The other work of Laugākṣibhāskara is the *Tarkakaumudī,* which also, like the Arthasaṅgraha, is a good prakaraṇa work in the Nyāya system. Anyhow it is not as popular as the Arthasaṅgraha, probably owing to the great popularity of the Tarkasaṅgraha of Annambhaṭṭa.

To the close of the sixteenth century belonged many great writers on Mīmāṁsā—Śaṅkarabhaṭṭa, Āpadeva, Khaṇḍadevamiśra, Rājacūḍāmaṇi Dīkṣita, Veṅkaṭādhvarin, Somanātha Dīkṣita and Yajñanārāyaṇa Dīkṣita.

Śaṇkarabhaṭṭa (*c.* A.D. 1550-1620)

Śaṅkarabhaṭṭa is known as the author of four works : (i) a commentary on the *Śāstradīpikā* known as *Prakāśa*;[247] (ii) the *Mimāṁsābālaprakāśa*[248] a *prakaraṇa* work containing a summary of the contents of the twelve Adhyāyas; (iii) the *Mimāṁsā-sārasaṅgraha*[249] in verse, and (iv) the *Vidhirasāyanadūṣaṇa*[250] —a refutation of the theories propounded by Appayya Dīkṣita in his Vidhirasāyana. Śambhubhaṭṭa, the famous commentator on the Bhāṭṭadīpikā, makes Khaṇḍadeva presuppose a work, called *Prakāśa*[251]; this might be in all probability Śaṅkarabhaṭ ṭa's *Śāstra-dīpikā-prakāśa* or *Bālaprakāśa*. So Śaṅkarabhaṭṭa might be placed between Appayya Dīkṣita and Khaṇḍadeva.

Śaṅkarabhaṭṭa is known as the son of one Nārāyaṇabhaṭṭ a,[252] the author of the Prayogaratna. This Nārāyaṇabhaṭṭa was the son of Rāmeśvarabhaṭṭa whose father was one Govinda-bhaṭṭa[253] of Benares. Śaṅkarabhaṭṭa had a brother Rāmakṛṣ ṇabhaṭṭa who also is known as a commentator on Kumārila's *Tantravārttika*.

Āpadeva (*c.* A.D. 1580-1650)

Āpadeva's pedigree can be known from the account given by his son, Anantadeva. In the introductory verses of his *Smṛti-kaustubha,*[254] Anantadeva called himself the descendant of the great Mahratha Saint Ekanātha who lived on the banks of the Godāvarī and performed many vedic sacrifices, worshipping God Kṛṣṇa. Anantadeva was the son of Āpadeva (our author) who was again the son of one Anantadeva and the grandson of Āpadeva and the great-grandson of Ekanātha (above described). Anantadeva II's time may be fixed at *c.* A.D. 1620-1690 and as Mr. P.V. Kane says he must have been patronised by Baig Bahadur Candra between A.D. 1645-1675. From this the date of Āpadeva, (Anantadeva's father and the author of the Nyāya-prakāśa) may be roughly fixed at *c.* A.D. 1580-1650.

His *Mīmāṁsānyāyaprakāśa*[255] is the standard prakaraṇa work elucidating the contents of the Dvādaśalakṣaṇī; it places greater emphasis on the contents of the first, third and fifth *adhyāyas*. No similar work exists dealing with the important topics—*atideśa, ūha, bādha, tantra* and *prasaṅga*—the contents of the latter half of the P.M. Śāstra. The style of the work is very simple and clear. It is polemic in some places, but it cogently argues the points dealt with. The dissertation on the injunction—'*somena yajeta*'; the exposition of the *artha-bhāvanā* as the chief import of the *ākhyātapratyaya*; the elucidation of the *prakaraṇapramāṇa on aṅgatva,* the detailed exposition of the *four pramāṇas on nāmadheya* and *of pravartanās as the liṅgārtha,*—these the author has handled in this work in an inimitable manner.

His other work is a commentary on the Vedāntasāra, a prakaraṇa work in the system of Advaita philosophy.

Khaṇḍadevamiśra (*c.* A.D. 1575-1665)

Just like Nārāyaṇabhaṭṭa of Kerala, Khaṇḍadevamiśra (probably of Bengal or Benares) was a younger contemporary of Appayya Dīkṣita, whom he has referred to in his Mīmāṁsā-kaustubha as *Mimāṁsakamūrdhanya.* At least for some time he should have lived at Benares where he had occasion to meet Appayya Dīkṣita when he was there.

Khaṇḍadeva was the son of Rudradeva.[256] He is known (from a reference made by Jagannātha Paṇḍita in his *Rasa-gaṅgādhara)* as the Mīmāṁsā teacher of Perubhaṭṭa, the father of Jagannātha Paṇḍita who flourished in the middle of the 17th century (in the courts of Shah Jehan and Darashukho at Delhi and of Prāṇanārāyaṇa of Kāmarūpa, a vassal under the then Mogul ruler, and the Lord of Kamatā, the modern Assam).[257] So, between Appayya Dīkṣita and Jagannātha Paṇḍita or his father Perubhatta *i.e.,* in the closing decade of the 16th century and in the first half of the 17th century, Khaṇḍadeva must have flourished. Mr. P.V. Kane says[258] that Khaṇḍadeva died in A.D. 1665.

He has written three important works on Mīmāṁsā—the *Bhāṭṭakaustubha,* the *Bhāṭṭadīpikā* and the *Bhāṭṭarahasya.* They are epoch-making works in Mīmāṁsā literature in that they clearly make out the foundation of the modern school— *navīna-mata*—in the history of the Bhāṭṭa school. They are again epoch-making in both language and the treatment of the subject-matter. Such of the students of Mīmāṁsā as are not well-versed in the terminology of the *Navya-nyāya,* introduced for the first time into the history of Indian Philosophy by Gaṅ-geśopādhyāya, the author of the *Tattvacintāmaṇi*, are apt to criticise that what is gained by the precision of thought is lost in language which is described as "spoiled by a huge overgrowth of inflated and hair-splitting logic-chopping.[259]" But those who are well-equipped with the *navya-nyaya* terminology gain much in the precision of thought that such terminology ensures.

In many places in his works Khaṇḍadeva criticises the Bhāṣyakāra, the Vārttikakāra, Pārthasārathimiśra, Bhavadeva-bhaṭṭa and Someśvarabhaṭṭa, who, according to him, were the representatives of the *prācīnas*[260] views in the Bhāṭṭa school, and elucidates his own views which are to a great extent *original.* In giving the *pūrvapakṣa*s and *siddhāntas* of each adhi-karaṇa he almost follows the Vārttikakāra, yet in some details he differs from him and his followers.

In his *Bhāṭṭakaustubha,*[261] (his first work, which is a very elaborate commentary on the *sūtras* extending only to the *Balabalādhikaraṇa* III.3.7) he not only explains the *sūtras* and gives the *adhikaraṇa-svarūpa* but also discusses many important questions. His method of treatment is almost perfect. His style is mostly argumentative like that of a *Navya-Naiyāyika*; and in his explanation of the *sūtras* and the *adhikaraṇas* he does not at all indulge in flowery language. The result is that his views can be easily understood from this work by a student of Mīmāṁsā knowing navya-nyāya. It is very elaborate, for it deals with the adhikaraṇārthas and other topics like the *śabdabodha-paddhati* as accepted by the Mīmāṁsakas.

According to his disciple Śaṁbhubhaṭṭa (the commentator on the Bhāṭṭadīpikā) Khaṇḍadeva has not commented on the *Tarkapāda* 1-1.1.7, both in his Bhāṭṭakaustubha and Bhāṭṭ adīpikā. But the late editor of the Bhāṭṭadīpikā[262] (in Mysore Government Sanskrit Series) has however published the *Tarka-pāda* of the Bhāṭṭadīpikā, the genuineness of which is question-able, in view of the fact that many passages in the *Jijñāsā-*

dhikaraṇa (I-1.1) and the *Vākyādhikaraṇa* (I-1.7) are found repeated in the *Arthavādādhi-karaṇa* (I-2.1) and in the *Mantrādhikaraṇa* (I-2.4). But the other two commentators on the Bhāṭṭa-dīpikā, Bhāskararāya and Vāñcheśvarayajvan, have commented on the *Tarkapāda* of the Bhāṭṭadīpikā.

The *Bhāṭṭadīpikā*[262] is his second work and is the most important of all, both from the standpoints of the author and of the students. It contains, on the model of the *Śāstradīpikā*, elucidations of the *adhikaraṇas* in a brief and measured language so that in many places his views cannot be made out without a commentary or without a reference to the Kaustubha. So, it is a good summary of the Kaustubha to the end of the *Balābalādhikaraṇa.* Though the style in the work is terse and to some extent obscure, it has attained the acme of perfection as an advanced work in Mīmāṁsā Śāstra. No advanced student would fail to master it. As a nibandhana work it has superseded both the Sāstradīpikā and the Nyāyamālāvistara, though the latter is still considered as a guide for beginners. Among his original contributions special mention may be made of Khaṇḍadeva's elucidation of the original definitions of the three-fold vidhis—*apūrvavidhi, niya-mavidhi* and *parisaṅkhyā-vidhi*—and refutation of the definitions as embodied in the Vārttika—

"*Vidhiratyantamaprāpte*
niyamaḥ pākṣike sati |
Tatra cānyatra ca prāptau
parisaṇkhyeti Kirtyate ||"

and also in the Vidhirasāyana of his elder contemporary Appayya Dīkṣita. His *jātiśaktivāda* in the *ākṛtyadhikaraṇa*; his explanation of the *tatsiddhipeṭikā*—six conditions under which *gauṇī, a śabdavṛtti separate from lakṣaṇā,* is to be employed; his exposition of *pravartanā* and *yatna* as the chief imports of the *liṅ-pratyaya* in its capacities as a *vidhipratyaya* and an *ākhyātapratyaya* respectively; his definitions of the six pramāṇas on the *karmabheda, aṅgatva* and *krama* with suitable illustrations in the second, third and fifth *adhyāyas*; his exposition of *puruṣārthatva* and *kratvarthatva* together with the *prayojakatva* and *prayojyatva* in the fourth *adhyāya*; his definitions and exposition of *atideśa, ūha, bādha* in the later *adhyāyas*— in these and other expositions Khaṇḍadeva shows his originality, clearness of thought and freedom from bias.

His *Bhāṭṭarahasya*[263] is a unique work in that it is completely devoted to the *śābdabodhapaddhati*. So, it stands on a par with Gadādhara Bhaṭṭācārya's *Vyutpattivāda* in the Navyanyāya school and with Kauṇḍabhaṭṭa's *Bhūṣaṇasāra* and Nāgeśa Bhaṭṭa's *Mañjūṣā* in the Navya Vaiyākaraṇa school. The topics discussed in these works are more or less the same, though each work follows its own method in arrangement and in the order of topics discussed.

The *Bhāṭṭarahasya,* a work on the Dharmamīmāṁsā, rightly begins with the nature and definitions of *dharma* and *adharma* as embodied in the *Sūtra*—'*Codanālakṣaṇosrtho dharmaḥ.*' Then the chief question—the meaning of the *vidhipratyaya* in the affirmative and negative propositions like '*agnihotraṁ juhuyāt svargakāmaḥ*' '*na kalañjaṁ bhakṣayet*' is taken up. While elucidating *pravartanā* and *nivartanā* as the meanings of the Vidhipratyaya '*lift*' in the affirmative and negative propositions respectively, the Naiyāyika view that *iṣṭasādhanatva, kṛtisāddhyatva* and *balavadaniṣṭānanubandhitva* constitute generally the meaning of the '*liṅ*' is refuted on the main ground that these, three ideas cannot be uniformly explained as related to their *Viśeṣyas* in all propositions (both affirmative and negative.) It is conceded that there is *lāghava* in explaining the relation of one idea to another in a sentence if we accept *pravartanā* as the meaning of '*liṅ pratyaya.*' After this the most important topic—*viz.* the *bhāvanā* as the meaning of the *Akhyātapratyaya* is the *leading concept* in the *śābdabodha*. Here he points out clearly that in a sentence the verb is the most important element and as such, it should convey the *leading concept* of the *śābdabodha*; and that in the verb, the personal suffix conveys the chief idea—*pradhānārtha*—as the elders have explained in their dictum—'*prakṛtipratyayau pratyayārtham saha brūtaḥ, tayostu pratyayaḥ prādhānyena'*; and that of the many ideas conveyed by the *liṅ* suffix—*viz.*, *pravṛtti, pravarttanā, saṅkhyā* (number), etc., the chief idea is *pravṛtti* which is in popular language known as *bhāvanā* (as instances vary), *cf.* Yāska's Nirukta—*'Bhāvapradhānamākhyātam'.* In this connection our author refutes the Naiyāyika and the Vaiyākaraṇa views that the leading concepts of the *śābdabodha* are *prathamāntārtha* (idea conveyed by a word in nominative case) and the *dhātvar-tha* (idea conveyed by the root of the verb). And then, the *lakārārtha,* the *dhātvartha,* the *ākhyātārtha, the chief imports of the seven cases* (with their usages in a sentence) are most scientifically elucidated in this work.

This particular literature known as '*Vyutpattivāda*' developed in India even from ancient days; but in the sixteenth and seventeenth centuries and onwards it has been further developed and systematised as a separate part of dialectical literature in Mīmāṁsā, Nyāya, and Vyākaraṇa. This branch of literature marks well also the development of that part of the modern science of Comparative Philology—*Semantics—on the speculative side;* and its explanations of the four kinds of words—*yaugika, rūḍha, yogarūḍha* and *yaugikarūḍha* and of the *śabdavṛttis* (significative potencies of words)—*abhidhā, lakṣaṇā, gauṇī, vyañjanā, etc.*, are of immense help for tracing the history of the meaning of a word or words in language and for a successful classification of the semantic changes under the *three* well-known heads—*specialisation* (or narrowing), *generalisation* (or widening) and *transference.*

Rājacūḍāmaṇi Dīkṣita (*c.* A.D. 1580-1650)

Rājacūḍāmaṇi Dīkṣita's genealogy and literary works are fully described by a descendant of his family, Bālayajñavedeśvara, in the introductory verses of the latter's commentary on the former's *Rukmiṇīkalyāṇa.*[264] One of the remote ancestors of Rājacūḍāmaṇi Dīkṣita is one Bhavasvāmin who had a son Śrīkṛṣṇa and a grandson Kumārabhavasvāmin. This Bhavasvāmin had a son Śrīkṛṣṇārya who had a son Bhavasvāmin. This Bhavasvāmin was the father of the famous Ratnakheṭa ṣrīnivāsa Dīkṣita whose mother was Lakṣmī. This Śrīnivāsa Dīkṣita had two wives and by the first wife, he had two sons, Keśava Dīkṣita and Ardhanārīsvara Dīkṣita, and by the second wife, Yajña-nārāyaṇa *alias* Rājacūḍāmaṇi. It seems that Rājacūḍāmaṇi lost his parents in his earlier days and his brother Ardhanārīśvara took care of the boy Rājacūḍāmaṇi. He educated him according to his family tradition and soon he began to display his genius. In the prologue to his Nāṭikā— *Kamalinikalahaṁsa*—it is said that he wrote it in his sixth year. In his *Kāvyadarpaṇa* he has mentioned 27 works of his. He was like Nlakaṇṭha Dīkṣita, another great literary celebrity of the age, a disciple of Veṅkateśvara Dīkṣita (already referred to) whom he has highly eulogised.

His works on Mīmāṁsā are three in number[265]:—the *Tantraśikhāmaṇi,* the *Saṅkarṣamuktāvali* and the *Karpūra-varttikā.* The Tantraśikhāmaṇi is a commentary on the Dvādaśa-lakṣaṇī, which was written by him at the bidding of his teacher Veṅkaṭeśvara Dīkṣita. The date of composition of this work is given by the author as 1559 Śaka which is equivalent to A.D. 1636.

Dhīmānmānye-śakasyābde
hāyane ceśvarābhidhe |
Cūḍāmaṇiḥ kalayate
yajvā Tantraśikhāmaṇim ||

His Saṅkarṣamuktāvali otherwise known as Nyāyamuktāvali is a commentary on the Saṅkarṣakāṇḍa—the supplement to the Dvādaśalakṣaṇī; this commentary is a positive proof of the genuineness of the Saṅkarṣakāṇḍa as a supplement to the Dvādaśalakṣaṇī. His other work Karpūravarttikā is a commentary on the *Śāstradīpikā*; and this and other great commentaries of this period speak well of the popularity of the *Śāstradīpikā* with all students of Mīmāṁsā.

Veṅkaṭādhvarin (*c.* A.D. 1590-1660)

Veṅkaṭādhvarin is known as a contemporary of Nīlakaṇṭha

Dīkṣita, the grandson of Āccān Dīkṣita, the brother of the famous Appayya Dīkṣita; so he must be a contemporary of Rājacūḍāmaṇi Dīkṣita (just referred to). He says in the introductory verses[266] of his famous literary work—the *Viśvaguṇādarṣa Campū*—that he belonged to the family of the famous Tātācārya who was well-known as the Ācārya of the great king, Veṅkaṭapati of Vijayanagar, and a rival of Appayya Dīkṣita; that his grandfather was one Appayya who is glorified as the nephew of the famous Tātārya, otherwise known as Tātācārya, and as a great literary scholar who performed many sacrifices; and that this Appayya had a son called Raghunātha Dīkṣita who was a poet of a very high order. His son was our author—Veṅkaṭādhvarin—who regarded himself to be well-versed in logic, Vedānta, Mīmāṁsā and Vyākaraṇa—the four great Śāstras. He belonged to the village *Arasāṇipāle* near Conjeevaram in the North Arcot District (Madras).[267] His two works on Mīmāṁsā are—the *Vidhitrayaparitrāṇa* and the *Mīmāṁsāmakaranda,*[268] the former explaining the necessity of the division of *Vidhi* into three—*apūrva, niyama* and *parisaṅkhyā*—and the latter dealing with the authoritativeness of the *arthavādas* on *dharma* as understood by the Mīmāṁsakas. His Viśvaguṇādarśa deserves high praise as a standard work and is second only to the Rāmāyaṇa Campū.

Rāghavendrayati (*c.* A.D. 1600-1670)

Rāghavendrayati is known as the second spiritual successor of Vijayīndra Tīrtha between A.D. 1623 and 1671 (Śaka 1545-93).[269] About fifty works are ascribed to him, including commentaries on the Vedas. One of the greatest works of his is the *Parimala* (on the model of Appayya Dīkṣita's Kalpataruparimala), a commentary on Jayatīrtha's Nyāya-sudhā. His only work in Mīmāṁsā is the *Bhāṭṭasaṅgraha,* a commentary on the *Pūrvamīmāṁsā Sūtras*[270] which was much appreciated by Nīlakaṇṭha Dīkṣita.

His father was Timmaṇṇabhaṭṭa, his mother, Gopammā, his grandfather, Kanakācalabhaṭṭa and great-grandfather, Kṛṣṇabhaṭṭa. His teacher was Sudhīndragurupāda. His original name was Veṅkaṇṇabhaṭṭa. His great-grandfather left Kumba-konam for Vijayanagar and was a famous Vaiyākaraṇa in the Court of Vijayanagar. After the ruin of Vijayanagar, he left for Kāñcī. Rāghavendrayati, *alias* Veṇī-(Vīṇā ?) Veṅkaṇṇa-bhaṭṭa is said to have married at Bhuvanagiri, five miles from Cidambaram. His mortal remains lie entombed at the Mantrālaya on the banks of the Tuṅgabhadrā in the Bellary District.

Rāmakṛṣṇa Dikṣita (*c.* A.D. 1600-1670)

To the seventeenth century might have belonged Rāmakṛṣṇa Dīkṣita, who is known to have written a commentary on the *Pūrva Mīmāṁsā Sātras—Mimāṁsānyāyadarpaṇa.*[271] He is the son of Dharmarājādhvarīndra, the celebrated author of the Advaita Vedānta Paribhāṣā and the Tarkacūḍāmaṇi (a commentary on the Tarkacintāmaṇi and an adverse criticism of the Daśaṭīkā.)[272] He belonged to the *Velaṅguḍi* village near Kumbakonam where flourished the great revered scholar Veṅkaṭanātha, the teacher and father of Dharmarājā-dhvarīndra. This Dharmarājādhvarīndra is later than Appayya Dīkṣita since he has presupposed his Parimala and Siddhāntaleśasaṅgraha, and anterior to Śrīnivāsadāsa, the author of the Yatīndramatadīpikā which contains the refutations of some sections of the Advaita Vedānta Paribhāṣā. So, Dharmarājādhvarin might have, as a younger contemporary of Appayya Dīkṣita, flourished towards the close of the 16th century and at the beginning of the 17th century, and his son Rāmakṛṣṇa Dīkṣita, in the middle of the 17th century.[273]

Rāmakṛṣṇa Dīkṣita is known to posterity as the famous commentator on his father's Vedānta Paribhāṣā, where he plays the part more of a Naiyāyika than of a true Advaitin.

Somanātha Dīkṣita (*c.* A.D. 1600).

Somanātha Dīkṣita is another famous writer of this period. He is the reputed commentator on the *Śāstradīpikā*, omitting the *Tarkapāda*. The earliest reference to him is made by Śambhubhaṭṭa in his Prabhāvali,[274] a commentary on Khaṇḍadeva's Bhāṭṭadīpikā. From the colophon,[275] the introductory verse[276] and an *ūha* passage[277] it is clear that he was the great-grandson of Sureśvarayajvaśarman of Niṭṭalakula (gotra), the grandson of Somanāthayajvaśarman and the son of Sūrabhaṭṭa-śarman, otherwise known as Sūrabhaṭṭamahopādhyāya. His mother's name is Mairammadā. His teacher was his own elder brother Veṅkaṭādriyajvan. His family is very famous for the performance of vedic sacrifices. He himself is known in the colophon as a *sarvatomukhayajvan.* The three *pravararṣis* of his family are *Yuvanāśva, Ambarīṣa* and *Aṅgiras.* His *Mayūkha-mālikā*[278] is a standard commentary on the *Śāstradīpikā.* He refers to most of the important authors and works in the Mīmāṁsā-śāstra—the Bhāṣyakāra (Śabarasvāmin), the Vārttikakāra, the author of the Mbandhana,[279] Bhavadeva,[280] Bhavanātha,[281] the Nyāyasudhākāra,[282] Varadarāja,[283] Appayya Dīkṣita's Vidhira-sāyana,[284] the Kāslkāṭīkā,[285] the Tantraratna,[286] and the Nyāya-ratnamālā.[287]

Yajñanārāyaṇa Dīkṣita (*c.* A.D. 1600)

To this period might also have belonged Yajñanārāyaṇa Dīkṣita, another great commentator on the *Śāstradīpikā.* In the colophon and the introductory verses of the work[288] he has described himself as the great-grandson of Tirumalayajvan, the grandson and disciple of Yajñeśvara Bhaṭṭopādhyāya, and the son of Kūrikoṇḍabhaṭṭopādhyāya. His mother's name was Gaṅgāmbikā. He had a paternal uncle Lakṣmaṇa whom he calls his *guru* and had an elder brother, Tirumala (*yajvan*). He belonged to the *Kāśyapa gotra* and studied the ṛg-Veda. His commentary on the *Śāstradīpikā* is known as the *Prabhā-maṇḍala.* It begins with the second pāda of the first Adhyāya. He calls himself a great writer of Nāṭakas and treatises on Alaṅkāraśāstra, Vedānta, Tarka and śabda (Vyākaraṇa). His commentary[289] is elaborate and is useful in tracing out the tenets of the Prābhākara school, which Pārthasārathimiśra has refuted in his *Śāstradīpikā.*

Nārāyaṇa (*c.* A.D. 1600)

Nārāyaṇa (or Nārāyaṇabhaṭṭa) has written the *meya* section

of the *Mānameyodaya* under the benevolent patronage of *King Mānaveda* of Calicut. From the introductory and concluding verses of his work[290] his teachers are known— *Subrahmaṇya* (the son of the daughter of one famous *Puruṣottama)* and *Rāma* for *Mīmāṁsā,* and *Kṛṣṇa* for *Sāhitya.*

Kamalākarabhaṭṭa (*c.* A.D. 1590-1660)

Kamalākarabhaṭṭa[291] is the son of Rāmakṛṣṇabhaṭṭa, brother of Śaṅkarabhaṭṭa (already referred to). He is known to have written two works on Mīmāṁsā, one, a commentary on the *Tantravārttika* and another, on the *Śāstradīpikā*, the latter known as *Āloka.*[292] Besides these two works, he is credited with 20 more works on different topics, mainly bearing on Dharmaśāstra. His famous work is the *Nirṇayasindhu*—a nibandhana work, or digest, in the Dharmaśāstra which is said to have been completed by the author in 1668 Vikrama era on the 14th day of the dark half of the month Māgha in the Raudra year, which is equivalent to 20th February A.D. 1612. So his literary career might have been between A.D. 1610 and 1640.

Dinakarabhaṭṭa *(c.* A.D. 1590-1660)

Kamalākarabhaṭṭa's brother is Dinakarabhaṭṭa who is also known as a great scholar on Mīmāṁsā. His work on Mīmāṁsā[293] is a brief commentary on the 12 chapters of the *Mīmāṁsā Sūtras* on the model of the *Śāstradīpikā.*

Anantadeva and Jivadeva *(c.* A.D. 1600-1670)

To the beginning of the 17th century belonged the two sons of Āpadeva—Anantadeva and Jīvadeva. Anantadeva is the author of a commentary on his father's Nyāyaprakāśa, called *Bhāṭṭālaṅkāra,* which Śambhubhaṭṭa has every now and then referred to and criticised.[294] This commentary[295] is no doubt good but cannot be regarded as his best work. His Smṛtikaustubha (already referred to) gives him a higher place among the great authors of his time. Jīvadeva, the younger son of Āpadeva, is the author of the *Bhāṭṭabhāskara,* which is also referred to by Śambhubhaṭṭa.[296] It deals with the pramāṇas on dharma —the contents of the first Adhyāya.[297] His other works are the *Grotrapravaranirṇaya* and the *Aśaucanirṇaya* bearing on the Dharmaśāstra.

Kavīndrācārya *(c.* A.D. 1600-1670)

To the beginning of the seventeenth century belonged Kavīndrācārya who is known to have written a commentary on the *Tantravārttika*. He is said to be a contemporary of Visvanātha Pañcānana, the author of the Nyāya*siddhānta*-muktāvali and other works in Nyāyaśāstra. Besides being a great scholar and an author of many works including commentaries on the Vedas,[298] he is known to have possessed a good collection of rare works carefully preserved; and this list of books has been published in the Gaekwad's Oriental Series, Baroda, No. 17.

Anantabhṭṭa (*c.* A.D. 1630-1730).

Anantabhaṭṭa, son of Kamalākarabhaṭṭa, is known to have written a work—*Śāstramālāvṛtti*.[299] It is a commentary on the *sūtras* on the model of the *Śāstradīpikā*. It is very brief and summarises the contents of the *adhikaraṇas*.

Gāgābhaṭṭa *(c.* A.D. 1630-1700)

Gāgābhaṭṭa also known as Viśveśvarabhaṭṭa, is the son of Dinakarabhaṭṭa (already referred to). He is known as the author of a commentary on the 12 chapters of the *Pūrva Mīmāṁsā Sūtras*, called *Bhāṭṭacintāmaṇi*.[300] He adopts every now and then the *navya-nyāya* terminology and his elucidation of many topics in the Tarka-pāda and other sections of his commentary is very precise. His other works on Mīmāṁsā are: a commentary on the *Ślokavārttika* called *Śivārkodaya* and a *Sūtravṛtti* called *Kusumāñjali* the latter he has referred to in his Bhāṭṭa-cintāmaṇi.[301] Mr.P.V. Kane says[302] in his History of the Dharmaśāstra that Gāgābhaṭṭa officiated at the coronation of the great Shivaji in 1674 A.D. So, he can well be assigned to the latter half of the 17th century.

Kollūr Nārāyaṇa Śāstri (*c.* A.D. 1630—1700)

Kollūr Nārāyaṇa Śāstri is known[303] as the disciple of

Somanātha Dīkṣita, the famous commentator on the *Śāstra-dīpikā*. His father was Kollūr Somayājin and mother, Āccamāmbā. He is the author of three works—(1) *Mimāṁsā-sarvasva* which is a commentary on the *Sūtras* explaining the *adhikaraṇas* in full; (2) *Vidhiviveka*—an independent treatise possessing nine main sections[304] chiefly dealing with the various aspects of *vidhi*—(i) *utpatti, viniyoga, prayukti,* and *adhikāra*; (ii) *nitya, naimittika* and *kāmya, etc.*; (3) *Vidhidarpaṇa*—another similar work dealing with the *vidhis* and its varieties. As he was the disciple of Somanātha Dīkṣita, he may be fairly placed soon after him *(i.e.)* A.D. 1630-1700.

Śambhubhaṭṭa *(c.* A.D. 1640-1700)

To the latter half of the 17th century belonged Śambhu-bhaṭṭa, the celebrated commentator on the Bhāṭṭadīpikā. He is known[305] as the direct disciple of Khaṇḍadevamiśra himself. His father was Bālakṛṣṇa, who is described by him as well-versed in the vedas and Śāstras, as a great sacrificer and an ardent devotee of Śiva. Śambhubhaṭṭa's only work so far known is the *Prabhāvali,* the commentary on the Bhāṭṭadīpikā. It is very elaborate and polemic. It does not in many instances explain the difficult text of the Bhāṭṭadīpikā, though it supplements it much. As a direct disciple of Khaṇḍadevamiśra he had the unique advantage of knowing fully the views of his teacher whom he calls *pūjyapāda,* and he has strengthened further the navya school in Mīmāṁsā founded by Khaṇḍadeva. As he himself has said,[306] he was asked by his teacher not to comment on the Bhāṭṭadīpikā to the end of the Balābalādhikaraṇa on the ground that students of Mīmāṁsā could understand the terse and brief language of the Bhāṭṭa dīpikā by a close study of the more elaborate Bhāṭṭakaustu-bha. But against the wishes of his revered teacher he has commented on those portions also with a fitting introduction dealing with the important topics in the *Tarkapāda*. It is a very elaborate commentary on the Bhāṭṭadīpikā and it further establishes the *navyamata* by refuting the views of the Prācīnas belonging to the Bhāṭṭa school—Pārthasārathimiśra,

Bhaṭṭasomeśvara, Khaṇḍanakāra (?)[307] Appayya Dīkṣita, Apadeva and his son Anantadeva, Śaṅkarabhaṭṭa and Somanātha Dīkṣita. At times he refutes also the views of the Prābhākaras.

Appayya Dīkṣita *(c.* A.D. 1650)

Appayya Dīkṣita is known as the author of the *Tantrasiddhāntadipikā,* a commentary on the *Pūrva Mīmāṁsā Sūtras*. As is stated in the colophon[308] he was the son of Appayya Dīkṣita (the author of Rukmiṇīpariṇaya and many other works) and grandson of Ayyā Dīkṣita (the brother of the famous Appayya Dīkṣita); so he may be assigned to the middle of the 17th century. There is another work—*Viṣayasaṅgrahadīpikā* from the pen of one Appayya Dīkṣita who might be the same as the author of the Tantra*siddhānta*dīpikā. The latter work is only a succinct summary of the contents of the 12 Adhyāyas of the *Pūrva Mīmāṁsā Sūtras*, omitting the *Tarkapāda*.

Annambhaṭṭa (*c.* A.D. 1700)

To the latter part of the 17th century belonged Annambhaṭṭa, one of the literary celebrities of this century. He is said to have belonged to some Āndhra district. He is known (from the colophons of his works)[309] as the son of Tirumalārya of Rāghava Somayāji family. A versatile scholar and a reputed polymath, he has written works in almost all important branches of Śāstraic literature. His works on Mīmāṁsā are (1) *Subodhinī*—a commentary on the Tantravārttika; (2) *Rāṇakojjīvinī—a* commentary on the Rāṇaka otherwise known as the Nyāya-sudhā of Bhaṭṭasomeśvara; and (3) the *Rāṇakabhāvanākarikāvivaraṇa*—containing 54 stanzas with commentary which investigates the import of the *vidhipratyaya* from the Mīmāṁsaka standpoint—probably an extract culled from Bhaṭṭa-someśvara's Raṇaka.[310] Among his other works mention may be made of (1) his advaitic commentary on the Brahmasūtras; (2) his commentary on the Aṣṭādhyāyī of Pāṇini; (3) an extensive commentary called Udyotana on Kaiyaṭa's-Bhāṣyapradīpa; (4) his learned commentary called *Siddhāñjana* on Jayadeva's Maṇyāloka; (5) the *Tarkasaṅgraha*—the most popular primer in Nyāya Śāstra; and (6) his own commentary *Dīpikā* on the Tarkasaṅgraha. These works well prove the versatility of our author.

Rāmakṛṣṇabhaṭṭa (*c.* A.D. 1700)

Rāmakṛṣṇabhaṭṭa, the author of the *Yukti-snehaprapūraṇī*, might have belonged to this period. His introductory verses[311] give his genealogy. In the Malwa country on the northern bank of the Narmadā (Revā) there flourished a brahmin family of *Parāśara gotra* where was born one Śivadāsa who was well-versed in the Vedas and Śāstras. He had a son Mitraśarman who was much revered by the scholars of his day for his learning in all Śāstras and for his magnanimous personality. He had in his turn a son called Janārdana, a great scholar and devotee of Viṣṇu. This Janārdana begot a son Bhairava by his wife Gaṅgā. This Bhairava was much patronised by the contemporary king of Śeṣavaṁśa. To him and Pūnādevī was born Nārāyaṇa who also was a reputed scholar in Śāstras and was patronised by the contemporary kings. He had by his wife Ramā a son called Mādhava who is said to have left his native place for Benares for his education. There he had by his wife Pr*abhāva*tī a son called Rāmakṛṣṇa (our author) who was much devoted to his parents and was known as an adept in all the Śāstras. He got the title '*Bhaṭṭa*' in an assembly of learned pandits and citizens and he made a name for himself by writing many works. By the composition of his *Pratāpamārtāṇḍa* he got the title *Paṇḍitasiro-maṇi* from Balabhadra, the preceptor of the then king (of Benares) in the *Gajapatisadas*. He says also that he wrote his commentary on the *Śāstradīpikā* (*Tarkapāda* only) in view of the fact that no commentary had been so far written on it.

His commentary—*Yuktisnehaprapūraṇi*—with his own Ṭīkā (gloss) elucidates the text of the *Tarkapāda* of the *Śāstradīpikā*; in addition, it quotes Umveka, Bhartṛmitra—two obscure and generally unknown authors in the *Pūrva* Mīmāṁsā Śāstra. It refers to the Bṛhaṭṭīkā as belonging to the Vārttika-kāra. It helps considerably in the establishment of the view that the Vṛttigrantha in the Śābarabhāṣya on I-1.5 extends to the end of the bhāṣya thereon.[312] It quotes profusely from Kumārila's *Ślokavārttika* and from Sucaritamiśra's Kāśikā.

It is very doubtful whether this same Rāmakṛṣṇabhaṭṭa is identical with Rāmakṛṣṇa, the author of the *Laghupūrva Mīmāṁsādhikaraṇa-kaumudī,*[313] for the latter contains many *apasiddhāntas*; so it cannot have been from the pen of the author of the *Yuktisnehaprapūraṇi*.

Bhāskararāya *(c.* A.D. 1700-1760)

To the beginning of the 18th century belonged Bhāskararāya, the son of Gambhīrarāya and the author of the commentaries on the Bhāṭṭadīpikā *(Candrodaya)*[314] and on the Saṅkarṣakāṇḍa *sūtras*, *(Candrika*[315] the latter giving only the *Pūrvapakṣa* and Siddhānta views very briefly. It is also believed that he is the author of a paper entitled '*Matvarthalakṣaṇāvicāra.*' Some scholars have opined that Bhāskararāya has based his commentary on Khaṇḍadevamiśra's commentary on the Saṅkarṣakāṇḍa. But it is proved beyond doubt from Bhāskararāya's own statements in his *Bhāṭṭacandrikā* that Khaṇḍadeva has not written any commentary on the Saṅkarṣa; and so it can be said that his commentary might not have been based on that of Khaṇḍadeva but as references show, on the Bhāṣya of Devasvāmin.[316]

Bhāskararāya's commentary on the Bhāṭṭadīpikā begins with the *Tarkapāda* of the Bhāṭṭadīpikā, the authenticity of which is however questioned. His commentary is better and more helpful than the Pr*abhāva*li in that it explains clearly the brief and enigmatic language of Khaṇḍadeva in his Bhāṭṭadīpikā.

Bhāskararāya seems to have been a prolific writer. Among his other works[317] mention may be made of his commentary on the *Lalitā-sahasranāma* and his *Vaidikakośa* with his Vṛtti.

Kṛṣṇayajvan *(c.* A.D. 1700-1760)

Most probably in the beginning of the 18th century flourished Kṛṣṇayajvan who has written a very good *prakaraṇa* work called *Paribhāṣa.*[318] It is of immense use for the beginners of Mīmāṁsā in that it succinctly summarises the most important tenets of Mīmāṁsā such as *Vidhi* with its important varieties, the *six pramāṇas of aṅgatva,* the division of *Karma,* the two kinds of *Bhāvanā,* etc. The style is simple and lucid and the exposition, though brief, is to the point. The author seems to be a Tamilian and as such it is popular in the Tamil countries.

Vāsudeva Dīkṣita ***(c.*** **A.D. 1700-1760)**

To this period belonged Vāsudeva Dīkṣita, the reputed author of the *Adhvaramīmāṁsākutūhalavṛtti.* He was the son of Adhvaryu Mahādevavājapeyin by Annapūrṇā. Mahādeva-vājapeyin was the adhvaryu (one of the four chief priests) in the sacrifices performed by Tryambakarāyamakhin, the famous minister of King Sāhaji *(C.* A.D. 1684-1710) and by Ānanda-rāyamakhin, the well-known minister and *Dalavoy* of the Mahratha kings of Tanjore—Serfoji I. and Tukkoji (Tulaja I.) between *C.* A.D. 1711-1735.[319] So he belonged to the 18th century. His chief work is the *Adhvaramīmāṁsākutūhalavṛtti,*[320] a voluminous and polemic commentary on the *Pūrva-*mīmāṁsāsūtras on the model of the Bhāṭṭakaustubha of Khaṇḍadevamiśra; and this marks the last of the series of this kind of commentaries in the history of the *Pūrva* Mīmāṁsā system. Very frequently he quotes the Saṅkarṣakāṇḍa *sūtras* together with Devasvāmin's Bhāṣya thereon, which help one considerably for the reconstruction of the lost *sūtras* of the Saṅkarṣakāṇḍa. This fact would also suggest that he might have had a full access to the Saṅkarṣasūtras (which are unfortunately lost to us) and might have written a commentary on them also.

In many places his interpretations of *sūtras* and vedic passages differ considerably from those of the Vārttikakāra and his followers. His interpretation of the *Svādhyāyavidhi* in the Arthavādādhikaraṇa (I-2-1) is a departure from those of his predecessors in the field. He says that the svādhyāyavidhi enjoins Vedādhyayana *not for Arthajñāna but for Akṣaragra-haṇa;* and he argues that if the former be the case, then all *traivarṇikas* would not have the necessity of studying all portions of the vedas, in view of the fact that a brahmin has not the utility of the knowledge of the text dealing with the Rājasūya sacrifice which a kṣatriya alone is allowed to perform. And he raises a technical objection to the fact that the *arthajñāna* is the *phala* (fruit) of the svādhyāyavidhi, *i.e.*, that the *phala* would be that which is already known to us and that nobody would desire to get a thing which is not known to him. So, on the authority of the *Puruṣārthānuśāsana sūtras* (quoted by Sāyaṇācārya in the introduction to his Ṛg-Veda Saṁhitābhāṣ ya)[321] and of the *Śruti* cited by Patañjali in his Mahābhāṣya,[322] he concludes that the *adhyayanavidhi* enjoins adhyayana for *akṣaragrahaṇa,* and that the arthajñāna is also made *nitya* by the smṛtis like '*sthāṇurayam bhārahāraḥ kilābhūt*' which condemn the person who after committing the Vedic texts to memory, does not understand the meaning of the Vedas, as a statue or pillar which bears a great burden on its head without knowing its nature and weight.

In many other places also he discards the views of his predecessors—the Vārttikakāra and others. In the *Abhyāsādhikaraṇa* (II-2.2) he concludes on the basis of an *adhikaraṇa* in the Sañkarṣakāṇḍa that the injunctions '*samidho yajati*', '*Tanūnapātam yajati*', etc., are *guṇavidhis.*

Among his other works, mention may be made of (i) the *Bālamanoramā,* a good and exhaustive commentary on the Siddhāntakaumudī, and (ii) the *Bodhāyanaśrautasūtra-vyākhyā.*[323]

Rāmānujācārya is known from the introductory verses[324] of his *Tantrarahasya* to have belonged to a place Dharmapurī on the banks of the Godāvarī and as a worshipper of God Narasiṁha, an incarnation of Viṣṇu. In that work he salutes *Sūtra*kāra Jaimini, Bhāṣyakāra Śabarasvāmin, the ṭīkākāra'[325] *alias* Guru, the author of the two commentaries on the Bhāṣya—the Bṛhatī and the Laghvī. He then pays his tribute to Śālīkanātha as a writer of the two commentaries on the two works of

Prabhākara—the Ṛjuvimalā on the Bṛhatī and the Dīpaśikhā on the Laghvī and of the prakaraṇa work—Prakaraṇapañcikā. This reference sheds considerable light on the contended question whether the Bṛhatī is the same as the Nibandhana and the Laghvī is identical with the Vivaraṇa. He refers also to Bhavanātha[326] as one who has summarised in his *Nayaviveka* the doctrines of the Prābhākara school as embodied in the two works of Prabhākara and the Pañcikās of Śālīkanātha.

His work *Tantrarahasya*[327] gives a summary of the important doctrines regarding *māna* and *meya* as found in the works of his predecessors. It contains five *paricchedas,* the first and second dealing with the *mānas* and *meyas* respectively; the third known as *Śāstrapariccheda* deals with the nature of *śabda* and the *anvitābhidhānavāda* in *Śābdabodha*; the fourth contains the exposition of *apūrva* as the import of the *liṅ* suffix which is one of the fundamental doctrines of the Prābhākaras; the fifth summarises the *Śāstramukha* section of the *Prakaraṇa-pañcikā* discussing the *adhyayanavidhi.* This work is, therefore, a good prakaraṇa work in the Prābhākara school, just as the *Mānameyodaya* of Nārāyaṇabhaṭṭa is in the Bhāṭṭa school. Its style is very simple, lucid and sometimes argumentative. In many places it refers to Kumārilabhaṭṭa as *ācārya* and *Vārtti-kakārapāda.* It also refers to a prakaraṇa work *Vimalāñjana*[328] and another work—*Nyāyaśuddhi*'[329] about which nothing is known.

The *Nāyakaratna*[330] is another work of his, which is a commentary on Pārthasārathimiśra's Nyāyaratnamālā. Though this author was a follower of the Prābhākara school, he has commented, as he says in one of the introductory verses,[331] on the Nyāyaratnamālā because of his great reverence for that great writer in the Bhāṭṭa school of the Mīmāṁsā Śāstra.

Vāñcheśvarayajvan *(c.* A.D. 1760-1830)

To the beginning of the 19th century belonged Vāñcheśvarayajvan, the author of the *Bhāṭṭacintāmaṇi,* a commentary on Khaṇḍadeva's Bhāṭṭadīpikā. From his introductory verses[332] and colophon[333] it is known that his great-grandfather Vāñcheśvarasudhī (of Viśvāmtra gotra and of Āśvalāyana *sūtra*)—otherwise known as Kuṭṭikavi, was a great poet who has written three famous śatakas—the *Mahiṣaśataka,* the *Dhāṭīśataka* and the *Aśīśśataka*; and was surnamed *śleṣakavi-sārvabhauma* (the emperor of the poets who indulged in *double entendre)*; that his grandfather was one Mādhavārya and his father, Narasiṁha who was well-versed in Vedas and Vedāṅgas. He studied Vedas and Śāstras under his revered father and wrote a commentary on the Mahiṣaśataka of his greatgrandfather on the lines suggested by his own father; he also commented on the Hiraṇyakeśiśrautasūtra; composed two smṛti digests in the Dattakacintāmaṇi and the Śrāddhacintāmaṇi, a commentary called *Brahmasūtrārthacintāmaṇi* on the Brahmasūtras, and an independent treatise known as *Kākatālīy-avādārtha* explaining the significance of the popular yet difficult *kākatāliyanyāya.*

Vāñcheśvara is known as a *protégé* of Serfoji, the last but one of the Mahratha kings of Tanjore in the first quarter of the 19th century. He belonged to a *karṇāṭaka* family, called Hosala, and from his great-grandfather Kuṭṭikavi, all learned members of his family were protected by the Mahratha Court at Tanjore and they settled finally in the village *Sāharājapura,* the modern *Thiruveśanellore,* near Kumbakonam— a village which is believed to have been gifted away to brahmins by the great Sahaji, the son of Ekoji *alias* Venkoji, the first Mahratha king at Tanjore.

He mentions in the introductory verses[334] of his *Bhāṭṭacintāmaṇi* and *Hiraṇyakeśiśrautasūtravyākhyā* three gurus—*Īśvara, Śrīnivāsa* and *Ahobala* under whom he studied Mīmāṁsā, Nyāya and Vedānta respectively. He also gives the date when he began to write the commentary on the Hiraṇyakeśiśautasūtras thus—

Vasvagnyadrikṣitimita-
śake vāñcheśvaraḥ sudhīḥ |
Hiraṇyakeśinām sūtraṁ
vyākhyātumupacakrame || [335]

It comes to 1738 Śaka, *i.e.,* A.D. 1816. So he may be fairly fixed to a period between A.D. 1760 and 1830.

In the fore-going pages I have endeavoured to give a brief survey of the history of the *Pūrva* Mīmāṁsā Śāstra and tried to notice nearly *seventy* authors, more than half of whom are practically unknown to the students of Sanskrit. The reason for this is obvious: their works are not published. In many such cases I have consulted the works of those authors preserved in the Madras Govt. and Adyar Mss. Libraries and given a brief account of their nature and value. Nearly *fifty* works more are noticed in an alphabetical order in Appendices I and II. The authors of many works in them are not known; nothing also is to be suggested about their dates. Besides the descriptive catalogues of the Sanskrit Mss. at Madras and Tanjore, I have consulted Mr. P.V. Kane's paper on 'The *Pūrva* Mīmāṁsā System' and 'The History of the Dharmaśāstra', both affording great help to me. Dr. A.B. Keith's Karmamīmāṁsā, Sir S. Radhakrishnan's Indian Philosophy, Vol. II and Prof. Das Gupta's 'A History of Indian Philosophy' Vol. I and many important papers contributed by many a scholar in the field were also of great avail to me; and all these I have acknowledged either in the body or in the References of my Introduction. As far as possible, I have made a note of the publications of those works already printed. The dates that are assigned are necessarily to be very tentative and any suggestion towards greater accuracy will naturally be very welcome. A full discussion of the doctrinal side of the history of the *Pūrva* Mīmāṁsā System I have purposely omitted in this short Introduction.

REFERENCES

* *Vide* MM. S. Kuppuswami Sastrigal's "*A Primer of Indian Logic*"—Introduction, pp. VI & VII.

1. Compare Pāṇini's *sūtra*—' *mānbadhadūnśānbhyo dirghaḥ ca abhyāsasya* ' III—1. 6; and Kātyāyana's Vārttika—' *māneḥ jijñāsāyām*'.

2. "The expounders of Brahman *discuss* (the question) whether (a day) should be omitted or not; on this (they) say that it must be left out."—(P. V. Kane, P. M. System, p. 2.)
3. 'One should not *discuss* the merits of a brāhmaṇa '—*(ibid)*.
4. 'Then follows the *discussion* of the Go and Āyus (in the Gavāmayana satra sacrifice)'—Keith.
5. "Now they *discuss* (this question)—'supposing some one in carelessness makes a blunder in a Śāstra or a recitation or if there is doubt, should one, thinking that the error has passed unnoticed, mentally considering the (place of) occurrence, having gone back and remedied the error, proceed immediately from the (place of) occurrence (of the error) ? "—Keith, p. 497.
6. 'Now begins the *discussion* of the Paridhāna itself. —KANE.
7. This, however, is mere *speculation*'.—[Eggeling's translation. (S. B. E. Vol. XXVI, p. 25.)]
8. "Several learned Vedic students like Prācīnaśāla Aupamanyava have assembled together and *discussed* the question 'Who is the Ātman ? ' 'What is Brahman?'"— (P. V. Kane's P. M. System).
9. "This is (the result of) the *discussion* on Bliss."— *(Ibid.)*
10. "Thou knowest indeed very little of Brahman's form if thou knowest 'I know it well'. What thou knowest of this brahman among the gods is also very little. Therefore the nature of brahman is still to be *ascertained* or *discussed* by Thee."
11. "The Brahmavādins *discuss* whether water can be drawn at sunset."
12. "(The scholars) discuss whether any expiatory ceremony is to be enjoined or not (when one utters falsehood, etc.)"
13. "When there is a conflict of two texts of equal authority, either may be accepted (as pramāṇa)."
14. "There is option between two or more objects which have the same utility or purpose."
15. '*Śruti* (a vedic text) is an authority more powerful than *ācāra* (custom), the authoritativeness of which is inferential.'
16. 'A vedic text, which is independent, is more authoritative than a smṛti text when there is a conflict.'
17. "When an action is due when one has ready pleasure therefrom, there is no inference of Śāstra."—(P. V. Kane's P. M. System, p. 3.)
18. '*Yasmin prītiḥ puruṣasya tasya lipsārthalakṣaṇū vibhaktatvāt.*'
19. "*Vivāhe duhitṛmate dānaṁ kāmyaṁ dharmārthaṁ śrūyate tasmāt*

duhitṛmate atiratham tad mithyākuryād iti tasyām krayaśabdaḥ saṁstutimātraṁ dharmāddhi sambandhaḥ."

20. '*Krayasya dharmamātralvam.*'

21. Jaimini quotes various *Ācāryas: Ātreya*—IV. 3. 18, V. 2. 18, VI. 1. 26; *Aitiśāyana*—III. 2. 43, III. 4. 24, VI. 1. 6; *Kāmukāyanā*—XI. 1. 56, XI. 1. 61; *Kārṣṇājini*—IV. 3. 17, VI. 7. 35; *Bādari*—III 1. 3, VI. 1. 27,' VIII. 3. 6, IX. 2. 33; *Lābukāyanu—VI* 7. 37; *Āśmarathya—VL* 5. 16, XVI. 2. 1 (2); *Ālekhana*—VI. 5. 17, XVI. 2. 1 (1).
Jaimini refers to some *Ācāryas* as '*eke*'—IX. 3. 4.

22. The Mahābhāṣya of Patañjali speaks of Mīmaṁsakas.—(Keilhokn Vol. I., p. 239); Patañjali instances a Brāhmaṇī who studied Kāsakrtsnī—Mīmāṁsā propounded by Kāsakṛstni: '*Kāśakṛtsī proktā mīmāṁsā Kāśakṛtsnī, Kāśakṛsnīm adhīte Kāśakṛtsnā brāhmaṇī '—(ibid.* Vol. II., pp. 205, 249, 325). P. V. Kane's P. M. System, p. 3.

23. '*Aṅgānām tu pradhānaiḥ avyapadeśa iti Nyāyavitsamaḥyah.*'

24. '*Athāpi nityānuvādam avidhim āhuḥ Nyāyavidaḥ.*'

25. Das Gupta's 'A History of Indian Philosophy' Vol. I. p. 370:—'Jaimini's *Mīmāṁsā Sūtras* were probably written about 200 B. C.' Sir S. RadhaKṛishṇan's Indian Philosophy Vol. II. p. 376 and footnote:— "The Fourth Century B.C. is the earliest period we can assign for Jaimini's work." Professor Jacobi in his contribution to 'Indian Studies in honour of Charles Rockwell Lanman' (1929) pp. 145-165, places the Mīmāṁsāsūtras of Jaimini between 300-200 B.C. on the assumption and belief that Jaimini is post-Paṇiniyan, a contemporary of Kātyāyana and prior to Patañjali. Professor Keith in his paper on 'Some Problems of Indian Philosophy ' (I.H.Q. 1932) does not, however, accept the reasons of Professor Jacobi, but has assigned the philosophical *sūtras* including the Mīmāṁsāsūtras to a date 'between the chief Upaniṣads and the third and fourth century A.D. (Sanskrit Literature p. 472.) In his Karmamīmāṁsā also he says that 'it is, then, a plausible conclusion that the Mīmāṁsā *Sātra* does not date after 200 A.D.' (p. 5.)

26. I. 3. 8-9 discuss whether *āryaprasiddhi* and *mleccha-prasiddhi* are equal authorities in the Śabdārthanirṇaya, and it concludes that the former is a greater authority than the latter, if there is conflict between them. I. 3. 10 decides, however, the authoritativeness of the mlecchaprasiddhi in instances where

there is no *āryaprasiddhi* e.g., *pika, nema,* etc.

27. I. 3. 1 (1-2) deals with the *prāmāṇya* of the *Smṛtis* on *dharma* and explains through the *pratyakṣaśrutī* which is now to be inferred. I. 3. 2 (3) decides the *aprāmāṇya.* of the *Smṛti* if it is in conflict with a *Śruti.*

28. I. 3. 11-14 decide the *prāmāṇya* of the *Kalpasūtras* on *dharma,* like other *Smṛtis.*

29. I. 3. 24-29 deal with the *sādhuśabdaprayoga* in vedic functions, which can be acquired only by a systematic study of the science of grammar. Hence the authoritativeness of Grammar on *dharma.*

30. Jaimini refers to Bādarāyaṇa in I. 1. 5; V. 2. 19; VI. 1. 8; X. 8. 44, and XL. 1. 63. Bādarāyaṇa refers to Jaimini in I. 2. 28; I. 2. 31; I. 3. 31; III. 2. 40; III. 4. 2; III. 4. 18; III. 4. 40; IV. 3. 12; IV. 4. 5, and IV. 4. 11. In these references Jaimini accepts Bādarāyaṇa's views *mostly* while Bādarāyaṇa does not approve of Jaimini's views.

31. "*Yadapi Jaiminīyaṁ vacanaṁ udghāṭayati, tadapi tadvivakḷāparijñānādeva udbhāuyate. kim kāraṇam. yato na jaimineḥ ayam abhiprāyaḥ—āmnāyaḥ sarva eva kriyārthaḥ—iti. Yadi hyayam abhiprāyosbhariṣyat 'athāio brahmajijñāsā, Janmādyasya yataḥ' ityevamādi brahmavastusvarūpamātrayāthāhaprakāśanaparam ganibhīranyāyasandṛbhdham sarvavedāntārtha-mīmāmsanam śrīmacchārrakam nāsūtrayiṣyat; asūtrayacca. Tasmāt Jaiminereva ayam abhiprāyo— yathaiva vidhivākyānām svārthamātre prāmāṇyam, evam aikātmyavākyānām api anadhi gatavastuparicchedasāmyāt iti."—Naiṣkarmyasiddhi,* P. 52. B. S. P. S. No. XXXVIII.

In Lecture IV—*Vedānta in the Brahmasūtras*—in his Shree Gopal Basu Mallik Lectures (1925), Professor S. K. Belvalker observes: "That a '*Sārīrakasūtra*' beginning with the first two *sūtras* of the present Brahmasūtra was actually composed by Jaimini, the author of the *Pūrva Mīmāṁsā Sūtras*, is unambiguously declared by no less a writer than Sureśvarācārya, author of the Naiṣkarmyasiddhi; and this *Śārirakasūtra* may very well have been the postulated 'Chāndogya' Brahmasūtra, not only for the reason that both the writer (Jaimini) and the Upaniṣad (Chāndogya) belong to the Sāma Veda, but also for the further reason that, with one solitary exception in all the other references to Jaimini in the Vedānta *Sātras*—where the references are directly to a textual exegesis—we find him discussing a passage from the several Prapāṭhakas of just the Chāndogya Upaniṣad." (P. 141). Thus, Professor S. K. Belvalker along with Deussen, believes that like ten pratiśākhlya Kalpasūtras, Jaimini's Vedānta *Sātras* belonged to the Śākhās of the Sāma Veda, particularly to that of the Chāndogyopaniṣad and that 'this *Śārīrakasūtra* was bodily incorporated within, and forms the main part of the contents of, the present text of the Brahmasūtra (of Bādarāyaṇa)'. (P. 142). It may be observed here that it is doubtful whether Jaimini and the predecessors of Jaimini and Bādarāyaṇa wrote *pratiśākhīya Brahmasūtras,* (like the Kalpasūtras) on the ground that the aims and function of the Brahmasūtras and the Kalpasūtras are different (i.e.) the former attempting a correct interpretation of doubtful or ambiguous passages in the Karmakāṇḍa and Upaniṣ ads, and the latter, cataloguing the duties of a sacrificer that are scattered in one or other of the Śākhās of the Vedas. That the Brahmasūtras attempt a synthetic study of the Upaniṣads is even accepted by Professor S. K. Belvalker when he says "that the original *Chāndogya* Brahmasūtra has undergone two radical overhaulings : first when the *pratiśākhīya* Brahmasūtra was enlarged in scope so as to be a *sarvaśākhīya* text giving a harmonious interpretation of the teaching of the Upaniṣads as a whole, and secondly by the addition of the controversial matter—and in particular the *Tarkapāda* (II. 2)— meant to carry the warfare into the enemy's own territory" (P. 144). It is possible to maintain that the *Tarkapāda* in the present Brahmasūtra is a new feature of its own; but it is to be accepted as an undeniable fact that all Brahmasūtras, like the *Pūrva Mīmāṁsā Sūtras*, as the Science of Exegesis, attempt a synthetic study of all Upaniṣ ads of all Śākhās of all Vedas so far known or were available to them.

32. Prof. K.A. Nilakantha Sastri in his paper on 'Jaimini and Bādarāyaṇa' duplicates Jaimini to differentiate the Mīmāṁsist from the Vedāntin. (*Vide* Indian Antiquary, Vol. L. 211 ff.) But, in some cases of Ācāryas, the Mīmāṁsist himself can be a Vedāntin. The Jaimini referred to in the Śābarabhāṣya on VI. 3. 1. may, however, be a different person other than the *Pūrva* Mīmāṁsā *Sātra*kāra. Hence no room for assuming a third Jaimini as a *darśanakāra*. (See Keith's Sanskrit Literature, p. 475 f. n.)

33. "*Siṁho nyākaraṇasya karturaharat prāṇān priyān pāṇineḥ. mīmāṁsākṛtamunmanātha sahasā hastī muniṁ jaiminim.*"

34. "*Sosyaṁ prājāpatyo vidhiḥ tarn imaṁ prajāpatiḥ bṛhaspataye provāca bṛhaspatiḥ nāradāya nārado viṣvaksenāya viṣvakseno vyāsāya pārāśaryāya vyāsaḥ pārāśaryo jaiminaye jaiminiḥ pauṣ -pīṇḍyāya pārāśaryāyaṇāya pārāsaryāyaṇo bāda-rāyaṇāya*"—(quoted by Prof. K. A. Nilakantha Sastri in his paper on 'Jaimini and Bādarāyaṇa.' P. 173, I. A. Vol. L. 1921.)

35. "*Brahmā prajāpataye mīmāṁsāṁ provāca sopīndrāya sopyagnaye, sa ca vasiṣṭhāya, sopi parāśarāya parāśaraḥ kṛṣṇadvaipāyanāya sopi jaiminaye sa ca svopadeśāt anantaram imam nyāyam granthe* nibaddhavān *iti.*" Another version of this *guruparamparā* is known with slight modification—'*Brahmā maheśvaro vā prajāpataye mīmāṁsām provāca prajāpatiḥ indrāya indra ādityāya sopyagnaye etc.*'—(*Yuktisnehaprapūraṇi*. P. 4. N. S. Ed.)

36. '*Parāśarāt satyavatyām aṁśāṁśakalayā vibhuḥ;*
avartīrṇo mahābhāga vedam cakre caturvidham.
× × ×
tāsāṁ sa caturaḥ śiṣyān upāhūya mahāmatiḥ;
ekaikām saṁhitām brahman ekaikasmai dadau vibhnḥ.
× × ×
sāmnāṁ jaiminaye prāha tathā chandogasaṁhitām.
(*Sri Bhāgavatam*, XII. 6. 49-55.)

37. "Prācīnāvītī *Sumantu- Jaimini-vaiśampāyana-paila sūtra-bhāṣyabhāratamahābhūratadharmācāryāḥ*"— (*Āśvalāyanagṛhyasūtra*. III. 4. 5.) Trivandrum Sanskrit Series No. (XXVIII 1923).

38. *Vide* the author's paper on '*Saṅkarṣakāṇḍa—a genuine supplement to the Pūrva Mīmāṁsā*' MM. Haraprasāda Śāstri Commemoration Volume, I. H. Q., Vol. IX, 1933.

39. Śabarasvāmin refers to the *Saṅkarṣakāṇḍa* in his Bhāṣya XII. 2. 11: '*iti Saṅkarṣe vakṣyati*' which proves that the *Saṅkarṣakāṇḍa sūtras* are from the pen of Jaimini and that they are genuine. The traditional belief that Śabarasvāmin has written a Bhāṣya on those chapters has not as yet been proved by literary or other evidences.

40. *Vide* the *Tantravārttika* I. 3. 2 (5)—'*etajjaimininaiva Chāndogyānuvāde.*'

41. *Vide* Keith's Karmamīmāṁsā: page 5.

42. *Vide* his paper on '*Bodhāyana and Dramiḍācārya— two old Vedāntins presupposed by Rāmānuja*' submitted to the Third Oriental Conference, Madras, (1924).

43. *Vide* his '*Maṇimekhalai in its historical setting*' pp. 91-92.
44. *Prapañcahṛdaya*—(T. S. S. XLV. P. 39).
45. *Vide* Dr. S. K. Iyengar's '*Maṇimekhalai in its historical setting*' p. 189.
46. *Ibid.*, p. 92.
47. *Vide* A. B. Dhruva's Introduction to Diṅnaga's *Nyāyapravesa*, p. xv. (G. O. S. No. xxxviii).
48. '*Maṇimekhalai in its historical setting*' p. 192.
49. See the writer's paper on the '*Doctrine of Sphoṭa*' in the Annamalai University Journal, Vols. I. (Part 2), and II. (Part 1).
50. Journal of Oriental Research, Vol. III. Part I. (1929).
51. For a detailed discussion of this point, see the writer's paper on '*Old Vṛttikāras on the Pūrva Mīmāṁsā Sūtras*' I. H. Q., September 1934.
52. Kumārila's *Vārttika* on I. 3. 2 gives us another instance:
"pramāṇāyāṁ smṛtau sparśanaṁ vyāmohaḥ
sparśane pramāṇe smṛtiḥ vyāmohaḥ" (Bhāṣya):
"pramāṇamayate yāti mūlabhūtāṁ śrutim yataḥ;
Kvibantādayateḥ tasmāt pramāṇā smṛtirucyate." (Vārttika).
53. Compare Appayya Dīkṣita's remark in his *Kalpataru-Parimala* I. 1. 1. See the writer's paper on '*Old Vṛttikāras on the P. M. Sūtras*' I. H. Q., September 1934 (foot-note p. 436).
54. See ibid *foot-note* pp. 436 & 437. For Upavarṣa's views as gleaned from Śabara's *Bhāṣya* and Kumārila's *Vārttika*, see *ibid.* pp. 437-448.
55. '*loka ityasya bhāṣyasya ṣaḍarthān sampracakṣate*' *Ś.* V. I. 1. 1.
56. "*Vṛttyantareṣu keṣāñcit laukikārthavyatikramaḥ;*
śabdānāṁ dṛśyate teṣām upālambhoyamucyate.
'athāta' ityayaṁ loke nānantarye prayujyate;
tasmāt tādarthyametasya paribhāṣādibhihiḥ bhavet.
prasiddhahāniḥ śabdānām aprasiddhe ca kalpanā;
na kāryā Vṛttikāreṇa sati siddhārthasambhave." (Ś. V. I. 1. 1. verses 33-35).

Pārthasārathimiśra in his *Nyāyaratnākara* comments on this Vārttika thus :—*upālambhapakṣam parigṛhṇāti– Vṛttyantareṣviti. Keṣāñcit—Bhavadāsādīnām—Vṛttyantareṣu. Kīdṛśaḥ punarupālambhaḥ iti tat svayam darśayati—athāta iti. Padadvayam arthadvayavāci lokaprasiddhamapi Bhavadāsena ekapadīkṛtya ānantaryamātrārtham vyākhyātam, tadayuktamiti—upālambha iti.* (Chaukhamba Edn., pp. 11 & 12).

Sucaritamiśra in his *Kāśikā* observes thus :—'*Vṛttyantareṣu iti; Keśāñcit hi Bhavadāsādīnāṁ Vṛttyantareṣu śabdānām alaukikortha upavarṇitaḥ............Kva punaḥ Bhavadāsena alaukikārthagrahaṇam kṛtam, yadevam upālabhyate; ata āha—athāta iti...........Bhavadāsena ca uktam—"athāta ityam śabda ānantarye prayujyate" iti.* (Kāśikā, T.S.S., pp. 13 & 14).

57. Ś.V. Chau. Edn., pp. 21 & 22.

58. '*Varṇyate sūtrabhedena yena pratyakṣalakṣaṇam.*' (Ś.V.) The *Nyāyaratnākara* on this observes :—'*Bhavadāsena etat sūtraṁ dvidhā kṛtvā 'satsamprayoge' ityādi 'pratyakṣam' ityevantaṁ pratyakṣalakṣaṇaparam; 'animittam' ityādi tasya dharmaṁ prati unimittatvaparam vyākhyātam, tat upanyasya dūṣayati—'Varṇyate' iti.* Pp. 133 & 134.

The *Kāśikā* also observes.—"*tadidaṁ vṛttyantare animittādavacchidya tat pratyakṣam ityevamantam lakṣaṇaparaṁ vyākhyātam; tat upanyasya dūṣayati—Varṇyate iti*". T. S. S., p. 204.

59. In I. 1. 5 Śabara mentions Pāṇini, and in X. 8. 1 (4) both Pāṇini and Kātyāyana with the honorific title '*bhagavān*'; but he asserts that Pāṇini is a greater authority than Kātyāyana. "*Sadvāditvcca Pāṇineḥ vacanam pramāṇam; asadvditvāt na Kātyāyanasya.*"

60. In I. 1. 5 he mentions Yāska by the title *Śāstrakāra,* Piṅgala as the author of the *Chandaśśastra*; in I. 1. 2, Manu and in VI. 1 cites one verse as a Smṛti passage which is more or less the same as the Manusmṛti IX. 416 and the Mahābhārata Udyogaparva—33. 64; in VI. 8. 18 he cites an Āpastamba *sūtra* as a smṛti passage; in I. 3. 3 he might have referred to by the phrase—*Vedabrahmacaryacaraṇa*—the Baudhāyana passage (I. 2. 1) which he also uses.

61. '*Brāhmaṇyāmabhavat varāhamihiro jyotirvidāmagraṇīḥ*
rājā bhartṛhariśca vikramanṛpaḥ kṣatrātmajāyāmabhūt;
vaiśyāyām haricandravaidyatilako jātaśca śaṅkuḥ kṛtī
śūdrāyām amaraḥ ṣaḍeva śabarasvāmidvijasyātmajāḥ.'

62. ' *iti saṅkarṣe vakṣyati.*'

63. This Bhāṣya was published first in the *Bibliotheca Indica* and then in the Chaukhamba Series at Benares. Two parts of its translation in English by MM. Dr. Ganganatha Jha were published in the Gaekwad Series, Baroda, (1934).

64. *Vide* the writer's paper on '*The Old Vṛttikāras on the P. M. Sūtras*' I. H.Q., September 1934

65. It is now accepted on all hands that the *Vṛttigrantha* in Śabara's *Bhāṣya* on I. 1. 5 goes to the end of that *adhikaraṇa* and that the ātmavāda therein is a *résumé* of Upavarṣa's Vṛtti on III. 3. 53 of the Vedānta *Sūtras*. For other details of Upavarṣa and of other Vṛttikāras, see the paper on '*The Old Vṛttikāras on the P. M. Sūtras.*'
66. *Vide* his Bhāṣya X. 8. 1.
67. '*nanu mīmānisāyāḥ cirantanāni bhartṛmitrādiracitāni vyākhyānāni vidyante, kimanenu ityata āha—prāyeṇeti. Mīmāṁsā hi bhartṛmitrādibhiḥ alokāyataiva satī lokāyatikṛtā nityaniṣiddhayoḥ īṣṭānīṣṭaṁ phalaṁ nāstītyādi bahvaprasiddhāntaparigraheṇeti tam āstikapathe kartuṁ vārttikārambhayatnaḥ kṛto mayā iti.*' (Chau. Edn., pp. 3-4)
68. *Vide* the Proceedings of the Second Oriental Conference, Calcutta, pp. 410-411.
69. Prabhākaravijaya (Sanskrit Sāhitya Parishad Series, PP. 1-4).
70. Benares Edition, pp. 4-5.
71. *Vide* MM. S. K. Sastrigal's paper on '*Further Light in the Prābhākara School of Karma Mīmāṁsā*' submitted to the Third Oriental Conference, Madras (1924); and MM. N. S. Anantakrishna Śāstri's Edition of the Prabhākara Vijaya.
72. '*imameva ca saṁskāram śabdagrahaṇakāraṇam;*
kecittu paṇḍitammanyāḥ śrotramityabhimanyate.'
Saṁjñāsañcaraṇāccaiṣām bahumānaḥ svacetasi;
mudhaiṣām bahumānoyam vastvanutpādya kiñcana.
Ś.V. L. 1. 6. 130-131.

    Pārthasārathimiśra while commenting on these *Vārttika* verses observes thus :—'*atha bhartṛmitro vadati—na śrotram nāma kiñtcit, tasya ca dhvanijanyaḥ saṁskāraḥ' iti dvayam Kalpyam; ādau dhvanijanyaḥ saṁskāra eva śrotram, tat upanyasya upālambhate—Imam iti.* (Chau. Edn., pp. 763.)
73. Vizianagaram Sanskrit Series, pp. 213, 226.
74. Nirnaya Sagara Edition, p. 14.
75. Bhartṛhari (who died about A.D. 600) is believed by eminent writers to have written *Vṛttis* or *Bhāṣyas* on both the *Pūrva* and the Uttara *Mīmāṁsā Sūtras*. None of them is however available to us. But, as there are strong evidences to show that he has elucidated many important doctrines of both the Mīmāṁsā systems in his famous *Vākyapadīya,* would it be far-fetched to suggest that he might not have written any commentary on

those *sūtras* ? (*Vide* the writer's paper on ' *The Doctrine of Sphoṭa'*, Annamalai University Journal, Vol. I., Part 2, p. 235, foot-note.)

76. Tradition says that Kumārila was an incarnation of God Subrahmaṇya. It would further have it that he was a scholar well-versed in the orthodox systems of philosophy and other allied branches of knowledge, and that later, in the guise of a Buddhist mendicant, he studied Buddhism first-hand under a Buddhist Ācārya and gave it its death-blow by writing his *Ślokavārttika* on the Tarka-pāda of the *Śābarabhāṣya* and that he burnt himself in a pyre of chaff-fire for his purification and release from the curse of his Buddhist teacher.

77. *Vide* the *Tantravārttika*, I. 3. 5 (10).

78. *Vide* his remarks on I. 3. 2 (4).

'Kaṭhamaitrāyaṇīyādipaṭhitaśrutimūlikāḥ;
dṛśyante smṛtayaḥ sarvāḥ bhadropanayanādiṣu.
tadā tanmadhyapātyekam vākyam kiñcidapasmṛtiḥ;
mūlāntarodbhavam vaktum jihvā no na pravartate.

× × ×

bādhitā ca smṛtirbhūtvā kācinnyāyavidā yadā;
śrūyate na cirādeva śākhāntaragatā śrutiḥ.
tadā kā le mukhacchāyā syānnaiyāyikamāninaḥ;
bādhābādhānavasthānam dhruvamevam prasajyate.'

He says also that the *sarvaveṣṭanasmṛti* is based on one *prakāśaśruti* : —*'etat Jaimininaiva chāndogyānuvade śāṭyāyanibrāhamaṇagataśrutimūlatvena audumbarīprakaraṇe ca śāṭyāyaninām tām ūrdhvadeśena ubhayatra vāsasi darśayatīti 'vaiṣṭutam vai vāsaḥ śrīḥvai vaśaḥ śriḥ sāma' iti darśite tatprasaṅgena audum-barīveṣṭanavāsasopi prakāśaśrutimūlatvameva anvākhyātam.'*

79. In the same *adhikaraṇa* Kumārila observes.— *'etaddhi Jaimininā atyantam hitopadeśinā jijñāsubhyaḥ pratipādyate—*
Yāvadekam Śrutau karma smṛtau, vānyat pratīyate;
tāvattayorviruddhatve Śrautānuṣṭhānamiṣyate.'

80. The *Ślokavārttika* was published at Benares with the commentary Nyāyaratnākara (1898) and a part of it at Trivandrum (T. S. S.) with the Kāśikā (1926). The *Tantravārttika* and Ṭupṭīkā were published at Benares and at Poona. The English translation of both the *Ślokavārttika* and the *Tantravārttika* by Dr. Jha were also published at Benares.

Mādhavasarasvatī in his *Sarvadarśanakaumudī* gives the list of works of Kumārila:—'*tatra sahasrādhikaraṇadvādāśalakṣaṇyā mīmāṁsāyāḥ caturviṁśatisahasram Śabarasvāmikṛtam bhāṣyam. Tadupari prasthānadvayam—Bhāṭṭam Prabhākaram iti. Tatra Bhaṭṭācāryāṇām pañca vyākhyānāni bhāṣyasya:—ekā bṛhaṭṭīkā, dvitīyā madhyamaṭīkā. tṛtīyā ṭupṭikā, caturthī Kārikā, pañcamam Tantratārttikam uktānuktadurukta-cintakam. Tatra Bṛhan-Madhyamaṭīke samprati na vartete.*'

81. The discovery that Kumārilabhaṭṭa has written a commentary called *Bṛhaṭṭīkū* has now led scholars to believe that such vārttika verses cited by Śālīkanātha and other authors of the Prābhākara school as are not found either in the *Ślokavārttika* or in the *Tantravārttika* may be traced to the *Bṛhaṭṭīkā,* and that the *Vārttikakāramiśra* mentioned by Śālīkanātha in his *Prakaraṇapañcikā* and other works may therefore be none other than Kumārila. If this view is accepted, there is no room for the assumption that there was a *Vārttikakūra* other than Kumārila as the *precursor of the Prābhākara school of the Mīmāṁsā Śāstra.*

82. Nyāyasudhā, I. 3. 10. pp. 329 & 330. Chaukambah Edition. Mānameyodaya. Arthāpatti Section, p. 126, T. P. H. Oriental Series, 1933.

83. *Vide* his *Prābhākara Mīmāṁsā:* a reprint from 'Indian Thought' pp. 12-17. Refer also Keith's A History of Sanskrit Literature, pp. 473-474.

84. *Vide* his paper 'Further Light on the Prābhākara Problem' in the Proceedings of the Third Oriental Conference, 1924, pp. 474-481.

85. *Vide* Dr. T. R. Chintamani's paper on 'The Works of Prabhākara': Journal of Oriental Research, Madras, Vol. Ill, pp. 281-291 (1929).

86. See Śālīkanātha's opening remark in his *ṛjuvimalīā*—'*loake' ityādi bhāṣyam 'yatnagauravam prasajyeta' ityevamantam athaśabda-dūṣaṇārtham aucityānubhāṣaṇaparam iti vārttikakāreṇa vyākhyātam. Tattu mandaprayojanamiti matvā ṭīkākāraḥ prayojanam darśayati—loka ityādi bhāṣyasyetyādinā.*' (Ṛjuvimalā, Madras Edition, pp. 1 & 2.) See also *ibid,* p. 116 which refers to 'Bhagavān Vārttikakāra' and 'ṭīkākāra' the latter refuting the former—'*tadetat ṭīkākāro na mṛṣyati.*'

87. *Vide* MM. S. Kuppuswami Sastri's A Primer of Indian Logic, p. 167.

88. *Vide* his History of Dharma Śāstra under Viśvarūpācārya, pp. 252-264.
89. The Vidhi Viveka was printed with the commentary *Nyāyukaṇikā* in the 'Pandit', at Benares (1907).
90. The Bhāvanāviveka was edited by MM. Dr. Ganganatha Jha (in two parts) with the commentary of Umveka in the Sarasvatī Bhavana Text Series, Benares.
91. The Vibhramaviveka was edited by MM. S. Kuppu-swami Sastrigal and Vedānta Śiromaṇi T.V. Ramachandra Dikshitar in the Journal of Oriental Research, Madras. Prof. MM. S. K. Sastrigal has dealt with the five *khyātis* in a learned introduction to that work.
92. The text of the Mīmāṁsāsūtrānukramaṇī was published at Benares; a second edition of the same has been published together with an elaborate commentary by Dr. Ganganatha Jha.
93. The *Sphoṭasiddhi* (with its commentary *Gopālikā)* was edited by Pandit S.K. Ramanatha Sastri under the auspices of the Madras University.
94. The *Brahmasiddhi* is in course of publication by the Madras Government under the editorship of MM. S.K. Sastrigal.
95. See his papers on 'The Prābhākara Schools of Karma Mīmāṁsā' and on 'Further Light of the Prābhākara Problem', submitted to the Second and Third Oriental Conferences, 1922 and 1924.
96. Citsukhācārya's Tattvapradīpikā, N. S. Edn., p. 265.
97. *'iti śrī bhaṭṭa-kumārilaśiṣyakṛte mālatīmādhave tṛtīyoṅkaḥ'. 'iti śrī kumārilasiāmiprasādaprāptavāgvaibhava śrīmadum-vekācāryaviracite mālatī mādhave ṣaṣṭhoṅkaḥ'.*
98. *'Yadvedādhyayanam tathopaniṣadām sāṅkhyasya Yogasya ca jñānam tatkathanena kim, na tu tataḥ kaṣcit guṇo nāṭake.*
[Prologue to the Mālatīmādhava].
99. His commentary on the *Ślokavārttika* is now in course of publication under the editorship of Pandit S. K. Ramanatha Sastrigal under the auspices of the Madras University.
100. It was published under the editorship of Dr. Ganganatha Jha as No. 6 of the Prince of Wale's Sarasvati Bhavana Text Series, Benares.
101. According to Parameśvara II (the commentator on the *Tattva-bindu)* we have to believe that Cidānanda. in the introductory portion of his Nītitattvāvirbhāva, has mentioned Umveka as a great *Nibandhanakāra*.

102. Rāmakṛṣṇa's *Yuklisnehaprapūraṇī* on I. 1. 2.—"*atra umvekabhaṭṭaiḥ :—'idantu vārttikakāriyam dūṣaṇam samarthanam ca sarvam eva ahīnaviśīrṇam' ityādinā 'syenādau no. kaśyacit anarthatvam, brahmahatyādaya eva tu anarthatvena arthapadavyāvartyāḥ; Śyenādīnāntu na sākṣāt, nāpyupacāreṇa, nāpi tatphalasyānarthatvam iti tasyānarthatvapratipādanaparam 'śyeno vajraḥ' ityādi bhāṣyam upekṣaṇīyam—*
'Gurorapyamliptasya kāryākāryamajānataḥ;
Utpatham pratipannasya 'parityāgo vidhīyate'".
ityantena aranthena vārttikam bhāṣyañca dūṣitam, (tadasmābhiḥ granthavistarabhayāt prakṛtānupayogācca na likliitam)."
—N. S. Edn., p. 30.

103. Śālīkanātha quotes in his Prakaraṇapañcikā (p. 178, Benares Edn.) two verses of Maṇḍana:—'*pumsām neṣlābhyu-pāyatvāt*', '*Karturiṣṭābhyupāye hi*'.—(Vidhiviveka, pp. 243 & 302, Benares Edition).

104. The passage in the *Nyāyakaṇikā* (p. 109, Benares Edition)—'*atraiva Juratprābhākaronnītārtham guroḥ vacaḥ saṅgacchata ityāha.......... navīnastūnnayanti— 'anirūpitaniyoga-vyāpārasyedam codyamityupakramya idam uktam—'Kurtavyatā-viṣayo niyogaḥ na punaḥ Kartavyatāmātram' iti. Yāgakarta-vyatānuṣṭhānam viṣayo niyogasya, tena niyogaḥ sādhyate na tu yāgasyānuṣṭhanam jñāpayati."* Here the reference to '*navīnas*' is, according to Professor MM. S. Kuppuswami Sastrigal, to Sālīkanātha whose explanation of this *Ṭīkāgrantha* in his *Ṛjuvimalā* (Madras Edition, p. 37) Vācaspati practically repeats *verbatim*. See MM. S. Kuppuswami Sastrigal's paper on 'Further Light on the Prābhākara Problem' (p. 479).

105. Its *Tarkapāda* with the Bṛhati and the Bhāṣya was edited by Pandit S. K. Ramanatha Sastrigal under the auspices of the University of Madras (1934).

106. It was published by the Chaukhamba Book Depot at Benares in 1903.

107. This is in course of publication by the Madras University.

108. *Vide* the Journal of Oriental Research, Vol. II, pp. 62-64. The *Candrikā* says '*mahodadhirnāma Śārīkanāma (Sālikanātha) sahabrahmācārī gurumate nibandhanakartā Bhavanātha-vat......... Mahāvrato nāma bhaṭṭamatānuvartī Muhodadhi-pratispardhī*'. N. S. Edition, p. 53.

109. *Vide* I. 1. 7 of the *Nayaviveka*.
110. See Das Gupta's History of Indian Philosophy, Vol. I, p. 107; Keith's Indian Logic and Atomism, p. 29.
111. See Keith's Indian Logic and Atomism, p. 31.
112. *Vide* his Tātparyaṭīkā, Benares Edition, p. 133. '*Trivikramagurūnnītamārgānugamanonmukhaiḥ; yathāmānam yathāvastu tyākhyātamidamidṛśam*'.
113. *Vide* Bhāmatī II. 1. 33 and the last verse.
114. The text and English translation by Dr. Ganganatha Jha were published at Benares.
115. It was published at Poona (together with the *Sātras* and Bhāṣ ya).
116. The *Nyāyakaṇikā* (with the *Vidhiviveka)* was published in the 'Pandit' at Benares.
117. The *Tattvabindu* was first published in the 'Pandit'. Another edition of the same (together with the *Tattvavibhāvanā)* now appears in the Annamalai University Sanskrit Series No. 3. (A. U.S.S. 3).
118. The *Brahmatattvasamīkṣā* is so far not known as available even in Mss.
119. Several editions of the *Bhāmatī* appeared together with Bhāṣya and commentaries at Bombay, Benares and Srirangam (Madraṣ). In the Bibliotheca Indica it was published separately. Its Catussūtrī with the Bhāṣya in English translation was published by Messrs. Dr. C. Kunhan Raja and S. Suryanarayana Sastri. (T. P. H.)
120. *Vide* the *Prapañcahṛdaya,* T. S. S. Edition, p. 39.
121. *'Asmin pāde 'apūrvāt tathā somaḥ' ityārabhya āpāda-parisamāpteḥ Bhāvadāsameva bhāṣyam' iti.* See Bhavadāsa above p. 20.
122. It is preserved in Ms. in the Madras Government Oriental and Adyar Mss. Libraries.
123. *Vide* Mr. P. V. Kane's 'History of Dharmaśāstra' p. 281.
124. '*Vārttikakāreṇa prāmāṇyavicārapūrvakam guṇavidhinā-madheyacintāpravartanena kṛstanasyādhyāyasya pramāṇa-vyutpādanārthatvam vārttikakārābhimatam ityavagamāt pramāṇa-vyutpādanārthatvam vārttikakārābhimatam ityavagamāt Sucaritamiśramatam Vārttikakārāsammatatvāt na yuktamityāha—'tadaneneti'. 'tadanena....ye manyante te nirākṛtāḥ....'.—Śāstradīpikā* with the Mayūkhamālikā, N. S. Edn.,

p. 53.

125. '*tathā ca Kāśikā....Seśvaramīmāṁsā*'—Conjeevaram Edition, pp. 64-65.
126. '*aprayogasya siddhim Kāśikoktām pariharannāha—'na cā yaugikānāmiti'*.— Nītitattvāvirbhāvavyākhyā—Yogarūḍhivāda. Adyar Ms. p. 431.
127. A part of the Kāśikā with the *Ślokavārttika* was published in Trivandrum Sanskrit Series.
128. See his *Nyāyaratnamālā,* Chaukhamba Edn., p. 212.
Bhuvanatrayavikhyātaśrīmadyajñātmasūnunā;
Tata eva śrutam prāpya viśrutaḥ Pārthasārathiḥ.'
129. *Vide* his introductory remarks in the *Nyāyamālā-vistara : 'yadyapi Śātradīpikādau kvacit kvacit saṅgraha-ślokossti, tathāpi na sarvatra vidyate. Yatrāsti tatrāpi viṣaya-saṁśayayorasaṅg-rahānna ślokapāṭhamātreṇādhikaraṇamu-panyasitum śakyute. Ato na kvāpi gatārthatvam śaṅkanīyam'.*— (London Edition, 1878, p. 4.)
130. *Vide* the Vivaraṇaprameyasaṅgraha, Vizianagaram Sanskrit Series, Benares, No. 7, pp. 107, 124.
131. *Vide* Bhaṭṭasomeśvara (below). Foot note.
132. A part of the Tantraratna was, for the first time, published in the Sarasvatī Bhavana Text Series No. 31, Benares, under the editorship of MM. Ganganatha Jha, (1930).
133. The *Śāstradīpikā* refers to the Tantraratna and the Nyāyaratnamālā N. S. Edition, pp. 62, 471; the Nyāyaratnākara (p. 845) refers to the Nyāyaratnamālā and the *Śāstradīpikā*.
134. The *Śāstradīpikā* was first published at Benares. A second edition appeared at Bombay (1915) together with the Yuktisneha-prapūraṇī for the *Tarkapāda* and the Mayūkhamālikā for the rest. The *Tarkapāda* with a very recent commentary called *Prakāśa* was published at Benares.
135. The sixth is omitted by some authors.
136. The *Nyāyaratnamālā* was published at Benares.
137. The *Nyāyaratnākara* was published at Benares together with the *Ślokavārttika*.
138. (1) *Nayaviveka*, Adyar Ms. Vol. I., p. 264 : '*Śrīkaroktam—anvitesbhidheye anvayo gamyo nābhidhānivișṭi iti na śakti-gauravam iti; tanna.*' (2) *Ibid*. Vol. II., p. 458 : '*Śrīkarastu—Prākaraṇikaśeṣatvamātre dvaitīyasyāpūrvabodhakaśāstrabheda-syāpekṣeti hetutāmāha; tanna.*' (3) *Ibid*. Vol. II, p. 508:

'Śrīkarastu—Śrutitaḥ somārthakrayānvaye tanmukhena somaśeṣ atvāt āruṇyasya padārthāntarbhāvāt vākyata idam iti saṅgatimāha; tanna.' (4) *Ibid.*, Vol. II, pp. 529-30:—*'Śrīkarastu—kārakācastliābhidhāne kāraṇādibhyo nivartayitum kriyāphalabhāgitopādhiḥ anujñeyaḥ tadā gauravamityāha; tanna.'* (5) *Ibid.*, Vol. II, p. 544:—*'Śrīkarastu—Vājapeyena yūpasyopakāryopayogakārakāsambandhāt ṣaṣṭhītyāha; tanna.'*

139. (1) *Nayaviveka*, Adyar Ms. Vol. I, pp. 240-241.— *'Tadavasthe ca yāge tṛtīyārthasambhāvaneti. Tatraike samā-dadhati.'* Dīpikā, Adyar Ms. Vol. II, pp. 42-43 : —*'Asya codyasya Prakāśoktam samādhānamāha—Tatraike iti.'* (2) *Nayaviveka*, Vol. I, p. 248.—*'Yattu Kecit samādadhati—Kriyākārye .... ato dharmamātre lakṣaṇā yukteti. Tadayuktam.'* N. V. Dīpika, Adyar Ms. Vol. II, pp. 62 and 63 : *'na ca kriyākārye muktiyatā liṅādeḥ, apūrve tu lakṣaṇeti kuto na viparītamiti codyam. Prakāsādayo anyathā samāhitavantaḥ. Tudanubhāṣate dūṣayitum—Yattviti.'* (3) *Nayaviveka*, Vol. I, p. 290.—*'Kecittu vediprasaṅyavaiṣamyam eiamāhuḥ.'* Dipikā, Vol. II, p. 152.—*'Prakāsādayattu anyathā vedipmsangamūcuḥ; tadāha—Kecittviti.'* (4) *Nayaviveka*, Vol. I,pp.348-349:—*'Tatra Pañcikāyāmupāṁśuyājādhi-karaṇatrayasyāpavādakatayā saṅ-gatiruktā. Tatra Kecittu paurṇamāsyām apavādakatoktā ityāhuḥ; Tadayuktam.'* *Nayaviveka*dīpikā, Vol. II, pp. 361-362:—*'Atra Prakāśena paurṇamāsyadhikaraṇamīlacintāyām 'ya evam vidvān' ityvam sajātiyavākyānām yat samudāyānuvāda-katvam uktam, tat 'upāṁśuyājamantarā yajati' ityasya na sambhavatītyasya sādhyam. Tathā āghārāgnihotranaye agni-hotrāghāravākyayoḥ. ataḥ upāṁśuyājādhikaraṇatrayasya paur-ṇamāsyapavādakatayā saṅgatiḥ pañcikoktetyuktam. Tadāha— Tatra Keciditi. Tadayuktamiti. Paurṇamāsyapatādakatve peṭikāsaṅgatimātram syāt, nādhyāyasaṅgatiḥ. Nāyam Pañcikā-granthārtha ityarthaḥ.'*

140. *Vide* Mr. P. V. Kane's History of Dharma Śāstra, pp. 266-68.

141. *Vide ibid.*, pp. 306-308.

142. *'Mahatā praṇidhānena śakyameva vidhāntaram;*
Lokānumitamityeva Śālīkoktam prasādhyate'.
(*Nayaviveka*, Adyar Ms. Vol. I, p. 1, verse 3.)
'Pañcikādvayatantrārthasammohavṛnivṛttaye;
Udgrāhiṇi Bhavenaiśā vakṣyate Śeṣalakṣanā'.
(*Ibid.* III-l. 1. Vol. II, p. 455).

143. *'Vihāya vistaram śabdasoundaryaparanindane;*
Vyajyate Bhavanāthena tattiam Nayavivekataḥ.

Granthesmin vismayo bhāvī na vā kim tasya duṣkaram;
Yo dadāti......sarvasvam sahasotpattiśāsanam,'
(Ibid. I-1. 1. verses 2 and 4).

144. See the *Abhikramanādhikaraṇa,* III. 1.

145. See the *Vākyādhikaraṇa,* I. 1. 7, Adyar Ms., pp. 270-272.

146. From this title we have to understand that Kumārila—and not Prabhākara—is known as '*tutāta*' and his school as '*lautātitamata*'. *Vide* Vidyāraṇya's Śaṅkaradig-vijaya, Canto X, Verse 119.

147. '*Iti Śrī Bālavalabhībhujaṅgāparanāmno Bhaṭṭaśri-Bhavadevasya kṛtau tautātitamatatilake dvitīyasyādhyāyasya prathamaḥ pādaḥ.*'

148. P. V. Kene, op. Cit., 304.

149. '*Yasya khalu Bālaralabhībhujaṅga iti nāma nādṛtam kena;*
Mīmāṁsāyūpi sa pulakamākarṇitavarṇitodgītam.'
(Epigraphica Indica, Vol. VI, pp. 203-5, verse 24).

150. See *History of Dharmaśāstra*, p. 305.

151. This is preserved in the Madras Govt. Oriental Mss. Library and in the Adyar Theosophical Mss. Library.

152. '*Jaimini-Śabara-Kumārila-Sucarita-Paritoṣa-Pārtha-sārathayaḥ;*
Umveka-Vijayakārau Maṇḍana-Vācaspatī ca vijayantām.'

153. '*Nyāyasudhāyāmapi na prayoganirūpyatvadatra nirākṛtā evālaukikī preraṇā iti pakṣassamarthitaḥ. Evamanyairapi. Ajitāyām tu iṣṭasādhanatapakṣam prathamam vyākhyāya paścāt abhidhaivetyayamapi pakṣassamarthitaḥ. Pārthasārathimiśreṇa tu abhidhāpakṣam ciramanusṛtya paścādiṣṭasādhanatāpakṣ-osṅgīkṛto Nyāyaratnamalāyām. Śāstradīpikāyāntu svarga-kāmādhikaraṇe abhidhāpakṣa evāṅgīkṛtaḥ. Evañca sati śabdatadvyāpāravidhitvaparityāge ko hetuḥ, ata āha—śabdatadvyā-pārayoriti.*'—(Nītitattvāvirbhāvavyākhyā, Adyar Ms., p. 237).

From this remark of Parameśvara II, it may be said that Cidānanda, the author of the Nītitattvāvirbhāva, has presupposed the Nyāyasudhā of Bhaṭṭasomeśvara, the Ajitā of Paritoṣamiśra, and Pārthasārathimisra's Nyāyaratnamālā and *Śāstradīpikā*.

154. *Vide* D. T. Tatacarya's Mīmāṁsābhyudaya, p. 50 and Appendix II, p. 22.

155. The supposition that Bhaṭṭa Someśvara, the author of the Nyāyasudhā, is identical with Someśvara Bhaṭṭa, son of Vāmana Bhaṭṭa and grandson of Mahādevabhaṭṭa of Maura family, (who was mentioned in the Gadag and other inscriptions as the

dānādhikārin under the Cālūkya King Vikramāditya VI. *Vide Epigraphica Indica*, Vol. XV. pp. 348-363) cannot be accepted, in view of the fact that our author was (as the colophon in the Nyāyasudhā states) the son of Mādhava Bhaṭṭa. It is also known from the same inscription that Someśvara (son of Vāmana Bhaṭṭa) founded an endowment for the popularisation of the Prābhākara school, and as such, he was a staunch Prābhākara, while our author, the Commentator on the *Tantravārttika*, was a close follower of the Bhaṭṭa school.

156. The Nyāyasudhā was published at Benares.
157. *Vide* Nyāyasudhā, p. 1285.
158. *Vide* Bhāṭṭadipikā, IV. 3. 9 and Adhvaramīmāṁsā-kutūhalavṛtti, I. 2. 4. Vani Vilas Edition, p. 46.
159. The Arthavādādhikaraṇa (I. 2. 1) and the Mantrādhikaraṇa (I. 2. 4) were published in the J. O. R. Madras, Vol. II, pp. 270-278 (1928) and Vol. V, Supplement pp. 1-5.
160. *Vide* 'Annals of Bhandarkar Research Institute', Vol. X. (1930) pp. 238-45.
161. *Vide* J. O. R. Madras, Vols. II and V (1928 & 1931).
162. See MM. Kuppuswami Sastri's 'A Primer of Indian Logic', Introduction, p. XLVIII, and Kāvyatīrtha Umesha Miśra's Note on 'Ekādaśādyādhikaraṇa of Murāri Miśra', A. B. R. I., Vol. X, p. 236.
163. See Dr. A. B. Keith's Sanskrit Drama, p. 225.
164. See the Sanskrit Introduction to the Prabhākaravijaya, p. 16, Saṁskṛta Sāhitya Pariṣat Series, No. 11, (1926) Calcutta.
165. The 21 topics are.—

1. Prayuktinirṇayaḥ	11. Paramāṇusamarthanam
2. Vaktṛjñānānumānatā	12. Kāryavyutpattisamarthanam
3. Akhyātisamarthanam	13. Arthāpattyanumānavaiṣamyam
4. Pramāṇalakṣaṇam	14. Abhāvapramāṇanirāsaḥ
5. Pratyakṣalakṣaṇam	15. Sattāsāmānyanirāsaḥ
6. Saṁvitsvaprakāśatā	16. Vedāpauruśeyatvam
7. Manassadbhāvata-tadaṇutvapra-karaṇam	17. Svarūpabhedasamarthanam
8. Jṅānānumeyatānirāsaḥ	18. I\śvarānumānikatānirāsaḥ
9. Kriyānumeyatā	19. Ātmanaḥ Śārīrādibhedaḥ
10. Atīndriyaśakti-samarthanam	20. Vyāptisamarthanam
	21. Bhedābhedanirāsaḥ

166. This work is preserved in the Madras Government Oriental and Adyar Mss. Libraries.

167. The 44 *vādas* into which the *Nītiattvāvirbhāva* is divided are:—

1. Adhyayanavādaḥ
2. Kāryavādaḥ
3. Svataḥprāmāṇyavādaḥ
4. Kālapratyakṣatāvādaḥ
5. Anyathākhyātivādaḥ
6. Sākṣātpratītinirāsavādaḥ
7. Kalpanāpoḍhanirāsavādaḥ
8. Yogarūḍhivādaḥ
9. Indriyavādaḥ
10. Manovaibhavavādaḥ
11. Ajasaṁyogavādaḥ
12. Pavanākāśapratyakṣatā-vādaḥ
13. Karmapratyakṣatāvādaḥ
14 Viśeṣanirākaraṇavādah
15. Samavāyanirāsavādaḥ
16. Tādātmyavādaḥ
17. Avayavavivādaḥ
18. Paramāṇuvādaḥ
19. Tamovādaḥ
20. Jātinirṇayavādaḥ
21. Mahāsāmānyavādaḥ
22. Avāntarajātivādaḥ
23. Bhedavādaḥ
24. Advaitavādaḥ
25. Anirvacanīyavādaḥ
26. Avidyāvādaḥ
27. Mithyātvavādaḥ
28. Vijñānavādaḥ
29. Svayamprakāśavādaḥ
30. Jñānapratyakṣanirāsa-[vādaḥ
31. Prākaṭyavādaḥ
32. Yogipratyakṣanirāsavādaḥ
33. Anumānaparīksāvādaḥ
34. śabda-parīkṣāvādaḥvādaḥ
35. U0pamānaparīkṣāvādaḥ
36. Arthāpattiparlkṣāvādaḥ
37. Abhāvaparīkṣāvādaḥ
38. Sphoṭavādaḥ
39. īśvaravādaḥ
40. śabdanityatvavādaḥ
41. Kṣaṇikavādaḥ
42. ātmavādaḥ
43. Anvitābhidhānanirāsa-vādaḥ
44. Vedāpauruṣeyatvavādaḥ

168. This work is preserved in the Madras Government Mss. Libraries.

169. For *Vedānta Deśika*'s personal history, date and works, see A. V. Gopalachari's Introduction to the Yāda-vābhyudaya on 'the Life of *Vedānta Deśika*' and '*Vedānta Deśika* as a Poet' (Vani Vilas Edn., Vols. I & III), and V. Rangachari's 'the Life and Times of *Vedānta Deśika*' (J. B. B. R. A. S. Vol. XXIV, 1917).

170. The Mīmāṁsāpādukā and a part of Seśvaramīmāṁsā were published at Conjeevaram (1902).

171. J. B. B. R. A. S., Vol. XXIV, pp. 278-9.

172. See Epigraphica Indica, Vol. III, p. 118.

173. See the Annual Report of Arch. Survey of India for 1907-8, p. 245.

174. See MM. R. Narasimhachariar's papers on 'Mādhavācārya and his Two Brothers'. Indian Antiquary, Vol. XLV, (1916); also Gopinatha Rao's Introduction to the Madhurāvijaya of Gaṅgā Devī.

175. *Vide* Indian Historical Quarterly, Vols. VI (1930), VII (1931) and IX (1934), and the Journal of Indian History, Vol. XII, Part II.
176. *Vide Nyāyamālāvistara*—Introductory verses, 2-5; the sixth verse runs thus .—
'Tām praśasya sabhāmadhye vīraśrī-, bukkabhūpatiḥ
Kuru vistaraimisyāstvamiti Mādhavamadiśat.'
177. See MM. R. Narasimhachariar's paper on 'Mādhavācārya and his Two Brothers'. Indian Antiquary, Vol. XLV.
178. This was edited by Theodor Goldstücker and Edward B. Cowell, London (Trūbner & Co.), 1878. It was published also in the Anandasrama Press, Poona (1916).
179. *'Bhavanāthaviviktasya nayatattvasya saṅgrahaḥ;*
Yathāmati yathābhyāsam varṇyate bhaṭṭa viṣṇunā.'
180. *'Atra caitanmatarūpasphoraṇāya asmābhiḥ Nayatattva-grantho likhyate—*
'Rūpaprayukiakāryārthī rūpāvacchinnarūpiṇī;
Ceṣṭate satyamithyātvasādhāraṇagatistviyam.'
(Nītitattvāvirbhāvavyākhyā, Anyathākhyātivāda, Adyar Mas., pp. 361-2).
In every probability this Nayatattva might be Viṣṇubhaṭṭa's Nayaiattvasaṅgraha. In another place, Nayatattvasaṅgraha is quoted with the prefatory note—'*Yathoktam Nayatattva-saṅgrahe'.* [*Ibid. Kāryavāda,* p. 230.]
181. This work is preserved in the Madras Government Oriental and Adyar Mss. Libraries.
182. This work is preserved in the Madras Mss. Library.
183. *'Atha buddhimatām kṛtesjitām*
Paritoṣāryakṛtim jigīṣatām;
Vijayākhyamidam vidhāsyate
nipuṇagrāhyaguṇam nibandhanam.'
'iti Śrīmanmahopādhyāyasya Ajitācāryāparanāmadheyasya Anantanārāyanāryasya kṛlau Ajitānibandhane Vijayākhye pra-thamasyādhyāyasya tṛlīyaḥ pādaḥ samāptaḥ.'
184. *'Yosau Dinakṛdivorvyāmavatīrṇaḥ Suryaviṣṇumiśra iti.*
Sūnustasya kanīyānajitāmevam yathāmati vyākhyat.'
185. This commentary together with the *Nayaviveka* for the *Tarkapāda* is now in course of publication by the Madras University.
186. See *Tattvavibhāvanā* (below) pp. 134-136.
187. *'Iti Śrīmadṛṣigaurīnandana-śrī Bhavadāsapītṛvya-Śrī-macc-*

haṅkarapūjyapādaśiṣya-Parameśvarakṛtau Svaditaṅkara-ṇyām tṛtīyaḥ Ślokaḥ. (Madras Government Oriental Mss. R. No. 3595, p. 68. See also the Sanskrit Introduction to the Sphoṭasiddhi (Madras).
'Juṣadhvaṅkaraṇīvyākhyā racitāssmābhiráditaḥ; Svaditaṅkaraṇīvyākhyā sampratīyam vitanyate.' Ibid. p. 1.

188. *'Iti Gopālikāsūnuḥ ṛṣeḥ pituranugrahāt; Antevāsī pitṛvyasya Bhavadāsasya dhīmataḥ.'* (Nītitattvāvirbhāvavyākhyā: the end of the prathamavāda).
189. *'Iti vyākhyāpayāmāsa kāryavādamimam sudhīḥ; Subrahmaṇyo yathārthākhyo bhrātureva ca sūnunā.'* (*Ibid,* the end of the Kāryavāda).
190. *'Evam svataḥpramāvādam vyākhyad Gopālikāsutaḥ; Vāsudevapitṛvyoktarītyā kevalayaiva tu.'* (*Ibid,* the end of the pramāvāda).
191. The *Kumārilayuktimālā* contains a narration of the principles of interpretation as explained by Kumārila in his Vārttika. It contains verses beginning with Vararuci's vākya.—*cf.* *'Gīrṇaśśreyaskarīyiha Śrutiriti paṭhanīyeti pitrādivācā Vipram sāṅgaśrutitam* (?) *gurunilayavataḥ snānato yātukāmam; Āpātajñātadharmaśrutiviṣayamṛṣirmārgamasyā vicāre Vaidhe dharmasya rūpādiṣu ca vividiṣuh sūtra āhetyatheti,' 'Bhadrakarosrthī nityo doṣopeto hitassatām mānyaḥ; Vedassaparikaro-syamprathamedhyāye pramāṇamiti siddham'* Colophon : "*Iti śrīmacchrutikāntārāvasthitavṛṣābhūtāryanandāyi* (?) .... *Maharṣi-Gopālīnandanakṛtiḥ Kaumārilayuktimālā* ....". This Vāsudeva is also credited with the authorship of other works: (1) *Devīcarita,* (2) *Satyatapaḥ-kathā,* (3) *Śivodaya,* (4) *Achyutalīlā.* All these are preserved in the Madras Govt. Oriental Mss. Library, R. No. 3060 *(a-d.)*
192. *'Vistareṇa cāyam pakṣo Vibhramavivekavyākhyāvasare Nayatattvasaṅgrahoktaprakāreṇa dūṣita ityasmābhiruparamyate'* Nītitattvavibhāvanāvyākhyā, Adyar Ms., p. 367. "*Asmābhiśca Vibhramavivekavyākhyāyām taduktasaṅkṣepo darśita iti na prakramyate*"—see the *Tattvavibhāvanā*, p. 43.
193. *'Yathā ca padavadvākyepi lakṣaṇasambhavaḥ tathoktam Tattvavibhāvanāyāmasmābhiḥ.'*— (Nītitattvāvirbhāvavyākhyā, Adyar Ms, p. 55).
194. See the Sphoṭasiddhivyākhyā (Gopālikā) (Madras Edition), p. 266.

195. A part of this work is preserved in the Madras Mss. Libraries.
196. See the *Tattvavibhāvanā* (below), p. 76.
197. This work is preserved (a part only) in the Madras Mss. Libraries.
198. See above under 'Anantanārāyaṇa'.
199. '*Pūrṇāṅgesdhyāpīti vaḥ praṇamāmi Vāsudevācāryān*' 'Sūtrārthasaṅgraha'.
200. See Pandit S.K. Ramanatha Sastri's Sanskrit Introduction to his Edition of the Sphoṭasiddhi, p. XVII-XX.
201. See K.R. Pisharoti's paper on 'the Glimpses of Cochin History'—J.O.R. Madras, Vol. IV, pp. 142-151 (1930).
202. See his Mayūkhamālikā, pp. 96, 183.
203. '*Yatpādapaṅkajdvandvaniranlaraniṣevuṇāt;*
Vidyānithiḥ śiṣyagaṇo namāmastam Sudarśanam.
Numāmi piturau vṛddhāvapi kalyāṇacetasau;
Yatprasādena, mūkopi bhavedvācaspatessamaḥ.
Namāmi Jaiminimunim Bhāṣyakāra-Prabhākarau;
Nātham Bhavam nibandhṛṁśca candrādīn samupāsmahe.
Purā Śukāvagātire Kiḍāmbikulabhūṣaṇam;
Yājñadroṇāt samabhavat Praṇarārtiharābhidhaḥ.
Tasmāt samabhavat prājño devarājo bahuśrutaḥ;
Tatra Śrī Raṅganāthākhyo vipaścitsattamosjani,
Tatsūnunā Varadarājabudhāgrimeṇa
Vyākhyāyate Nayaviveka iti prabandhaḥ.'
Colophon :—'*Ityātreyasudarśanācāryaśiṣyasya ŚrīRaṅga-rājādhvarisūnoḥ Varadarājasya kṛtau Nayavivekadīpikāyām prathamādhyāyasya caturthaḥ pādaḥ.*'
204. It is preserved in the Madras Mss. Libraries.
205. See the *Sarvadarśanasaṅgraha*, p. 152, V. S. Abhyankar's Edition (Poona), 1924.
206. See the *Sphoṭasiddhi* with the Gopālikā (Madras Ed.), p. 45.
207. *Vide* MM. S. Kuppuawami Sastrigal's 'A Primer of Indian Logic' Introduction, p. XLV.
208. See the Kalpataruparimala (Bombay Edition), p. 789.
209. See Mr. A.V. Gopalachari's 'Life of Appayya Dīkṣita'—Introduction to the Yādavābhyudaya, Vol. II, (Vani Vilas Edition, Srirangam).
210. See his introduction to the Yādavābhyudaya, Vol. II, p. II-IV.
211. *Vide* J. O. R., Madras, Vol. II, pp. 225-237.
212. '*Vaṁśe mahati sudhāṁśoḥ Pāṇḍusutapravaracaritaparipūte;*

Āsīdaparamahimā Mahīsvaro Rāmarāja iti.
Udapādi Timmarājaḥ talombudheriva sudhāmayāt Maṇirājaḥ;
Hṛdayaṅgamam Murāreḥ yamalañcakre prabheva
* * * * * *Gopīdevī*
Teṣu mahiteṣu jayati tridivādhīśeṣu padmabandhuriva;
Śrī Cinna-Timmarājaḥ pratāpanirājitakṣamāvalayaḥ.'
[The commentary on the Yādavābhyudaya, Verses 2, 3 and 5, Vani Vilas Edition, Srirangam.]

213. *'Bhāṣyametadanagham vivṛṇviti*
svapnajāgaraṇayossamam prabhuḥ;
Cinna Bommanṛparūpabhṛtsvayam
mām nyayuṅkta mahilārdhavigrahaḥ.
Śrī Cinna Bomma nṛpatiḥ Śritapārijātaḥ
sarvātmanā Paśupatim Śaraṇam prapannaḥ;
Yaḥ sārvabhaumapadavīmadhigamyadhīra-
statpūjayaiva manute saphalatvamasyāḥ.'
Śivārkamaṇidīpikā, verses 12 and 13.

214. Nalacarita Prologue, Balamanorama Edition, p. 4.

215. See also Heras' 'the Araviḍu Dynasty of Vijayanagar', p. 303.

216. *'Ayam Kuvalayānandamakarodappadīkṣitaḥ;*
Niyogādveṅkata-paternirupādhikrpānidheḥ.'
Kuvalayānanda, last verse.

217. *Kintu vyāpārameṣa prathayati*
phalasamyojanārtham pareṣām;
Prāptaḥ puṇyairagaṇyairiva
vibudhāgaṇo Veṅkaṭakṣonīpālam.
Vidhirasāyana.

218. For a short account of Tātācārya, see Heras' 'the Aravidu Dynasty of Vijayanagar', pp. 304-306.

219. See the Report of the Mysore Archaeological Dept., (1917). See also Heras' 'the Aravidu Dynasty of Vijayanagar,' pp. 521-22.

220. Three more works of his in Mīmāṁsā are said to be available in Ms.: (1) *Pūrva*mīmāṁsāviṣayasaṅgrahadīpikā, (2) Dharmamīmāṁsāparibhāṣā, and(3) Atideśalakṣaṇapunarākṣepa. Whether they are included in his 108 works is not definitely known.

221. It was published at Benares.

222. See the Bhāṭṭadīpikā, I. 2. 4. (N. S. Edition), p. 41.

223. It was published at Benares.

224. It was published by the Vani Vilas Press, Srirangam.

225. A part of it is preserved in Ms. at Madras Govt. Ms. Library.

226. It is now in course of publication in parts in the J.O.R. Madras (1934 and 1935).
227. See the Report of the Mysore Archaeological Dept., 1917.
228. See Epigraphica Indica, Vol. XII, p. 357.
229. The three works are preserved in the Mss. Libraries at Madras.
230. See Epigraphica Indica, Vol. XII, p. 344. See also Heras' 'the Araviḍu Dynasty of Vijayanagar', p. 521-22.
231. For Govinda Dīkṣita, see Heras' 'The Araviḍu Dynasty of Vijayanagar', pp, 288 and 522.
232. "*Asti Govindayajvendra-Nāgamāmbātapaḥphalam;*
Śrī Veṅkaṭeśvaramakhī sarvatantrasvatantradhīḥ.
Yeneṣṭam sāgnicityāptavājapeyādibhirmakhaiḥ;
Kṛtam Sāhityasāmrājyanāmakāvyamanuttamam.
Vyatāni Sulbamīmāṁsā tathā Karmāntavārttikam;
Ṭupṭīkāyāḥ kṛtā ṭīkā Vārttikābharaṇābhidhā."
Tantraśikhāmaṇi.
233. The Karmāntavārttika is described by the author in this verse :—
'Kalpādyanuktārthaviśeṣarūpa-
pravṛttakarmāntanibandhadīpakam;
Mīmāṁsāyā māmsalitañca vārttikam
Śrī Veṅkaṭeśādhvariṇā vitanyate.'
234. '*Umāpatim Ramānātham Bodhāyanamunīśvaram;*
Govindādhvariṇam tātam vande sarvārthasiddhaye.'
Karmāntavārttika, First verse, T.M.S.S.M. Library
Sanskrit Catalogue, Vol. IV, p. 1669.
235. '*Iti Śrīmadadvaitavidyācāryasāgnicityasarvatomukhātirātrasāgnicityāptavājapeyayāji-Govindadīkṣitasya varanandanasya Śrī Veṅkaṭeśvaradīkṣitasya kṛtiṣu Karmāntasūtravārttike sāmānyasūtravārttikam samāptam.' (Ibid.* p. 1672).
236. See Prof. Pisharoti's paper on 'Meppattur Nārāyaṇa Bhaṭṭatiri' I. H. Q., Vol. IX, 1933.
237. The *Meya* section now available is composed by another Nārāyaṇa, a *protāgā* of King Mānaveda (of Calicut) in the 17th century. See the beginning and end of the Meya section.
238. '*Taduktam Bṛhaṭṭikāyām—*
Tasmādyo vidyamānasya gṛhābhāvovagamyate;
Sa hetuḥ sa bahirbhāvam nāgṛhītvā ca gṛhyate.'
Mānameyodaya (Adyar Edition), p. 126.
239. *Ibid.*, p.; 91.
240. *Ibid.*, p. 146.
241. This was first published in the Trivandrum Sanskrit Series No.

XIX (1912) and was for the second time, published with English Translation in the Theosophical Publishing House Oriental Series (1933).

242. It is preserved in the Madras Mss. Libraries.

243. The first part of this work was published in the Trivandrum Sanskrit Series. The commentary on the Unādi *Sūtras* was edited by Dr. T. R. Chintamani under the auspices of the University of Madras (1933).

244. The Trivandrum Editor of the Prakriyāsarvasva believes that Nārāyaṇabhaṭṭa might have flourished between A.D. 1560 and 1666, while Prof. Pisharoti places him 10 years earlier *(i.e.),* A.D. 1550-1656.

245. Several editions of this work have appeared in India; the earliest, probably, is that of Dr. G. Thibaut with his English Translation. (Benares, 1882); another, with the commentary Kaumudī by Rāmeśvara Śivayogin at Benares (about 1900) and at Bombay 1922; another with a commentary by D.T. Tatachari (a reprint from his Monthly Journal '*Udyānapatrikā*' (1922); another with the Kaumudī and English Translation of the Text by D. V. Gokhale, B.A., Poona (1932).

246. See Pandit A. Chinnaswami Sastri's Sanskrit introduction to his edition of the Nyāyaprakāsa with his commentary, Benares (1925) and also Prof. F. Edgerton's Introduction to his edition with English Translation, p. 20.

247. This work is preserved in the Madras Mss. Libraries.

248. This work was published by the Chaukambha Book Depot, Benares (1902).

249. This was also published at Benares (1904).

250. This work is preserved in the Madras Mss. Libraries.

251. '*Yattu prakāśakārāḥ Kalpasūtraprāmāṇyasādhanādhikaraṇe ittham prāmāṇyaprakāramāhuḥ .... tat tadadhikaraṇa Kaustubha eva dūṣitam draṣṭavyam.*' '*Prabhāvali*', (N.S. Edition), pp. 42-43. The Prakāsakāra is identified with the author of Vidhirasāyanakhaṇḍana.' *Tadetat prakāśakārā na kṣamante, ittham hi Vidhirasāyanakhaṇḍane tairupapāditam.*' *ibid.*, p. 36, See also *ibid.*, pp. 102, 240, 305 where Śambhubhaṭṭa makes Khaṇḍadeva presuppose the Prakāśa.

252. '*Iti Śrīmatpadavākyapramāṇapārāvārapārīṇadhurīṇa-Mīmāṁsāsāṁrājyadhurandhara Śri Bhaṭṭanārāyanātmaja Bhaṭṭa Śaṅkarakṛtam Vidhirasāyanadūṣaṇam samāptam.*'

(Vidhirasā-yanadūṣaṇa). See also P. V. Kane's *History of Dharmaśāstra*, pp. 300, 350 and 438.

253. See Kamalākarabhaṭṭa in Mr. P.V. Kane's History of *Dharmaśāstra,* p. 432.

254. See verses 13-18 :—

Ekanātha
| (son)
Āpadeva
| (son)
Ānantadeva
| (son)
Āpadeva (the author of the Nyāyaprakāśa)
| (son)
Anantadeva (the author of the Smṛtikaustubha)

That Anantadeva II wrote the *Smṛtikaustubha* in order to please his royal patron Baig Bahadur Candra is known from his verses at the end of the Smṛtikaustubha:—"

Srībāgabahaduracandran-ṛpaśya tasya
vācā himācalagatāvanidevatuṣṭyai.
Yosnantade-vakṛtamanthanasannibandha
kṣīrabdhijostha satatam hariṇā dhṛto yaḥ;
Nityam nije hṛdi satām pramudestu tasya
sarvābdadīdhitirayam Smṛtikaustubhasya."

See P. V., Kane's History of Dharmaśāstra, pp. 450-453.

255. The earliest edition of this work (along with the Arthasaṅgraha) was in Telugu script (Mysore). It was afterwards published by the N.S. Press, Bombay (1911); another with a commentary by Pandit A. Chinnaswami Sastri at Benares. Later on, it was edited in Roman script with English translation by Professor F. Edgerton.

256. '*Śaśvadbodhataraṅgā vidyāgaṅgottamāṅke yasya;*
Śrirudradevasaṁjñam Janakam vande sadā sphūrtyai.'
Kaustubha, verse 3.

Vide also the colophon :—' *Iti Śrīmat-pūrvottaramīmāṁsā-pārāvārapārīṇadhurīṇa-Śrī-Rudradevasūnu-Khaṇḍade-vaviracite Mīmāṁsakaustubhe dvitīyasyādhyāyasya dviūyaḥ pādaḥ.'*

257. *Vide* the writer's paper on 'Jagannātha Paṇḍita', Annamalai University Journal, Vol. II, pp. 201-208.

258. See the P. M. System, p. 19.

259. See MM. S. K. Sastrigal's 'A Primer of Indian Logic'—

Introduction, p. XLVII.

260. It was published—three *pādsa* at Conjeevaram (1902, 1904, 1911), and the rest at Benares (1924, etc.).

261. See also MM. Ramasubba Sastrigal's *Bhāṭṭakalpataru* —a gloss on the Bhāṭṭadīpikā.

262. It was first published (in parts) by the Asiatic Society of Bengal omitting the *Tarkapāda*; a second edition appeared in the Mysore Government Oriental Library Series in four volumes (with late Pandit Kasturirangacarya's *Sūtravṛtti Sārāvali* from the beginning to the end of the fourth pāda of the third *adhyāya*) (1911, 1914, etc.); a third edition appeared with Śambhubhaṭṭa's *Prabhāvali* to the end of the third pāda of the third *adhyāya*, Bombay (1922); a fourth edition appeared with Vāñcheśvara's *Bhāṭṭacintāmaṇi* to the end of the third pāda of the third *adhyāya* (Madras, 1934).

263. It was twice published at Conjeevaram.

264. *Vide* Dr. T. R. Chintamani's Introduction to the Rukmiṇīkalyāṇa, pp. XXIII-XXXVI (Adyar Edition, 1929).

265. The Tantraṣikhāmaṇi and the Karpūravarttikā are preserved in the Madras Mss. Libraries, while the Saṅkarṣamuktāvali is not available in those collections.

266. '*Kāñcimaṇḍḍalamaṇḍanasya makhinaḥ*
Karṇāṭabhūbhṛdguroḥ
Tātāryasya digantakāntayaśaso
yam bhāgineyam viduḥ;
Astokādhvarakarturappayaguro-
rasyaiṣa vidvanmaṇeḥ
Putraḥ Śrī Raghunāthadīkṣitakaviḥ
pūrṇo guṇairedhate.
Tatsutastarkavedāntatantravyākṛticintakaḥ;
Vyaktam Viśvaguṇādarśam vidhatte Veṇkatādhvarī.'

The colophon at the end of this work gives additional matter that he belonged to the Ātreya Gotra and his mother was called Sītā:— "*Iti Śrīpañcamatabhañjananibandhanavikhyāla Tātayajvabhāgineya—Vājapeyasarvapṛṣṭhāptoryāmādiyājyātreyavaṁśamauktikībhavadappayyāryatanūbhavaśleṣayama-kacakravarti-Raghunāthācāryatanayasya Śrīnivāsakṛpātiśayasaṁviditanayasya Sītāmbāgarbhasambhavasya Śrīmat-Kāñcīnagaravāstavyasya Mahakavi-Śrī-Veṅkaṭādhvariṇaḥ kṛtau Viśva-(Guṇādarśacampuḥ samāptimagāt).*"

267. See the Sanskrit Introduction to the Visvaguṇādarśa, (N.S. Edition), p. 6, (1915).

268. Both the works are preserved in the Madras Mss. Libraries.
269. See Epigraphica Indica, Vol. XII, pp. 344-7.
270. See colophon of this work:—"*Iti Bhāṭṭasaṅgrahe sarvatantrasvatantra-Sudhīndragurupādaśiṣya-Rāghavendra-yatikṛte dvādaśādhyāyasya caturthaḥ pādaḥ.*' This work is preserved in the Madras Mas. Libraries.
271. This work is preserved in the Madras Mss. Libraries.
272. See the introductory verses of the Vedānta Paribhāṣā.
273. See MM. N. S. Anantakrishna Sastrigal's Sanskrit Introduction to his edition of the Vedānta Paribhāṣā, p. 64, and also Sir S. Radhakrishnan's English Foreword (Calcutta 1927).
274. See the Pr*abhāv*ali, pp. 66, 88, 92, 95, 97, 108 (N. S. Edition.)
275. '*Iti Śrī Niṭṭalakulatilaka-Sūrabhaṭṭa-mahopādhyāyatanū-bhavasya Veṅkaṭādriyajvagurucaraṇānujasya Somanāthasarva-tomukhayājinaḥ kṛtau Śāstradīpikāvyākhyāyām Mayūkhamāli-kāsaṁjñāyām prathamādhyāyasya caturthaḥ pādaḥ.*' (p. 92, N. S. Edition.)
276. '*Athigalya kalāmakhūām*
agrabhavād-Veṅkaṭādriyajvaguroḥ;
Vacanaiḥ anatipracuraiḥ-vyākurve Śāstradīpikām viṣadām.'—
Verse 2.
277. '*Agnirdevo hoteti mantre Yuvanāśvavadambarlṣavadaṅgirovat ittham yajamānārṣeyam pravaraḥ Subrahmaṇyānigade Sūrabhaṭ ṭasarmaṇaḥ putro yajate Somanāthayajvasarmaṇaḥ pautraḥ Sureśvarayajvasarmaṇo naptā yajate Mairammadāyāḥ putro yajate ityevam prakṣipyamāṇāni, etc.* p. 113. It is likely that the author has given his own *gotrarṣis* and *pravrararṣis* in the Ūha passage when he had to illustrate it,
278. This was published (together with the *Śāstradīpikā*) in the Nirnaya Sagara Press, Bombay, in 1915.
279. See page 12.
280. P. 33, 52, 127.
281. P. 11, 183.
282. P. 86, 106, 131, 274.
283. P. 75, 96, 183.
284. P. 728.
285. P. 50.
286. P. 105.
287. P. 110.
288. '*Vandesmatprapitāmaham*

Tirumalaśrīyajvarājam tathā
Yajñeśam ca pitāmaham
svapitaram Śrīkoṇḍubhaṭṭārakam;
Tacchi(ṣyā)nujanim pitṛvyatilakam
Śrīlakṣmaṇāryam gurum
Jyeṣṭham śreṣṭhaguṇānvitam
Tirumalākhyānam varam yajvanām.

Kadalikapotamaheśaprītiparipräptabhāraliśrīkau;
Ācārakūrikulendūnapi...naumi puruṣadhaureyān.

Nutyeha Gautamāmbā tanayoslaṅkāranāṭakādikaraḥ;
Vedānta-tarka-śabda-granthakṛdābhāti jagati Yajñeṣaḥ.

Prabhinnatamasam Śāstradīpikārthaprakāṣakam;
Prabhāmaṇḍalanāmānam prabandham sohamārabhe.'
Colophon :—' *Iti Śri sakalapaṇḍitamaṇḍakākhaṇḍalacala-Kūri-Koṇḍabhaṭṭopādhyāyatanayena Śrī-pitāmaha-Yajñesvarabhaṭṭopādhyāyaśiṣyeṇa Kāśyapagotrabahvṛcāgresareṇa Tirumalayajvapriyasodareṇa Gāṅgāmbikeyena Śrī Yajñanārāyaṇadikṣitena viracite Śāstradīpikāvyākhyāne Prabhāmaṇḍalākhyāne prathamasyādhyāyasya dvitīyaḥ pādaḥ.*

289. This work is preserved in the Madras Mss. Libraries.
290. See the Meya Section of the Mānameyodaya, (T. P. H.), pp. 146-147; 306-309.
291. See P. V. Kane's 'History of Dharma Śāstra' pp. 432 and 437. *Vide* also his P. M. System, p. 19.
292. Both the works are preserved in the Madras Govt. Mss. Library.
293. This work is preserved in the Madras Mss, Libraries.
294. See the Pr*abhāva*li, (N. S. Edition), pp. 3, 6, 15, 19, 21, 32, 80, 282.
295. It was published (together with the text) at Benares.
296. See the Pr*abhāva*li, pp. 14, 18.
297. It is preserved in the Madras Mss. Libraries.
298. *Vide* the Introduction.
299. This work is preserved in the Madras Govt. Mss. Libraries.
300. The *Tarkapāda* was published at Benares and the rest are preserved at Madras and Tanjore Mss. Libraries.
301. See the Bhāṭṭacintāmaṇi, page 67, Benares, 1934.
302. See his History of Dharma Śāstra, p. 437. See his P. M. System, p. 19.

303. *Vide* the colophon in his Mīmāṁsāsarvasva—'*Iti Śrī Niṭṭhalakulatilaka-Somanāthadīkṣitamahopādhyāyacaraṇaparicaraṇasamuditamanonairmalyaviśadlkṛtasakalaśāstratattvasya Kollūri-Somayājitanūbhavasya Āccamāmbāgarbhasambhavasya Nārāyaṇaśāstriṇaḥ kṛtiṣu Mīmāṁsāsarvasvasamākhyā-yām dviūyasya caturthaḥ pādaḥ.*' All his three works are preserved in the Madras Mss. Libraries.

304. The nine main sections of this work are:—

1. Sāstrārambhavicāraḥ
2. Kāmyanityavivekaḥ
3. Śrutiviniyogavidhiḥ
4. Liṅgādiviniyogavidhiḥ
5. Prayukticintā
6. Kramapramāṇanirūpaṇam
7. Vidhyadhikāranirūpaṇam
8. Atideśavicāraḥ
9. Atideśabādhavicāraḥ

Colophon of this work :—'*Iti Śrī Kollūrikulatilaka-Somayājitanayasya Āccamāmbāgarbhasambhūtasya Kollūri Nārāyaṇa Sāstriṇah kṛtau Vidhivivekasamākhyāyām praihamaḥ paricchedaḥ.*' This work has also got a division into Pariccheda.

305. See his introductory verses of his Pr*abhāva*li:—

'*Yo vedaśāstrārṇavapāradṛśvā*
yajñādikarmā ca raṇestidakṣaḥ;
Sadāśivārādhanaśuddhacittaḥ
tam Bālakṛṣṇam pitaram namāmi.
Śrī Khaṇḍadevam praṇipatya sadgurum
Mīmāṁsakasvāntasarojabhāskaram.'

The colophon of this work may also be noted with advantage:—'*Iti Śrīmatpūrvottararmīmāṁsāpārāvārīṇadhuriṇaśrī Khaṇḍadevāntevāsi Kavimaṇḍana-Śambhubhaṭṭaviracitāyām Bhāṭṭ adīpikāprabhāvalyām prathamādhyāyasya caturthaḥ pādaḥ.*' P. 131, (N. S. Edition).

306. See the Pr*abhāva*li, p. 295, (N. S. Edition).

307. See the Pr*abhāva*li, p. 41. Who is this Khaṇḍanakāra (Śrī Harṣa?) is not known.

308. '*Iti Śrīmadbhāradvājakulajaladhikaustubha-Śrīkaṇṭha-matapratiṣṭhāpaṇācārya-caturadhikaśataprabandha-nirmāṇadhurandhara-mahāvratayāji - Śrīmadappayyadīkṣita-sodarya - Śrīmadayyādīkṣitapautreṇa Rukmiṇīpariṇayālaṅkāra-tilakādyaneka-prabandhanirmātuḥ Appayyadīkṣitasya putreṇa Appayyadīkṣitena kṛtāyām Tantrasiddhāntadīpikāyām prathamādhyāyasya caturthaḥ pādaḥ.*' This and the Viṣaya-saṅgrahadīpikā are preserved in the Madras Mss. Libraries.

309. '*Iti Śrīmahopādhyāyādvaitavidyācārya-Rāghavasomayājikulāvataṁsaśrī—Tirumalāryavaryasya sūnoḥ Annambhaṭṭasya kṛtau Tantravārttikaṭṭkāyām Subodhinyām tṛtīyādhyāyasya prathamaḥ pādah`.*'
310. The three works are preserved in the Madras Mss. Libraries.
311. Yuktisnehaprapūraṇī, verses 4-19, (N. S. Edn., 1915).

Śivadāsa (of Parāśara Gotra)
|
Mitrasarman
| (son)
Jaṇārdana—m. Gaṅgā
| (son)
Bhairava—m. Pūnādevī
|
Nārāyaṇa—m, Ramā
|
Mādhava—m. Pr*abhāvat*ī
| (who left to Benares)
Rāmakṛṣṇa (the author of the Yuktisnehaprapūraṇī).

312. See the writer's paper on 'Old Vṛttikāras on the *Pūrva*mīmāmsā *Sātras*' I. H. Q., September 1934.
313. This work was published at Benares,
314. It is preserved in the Madras Mss. Libraries.
315. It was published in the 'Pandit'.
316. See the writer's paper on 'The Saṅkarṣakāṇḍa—a Genuine Supplement to the P. M. Śāstra' I. H. Q.
317. *Vide* the English Introduction to the Lalitāsahasranāma Translation by B. Anantakrishna Sastri.
318. It was published at Bombay. It was also published with a commentary by Pandit D. T. Tatacharya, M. O. L., at Tanjore.
319. *Vide* the colophons in his Adhvaramīmāṁsākutūhalavṛtti and Bālamanoramā.
320. The first three *adhyāyas* of this work (with a Summary by MM. Prof. S. Kuppuswami Sastrigal) were published in the Vani Vilas Press, Srirangam (Trichy Dt.)
321. *Vide* Sāyaṇa's Upodghāta to his Ṛg-Vedabhāṣya, pp. 46-52. Dr. Paśupatinātha Śāstri's Edition (Sanskrit Sāhitya Parishad Series No. 9).
322. *Cf.* Mahābhāṣya Paspaśāhnika, N. S. Edition, p. 21. "*Āgamaḥ khalvapi—*

'Brāhmaṇena niṣkāraṇo vedaḥ ṣaḍaṅgosdhyeyo jñeyaśca.'"

323. *Vide* T. M. S. S. M. Library Descriptive Catalogue Vol. IV, pp. 1664-1669.

324. *Vide* verses 1-10 :—
'Godāvarīrodhasi sanniviṣṭā
garīyasī dharmapurī cakāsti;
Tatrāvatīrṇasya Nṛsimhamūrteḥ
Viṣṇoḥ padam cetasi saṁsmarāmi.—Verse (2)

325. *Ālocya śabdabalamarthabalam śrutīnām*
ṭīkādvayam vyaracayad Bṛhatīm ca Laghvīm;
Bhāśyam gabhīramadhikṛtya mitākṣaram yaḥ
sopi Prabhākaraguroḥ jayati trilokyām.
Bṛhatīm tathaiva Laghvīm
ṭīkāmadhikṛ tya Śālikānāthaḥ;
Ṛjuvimalām Dīpaśikhām
viśadārthāmakṛta Pañcikām kramaśaḥ.
Tathānyām Śālikānātho nānāprakaraṇātmikām;
Mānameyavivekārtham prabandham sarvasammatam.'
verses 5, 6 and 7

326. *'Tīkādvayam Pañcikām ca Bhavanāthastu saṅkṣipan;*
Cakre Nayavivekākhyam prabandham sarvasammatam.'

327. This was published in 'Gaekwad Oriental Series No. XXIV' (1923) under the editorship of Dr. R. Sama Sastri.

328. *Ibid.*, p. 28.

329. *Ibid.*, p. 27.

330. A transcript of this Ms. is preserved in the Annamalai University Library. It is also preserved in the Madras Mss. Libraries.

331. *'Avibhaktavibhaktamārgayoḥ*
matayorbhaṭṭagurūpadiṣṭayoḥ;
Ubhayorapi Pārthasārathiḥ
prathitopyādyamatesbhiyogavān.
Aspaṣṭabhāvamaparlkṣakaduṣpraveśam
ācāryatantramadhikṛtya dṛḍhaprakāśam;
Nyakkṛtya Pārtharathasārathiranyatantram
satprītaye grat.hitavān navaratnamālām.
Gurutantraniyantritopyaham
bahumānādiha Pārthasāratheḥ;
Vivṛṇomi matāntarāśritām
sthirabhāvām Nayaratnamālikām.'
—Nāyakaratna, verses 3-5.

332. *Vide* the Bhāṭṭacintāmaṇi, verses 1-10 :—

'Śrī Saharājendrapure Śrīsaharājendraviṣṭapaiḥ sadṛśe;
Kṛtavāso vimalamatiḥ hośanikarṇāṭakassudhīḥ brīmān.
Cakre Māhiṣaśatakam Dhāṭīśatakam tathāśiṣām śatakam;
Śleṣakavisārvabhaumaḥ śrīmān Vāñcheśvaraḥ svatantrosau.
Tasya naptā Mādhavārya-pautraḥ Śrī-Narasimhataḥ;
Vedavedāṅgatattvajñāt sarvaṣṭtāgrapūjitāt.
Labdhajanmāsdhītaśāstro vedārthaikaniviṣṭadhīḥ;
Māhiṣam śatakam yena prapitāmahanirmitam.
Vyākhyātamatigambhīram pitṛproktena vartmanā;
Hiraṇyakeśisūtrañca vyākhyātam kṛstnameva hi.
Dattacintātmaṇiñcaiva Śrāddhacintāmaṇim tathā;
Kṛtavān Brahmasūtrārthacintāmaṇimanuttamam.
Kākatāliyavādārthaḥ kṛto yenātidurghaṭaḥ;
Śrī Vāñcheśvaranāmāsau tametedya yathāmati.
Śrī-Bhāṭṭadīpikāvyākhyām Bhāṭṭacintamaṇim mudā;
Doṣasattvepi kṛpayā guṇam gṛhṇantu paṇḍitāḥ.—Verses 3-10.

333. Colophon:— *"Iti Śrī-Coladeśāgrapūjyavidvatsamājavirājamāna-Sāhajendrapuranivāsi-Kāmakāyana-Viśvāmitragotra jaladhikaustubha-Śrīman Nṛsiṁhasūrivarasūnvāśvalāyanasūtra-Hośani-Karṇāṭakajātīya- Vāñcheśvarayajvanaḥ kṛtiṣu Bhāṭṭadīpikāvyākhyāne Bhāṭṭacintāmaṇau prathamasyādhyāyasya prathamaḥ pādaḥ." Ibid.*, p. 34.

This work (to the end of the first *adhyāya*) was published by my revered teacher of Mīmāṁsā, the late MM. T. Venkatasubba Sastrigal (Madras, 1928); it is now recently published by the Law Journal Press, Madras, to the end of the third pāda of the third Adhyāya.

334. *'Iśvaraśrīnivāsāryāhobalākhyagurūttamān'*—Verse 1.

335. *Vide* T. M. S. S. M. Library Descriptive Catalogue of Sanskrit *Mss.*, Vol. IV, Serial No. 2072, pp. 1682-1687. In one of the introductory verses of his *Hiraṇyokeśiśrautasūtravyākhyā,* Vāñcheśvara refers to one Mātṛdatta, who, most probably a commentator or a Nibandhanakāra on the *Śrauta Sūtras,* is not considered by this author as a reliable authority, *cf.*— *'Mātṛdattaprayogastu naitatsūtrārthasammataḥ.'*

PART II

ANALYSIS OF THE TATTVABINDU

What is the nimitta or efficient cause of śābdabodha is the main theme of the Tattvabindu. A full elucidation of this question obliged Vācaspatimiśra to discuss elaborately the five traditional views on *śābdabodha:* (1) The *Vaiyākaraṇas* (the sphoṭavādins) hold that the *Vākyasphoṭa*[1] *conveys the vākyārtha* (the meaning of sentence); and they describe the Sphoṭa as *being devoid of parts (avayavas) though it is experienced as possessing avayavas through our avidya* (Ignorance). (2) The *old school of Mīmāṁsakas* explain it thus[2]: *The cognition of the last varṇa (of the sentence) coupled with the impressions produced by the experiences of the previous words with their meanings is the cause of the Vākyārthajñāna.* (3) *Some*[3] however among them hold that the cause of the *Vākyārthajñāna* is the *Varṇamālā—the group of varṇas which are reflected in the mirror of recollection produced by the family of impressions generated by the experiences of each varṇa, pada and the meanings of words.* (4) The *Ṭīkākāra (Prabhākara)*[4] maintains that *the cause of the Vākyārthapratīti is the Cognition of the padas themselves which convey meanings related to one another on the basis of ākāṅkṣā, yogyatā and sannidhi.* (5) *Ācārya Kumārila*[5] whom Vācaspatimiśra closely follows in this work, suggests that *words convey their meanings (padārthas) which, in their turn (while mutually related) generate the śabdabodha —the cognition of the vākyārtha.*

I

According to the Sphoṭavādins[6] the *vākyasphoṭa* which is an *akhaṇḍavastu*—an object devoid of parts and properties—*is the efficient cause of Śābdabodha.* The division of *vākya* into *varṇas* and *padas* is not real but is based on a *super-imposition* caused by eternal Ignorance *(anādyavidyā).*

In the elucidation of this Sphoṭavāda Vācaspatimiśra first puts a question with two alternatives[7]—whether the akhaṇḍasphoṭa is to be accepted as the Vākyārthavācaka on the basis of the time-honoured experience of the world, or on that of the difference of the imports of words and sentences which cannot be otherwise explained. Again, in the first alternative another question is raised[8]—whether the *vākya* is to be considered as one unit possessing many parts like *varṇas* and *padas*, or whether it is completely devoid of any such parts. Of these three, the alternative that *the vākya possesses parts is unsound,*[9] because it is accepted by the Vaiyākaraṇas even that the varṇas are *Vibhus* (possessing *paramamahattva),* and that no *avayavin* (whole) bigger than the *paramamahat avayavas* (parts) can therefore be produced. Even according to the Naiyāyika theory that śabda is a *quality (guṇa)* of *ākāśa,*[10] the varṇas or padas as qualities cannot be the *material cause* of the vākya, since it is held unanimously that only a *substance (dravya)* and not a *quality (guṇa)* is a *samavāyikāraṇa* (material cause). If one takes the view of the *Śikṣākāras*[11] that *varṇa* is produced from the particles of *Vāyu* (wind), these wind-particles are to be associated with one another for the production of *vākya,* but since *varṇas* are experienced as perishing after a moment's existence,[12] the contact or association of one *varṇa* with another, cannot be possibly conceived of; if the varṇas succeed one another, they cannot produce any *avayavin —kārya* (effect); nor do they possess the contact which (as the *asamavāyikāraṇa* (non-inherent cause) is very essential to the production of effect. The supposition[13] that the *part* is one and produces the *whole* is absurd, in view of the fact that there is no *kāryadravya* (substance as effect) conceivable, if two or more *parts* do not produce the effect. And it is not possible to maintain that the cognitions of *varṇas,* associated with one another,[14] become the cause of the *vākya,* since the cognitions of varṇas or varṇas themselves do not co-exist. *So, it cannot be held that vākya is one avayavin with many parts—varṇas and padas.*

The other alternative that *vākya is one unit devoid of parts*[15] *is equally unsound.* According to this view, *vākya* conveys the meaning, but *varṇas* or padas do not, as they are not unitary. Moreover, varṇas and padas have no real existence in language. *Vākya* (sentence) alone really exists; it is *nitya* (eternal) and as such is to be manifested. The successful manifestation of this real element in speech— the *sonant substratum*—is effected by *dhvanis* which, owing due to their different places and modes of articulation, generate an (invalid) cognition of the real *śabda—sphoṭa—*as possessing many parts like varṇa and *pada.*[16] This resembles the experience of a person who looks at his own face through a gem or mirror of varied shape.[17] The question that the second and succeeding *dhvanis* in a *pada* or *vākya* are superfluous since the first *dhvani* itself is capable of manifesting the sphoṭa, does not arise, in view of the fact that the manifestation by the first *dhvani* is not so successful and complete as it would be at the end of the series of manifestations by different *dhvanis.* Similarly, it cannot be held that the last *dhvani* manifests the unitary *sphoṭa* since the last *dhvani* has not the full capacity to manifest it unless it is strengthened by the *saṁskāras* (impressions) produced by the experiences of the previous *dhvanis.* The manifestation of sphoṭ a by *dhvanis* bears comparison to the examination of a gem by an expert jeweller who satisfies himself as to its genuineness, after a series of detailed examination.[18]

The question how the dhvani-cognitions (which are invalid in that they present the non-existing properties like *hrasvatva* of the *varṇas*) manifest sphoṭa, can be easily answered by the fact that *invalid cognitions sometimes lead one to a valid knowledge.*[19]

Again, the Sphoṭavādin advances his arguments in favour of the acceptance of *sphoṭa as a unitary śabda.*[20] The unitary experience of '*a word*' and '*a sentence*' cannot be satisfactorily explained unless *a unitary śabda* called *sphoṭa* is accepted. He asks—do the varṇas *each separately* produce the cognition of the unitary śabda or *in their combination* ?[21] The first alternative is untenable, since it goes against our ordinary experience and since it makes other *varṇas superfluous*. The second is treated as consisting of two alternatives—whether *varṇas* are *in reality associated* with one another or they *are cognised together.* Since the *varṇas* are both *nitya* (eternal) and *vibhu* (all-pervading), they are not associated with one another; and since they are also to be cognised *separately* and with some *time-sequence* (due to the generations of different cognitions), it is not possible to maintain that *varṇas* are cognised together.[22]

Again, the Varṇavādin maintains his position by saying that the last *varṇa* in combination with the impressions produced by the experiences of the previous sounds in a word or sentence conveys the idea, and that thus, the popular experience of the *unitary śabda as the conveyor of ideas— 'śabdāt arthadhīḥ udīyate'*—can be explained.[23] Here the Sphoṭavādin questions the nature of the impression *(saṁskāra)* cited by the Varṇavādin—is it *that saṁskāra which produces a smṛti* (recollection), or is it of *that type which one finds in corns (vrīhis) by sprinkling (prokṣaṇa)* on the basis of the *Śruti—'Vrīhīn prokṣati'* ? The second is inexplicable[24] in view of the fact that the uncombined *varṇas* cannot produce in themselves one *saṁskāra;* nor can it be said that each *varṇa* produces *a saṁskāra* and that all these *saṁskāras* of different *varṇas* and the *experience* of the last *varṇa* generate the *arthapratīti,* for, it accepts many *adṛṣṭas* which are not known by popular means of knowledge like *pratyakṣa.* The citation of the well-known *āgneya* and other vedic sacrifices, which, being enjoined by *Śrutis,* compel us to accept such *adṛṣṭas* in the instance of *vrīhis* does not favour our acceptance of many *saṁskāras* for the production of the arthapratīti; (for, here no such injunction is known to us.[25]) The first alternative[26] that the *saṁskāra* otherwise known as *vāsanā,* the cause of recollection, helps much the last *varṇa* in a *pada* not only in recollecting the *śabda* but also in understanding the idea by the last *varṇa*, so much so that there is no additional *adṛṣṭa* excepting the assignment of an additional function to the existing *saṁskāra*, is also untenable, on the ground that such a thing (as described above) goes against the very nature of *saṁskāra.*; and it also drags us to accept another *adṛṣṭa,* for, the saṁskāra which rests in *ātman* produces the recollection in *him (ātman)* and in none else; otherwise we will have to accept that all will remember an object which one alone has previously experienced. Moreover, the *saṁskāra, vāsanā* or *bhāvanā* is only the capacity of *ātman* for recollecting an object which *he* has experienced; and this capacity we have preferably to posit in *ātman* and *not* in the *saṁskāra* (according to the pūrvapakṣin), for,[27] its very existence is based on the cognition of ideas (from the words in sentence) by the *same ātman.* The argument that no additional *adṛṣṭa* is accepted except an additional function for the existing *saṁskāra,* falls to the ground, since it also involves the acceptance of another *adṛṣṭaśakti* and so on *ad infinitum.*[28]

The Varṇavādin again comes forward with his explanation[29] that all varṇas in a pada or vākya being recollected together convey the idea, so that there is no necessity for accepting the *unitary śabda, viz.,* sphoṭa. The Sphoṭavādin rejects[30] this explanation as unsatisfactory, in view of the fact that the varṇas in words— *nadī, dīna, etc.*—being the same in one recollection, do not convey the same idea. It cannot also be held[31] that the different *saṁskāras* produced by the experiences of the various varṇas produce one *smṛti* which has all varṇas as its object with the same sequence as they were in the previous experiences, so that these varṇas together with their individual traits being bound by one *recollection* constitute different padas and as such, convey different ideas; for, the bundle of the *saṁskāras* cannot produce one recollection of different *varṇas*. Moreover, *varṇas*, being *vibhudravyas,*[32] do not possess any *krama* (sequence), and if they are spoken of as possessing that, it is only in reference to a cognition which presents them as such; and if the cognition is one, how can one explain any sequence to varṇas on the basis of cognitions ?

The Sphoṭavādin therefore concludes[33] that a *unitary śabda* called *Sphoṭa* is to be accepted for satisfactorily explaining the popular experience that *'śabda conveys idea'*, and that *this śabda* cannot be the *varṇas* (as explained above) and it being *nitya* (eternal) is to be accepted as manifested by *dhvanis* which we experience. The successful manifestation and full experience of Sphoṭa is possible only when all dhvanis separately manifest it; and as the manifestation or experience of Sphoṭa being a perception *(pratyakṣa)* can have various degrees, there is no reason for placing the *arthapratīti* by *varṇas* on a par with the manifestation of sphoṭa by dhvanis. So, *the unitary sphoṭa is to be accepted.*

The Varṇavādin begins[34] his refutation of the Sphoṭavāda by raising a question[35]—whether the cognitions of *varṇas* present only those *varṇas* or a *sound-element* devoid of any form or property in addition to those *varṇas*. In the former,[35] no *sphoṭa* is known in addition to the *varṇas*, which, as different elements in themselves, cannot be spoken of as the *vivartas* (manifestations) of another sound-element. In the latter, a sound-element apart from varṇas is to be accepted, which, while cognised, is known as *śabda—the conveyor of ideas. What is this sonantal element ?* Is it *śabdatva*[37] (the generality of śabda) which is to be considered as the conveyor of ideas ? If so, *śabdatva* being a common property of all śabdas, all ideas, it may be objected, may be known to the hearers from each and every śabda. But the experience of differences in ideas is to be explained only by the differences in their *expressions,* viz., *śabdas.* The explanation that *śabdatva,* though one and devoid of any form or properties, has got its own different *vivartas* (manifestations) like *gakāra, aukāra* and *visarga* in the word '*gauḥ*', which, however, produce the cognitions of different ideas, is unsatisfactory[38] on the ground that the same can be well explained by *śabdas* themselves, which are acceptable to both parties. Moreover, just like *śabdatva, other generalities—sattā, varṇatva,* etc.—may be taken as the conveyor of ideas through their own *vivartas.* Hence, there is *vinigamanāviraha*—no means to prefer one generality to others.

The Varṇavādin adds[39] that *śabdatva,* being an eternal generality, exists in varṇas that are cognised previously in a word or sentence; it may not necessarily depend on the *anusaṁhārabuddhi* of the last *varṇa* to convey the idea, so much so that it will have to be accepted that even the first sound or sounds in a word, while cognised, may convey the idea.[40]

Can the term *śabda* then mean *śrotra-grahaṇa*[41]—that which can be experienced by ear ? Since like *varṇas, grahaṇas* (cognitions of those *varṇas*) also are different, nothing can be said about the *unitariness of śabda* (which is so experienced generally). The *ear* also[42] (being *ākāśa)* is *inferable* and as such, is beyond senses; and the cognition of ear, like all cognitions, is inferable (according to the Bhāṭṭas), so that nothing can be regarded as the object of the unitary experience of śabda by the senses *(aparokṣāvabhāsa).* If the ear *(śrotra)* and its cognition *(grahaṇa)* in the body of *śabda* (as explained above) are not cognisable by the senses, how can the cognition of such a qualified thing (*śabda*) arise as conveyed by the word *śabda?*

Is it then the *sphoṭa*[43] which is cognised as uniform in all varṇas in a word or sentence, but different in different words and sentences ? And are the varṇas, the seeming manifestations of the unitary *sphoṭa,* to explain the difference in the cognition of sphoṭa ? The Varṇavādin again puts a question to the Sphoṭavādin[44]—do the cognitions of the previous *varṇas* help that of the last varṇa in its combination with the previous varṇas ? If so, the cognitions of the previous *varṇas* do not exist when the cognition of the last *varṇa* arises, and so the non-existing things are said to be helping in producing a real thing[45]—a fact which always goes against popular experience. It is an accepted fact that all cognitions do arise, exist for a while, perish and are never brought back to life. So, even if they are supposed to be existing at the time of the cognition of the last *varṇa* in a word, they do not function at all in colloboration with that of the last varṇa.[46] The argument that the varṇas, while cognised, manifest separately the *sphoṭa* without depending on their mutual combination in one *anusaṁhārabuddhi,* falls to the ground[47] since it does not help us to propound the existence of an *akhaṇḍapadārtha* separate from the experienced *varṇas*; in other words, the *akhaṇḍasphoṭa* does not exist like the horn of a man or rabbit. So, it is to be accepted on the basis of valid experience, the Varṇavādin contends, that the perceptions of different *varṇas* produce an *anusaṁhārabuddhi* with those *varṇas* as its object and none else.

Again, the Sphoṭavādin[48] raises many objections to the Varṇavādin's view. The experience —'*gauḥ*' is *one word*—well speaks of the unitary aspect of the word '*gauḥ'*, and this unitariness cannot be satisfactorily explained[49] if we accept only *varṇas* as its object *(viṣaya)*. Nor can it be argued that this unitariness is based on an *upādhi*[50] (limitation) like that of the experiences of 'army', 'forest', etc., because nothing is to be said as the *upādhi* in this instance. Here two *upādhis* are suggested and refuted: (1) *Ekavijñānaviṣayatā*—being the object of one cognition, and (2) *ekābhidheyapratyaya-hetutā*—being the cause of the cognition of one idea. The former cannot be accepted, for, the cognition in the body of upādhi must be known[51] before the delimited object is cognised through that *upādhi*; and that cognition is not cognised when its object is known and it is either to be cognised by a perception called *anuvyavasāyajñāna* or by *inference*. So, the *anusaṁhāra-buddhi* does not bear the cognition as its object *(viṣaya),* much less its unitariness. The second also is untenable[52] since, it involves the fallacy of *interdependence (itaretarāśraya)*. The argument that the distinction of a word from another is known by that of the idea conveyed by it leads to the fallacy of *interdependence* between cause and effect: the conception of *one word* is based on that *of its conveying an idea* and *vice versa*. So, the capacity of *vācakatva* of a word is to be explained only in reference to the *unitary sphoṭa*. Moreover, if we explain the cognition of *unitariness (ekāvabhāsa)* as due to *some upādhi,* nothing would be possibly explained as a real and unitary object, for, some *upādhi* may be invented to explain the same. If so, it can also be suggested, the Sphoṭavādin concludes, that there will be no plurality among objects, since the plurality of objects is only a manifestation of one real object or entity.

The Varṇavādin refutes the Sphoṭa theory thus[53]:—The cognition of unitariness is not an authority to prove the existence of a unitary object, viz., *Sphoṭaśabda* but only the possibility of a usage which bears out the oneness of the object cognised. Though *elephants, horses, chariots* and *foot-men* are different entities and though the *campaka, aśoka, kiṁśuka,* etc., are different species of trees,[54] they become objects of the unitary cognitions—'*It is an army*', '*it is a forest*', etc., which (through some limitation) present unitary objects like 'army' and 'forest'. It cannot be held that the experiences—'*It is an army*', '*it is a forest*', '*it is a śabda*'—have as their objects another entity—*a whole*—separate from the *parts (avayavas)*; (for, no separate entity is accepted in such cases). Nor can it be argued that for the lack of a limitation *(upādhi)* as explained above, the unitary śabda may be accepted, for, it can be held that the three *varṇas* in the word '*gauḥ*' while they become the objects of one recollection, become the cause of the knowledge of one idea, just like three or more stones supporting one *piṭhara* (oven).[55] The fallacy of interdependence (cited above) does-not arise, in view of the fact that the conception of *one word* is based on that of its capacity to convey *one idea.* The word '*pada*' connotes that particular kāraka—*karaṇa*—in relation to the knowledge, since[56] it is derived from the root *pad—to know,* in the sense of *instrument* (*karaṇa*); and as it is a *kāraka,* it ought to be related to a *kriyā viz., knowledge*. The difference between one word and another found in the pairs (1) *gauḥ* and *aśvaḥ*; (2) *vṛṣa* and *vṛṣabha*; and (3) *nadī* and *dīna,* etc., is not possible to explain before it becomes the object of one cognition and conveys a unitary idea. So, it is maintained that *the unitary conception of pada is based on that of the idea conveyed by it.*[57]

Again the Varṇavādin criticises the conception of Sphoṭa by pointing out some gross absurdities involved in it.[58] The view that the previous dhvanis manifest *sphoṭa not so clearly* as the last *dhvani*, does not hold good, in view of the fact that the *sphoṭa*, devoid of any parts, cannot be spoken of as being partly or fully manifested by *dhvanis*. The full or clear manifestation is possible only for a thing which has got parts or qualities, both common and special. The *sphoṭa* cannot be said to have a full or partial manifestation. It should or should not be fully manifested and cognised. The middle course is not possible.

The view that the manifestation of *sphoṭa* is based on superimposition cannot be held, since no superimposition can be explained in reference to an object—the substratum of it—previously unknown.[59] Even if it is held that the *sphoṭa* can be and is previously cognised, it is not possible to maintain that it is devoid of any parts. So the Sphoṭavādin's view that the *padatattva* (the essence or entity of *śabda*) is experienced as one devoid of parts, contains no truth and as such, is not reliable. The popular experience—*we learn idea from śabda*—has no special significance in favour of the Sphoṭavādin's view.[60] The popular experience is sometimes acceptable and sometimes, unacceptable. If it is argued that the validity of the popular experience is anyway to be accepted, it can be maintained in *one way only*—that the unitariness or oneness of śabda (which conveys idea) belongs to the varṇas themselves when they become the object of *one recollection,* and as they form one group (with the name '*pada*'), they convey one idea. This explanation is possible in the case of *śabda*, since it is so experienced in the world, but it is not possible in other instances (since no such popular experience exists).[61]

The Varṇavādin now begins to condemn the second main alternative of the Sphoṭavādin's view'[62]—that the unitary *sphoṭa* is to be accepted on the basis of the difference in ideas, which cannot be otherwise explained. The *Sphoṭa* which is not perceptible, cannot be known by inference from its function, *viz.*, its conveying an idea, for, it involves the fallacy of interdependence.[63] It is this :—the *śabda* by itself cannot convey the idea but only through its knowledge; otherwise it being eternal, it may have to be accepted that all people know for ever ideas from śabdas. But its knowledge is derived, as has been already said, by inference from the middle term, *viz.*, the cognition of idea derived from it, so much so, that the *śabdajñāna* is depending on the *arthapratyaya,* which again depends on the *śabdajñāna.*

Moreover, there is no need for accepting a *unitary śabda* like *sphoṭa.* The knowledge of idea is well brought about by the single cognition of *varṇas* (in words), which, as they appear different on account of the order, sequence or properties like *hrasvatva,* convey different ideas, as in the instances—*nadī, dīna,* etc.[64] The Varṇavādin mentions many conditions—*krama, nyūnātiriktatva, svara, vākya, śruti* and *smṛti*—for differentiating one pada from another. If the *varṇas* or *padas* are uttered at a time by different persons, there arises no cognition of the idea *(artha).* So, it is held that these padas are to be uttered in a particular *sequence by one and the same person,* and that this *ekavaktṛtva* is necessarily cognised by the person who knows ideas from words. Moreover, this *ekavaktrtva* is a *jñāpakahetu*—cause of cognition, and so, it need not be necessarily cognised just like the mind which, as uncognised, becomes the cause of inference.[65]

So, the Varṇavādin concludes that since the sense or meaning of the sentence or word can be well cognised from the knowledge of the words in the combination of *varṇas*, it does not drive one to the necessity of establishing the *akhaṇḍa-padatattva* viz., *sphoṭa,* devoid of any parts and properties.[66]

II

After the refutation of the *sphoṭavāda,* the second view is taken up for discussion. Its superiority to the sphoṭa doctrine lies in the fact that it does not postulate a thing like sphoṭa which goes beyond one's easy comprehension; and it lays[67] stress on the *varṇas* and padas as the cause of the *arthapratīti* (i.e.), the cognition of the meaning of sentence arises from the cognition of the last varṇa in it by the sensory organ—ear, which is much helped to do its function by the impressions produced by the cognitions of words and their meanings, just as the cognition of the last *varṇa* of a word coupled with the impressions produced by the cognitions of the preceding *varṇas* of the word generates the recollection of the *padārtha.*

This view is rejected with the question[68]— does the last *varṇa* generate the *vākyārthapratīti* after producing the recollection of the relation between the last word (of the sentence) and its sense ? If this is accepted, the Siddhāntin says, at the time of the mental impression ready to produce its effect, *viz.,* the recollection (of the *padārtha*), the perception (of the *pada*), the cause of the impression, does not exist[69]; and no one can explain the existence of the cognition of the last *varṇa* in a *pada* or a *vākya* when one recollects the relation between *pada* and *padārtha*, (since it is to be explained that the recollection of the last varṇa arises first, then that of the pada containing the last *varṇa* and then that of the *padārtha*). It cannot also be argued[70] that the *vākyārthapratīti* arises from the cognition of the last *varṇa* even without the recollection of the relation between the pada and padārtha, for, the experience of the *padapadārthasambandha* is of no use if it does not produce a recollection (of the same). Hence, it cannot be explained why one does not have the verbal cognition if one does not get oneself sufficiently acquainted with the import of words which one hears. Nor can it be said that these three—the cognition of the last *varṇa*, the impression of the *padārtha* and the recollection of the *padārtha* are *simultaneous,* in view of the fact that cognitions do arise in *ātman* only one succeeding another. The cognition of the last *varṇa* does not arise a second time *(i.e.)* at the time of the recollection of the *padārtha*, for want of its cause, *viz.*, the *saṁskāra* (produced in the ear of the hearer by the speaker) which is characterised as so *fleeting* and *transient* as the flash of lightning in a dark cloudy night.[71] It cannot also be said that the last varṇa or śabda by itself cannot convey the import of the sentence, except through its cognition; and since the cognitional unity of the last *varṇa* along with the impressions of the previous *varṇas,* padas and padārthas cannot be explained, this view also is described as wholly untenable.

III

Then the third view—the group of *varṇas* or *varṇamālā* in one mirror-like recollection is the cause of the *arthapratīti*—is taken up. It is explained thus[72]: The relation between pada and *padārtha* depends upon the time-honoured usage. Our elders have not used *varṇas* and *padas* alone for the inter-communication and exchange of ideas, but have used *vākya* (sentence). It is not the *sphoṭa* (already described) but the *varṇas*. When it becomes the object of one recollection, it produces the verbal cognition (of the *vākyārtha*). The *padārthasmṛti* arising from the knowledge of *padas* in a *vākya* is an accessory to this varṇamālā in the production of the *vākyārthapratīti*.

This view also is refuted on various grounds. The first defect is *gaurava.*[73] It consists in this: if the *varṇamālā* is accepted as the cause of the *vākyārthapratīti,* then in the sentences— '*arbhaka ! gām ānaya, arbhaka! gām badhāna, Śiśo I gām ānaya, Śiśo! gām badhāna, etc.*', each of which possesses at least one different word, one has to accept that each varṇamālā which is a vākya, possesses different *śaktis* to convey the *vākyārtha*, so that numerous *śaktis* are to be accepted. But for the padavādin the *śakti* is to be accepted over the *padas* only and the *śakti* of one word in different sentences is not different; hence there is no *anavasthā.*

Another defect described is *viṣayābhāva.*[74] It is explained thus:—the *varṇamālā* cannot express the *vākyārtha*, *viz.*, the *padārthasaṁ-sarga,* without *padārthas*, since the latter being the *saṁsargin* (the related object) is to be known before the *saṁsarga* (relation) is cognised. So, the cognition of the *padārthas* as expressed by the *padas* is indispensable for the cognition of the relation of the *padārthas*. And since the very same *padārthajñāna* is capable of producing *vākyārthajñāna,* the *varṇamālā* is said to be superfluous.

Moreover, it is very difficult to maintain[75] that the *varṇamālā* in a long sentence becomes the object of one *anusaṁhārabuddhi*. It is therefore possible to maintain the *abhihitānvayavāda* as explained by Kumārilabhaṭṭa, *viz.*, that *words convey their ideas—padārthas—which however produce the cognition of vākyārtha.*[76]

IV

Now, the *Anvitābhidhānavādin,* the follower of the Ṭīkākāra *alias* Prabhākara, puts forward his view that *words themselves convey the anvitapadārthas,* viz., *their meanings and their mutual relation, so that the padārthas conveyed by padas do not convey the vākyārtha* (i.e.) *there is no abhihitānvaya.*[77]

The Vākyārtha is said to be *one* and *viśiṣṭa*. It is related to many subordinate ideas conveyed by padas. So, it can be well said that the *padas* themselves while they convey the *padārthas*, convey them only as related to one another on the strength of the three well-known accessories —*ākāṅkṣā* (verbal expectancy), *yogyatā* (congruity) and *sannidhi* (proximity).[78] Hence, there is no necessity to accept the Sphoṭaśabda, the last *varṇa* or the *varṇāvalī* as the cause of the cognition of the *vākyārtha*.

Now, the *Abhihitānvayavādin* comes forward with certain objections to the *anvitābhidhanavāda.*[79] First he puts a question to the *anvitābhidhānavādin*: when a word, say the first, in a sentence conveys its idea and the relation (to the other ideas), are the other ideas conveyed or not by their own expressions (in the sentence) ? If other ideas are not conveyed by their own expressions, it is to be admitted that ideas that are to be generally conveyed by words in a sentence are conveyed by the first word itself and so, there is the *superfluity* of the second and other words in the sentence. If it is argued that other words also convey their own ideas and that all words convey them and their relation as conveyed by other words, then in the sentence '*ukhāyām pacet*' for example, till the word '*pacet'* does not convey the idea '*cooking'* as related to *ukhā,* the word *ukhāyām* does not convey the *adhikaraṇa ukhā*; so also, the word '*pacet* does not convey its idea till the word '*ukhāyām*' conveys its meaning. Hence *the fallacy of interdependence.*[80]

The argument that words *first* convey their ideas *(padārthasvarūpas)* and *then* those *padārthas* as *related (anvitārthas),* so that there is no *fallacy of interdependence (parasparāśrayadoṣa),* involves the acceptance of *two abhidhānaśaktis* for words—a fact which is not warranted *or* accepted on authority. It cannot also be argued that words convey *only ideas with their relation (anvitapadārthas)* but those ideas were first recollected by their mere *juxtaposition (sāhacarya)* (and not by words themselves with any significative potency), so that there is *no double śabdaśakti* in words; for, the recollection of the meanings of words is to be based on their *anubhavas* which present them as *not isolated* but *as related to one another.* So in the example '*gām ānaya*' the *gośabda* conveying the *go padārtha* (cow) as related to the *ānayanakriyā* (bringing) produces in the hearer a recollection of *ānayanānvitagopadārtha* (cow as related to the action—bringing) and not of a mere cow.[81] This explanation would land us in the difficulty that the same *gośabda* in the sentence '*gām paśya*' would not convey *darśanānvita-go (cow* as related to the action—*seeing),* since it had been originally related to the *ānayanakriyā.* So also in the example—'*prāsādam paśya*', the word *paśya* conveys *darśanakriyā* (seeing) as related to the *prāsādapadārtha* (palace), and it does not convey the same as related to the *gopadārtha* (cow). This would set aside the possibility of explaining the *padārthas* (and vākyārthas) in all verbal propositions.[82]

The argument that the *gośabda* on the basis of *avyabhicāra* (invariability) generates in the hearer a recollection of its meaning only, *viz.*, *cow,* and not the meanings of other words, falls to the ground since *avyabhicāra* is not recognised as the cause of recollection. It is *bhāvanā* (mental impression) that when it is deep-rooted on account of the strong and constant previous experiences *(anubhavapaunaḥpunya),* is roused and produces *smṛti* (recollection). And *avyabhicāra* has no place among the causes of *bhāvanodbodha* (rousing the mental impression), since among the causes of *bhāvanodbodha, praṇidhāna* (meditation) and others are mentioned and *not avyabhicāra.*[83] *Sāhacarya* is however accepted as one of the causes of the *bhāvanodbodha,*[84] since *sambandha* in the list includes *sāhacarya* and not *avyabhicāra.* And this *sāhacarya* is common to both *svārtha* and *padāntarārtha* (the meaning of one word and those of others), so that there arises from words a recollection of *anvitapadārthas (i.e.)* both *svārtha* and *padāntarārtha.* So, the *gopadārtha* cannot be said as related to *darśañakriyā* by *ākāṅkṣā.* Hence, there is no possibility of cognising the vākyārtha from a verbal proposition, if anvitābhidhāna is accepted.[85]

So words, the Abhihitānvayavādin contends, convey only their own meanings, and those meanings, incomplete and incoherent in their isolation, are related to one another by the threefold conditions—*akāṅksā, yogyatā* and *āsatti* —and convey the *vākyārtha.*

The Anvitābhidhānavādin answers[86] all charges levelled against him by the Abhihitānvayavādin. He says first that there is no fallacy of *interdependence* (as explained above, if *anvitābhidhāna* is accepted), for, though the words through *abhidhāna-śakti* convey the *anvitapadārthas* (their meanings and their mutual relation), the meanings of other words are not invariably recollected from one word for want of *abhyāsa,* so much so that there arises from a *pada* a recollection of its own meaning *(svārtha)* and its *anvaya* (relation). It can be therefore said that words invariably convey only their own meanings *(svārthas)* along with the *anvaya* and not the meanings of other words also.

In support of this argument the Anvitābhidhānavādin puts a question to his opponent—*what kind of cognition is that which one derives from words ?* Only *four* kinds of cognitions are recognised—*pramāṇa* (valid experience), *saṁśaya* (doubt), *viparyaya* (misapprehension) and *smṛti* (recollection). The cognition of the meanings from words is not a *pramāṇajñāna,* since it does not possess as its object anything previously unknown. To say that it is a *doubt* or *viparyaya* is out of place.[87] As there is no *fifth* variety, it is to be accepted that it is a *recollection* and that words, like *praṇidhāna,* are the conditions of *saṁskārodbodha* (rousing mental impressions). And this recollection of the meanings of words presents both objects and their relation.

Again, the contention (of the Abhihitānvayavādin) that the padārthas recollected by the *abhidhānaśakti* of words—and not by mere *sāhacarya*—become the objects of the vākyārthajñāna, is of no avail, in view of the fact that in instances like '*Gaṅgāyām ghoṣaḥ prativasati*' the 'bank' which is only a secondary meaning of the word *gaṅgā,* is related to '*dwelling*', the primary meaning of the word '*prativasati.*'

Moreover, one padārtha recollected by the *abhidhānaśakti* of one word can be related to another recollected by mere *sāhacarya* on the basis of *ākāṅkṣā,* so that it may not be again related to (the other or) last idea conveyed by its own word with its *abhidhānaśakti.* If this is possible, the whole *vākyārtha* would not be cognised at all. So, it is to be admitted that there arise *first* the recollection of the *isolated ideas (ananvitārthas)* by the mere *sāhacarya* of words[88] and *then* that of the *anvitapadārthas* from words.[89] It cannot be said that the padārthas are not mutually related for want of *ākāṅkṣā*[90] (verbal expectancy), for, expectancy is said to be *nothing but the knower's desire for knowledge.* It is explained on the basis of the *incompleteness of abhidhāna (abhidhānāparyavasāna)* as in the example— *dvāram*—which, being in nominative case, does not convey any new idea other than that of the stem *(prātipadika)*; so, the knower seeks some other idea, which can be well related to the *padārtha,* viz., *dvāra.*[91] It is also explained on the basis of the *incongruity or incompatibility of the idea already known from a word (abhihitāparyavasāna).* In the vedic passage— *Viśvajitā yajeta*—the sacrifice *Viśvajit* is known by the instrumental case as the *karaṇa* (instrument) of the *kārya,* which (an *abhihita)* is incompatible with the *karaṇa* without a *niyojya-puruṣa* and as such, leads to the explanation of a *niyojya-viśeṣa* (like the *svargakāma).*[92]

The argument of the Abhihitānvayavādin[93] that words convey their meanings without their mutual relation and that those meanings produce *vākyārthajñāna* on the strength of the threefold accessories—*ākāṅkṣā,* etc., so that words have no direct capacity to generate *Śābdabodha,* falls to the ground, in view of the fact that unless those ideas are conveyed by words, they are not considered as the cause of the *vākyārthajñana.*[94]

The Abhihitānvayavādin further argues that one who perceives a *white object* and hears the *heṣā* sound (neighing) and the *noise of galloping* experiences that '*a white horse gallops'* even without the cognition of words expressing them. The Anvitābhidhānavādin answers that this knowledge is arrived at either from *inference (anumāna)* or from *presumption (arthāpatti)* and *not from words (śabda).* In the explanation of the same he raises a question—whether in this instance one experiences the *heṣā sound* and the *noise of galloping* as *co-existing* in the white object, or whether all the *three* are *independently* known. In the former, the knowledge is *inferential* on the basis of *probans*; in the latter, it is a knowledge from *presumption,* in case no other object (possessing these qualities) is definitely known.

Moreover, if śābdabodha is generated by *padārthas*, it would be *aśābda* (i.e.) *not based on śabdas*; and as it is not definitely known whether the *arthas* seek the help of the mind which does not operate on the external objects, it would result in the acceptance of a *seventh pramāṇa* (called *padārtha* separate from the six well-known pramāṇas). It is therefore to be accepted that the *padārthas* not conveyed by words do not become the *cause of vākyārthajñāna,* and that the ideas conveyed by words do possess the power to generate the *same (śābdabodha).*[95] This would mean for the Abhihitānvayavādin the acceptance of *two śaktis— one* over the *padārthas* to generate the *vākyārtha-jñāna* and *other* over words capable of creating (the *first) śakti* over the padārthas. But for the Anvitābhidhānavādin, *only one śakti* is to be accepted over words which convey *padārthas* on the basis of the intention of the speaker, and through that *śakti* one word conveys its meaning as related to the meanings of other words (in the sentence) on the strength of the three accessories—*ākāṅkṣā,* etc. *Hence, it is appropriate to say that words which convey padārthas are the cause of the cognition of the vākyārtha.*

V

The Abhihitānvayavādin begins the refutation of the anvitābhidhānavāda with an introductory remark that it is a general rule that in the absence of any strong objection *(bādhaka),* that which stands very near to the effect becomes the cause of it; hence, the recollection of the *padārthas* which are nearer to the *vākyārthajñāna* than the padas, can be well considered as the cause of the *vākyārthajñāna.* He adds that one would never know *vākyārtha* from the mere knowledge of words without recollecting the *padārthas* therefrom, but knows it invariably after recollecting the *padārthas* from the juxtaposed words.

On the basis of this observation he puts forth his view of

the abhihitānvayavāda that the recollections of the *padārthas* associated with one another become the cause of the *vākyārtha-jñāna,* on the strength of the three accessories— *ākāṅkṣā* (expectancy), *yogyatā* (congruity) and *āsatti* (proximity).[96]

It is again argued[97] (by the Anvitābhidhānavādin) that the recollections of the meanings (of words) which are in reality associated with those (of other words in a sentence) do not bear them as objects in their isolation. For example, if one recollects a *palace* without its locality, *viz., Pāṭalīputra* and *Māhiṣmatī* (another place which has nothing to do with the palace referred to), one is not capable of understanding these two *padārthas (—palace* and *Māhiṣmatī—)* as related to each other. So, words have no inherent capacity to denote their meanings as unrelated to one another. This is considered to be the main objection—*bādhaka*—viz., *sāmarthyābhāva* to the assumption that the *padārthas* (the immediate neighbour of the *vākyārthajñāna)* are the cause of the *vākyārthajñāna.*

The Abhihitānvayavādin answers this easily. He says[98]: the mental impression has no such capacity to produce a valid recollection as would invariably present those objects which had and had not been previously experienced (as related to one another); but (it possesses a capacity) to generate *padā-rthasmṛtis'*[99] (recollections of the meanings of words) from the group of words in *juxtaposition.* These *padārthasmṛtis* have the support of the three accessories—*ākāṅkṣā,* etc., and as such, become *karaṇa* (of the *vākyārtha-bodha)* in that they immediately produce the valid cognition of the mutual relation of the *padārthas,* viz., the *vākyārtha.*

If such a *vākyārthajñāna* is not *pramāṇa,* then the cognition known as *recognition (pratyabhijñā)*[100] will never arise (valid, since it is generated by recollection or mental impression). And it may be objected how a mental impression or recollection produced by the impression which owes its existence to an experience presenting an object with certain limitations of space, time, etc., would generate another cognition presenting the same object with the limitations of different space, time, etc. To answer this objection it is to be accepted that the mental impressions or recollections do possess an extraordinary power to produce *recognition* which would present objects uniformly existing at different times and places when they attain new features by their association with the accessories like the senses.[101] Such an explanation, *viz.*, the possession of a power by the *padārthasmṛtis* and *saṁskāras,* is possible here also if one views it without any prejudice.[102] It is also explained in the Nyāyakaṇikā that no object becomes varied or different through the difference of time, space and the various stages[103] of the object.

It is argued again[104] by the Anvitābhidhānavādin that as has been already said, the *padārthas,* if they are recollected from any source (other than words), do not possess the power to produce the *vākyārthajñāna.* If it is said that they have such a power, they would be recognised as the seventh *pramāṇa* (means of knowledge); or *āgama* (verbal testimony) would merge in the *padārthas.* And they (padārthas) should have been explained (by the *Vṛttikāra* and others) along with *pratyakṣa* and other (means of knowledge), and *āgama* should not have been mentioned (as a separate pramāṇa), since it is only a subdivision of the *pramāṇa*, *viz., padārtha.* Experienced people do not use[105] words denoting unequal divisions (in a *dvandva* compound) as '*Brāhmaṇa and Yudhiṣṭhira*' (one a caste-name and other the name of an individual) but use such words expressing equal divisions as '*Brāhmaṇa and Rājanya*' (two caste-names) and '*Vasiṣṭha and Yudhiṣṭhira*' both being the names of two persons. By the mention of one sub-division, another sub-division (of the same class) cannot be taken as mentioned. So, the *genus— padārthas*—should have been enumerated in the list of *pramāṇas.* To say that the Vṛttikāra and the Bhāṣyakāra who began to elucidate all means of knowledge, left out some little *pramāṇa* unexplained would be attributing to them unsound scholarship[106]; so (to avoid that) it is to be stated that *padārthas* which become objects of experiences or recollections resulting from words, do possess a special power to generate the cognition of the *vākyārtha*. If this is accepted, *three* or *two śaktis*[107] are to be explained—*two śaktis* on words and *one* on their meanings[108] (if words generate the experience *(anubhava)* of their meanings), or *one śakti* over words and *one* over their meanings,[109] (if words generate a recollection of their meanings). But, if anvitābhidhānavāda be accepted, only *one śakti* over words is to be accepted; and (as there is no *śakti* over the *padārthas*), there is much saving of labour. *Hence the anvitābhidhānavāda is acceptable.*

The Abhihitanvayavādin while replying to this accepts first the principle of *lāghava* enunciated by his opponent and remarks that in order to find out that, an impartial investigation is to be made.

The one *padaśakti* accepted by the Anvitābhidhānavādin has reference to the meanings of words as mutually related *(i.e.)* words convey by their *abhidhānaśakti* both *padārthas* and their relation. This *śakti* cannot be said as having reference to the *anvaya* only. If so, the *anvaya*—relation—being one and the same, all words would become *synonymous*.

Again, it is argued: words convey the related things *(vyatiṣakta)*[110] and do not convey their relation also, just as words connoting generalities do not convey the idea of individuals. The relation is known when the related objects are cognised, and since the related objects are different, there is no fallacy of all words becoming *synonymous*.

This is also refuted as *inconclusive*. In the refutation of the same a question is raised— whether by the word *vyatiṣakta* (related thing) is to be understood only the object or the object as well as the relation. Words which convey by *abhidhāna* the *concepts (padārthasvarūpa)* cannot convey the relation also, just as a word connoting a generality by its *abhidhāśakti* does not convey the idea of individual. A quality like colour cannot exist without a substance; so, a word connoting a quality expresses its own *āśraya* (substance). Can a similar thing be spoken of *padārthas* ? No; it is held that the *padārthas* can be well known (by words) even without their mutual relation. If it is said that the *padārthas* are not known without their relation, it will have to be accepted that the *liṅga (probans)* cannot be known[111] without the cognition of the *liṅgin* (the major term) in the *pakṣa* (the minor term); so also *liṅgatva* (invariable concomitance) cannot be known. Hence the whole domain of inference would become very difficult to explain. So, to say that the *anvita* is known by words would mean that both *padārthas* and their relation are conveyed by words.

Now the Abhihitānvayavādin questions[112]— whether one is contented with the fact that on the basis of *lāghava* (labour-saving), words by their *śakti* or *sāmarthya* do not convey the *relation* but only the *padārthasvarūpa,* which however generates the cognition of the *vakyārtha,* (so that one would refrain from attributing to words the power to convey the relation of the padārthas), or whether they by their *śakti* convey both the *padārthasvarūpa* and their relation, without which no cognition of vākyārtha would possibly arise even though one makes a thousand and one efforts to obtain it.

Of these two, which is to be accepted ?

On the strength of *samabhivyāhāra*[113] words become capable of conveying the relation between one *padārtha* and another; or the juxtaposition or co-utterance would be of no avail. Any object is said to possess a particular *sāmarthya* (capacity) if its effect cannot take place without that object. The knowledge of the relation (between one *padārtha* and another) arises from a visible or invisible thing other than words; so there is no authority for us to attribute it to words. The learned in the Three Vedas observe that the śabdārtha—the meaning of a word—is that which is not known from any other source. On the basis of this observation they have held the view that the personal termination *(ākhyātapratyaya),* etc., do not convey by *abhidhā,* the agent *(kartā)* of the action, etc. On the basis of the juxtaposition or expectancy, again, words by their secondary significative power convey the mutual relation of their meanings *(anvitāvasthā),* since they are uttered by the speaker with the intention of conveying the *anvaya.* Even unjuxtaposed words do not stop their functioning with generating the knowledge of their own meanings. The learned people in the world do not use words for conveying the padārthas merely; on the other hand, they utter words[114] with the intention of conveying (to the hearers) their ideas through those words. If words do not convey the intended ideas of the speakers, then those speakers are to be considered as men without the knowledge of the world or true judgment. Nobody seeks to know padārthas which have already been known. So, the (learned) use words in a particular order so as to make others know an idea already unknown. Hence, the particular order or juxtaposition of words which have the sole object to convey an idea hitherto unknown, without which the co-utterance of words in a particular order or the sentence itself would be impossible, helps (the words) to convey by the secondary significative potency the relation that subsists between one padārtha and another. To this effect the Vārttika says that the cognition of the *viśiṣṭārtha, viz.,* the mutual relation of the padārthas, is generated by the *samabhivyāhṛti* (co-utterance of words).[115]

So on the basis of the recollection (of the *padārthas*) produced by words in juxtaposition which cannot be otherwise explained and strengthened by the expectancy and congruity of the *padārthas*, words, therefore, convey by lakṣaṇā the *anvitāvasthā* (the relation between one *padārtha* and another), which does not therefore impose on words any special *śakti* for its own knowledge.[116]

Words that are used by honest people with the intention of conveying certain ideas to the hearers may bring out the unknown idea *viz., vākyārtha* by the secondary significative potency which is generally adopted on the basis of the incompatibility of the intended idea of the speaker; but words in the vedas which are believed to be *self-revelations,* cannot convey the *vākyārtha* by lakṣaṇā, since there is no *puruṣa* (author) in the case of the vedas and since there is no possibility for the explanation of the *tātparyānupapatti.*[117] It may be accepted that (on the basis of the *lokavedādhikaraṇa)* there is no difference between *laukika* and *vedic* words (so that there will arise valid *śābdabodha* from the *Vaidika* words just like from other words). This does not hold good in view of the fact that (if such a comparison be held between the *loka* and the *vedas),* another similar thing would have to be accepted in the *laukika* words used, *i.e.,* that the word *gaṅgā* (in the sentence '*gaṅgāyām ghoṣaḥ*') which means *bank* by the secondary significative potency, would have to mean the same in the sentences— '*gaṅgāyām payāṁsi, yādāṁsi gaṅgāyām' (waters of the Ganges, animals in the Ganges).* The argument that there is no *anupapatti* (incompatibility of the primary sense in the context, so that there is no basis for lakṣaṇā) does not any way favour the position of *laukika* words in as much as the same might be said of the vedic words.[118]

The Abhihitānvayavādin argues that if anvitābhidhānavāda be accepted, the vedic words (in a sentence) would not generate an unknown kind of *jñāna,* viz., *vākyārthajñāna* (since it emphasizes only the recollection of *anvitāvasthā* from words). To this Anvitābhidhānavādin however replies that just as *laukika* words *(i.e.)* used in ordinary conversation convey even ideas with the relation (of those ideas), so also the vedic words convey both their ideas and relation (since the *laukika* and *Vaidika* words are said to be identical). This is again refuted by the Abhihitānvayavādin on the main ground of *lāghava* (already explained) and also on the ground that words, while used by speakers, convey invariably the intended ideas (on their individual capacity) and as such, are not capable of conveying the *anvitāvasthā,* so that there is no room for attributing to words the power of conveying their own ideas as associated with the ideas of other words *(arthāntarānvitasvārtha-kalpanā).*[119]

Again, the Anvitābhidhānavādin contends[120] that the authoritativeness of the vedas cannot be accepted in view of the fact that the complete understanding of the import of the Vedas would be impossible (if anvitābhidhānavāda is not accepted). At this the Abhihitānvayavādin coolly remarks: if such a thing happens, well and good! Nothing is lost to them who accept everything on sound reason.[121] So, it is to be ascertained without any prejudice but following the path of a true *āstika* what is acceptable as an indispensable factor[122] which contributes to our understanding of the meanings of the *Vaidika* words. It is an admitted fact that the means of the knowledge of the relation between words and their meanings is the beginningless tradition of the old (who used words to convey certain definite ideas); so even without a person responsible for that relation, the knowledge of the meanings of words (*padārthas*) can arise. *Hence, the relation between words and their meanings is considered to be but natural.*

It is questioned—does that relation (of words *viz., śakti* pertain to) the meaning of one word related to the meaning (of another) or to the meaning of one word only ? In the second, do words convey (by their *śakti)* their meanings alone or the mutual relation also ? If words convey their meanings only, they do not produce the cognition of the vākyārtha, and as such, cannot be considered to be the efficient cause of the cognition of the *padārthasaṁsarga (vākyārtha). Hence the two other alternatives are open to explain that words have the utility for generating the cognition of the relation of the padārthas.*

Now, the Abhihitānvayavādin[123] says that though words bear out the intention of conveying the relation of *padārthas*, they convey by their *abhidhānaśakti* the *padārthasvarūpa* only, and since the relation of the *padārthas* is known (by other means of knowledge), there is no room for *presumption* (*arthāpatti*), on the authority of which words are said to possess a peculiar power to convey (not only *padārthas* but also) the *vākyārtha.* When we hear a particular statement from a reliable person, we are sometimes prompted to action or to keep ourselves aloof; sometimes we realise pleasure, pain or fear; and from this a careful observer infers our knowledge—the cause of our mental state. He verifies also that such a thing does not take place in the presence of other things *but words*. And this knowledge does not present *padārthas merely* to produce such effects as *action* but the *qualified padārthas—padārthas* and their relation. So, words used by the learned bear out the intention of conveying the *qualified padārthas*; and this cannot be explained without the recollection of the *isolated padārthas* (through words), which may be inferred from the experience of the *viśiṣṭavākyārtha* arising therefrom. The capacity of words to produce a recollection of padārthas, does not dare to destroy (the power of) their being the vehicle of the intended *viśiṣṭārtha,* since nothing (in this world) will destroy its own *nimitta* (cause), much less its *own self.* So, words do not convey by *abhidhāna* the qualified padārthas. Hence as in the *laukika* words,[124] the *vaidika* words in a sentence do by *lakṣaṇā* generate a cognition of the *qualified padārthas* on the basis of their conveying (by abhidhāna) unqualified or isolated ideas. To say that words bear out the intention of conveying the isolated ideas only, which by themselves do not bear any fruit to the hearer, would be denying one's understanding of the *vākyārtha* through the cognition of words.

To this effect says the revered *Vārttikakāramiśra*— '*Varṇas* (words) directly however convey *padārthas* (concepts), yet they do not stop with them, the mere knowledge of which is of no use to the hearer. The conveying of *padārthas* by words is indispensable for the cognition of *vākyārtha*, just like fire for cooking by means of pieces of wood'.

So, also (says he)—

'That *vākyārtha* is everywhere conveyed by words by *lakṣ -aṇā* (secondary significative potency) only is an accepted fact for us.'

It cannot be argued that words which bear out the intention of conveying their meanings and their relation, convey both by *abhidhāna*; if this be accepted,[125] one will have to accept that the word *gaṅgā* in the sentence '*gahgāyām ghoṣaḥ*' would on the basis of *tātparya* convey the idea of *bank* by its *abhidhāna*. To say that the idea of *bank* is conveyed by the word *gaṅgā* (by *lakṣaṇā*) on the basis of its relation (proximity) to the *svārtha* viz., *current,* and as such, is not, *in spite of the tatparya,* conveyed by its *abhidhāna,* is favourable to what has been said with reference to words. So the *tātparya* does not invariably prove the existence of a special *padaśakti* for conveying the *vākyārtha*. The pieces of wood though they are intended for cooking, never directly accomplish their fruit; but fire alone (accomplishes it); and through that, they also accomplish it. The priority of words to meanings in generating the *vākyārthajñāna* has no special significance and as such, would not anyway indicate the existence of a special *padaśakti*. That both words and their meanings stand on a different footing has been already explained by the fact that words convey by *abhidhāna* their meanings and not their relation, for there is the objection of *gaurava*. It need not be said that the *padārthas* even with the support of the accessories like *expectancy,* do possess a special power to generate the cognition of the *viśiṣṭārtha,* for, even without it, such a cognition arises from the *padārthas*.

Not only the *padārthas* recollected through words but also others (recollected) through other means of knowledge are capable of generating the *viśiṣṭārthabuddhi*. Just as *presumption (arthāpatti)* and *inference (anumāna)* produce a *viśiṣṭārthabuddhi,*[126] so also padārthas recollected through words which are considered as bearing out the intention of the speaker, generate a *viśiṣṭārthabuddhi*. The *tātparya* which is known from the incompatibility (of the primary sense) and the relation to the *vākyārtha* does not any way explain or suggest the existence of a new *śabda-śakti,* in view of the fact that such an explanation would result in our acceptance of the śakti over words like *gaṅgā* and over objects like *kaṣṭha* (pieces of wood), in the senses of *bank* and *cooking* respectively.

Lakṣaṇā is not always adopted in a sense on the exclusion of the primary sense of a word; but there are both *acceptance* and *abandonment* of the primary sense according to the nature of the secondary sense. For example, in the sentence—'*gaṅgāyām ghoṣaḥ'* the primary sense of the word *gaṅgā* is abandoned on the adoption of *lakṣaṇā* in the sense of *bank* capable of locating a hamlet; but in the example—'*daṇḍino gacchanti,'* the primary sense of the word *daṇḍin* merges into the body of the secondary sense—the group of both sets of people with and without sticks. In the vedic example also—'*sṛṣtīrupadadhāti*', the word *sṛṣṭi* by *lakṣaṇā* means the *bricks* that are associated with a group of *mantras* with and without the word *sṛṣṭi.* Similarly, when the relation of the padārthas is conveyed by words by *lakṣaṇā,* the *padārthas* (the primary meanings) also are included in the body of the secondary sense, for, without them, the secondary sense is of no avail and as such, will have to be discarded.

It cannot be argued[127] that words convey the *vākyārtha* by *lakṣaṇā* in as much as it does not satisfy its own definition; for, *lakṣaṇā* is to be so defined as to include within its scope the present instance also.

Can this be then the *lakṣaṇā* as explained by one author:—that which is adopted to convey a new sense that can be related to the *vākyārtha* through the cognition of its relation to the primary sense, when the primary sense (of the word) is incompatible with the intended sense of the sentence ? In the sentence—'*Odanam pacati Caitraḥ pithāre'* (Caitra cooks food on an oven) the ideas of Caitra, pithāra, etc., have nothing unrelated to the *vākyārtha.* Nor has the *anvitāvasthā* which is to be conveyed by words by lakṣaṇā, been related to another *anvaya* (just as the secondary sense of the word *gaṅgā* possesses the relation to the *vākyārtha).* So no *lakṣaṇā* is to be adopted in words in the sense of the *anvitāvasthā.*

To this the Siddhāntin replies in a jeering tone: if there be no *lakṣaṇā*, then, are the things that can be known by other means of knowledge accepted to be conveyed by words ? Nobody accepts *abhidhānaśakti* in the word *agnihotra* in the vedic passage—'*Māsamagni hotram juhoti*', though it cannot convey the idea of the *Māsāgnihotra* by *lakṣaṇā*. If it is said that on the basis of *similarity* (between the *Nityāgnihotra* and the *Māsāgnihotra)* the word is *gauṇa* (metaphorical) and that, there is no necessity for accepting *abhidhāna* in the sense of *Māsāgnihotra,* it may be asserted even here that without any special *abhidhāna* the *anvitāvasthā* may be well cognised as explained above. If the *padavṛtti* (by which words convey the *anvitāvasthā)* does not satisfy the definition of *lakṣaṇā, a fourth kind of padavṛtti*[128] may be accepted on the basis of experience; or it may be asserted as *lakṣaṇā* itself which may be given a different definition, simply to avoid an *unknown padavṛtti*. Two conditions of *lakṣaṇā* as given in the definition cited above may be well accepted, *viz.*, (1) the incompatibility of the primary sense and (2) the relation of the secondary sense to the primary sense; but not other conditions like the incompatibility of the primary sense *with the vākyārtha.*

It is experienced that words that are juxtaposed or co-uttered with the intention of their conveying a *viśiṣṭārtha* will have no significance if they convey only the *padārthas*, so that they convey (by *lakṣaṇā*) the *anvitāvasthā* as related to the padārthas. This definition is applicable to both *laukika* and *Vaidika* instances without any violence. Though words by *abhidhāna* express the *padārthasvarūpas* (concepts) only, yet they do not stop with them; they directly express the *padārthas* for the sake of the *vākyārthajñana,* and so they convey the *vākyārtha* by *lakṣaṇā*.

The objection that the *anvitāvasthā* cannot be taken as the secondary sense of words for the reason that it is not previously known as associated with the *padārthas*, may be answered easily. It is said that the *anvitāvasthā* is previously known in its general capacity, though it is known afterwards in its special feature at the time of its association with the *padārthas*. The *anvitāvasthā* is said to be nothing but the *anvitapadārthas*—concepts with their relation, so that no duplication in the capacity *(sāmarthya)*[129] other than that to convey the *padārthas* is to be accepted. Words do not convey by *abhidhānaśakti* the *anvaya* also, since the *anvaya* is cognised even when the padārthas alone are known by *abhidhānaśakti*.

If the cognition of the padārthas generated by the potency of words does not come under the kinds—valid cognition, doubt, and misapprehension, and if no kind of cognition other than recollection is recognised, it may be by all means recollection itself, which however arises not on merely rousing up the impressions, but on those impressions roused up by words by *abhidhānaśakti*. To say that words have utility in rousing up the impressions (and as such, possess a power to convey the relation of padārthas), would lead us to accept a similar power over *arthas*; for, they also by their *śakti* become the condition to rouse the impressions of their own words and as such, may be well considered as expressing the words also. It is therefore to be asserted that words do not convey by *abhidhāna* the *anvaya* which is not known by other means of knowledge.

Now, a question is raised (against the Anvi-tābhidhāna-vādin)—what is that *abhidhā power* of *śabdas* which convey also the *anvaya* by it ? It is not movement *(parispanda)* which exists in objects possessing form. And *śabda* either as a *vibhudravya* or a *vibhuguna* does not possess any form. The *mūrti* (form) is defined by those who have understood (the essence of) the phenomenal world as the *measurement of a substance not all-pervasive*. And there is no authority to say that it is an invisible kind of movement like the *volition*. The cognition of *anvaya* (the relation of the padārthas) will arise from that of *śabdas*[130] when that relation (between *śabdas* and arthas) has been already known (and recollected). So, this cognition presenting *śabda* as such is the *vyāpāra* (immediate cause) of the cognition of *svārthas*. To this effect says the revered Bhāsyakāra—

'śāstra (verbal cognition) is the cognition presenting an object having no contact with the senses by the cognition of *śabda*.'

That alone is called *abhidhā* in that *śabda* possesses an inborn potency and generates the cognition of the *padārthas* by that power. It does not independently produce the cognition of *arthas* but through rousing the mental impressions (of those arthas previously known). So, there is no room for the presumption that the cognition of arthas first rouses the impressions of words and then produces the recollection of words and as such is called *abhidhā*. But it is the cognition of *śabda*, which invariably generates the recollection of the padārthas. So, have the experienced people in this world explained the use of words (for communicating one's thought to another).

It may be objected that *śabda* never rouses the mental impressions, since it is not studied in the list beginning with *praṇidhāna* (meditation). This is answered thus: *śabda* also may be said to be included in the list.[131] The conditions of recollection are enumerated by *Prāmāṇikas* (authoritative people)—*praṇidhāna, nibandhana, abhyāsa, liṅga, lakṣaṇa, sādṛsya, parigraha, āśraya, āśrita, sambandha, ānantarya, viyoga, ekakārya, virodha, atiśaya, prāpti, vyavadhāna, sukha, duḥkha, icchā, dveṣa, bhaya, arthitva, kriyā, rāga, dharma, adharma*. Though *pada* is not found (in the list), *sambandha* (relation) is studied in the list of the conditions of recollection; and it includes well the *padas* (as the related object), just as the pupil reminds one of the teacher and the priest, of the sacrificer. The relation between words and ideas is eternal and it is nothing but *vācyavācakabhāva*—the relation that subsists between the conveyor and the conveyed. The cognition of śabda coupled with the impression produced by the experience of the *artha* will generate the recollection of the *svārtha* (its concept), since *śabda* is uttered with the intention of generating the *arthajñāna* (in the hearer). The relation between the conveyor and the conveyed is nothing but that between the cogniser and the cognised, or strictly speaking, that between the recollector and the recollected.

It is again objected that the disciple reminds one of his

teacher through the *relation between the teacher and the pupil* and not necessarily by that between the recollector and the recollected, and that, in the instance of *śabda* some other relation should therefore be found out; that since there is no other suitable relation, *viz., abhidheyasāhacarya* (the association with the *abhidheyārtha)* and as such, the power or capacity of *śabdas* for reminding the hearer of the ideas may be established.

Now, the Siddhāntin retorts that if anvitābhidhāna be accepted, is there any other relation on the basis of which words would convey the *anvitārtha* (ideas and their relation) ? The eye and other (senses) and the smoke and other *(probans)* are observed as generating cognitions of such objects as invariably associated with them, through the relations such as their *contact* with the objects in vision and the invariable concomitance.[132] If it is said that even without any other relation there may arise from words the cognition of ideas through the eternal significative potency *(śakti),* the existence of which is well inferred from their time-honoured usage, the same may be said here also. The relation between *śabda* and *artha* may be that between the recollector and the recollected, since it is observed that words do possess a potency to generate a recollection of arthas; and that relation is nothing but the cognition of śabda which is also known as *abhidhā,* as explained above.

So, the capacity of words to convey the ideas *(abhidhātṛtva)* cannot be satisfactorily explained if anvitābhidhāna be followed. It is therefore appropriate to say that on the ground of *lāghava* (saving labour) *vākyārtha* is known from words by their secondary significative potency in that it is generated by the *padārthas* recollected by the means of words co-uttered or juxtaposed and associated with the accessories like expectancy.

So, it has been well said—"Words convey their ideas (concepts) and refrain from any other functioning; and then the *padārthas* being cognised produce the cognition of the *vākyārtha.*"

REFERENCES

1. See the Tattvabindu (below) p. 6.
2. See *ibid.*, and the *Tattvavibhāvanā*, p. 6.
3. *Ibid.*, p. 7.
4. *Ibid.*
5. See the Tattvabindu (below), p. 8.
6. As he has observed in his Devatādhikaraṇabhāṣya-Bhāmatī (I. 3. 28)—'*diṅmātramiha darśitam, vistarastu Tattva-bindāvavagantavyaḥ*'—Vācaspatimiśra has in this section of the work dealt with and refuted the Sphoṭavāda in a most elaborate and inimitable manner. Here he anticipates and replies to (as the *Tattvavibhāvanā* goes) many attacks made by Maṇdanamiśra in his Sphoṭasiddhi against Kumārila. [See the *Tattvavibhāvanā* (below) pp. 17, 18, 19, 20, 22, 23, 26, 29, 34 36, 44, 49 & 50, 58, 59 & 60, 68, 70 & 71.]
7. See the Tattvabindu (below) p. 9.
8. *Ibid.*
9. See the Tattvabindu (below) p. 9.
10. See *ibid.*, p. 10. *Cf.* Kārikāvali, verse 23. '*Sama-vāyīkāraṇatvam dravyasyaiveti vijñeyam.*'
11. *Cf.* '*Vāyurapadyate śabdatām.*'
12. See the Tattvabindu (below) p. 11.
13. *Ibid.*, p. 12.
14. See the Tattvabindu (below) p. 13.
15. See *ibid.*, p. 14. *cf.* The theory current among Modern Philologists—'Sentence is the Unit of Language.'
16. *Vide* the Tattvabindu (below) p. 18.
17. *Ibid.*, p. 19.
18. See the Tattvabindu (below) pp. 20 and 21.
19. The (invalid) cognition of trees at a distance as a row of green grass *(haritapravāha)* leads one to that of green trees (which do not exist there). *Ibid.*, p. 21.
20. *Ibid.*, pp. 23 and 24.
21. *Ibid.*, p. 25.
22. See the Tattvabindu (below) p. 25.

23. *Ibid.*,
24. *Ibid.*, p. 26.
25. *Ibid.*,
26. See the Tattvabindu (below) p. 26.
27. *Ibid.*, p. 28.
28. *Ibid.*,
29. *Ibid.*, p. 29.
30. See the Tattvabindu (below) p. 30.
31. *Ibid.*, p. 31.
32. *Ibid.*, p. 32.
33. *Ibid.*, pp. 35 & 36.
34. See the Tattvabindu (below) p. 36.
35. *Ibid.*, p. 37.
36. *Ibid.*
37. *Ibid.*, p. 38.
38. *Ibid.*, p. 39.
39. See the Tattvabindu (below) p. 41.
40. In this connection Vācaspatimiśra hits the Prābhākaras who have denied the existence of *śabdatvajāti,* lest they should have to attribute to it the function of conveying ideas. He says that *śabdatva* never stands in the way of the reality of the different varṇas which are to be accepted as eternal. Just as *śābaleyatva* (a narrower generality) is found along with *gotva* (a wider generality) in a black cow, so in śabda properties like *actva* and *haltva* are found along with *śabdatva* on the basis of the popular experiences—'*gakāraḥ śabdaḥ'*, etc. Nor can this experience be explained without the generality—*śabdatva.* [See the Tattvabindu (below) pp. 40 and 41.]
41. See the Tattvabindu (below) p. 41,
42. *Ibid.*, p. 44.
43. See the Tattvabindu and the *Tattvavibhāvanā*, (below) p. 45.
44. *Ibid.*, p. 46.
45. *Ibid.*, p. 47.

46. See the Tattvabindu (below) pp. 47 and 48.
47. See the Tattvabindu (below) p. 48.
48. *Ibid.*, p. 49.
49. *Ibid.*, p. 50.
50 *Ibid.*, p. 51.
51. *Ibid.*,
52. *Vide* the Tattvabindu (below) p. 51.
53. *Ibid.*, p. 51.
54. *Ibid.*, pp. 52 and 53.
55. *Vide* the Tattvabindu (below) p. 54.
56. *Ibid.*, p. 56.
57. *Ibid.*, pp. 56 and 57.
58. *Ibid.*, p. 58.
59. *Vide* the Tattvabindu (below) p. 59.
60. *Ibid.*, p. 60.
61. *Vide* the Tattvabindu, pp. 61-64.
62. *Ibid.*, p. 64.
63. *Ibid.*, pp. 65 and 66.
64. *Ibid.*, pp. 67 and 68.
65. *Vide* the Tattvabindu, pp. 72 and 73.
66. *Ibid.*, pp. 74 and 76.
67. *Ibid.*, p. 77.
68. *Vide* the Tattvabindu, p. 78.
69. *Ibid.*, p. 79.
70. *Ibid.*, p. 80.
71. *Vide* the Tattvabindu, p. 82.
72. *Ibid.*, pp. 83 and 84.
73. *Vide* the Tattvabindu, pp. 84 and 85.
74. *Ibid.*, pp. 86-88.
75. *Ibid.*, pp. 89 and 90.
76. *Ibid.*, p. 90.
77. *Vide* the Tattvabindu (below) p. 91.
78. *Ibid.*, p. 92.
79. *Ibid.*, p. 93.
80. *Vide* the Tattvabindu (below) p. 94.
81. *Ibid.*, p. 95.

82. *Vide* the Tattvabindu (below) p. 96.
83. *Ibid.*, p. 97.
84. *Ibid.*, p. 98.
85. *Vide* the Tattvabindu (below) p. 99.
86. *Ibid.*, p. 100.
87. *Vide* the Tattvabindu (below) p. 101.
88. *Ibid.*, p. 102.
89. *Ibid.*, p. 104.
90. *Ibid.*, p. 105.
91. *Vide* the Tattvabindu (below) p. 106.
92. *Ibid.*, p. 107.
93. *Ibid.*, p. 108.
94. *Ibid.*, p. 110.
95. *Vide* the Tattvabindu (below) p. 111.
96. *Vide* the Tattvabindu (below) p. 112.
97. *Ibid.*, p. 113.
98. *Vide* the Tattvabindu, p. 114.
99. *Ibid.*, p. 115.
100. *Ibid.*, p. 116.
101. *Vide* the Tattvabindu (below) p. 117.
102. *Ibid.*, p. 118.
103. *Ibid.*, p. 119.
104. *Ibid.*, p. 120.
105. *Ibid.*, p. 121.
106. *Vide* the Tattvabindu (below) p. 122.
107. *Ibid.*, p. 123.
108. Words possess a *śakti* called *abhidhāna* to convey their meanings; the meanings possess a *śakti* to convey their mutual relations and words have another *śakti* to give power to the *padārthas* (to convey their relation).
109. The *padārthas* have one *śakti* to convey the *vākyārtha,* while words possess a *śakti,* which enables the *padārthas* to generate the *vākyārthajñāna*. *Vide* the Tattvabindu, p. 123.
110. *Vide* the Tattvabindu (below) p. 124.
111. *Vide* the Tattvabindu (below) p. 129.

112. *Ibid.*, p. 130.
113. *Ibid.*, p. 131.
114. See the Tattvabindu (below) p. 132.
115. *Vide* the Tattvabindu (below) p. 132.
116. *Ibid.*, p. 133.
117. *Ibid.*, p. 135.
118. *Vide* the Tattvabindu (below) p. 136.
119. *Vide* the Tattvabindu (below) p. 137.
120. *Ibid.*, p. 149.
121. *Ibid.*, p. 150.
122. *Ibid.*, p. 151.
123. *Vide* the Tattvabindu (below) p. 152.
124. *Vide* the Tattvabindu (below) p. 153.
125. *Ibid.*, p. 154.
126. *Ibid.*, p. 155.
127. *Ibid.*, p. 156.
128. *Ibid.*, p. 157.
129. *Ibid.*, p. 158.
130. *Ibid.*, p. 159.
131. *Ibid.*, p. 160.
132. *Vide* the Tattvabindu (below) p. 161.

तत्त्वबिन्दुः

'तत्त्वविभावना' टीकासहिता

TATTVABINDU

WITH TATTVAVIBHĀVANĀ COMMENTARY

ॐ

॥ तत्त्वबिन्दुः ॥

[१]अहये बुध्न्याय नमो ब्रध्नाय नमो नमोऽस्तु गणपतये।
आर्यायै भारत्यै नमो नमो[२] विष्टरश्रवसे॥

॥ तत्त्वविभावना ॥

अभिवन्द्य हरं. . . . . .।
हरिं गुहं गुरुञ्चैव कायेन मनसा गिरा॥
(वाचस्प)तिकृतौ तत्त्वबिन्दौ व्याख्यानमञ्जसा।
करिष्ये विदुषामाज्ञां पुरस्कृत्य यथामति॥

ग्रन्थारम्भेऽभिमता देवताः. . . . . (काय)वाङ्मनः प्रह्वतालक्षणया प्रणत्या पूजयति–

अहये बुध्न्याय नमो ब्रध्नाय नमो नमोऽस्तु गणपतये।
आर्यायै भारत्यै नमो नमो विष्टरश्रवसे॥

अत्र च प्रमाणं प्रयोजनं न 'विशुद्धज्ञानदेहाय' इत्यत्र वार्तिककारीयैरुक्त-मनुसन्धेयम्। यथोक्तं–'अस्य च कर्तव्यतायां शिष्टाचारः प्रमाणं; प्रयोजनं च विघ्नोपशम' इति। एवञ्च व्याचक्षते–**'ज्ञानं महेश्वरादिच्छेत्'** इति

---

१. 'अहये बुध्न्याय=शिवाय। 'अष्टमूर्तिरहिर्बुध्न्य' इति कोशः। नामान्तराण्यनु-पादायैतस्यैवोपादानं तु "अहे बुध्निय मन्त्रं मे गोपाय। यमृषयस्त्रयी (स्त्रयि) विदा विदुः। ऋचस्सामानि यजूंषि। सा हि श्रीरमृता सताम्" (तैत्तिरीयब्राह्मणे अ० १. प्र० २०, खं० २६, मन्त्रः २) इति मन्त्रानुसन्धापनेन शिवस्य वेदत्रयेगोप्तृत्वद्योतनायास्य मन्त्रस्य शाबरभाष्ये (अ० २. पा० १. सू० ३५) उदाहृतत्वेन।

२. 'नमश्चास्तु विष्टरश्रवसे' इति मुद्रिततत्वबिन्दौ पाठः।

स्मृतिमनुविदधानो ज्ञानपुरस्सरत्वाद्ग्रन्थनिर्माणस्य ज्ञान (काम)स्तावन्महेश्वरं नमस्यति–'**अहये बुध्न्याय नमः**' **इति**।। विश्वे देवा इतिवदहिर्बुध्न्य इति पदद्वयं संहत्य भगवतो वाचकमिति द्रष्टव्यम्। न केवलं ज्ञानोत्पत्तिरेवाभ्यर्थनीया किन्तु ज्ञातस्याविस्मरणमप्यर्थनीयमेवेति मन्यमानो विद्यापरिपालनस्वभावतया प्रसिद्धस्य रुद्रविशेषस्य नमस्कारं कृतवानित्यवसेयम्। तथा च श्रूयते–'अहे बुध्निय मन्त्रं मे गोपाय, यमृषयस्त्रै(स्त्रयि)विदा विदुः' इत्यादिमन्त्रे अस्या देवतायाः मन्त्ररक्षणप्रार्थनेति। रुद्रविशेषता च वैष्णवे पुराणे–

"अजैकपादहिर्बुध्न्यस्त्वष्टा वीर्यश्च बुद्धिमान्।
हरश्च बहुरूपश्च त्र्यम्बकश्चापराजितः।।
वृषाकपिश्च शङ्कुश्च कपर्दी रैवतस्तथा।
एकादशैते कथिता रुद्रास्त्रिभुवनेश्वराः।।"

इति वर्ण्यते। महेश्वरव्यष्ट्यात्मकत्वाच्च रुद्राणां रुद्रविशेषनमस्कारेणैव तत्समष्टिभूतमहेश्वरनमस्कारफलमपि सेत्स्यतीति भावः। केचित्तु समष्टिरूपस्यैव महेश्वरस्याभ्यां पदाभ्यां उपादानमित्याहुः। तद्वाचकता चास्य पदद्वयस्य लोके प्रसिद्धा। उक्तं च लोकविद्भिः–

अहिर्बुध्न्यो विरूपाक्षश्शिपिविष्टो गणाधिपः।
गङ्गाधरो महादेवः' इति।

फलद्वयपि पूर्ववत्तत एव सेत्स्यति, समष्टिव्यष्ट्यात्मनोरेकत्वात्। केचित्तु मन्त्रेऽपि समष्ट्यात्मैवोच्यत इत्याहुः। तद्यथा तथा नामस्तु।।

अथ 'आरोग्यं भास्करादिच्छेत्' इति स्मृत्यनुसारेण नीरोगत्वाय सूर्यं

ऋक्त्वादिज्ञानोपयुक्तेक वाक्यत्वलक्षणे (सू० ४६) बहुत्वात्पदार्थानामिति शाबरभाष्योक्तेरन्विते पदानां न शक्तिरिति व्यवस्थापयिष्यमाणसिद्धान्तस्य भाष्यकाराभिमतत्वस्फोरणाय चेति बोध्यम्। तथैवोसंहरिष्यति। ब्रध्नः=सूर्यः। 'भस्कराहस्करब्रध्न' इति कोशः। आर्यायैः भारत्यै= सरस्वत्यभिन्नायै गौर्यै। ग्रन्थारम्भे सरस्वतीमनमस्यौचित्यात्पञ्चायतने गौर्या एव शास्त्रेषूपदेशात्तथोक्तिः। सरस्वतीगौर्योरभेदश्च देवीमाहात्म्योत्तमचरिते स्पष्टः। 'आर्या दाक्षायणी चैव' इति कोशः। विष्टरश्रवसे=विष्णवे। 'वैकुण्ठो विष्टरश्रवा' इति कोशः। अनेन 'आदित्यमम्बिकां विष्णुं गणनाथं महेश्वरम्' इति स्मार्तैरवश्योपस्यते- वतापञ्चकनमस्काररूपं मङ्गलमनुष्ठितं भवति।' इति टिप्पणी।

नमस्यति–**ब्रध्नाय इम इति।।** 'ब्रध्नो हंसः खगो मित्रश्चित्रभानुरहर्पतिः' इत्येकार्थाः। आधिव्याधिरहितेनैव हि ग्रन्थः सम्यक्कर्तुं शक्यत इति भावः।।

अथ प्रत्यूहनिवृत्तये विघ्नेश्वरं नमस्यति–**नमोऽस्तु गणपतये इति।।** यथाहुः–'सिद्धिकामो विनायकम्' इति सम्प्रति वाग्वश्यतायै वागीश्वरीं नमस्यति–**आर्यायै भारत्यै नम इति।।** 'ऋ गतौ' इत्यस्येदं रूपं आर्येति। अधिगन्तव्याया इत्यर्थः। समुदायप्रसिद्धिमाश्रित्योत्कृष्टाया इति वार्थो द्रष्टव्यः। शब्दरचना हि अस्माभिरेवमुपक्रान्ता अतस्तधिदेवतैवात्रोत्कृष्टतमा, सम्प्रति विशेषत उपासनीया वा इति।। यथोक्तं–

'ये त्वामम्ब!' न शीलयन्ति मनसा तेषां कवित्वं कुतः' इति। 'मेधाकामः सरस्वतीं' इति च। मेधेति कवित्वबीजभूता प्रतिभा विवक्षिता। अथवा–परिपन्थिनरासाय दुर्गां नमस्यति–**आर्याया इति।।** नमसस्त्वाकर्षोऽनुषङ्गो वा द्रष्टव्यः। यथोक्तं–

'ये त्वामार्येति दुर्गेति वेदगर्भाम्बिकेति च।
भद्रेति भद्रकालीति क्षेम्या क्षेमंकरीति च।।
प्रातश्चैवापराह्णे च स्तोष्यन्त्यानम्रमूर्तयः।
तेषां हि प्रार्थितं सर्वं त्वत्प्रसादाद्भविष्यति।।' इति।।

अन्यत्राप्युक्तम्–

'तस्याहं सकलां बाधां नाशयिष्याम्यसंशयम्' इति।

अथवा–

भवान्या नमस्कारमनेन करोति–भवान्या अपि आर्येति संज्ञा। यथोक्तं–

'आर्याम्बिका मृडानी हैमवती पार्वती गौरी'। इति।।

यथोक्तं वायुसंहितायां ब्रह्मणा स्वयमेव देवीं प्रति–

'त्वामृते परमां शक्तिं संसिद्धिः कस्य कर्मणः' इत्यारभ्य,

'त्वामनाराध्य देवेशे पुरुषार्थचतुष्टयम्।
लब्धुं न शक्यमस्माभिरपि सर्वसुरोत्तमैः।।
व्यत्यासोऽपि भवेत्सद्यो ब्रह्मत्वस्थावरत्वयोः।
सुकृतं दुष्कृतं चापि त्वय्यवस्थापितं यतः।।

इह खलु [१]पदकदम्बकश्रवणसमनन्तरमिविवादं विदि[२]त-

त्वं हि सर्वजगद्भर्तुः शिवस्य परमात्मनः।
अनादिमध्यनिधना शक्तिराद्या सनातनी।।
समस्तलोकयात्रार्थं मूर्तिमाविश्य कामपि।
क्रीडसे विविधैर्भावैः कस्त्वां जानाति तत्वतः।।' इति।।

अतस्त्वदधीना सर्वलोकयात्रेति तत्प्रसादायावश्यकर्तव्यस्तन्नमस्कार इति। सम्प्रति कृतस्य ग्रन्थस्य प्रचयगमनादिपरिपालनसिद्धये स्थित्यधिकृतां देवतां नमस्यति–**नमो विष्टरश्रवस इति।।** यथोक्तं–

'न हि पालनसामर्थ्यमृते सर्वेश्वरं हरिम्।' इति।।

'अथ यदसन्दिग्धप्रयोजनं च न तत्प्रेक्षावत्प्रतिपित्सागोचरः, यथा समनस्केन्द्रियसन्निकृष्टस्स्फीतालोकमध्यवर्ती घटः करटदन्ता वा' इति मन्यमानः प्रकरणस्य सन्दिग्धं प्रयोजनवन्तं च विषयं दर्शयति–**इह खल्विति।।** लोक इत्यर्थः। लौकिकेष्वेव वाक्येष्वत्र तथा वर्तिष्यते, लोकोपायत्वाच्च वैदिकेषु निर्णयस्य, लौकिकेषु कृतो निर्णयो वैदिकेषु भविष्यतीति भावः।।

'. . . .अतोऽस्ति वाक्यधीमूलसम्भवः।
ततश्चार्थाद्भवेल्लोके वेदार्थस्त्वप्रमाणकः।।' इति।।

तथा सिद्धान्तेऽपि–

'भावनावचनस्तावत्तां स्मारयति लोकवत्' इति लौकिकेषु वर्णितं वैदिकेष्वतिदिष्टम्। **पदकदम्बकश्रवणसमनन्तरमिति।।** प्रत्येकं पदानां वाक्यार्थबोधकत्वाभावात्कदम्बकग्रहणम्। न हि प्रत्येकं पदेभ्यो वाक्यार्थप्रतीतिर्दृश्यते। न च सम्बन्धग्रहणमन्तरेण पदानां प्रत्यायकत्वम्। न च सम्भवति। अनन्तत्वाद्वाक्यार्थानाम्। वेदार्थस्य च प्रमाणान्तरागोचरत्वात्तेन सम्बन्धग्रहणमत्यन्तासम्भाव्यम्। अनेकवाक्यार्थसाधारणत्वाच्च पदानां प्रत्येकं वाक्यार्थविशेषप्रतिपादनमनुपपन्नमित्येतदविवादसिद्धमेषां हि वादिनामिति भावः।

---

१. 'पदकदम्बश्रवण' इति मुद्रितपुस्तके पाठः।
२. 'विदितपदतदर्थसङ्गतीनां' इति मुद्रितपुस्तकपाठः।

सङ्गतीनां अनधिगतार्थविषयो[१] धीरुदयमासादयति पुंसाम्। [२]अस्या

शब्दविज्ञानादिति स्थितत्वात् **श्रवण**ग्रहणम्। अन्वयव्यतिरेकाभ्यां धियः शाब्दत्वबोधनाय **समनन्तर**ग्रहणम्। न च शाब्दत्वेऽपि तेषां कश्चिद्विवाद इति भावः। **अविवाद**मिति क्रियाविशेषणम्। यदि शब्दोऽर्थस्य प्रत्यायकः किमिति तर्हि प्रथमश्रवणे न प्रत्याययति इत्यत उक्तं–**विदितसङ्गतीनामिति।।** संज्ञात्वग्रहणमपि हि शब्दस्यार्थं प्रतिपादयतोऽङ्गं नेत्रस्येवालोकः, येन यः पुरुषान्तरेभ्योऽयं शब्दोऽस्य संज्ञेयत्वगतवान्, तस्यैव प्रत्याययति नान्यस्येति न दोषः। यथोक्तम्–

"वाच्यवाचकशक्त्योश्च नियमः सहजो यदि।
प्रथमश्रवणेऽप्यर्थः शब्दात्किं न प्रतीयते।।
उच्यते, यद्यथा दृष्टं तत्ताभ्युपगम्यते।
सम्बन्धज्ञानसापेक्षश्शब्दश्चार्थं ब्रवीति नः।।
न च सापेक्ष इत्येवं वाचकत्वास हीयते।
ज्योतिष्ठोमोऽङ्गसापेक्षो न स्वर्गादेर्न साधनम्।।
यथैव श्रवणपेक्षश्शब्दः स्वार्थं ब्रुवन्नपि।
नावाचकस्तथा शक्तिविज्ञानापेक्षयापि नः।।" इति।।

अनधिगतार्थविषया धीरुदयमासादयति पुंसामिति।। उदयमासादयतीत्यनेनानुत्पत्तिलक्षणमप्रामाण्यं निराकरोति। न चेयं निरालम्बना स्वांशावलम्बना वेति दर्शितम्–**अर्थविषयेति।।** न चास्या ज्ञातविषयत्वात्स्मृतित्वेनाप्रामाण्यमिति दर्शितम्–**अनधिगतेति।।** न चास्या देशान्तरे कालान्तरे पुरुषान्तरेऽवस्थान्तरे वा विपर्यय इति दर्शितं **पुंसा**मिति बहुवचनप्रयोगेण। **अनधिगतार्थविषये**त्यनेनैव संशयात्मकत्वमपि निरस्तं वेदितव्यम्। न चैवंविधा धीर्नियतनिमित्तमन्तरेणोत्पत्तुमर्हतीति भवितव्यमस्या नियतेन निमित्तेन। व्यभिचारार्थं ह्यनिश्चयात्मकमनैकान्तिकलिङ्गप्रसूतं संवेदनं प्रतिभेति प्रतिभाविदः। न चेयमेवंविधेत्यस्या नियतं निमित्तं कल्पनीयमित्यत्र न कश्चित्तेषां विवाद इति। निमित्तस्वरूपे तु बहुधा विवाद इत्याह–**अस्या निमित्तं प्रति विवदन्ते**

१. 'अनधिगतार्थगोचरा' इति मुद्रितपुस्तकपाठः।
२. 'तस्या' इति मुद्रितपुस्तकपाठः।

निमित्तं प्रति विवदन्ते वादिनः। [१]**अनवयमेव वाक्यमनाद्यविद्योपदर्शितालीकवर्णपदविभागमस्यानिमित्तमिति**[२] **केचित्।**

पारमार्थिकपूर्वपूर्वपदपदार्थानुभवजनितसंस्कारसहितमन्त्यवर्णविज्ञानमित्येके।[३]

वादिन इति।। विवादमेव दर्शयति–**अनवयवमेव वाक्यमनाद्यविद्योपदर्शितालीकवर्णपदविभागमस्यानिमित्तमिति केचित्।।** अत्र सर्वत्र वदन्तीत्यर्थसिद्धं द्रष्टव्यम्। विवदन्त इत्युक्तत्वात्। क्वचित्तु '**केचिदाहुः** अनवयवम्' इत्यादि दृश्यते। तत्रोत्तरेषु चतुर्ष्वपि आहुरित्यनुमन्त(षक्त)व्यम्। वैयाकरणमतमुपन्यस्तम्।।

मीमांसकेष्वेव केषाञ्चिन्मतमुपन्यस्यति–**पारमार्थिकपूर्वपूर्वपदपदार्थानुभवजनितसंस्कारसहितमन्त्यवर्णविज्ञानमित्येके।।** एतच्च 'पूर्वपूर्वर्णजनितसंस्कारसहितोऽन्त्यो वर्णो वाचक इत्यदोष' इति भाष्यमनुशीलयतां मतम्।।

तेष्वेवान्येषां मतमुपन्यस्यति–**प्रत्येकवर्णपदपदार्थानुभवभावितभावनानिचयलब्धजन्मस्मृतिदर्पणारूढा वर्णमालेत्यन्ये।।**

---

१. 'केचिदाहुरनवयवमेव......निमित्तम्' इति मुद्रितपुस्तकपाठः।

२. (केचित्)–'**वैयाकरणाः**। तथा च वाक्यपदीये काण्डे १. श्लोक ७३.

'पदे न वर्णा विद्यन्ते वर्णेष्ववयवा इव।
वाक्यात्पदानामत्यन्तं प्रविवेको न कश्चन।।' इति।

काण्डे २० श्लोक २३४

'शास्त्रेषु प्रक्रियाभेदैरविद्यैवोपवर्ण्यते।' इति।

उपपादयिष्यते चेदमग्रे। एवं मतान्तराण्यपि।' इति टिप्पणी।

३. (एके)–'**नैयायिकाः**। वात्स्यायनभाष्ये अ० ३. आ० २ सू० ६२ 'वाक्यस्थेषु खलु वर्णेषूच्चरत्सु प्रतिवर्णं तावच्छ्रवणं भवति श्रुतं वर्णमेकमनेकं वा पदभावेन न प्रतिसन्धत्ते प्रतिसन्धाय पदं व्यवस्यति पदव्यवसायेन स्मृत्या पदार्थं प्रतिपद्यते पदसमूहप्रतिसन्धानाच्च वाक्यं व्यवस्यति सम्बद्धांश्च पदार्थान्गृहीत्वा वाक्यार्थं प्रतिपद्यत' इति। सिद्धान्तमुक्तावल्यां शब्दखण्डे च 'प्रत्येकपदानुभवजन्यसंस्कारैश्चरमतावद्विषयकस्मरणस्याव्यवधानेनोत्पतेः तावत्पदसंस्कारसहितचरमवर्णज्ञानस्योद्बोधकत्वात्' इति। एवं पदवाक्यरत्नाकरादिष्वपि।' इति टिप्पणी।।

प्रत्येकवर्णपदपदार्थानुभवभावितभावनानिचय[१]लब्धजन्म-स्मृतिदर्पणारूढा वर्णमालेत्यन्ये।।[२]

पदान्येवाकाङ्क्षितयोग्यसन्निहितपदार्थान्तरान्वितस्वार्थाभिधा-यीनीत्यपरे।।[३]

एतच्च–

'यद्वा प्रत्यक्षतः पूर्वं क्रमज्ञातेषु यत्परम्।
समस्तरूपविज्ञानं तदर्थज्ञानकारमणम्।।

इति वार्तिकमनुशीलयतां मतम्। एतत्तु मतद्वयं सम्भावनामात्रेणोपन्यस्तमिति केचित्। प्राचां मीमांसकानामित्यन्ये। अन्येषां केषाञ्चित्तीर्थिकानामित्येके। तद्यथा तथा नामास्तु।।

टीकाकारीयं मतमुपन्यस्यति–**पदान्येवाकांक्षितयोग्यसन्निहितपदार्था-न्तरान्वितस्वार्थाभिधायीनीत्यपरे।।**

सिद्धान्तमुपन्यस्यति–**पदैरेव समभिव्याहारवद्भिरभिहिताः स्वार्था आकाङ्क्षायोग्यतासत्तिसध्रीचीना वाक्यार्थधीहेतव इत्याचार्याः।।** एते च पक्षा यथास्वमवसरे विवरिष्यन्त इति नेह प्रपञ्च्यन्ते।।

अत्र चेदमाकूतम्–'तथा भू (द्भू)तानां क्रियार्थेन समाम्नायोऽर्थस्य तन्निमित्तत्वात्' इति वाक्यार्थधियः समूलत्वं प्रतिपादितम्। तच्च वादिविप्रतिपत्तेः संदेहमापातिदं सत्प्रतिपित्सितं शङ्कितसमारोपितव्यवच्छेदेन प्रकरणेन प्रतिपाद्यते। प्रकरणस्य च यत्प्रकरणिनः प्रयोजनं तेनैव फलवत्तेति न पृथक् प्रयोजनापेक्षेति

---

१. 'निचयजन्मलब्धजन्म' इति मुद्रितपुस्तकपाठः। 'जन्मेति पदमधिकमपि पुस्तकक्रये सत्वात्स्थापितम्'। इति टिप्पणी।।

२. (अन्ये)–'उपवर्षप्रभृतयो मीमांसकाः। ब्रह्मसूत्रशाङ्करभाष्ये अ० १ पा० ३. सू० २८, 'वर्णा एव तु शब्दा इति भगवानुपवर्ष' इति। शाबरभाष्येऽपि अ० १. पा० १. सू० ५. 'अथ गौरित्यत्र कः शब्दः? गकारौकारविसर्जनीया इति भगवानुपवर्षः' इति। योगभाष्ये व्यासदेवोऽपि पा० ३. सू० १७. 'गकारौकारविसर्जनीयाः सास्नादिमन्तमर्थं द्योतयन्ति'। इति।' इति टिप्पणी।

३. (अपरे)–'अन्विताभिधानवादिनः प्राभाकराः।' इति टिप्पणी।

पदैरेव समभिव्याहारवद्भिरभिहिताः स्वार्था आकाङ्क्षा-योग्यताऽऽसत्तिसध्रीचीना वाक्यार्थधीहेतव इत्याचार्याः[१]।। तत्र

मीयमानपरित्यागो बाधके नासति स्फुटे।
दृष्टात्कार्योपपत्तौ च नादृष्टपरिकल्पना।।

स खल्वयमेको वाक्यात्मा वाक्यार्थधीहेतुरनुभवाद्वा

सन्दिग्धत्वं प्रयोजनवत्त्वं च प्रकरणविषयस्य सिद्धमिति। वाक्यार्थधियः समूलत्वप्रतिपादनं च तद्भूताधिकरणप्रयोजनम्। यथोक्तमारम्भे–

'पदार्थपदसम्बन्धनित्यत्वे साधितेऽपि वा (वः)।
नैव वेदप्रमाणत्वं वाक्यार्थं प्रति सिद्ध्यति।।' इति।।

तथा सिद्धान्तेऽपि–

'शब्दप्रामाणण्यनिर्णीत्यै पदार्थेभ्यो यथेष्यते।
अत्यन्तादृष्टवाक्यार्थप्रतिपत्तिस्तथोच्यते।।' इति।।

परेषां तु चतुर्णामपि प्रतिपक्षत्वेन प्रथमोपन्यस्तं स्फोटपक्षं तावन्निराकरोति–

'मीयमानपरित्यागो बाधके नासति स्फुटे।
दृष्टाकार्योपपत्तौ च नादृष्टपरिकल्पना।।'

कारिकां व्याचष्टे; तत्र पूर्वार्धोत्तरार्धयोः विषयभेदप्रदर्शनाय विकल्पयति– **स खल्वयमेको.......अन्यथाऽनुपपद्यमानात्।। अर्थधीभेदादिति।।** पदार्थधीभ्यो भिन्नाया वाक्यार्थधिय इत्यर्थः। अन्यथानुपपत्तिश्च **'यस्तु स्वतन्त्रसिद्धान्ताभ्यासाहितव्यामोहापस्मारः'** इत्यत्र स्पष्टीभविष्यतीति। पूर्वार्धव्यावर्त्यमपि पक्षमर्थतः शब्दतश्च निराकरणं दर्शयितुं विकल्पयति–**अनुभवोऽपि च .. ..विभागं वा।** अङ्गानि करचरणादीनि, प्रत्यङ्गानि कूर्परादीनि, **वर्णपदव्या-**

---

१. (आचार्याः)–''भाट्टाः शबरस्वामिप्रभृतयश्च। तन्त्रवार्तिके अ० २. पा० १. सू० ४६. 'पदार्थैः पदविज्ञातैः वाक्यार्थः प्रतिपाद्यते इति। शाबरभाष्ये अ० १. पा० १. सू० २५ 'पदार्था अवगताः सन्तो वाक्यार्थं गमयन्ति' इति।' इति टिप्पणी।

व्यवस्थाप्यते, अर्थधीभेदाद्वा अन्यथाऽनुपपद्यमानात्। अनुभवोऽपि च वाक्यात्मानमेकमवयविनमनेकव[1]र्णपदव्यासङ्गिनमङ्गप्रत्यङ्ग-वर्तिनमिव देवदत्तमनुभवेत्यप्रत्यस्तमितवर्णपदविभागं वा।।

वर्णाः पदानि चास्यावयवाः सत्तामात्रेण अनुभूयमानतया वा भवेयुः। न तावत्पूर्वः कल्पः। अवयविन्यूनपरिमाणत्वा-दवयवानाम्। परममहताञ्च वर्णानां तदनुपपत्तेः। गगनगुणत्वे चाऽद्रव्यतया समवायिकारणत्वाभावेनावयवभावा[2]भावात्।।

सङ्गिनमित्यङ्गप्रत्यङ्गवर्तिनमिवेत्यनयोः प्रत्यङ्गोपमेयता वर्णानां, अङ्गोपमेयता पदानामिति द्रष्टव्यम्।।

अर्थतोऽपि निराकार्यमपि पक्षं विकल्पयति—**वर्णाः पदानि चास्या-वयवाः.....भवेयुः।।** तत्र 'वर्णाः पदानि च सत्ता मात्रेण वास्यावयवा भवेयुः' इत्यमुं पक्षं दूषयति—न **तावत्पूर्वः कल्पः।।** हेतुमाह—**अवयविन्यूनपरिमाणत्वादवयवानाम्।।** ततः किमित्यत आह—**परममहतां च वर्णानां तदनुपपत्तेः।।** अयमर्थः—सर्वत्र हि कारणपरिमाणाधिकं कार्यपरिमाणं तन्तुपटयोरिव। न च विभुभ्यो वर्णेभ्यः परिमाणाधिक्यं कस्यचित्सम्भवति। अतो नास्ति गोशब्दावयवी नाम कश्चिदिति। परममहत्वं च वर्णानां—

'वर्णात्मकाश्च ये शब्दा नित्यास्सर्वगतास्तथा।
पृथग्द्रव्यतया ते तु न गुणाः कस्यचिन्मताः।।'

इति स्थितमेवेति। ननु गुणवादिनां दर्शने कथमवयवभावो वर्णानां, अत आह—**गगनगुणत्वे.....अवयवभावाभावात्।।** इदमाकूतम्—गुणवादिनोऽपि ये नित्यतया यावद्गगनवर्तिनं शब्दमाचक्षते, न तन्मते वर्णानां परममहत्व-परिहारः। ये पुनः "वीचीतरङ्गवृत्त्यैवमन्त्यः श्रोत्रेण गृह्यते" इति क्षणिकयाचक्षते, तन्मते वर्णानामाशुतरविनाशितेति वक्ष्यमाणमपि दूषणं यद्यपि सम्भवति, तथापि तन्नोच्यते, पर्यनुयोज्योपेक्षणप्रसङ्गात्। गुणस्य समवायिकारणत्वाङ्गीकरणशङ्का-

---

१. 'अनेकपदवर्णव्यासङ्गिनम्' इति मुद्रितपुस्तकपाठः।
२. 'अवयवभावानवकल्पनात्' इति मुदित्रपुस्तकपाठः।

[१]वाय[२]वीयावयवारब्धवर्णवादिनामपि वर्णानामाशुतरविनाशितया परस्परमसम्भवामवयव्यारम्भासम्भवात्। न खल्वेते क्रमभाविनोऽवयविनं वा तदसमवायिकारणं वा व्यतिषङ्गं[३] बिभ्रति। अबिभ्राणाश्च कथमवयवा व्यतिषक्ता वा।।

प्रसङ्गाच्च। किन्तूभयेषां साधारणं दूषणं ब्रूमः–'शब्दो गुणः बहिरिन्द्रियग्राह्यव्यवस्थाहेतुत्वात् (?) गन्धवत्' इत्यनुमानात्,

'पुराणमानवादेश्च, व्योम्नः शब्दं गुणं विदुः।' (इति)

न च गुणस्य सम्भवतः क्वचिदप्यवयवभावः सम्भवति, समवायिकारणत्वाभावात्। समवायिकारणं हि तन्त्वादि अवयव इत्युच्यते नार्थान्तरम्। समवायिकारणञ्च द्रव्यमेव न गुणादीत्यवस्थितमेव। यथोक्तं **कणादतन्त्रे**–'क्रियावदरगुणवत्समवायिकारणं द्रव्यमिति द्रव्यलक्षणम्' इति। अतो गुणत्वे सति प्रसज्यमानादद्रव्यत्वाद्द्रव्यत्वव्याप्यं समवायिकारणत्वं निवर्तमानं स्वाव्याप्यमवयवत्वमपि निवर्तयतीति।।

ननु वायवीयपरमाण्वारब्धा वर्णा इति केचिद्वदन्ति। अतो वर्णानां द्रव्यत्वात्परमहत्वाभावाच्च युक्तोऽवयवभाव इति चेदाह–**वायवीयावयवारब्धवर्णवादिनामपि....अवयव्यारम्भासंभवात्।। असम्भवतामिति।।** युगपदसतामित्यर्थः। असहभुवामिति क्वचित्पादः। ननु क्रमभाविनोऽप्याग्नेयादयः उत्पत्त्यपूर्वद्वार यथा परमापूर्वमारभन्ते एवमेतेऽपि व्यतिषङ्गद्वाराऽवयविनमारभन्तामित्याङ्क्योपपादयति–**न खल्वेते. . . .व्यतिषक्ता वा।।**

---

१. (वायवीयावयवारब्धवर्णवादिनां) वाक्यपदीये काण्डे १. श्लोक १०९–१०.
'लब्धक्रियः प्रयत्नेन वक्तुरिच्छानुवर्तिना।
स्थानेष्वभिहतो वायुः शब्दत्वं प्रतिपद्यते।।
तस्य कारणसामर्थ्याद्वेगप्रचयधर्मिणः।
सन्निपाताद्विभज्यन्ते सारवत्योऽपि मूर्तयः।।' इति टिप्पणी।

२. 'वायवीयावयवारब्धवर्णवादिनामप्याशुतरविनाशशीलतया वर्णानां परस्परमसहभुवां असम्बद्धानां अवयव्यारम्भासम्भवात्। नो खल्वेते' इति मुद्रितपुस्तकपाठः।

३. 'व्यतिषङ्गोऽसमवायिकारणीभूतः संयोगः।' इति टिप्पणी।।

[१]एकद्रव्यस्य च कार्यद्रव्यस्यानुपत्तेः। [२]कारणद्वयाभावे तदविश्लेषात्, द्रव्याविनाशे कृतकनित्यत्वप्रसङ्गात्।।

अयमर्थः—वायवीयारब्धवर्णवादिनोऽपि वर्णानां क्षणिकतामेवाभिमन्यन्ते। ततश्च वर्णानां क्रमेण सत्तावाभाजनत्वान्नैकावयविभरणक्षमत्वम्। एकदेशकालवर्तिनो हि तन्तवः पटं बिभ्रति। न चावयविनोऽसमवायिकारणं परस्परव्यतिषङ्गं बिभ्रति। अवयविव्यतिषङ्गावबिभ्राणाश्च वर्णा यथाक्रमं कथमवयवा व्यतिषक्ता वा भवेयुरिति।

इदञ्चाकूतम्—आग्नेयादयो हि क्रमभाविनोऽपि स्थिराण्युत्पत्त्यपूर्वाण्यात्मन्युत्पादयन्तः तद्द्वाराऽऽत्मनि परमापूर्वमेकमुत्पादयन्तीति युक्तम्। न हि तेऽवयवाः। न च परमापूर्वमवयवि। (अवयवी?) पुनर्नावयवेभ्योऽर्थान्तरं तेभ्यः पृथक्सिद्धम्। किन्तु तेषु समवेतं तदारब्धं द्रव्यान्तरम्। अवयव्यारम्भश्चावयवैरसमवेत(वायि)कारणं परस्परव्यतिषङ्गमन्तरेण न सम्भवतीति स्थितम्। न च व्यतिषङ्गस्तुल्यदेशकालानां सम्भवतीति कथमवयव्यारम्भाय व्यतिषङ्गं बिभ्रति आरब्धं वाऽवयविनं कथं बिभ्रति, अबिभ्राणाश्च कथं तादृशा इति। क्रियाफलस्य कर्त्रभिप्रायत्वद्योतनार्थमात्मनेपदप्रयोगः। न हि कारणाभावे कार्यं भवतीति भावः। भवति च प्रयोगः—वर्णा नावयविनमारभन्ते विभुत्वात् गगनवत्, गुणत्वाद्वा शौक्ल्यवत्, क्रमभावित्वाद्वा विनष्टवर्तमानाजातवस्त्वन्तरवत्।। न च वर्णा अवयविनं बिभ्रति क्रमभावित्वात् भूतभविष्यद्वर्तमानवत्; न वा वर्णास्तमारभन्ते, असमवायिकारणाभावात्, एकतन्तुवत्। न चैतेऽवयविनं बिभ्रति, क्रमभावित्वात् भूतभविष्यद्वर्तमानवस्त्वन्तरवत्। वर्णाश्चावयवा न भवन्ति अवयविसमवायाभावात् आकाशवत्। न च वर्णाः परस्परव्यतिषक्ताः व्यतिषङ्गाधारत्वाभावात् हिमवद्विन्ध्यवत् इति।।

---

१. (एकद्रव्यस्य च)—'अवयवद्वयानारब्धस्य परमाणुगगनादेर्द्रव्यस्य कार्यताया अनङ्गीकारात्। द्रव्यनाशस्यासमवायिकारणनाशजन्यत्वनियमात् द्रव्योत्पत्तौ असमवायिकारणसंयोगस्यापेक्षितत्वेन चाद्यहेतुनाऽलीकत्वरूपकृतकत्वस्य द्वितीयहेतुना नित्यत्वस्य चेति विरुद्धयोर्द्वयोरापत्तेरित्यर्थः।' इति टिप्पणी।।

२. 'अनुपपत्तेः, द्रव्यविनाशकारणद्वयाभावेन कृतकनित्यत्वप्रसङ्गात्'—इति मुद्रितपुस्तकपाठः।

असहभावित्वादेव चानुभूयमानतयाप्यवयवभावः परास्तो वेदितव्यः। [1]**आशुतरविनाशित्वेनानुभवानामेतत्कर्म**[2]**भूतानामपि तथात्वेन सहभावाभावात्।**

ननु मा भूवन्ननेकेऽवयवभूता वर्णा एकस्यावयविन आरम्भकाः, एक एव वर्णः एकं पदावयविनं वाक्यावयविनं वाऽरभतामित्यत आह—**एकद्रव्यस्य च कार्यद्रव्यस्यानुपपत्तेः॥** एकं द्रव्यं कारणं यस्येति बहुव्रीहिः। कार्यद्रव्यस्येति कर्मधारयः। 'न तावत्पूर्वः कल्प' इत्येतदेव साध्यम्। कथमनुपपत्तिरित्यपेक्षयामाह—**कारणद्वयाभावे तदश्लिेषात् द्रव्याविनाशे कृतकनित्यत्वप्रसङ्गात्॥** चतुर्णामपि पदानां यथाक्रमं हेतुहेतुमद्भावने सम्बन्धः। न कारणमात्रस्यैकत्वेऽनुपपत्तिरुच्यते। किन्तु समवायिकारणभूतद्रव्यस्यैकत्व इति दर्शितं—**एकद्रव्यस्येति द्रव्य**ग्रहणेन। न च कार्यमात्रं प्रति, किन्त्वयविद्रिव्यं प्रत्येवेति दर्शितं—**कार्यद्रव्यस्येति च द्रव्य**ग्रहणेन। भवति। चात्र—नैको वर्णोऽवयविनमारभते एकद्रव्यत्वात् आकाशवत्; यत्कार्यद्रव्यं तदवयवविश्लेषादेव विनश्यति कार्यद्रव्यत्वात् अवयवित्वाद्वा पटवत्। यच्चैकद्रव्यं न तस्य कारणविश्लेषः कारणद्वयाभावादाकाशवत्। तथा यस्य न विनाशः तन्नित्यं यथाऽऽकाशः इति। एष एव न्यायः पदेष्वप्यारम्भकेषु दर्शनीयः वर्णव्यतिरिक्तपदाभावात्। वायवीयावयवारब्धवर्णैश्च वाक्य- वत्पदस्याप्यनारम्भात् अनारब्धैश्च पदैर्वाक्यारम्भस्य बन्ध्यासुतोत्पत्तितुल्यत्वादिति। **एवं प्रथमः कल्पो निरस्तः॥**

'वर्णाः पदानि वास्यावयवा अनुभूयमाना भवेयुः' इति **द्वितीयं कल्पमपि** निराकरोति—**असहभावित्वादेव चानुभूयमानतयाप्यवयवभावः परास्तो वेदितव्यः। . . . . .सहभावाभावात्॥** इदमाकूतम्। पूर्वपूर्वोक्तदोषपरिहारेण प्रत्यवस्थीयते—न वयं सत्तयावयवभावं वर्णानां सङ्गिरामहे, येन पूर्वोक्तदोषाः प्रसज्ये(जे)युः; किन्त्वनुभूयमानतया, परममहत्त्वं वा वर्णानामस्तु क्षणिकत्वं वा, उभयथापि पदं वाक्यं वाऽनुभूयमानावस्था आरभन्त इति न कश्चिद्दोष

---

१. (आशुतरविनाशित्वेन)—'अनुभवकर्मत्वेऽप्याशुतरविनाशित्वेनैककालिकत्वाभावादसमवायिकरणसंयोगाश्रयत्वानुपपत्तेः।' इति टिप्पणी॥

२. 'अनुभवानां तत्कर्मतयापि तथात्वेन—' इति मुद्रितपुस्तकपाठः।

स्यादेतत्; अनवयवमेव वाक्यं [१]वाक्यार्थस्य वाचकम्। न

इति।। अत्रोच्यते—यत्तावदुक्तं क्षणिकत्वपक्षेऽनुभूयमानतयाऽवयवभाव इति तदयुक्तम्। वर्णानामाशुतरविनाशितया यदसहभावित्वं तस्मादेव कारणादनुभूमान-तयापि योऽप्यवयवभावः सोऽपि परास्तो वेदितव्यः। कथं वर्णानामसह-भावित्वादनुभूयमानतयाऽवयवभावस्य परासः? अनुभवानां क्रमोत्पत्तिद्वारेणेति ब्रूमः। न च क्रमोत्पत्तित्वेऽप्यनुभवा-नामनुभूयमानतया अवयव्यारम्भसम्भव इति वाच्यम्। यतः क्रमोत्पत्तयोऽनुभवा आशुतरविनाशिनः। 'न हि तत्क्षण-मप्यास्त' इति न्यायात्। एतेषामनुभवानाञ्च ये कर्मभूता वर्णाः तेऽपि पूर्वोक्तक्रमेणाशुतरविनाशिन इति कथमुभयेषामपि सहभावसम्भवः। अनुभवानां तत्कर्मणाञ्चासहभावित्वे कथमुभयसम्बन्धरूपानुभूयमानतापि प्रत्येकवर्णवृत्ति-कार्यारम्भायावतिष्ठेतेति भावः। अथवा—यद्वत्सत्तयावयव्या रम्भाभावे वर्णानां कारणमसहभावित्वं सत्तायाः, तद्वदनुभूयमानतया तदारम्भाभावेऽपि कारणमनु-भूयमानताया असहभावित्वमित्युचितं (क्तं)—**असहभावित्वादेवेति।** अनुभूयमानताया एवासहभावित्वं दर्शयति— **आशुतरेति।।** 'न हि तत्क्षणमप्यास्त' इत्याशुतरविनाशित्वेनानुभवानां कारणेन, यत्खल्वेतत्कर्मभूतानां वर्णानां तथात्वमाशुतरविनाशित्वं तेन कारणेनानुभवकर्मभूतानां सहभावाभावः, तस्मादिति। कर्मभूतानामिति विशेषणप्रधानो निर्देशः। अनुभवकर्मभूतया (?) (कर्मतया) इति यावत्। अनुभूयमानता च क्षणिकैव। यथाहुः—[२]. . . . . .का पुनरियं प्राप्तिः प्रतीतिरर्थधर्मः कञ्चिदेव प्रमातारं प्रति द्वित्वादिसङ्ख्येवापेक्षाबुद्धिमन्तं प्रति बुद्धिध्वंसाच्च ध्वंसते द्वित्वादिक-मिवापेक्षाबुद्धिविनाशादिति। ज्ञातुरात्मनो ज्ञेयसम्बन्ध एव ज्ञाततेत्यत्रापि पक्षे तस्याः क्षणिकत्वमस्त्येव। यथोक्तं—'कुतः पुनरनुभवावगतिः। अस्मादेव तु सम्बन्धलक्षणात्फलात्कादाचित्कात्' इति। विभुत्वेऽपि वर्णानामेषैव व्याख्येति।।

एवं पूर्वस्य विकल्पशिरसः श्लोकाभिप्रेतो निराकरणमार्गो दर्शितः। सम्प्रति पूर्वार्धव्यावर्त्यं प्रत्यस्तमितवर्णपदविभागं वेति द्वितीयं पक्षमुपक्षिपति—**स्यादेतत्; अनवयवमेव वाक्यं वाक्यार्थस्य वाचकम्।।** एवकारेण सावयववाक्यपक्षो न **शब्दतत्त्वविदां** सम्मत इति दर्शयति। यथोक्तं—

१. 'वाक्यार्थस्य च वाचकम्।' इति मु० पु० पाठः।

२. अत्र व्याख्याने ग्रन्थपातः।

च वर्णा एवानुभूयन्ते न तु तदतिरिच्यमानशरीरमपि[१] वस्त्वति साम्प्रतम्। पदमिति वाक्यमिति[२] वानुसंहारबुद्धावभिन्नस्य[३] वस्तुन उपारोहात्। न खल्वियं बुद्धिरभिन्नवस्तुनिर्भासा परस्पर[४]

'अनेकावयवात्मदोषाभिधानं तावन्नभोरोमन्थनप्रायम(न)भ्युपगमात्' इति। तथा–'नानेकावयवं वाक्यं पदं वा स्फोटवादिनाम्' इति। इमानि पदानि, एते पदार्थाः, एतद्वाक्यं, अयं वाक्यार्थ इत्यस्ति विभागेन बुद्धिः; अतो यथा पदं पदार्थस्य वाचकं एवं वाक्यं वाक्यार्थस्य वाचकमित्युचितं, न तु वर्णानां पदानां वा वाक्यार्थवाचकत्वमुचितम्। पदपदार्थाभ्यां वाक्यवाक्यार्थयोः भेदाभावप्रसङ्गात्। न च पदाभिहिता वा पदार्था वाक्यार्थधीहेतव इति साम्प्रतम्। अशाब्दत्वप्रसङ्गात्, इति वाचकत्वं वाक्यस्याङ्गीकर्तव्यमित्यर्थः। वाक्यमित्यनेनैव प्रत्यक्षानुभववेद्यता स्फोटात्मनो दर्शिता। वर्णविज्ञानविलक्षणस्य पदकदम्बकविज्ञानविलक्षणस्य वा पश्चाद्गौरिति विज्ञानस्य गामानयेत्येकं वाक्यमिति विज्ञानस्य निरालम्बनत्वायोगात्। न तावद्वर्णा (आ)लम्बनं, तद्बुद्धिविलक्षणत्वात्। तस्मादर्थान्तरमवलम्बितुमर्हतीति भावः।।

ननु अस्त्विदं पश्चादेकैकवर्णविज्ञानविलक्षणमेकैकपदविज्ञानविलक्षणं वा विज्ञानं, न तु तदर्थान्तरावलम्बनम्। वर्णरूपानुविद्धत्वात् रूपान्तरानवभासनाच्च। तदुक्तं भाष्ये–'न च प्रत्यक्षेभ्यो गकारादिभ्योऽन्यो गोशब्दः भेदर्शनाभावाद-भेददर्शनाच्च' इति।। वार्तिके च–

'वैलक्षण्यं च तस्येष्टं एकैकज्ञानतः स्फुटम्।
वर्णरूपानुविद्धाच्च न तदर्थान्तरं भवेत्।।
इति चार्थान्तरत्वं स्यादेकैकस्मात्त्रयस्य तु।
वर्णत्रयपरित्यागे बुद्धिर्नान्यत्र जायते।।' इति।।

अत आह–**न च वर्णा एव . . . . . .वस्तुन (उपारोहात्)।।** उपारोहमेव स्फोरयति–**न खल्वियं. . . . गोचरयितुमर्हति।।**

---

१. 'वस्त्विति वाच्यम्।' इति मु० पु० पाठः।

२. 'वाक्यमिति च' इति मु० पु० पाठः।

३. (अनुसंहारबुद्धौ)='साहित्यावगाहिज्ञाने'। इति टिप्पणी।

४. 'व्यतिरिच्यमान' इति मु० पु० पाठः।

व्यतिभिद्यमानात्मनो वर्णानेव गोचरयितुमर्हति। एकत्वनानात्वयोरेकत्रासमवायात्। न च वर्णात्मनस्तत्समवायिनी वाक्यस्य कुतस्तदुपरागवती प्रख्येति वाच्यम्। तदतिरिच्यमानमूर्तीनां

बुद्धिवर्णविशेषणाभ्यां सूचितमेव हेतुं दर्शयति–**एकत्वनानात्वयोरेकेत्रासमवायात्।।**

एवं तावत् 'अनवयवमेव वाक्यम्' इत्ययमंशो निरूपितः। 'अनाद्यविद्योपदर्शितालीकवर्णपदविभागम्' इत्यस्यापि व्याख्यानाय प्रस्तूयते। ननु यदनुसंहारबुद्धिबोध्यमभिन्नं वसतु तद्वर्णेभ्यो भिन्नं अभिन्नं वा, भिन्नत्वेऽपि वर्णेषु समवेतं असमवेतं वा। न तावदभिन्नं; एकत्वनानात्वयोरेकत्रासमवायात्। भिन्नं चेत्कथं तद्वर्णोपरागवती तस्मिन्प्रख्योपपद्यते। न हि भिन्नं वस्तु भिन्नरूपेणापरेणोपरज्यते घट इव पटेन। न च समवायादुपपद्यते। तदसम्भवात् समवायनिराकरणात्। अतः शब्दत्वमेव वर्णोपरागेण मीमांसकमते तादात्म्यात्, तार्किकमते समवायादवबोध्यत इति कल्पयितव्यं, न तु वैयाकरणसम्मतस्य शब्दतत्त्वस्य तादात्म्यसमवाययोरभावाद्वर्णोपरक्तप्रत्ययोपपत्तिरित्यत आह–**न च वर्णात्मनः तत्सम(वायिनो वाक्यस्य) कुतस्तदुपरागवती प्रख्येति वाच्यम्।** हेतुमाह–**तदतिरिच्यमानमूर्तीनां परमार्थसतां वर्णानामभावात्।।** तच्छब्देन वाक्यपरामर्शः। 'अलीकवर्णपदविभागम्' इत्ययमंशो व्याख्यातः। 'अनाद्यविद्योपदर्शिते'त्यस्य व्यख्यानायोपक्रमते। ननु विपरीतं कस्मान्न स्यादत आह–**तथाहि? (तदेव हि). . . . .प्रत्येकप्रव्यञ्ज्नीयं तत्त्वम्।।** सर्वजनीनैः मानसप्रत्यक्षैः प्रवेदनीया ये प्रत्यत्नभेदास्तैर्भिन्ना नाना च विलक्षणाश्च ये ध्वनयः तैः। प्रत्येकमेवोत्तरोत्तरप्रकर्षयोगितया व्यञ्जनीयम्। तदेकमपि भवच्छब्दतत्त्वमिति। सार्वजनीशब्देन प्रयत्नविशेषणं वा। 'नन्वर्थाभिव्यक्ताविव शब्दाभिव्यक्तावपि तुल्यः प्रसङ्ग।'

तदुक्तम्–

> 'यस्यानवयवस्स्फोटो व्यज्यते वर्णबुद्धिभिः।
> सोऽपि पर्यनुयोगेन नैवानेन विमुच्यते।।' इति।।

'अत्रोच्यते–

परमार्थसतां वर्णानामभावात्। [१]तदेव हि [२]सार्वजनीनमान-सप्रत्यक्षप्रवेदनीयप्रयत्नभेदभिन्ननानाध्वनिभिः प्रत्येकप्रव्यञ्जनीयं तत्त्वम्।

'प्रयत्नभेदतो भिन्ना ध्वनयोऽस्य प्रकाशकाः।
प्रत्येकमनुपाख्येयज्ञानतद्भावनाक्रमात्।।

अनुपाख्येयरूपविषयज्ञानानां तज्जन्यानां भावनानाञ्च क्रमादिति विग्रहः। 'न तावत्कैवल्ये यौगपद्येऽभिमतानुपूर्व्यभेदे वा विशेषादर्थाभिव्यक्ताविव शब्दाभिव्यक्तावपि तुल्यः प्रसङ्गः'। अस्माभिर्वर्णवादिनं प्रति–

'यद्वा प्रत्यक्षतः पूर्वं क्रमज्ञातेषु यत्परम्।
समस्तवर्णविज्ञानं तदर्थज्ञानकारणम्।।'

इत्यस्य पक्षस्य,

'पूर्वोपलब्धिभेदेऽपि भवेदर्थस्य दर्शनम्।
एकोपलब्धौ नैतेषां भेदः कश्चन दृश्यते।।'

'पूर्वोपलब्धयो हि क्रमविशेषवत्यः परिगृहीताभिमतविपरीतानुपूर्व्या अक्रमाश्चैकवक्तृप्रयुक्तवर्णविषया विपरीताश्च न पश्चाद्भाविन्यामुपलब्धावपि परिवर्तमानान्वर्णात्मनो भिन्दन्ति' इत्यादिना यः प्रसङ्ग उक्तः स न शब्दाभि-व्यक्तौ सम्भवतीति। कैवल्य इति। वक्तृभेदादेकैकस्य ग्रहणमित्यर्थः। यौगपद्य इति। अक्रम इत्यर्थः। अभिमतस्यानुपूर्व्यस्य भेद इति विग्रहः। 'तथा हि– सर्वत्र शब्दसमुत्थापकप्रयत्ननिरूपणचित्तवृत्त्याध्यक्षमुपगृह्यमाण-

१. (तदेव) 'वाक्यमेव'। (तत्त्वं) 'मानसज्ञानविषयप्रयत्नभेदेने जनितैर्भिन्नैर्नानाध्वनिभिः प्रत्येकमभिव्यङ्ग्य स्फोटरूपं परमार्थसदित्यर्थः। तथा च वाक्यपदीये काण्डे १. श्लोक ८८।

शब्दस्योर्ध्वमभिव्यक्तेर्व्यक्तिभेदे तु वैकृताः।
ध्वनयः समुपोहन्ते स्फोटात्मा तैर्न भिद्यते।।

श्लोक ८९

प्रत्येक व्यञ्जका भिन्ना वर्णा वाक्यपदेषु ये।
तेषामत्यन्तभदेऽपि सङ्कीर्णा इव शक्तयः।।' इति टिप्पणी।

२. 'सर्वजनीन. . . . नानाध्वनिप्रत्येक' इति मु० पु० पाठः।

ध्वनयस्तु तुल्यस्थानकरणलब्धजन्मतया परस्परविसदृशतत्तत्पदवाक्यव्यञ्जकानेकविधध्वनिसादृश्येनान्योन्यविसदृशतत्त्पदवाक्यसादृश्या[1]न्यापादयन्तः[2] [3]सादृश्योपधानभेदादेकमप्यवयमपि नानावर्णात्मेवावयवीव चावभासयन्ति, मुखमिव मणिकृपाणदर्पणादयो निय[4]तस्थानमनुपप्लवं एकमनेकमिवानेक-

---

रूपभेदाः प्रयत्ना आत्मन्यायतमानाः स्वभावभेदहेतुतया ध्वनीन्व्यावर्तयन्ति। ततो नियतनादनिबन्धनोपव्यञ्जना न सर्वत्र शब्दभेदाः प्रकाशन्ते' इति यन्**मण्डनमिश्रै**रुक्तं, तस्य सङ्ग्रहोऽयमिति द्रष्टव्यम्॥

एवमनादिपदव्याख्यानं कृतम्। अविद्यात्वं वर्णावग्रहस्य दर्शयितुमारभते–**प्रत्येकेति॥** अस्यापि व्याख्यानाय ग्रन्थो लिख्यते–'नापि प्रत्येकमवद्योतनादुत्तरवैयर्थ्यप्रसङ्गादवयवशो व्यक्त्यनुपपत्तेस्तदभावात् प्रत्येकमशक्तौ समुदायेऽप्यशक्तेः क्रमजन्मनामनवाप्तयौगपद्यानां समुदायाभावात्पदाभिव्यक्तिर्दुर्लभेति साम्प्रतम्। यतः प्रत्येकमपि तेऽविकलं स्फोटमभिव्यञ्जयन्ति' इति। अत्राविकलशब्दार्थकथनं **प्रव्यञ्जनीय**मिति प्रशब्देन। अस्तु प्रत्येकं शब्दात्मनोऽभिव्यक्तिः तथापि कथमविद्यात्वम्; किञ्च तन्निमित्तं? तद्दर्शयति–**ध्वनयस्तु. . . . .चावभासयन्ति॥** तुल्यस्थानकरणलब्धजन्मतया परस्परविसदृशानां तत्तत्पदवाक्यानां व्यञ्जका येऽनेकविधा ध्वनयः तैः। सादृश्ये हेतुः। **सादृश्यं** पुनः **आपादयन्त** इत्यत्र हेतुः। **इव**शब्देनापारमार्थिकत्वं

---

१. 'सादृश्यापादयन्त?' इति मु० पु० पाठः।

२. (आपादयन्तः)–'परस्परं विसदृशनामपि तेषां पदानां वाक्यानां वा व्यञ्जका येऽनेकविधा ध्वनयस्तेषां तुल्यस्थानकरणजत्वेन सादृश्यात्तदभिव्यञ्जनीयपदवाक्ययोरभेदेन भिन्नयोरपि सादृश्यप्रयोजका इत्यर्थः। अर्थभेदाच्छब्दभेदस्य नित्यस्फोटवादिनः शब्दार्थतादात्म्यवादिनश्चेष्टतया हर्यादिपदेषु 'श्वेतो धावती' इत्यादिकेषु च द्व्यर्थकेषु पदेषु वाक्येषु चाभिव्यञ्जकध्वनिसादृश्यमूल एव तथा व्यवहार इति भावः॥' इति टिप्पणी।

३. (सादृश्योपधानभेदात्)–'हकाराद्यभिव्यङ्ग्यत्वेनैव सादृश्यस्य निरूपणीयतया हकारादिवैशिष्ट्यज्ञाने नानाध्वनिविषयकतया तद्‌तनात्वस्यापि प्रतिभासात्स्फोटस्य नानात्वसावयवत्वयोः प्रतिभास इति भावः।' इति टिप्पणी।

४. 'नियतस्थानवर्णपरिमाणसंस्थानमनुपप्लवं' इति मु० पु० पाठः।

विधस्थान[१]मिव [२]वर्णपरिमाणसंस्थानभेदोपप्लवमिव दर्शयन्ति। न च प्रत्येकमभिव्यञ्जकत्वेऽपि[३] ध्वनीनां प्रथमादेव ध्वनेर्वाक्यस्य प्रतीतेरुप[४]पत्तेस्तन्मात्रनिबन्धनत्वाच्चार्थप्रत्ययोत्पादस्य द्वितीयादीनामानर्थक्यं ध्वनीनामिति युक्तम्। व्यञ्जयन्तोऽपि हि प्रत्येकमिमे ध्वनयो न द्रागित्येव स्फुटतरं स्फोटात्मानमवभासयितुमीशते, अपि [५]त्वारूपमव[६]भासयन्ति। पूर्वपूर्वाभिव्यक्तिजनितसंस्कारा-

---

दर्शितम्। यथोक्तं–'यद्यपि वर्णपदवाक्यविषया भिन्नात्मानः प्रयत्ना मरुतश्च तदुदीरिताः स्थानाभिघातिनः स्थानाभिघातलब्धात्मानश्च ध्वनयः शब्दाभिव्यक्तिहेतवः, तथापि स्थानकरणादिसाम्येन कथञ्चिल्लब्धसादृश्याः सङ्कीर्णा इव। तन्निबन्धनोऽयं शब्दान्तरेषु शब्दान्तरग्रहणाभिमानः' इति। **परस्परविसदृशे**ति ध्वनिविशेषणं वा। वैसादृश्यसम्भवाया**नेकविधे**त्युक्तम्। अनेकविधत्वस्य वैसादृश्यपर्यवसाने तत्तदितिवत्पदवाक्यविशेषणम्। न चैतच्छ्रोत्रप्रत्यक्ष एवास्माभिरारोप्यते चाक्षुषेऽपि दृष्टवादित्यभिप्रायेणाह–**मुखमिव. . . .दर्शयन्ति॥ अनेकमिवे**त्यादीनां त्रयाणां पूर्वै**र्नियतस्थान**मित्यादिभिर्योग्यतया सङ्गतिः। प्रत्येकं व्यञ्जकत्वे केनचिदेकेन तत्सिद्धेरितरानर्थक्यापत्तेर्वर्णा व्यङ्ग्या

---

१. 'अनेकस्थानवर्णपरिमाणसंस्थानेभेदोपप्लवमिव।' इति मु० पु० पाठः।

२. (अनेकस्थानवर्णपरिमाणसंस्थानेभेदोपप्लवमिव)–'अनेके स्थानं वर्णः परिमाण संस्थानभेदः उपप्लवश्च यस्य तम्। मुखस्यैकत्वेऽपि दर्पणाद्याधारभेदाद्यथा सामीप्यदूरस्थत्वादिस्थानस्य मालिन्यादेर्वर्णस्याल्पत्वमहत्वपरिमाणस्य वक्रत्ववर्तुलत्वादेः संस्थानभेदस्यावयवसन्निवेशविशेषरूपस्य दर्पणादिनाशेन नाशस्य चारोपः तथा स्फोटेऽपीति।' इति टिप्पणी।

३. 'अपि' मु० पुस्तके नास्ति।

४. 'उत्पत्तेः' इति मु० पु० पाठः।

५. (आरूपमाभासयन्ति) (अवभासयन्ति)–'ईषद्रूपमस्फुटम्' इति यावत्। तथा च शास्त्रदीपिकायां–'न कश्चिदपि नादोऽस्य स्फुटाभिव्यक्तिं करोति। किन्तु सर्वे ते प्रत्येकं व्यञ्जकाः। स तु न द्रागेव स्फुटमवभासते प्रथममस्फुटावभासितः सन् पुनःपुनः श्रूयमाणः स्फुटो भवतीति।' (अ० १. प० सू० १. सू० ५) इति टिप्पणी।

६. 'आरूपमाभासयन्ति' इति मु० पु० पाठः।

सचिवोत्तराभिव्यक्तिक्रमेण त्वन्त्यो ध्वनिः स्फुटतरं[१] विशिष्ट-स्फोटविज्ञानमाधत्ते इति न वैयर्थ्यं द्वितीयादिध्वनीनाम्। नापि पूर्वेषां; तदभावे तदभिव्यक्तिजनितसंस्काराभावेनान्त्यस्य ध्वनेरसहायतया व्यक्त्यवभासवाक्यधीहेतुभावाभावात्। तद्यथा रत्नपरीक्षिणः पुनः पुना[२] रत्नतत्वमीक्षमाणस्य रत्नदर्शनानि प्रत्येकं रत्नस्वरूपमवगाहमानान्यपि सहसैव न समानासमानजातीय-व्यावृत्तं रत्नतत्वमवभासयन्ति, किन्तु पञ्चषदर्शनजनितभावना-सचिवचेतोलब्धजन्मनि चरमे चेतसि चकास्ति रत्नतत्वम्। न[३] च वर्णावभासा मिथ्याप्रत्ययाः तत्संस्कारा वा कथं व्यक्तया

न तदतिरिक्तमेकमिति चेदत आह—**न च प्रत्येकमभिव्यञ्जकत्वेऽपि. . . . .व्यक्त्यवभासवाक्यधीहेतुभावाभावात्।।** एतदप्युक्तम्। 'न चेतर-नादवैयर्थ्यम्। अ(भि)व्यक्तिभेदात्। तथा हि—पूर्वे ध्वनयोऽनुपजातभावना-विशेषमनसः प्रतिपत्तुरव्यक्तरूपोपग्राहिणीरुत्तरव्यक्तिपरिच्छेदोत्पादानुगुण-भावनाबीज भाविनीः प्रख्याः प्रादुर्भावयन्ति, उत्तरस्तु पुरस्तनध्वनिनिबन्ध-नाव्यक्तपरिच्छेदप्रभाविसकलभावनाबीजसहकारी स्फुटतरविनिविष्टस्फोटबिम्ब (मिव)प्रत्ययमभिव्यक्ततरपरिच्छेदमुत्पादयति' इति। विनिविष्टशब्देन(स्व) रूपावस्थितत्वं दर्शयति। अत एव गकारादीनामविनिविष्टत्वेनागन्तुकत्वं दर्शितं भवति। अत एव वैयाकरणग्रन्थे 'विनिविष्टस्फोटबिम्बप्रतिबिम्बप्रत्ययं' इति बिम्बग्रहणं कृतम्। प्रतिबिम्बस्थानीया गकारादयः, बिम्बस्थानीयः स्फोटात्मेति भावः। द्वितीयादीनां पूर्वेषां वाऽऽनर्थक्याभावे दृष्टान्तमाह—**तद्यथा रत्नपरीक्षिणः. . . . .चकास्तिरत्नतत्त्वम्।।** पूर्वश्चेतश्शब्दो मनोविषयः उत्तरस्तु ज्ञानविषयः इति। एतदप्युक्तम्। 'यथा रत्नपरीक्षिणः परीक्षणमाणस्य प्रथमसमधिगमानुपाख्यातमनुपाख्येयरूपप्रत्ययोपजनितसंस्काररूपाहितविशेषायां

---

१. 'स्फुटतरविनिष्टस्फोटबिम्बज्ञानमाधत्ते' इति मु० पु० पाठः।

२. 'रत्नस्वरूपं वीक्षमाणस्य' इति मु० पु० पाठः।

३. 'न च वर्णावभासा' इत्यारभ्य 'अर्थधीभेदोपलम्भात्' इतिपर्यन्तं मुद्रितपुस्तकपाठ एव दीयते, व्याख्याने ग्रन्थपातात्।

परिच्छित्तिहेतव इति साम्प्रतम्। आराद्वनस्पतौ [1]हरितप्रवाहस्य व्यक्ततरं वनस्पतितत्त्वप्रतीतिहेतुत्वदर्शनात्। वर्णाच्च समारोपितदीर्घत्वादिधर्मभाजः पारमार्थिकार्थधीभेदोपलम्भात्। तथा हि—लौकिका नग इति गिरिमपदिशन्ति, नाग इति दन्तिनं; अजिनमिति चर्म, अजीनमिति ज्यानिहीनं[2]; शुन इति तु कर्मभूतान्सारमेयान्, शून इति तु वृद्धिमापन्नम्। न[3] च ते प्रत्यया भ्रान्तयः, व्यवहाराविसंवादात्।।

बुद्धौ क्रमेण चरमे चेतसि चकास्ति रत्नतत्त्वम्; न ह्य(न्यथा स्फुटप्रकाश उपपद्यते पुर इव पश्चादपि, विशेषाभावात्।)[4]. . . हेतुतया योजने सामानाधिकरण्यप्रतीतिभङ्गः। व्याख्यानञ्चास्य ग्रन्थस्य पूर्ववदेव कृतप्रायम्। उपलम्भादित्यपि पूर्ववत्। उभयसिद्धश्चैतत्। अस्माभिस्तावदुक्तं समारोपिततत्त्वं; भवद्भिरपि।।

> 'दीर्घादेर्नन्वनङ्गत्वंवाचकाः धर्मतो भवेत्।
> इत्थं प्रतीयमानाः स्युः वर्णा नः प्रतिपादकाः।।
>
> यादृशा पूर्वदृष्टोऽसावर्थो गम्येत तादृशा।
> भ्रान्त्या कथं प्रतीतिश्चेन्नासावर्थमितिं प्रति।।' इति।।

यतः। एतदुक्तं भवति। तवारोपितधर्मभाजो वर्णा वाचकाः, ममापि आरोपितदीर्घादिधर्मकवर्णरूपभाजः स्फोटा इत्येव विशेषः। समारोपितधर्मभाजः शब्दाः प्रतिपादका इत्युभयसिद्धमिति। उपलम्भमेव स्फोरयति—**तथा हि लौकिकाः. . . . .व्यवहाराविसंवादात्।। लौकिका इति।।** लोकप्रमाणको हि शब्दार्थनिर्णय इति भावः। यथोक्तं—'लोकतोऽप्रयुक्ते' इति। **गिरिमिति।।** 'हिमाचलो नाम नगाधिराजः' इत्यादौ। **अपदिशन्तीति।।** अपदेशतो

---

१. (हरितप्रवाहस्य)—'दूरस्थवृक्षे हरिततृणसमूहज्ञानधाराया इत्यर्थः।' इति टिप्पणी।।

२. 'ज्यानिविहीन' इति मु० पु० पाठः।

३. 'न चैते भ्रान्तयः' इति मु० पु० पाठः।

४. अत्र व्याख्यानमातृकायां ग्रन्थपातः

यस्तु स्वतन्त्रसिद्धान्ताभ्यासाहितव्यामोहापस्मारः सार्वजनीन-

ह्युपलम्भसिद्धिरिति भावः। **दन्तिनमिति।।** 'नागं नागोऽधावत्' इत्यादौ। एवमकारे दर्शितम्। इकारेप्याह–**अजिनमिति चर्म।।** ऐणेयेन वाजिनेन ब्राह्मणमिति। **अजीनमिति।** 'ज्या वयोहानौ' इति धातोर्निष्ठान्तं पदम्। जीनमिति 'रदाभ्यां निष्ठातो नः पूर्वस्य च दः' 'संयोगादेरातो धातो र्यण्वतः' इति निष्ठातो नत्वम्। नञ्समासः। जीनमिति भावे चेन्निष्ठा तदा बहुव्रीहौ नञ्। कर्तरि चेत्तत्पुरुष इति विवेकः। **ज्यानिहीनमिति।।** 'ग्लाज्याम्ला- हाभ्यो निः' इति क्तिन्प्रकरणे निः। ज्यनिर्हानिः तद्रहित इत्यर्थः। ज्यनिशब्दप्रयोगात्तु जीनमिति भावे निष्ठेति गम्यते। नञ्समासे बहुव्रीहेस्तत्पुरुषस्य भावनिष्ठायाश्च कर्तृनिष्ठायाः प्रथमप्रतीतत्वादङ्गीकरण इदं ज्यानिहीनमित्यर्थकथन- मात्रमिति द्रष्टव्यम्। ज्यानिशब्देन धात्वर्थकथनं हीनशब्देन ततोऽपगतं तस्या अकर्तारं निर्दिशतीति। **शुन** इति 'पूर्णक! लगुडेन शुनो वारय' इति कर्मभूतान्। शून् इत्यत्र प्रातिपदिकार्थमात्रविवक्षा। अत्र तु कर्मत्वमपीति सूच्यते। तथा तत्र तदेव कर्मत्वं (देवकत्वं), अत्र बहुत्वमिति च। **सारमेयानिति।।** तत्र गुणवत्वमात्रं (अत्र) जातिभेदोऽप्यस्तीति भावः। **शून इति।।** 'टुओश्वि गतिवृद्ध्योः' इति धातोर्निष्ठान्तं पदम्। 'ओदितश्च'। इति निष्ठातो नत्वम्। **वृद्धिमापन्नमिति।।** उपलक्षणमेतद्गतिमतोऽपि। अथ वा, विवक्षितत्वाद्वृद्धिमत्वस्य तथा निर्देशः। अथ वा, 'हन हिंसागत्योः' इतिवद्गतौ प्राचुर्याभावाद्वृद्धावेव प्राचुर्यादेवं निर्देशः। तुशब्दौ परस्परापेक्षयेति। पारमार्थिकार्थविशेषणस्यासिद्धतां परिहर्तुं **'न च'** इत्यदि। **'व्यवहाराविसंवादात्'।।** यथाहुः बाह्या अपि–'प्रमाणमविसंवादि- ज्ञानमर्थक्रियास्थितिः। अविसंवादनम्' इति। न चाविसंवादोऽसिद्ध इति वक्तव्यम्। प्रत्यक्षविरोधात्। न हि सारमेयादिप्रत्ययाद्वृद्धिमदादिप्रत्ययो विशिष्यत इति। उक्तञ्च–'नासावर्थमितिं प्रति' इति। एतच्चोक्तं **मण्डनमिश्रैः**– 'भेदेनान्वीयमानमपि मणिकृपाणदर्पणादिषु तत्त्वस्य भेदविरोधात्तत्त्वप्रत्ययेन समुत्सारितसकलभेदं मुखमवसीयते तथा दीर्घादिभेदानुगमेऽप्यवर्णात्मा प्रत्यभिज्ञा- बलेन विधूतभेद एको गम्यते। तथा पदमपि स्वप्रत्ययावगम्यमानैकस्वभावं किञ्चिद्भेदपरामर्शेऽप्यभिन्नं निश्चीयते' इति।।

मपि पदमिति वाक्यमिति चैकविषयमनुभव[1]मवजानीते स[2] इत्थं शिक्षणीयः—'वत्स, वेत्सि तावच्छब्दार्थधीरु[3]दीयत' इति।।

ननु अनुभव एव तावत्परेषामसिद्धः। स एव हि भावता समर्थनीयः। तद्विहायान्यदुच्यमानमजातराजपुत्रक्रीडनकोपमामापद्यत इति चेत्तत्राह—**यस्तु स्वतन्त्रसिद्धान्ताभ्यासाहितव्यामोहापस्मारः. . . .नै?(चै)कविषयमनुभवमवजानीते।।** स्वतन्त्र एवाश्रितस्य सिद्धान्तस्याभ्यासेनाहितो व्यामोह एवापस्मारो यस्येति विग्रहः। ईदृशी चावज्ञाभिप्रेता।।

नन्वस्तीदं पश्चादेकैकवर्णविज्ञानविलक्षणं विज्ञानं न तु तदर्थान्तरावलम्बनं वर्णरूपानुविद्धत्वात्, रूपान्तरानवभासाच्च। तथा हि—त एव वर्णात्मानं(त्मानः) पुनः पुनः परिगतपरिच्छेदाः तत्रैवाप्यवभासन्ते न तु रूपान्तरम्। अर्थान्तरविषयत्वे तु यथा वर्णविज्ञानानि परस्परविषयरूपप्रत्यवमर्शशून्यानि प्रकाशमानरूपान्तराणि प्रकाशन्ते तथेदमपि स्यात्। वैलक्षण्यं तु पूर्वोपलब्धीनामेकैकवर्णगोचरत्वादस्यैव समुचितविषयत्वादिति नार्थान्तरविषयत्वं वैलक्षण्यमात्रात्सिद्ध्यति। यदि चैकस्मात्रयमर्थान्तरमस्तु (सः) प्रत्ययस्य विषयो न तदतिरिक्तः कश्चिदर्थात्मा, वर्णपरित्यागेन बुद्धावप्रतिभासनात्। अथ मतं गौरित्येकं विज्ञानं; को वाहान्यथा। ज्ञेयनतु नैकं ज्ञेये तु तद्ग्रह्यतयैकार्थकारितया चैकत्वभ्रमः एकत्वोपचारो वा वनादित्। अपि च शैघ्र्यात् (अल्पाक्षरत्वाद्वा) गोशब्दे भवेदप्येकत्वभ्रमः। देवदत्तादिशब्दे तु स्पष्ट एव भेदः प्रकाशते। तदुक्तं—'न च प्रत्यक्षेभ्यो गकारादिभ्योऽन्यो गोशब्दः, भेददर्शनाभावात् अभेददर्शनाच्च।।'

'वैलक्षण्यञ्च तस्येष्टमेकैकज्ञानतः स्फुटम्।
वर्णरूपानुविद्धाच्च न तदर्थान्तरं भवेत्।।
यदि चार्थान्तरत्वं स्यादेकैकस्मात्रयस्य तु।
वर्णत्रयपरित्यागे बुद्धिर्नान्यत्र जायते।।

---

१. 'अपजानीते' इति मु० पु० पाठः।

२. 'स इत्थं शिक्षयितव्यः' इति मु० पु० पाठः।

३. 'उदयते' इति मु० पु० पाठः। 'उदीयते' इति ३. पु० पाठः।' इति टिप्पणी।।

[1]सेयं वर्णातिरिक्तैकपदवाक्यानुभवमन्तरेण नोदेतुमर्हति। नो खल्विमां विधातुमुत्सहन्ते वर्णाः, विकल्पासहत्वात्। ते हीमां प्रत्येकं वा विदधीरन्नागदन्ता इव शिक्यावलम्बनं, मिलिता वा ग्रावाण इव पिठरधारणम्। न तावत्त्वप्रत्येकम्; अनुपलम्भविरोधात्, वर्णान्तरोच्चारणानर्थक्यप्रसङ्गाच्च। नापि मिलिताः, तथाभावाभावात्। तथा हि—वास्तवो वा समूह एतेषामाश्रीयते? अनुभवोपाधिको वा? तत्र सर्वेषामेव वर्णानां नित्यतया विभुजतया च वास्वती सङ्गतिरतिप्रसङ्गिनी केषाञ्चिदेव पदवाक्यभावं नापादयितुमर्हति। अनुभूयमानानान्त्वनुभवानुसारिणी तत्पर्यायेण पर्यायवती न समूहभाग्यभवति। न खल्वेकदेशेकालनवच्छिन्नाः समूहवन्तो भवन्ति भावाः, अतिप्रसङ्गात्।।

पूर्वपूर्ववर्णानुभवजनितसंस्कारसहितोऽन्त्यो वर्णः [2]प्रत्यायकोऽर्थस्य। तेन तथैवैकानुभवकल्पनेति चेत्—न; विचारासहत्वात्। को नु खल्वयं [3]संस्कारोऽभिमतआयुष्यमतः—किं स्मृतिबीजं? अन्यो वा प्रोक्षणादिभ्य इवं व्रीह्यादेः? न तावदन्त्यः। न ह्यसावसहभुवां वर्णानां जन्य एकः सम्भवति, उक्तादेव

गौरित्येकमतित्वन्तु नैवास्माभिर्निवार्यते।
तद्ग्रह्यैकार्थताभ्यां च शब्दे स्यादेकतामतिः।।
शैघ्र्यादल्पाक्षरत्वाद्वा गोशब्दे सा भवेदपि।
देवदत्तादिशब्दे तु स्फुटो भेदः प्रतीयते।।' इति।।

---

१. 'सेयं' इत्यारभ्य 'शक्या कल्पयितुं' इति पर्यन्तो ग्रन्थः यथामुद्रितपुस्तकं दीयते, व्याख्याने ग्रन्थपातात्।

२. (प्रत्यायकोऽर्थस्य)—'तथा च वाक्यपदीये काण्डे १. श्लोक ८५।
'नादैराहितबीजायामन्त्येन ध्वनिना सह।
आवृत्तिपरिपाकायां बुद्धौ शब्दोऽवर्धायते।।' इति टिप्पणी।।

३. 'अर्थसंस्कारः' इति ३. पु० पाठ इति टिप्पणी।

प्रकारात्। वर्णैर्यथास्वं क्रमविशेषशालिभिरन्येऽन्ये जन्यन्ते संस्काराः, तेषाञ्च स्थेम्ना सम्भवत्यन्त्यवर्णसाचिव्यमभिधेयप्रत्ययजननायेति चेत्—अहो! बतास्य [१]स्वपक्षदृष्टिपक्षपातः, यद्बहुतर दृष्टसम्भारकल्पनाक्लेशमपि न चेतयते संस्कार एव तावदनुमपलब्धपूर्वस्तस्य च नानात्वमिति। आग्नेयादिवत्कल्पनागौरवं न [२]कल्पकगर्हिततामावहतीति चेत्—न; इहान्यथासिद्धेः। आग्नेयादयो हि विशरारवो 'दर्शपूर्णमासाभ्यां स्वर्गकामो यजेत' इति चिरभाविने फलाय विहिताः समिदादयश्च प्रोक्षणादयश्च तदङ्गान्यसहभावीनि इति बह्वपूर्वकल्पनां विना नोपपद्यत इति नासौ प्रमाणमार्गागतो दोषमावहति। इह पुनरेकगोचरानुभवमात्रादभिधेयप्रत्ययोत्पत्त्युपपत्तेरप्रामाणिकानेककल्पना न दोषमावहतीत्यचतुरस्रम्।।

वासनापरनामा संस्कारः स्मृतिबीजमन्त्यवर्णसहकारी, तस्य च स्मरणफलप्रसवोन्नीतसद्भावस्यार्थधीजन्मनि सहकारितामात्रं कल्पनीयम्; तन्न गौरवमिति चेत्—न; स्वभावविपर्यासानुपपत्तेः, अदृष्टान्तरकल्पनाप्रसङ्गाच्च। तथा हि—यो यद्गोचरानुभवयोनिः

समर्थनमारभते—**स इत्थं शिक्षणीयः।।** इदमाकूतम्—नानुभवः समर्थनीयः सार्वजनीनत्वात्। स्वतन्त्रसिद्धान्ताभ्यासाहितव्यामोहापस्मारत्वात्तु स केवलमस्माभिर्व्यामोहापस्मारवारणाय कारुणिकैर्भूत्वा वक्ष्यमाणप्रकारेण शिक्षणीयो निजशिष्यवत् इति। शिक्षामेवाह—**वत्स वेत्सि तावच्छब्दादर्थधीरुदीयत इति।।** उदयत इति ग्रन्थः। इण् गतौ अस्मादुदेति स्यात्। अथवा 'इ गतौ' इत्यस्येदं रूपम्। तत्र कर्तरीयत इति सिद्ध्यति इदमाकूतम्—एवमयं प्रष्टव्यः **'शब्दादर्थधीरुदीयत'** इत्येतत्त्वयाऽवगम्यते वा न वा। यदि नावगम्यते, हन्त! अयमचिकित्स्योऽयमपस्मार इत्युपेक्षणीयं शिक्षणम्।

---

१. 'स्वदृष्टिपक्षपाः' इति २ पु० पाठ० इति टिप्पणी।

२. 'लोकगर्हितताम्' इति ३. पु० पाठः इति टिप्पणी।

संस्कारः स तत्रैव धियमाधत्त इति तस्य स्वभावः; यद्यन्यस्मिन्नप्यादधीत किञ्चिदेवैकमनुभूय सर्वः सर्वमर्थं [१]विजानीयात्। अपि च, संस्कार इति च वासनेति च भावनेति च प्राचीनानुभवजनितमात्मनः सामर्थ्यभेदमेव स्मृतिज्ञानप्रसवहेतुमाचक्षते। न [२]चास्यैवार्थप्रत्ययप्रसवशक्तिः शक्या कल्पयितुम् । सा खल्वभिधेयधीप्रसवोन्नीतसद्भावा फलवत्यात्मन्येव युक्ता कल्पयितुं न पुनरतद्वत्यामस्य [३]स्मृतिजनन[४]शक्तौ। यथा[५] खल्वियं

यद्यवगम्यते ततश्चिकित्स्योऽयमिति प्रयत्यते। त्वं च वत्स! **'शब्दादर्थधीरुदीयत'** इत्येतद्वेत्स्येव तावन्न संशयः, यतः त्वयास्मान्प्रति साधनदूषणवाक्यानि प्रयुज्यन्ते। अस्मत्प्रयुक्तानि च परिजिहीर्षसीति। अप च **'अर्थधीरुदयमासादयति'** इति यदादावेव वर्णितं तस्येदं फलं प्रदर्शितमिति वेदितव्यम्। अनेन च **'अर्थधीभेदाद्वा अन्यथानुपपद्यमानात्'** इति द्वितीयार्धव्यावर्त्यः पक्षः समर्थयितुमुपक्रान्तो वेदितव्य।[६]. . . 'शक्त्यन्तरकल्पनामात्रन्त्विह विषये, कार्यान्तरदर्शनात्; न तु स्फोटपरिकल्पना युक्ता, क्लृप्तवस्तुशक्तिमात्रपरिकल्पनया कार्योपपत्तौ अर्थापत्तिक्षयात्' इति। उक्तञ्च वार्तिके–

'अथवा वासनैवास्तु संस्कारात्स(रः, स)र्व एव हि।
दृढज्ञानगृहीतेऽर्थे संस्कारोऽस्तीति मन्वते।।
तस्यार्थबुद्धिहेतुत्वे विसंवादोऽत्र निर्णये।

---

१. (विजानीयात्)–'तथा च वर्णस्मरणमेव स्यान्न त्वर्थस्मरणमिति भावः।' इति टिप्पणी।।

२. (अस्यैवार्थप्रत्ययप्रसवशक्तिः)–'संस्करस्यैव शक्तिरूपत्वेन तत्र शक्त्यन्तरकल्पनानवकाशादिति भावः।' इति टिप्पणी।।

३. (स्मृतिजननशक्तौ)–'बोधरूपफलरहितायां शक्तौ संस्कारस्य स्मृतिजनकत्वमनुयोगात्कल्पयितुं न युक्तमित्यर्थः।' इति टिप्पणी।।

४. 'स्मृतिजननम्' इति २ पु० पाठ इति टिप्पणी।।

५. 'यथा चेयं' इति मु० पु० पाठः।

६. अत्र व्याख्यानमातृकायां पत्रषट्कपरिमितग्रन्थपातः।

मानान्तरसिद्धा, एवमसावपि। न चात्मनि शक्तिकल्पनायां[1] सा च, तस्याश्चान्या, अशक्तायाः कार्यकरत्वाभावादिति शक्त्यन्तरकल्पना, न तु स्मृतिप्रसवशक्ताविति साम्प्रतम्। न हि कल्प्यमाना शक्तिः शक्त्यन्तरयुक्ता कल्प्यते, तन्मात्रादेव सम्भवे शक्त्यन्तरकल्पनायामनवस्थापातात्, स्मृतिप्रसव-शक्तावपि च साम्यासाम्यात्।[2] तथा चादृष्टान्तरं नाम परि-कल्पनीयमिति। तदेवं [3]महद्गौरवमापन्नमिति।।

तद्भावभावितो(ता) हेतुरन्यत्रेव प्रतीयते।।' इति

'तदिदमसमञ्जसमिव लक्ष्यते' स्फोटं विहायार्थप्रसवशक्तेरन्यत्र कल्पने संस्कारविषयत्वपारिशेष्यासम्भव इति। **अस्यैवेति।।** संस्कारविषयत्वमेव कल्पनाया दुरुपपादम्। दूरे क्लृप्तशक्तिकतयोपपत्तिरित्यर्थः। एतदेव प्रकटयति–**सा खल्वभिधेयधीप्रसवोन्नीतसद्भावाफलवात्यात्मन्येव युक्ता कल्पयितुं न पुनरतद्वत्यामस्य स्मृतिजननशक्तौ।।** सेति। शक्तिः। **फलवति**–धीमति। **अस्य**–आत्मनः। **फलवती**–त्यनेनौचित्यान्तरङ्गत्वे सूचिते। **अतद्वत्या**मित्यनेनानौचित्यहिरङ्गत्वे। अतद्वतीत्वमेव व्यक्तिकृत्योक्तं–**अस्य स्मृतिजननशक्ताविति ।।** उक्तं हि–'प्राचीनानुभवजनितमात्मनः सामर्थ्ये'त्यादिति भावः।।

यच्च संस्कारकल्पनायां भवतां निबन्धनं तदविकलमात्मन्यपीति दर्शयन्नाह–**यथा खल्वियं मानान्तरसिद्धा एवमसावपि।।** मानान्तरसिद्ध इति विपरिम्यानुषङ्गः। फलवत्त्वन्त्वधिकमात्मनीति भावः। एवं द्वितीयो हेतुर्व्याख्यातः। स्मृतिहेतोरदृष्टाददृष्टान्तरमात्मनि कल्पयितुमुचितमिति।।

ननु नादृष्टान्तरं कल्पनीयं, गौरवात्। स्मृतिबीजे हि धर्ममात्रं कल्प्यम्।

---

१. 'शक्तिकल्पनायां सत्यां तस्याश्चाशक्तायाः कार्यकरणाभावाच्छत्तयन्तरकल्पना' इति मु० पु० पाठः।

२. **'साम्यात्, यथा वा अदृष्टान्तरं मा नाम कल्पनीयमिति तदेव गौरवमापन्नम्'** इति मु० पु० पाठः। 'तथा चादृष्टान्तरं नाने(मे)'ति ३. पु० पाठ इति टिप्पणी।।

३. (गौरवं)–'शक्तिरूपे संस्कारे शक्त्यन्तरकल्पनारूपम्' इति टिप्पणी।

[१]**तावत्स्मृतिसमारोहिणी वर्णा वाचकाः, ततो न गौरवमिति चेत्–**

अदृष्टान्तरे तु धर्म्यपि। अतोऽन्तरङ्गत्वादिकमपहाय लाघवपक्षपातिन्यार्थापत्त्या स्मृतिबीजे धर्ममात्रं कल्प्यते नादृष्टान्तरमित्याशङ्क्याह–**न चात्मनि शक्तिकल्पनाया. . . .साम्प्रतम्।।** **न चेति साम्प्रतं** युक्तमित्यन्वयः। इतिशब्दनिर्दिष्टं दर्शितम्–**आत्मनीत्यादिना।।** एवं शङ्कां प्रतिषिध्य हेतुमाह–**न हि कल्प्यमाना. . . .तदेवं महद्गौरवमापन्नमिति।।** वासनापक्षसमाप्ता-**विति**शब्दः। **अदृष्टान्तरमिति।।** अदृष्टान्तरवर्जनाय हि वासनापक्षः प्रस्तूयते, तस्मिन्नाश्रीयमाणेऽपि ततो न मुच्यसे, शक्तेः शक्त्यन्तरस्यात्यन्तादृष्टस्य कल्पनात्। एतच्च द्वितीयस्य हेतोर्व्याख्यानान्तरमिति द्रष्टव्यम्। अथवा–पूर्वो ग्रन्थोऽस्यैवाङ्गीकरणद्योतनाय। एष एव व्याख्यानग्रन्थः। एतच्चोक्तं–'शक्तेः शक्त्यन्तरायोगः' इति।।

सिद्धान्तारमपि वर्णवादिनां दूषयितुमाशङ्कते–**तावत्स्मृतिसमारोहिणो वर्णा वाचकाः ततो न गौरवमिति चेत्।।** इदमाकूतम्–'न खलु साक्षाद्भावनानां व्यापारमभिधेयप्रत्ययहेतुमुपेमः। अपि तु ताभ्यः स्थायित्वेन प्रतिलब्धयौगपद्याभ्यः प्रत्यवमृष्टसकलवर्णरूपात्मा एकः प्रत्यय उदेति। (तत्र) स एव वा तद्विपरिवर्तिनो वा वर्णाः तत्र समधिगतसहभावाः जनयन्त्यर्थावबोधमिति वृथा शब्दपरिकल्पनाश्रमः। स्मृतौ च सहभावः न स प्रत्यक्षे इति चेत्–किमत्र प्रत्यक्षवर्तिना यौगपद्येन? सर्वथा ज्ञानविषयं तदर्थ्यते, तच्च स्मरणज्ञानेऽस्त्येव। स चैष प्रत्ययः स्मरणप्रत्यक्षरूपाभ्यामु-भयात्मा सदसद्वर्णावभास्यन्त्यवर्ण(गोचर) इष्यते कैश्चित्। अन्यैस्तु सकलवर्ण-पदोपलब्धिनिबन्धननिखिलभावनाबीजजन्मा युगपदखिलवर्णरूपरामर्शी चरमवर्णप्रत्यक्षोपलब्धिसमनन्तरं स्मरणैकरूपः सङ्गीयते। क्रमसमधिगतात्मसु न युगपदनुस्मरणमित्यपि मिथ्या, यतः सकलवादिनामभिमतं पौर्वापर्यालो-चितेष्वपि भावेषु समुच्चयावग्राहि विज्ञानम्। तदनुपगमे हि तत्प्रकारपातिषु शतं विंशतिरिति समुच्चयदर्शनं विहन्येत। तस्माच्छ्रोत्रमनोजन्मभिः क्रमवतीभिरपि

---

१. 'स्मृतिसमारोहिणी वर्णा वाचकास्तन्न गौरवमिति चेत्' इति मु० पु० पाठः।

न; [१]अक्रमानुक्रमविपरीतक्रमाणां तत्राविशेषेणार्थधी-समुत्पादप्रसङ्गात्[२]। अथापि स्यात् [३]ये यथास्वं वर्णानुभवैराहिताः

बुद्धिभिरवधृतेष्वपि भावेषु वर्णात्मसु पुरस्तात्, परस्ताद्भवक्रम (स्तादद्व्यमक्रम) मखिलवर्णरूपावगाहि स्मरणमवकल्पते। तत्र च सङ्क्रान्तप्रतिबिम्बा वर्णाः समीहितकार्यं प्रत्यनन्तरतां नातिक्रामन्तीति। लौकिकवचनमपि समञ्जसं–'शब्दादर्थं प्रतिपद्यामहे' इति। शास्त्रकारवचनमपि–'भावमाख्यातेनाचष्टे' इति। तदिदमुक्तम्–

'यद्वा प्रत्यक्षरं (तः) पूर्वं क्रमज्ञातेषु यत्परम्।
समस्तवर्णविज्ञानं तदर्थज्ञानकारणम्।।' इति।।

'तत्र ज्ञाने च वर्णानां यौगपद्यं प्रतीयते।
नावश्यं यौगपद्येन प्रत्यक्षस्थेन तद्भवेत्।।

चित्ररूपाञ्च तां बुद्धिं सदसद्वर्णगोचराम्।
केचिदाहुर्यया वर्णो गृह्यतेऽन्त्यः पदे पदे।।

अन्त्यवर्णे च विज्ञाते सर्वसंस्कारकारितम्।
स्मरणं यौगपद्येन सर्वेष्वन्ये प्रचक्षते।।

सर्वेषु चैतदर्थेषु मानसं सर्ववादिनाम्।
इष्टं समुच्चयज्ञानं क्रमज्ञातेषु सत्स्वपि।।

न चेत्तदभ्युपेयेत क्रमदृष्टेषु नैव हि।
शतादिरूपं जायेत तत्समुच्चयदर्शनम्।।

तेन श्रोत्रमनोभ्यां स्यात्क्रमज्ञातेषु यद्यपि।
पूर्वज्ञानं परस्तात्तु युगपत्स्मरणं भवेत्।।

तदारूढास्तदा वर्णा न दूरेऽर्थावबोधनम्।
शब्दादर्थमतिस्तेन लौकिकैरभिधीयते।।' इति।।

---

१. 'क्रमाक्रमविपरीतक्रमाणां' इति मु० पु० पाठः।

२. 'समुत्पादनप्रसङ्गात्' इति मु० पु० पाठः।

३. 'ये' इति मुद्रितपुस्तके नास्ति।

संस्कारा: (ते) सम्भूय निखिलवर्णविषयमेकमेव स्मरणफालं प्रसुवते, तदा[१] रोहिणी वर्णा अव्यवधाना अभिधेयधियमादधति। न चैकैकवर्णोपलब्धिप्रतिलब्धजन्मान: संस्कारा: प्रतिवर्णगोचरास्तावतीरेव[२] तत्क्रमवती: [३]स्मृतीरपि भावयितुमीशते। तत्र तत्र[४] नि[५]रपेक्षणां कारणभावोपलम्भात्। न पुनर[६]खिलवर्णगोचरमेकमिति रमणीयम् ; तत्र तत्रानपेक्षाणां कारणत्वेऽपि मिलितानाम-

---

एतदपि दूषयति–**नेति**।। करणमाह–**अक्रमानुक्रमविपरीतक्रमाणां तत्राविशेषेणार्थधीसमुत्पादप्रसङ्गात्**।। अत्र वर्णानामिति विशेष्यं द्रष्टव्यम्। तत्रेति स्मृति परामृशति। एवं चोद्यपरिहारौ संक्षिप्य दर्शयित्वा चोद्यं तावद्व्याचष्टे–**अथापि स्यात् . . . न कदाचिददृष्टकल्पनेति**।। **संस्कारास्सम्भूये**त्यनयोर्मध्ये त इति पदमध्याहार्यं यदि न दृश्यते। **स्मरणफलमिति** कर्मधारय। **तदारोहिण:**–तादृशस्मरणफलारोहिण:। **अव्यवधाना इति**। अनेन लौकिकवयस: शास्त्रकारवचनस्य चोपपत्तिस्सूचिता। पूर्वोक्तं **'स्मृतिसमारोहिणो वर्ण वाचका:'** इत्येतद्व्याख्याय 'ये यथास्व'मित्यादेरर्थस्य कृत्स्नस्यासिद्धिं परिहर्तुं न चेत्यारम्भ:। **न चेति रमणीय**मित्यन्वय। **निरपेक्षाणां कारणभावोपलम्भादिति**।। यत्र यत्र कारणकार्यभाव: तत्र तत्र निरपेक्षाणामेव कारणभाव उपलब्ध:, यथा–बीजाङ्कुरयो:। न हि माषबीजसापेक्षं मुद्गबीजं स्वाङ्कुरं जनयति, चक्षुरादयो वा रूपानुविद्धम्। अतस्संकाराणामपि निरपेक्षाणामेव कारणत्वमिति न प्रत्येकवर्णानुभवजनितसंस्काराणां युगपदेकस्मरणफलप्रसवसम्भव इति।

---

१. 'तदुपारोहिणो वर्णा:' इति मु० पु० पाठ:।

२. 'तावतीरेव क्रमवती:' इति मु० पु० पाठ:।

३. 'स्मृतीर्भावयितुं' इति मु० पु० पाठ:।

४. (निरपेक्षाणां)–'कारणत्वेऽपि भावोपलम्भात्' इति २. पु० पाठ:। 'संस्कारान्तरनैरपेक्ष्येण प्रत्येकं संस्काराणां कारणत्वेन स्मृतिरूपफलदर्शनादित्यर्थ:। इति टिप्पणी।।

५. 'निरपेक्षकारणभावोपलम्भात्' इति मु० पु० पाठ:।

६. 'अखिलवर्णगोचरं स्मरणमेकमिति' इति मु० पु० पाठ:।

प्येक[1] (प्यनेक) गोचरैकविज्ञनाजननदर्शनात्। तथा हि– [2]संस्काराश्चक्षुराद्यनपेक्षाः स्मरणकारणं, चक्षुरादयश्च तदनपेक्षा आलोचनकारणं, प्रत्यभिज्ञाने तु संस्कारापेक्षाश्चक्षुरादयः कारणमित्यवश्यं तत्र तत्रोहनीयमिति न कदाचिददृष्टकल्पनेति। [3]तन्नास्ति; [4]क्रमयुक्तेभ्य इव युगपद्विपरीतक्रमयुक्तेभ्योऽप्यभिधेयप्रत्ययप्रसङ्गात्। न खल्वेकोपलब्धिवर्तिनामस्ति कश्चिद्विशेषो वर्णानाम्। न हि

अरमणीयत्वे पूर्वोक्तहेत्वसिद्धिरेव कारणमुक्तम्–**तत्र तत्र निरपेक्षाणां कारणत्वेऽपीति**। क्व पुनर्दृष्टमिति चेदित्याशङ्क्योपपादयतोक्तं–**तथा हीत्यादि।। आलोचनकारणमिति।।** अपरोक्षज्ञानसाधनमित्यर्थः। **इत्यवश्यं तत्र तत्रोहनीयमिति**। एवं प्रत्यक्षज्ञानमधिकृत्य दर्शितम्; एवमेवान्यत्रापि यत्र यत्र कारणभावः तत्र तत्रावश्यमेव शिष्यैरूहनीयमेव निरपेक्षाणां कारणत्वेऽपि मिलितानामपि एककार्यजननमित्यर्थः। ततो न गौरवमित्यस्यानुसन्धानम्–इति **न कदाचिददृष्टकल्पनेति।** इतिशब्दो व्याख्यानसमाप्तौ। एवं चोद्यं व्याख्याय परिहारमपि व्याचष्टे–**तन्नास्ति; क्रमयुक्तेभ्य इव युगपद्विपरीतक्रमयुक्तेभ्योऽप्यभिधेयप्रत्ययप्रसङ्गात्।। युगपदिति।।** भावप्रधानो निर्देशः। यौगपद्ययुक्तानां विपरीतक्रमयुक्तानां चेति विग्रहः। क्वचित्तु यौगपद्येत्येव पाठः। अनेन च पूर्वत्राक्रमाणां अनुक्रमाणां विपरीतक्रमाणां चेति विग्रहो दर्शितः। अनुगतः क्रमो येषु तेऽनुक्रमाः; विपरीतः क्रमो येषां ते विपरीतक्रमाः। क्रमराहित्यं यौगपद्यम्; अनुक्रमग्रहणं च दृष्टान्तार्थम्। **अर्थ**शब्दश्चाभिधेयवचन इति दर्शितं वेदितव्यम्। तत्र**विशेषेणे**त्येतव्द्याचक्षाणः एतदेव प्रतिपादयति–**न**

---

१. 'मप्यनेकगोचैरकविज्ञानं' इति मु० पु० पाठः।

२. 'संस्कारश्चक्षुराद्यनपेक्षः स्मरणकारणं चक्षुरादयस्तन्निरपेक्षा आलोचनकारणम्; प्रत्यभिज्ञाने तु संस्कारसापेक्षाः चक्षुरादयः। एवं तत्र तत्रोहनीयमिति न काचिददृष्टकल्पनेति'। इति मु० पु० पाठः।

३. 'अदृष्टकल्पनेति तत्रास्ति' इति मु० पु० पाठः। 'तन्नस्तीति २ पु० पाठः। तथा च सकलवर्णविषयकमेकं स्मरणं सम्भवतीति भावः। एतावत्पर्यन्तमाक्षेपः; उत्तरस्तु परिहारः।' इति टिप्पणी।।

४. 'क्रमाभिव्यक्तेभ्य इव यौगपद्यविपरीतक्रमाभिव्यक्तेभ्यः' इति मु० पु० पाठः।

वास्तवः क्रमो नित्यानां विभूनां तेषाम् उपलब्धिनिमित्तत्त्व? (स्त्वाश्रीयते।) सा चेदेका कुतस्त्यस्तर्हि क्रम एषाम्?

न च [१]प्राचीनप्रत्येकवर्णानुभवनिवयवर्तिनी [२]परापरतापि प्रभासत इति साम्प्रतम्। वर्णस्वरूपमात्रगोचरतया स्मृतिरियं न [३]तदनुभवानि गोचरयितुमर्हति प्रागेव तत्परापरतामिति। इति युगपद्विपरीतक्रमाभिव्यक्तानामनुक्रमाभिव्यक्तेभ्यो विशेषाभावादेकोपलब्धौ सर्वार्थप्रत्ययप्रसङ्गः।।

खल्वेकोपलब्धिवर्तिनामस्ति कश्चिद्विशेषो वर्णानाम्।। कश्चिदिति।। यौगपद्यं वा क्रमो वा विपरीतक्रमत्वं वेति। **वर्णा**नामित्यनेन पूर्वत्र विशेष्यञ्च सूचितम्। विशेषाभावञ्च स्फोरयति–**वर्णा**नामित्यनेन। सूचितमेवार्थं स्फोरयति–**न हि वास्तवः क्रमो नित्यानां विभूनां तेषाम्; उपलब्धिनिमित्तत्वा(?) (स्त्वाश्रीयते)** ।। अस्तु तर्हि स एवेति चेदत आह–**सा चेदेका, कुतस्त्यस्तर्हि क्रम एषाम्।।**

नन्वेका स्मृतिरुपलब्धिरभिप्रेता। सा च पूर्वानुभवनिचयजनितसंस्कारनिचयजन्या स्वकारणद्वारा कारणकारणवर्तिनीं परापरतामपि लप्स्यत इत्याशङ्क्याह–**न च प्राचीनप्रत्येक. . . . इति साम्प्रतम्।।** प्रत्येकग्रहणमनुभवनिचयवर्तित्वस्फोरणाय असाम्प्रतत्वे कारणमाह–**वर्णस्वरूपमात्रगोचरतया. . . .तत्परापरतामिति।।** धर्मिणोऽप्यविषयीकरणे धर्मविषयीकरणस्य दूरापास्तत्वादिति भावः। **इति**र्हेतौ। इतिशब्द उत्तरत्राप्यनुवर्तते। उपसंहरति–**इति युगपत्. . . . सर्वार्थप्रत्ययप्रसङ्गः।।**

---

१. 'प्राचीनप्रत्येकवर्णानुभवनिचयमनुवर्तनीयं परापरता प्रतिभासत इति साम्प्रतम्।' इति मु० पु० पाठः।

२. 'पदज्ञाने वर्णपौर्वापर्यपतिभासादनुभवगतक्रमविषयकत्वं स्मृतावङ्गीकार्यमिति भावः।' इति टिप्पणी।।

३. 'तत्तदनुभवानपि गोचरयितुमर्हति तत्परापरतां तु प्रागेवेति युगपद्विपरीतक्रमाभिव्यक्तानां क्रमाभिव्यक्तेभ्यो विशेषाभावादेकोपलब्धौ सर्वेषामर्थप्रत्यायनप्रसङ्गः।' इति मु० पु० पाठः।

अत्र चाक्रमानुक्रमविपरीतक्रमाणां मध्येऽनुक्रमाणामवधित्वं, इतरेषा-मवधिमत्त्वं, अर्थधीसमुत्पादप्रसङ्गश्च यद्विवक्षया ये वर्णा येन क्रमेण प्रयुक्ताः तस्य तत्क्रमान्यथात्वेऽपि प्रसङ्गमात्रमिति न मन्तव्यं, किन्त्वन्येषामप्यर्थानां प्रतीतिप्रसङ्गो विवक्षित इति दर्शितम्। **एकोपलब्धौ**–एकस्य पदस्य वाक्यस्य वोपलब्धौ। **सर्वार्थेति।।** वर्णानामेव पदवाक्यत्वात्तेषाञ्च भेदाभावात्क्रमस्य चाभावादिति भावः।।

एतदप्युक्तम्–

> 'पूर्वापलब्धिभेदेऽपि भवेदर्थस्य दर्शनम्।
> एकोपलब्धौ नैतेषां भेदः कश्चन दृश्यते।।' इति।।

'पूर्वोपलब्धयो हि क्रमविशेषवत्यः परिगृहीताभिमतविपरीतानुपूर्व्याः अक्रमाश्चैकवक्तृप्रयुक्तवर्णविषयाः विपरीताश्च न पश्चाद्भाविन्यामुपलब्धौ अनुविपरिवर्तमानवर्णात्मनो भिन्दन्ति, असम्प्राप्तनिरन्वयनिरुद्धयोर्विशेषा-भावादित्युक्तम्। एकोपलब्धौ तु यौगपद्यानन्नानुपूर्वीतो विशेषः। न चेदमिह समीचीनम्–उपलम्भगोचरमिदं यौगपद्यं नोपलभ्यविषयं, उपलभ्या वर्णाः क्रमभाज एवैकया प्रख्यया प्रख्यायन्त इति। तथा हि–स्वतो वर्णा नित्यतया विभुतया च (न) देशनिबन्धनं नापि कालनिबन्धनं परापरभाव- मनुपतन्तीति प्रख्यानिबन्धन एष समाश्रीयते। तच्चेदमद्वयमक्रमं यद्विपरिवर्तिनः (तेन?) ते प्रत्ययहेतवः। न चेदं पूर्वोपलब्धिसम्बन्धिनीं परापरतां गोचरयति वर्णावलम्बितया तदुपलब्धीनाविषयीकरणेन। न च समीहितावध्यवधिमद्भावं पौर्वापर्यं प्रत्येतुमर्हति। न चैकस्मिन्नानावर्णावयवात्मनि भिन्ने पदे भिन्नमवध्य- वधिमद्भामवपेक्षितुं क्षमते । प्रतिवर्णोपलम्भप्रभावितानि च भावनाबीजानि कामं संहतिसमापादनादेकमनेकावलम्बि स्मरणं जनयेयुः। तावतां चरितार्थेभ्यो न परो वर्णात्मसु विशेषो लभ्यते। तथा च सति यथाकथञ्चित्परस्तादधि- गतसंवेदनेभ्यो निखिलसंस्कारजन्मनि चरमसमधिगमेऽतिशयविरहादर्थपरिच्छेदः स्यात्। न चैवं दृश्यते। अतस्तदतिरिच्यमाननिमित्तावाप्तजन्मायमित्यनुमीयते' इति।।

युगपदभिव्यक्तानां विपरीतेन क्रमेणाभिव्यक्तानाञ्चेति विग्रहः। अनुसृतः क्रमोऽनुक्रमः, तेनाभिव्यक्तेभ्य इति। इमामुक्तिमनुसृत्य पूर्वं 'अक्रमानुक्रम-विपरीतक्रमाणां' इत्यत्रापि तत्पुरुषसमास एव न बहुव्रीहिरित्यूह्यते। किन्तु

तस्मात्स्व[१]सिद्धान्तव्यामोहमपहाया [२]भ्युपेयताम[३]नुसंहार-बुद्धेरेकपदवाक्यगोचरता। न चास्या गोचर इव प्रत्येक[४]ध्वनि-व्यञ्जनीयः तदर्थोऽपि [५]प्रत्येकवर्णव्यञ्जनीयः इति साम्प्रतम्। प्रथमादेव वर्णादभिधेयधीसमुत्पादादानर्थक्यं द्वितीयादीना-

---

'क्रमयुक्तेभ्यः' इति निर्देशात् **'एकोपलब्धिवर्तिनामस्ति कश्चिद्विशेषो वर्णानां'** इति च दर्शनाद्बहुव्रीहित्वमाश्रितमिति वेदितव्यम्। केचित्तु-तत्पुरुषत्वमाश्रित्याक्रमानुक्रमविपरीतक्रमाणामेकोपलब्धौ विशेषाभावेनासत्त्वस्य तुल्यत्वेनेति व्याचक्षते, तत्र **'अर्थधीसमुत्पादप्रसङ्गः'** इत्यस्य **'क्रमयुक्तेभ्यः'** इति, **'अविशेषात्'** इत्यन्तस्य **'परापरतां'** इति व्याख्यानमवशिष्टेनोपसंहार एवेति। एवन्तावत् **'नो खल्विमामाधातुमुत्सहन्ते वर्णाः'** इत्येतत्प्रसाधितम्। सम्प्रति तदेव **'सेयं वर्णातिरिक्तैकपदवाक्यानुभवमन्तरेण नोदेतुमर्हति'** इत्यत्र पर्यवसाययति–**तस्मात्स्वसिद्धान्त. . . .वाक्यगोचरता।।** यस्मान्ना-न्यावग(न्या ग)तिर्विद्यते तस्मादित्यर्थः। तथा च **'सार्वजनीनमानसप्रत्यक्ष-प्रवेदनीयनानाध्वनिभिः प्रत्येकव्यञ्जनीयं तत्त्वम्'** इत्येतदेवावस्थितम्।।

यद्यत्र कश्चिद्ब्रूयात्–यथा भवतामनुसंहारबुद्धेर्विषयः प्रत्येकध्वनिभिर्व्यज्यते एवमस्माकं वर्णैरर्थ इति व्यर्था स्फोटकल्पनेति; तत्राह–**न चास्या गोचर इव. . . .इति साम्प्रतम्।।** इदंशब्देनानुसंहार-बुद्धेः तच्छब्देन च गोचर(स्य) परामर्शः। हेतुमाह–**प्रथमादेव. . . .इत्युक्तम्।।** उक्तिः **'न तावत्प्रत्येकम्'** इत्यत्र। **अस्याः गोचर इवेति** वदतोऽभिप्रायं निषेधति–**न चैतत्पदेऽपि तुल्यम्।।** पदशब्दो वाक्यस्याप्युपलक्षणम्। अतुल्यत्वे कारणमाह–**तस्य हि प्रत्यक्षस्य. . . .सम्भविनी।।** प्रत्यक्षाप्रत्यक्षशब्दाभ्यां सूचितमर्थं सूच(स्फोर)यति–**प्रत्यक्षगोचरो. . . न मानान्तरगोचरः।।** 'न मानान्तरगोचरः'

---

१. 'स्वसिद्धान्ताभ्यासव्यामोह' इति मु० पु० पाठः।

२. (अभ्युपेयतां)–'अभ्युयेतां' इति ३ पु० पाठः। इति टिप्पणी।।

३. 'अनुसंहारबुद्धिरेकपदवाक्यगोचरा' इति मु० पु० पाठः।

४. 'ध्वनिशब्दो नास्ति ३ पु० पाठः' इति टिप्पणी।

५. 'प्रतिवर्णव्यञ्जनीय' इति मु० पु० पाठः।

मित्युक्तम्। न चैतत्पदेऽपि तुल्यम्। तस्य हि प्रत्यक्षस्य प्रतिध्वनिव्यञ्जनीय- स्याभिव्यक्तितारतम्यं नानाध्वनिष्वायतत इति नानर्थक्यमुत्तरेषाम्। न चेयमप्रत्यक्षेऽभिधेये विधा [१]सम्भविनी। [२]प्रत्यक्षगोचरोऽपि (ह्यभिव्यक्ति)तारतम्यभाक् न मानान्तरगोचरः। स खलु गृह्यते वा न वा, न पुनर्व्यक्तोऽव्यक्तश्चेति।।

तदिदमसमञ्जसम्। तथा हि—चक्षुषी निमील्य डिण्डिकरागं[३] परित्यज्य निरूपयत्वत्रभवान् [४]पूर्वा बुद्धीरेकैकवर्णगोचराः,

---

इत्येतदेव व्याचष्टे—**स खलु. . . .अव्यक्तश्चेति।।** एतदप्युक्तं—'अथ कस्मादेष स्फोटोलब्धिक्रमोऽर्थोपलब्धावेव नाश्रीयते, यतः—

'प्रत्यक्षज्ञाननियता व्यक्ताव्यक्तावभासिता।
मानान्तरेषु ग्रहणमथवा नैव हि ग्रहः।।'

इन्द्रियं हि व्यक्तावभासिनोऽव्यक्तावभासिनश्चार्थप्रत्ययस्य हेतुः; यथा—दूराद्ग्रहणे सूक्ष्मार्थनिरूपणायाञ्च। लिङ्गशब्दादयस्तु निश्चितात्मानं प्रत्ययमुपजनयन्त्येकरूपं, नैव वा; न तत्र व्यक्ताव्यक्तग्रहणबुद्धिभेदः; अर्थश्च शब्दप्रत्ययादवसेयः, स्फोटात्मा तु प्रत्यक्षवेदनीय इति निरवद्यम्' इति।।

अत्र प्रतिविधत्ते—**तदिदमसमञ्जसं. . . .अत्र भवान्।। चक्षुषी निमील्येति** सावधानत्वाय। **डिण्डिकरागं परित्यज्येति।।** डिण्डिकानां यादृशो भवति रागः तादृशं रागं परित्यज्य मध्यस्थतामवलम्ब्य निरूपयतु। रागान्धचित्तो हि परमार्थनिरूपणायाशक्त इति। यथोक्तं—'दोषे(षो)ऽप्य(ह्य)विद्यमाने(नो)ऽपि

---

१. 'सम्भवति' इति मु० पु० पाठः।

२. (प्रत्यक्षगोचरो हि)—'प्रत्यक्षगोचरो ह्यभिव्यक्तितारतम्यभाग् न मानान्तरगोचरः स खलु' इति ३ पु० पाठः श्लिष्टः। २ पु० भाग् मानान्तरगोचरगोचरः। न खल्विति पाठः' इति टिप्पणी।।

३. 'डिण्डिकमतरागं' इति मु० पु० पाठः।

४. 'पूर्वबुद्धीः' इति मु० पु० पाठः।

[१]उत्तराश्च विशदपदवाक्यावगाहिनी:; किमेता गादिबुद्धयो गकारादिमात्रनिर्भासा: आहोस्वित् गकाराद्याकारं किञ्चिदेकमनाकारमासु[२] सम्प्लवते, मुखमिव मणिकृपाणदर्पणादिषु[३] विभिन्नवर्णपरिमाणमप्येकम्।[४] इतरथा [५]हि तत्र मुखमिति बुद्धिव्यपदेशावभिन्नवस्त्ववगाहिनौ[६] न स्याताम्। न सम्प्लवते चेद्गोदय एव परस्परं[७] नानात्मान: प्रकाशन्ते न पुनस्तदाकारं पदतत्त्वमेकं प्रकाशत इति सिद्धति। न जातु [८]गगवयकरभरुख: परस्पर-

---

तच्चिन्ता(त्ता)नां प्रकाशते' इति।। यथा–'रागाद्युपप्लुते चित्ते दृष्टा विस्मरणात्मनि'। इति।

अत्रभवान्–तत्रभवानित्यर्थ:। निरूपणकर्म दर्शयति–**पूर्वा बुद्धी: . . . वाक्यावगाहिनी:।।** नन्वेतादृशीरुभयोरपि बुद्धीरुक्तरीत्या निरूप्यैवास्माभिरेवमुच्यते; भवतस्तु किं तत्र प्रष्टव्यं तत्पृच्छ्यतामिति चेदत्राह–**किमेता गादिबुद्धयो. . . विभिन्नवर्णपरिमाणमप्येकम्।।** दृष्टान्तसिद्धिमप्याह–**इतरथा हि मत्र. . .न स्याताम्।।** एवं विकल्प्य प्रथमे पक्षे दूषणमाह–**न सम्प्लवते चेत् . . . . इति सिद्ध्यति।।** एवञ्चति सति पदतत्त्वस्यैवैकस्य विवर्ता गकारादय: इत्येतन्न सिद्ध्यतीति दृष्टान्तेनाह–**न जातु. . . विवर्ता भवन्ति।।** अथ वा–**न पुनस्तदाकारं पदतत्त्वमेक**तित्यत्र भवतीति सिद्ध्यति, 'अस्तिर्भवन्तीपर:' इति न्यायात्। तेन न पुनरेकस्य पदतत्त्वस्य विवर्तकारितेत्यर्थ:। अत्रैव दृष्टान्तदानमुत्तरेण। गकारौकारविसर्जनीया नैकस्य

---

१. 'उत्तरां च विशदपदवाक्यावगाहिनीं' इति मु० पु० पाठ:।

२. 'अनाकारं' इति मु० पु० नास्ति।

३. 'मानकृपाणेति ३ पु० पाठ:' इति टिप्पणी।

४. 'भिन्नवर्णपरिमाणसंस्थानमेकं' इति मु० पु० पाठ:।

५. 'हि' इति मु० पु० नास्ति।

६. 'अभिन्नवस्तुग्राहिणौ' इति मु० पु० पाठ:।

७. 'परस्परानात्मान:' इति मु० पु० पाठ:।

८. 'गजगवयहयरासभरुरव:' इति मु० पु० पाठ:।

व्यतिभिद्यमानमूर्तयो भासमाना रासभादिविवर्ता भवन्ति। सम्प्लवते चेदस्ति[1] तर्हि गकारादिषु भिन्नेष्वप्यभिन्वस्तुनिर्भासा[2] शब्दः शब्द इति प्रख्या लौकिकपरीक्षकारणाम्। तत्किं शब्दत्वमेव वाचकमभिधेयभेदानाम्। तथा च तस्य सर्वस्या[3](र्वत्रा) विशषात्सर्वेऽर्थाः सर्वशब्देभ्यः प्रतीयेरन्। न खलु कारणानियमे कार्यभेदनियमो भवितुमर्हति, तस्याकस्मिकत्वप्रसङ्गात्। [4]गकाराद्याकारभदेविवर्तं [5]शब्दत्वमभिधेयभेदानामभिधायकं, तन्नाति-

---

पदतत्त्वस्य विवर्ताः। एकपदात्मना प्रत्येकमप्रतिभासात्। रासभादेरिव गजादय इति विवर्तपक्षे गकारादयो गोपदात्मना प्रथेरन्, तद्विवर्तत्वात्, मणिकृपाण-दर्पणादिषु मुखवत्। अतस्तदात्मना भासनं निवर्तमानं स्वव्याप्यं विवर्तत्वमपि निवर्तयतीति प्रतिबन्धसिद्धिः। द्वितीयं कल्पं दूषयति–**सम्प्लवते चेत्. . .परीक्षकाणाम्।।** यदि सम्प्लवोऽस्ति तर्ह्येषैव प्रख्या ससम्प्लवा नान्येत्यर्थः। अस्या उभयवादिसिद्धत्वादिति भावः।।

अयञ्च शब्दत्वादेर्वाचकत्वस्योभयवाद्यनभिमतस्यापि शिष्याणां हितकाङ्क्षया दूषणाय प्रस्तावः। सम्प्रति स्फोटवादिनं प्रत्युपहसन्नाह–**तत्किं शब्दत्वमेव वाचकमभिधेयभेदानाम्।** सुगमो ग्रन्थः। न चैतत्त्वयाऽभ्युपगम्यते, स्पष्ट-दोषत्वादित्यभिप्रायेणाह–**तथा च तस्य. . .आकस्मिकत्वप्रसङ्गात्। तथा चेति।।** यदि शब्दत्वमेव वाचकं तदेत्यर्थः। **तस्य**–शब्दत्वस्य, **सर्वत्र**–सर्वेषु शब्देषु; **तस्य**–कार्यभेदनियमस्य; **आकस्मिकत्वं**– निष्कारणत्वम्। अत्र पाश्वस्थश्चोदयति–**गकाराद्याकारभेदविवर्तं. . . तन्नातिप्रसङ्ग इति चेत्।।** गकाराद्यकाराभेदा विवर्ता यस्येति बहुव्रीहिः। एकस्यापि शब्दत्वस्य विवर्तभेदेन

---

१. 'अस्ति हि गकारादिषु' इति मु० पु० पाठः।

२. 'भिन्नेष्वभिन्न' इति मु० पु० पाठः।

३. 'सर्वत्राविशेषात्' इति मु० पु० पाठः।

४. 'गकाराद्याकारविवर्तभेदं शब्दत्वमभिधेयभेदाभिधायकं' इति मु० पु० पाठः।।

५. (शब्दत्वं) –'भेदशब्दमिति २ पु० पाठः। गकाराद्याकारैरारोपितैर्भिद्यमानः शब्दो यत्र तादृशं पदं वाक्यं वेति तस्यार्थः। इति टिप्पणी।।

प्रसङ्ग इति चेत्—न। प्राप्ताप्राप्तविवेकेन गादीनामेवाभिधेयधीहेतुभावात्।[१] अन्यथा सत्त्वगुणत्वादीनामपि तत्प्रसङ्गात्। अत्यल्पमिदम्, अखिलमेव [२]कार्यजातं सत्त्वसामान्यनिर्माणं प्रसज्येत। अपि च, शब्दत्वं चरमविज्ञान इव पूर्वेष्वपि प्रत्ययेषु प्रथत इति नास्ति तिरोहितमिव किञ्चनेति तेभ्योऽप्यर्थप्रत्ययप्रसङ्गः। एतेन वर्णत्वमपि परास्तमभिधेयधीहेतुभावेनेति[३] वेदितव्यम्।

भेदात्कारणभेदनियमे कार्यभेदनियमोप- पत्तिरित्यर्थः। क्वचित्तु—**गकाराद्याकाराविवर्तेनेदं शब्दत्व**मित्येव पाठः। परिहरति—**नेति**।। कारणमाह—**प्राप्ताप्राप्तविवेकेन. . .हेतुभावात्**।। 'तदागमे हि दृश्यते' इति न्यायोऽनेन दर्शित इति वेदितव्यम्। एतमेव हेतुं साधयति—**अन्यथा सत्त्वगुणत्वादीनामपि. . . प्रसज्येत**।। **अन्यथेति**।। प्राप्ताप्राप्तविवेकाभाव इति। तच्छब्देनार्थधेयहेतुभावं परामृशति। आदिशब्देन श्रोत्रग्राह्यतादेरुपादानम्। **इदं**—अन्यथेत्यादिकमुक्तमिति। निर्मीयत इति निर्माणशब्दव्युत्पत्तिः। अथ वा निर्मीयतेऽऽनेनेति व्युत्पत्त्या सत्त्वसामान्यं कारणं यस्येति बहुव्रीहिः। एवं गकारौकारविसर्जनीयात्मकं विवर्तरूपमेव कारणं स्यात् न शब्दत्वमित्युक्तम्। शब्दत्वस्य विवर्तद्वारा कारणत्वेऽनुसंहारबुद्धिप्रतीक्षणेऽपि न कारणं स्यादित्याह—**अपि च शब्दत्वं . . . अर्थप्रत्ययप्रसङ्गः**।। इतिरुभयत्रापि हेतौ। तच्छब्देन पूर्वप्रत्ययपरामर्शः। केचित्तु—शब्दत्वस्य समुद्रघोषादौ व्यभिचाराद्वर्णत्वमेवाभिधेयधीहेतुभावं भजत इत्याहुः। तान्प्रत्याह—**एतेन वर्णत्वमपि. . . वेदितव्यम्**।। तत्रापि साम्यं शब्दत्वोक्तस्य कृत्स्नस्य प्रसङ्गस्येति भावः। एवञ्च सति यत्**प्राभाकरै**र्वर्णानां वाचकत्वं साधयितुं शब्दत्वसामान्यनिराकरणं कृतं तस्मिन्सति तदेव वाचकं स्यादिति मन्यमानैः, तदपि मुधैवेत्याह—**तदिह कृतं. . . निराकरणेन**।।[४] तस्मिन्सत्यप्युक्तेन क्रमेण वर्णानामेव वाचकत्वात्। अपि च निष्प्रमाणकमेव

---

१. 'हेतुत्वात्' इति मु० पु० पाठः।

२. 'कार्यसामान्यजातं' इति मु० पु० पाठः। 'सामान्येति ३ पु० नास्ति' इति टिप्पणी।

३. 'हेतुभावेन वेदितव्यम्' इति मु० पु० पाठः।

४. 'निराकरणेन' इत्यतः परं 'तावदलम्' इत्यधिकं दृश्यते व्याख्यानमातृकायाम्।

तदिह कृतं कृतधियामप्रामाणिकेन शब्दत्वसामान्यनिराकरणेन। न च शब्दत्वमेकं वस्तु सत् गकारादिनानात्वभाविकत्वविरोधि, येन [१]तद्भाविकत्वाय शब्दत्वमपाक्रियते। शाबलेयादिभेदव्यवस्थापनाय गोत्वादिनोऽपि सामान्यस्यापाकरणप्रसङ्गात्। [२]शाबलेयादिषु भिन्नेषु गौरित्येकावभासादशक्यापह्नवमिति चेत्–न। इहापि समानत्वात्। नो[३] खल्वक्षु व्यञ्जनेषु च शब्दः शब्द इत्येकनिर्भासनमतिः[४] नाविरस्ति लौकिकपरीक्षकाणाम्। न चैषा श्रोत्रग्रहणोपाधिर्विनापि[५] शब्दत्वमिति साम्प्रतम्।

तन्निराकरणमित्यर्थः। निष्प्रमाणकत्वमेव स्फोरयति–**न च शब्दत्वमेकं. . .विरोधि।** गकारादीनां नानात्वस्य यद्भाविकत्वं पारमार्थिकत्वं तस्य विरोधीति विग्रहः। विरोधित्वेन किमनिष्टं प्रसज्यते, तदाह–**येन तद्भाविकत्वाय शब्दत्वमपाक्रियते।।** इदमाकूतम्–एकत्वनानात्वयोरेकत्रासमवायादन्यतरत्पारमार्थिकमन्यतरन्मिथ्येत्यापतति। तत्र च 'विप्रतिषिद्धधर्मसमवाये भूयसां स्यात्सधर्मत्वम्'। तत्र च 'विप्रतिषिद्धधर्मसमवाये भूयसां स्यात्सधर्मत्वम्' इति न्यायेन शब्दत्वस्यैकस्य हानेन भूयांसो गकारादयोखखनुगृह्यन्त इति। तच्छब्देन गकारादिनानात्वं परामृश्यते न विरोधीत्यत्र कारणमाह–**शाबलेयादि–भेद. . . प्रसङ्गात्।।** हेतुसाम्यादिति भावः। परस्तु वैषम्यमाशङ्कते–**शाबलेया–दिषु. . . अशक्यापह्नवमिति चेत्।।** गोत्वादिसामान्यमिति सिद्ध्यति। परिहरति–**नेति।।** कारणमाह–**इहापि........समानत्वात्।।** एवमेव दर्शयति–**नो खल्वक्षु. . . लौकिकपरीक्षकाणाम्।।** इहान्यथासिद्धिचोद्यवादिनोऽभिप्रेतं निराकरोति–**न चैषा. . . .इति साम्प्रतम्।।**

अत्रेयमाशङ्का–किं पुनरिदं शब्दत्वं नाम? ननु नेदमपि श्रोत्रग्राह्यत्वाद–

---

१. (भाविकत्वाय)–'गत्वादेर्वस्तुत्वसिद्धये'।

२. 'शाबलेयादिभेदेषु गौर्गौरित्येकाकारावभासादशक्यापह्नवं तदिति चेत्' इति मु० पु० पाठः।

३. 'नो खल्वचि' इति मु० पु० पाठः।। 'अक्ष्विति ३ पु० पाठः' इति टिप्पणी।

४. 'एकनिर्भासः प्रकाशो नास्ति' इति मु० पु० पाठः।

५. 'विनापि शब्दत्वमेकमिति साम्प्रतम्' इति मु० पु० पाठः।

न्यदुपलभ्यतेन। न हि गकारादिष्वेकवणग्रहणे वर्णान्तरावमर्शो भवति पाचकादिष्विव। तस्मात्क्रियाबिन्धनैवेयं शब्दशब्दवाच्यता। यथोक्तं–'श्रोत्रग्रहणे ह्यर्थे लोके शब्दशब्दः प्रसिद्धः' इति। यत्र त्वेकत्र पदार्थेऽनुभूयमाने पूर्वदर्शन-सम्बन्ध्यवमर्शो भवति तत्र सामान्यमिष्यते। यथा शाबलेयमुपलब्धवतो बाहुलेयं पश्यतः पूर्वाकारावमर्शः। एकशब्दवाच्यता त्वेकनिमित्ता न पुनरेकताकृता। न ह्येकसामान्यशब्दवाच्यतया गोत्वादिसामान्यानामितरेतरानुप्रवेशः। यथा च गोत्वेऽप्येकाकारबुद्धिजननोपाधिको भिन्नेष्वप्येकसामान्यशब्दप्रयोगः एवमत्रापि एकेन्द्रियग्रहणोपाधिको नानात्मस्वेव गकारादिष्वेकशब्दशब्दप्रयोगो नो(ग उ)पपद्यत इति। **एषा** मतिः। श्रोत्रग्रहणमुपाधिर्यस्या इति बहुव्रीहिः। एष इति पुल्लिङ्गपाठे अवभास इति विशेष्यं द्रष्टव्यम्। शब्दशब्द इति वा। **न चेति साम्प्रत**मित्यन्वयः। कारणमाह–**तद्ग्रहणानामपि. . .सामर्थ्यात्।।** वर्णवदेव ग्रहणानामपीत्यर्थः। ननु 'श्रोत्रग्रहणे' इतायत्र भाष्ये तद्योग्यत विवक्षिता। यथोक्तशब्दपदानुवृत्तिस्तु श्रोत्रेत्थधीक्रियोपलक्षितयोग्यतात एवेत्यस्तु। **निबन्धने**ऽपि तद्ग्रहणशब्देन योग्यते विवक्षिते इत्यदोषः। तथा च श्रोत्रग्रहणयोग्यतात्मकमेकमिह निमित्तं नास्तीति कथमेकशब्दानुवृत्तिरेक-प्रत्ययजनकत्वं वेत्यर्थः।।

ननु

> 'श्रोत्रधीलक्षिता वर्णाः पञ्चाशदिति गोचराः।
> व्यक्तयश्शब्दशब्दस्य न सामान्यमबोधनात्।।'

इति स्थितिः। यथोक्ततद्योग्यता तु केषाञ्चिदेव तद्धीवेद्यत्वदर्शनात् स्थितेति तद्ग्राह्यवर्णानामानन्त्याभावात्पृथक्पृथगेव योग्यतामवधार्य तदनुसन्धानपूर्वकः शब्दप्रयोगो नानुपपन्न इत्यर्थः। हन्त! एवं बहूनां निमित्तत्वाश्रयणमेव दोष इति।।

ननु जातिवादिनोऽपि तुल्योऽयं दोषः। यथोक्तशब्दत्वजातिमनुजानतापि केचिदेव जात्यन्वयिनो वाच्या इति। जात्युपगमेऽपि तत्समवायप्रयोजकत्वेन तदाश्रयणं दुर्वारमिति तुल्यत्वान्न दोष इत्यर्थः। पुनश्च, ननु तत्समवायप्रयोजक-त्वेऽपि जातिवादिनो न तज्ज्ञानापेक्षा। शब्दप्रयोगानिमित्ततोपगमे तदपेक्षेति विशेष इत्याशङ्क्योक्तम्–ननु जातियोगः केषामिति पृष्टो जात्युपलक्षणेनैव

प्रतिवक्तीति युक्तमिति। जात्युपगमेऽपि गवादिवत्सर्ववर्णानुवृत्ततया स्फुटदृष्ट्य-भावाच्छब्दप्रवृत्त्युन्नेयतया तद्व्युत्पत्तिः प्रत्येकप्रयोगमूलैवोपेयेति साम्यमित्यर्थ इति। अत**स्तद्ग्रहणानां नानात्वे**नेत्ययुक्तमिति।।

अत्र ब्रूमः–युक्तमेवोक्ते, उक्तं हि बहूनां निमित्तताश्रयणमेव दोष इति। यथाहुः–'अन्यायश्चानेकार्थत्वम्' इति। सत्यं स्वारसिकी स्थितिरेषा। अगत्या त्वर्थादिवदनेकार्थत्वमप्यङ्गीक्रियमाणं न दोषमावहति। इह च गतिर्नास्त्येव। यथोक्तं–ककारगकारादावेकधीविरहाच्छब्दत्वजातिरप्युक्तेति चेत्, तन्न। असिद्धत्वात्। तथा हि–यत्तावदुक्तं पूर्वककारावमर्शो गकारादिषु नास्तीति; तत्केनाभिप्रायेण? अस्ति हि तत्रापि व्यावृत्तमनुगतं च रूपं तद्यदि गकारादीनामितरेतरव्यावृत्तः आत्मा नान्यत्र प्रतिसन्धीयत इत्युच्यते तदिष्यत एव। न हि गवादिष्वपि व्यावृत्तात्मप्रतिसन्धानमस्ति। यथा तु तत्र स एवायमित्यनुगतं रूपमाभासते एवमिहापि भावान्तरेभ्यो व्यावृत्तमनुगतं च गकारादिषु रूपमुपलभमाना न सामान्यान्तरवच्छब्दत्वसामान्यापह्नवं कर्तुमुत्सहामहे। एतच्च **नो खल्विति** पूर्वमेवोक्तम्। तस्मात्ककार-गकारादवेकधीविरहादित्यस्य कोऽभिप्रायः? अनुवृत्तस्य व्यावृत्तरूपत्व-भानाभावादिति।। यथोक्तं–

'भेदोत्थप्रतिभासेऽस्ति यद्येकाकारबोधनम्।
तत्र जातिरुपेता स्यान्नैकशब्दप्रयोगतः।।' इति।

तदयुक्तम्। असिद्धेः; गकारादिष्वपि गोशब्दो गकारौकारविसर्जनीयाश्शब्द इति तादात्म्यबोधादुपदेशाच्च। तथाहि–प्रत्येकमकारादिष्वयं शब्दोऽयं शब्द इति समानाधिकरणबोधो दृश्यते इत्यसिद्धं व्यावृत्तरूपत्वाभानमित्यनुसन्धेयम्। यथोक्तं–

'इदङ्क्वोरपर्यायसामानाधिकरण्यतः।
मिथस्तदर्थयोर्वाच्यो भेदाभेदसमुच्चयः।।' इति।

तस्मात्प्रत्यक्षसिद्धत्वाद्गकारादिष्वनुवृत्ताकारस्य शब्दशब्दस्यापि तन्निमित्तत्वोपपत्तौ तस्य निमित्तान्तरकल्पनायां नावकाश इत्यतः स्थितं बहूनां निमित्तत्वाश्रयणमेव दोष इति। ननूक्तं जात्युपगमेऽपि तत्समवाय-प्रयोजकत्वेन तदाश्रयणमिति। सत्यमुक्तम्; अयुक्तन्तु तत्, समवायस्यैवाभावात्

तद्गहणानामपि नानात्वेनैकप्रत्ययसमुत्पादासामर्थ्यात्। [१]श्रोत्रस्य चात्यन्तपरोक्ष तयां [२]तत्प्रतीतेरग्रहे शब्दः शब्द इत्येकावभास-

---

दूरे तत्पश्नप्रतिवचने इति। यथा च समवायस्यैवाभावः तथा वार्तिककारेण वार्तिककारीयैश्च पराक्रान्तम्। अस्माभि; **विभ्रमविवेकव्याख्यायां** तदुक्तसंक्षेपो दर्शित इति न प्रकम्यते। किञ्च, गोत्वादिष्वपि जातियोगः केषामिति पृष्टे येन प्रकारेणोत्तरं दीयते तेनैवात्रापि। यदि ह्येवमेव तत्रापि, तर्हि तवानेकनिमित्तता सर्वजातिसमाना कुतो हेतोरत्र दूषणतयोपन्यसितव्या। अथोच्येत गवादौ जात्युपलक्षणेनैव प्रतिवक्तीति युक्तम्। गोत्वादेर्निजव्यक्त्यनुवृत्ततया स्फुट-दर्शनात्। इह तु सर्ववर्णानुवृत्ततया स्फुटदृष्ट्यभावाच्छब्दप्रवृत्त्युन्नेयतया तद्व्युत्पत्तिः प्रत्येकप्रयोगमूलैवोपेयेति विशेष इति। अत्र ब्रूमः–अयमपि विशेषो नास्ति। यतो गोत्वादिवच्छब्दत्वेऽपि स्फुटमेव दर्शनमिति। यथोक्तम्–

> 'अल्पीयसापि यत्नेन शब्दमुच्चरितं मतिः।
> यदि वा नैव गृह्णाति वर्णं वा सकलं स्फुटम्।।' इति।

अतस्सूक्तं तद्ग्रहणानामपीति। हेत्वन्तरमाह–**श्रोत्रस्य चात्यन्तपरोक्षतया. . . .प्रकाशानुपपत्तेः।।** इदमाकूतम्–अस्ति तावच्छब्दः शब्द इत्यपरोक्षावभास इत्युक्तम्। अस्य च तावदपरोक्षो विषय इत्यङ्गीकरणीयम्। स च श्रोत्रग्राह्यता चेत्कथं श्रोत्रस्य नित्यानुमेयत्वे तद्ग्रहणं तद्ग्राह्याता वाऽपरोक्षज्ञानविषयता-मश्नुवीत। न च ग्रहणं तद्योग्यता (वा) प्रत्यक्षं, ग्रहणस्यानुमेयत्वात् स्वयंप्रकाशत्वाद्वा । योग्यतायाश्च शक्त्यात्मकत्वेनार्थपत्तिप्रमेयत्वात्। न च प्राकट्यं त्वयाभ्युपगम्यते, येन तदेव विषय इत्युच्येतेति। कुतः पुनस्तद्गृहीतेरग्रहे तादृक्प्रत्ययानुपपत्तिरत आह–**अगृहीतस्योपाधेरुपहितप्रत्ययाधानासहत्वात्।।** न हि रागमनवगम्य रक्तता ज्ञातुं शक्यत इति भावः। बुद्धेरप्यपलापे उपेक्षैवोत्तरमिति वेदितव्यम्।।

प्रामाणिकाश्चाहुः–'श्रोत्रग्राह्यतापि च शब्दत्वगुणत्ववर्णत्वातिव्यापिनी न

---

१. 'श्रोत्रग्राह्यत्वोपाधेश्च' इति मु० पु० पाठः। 'श्रोत्रस्य चेति ३ पु० पाठः इति टिप्पणी।।

२. 'तद्गृहीतिविरेह शब्दः शब्द इत्येकनिर्भासप्रकाशानुपपत्तेः' इति मु० पु० पाठः।

प्रकाशानुपपत्तेः। अगृहीतस्योपाधेरुपाहितप्रत्ययाधानासहत्वात्।[1] **न च गकारादिष्वनुस्यूतमश्वादिपदव्यावृत्तमेकैकवर्णावगाहिनीषु प्रख्यासु तिरोहितमिव प्रथते ।** [2]**किं न प्रथते यदा विशदपदावभासिनि गौरित्येकं पदमिति चरमे चेतसि चकास्ति पूर्वोपलभ्य-**

शब्दत्वलक्षणम्। तथा हि–न शब्दत्वसमवायिनः सत्त्वादयो न श्रोत्रावसेयाः। न च श्रोत्रेणैवेत्यवधारणं, वर्णानां मनसाप्यवधारणात्। वर्णत्वे च प्रसङ्गानतिवृत्तेः। न च सत्त्ववर्णत्वाद्यपह्नवः साधुः, सर्वसामान्यापह्नवापातात्। न हि सामान्य-विशेषान्तरपरिकल्पनेपि निबन्धनमस्त्यन्यत् अतोऽनुवृत्तव्यावृत्तावभासिनः प्रख्यानात्' इति। ननु सम्प्लवत एव। न खल्वेता गादिबुद्धयो गकारादि-मात्रनिर्भासाः, किन्तर्हि गकाराद्याकारं किञ्चिदनाकारं आसु सम्प्लवते। न च तच्छब्दत्वमेव, उक्तदोषात्। अपि तर्हि स्फोटात्मैव। स च न शब्दत्ववत्सर्वसाधारणः। अश्वादिभ्यो व्यावृत्तो गकारादिष्वेवानुवृत्त इति। मुखस्येव मणिकृपाणदर्पणादिषुदा तस्य विवर्ता गकारादय इत्युपपन्नमित्यत्राह–**न च गकारादिषु. . . .प्रथते।।** न प्रथते इत्येतदसहमानश्चोदयति–**किं न प्रथते यदा . . . .चकास्ति।।** पूर्वोपलभ्यभागप्रतिसन्धानवति यदैवं भूते ज्ञाने चकास्ति तदा किं न प्रथत इति योजना। **तिरोहितमिवे**त्यस्य संवादाय **विशदपदावभासिनी**त्युक्तम्। गकारादिष्वनुस्यूतमिति दर्शयतोक्तं–**पूर्वोपलभ्य-भागप्रतिसन्धानवतीति।।** वर्णसमूहमात्रावलम्बनाय पदप्रख्येति चेत्तत्राह–**न चास्यैते भागा इत्यायुष्मतैवोपपादितम्।।** इदमाकूतम्–उक्तं हि–**'तस्मात् स्वसिद्धान्त-व्यामोहमपदायाभ्युपेयतामनु- संहारबुद्धेरेकपदवाक्यागोरचता'** इति। न च स्फोटात्मनो भागा वर्णा इति साम्प्रतम्। 'न तावत्पूर्वः कल्पः; अवय-विन्यूनपरिमाणत्वादवयवानाम्' इत्यादिना भवतैव साधितत्वादिति। एवन्तर्हि वर्णोपरागवती पदप्रख्या किन्निबन्धनेति चेत्तत्राह–**अतस्तद्विवर्ताः।।** वर्णा इत्यधिकारात्सिद्ध्यति। एवञ्च 'गकारादिष्वनुस्यूतमश्वादिपदव्यावृत्त-

१. 'प्रत्ययाधानासामर्थ्यात्' इति मु० पु० पाठः।

२. 'कथं न प्रथते यदा विशदपदावगाहिनि गौरित्येकं पदमिति चरमे चेतसि पूर्वोपलब्धभागप्रतिसन्धानमस्ति' इति मु० पु० पाठः।

भागप्रतिसन्धानवतीति । न चास्यैते भागा इत्यायुष्मतैवोपपादितम्। अतस्तद्विवर्ता:।।

तथा च तदेव तेन तेनापरमार्थसता गकाराद्याकारेण प्रतिभासत इति प्रमाणमार्गागतम्।

तत्किमिदानीमनुसंहारबुद्धिप्रतिसन्धानापेक्षाः प्राञ्चः प्रत्यया यथास्वं गकाराद्यनुविद्धमेकमवभासयन्ति? ओमिति चेत्—न।[1] तत्र तत्र चरमविज्ञानसमये प्राचां प्रत्ययानामतिवृत्तवां[2] तत्काले

मेकैकवर्णावगाहिनीषु प्रख्यासु तिरोहितमिव प्रथते' इत्येतत्सिद्धमित्याह **तथा च तदेव. . .प्रमाणमार्गागतम्।।** प्रमाणमार्गेणागतमिति विग्रहः। नान्या गतिरस्तीति भावः। एष च पूर्वोक्तसङ्क्षेप इति द्रष्टव्यम्।।

अत्र परिहराय प्रक्रम्यते। ननु **'यदा विशपददावभासिनी'**त्यत्र चरमस्य चेतसो भवतां प्राक्प्रत्ययेष्वेकानुव्याधं प्रति कारणत्वमभिमतं, ज्ञापकत्वं, वा; कारणत्वञ्चोपकार्यत्वं अभिमतं, उपकारकत्वं वा। तत्रोपकारकत्व-मुत्थापयन्नाह—**तत्किमिदानीं. . . अवभासयन्ति।।** अनुसंहारबुद्धिं प्रतिसन्धायाभिवीक्ष्येत्यर्थः। एतदेवाङ्गीकारयन्नाह—**ओमिति चेत्।।** दूषयति—**नेति।।** कारणमाह—**तत्र तत्र . . . बतापतितम्।।** यदि स्वकाले सतां प्राचां प्रत्ययानामुपकार्यत्वं तदा चरमस्य चेतसोऽनागतत्वेनासत्त्वादसन्तः पदार्था उपकुर्वन्तीत्यङ्गीकृतम्। अथ स्वकाले सदेव चरमं चेत उपकरोति तदा प्राचां प्रत्ययानामतिवृत्तत्वादसतोऽपि वस्तुन उपकार्यत्वमस्तीत्यङ्गी-कर्तव्यमिति कष्टमस्यापन्नमिति। अत्रैव दूषणान्तरमाह—**अपि च जन्मात्रव्यापारत्वेन. . .विरम्य व्यापारायोगः।।** ततः किमित्याह—**तद्विपरीतं चाप्युपेतम्।।** परमार्थतः सतामेवोपकार्यत्वादसतश्च तदभावात्सत एव

---

१. 'ओमिति चेत् हन्त तत्र तत्र' इति मु० पु० पाठः।

२. (तत्काले)—'आद्यवर्णज्ञानकाले। चरमनादाभिव्यञ्जनीयस्य स्फोटस्याद्य वर्णप्रत्यक्ष-कालेऽसत्वादसत उपकार्यत्वं चरमवर्णकाले चाद्यानां नाशादसत उपकारकत्वं चापद्यत इत्यर्थः।' इति टिप्पणी।

चरमस्य चेतसोऽनु[१]वृत्तत्वादुपकुर्वन्त्यसन्तो वा सतोऽसतो वेति बतापतितम्। अपि च जन्ममात्रव्यापारत्वेन विज्ञानस्य [२]जातस्य जन्माभावेन विरम्यव्यापारायोगः, तद्विपरीतं [३]चाभ्युपेतम्।।[४]

[५]अनपेक्षाश्च प्राञ्चः प्रत्ययाः स्तम्भकुम्भाम्भोरुहाद्यवगाहिन इवाभिन्नानुव्याधविरहिताः[६] स्वानुभवाद्भासमानाः न परस्परं

वोपकारकत्वाच्चरमज्ञानसमये विरतव्यापाराणमपि प्राचामुपकारग्रहणाय पुनर्व्यापारोऽ-स्तीत्यभ्युपगन्तव्यत्वात्। तस्य विरम्यव्यापाराभावस्य विपरीतं वैपरीत्यं वस्तु वोऽभ्युपेतमेवेत्यक्षरम्(रार्थः)। अथ वा 'तद्विपरीत'मिति पदद्वयम्। तच्छब्देना-योगस्य सामान्यविवक्षया निर्देशः। अस्मिन्नेव कल्पे दूषणान्तरमाह–**अनपेक्षाश्च. . . सम्भिन्दन्ति।।** पदमार्थतोऽनुसंहारबुद्धिप्रति-सन्धानानपेक्षा इत्यर्थः। **न परस्परं सम्भिन्दन्ति** मेलयन्तीति। एतच्च सर्वं स्वसंवेद्यमित्युक्तम्। **स्वानुभवाद्भासमाना** इति। चरमस्य चेतसः उपकार्यत्वमप्यनेनैव निराकार्यमिति। तत्रापि व्याख्यायते–**अनुसंहारबुद्धि-प्रतिसन्धानापेक्षा** इति। अनुसंहारबुद्धौ निजविषयाणां वर्णानां प्रतिसन्धानं तदपेक्षमाणाः कामयमाना इत्यर्थः। **यथास्वं ये गकारादयः तैरनुविद्धमेकं** पदतत्त्वं प्रत्येक**मवभासयन्ती**ति। अनुसंहार्या-भावेऽनुसंहाराभावादिति भावः। अत्र **चोपकुर्वन्त्यसन्तो वा सतो** वेत्यत्र यथाक्रमं हेत्वोरन्वयः। **अपि चे**त्यादिकञ्च समञ्जसम्। **जन्ममात्रव्यापारत्वेने**ति। यथोक्तं–

---

१. 'अनागतत्वादुपकरोति असतामसन्निति चैवमापतितम्' इति मु० पु० पाठः।

२. 'ज्ञातस्य' इति ३ पु० पाठ इति टिप्पणी।।

३. (अभ्युपेतं)–'ज्ञानानामुत्पत्त्यैवार्थप्रकाशकतृतीयक्षणे नाशाच्च प्रथमवर्णज्ञानस्या-स्फटपदत्वाभिव्यञ्जकत्वं चरमवर्णज्ञानसाचिव्येन तस्यैव स्फुटाभिव्यञ्जकत्वमिति न युक्तमिति भावः।' इति टिप्पणी।।

४. 'स्यात्' इत्यधिक दृश्यते मु० पुस्तके।

५. (अनपेक्षाः)–'अनुसंहारबुद्धिप्रतिसन्धाननिरपेक्षाः। समुदायबुद्ध्यसहकृता इति यावत्।' इति टिप्पणी।।

६. 'विरहिणः' इति मु० पु० पाठः।

स्वगोचर [१]सम्भिन्दन्ति।[२] नाप्यननुभाविकः प्रत्ययेष्वेकानुव्याधः शक्यानुमानः, नरविषाणवदनुपलब्धि विरोधात्।।

तथा च परस्परव्यावृत्तवर्णमात्रगोचरा अनुभूतयो भावनोपजननद्वारा नाना वा एकं वा स्मृतिप्रत्ययं स्वगोचर एवादिध

'तेन जन्मैव विषयं(?)बुद्धेर्व्यापार इष्यते।' इति।

जातस्य जन्माभावेनेति। जननानन्तरमस्त्विान्वयात्सतश्चासत्वेनोत्पत्तिप्राक्कालीने सम्बन्धाभावादिति। अथ वा–जनिक्रियायाः स्वफलस्य तस्मिन्ननाधेयत्वेन तत्रासमवायादिति। **अनपेक्षाश्चेति।** अनुसंहारबुद्धौ प्रतिसन्धानमकामयमाना इत्यर्थः। ज्ञापकत्वमपि पराणुदन्नाह–**नाप्यननुभाविकः . . . अनुपलब्धिविरोधात् इति।।** यदा विशदपदावभासिनीत्येवं वदता किमनुसंहारबुद्धिप्रतिसन्धानापेक्षास्तेन मिश्रीभूयैकमवभासयन्तीत्यङ्गीक्रियते आहोस्विदनपेक्षाः पृथगवस्थित्येति विकल्पः; यथास्वं गकाराद्यनुविद्धमेकमव-भासयन्ति। यदानुसंहारबुद्धिरेकमवभासयति तदा स्वगोचरैर्भावैः तं विशिष्टतया बोधयन्तीत्यर्थः। द्वितीयं शिरो दूषयति–**अनपेक्षाश्चेति।।** पृथगेव स्थिता इत्यर्थः।।

ननु पृथगेव प्राञ्चः प्रत्यया यथास्वं गकाराद्यनुविद्धपदतत्त्वमवभासयन्ति अनुसंहारबुद्धौ गकाराद्यनुविद्धपदावभासनात् यथा धवखदिराशोकचम्पका वृक्षा इति पश्चादनुसंहारबुद्धिर्धवोऽयं खदिरोऽयं इत्यादिधवादिविशिष्टवृक्षावगमपूर्विकेति; तत्राह–**नापीति।।** अनुपलब्धिविरोधश्च मीमांसकमते पक्षदूषणं, नैयायिकमते कालात्ययापदिष्टाख्यो हेत्वाभास इति। दूषणान्तरानुपन्यासस्तु निष्फलत्वात्। न ह्यनुसंहारबुद्धीनामपि चम्पकाशोकपुन्नागा वनमित्यत्र चम्पकानुविद्धवनविषयत्वमिति व्यभिचार इति।।

एवन्तावत्पूर्वबुद्धीनां निरूपणम्। सम्प्रत्युत्तरबुद्धीनां निरूपणमुपक्रमते–

---

१. (न भिन्दन्ति) –'न व्यावर्तयन्ति। तथा च गोगवयगोतादिप्रत्ययेष्वाद्यप्रत्ययैरस्फुटत्वेनेष्टा अपि परस्परव्यावृत्तरूपगवादिपदस्फोटाभिव्यक्तयोऽनुपपन्ना इति भावः।' इति टिप्पणी।

२. 'भिन्दन्ति' इति मु० पु० पाठः।

(वाधि) त्सन्ति, नान्यगोचरे नाप्यगोचर इत्य [१]नुसंहारबुद्धिरपि परस्परव्या वृत्तवर्णमात्र[२](र्णत्रि)तयावगाहिनी, न तु वर्णा-नुव्याधवदेकपदगोचरेत्यनुभवमार्गायातम्। [३]कथमायातम्? यथा- गौरित्येकमिदं पदमित्येकपदावभासिनी धीरस्ति लौकिक-परीक्षकाणाम्। न चेयमनालम्बना, नापि वर्णालम्बना; तेषां

तथा च परस्परव्यावृत्त. . . अनुभवमार्गायातम्॥ वर्णमात्रेति पदतत्त्वस्यैक-स्यानुस्यूतिं व्यवच्छिनत्ति। **भावनोपजननद्वारा** न तु साक्षादेव पूर्ववदनु-संहारबुद्धिप्रतिसन्धानापेक्षेति। **नाना वा एकं वे**ति। तत्र तत्रानपेक्षाणां कारणत्वेऽपि मिलितानामपीत्युक्तत्वात्। **स्मृतिप्रत्ययम्।** नानुभवमिति। **स्वगोचर एवे**त्युक्त्वा (क्त्या) स्वपद व्यावर्त्यं **नान्ये**ति, गोचरपदव्यावर्त्त्यं **नापी**ति दर्शितवा-नित्यनुसन्धेयम्। **अनुसंहारबुद्धिरपी**त्यापिशब्देन पूर्वबुद्धिवदिति दर्शयति। **परस्परव्यावृत्ते**त्यस्य **वर्णानुव्या**धादिति, **वर्ण(त्रि)तये**त्यस्यै**कपदे**ति व्यावर्त्त्यमित्यपि द्रष्टव्यम्। **अनुभवमार्गायातम्**—अनुभवमार्गादायातम्। एव-मुत्तरबुद्धिनिरूपणेऽपि वर्णा एव पदमित्युक्तम्। तदेतदसहमानश्चोदयति-- **कथमायातम्? यथा. . .तेषां नानात्वात्॥** यथा(दा) धीरस्ति तदा कथं ह्यनुभवमार्गायातमिति योजना। न चेयमनालम्बना, विज्ञानवादे सालम्बनत्वस्य स्थितत्वात्। **नानात्वात्**—एकविषयबुद्धिग्राह्यत्वायोगात्। एकत्वनानात्वयो-र्विरोधादिति भावः। तदुक्तं–'कथं प्रत्यक्षवेद्यता स्फोटात्मनः? [४]वर्णविज्ञान-विलक्षणस्य पश्चद्गौरिति विज्ञानस्य निरालम्बनत्वायोगात्। न ताव(त) द्वर्णालम्बनम्, तद्बुद्धिविलक्षणत्वात्। तस्मादर्थान्तरमेवालम्बितुमर्हति। ननु अस्तीदं पश्चादेकैकवर्णविज्ञानविलक्षणविज्ञानं, न तु तदर्थान्तरावलम्बनम्। वर्णरूपानुविद्धत्वाद्रूपान्तरा(न)वभासनाच्च। तथा हि–त एव वर्णात्मानः पुरः

---

१. (अनुसंहारबुद्धिरपि)–'समुदायात्मकदस्वरूपज्ञानमपि' इति टिप्पणी।

२. 'व्यावृत्तवर्णरूपावगाहिनी एकगोचरेत्यनुभवमार्गागतम्' इति मु० पु० पाठः।

३. 'कथं गौरित्येकं पदमित्येकपदावभासिनी' इति मु० पु० पाठः।

४. 'वर्णविज्ञानाविलक्षणस्य पश्चाद्गौरिति विलक्षणस्य विज्ञानस्य' इति मातृकाग्रन्थपाठः।

नानात्वात्। न च सेनावनवत्[१] औपाधिकी। उपाधिः खल्वेक-विज्ञानविषयता वा भवेदेकाभिधेयप्रत्ययहेतुता वा। न तावत्पूर्वः पक्षः। [२]अप्रतीतोपाधेरुपहितप्रत्ययायोगात्। स्वसंवेदनं संवेदन-मनिच्छतामनुसंहारबुद्धा [३]स्वरूपाग्रहणात्तदेकत्वाग्रहात्तदु-पाध्येकपदप्रतिभासानुपपत्तिः। उत्तरस्मिन्नपि पक्षे परस्पराश्रय-प्रसक्तिर्दुर्वारा। न खल्वविदितपदरूपावधिरर्थमवैति। अवध्यन्तर-परिग्रहे तत्त्वेऽपि वर्णानां [४]तदर्थभेदानध्यवसायात्। तत्रार्थप्रति-

---

परिगतपरिच्छेदाः तत्राप्यवभासन्ते न तु रूपान्तरम्। अर्थान्तरविषयत्वे तु यथा वर्णविज्ञानानि परस्परविषयरूपप्रत्यवमर्शशून्यानि प्रकाशमानरूपान्तराणि प्रकाशन्ते तथेदमपि स्यात्। वैलक्षण्यन्तु पूर्वोपलब्धीना मेकैकवर्णगोचरत्वादस्य च समुच्चितविषयत्वादिति नार्थान्तरविषयत्वं वैलक्षण्यमात्रात्सिद्ध्यति। यदि चैकैकस्मात्त्रयमर्थान्तरम्, अस्तु प्रत्ययस्य विषयः न तु तदतिरिक्तः कश्चिच्छब्दार्थः (ब्दात्मा), वर्णपरित्यागेन बुद्धावप्रतिभासनात्। अथ मतं–गौरित्येकं विज्ञानं; को वाहान्यथा? ज्ञेयन्तु नैकम्। ज्ञेये तु तद्ग्राह्यतयैकार्थकारितया वैकत्वभ्रमः एकत्वोपचारो वा वनादिवत्' (इति)। अत्राह–**न च सेनावनवदौपाधिकी।।** अयमर्थः। यथा खलु भिन्नेष्वेव हस्त्यश्वरथपादातेष्वेककार्यकारितया सेनेयमेकेति, यथा वा धवखदिरादिषु नानाभूतेषु वनमिदमेकमिति धीरौपाधिकी, नैवमेकमिदं पदमिति धीरौपाधिकी। वनेऽपि, 'यद्वैककार्यहेतुत्वादेकं गोशब्दवद्वनम्' इत्यादा-वुक्त उपाधिरनुसन्धातव्यः। उपाध्य(सं)भवादिति भावः। प्रत्येकासम्भव-

---

१. 'नापि सेनावनादिवत्' इति मु० पु० पाठः।

२. 'अप्रतीतोपाधेः' किन्तु व्यपदेशमात्रम्' इति प्रयन्तं मुद्रितपुस्तकपाठो दीयते। व्याख्याने ग्रन्थपातात्।

३. (स्वरूपाग्रहणात्)–'ज्ञानेन स्वस्याविषयीकरणात्तस्यानुव्यवसायग्राह्यत्वात् ज्ञाततालिङ्गानुमेयत्वाद्वेति भावः।' इति टिप्पणी।

४. (तदर्थभेदानध्यवसायात्)–'पदत्वमनपेक्ष्य समुदायत्वादिधर्मान्तरपुरस्कारेण पदज्ञानेऽपि अर्थानां व्यावृत्तानामनुस्थितेः। सामान्यतः पदत्वज्ञानेनार्थवेनार्थेपस्थितिः स्यादपीति भावः।' इति टिप्पणी।।

पत्त्या पदरूपाविशेषमुपकल्पयतो दुरुत्तरमितरेतराश्रयं प्रसज्येत। न चैकार्थसम्बन्धाख्यानमेकपदत्वमापादयति। वर्णानामनाश्रितपदरूपाणामप्रत्ययाकत्वेनासम्बद्धानां [१]सम्बद्धाख्यानानुपपत्तेः। सम्बन्धाख्यानात्तु पदभावे तदेवेतरेतराश्रयत्वमापद्यते। पदत्वाद्धि सम्बन्धित्वे सत्याख्यानमाख्यानाच्च पदत्वे सति सम्बन्धितेति। व्यवस्थितं हि वाचकत्वमाख्यायते। अपि च एकावभासस्य प्रत्ययस्यौपाधिकत्वमिच्छतो न किञ्चिदेकं भवेत् सर्वत्रैव कथञ्चित्कस्यचिदुपाधेः सम्भवात्। तथा च नानापि न स्यात् एकसमाहारात्मकत्वान्नानात्वस्य।।

अत्र ब्रूमहे–न वयमेकावभासप्रत्ययमेकवस्तुव्यवस्थितौ प्रमाणयामः; किन्तु व्यपदेशमात्रम्। भवति हि [२]करितुरगरथपदातिषु चम्पकाशोककिंशुकादिषु च नानात्वेऽपि कञ्चिदुपाधि-

---

प्रतिपादनायोपाधिं विकल्पयति–**उपाधिः खलु. . .प्रत्ययहेतुता वा।।** भवेदिति सम्बद्ध्यते। तत्राद्यं शिरो दूषयति–न **तावत्पूर्वः कल्पः।।** कारणमाह–**अप्रतीतोपा([३]धेः उपहितप्रत्ययायोगात्). .** .नाद्रियामहे इत्येतदेव व्याचष्टे–**भवति हि . . .लौकिकानां सेनेति वनमिति च।।** एवं व्यपदेशमात्रमित्येतद्व्याख्यातम्। नाद्रियामहे इत्येतदपि प्रामाणिकं दर्शयन्नाह–**न च तत्सेना. . .प्रसिद्ध्यति।। तदेकोऽवयवी प्रसिद्ध्यतीत्यन्वयः।** तदित्यस्य व्याख्यानं–**सेना वनं वेति।** एतदेव प्रकृते उपयोजयन्नाह–**तथैव गकारादयोऽपि. . .भवितुमर्हन्ति।। 'तत्किमिदानीमनुसंहारबुद्धी'** त्यत्र **'परस्पर-**

---

१. 'असम्बन्धानां सम्बन्धाख्यानानुपपत्तेरिति ३ पु० पाठः।।' इति टिप्पणी।

२. 'करितुगादिष्वश्वत्थचम्पकाशोकखदिरधवकिंशुकादिषु नानात्वेऽपि कथञ्चिदेकमुपाधिमाश्रित्य सेना वनमिति व्यपदेशमात्रं लौकिकानाम्।' इति मु० पु० पाठः। 'अश्वत्थेति ३ पु० नास्ति' इति टिप्पणी।

३. अत्र मातृकाग्रन्थे पत्रचतुष्कपरिमितग्रन्थपातः।

माश्रित्य व्यपदेशो लौकिकानां सेनेति वनमिति च।[1] न च तत्सेना वनं वा करिचम्पकाद्यनेकसमवाय्येकोऽवयवी प्रसिद्धयति। तथैव गकारादयोऽपि पूर्वोपलब्धिविपरिवर्तिनो रूपादन्यूनाधिका[2] [3]एकस्यामेव स्मृतौ प्रथमानाः सत्यपि पदमिति व्यपदेशाभेदे नैकानुव्याधवन्तो भवितुमर्हन्ति। उपाधिविरहात् एकानुव्याधमुपकल्पयति[4] व्यपदेशभेद इति चेत्–न; इतरेतराश्रयापत्तेः। एकानुव्याधवती हि प्रख्या तादृशव्यप–

व्यावृत्तवर्णमात्रगोचरा अनुभूतयः' इत्यन्तस्य 'पूर्वोपलब्धिविपरिवर्तिनो रूपादन्यूनाधिका' इति संग्रहः। **'भावनोपजननद्वारा'** इत्यादेः **'नाप्यगोचरे'** इत्यन्तस्य **'एकस्यां'** इत्यादि **'व्यपदेशाभेदे'** इत्यन्तं शेषस्य च शेषः सङ्क्षेप इति द्रष्टव्यम्। अत्र चोदयति–**उपाधिविरहात्. . .** इति चेत्।। एतच्च **'कथमायातं'** इत्यादेश्चोद्यस्य सङ्क्षेपः। परिहरति–**नेति।।** कारणमाह– **इतरेतराश्रयापत्तेः।।** एतदेव व्याचष्टे–**एकानुव्याधवती हि प्रख्या. . . अन्योन्याश्रयमावहति।।** इतरेतराश्रयापत्तेरित्यत्राशङ्का, कथं इतरेतराश्रयापत्तेः। न हि व्यपदेशं प्रत्यक्षतो गृहीत्वा तन्मूलभूतामेकानुव्याधवर्ती प्रख्यातो(ख्यां ततो)ऽनुमित्सतां अन्योन्याश्रयसम्भव इति, सानेन निवार्यते। मा भूदनुमानमि(मान इ)तरेतराश्रयं, उत्पत्तौ तु भविष्यति। तथा हि–वक्तृणामेव तावदसिद्धा बुद्धिर्न व्यपदेशोत्पादिनी, सिद्धिश्च ज्ञानमेव, स्वयम्प्रकाशत्वाभ्युपगमात्। स्वयम्प्रकाशवादिनो हि ज्ञातैव बुद्धिः स्वकार्यक्षमेति मन्यन्ते। न च पूर्वासु बुद्धिष्वकानुव्याधोऽस्तीत्युक्तं, अनुपलब्धिनिरस्तत्वात्। ततश्च व्यवदेशादेव बुद्धिसिद्धिः, अन्यस्य प्रकारस्याभावात्। तदपेक्षा च व्यपदेशोत्पत्तिरि(ती)तरेतराश्रयमिति। एतच्च **व्यपदेशोत्पादिनीत्यनेन** सूचितमिति वेदितव्यम्। अथवा–एकमिदं पदमिति व्यपदेशस्यैकानुव्याधोप–

---

१. 'न चैतावता सेना वनं वा करिचम्पकाद्यवयवसमवाय्येकमवयवि प्रसिद्धयति।' इति मु० पु० पाठः।

२. 'अन्यूनानधिकाः' इति मु० पु० पाठः।

३. 'एकस्यां स्मृतौ' इति मु० पु० पाठः।

४. 'उपकल्पयति व्यपदेश' इति मु० पु० पाठः।

देशोत्पादिनी, [१]बुद्धिनिबन्धनत्वाद्व्यपदेशस्य। ततस्तु तामर्थयमानो [२]व्यक्तमन्योन्याश्रयमावहति।।

कल्पकत्वं केवलस्य वोपाधिविरहसहितस्य वा। उपाधिविरहश्चोध्यसम्भवादेकानुव्याधवत्त्वाद्वा। यद्येकानुव्याधवत्त्वादित्युच्यते तत इतरेतराश्रयः। एकानुव्याधवत्त्वज्ञानादुपाधिविरहवद्व्यपदेशोत्पत्तिविज्ञानं, सामान्यतो बुद्धिनिबन्धनत्वाद्व्यपदेशस्य। तद्विशेषस्यापि तद्विशेषनिबन्धनत्वात्तादृशेनोपाधि विरहवव्द्यपदेशाच्च तादृशीं बुद्धिमनुमिमानोऽन्योन्याश्रयमाविशतीति। उपाध्यसम्भवस्तु नास्त्येवेति वक्ष्यते। न च केवलस्याङ्गीकृतम्। उपाधिविरहादित्युक्तत्वात्। न च सम्भवति, सेनावनादौ व्यभिचारादिति। अथवा अन्या व्याख्या–एवं पूर्वासु बुद्धिषु एकानुव्याधवत्त्वं उत्तरबुद्धिगतव्यपदेशादिति कृत्वा व्याख्यातम्। सम्प्रत्युत्तरास्वेव तदनुमीयते इत्यत्र व्याख्यायते। एकस्यामेव स्मृतौ प्रथमाना नैकानुव्याधवन्त इत्युक्तम्। तत्र चोद्यं–व्यपदेशो ह्येकविषयोऽयं भ्रान्तिमूलो वा स्यात्, अभ्रान्तत्वेऽप्यौपाधिको वा स्याद्वनादिवत्, एकानुव्याधवान्वा जात्यादिवत्। तत्र भ्रान्तिमूलत्वं तावन्निर्निबन्धनत्वादनाशङ्कनीयमेव। उपाधिश्च न कश्चिद्रूप्यत इत्युक्तम्। अतः परिशेषादयं व्यपदेश एव स्वस्मिन्नेकानुव्याधमापादयतीति। उपकल्पयन्तीति बहुवचनदर्शने गकारादय इत्यनुषज्यते। व्यपदेश इतीत्यत्र सप्तम्यन्तपरिच्छेद इति योज्यम्। सर्वथायमेकानुव्याधवान्व्यपदेशो जायत इत्यर्थः। अत्रोत्तरं–बुद्धिनिबन्धनो व्यवपदेशभेद इत्यविवादम्। ततश्च गौरित्येकं पदमिति व्यपदेशोत्पत्तिरेकपदानुभवनिबन्धना स्यात्, एकानुभवोत्पत्तिश्च व्यपदेशोत्पत्त्यधीनेतीतरेतराश्रयं स्यात्। **व्यक्त**मिति। नेतरेतराश्रयप्रकारोऽत्र पृथगेव दर्शयितव्य इति भावः। अथवा–दुरुत्तरमिति भावः। एकानुव्याधवत्त्वं च व्यपदेशस्य कार्यतया वा स्यात् समकालतया वा। सर्वथाऽनुपलब्धिनिरस्तत्वान्नानुमातुं शक्यमिति पूर्वमेवोक्तमिति कृत्वेतरेतराश्रयमात्रमुक्तमिति द्रष्टव्यम्।।

---

१. (बुद्धिनिबन्धनत्वात्)–'बुद्धिनिमित्तत्वादिति ३ पु० पाठः' इति टिप्पणी।

२. 'व्यक्तमितरेतराश्रयत्वमाविशति' इति मु० पु० पाठः।। 'इतरेतराश्रयमिति ३ पु० पाठः' इति टिप्पणी।

न चात्रोपाधिविरहोऽपि। अस्ति खल्वेकाभिधेय[१] धीहेतु (भाव)स्त्रयाणामपि वर्णानामेकस्मरणसमारोहिणां ग्राव्णा मिवैकपिठरधारणे, यस्मात् पदमिति व्यपदेशः।[२] न चैवमन्योन्यायश्रयम्। न हि पदावधारणाधीनः सम्बन्धबोधः, किन्तु तदधीनं

अथवा–मा भूच्छ्रोत्रप्रत्यक्षेणैकानुव्याधवती प्रख्या व्यपदेश एव स्वयमौपाधिककत्वसम्भवात्तादृशीमेकानुव्याधवतीं प्रख्यां भावयिष्यति, किं श्रोत्रेणेति चेत्–न। अन्योन्याश्रयात्। बुद्धिनिबन्धनो हि व्यपदेशः, पौरुषेयेषु तथा दर्शनात्; तत्रैकानुव्याधवत्या प्रख्यया व्यपदेशोत्पत्तिः तया च सेतीतरेतराश्रयमपरिहार्यमिति। एवमभ्युपेत्योपाधिविरहं उक्तम्। परमार्थतस्तु सोऽपि नास्त्येवेति दर्शयन्नाह–**न चात्रोपाधाधिविरहोऽपि।।** अनेन च **'न च सेनावनवदौपाधिकं(की)'** इत्यादेः परिहारप्रक्रम इति वेदितव्यम्। कारणमाह–**अस्ति खल्वेकाभिधेयधीहेतुः . . .व्यपदेशः।।** अनेन चैकार्थतादूषणदुद्धर्तुमुपक्षिप्तेति वेदितव्यम्। उद्धरति–**न चैवमन्योन्याश्रयम्।।** अत्र कारणं प्रसक्ति हेतुविपर्ययं दर्शयन्नाह–**न हि पदावधारणाधीनः. . . पदज्ञानम्।।** तच्छब्देन सम्बन्धबोधं परामृशति। अनेन च **'न चैकार्थसम्बन्धाख्यानमेकपदतामापादयती'** त्यस्य प्रतिप्रसवः कृत इत्यनुसन्धेयम्। अत्र च **'न चैवमन्योन्याश्रय'**मिति पूर्वोपन्यस्तमन्योन्याश्रयद्वयमपि निषिद्धम्। **'न हि'** इत्यादिना पश्चादुक्तं एव प्रयत्यते, तत्परिहारद्वारेणैवेतरपरिहारसम्भवादिति वेदितव्यम्।।

ननु किमिदमुच्यते–**न हि पदावधारणेत्यादि।।** न हि जातुचित्सम्बन्धज्ञानाधीनं सम्बन्धिज्ञानम्। न खलु कुण्डं बदरं वा सम्बन्धग्रहणादवेति। किन्तु कुण्डबदरज्ञानाधीनं तत्सम्बन्धज्ञानमेव। तथा चोक्तं–'अनाश्रितपदरूपाणामप्रत्यायकत्वेनासम्बन्धिनां सम्बन्धाख्यानानुपपत्तेः' इति।।

अथान्यदेव भवतां पदशब्दवाच्यं न सम्बन्ध्येवाभिमतं, तर्हि तदुच्यतां,

---

१. 'अभिधेयधीहेतुभावः' इति मु० पु० पाठः।। 'हेत्वभाव इति ३ पु० पाठः' इति टिप्पणी।

२. 'व्यपदेशः प्रभवति' इति मु० पु० पाठः।

[1]**पदज्ञानम्।** [2]**कारकभेदाभिधेयि हि पदं, पद्यतेऽनेनेति व्युत्पत्त्या। तच्छब्दाश्च** [3]**कार्यसम्बन्धोपहितसीमानो नासति तस्मिन्प्रवर्तितु-**

अत आह–**कारकभेदाभिधायि हि पदम्।।** अयमर्थः–नास्माकं सम्बन्ध्येवाभिमतं पदशब्दवाच्यम्। किन्तु सम्बन्धिगतो धर्मभेदः, स च कारकविशेष इति। किं (कः)पुनः कारकविशेषः? करणत्वं नाम। तच्च ज्ञानक्रियायामिति दर्शयन्नाह–**पद्यतेऽनेनेति व्युत्पत्त्या।।** इदमाकूतम्–'पद गतौ' इत्यस्माद्धातोर्निष्पन्नोऽयं करणे शब्दः। 'गत्यर्थाश्च ज्ञानार्थाः' इति ज्ञानकारणमनेनाभिधीयते। न च धूमादिषु प्रसङ्गः, पङ्कजादिवद्रूढत्वस्याप्यङ्गीकरणादिति। 'अवध्यन्तरपरिग्रहेऽपि तत्त्वे वर्णानाम्' इति यदुक्तं तत्परिहरन्नाह–**तच्छब्दाश्च कार्यसम्बन्धोपहितसीमानो नासति तस्मिन्प्रवर्तितुमीशते।।** तच्छब्दाः कारकशब्दाः। **तस्मिन्** कार्यसम्बन्धे। **प्रवर्तितुं** स्वार्थेष्विति। इदमाकूतम्–'**न खल्वविदितपदरूपावधिः अर्थमवैती**'त्यप्यसिद्धम्। (सम्बन्धज्ञाना)भावादेव तत्राप्यर्थप्रतीतिर्न पदत्वाज्ञानात्। सम्बन्धज्ञानानन्तरन्तु [4]तन्निबन्धनस्य पदत्वस्यापि। तेन प्रत्यासत्तिमोहितधियां पदत्वाज्ञानादिति भ्रमो जायत इति। 'वर्णानामनाश्रितपदरूपाणां अप्रत्यायकत्वेनासम्बन्धिनाम्' इत्येतदपि परिहरन्नाह –**न च स्वरूपभेदः. . .प्राक् न प्रथते।।** अनेन च '**स्मृतिसमारोहिणो वर्णा वाचकाः ततो न गौरवम्**' इति चोद्यस्य परिहृत्य पश्चाद्विवृतस्योपन्यासः पश्चाद्विवृतस्य परिहारस्यासाधुत्वज्ञापनायेति द्रष्टव्यम्। **तादृश इति।।** यादृशेन भेदेन सम्बन्धितामापाद्यत इति। **तावतां**–यावतां पदत्वमभिहितम्। **वर्णान्तरेभ्यः**–यथा गौरित्यस्य पचतीत्यस्मात्। **तेभ्यो वाऽतावद्भ्यः**–यथा

---

१. 'पदविज्ञानं' इति मु० पु० पाठः।

२. 'कारकभेदावधायि हि पदपदं' इति मु० पु० पाठः। 'कारकभेदाभिधायी'ति ३ पु० पाठः। 'कार्यविशेषाभिधायकम्' इति टिप्पणी।

३. 'कार्यसम्बन्धोबोधपहितसीमानः' इति मु० पु० पाठः। 'कार्यो यः सम्बन्धबोधः तेन प्रापिता पदभेदरूपा सीमा अवधिर्येषां तादृशा इत्यर्थः।' इति टिप्पणी।

४. 'तन्निबन्धनत्वस्य पदस्य क्वापि' इति दृश्यते मातृकायाम्।

मीशते। [१]न च स्वरूपभेदस्तादृशस्तावतां वर्णानां वर्णान्तरेभ्यो तेभ्यो)वा[२]ऽतावद्स्भ्यस्तावभ्द्यो ऽता[३]दृग्भ्योऽन्त्यविज्ञानोपरोहिणामर्थप्रत्ययात् प्राक् न प्रथते। येन सम्बन्धिभेदाग्रहे न सम्बन्धिभेदो निरूप्येत। प्रकारान्तरवद्भयस्तु तेभ्यः तेषामेव चरमविज्ञाननिवेशिनां विशेषमग्रे [४]वक्ष्यामः। [५]तथा च सम्बन्ध-

---

वृष इत्यस्य वृषभ इत्यस्मात्। **तावद्भयो वाऽतादृग्भ्य इति**—यथा नदीत्यस्य दीनेत्यस्मात्। **न प्रथत** इति **न** किन्तु प्रथत एवेति। यदि न प्रथते ततः किं स्यात्? तदाह—**येन सम्बन्धिभेदाग्रहे न सम्बन्धिभेदोनिरूप्येत**।। येनाप्रथनेन सम्बन्धिनां सम्बन्धख्यानानुपपत्तेरित्येतत्सत्यं स्यादित्यर्थः। नन्वत उत्तरमप्युक्तं—'तन्नास्ति; क्रमयुक्तेभ्य इव युगपदद्विपरीतक्रमयुक्तेभ्योऽप्यर्थप्रत्ययप्रसङ्गात्' इत्यत आह—**प्रकारान्तरवद्भयस्तु. . . विशेषमग्रे पश्यामः (वक्ष्यामः)**।। इदानीं वर्णातिरिक्तदूषणाधिकारादुपेक्ष्यते। पश्चात्तु वर्णानां वाचकत्वं प्रतिज्ञाय 'अपि च वर्णेभ्यो नार्थप्रत्ययो नोपपद्यत इति। न चास्यां क्रमाक्रमविपरीतक्रमानुभूतानामविशेषो वर्णानाम्' इति प्रस्तावात्तत्रैव वक्ष्याम इत्यर्थः। अतो नास्त्येवेतरेतराश्रयत्वं सम्बन्धाख्यान इत्याह—**तथा च सम्बन्धः— ईषत्करम्। बोधनं** बोधो ज्ञातृव्यापारः, **आख्यानं** वचनं वक्तृव्यापारः, तयोर्द्वन्द्वैकवद्भावः। एवं च 'तत्रार्थप्रतीत्या पदरूपविशेषमुपकल्पयतो दुरुत्तरमितरेतराश्रयं प्रसज्येत' इत्यप्यपहस्तिततमित्याह—**समवधृत. . .नानुपपन्नम्(न्नः)**।। **पश्चात्** सम्बन्धबोधनाख्यानानन्तरम्। **तेषां** वर्णानाम्। **'समवधृत'** इत्यादि वर्णविशेषणम्।।

---

१. 'न च स्वरूपभेदस्तावतां तादृशां वर्णानां वर्णान्तरेभ्यस्तेभ्य एव वाऽताद्भयस्ताद्भयो वाऽतादृशेभ्योऽन्यविज्ञानोपारोहिणां' इति मु० पु० पाठः।

२. (अतावद्भयस्ताबद्भयो वा)—'भिन्नानुपूर्वीकेभ्यः। अर्थज्ञाननैरपेक्ष्येणैव नदीदीनादिपदेषु स्वरूपभेदः प्रत्यक्षसिद्ध एवेति भावः।' इति टिप्पणी।

३. 'अतादृग्भ्यः' इत्यतः परं 'अतः' इत्यधिकं दृश्यते मातृकायाम्।

४. 'वक्ष्यामः' इति मु० पु० पाठः।

५. 'तथा सम्बन्धबोधनाख्यानमप्यमीषामीषत्करं समधिगतैकाभिधेयधीहेतुभावानां च तेषां पश्चात्पदमिति व्यपदेशो नानुपन्नः।' इति मु० पु० पाठः।

बोधनाख्यानमप्यमीषामीषत्करम्। समवधृतैकाभिधेयधीहेतुभावानां च पश्चात्तेषां 'पदम्' इति व्यपदेशो नानुपपन्नः।।

अपि चानंशस्य वैशद्यावैशद्ये न युज्येते। [१]सामान्यविशेषतद्वतामनुभूयमानता हि वैशद्यं, सामान्यमात्रस्य विशेषमात्रस्य वा वेदनमवैशद्यम्। न च निखिलसामान्यविशेषविरहिणः स्फोटस्यास्फुटस्य दर्शनमुपपद्यते। [२]स खलूपलभ्येत, न वोप-

---

एवन्तावत्पूर्वासु बुद्धिषूत्तरासु च क्रमेण स्फोयत्मनो न प्रकाशभागितेत्युक्तम्। सम्प्रति प्रकाशभागित्वे यः प्रकारभेदोऽभिमतः सोऽपि नोपपत्तिभागित्युभयीष्वपि सम्भूय दूषणमाह–**अपि चानंशस्य वैशद्यावैशद्ये न युज्येते।।** पदस्य वाक्यस्य वेति सिद्धयति। यदि पदस्येति क्वचिदृश्यते तदापि तद्वाक्यस्योपलक्षणम्। कथं न **युज्येते** इत्यत आह–**सामान्यविशेषतद्वतां. . . अवैशद्यम्।।** अतः किमित्याह–**न च निखिल. . .न दृश्यन्ते चेति।।** अंशशब्देनावयवा निर्दिश्यन्ते। **सामान्य**शब्देन साधारणावयवा गवाश्वादीनां पादादयो गृह्यन्ते, **विशेष**शब्देन सास्नादयः, तद्वच्छब्देन तदाधारा इति। **वैशद्यमिति**–यथा करतलामलकस्य। **सामान्यमात्रस्य**–यथोर्ध्वत्वादेः। **विशेषमात्रस्य वेति**–यथा दत्तादेः तमसि गजादीनाम्। **निखिलसामान्यविरहिण** इति। 'अनवयमेव वाक्यं वाक्यार्थस्य वाचकम्' इत्युपक्रमात्। तथा च सिद्धान्तस्थितेः। यथोक्तं–

'निरस्तभेदं पदतत्त्वमेकं
व्यादर्शि युक्त्यागमसंश्रयेण।

---

१. 'सामान्यविशेषतत्त्वाभ्यां अनुभूयमानता हि वैशद्यम्। सामान्यमात्रस्य तद्वन्मात्रस्य वा वेदनमवैशयम्। न च निखिलसामान्यविशेषविरहिणः स्फोटस्यास्फुटं दर्शनमुपपद्यते।' इति मु० पु० पाठः।

२. **'स खलूपलभ्यते नोपलभ्यते।** न ह्यस्य दृश्यमानस्यास्ति किञ्चिददृश्यमानम्। न चास्ति सम्भवः। **स एव** तेनैव तदैव दृश्यते न चेति' इति मु० पु० पाठः। 'न खलूपलभ्यते न वोपलभ्यते' इति ३. पु० पाठः। 'नोपलभ्यते वेति विकल्प्य वक्ष्यमाणं दूषणद्वयं योजनीयम्' इति टिप्पणी।

लभ्यते। न ह्यस्य दृश्यमानस्यास्ति किञ्चिददृश्यमानम्। न नास्ति सम्भवः—[1]स एव तेनैव तदैव दृश्यते न दृश्यते चेति। अत एव न समारोपः, [2]सर्वथाऽननुभूते तदयोगात्। [3]कथञ्चिदनुभवे निरंश-त्वानुपपत्तेरपसिद्धान्तप्रसङ्गात्। तस्मादनवयवमेवानुभूयते पदतत्त्व (मेक?) मिति रिक्तं वचः॥

विधूतभेदग्रहमेव वैदिशा(मेतयैव)
दिशा परं सम्प्रतियन्त्वभेदम्॥' इति॥

परमिति वाक्यं निर्दिशति। अनेन चांशशब्देन सामान्यांशा विशेषांशाश्च दिश्यन्त इति व्याख्यातम्। हेतुश्चायमिति। साध्यं त्वस्फुटस्येति। **स खल्विति॥** सर्वथोपलम्भस्य वा सर्वथानुपलम्भस्य वा प्रसङ्गात्कथञ्चित्त(त्कथं त) दुभयसम्भव इति। तच्छब्देन निखिलसामान्यविशेषविरहिततयोपेतस्फोटपरामर्शः। एवं '**न ह्यस्ये**'तीदंशब्देन (स एव) परिदृश्यते (परामृश्यते)। न हि किञ्चिद्रूपमस्य दृश्यते स्थाण्वादिवदिति सद्भावासद्भावमात्रमुपलम्भस्येति। **न चास्तीति॥** तर्ह्युपलम्भमात्रत्वमेव स्फुटत्वं अनुपलम्भमात्रत्वमस्फुटत्वं सम्भवादी(स्तम्भादी)नामङ्गीक्रियतामित्यपि न वक्तव्यम्—**सम्भवा इति(?)॥** 'तेनैव तदैव दृश्यते न दृश्यते'त्यस्य वस्तुभेदे सति सम्भवात् **स ऐवेत्युक्तम्।**[4] . . **एकमिति रिक्तं वचः॥ अत्राह**—

'वस्त्वन्तरं प्रसिद्धं स्याद्विना शब्दप्रसिद्धितः।'

इति वार्तिके। यदप्युक्तम्—'सतोऽपि वर्णातिरेकिणोऽर्थधीहेतोर्न शब्दशब्दवाच्ये'ति। अहो! लोकशास्त्रप्रसिद्ध्योः परः परिचयः यदिदमपि न दृष्टं 'शब्दादर्थं प्रतिपद्यामहे' इति। 'भावार्थाः कर्मशब्दाः तेभ्यः क्रिया प्रतीयते' इति

---

१. (**स एव**)—'अत एवेति ३ पु० पाठः' इति टिप्पणी।

२. 'अत एव न समागेपः' इत्यारभ्य 'रिक्तं वचः' इति पर्यन्तो ग्रन्थः यथामुद्रितपुस्तकं दीयते; व्याख्यान ग्रन्थपातात्।

३. (कथञ्चिदनुभव)—'एकदेशावच्छेदेन प्रत्यक्षत्वाङ्गीकारे' इति टिप्पणी।

४. व्याख्याने एकपत्रपरिमितग्रन्थपातः।

अत एव च[१] 'शब्दार्थं प्रतिपद्यमाहे' इति वन्ध्यापत्येति-वदनुपपन्नार्थवचनम्; अनुभवाभावात्। अनुभव एव हि प्रमाण-

---

'भावमाख्यातेनाचष्टे' इति।' 'न च समुच्चयज्ञानावरोहिवर्ण निबन्धनार्थावबोधाभिप्रायं 'शब्दादर्थं प्रतिपद्यामहे' इति। नापि शब्दजात्यभिप्रायम्। तथा हि–

''नेक्षिता जातिशब्दानां समुदायानुपातिता।

जातिमाचक्षते ते हि व्यक्तीर्वा जातिसङ्गताः।।

न तावदिदं शब्दजात्यभिप्रायम्। न शब्दजातितोऽर्थप्रतीतिः। गवाश्वादिपदेषु तदविशेषात् अभिधेयाविशेषप्रसङ्गात्। न चानुपाश्रितव्यावृत्तयो व्यक्तयः जात्यात्मना निर्दिश्यन्ते इति साम्प्रतम्; वर्णव्यक्तिसमानाधिकरण्यदर्शनात्– 'गोशब्दादर्थं प्रतिपद्यामहे'इति। नापि शब्दव्यक्त्यभिप्रायम्, तद्भेदात् गोशब्दादित्येकवचनानुपपत्तेः। न हि व्यक्तिविशेषपरास्तभिधायिसमानाधि-करणवृत्तयो जातिशब्दा जातिसङ्ख्यामनुरुध्यन्ते। न जातु भवति 'देवदत्तयज्ञदत्तौ ब्राह्मणः' इति, 'धवखदिरा(रौ) वृक्षः' इति वा। नापि समुदायाभिप्रायम्, जातिशब्दानामेकैकव्यक्तिसमवायेन जातेः समुदायनिवेशशून्यतया तदनुपातसामर्थ्याभावेन; ते हि जातीस्तद्वतीर्वा व्यक्तीः निमित्तरूपोपादानेनाचक्षते न समूहम्। न हि भवति, यथा–धवादीनां वनं धवादिवनामिति वा तथा धवादीनां वृक्षो धवादिवृक्ष इति वा।।

ननु दृष्टः समुदायानुपाती जातिशब्दः, 'सहकारो(रा)वन'मिति सामानाधिकरण्यदर्शनात्। न। समूहसमूहिनीर्व्यक्तीराचक्षाणस्य समूहसमूहि-नोरभेदविवक्षायां सामानाधिकरण्यम्। तथा च बहुवचनम्। अन्यथा तदनुपातिन एकवचनं स्यात् वनशब्दवत्। न चेह तथा, समुदायशब्दाभावात्, गौरिति गकारादीनां विभक्तैरात्मभिरुपादानात्, बहुवचनाभावाच्च। अत एव न समारारनिर्देशः। न हि भवति 'धवखदिरं वृक्षमानये'ति, अपि तु, 'धवखदिरौ वृक्षा'विति, समूहसमूहिनोरभेदोपचारात्। नाप्यन्त्यवर्णाभिप्रायम्, पूर्ववर्णपरामर्शात्। तस्मान्नैकं शब्दात्मानमन्तरेण लौकिकवचनोपपत्तिः'' इति। तामेतामाशङ्कां

---

१. 'शब्दार्थ इति ३ पु० पाठः' इति टिप्पणी। 'च' नास्ति मु० पुस्तके 'प्रतिपाद्यमह इति सपिशाचवटैतिह्यवदनुपपद्यमानार्थवचनं' इति मु० पु० पाठः।

मार्गागतो लोक[१]; तत्त्वावलोकनात्। न [२]पुरुषप्रवादमात्रं, वृथावादोऽपि हि सम्भवति वटयक्षवत्। यदि त्ववश्योपपादनीयं

परिहरति—**अत एव च. . . अनुपपन्नार्थवचनम्।।** इदमाकूतम्—'मोपपादि लौकिकं वचनम्। उभयथापि दर्शनात् उपपन्नार्थानामनुपपन्नार्थानाञ्च। न हि वचनानुपपत्तिमात्रेण प्रमाणरहितोऽर्थः शक्यतेऽवसातुम्' इति। **अत इति।।** '**अनवयवमनुभूयते**' इति वचनस्य रिक्तत्वादेवेत्यर्थः। **वन्ध्यापत्य**शब्दयोः समासमात्रस्योदाहार्यत्वाद्वन्ध्यापत्यादिव(त्येतिव)दिति विभक्त्यापि विना निर्देशः।।

ननु—'असदेतत्, अनुपपन्नार्थत्वाप्रतीतेः। भवति हि जरद्गवादि-शब्देष्वनुपपन्नार्थप्रतीतिः। न त्विह तथा। न हि सार्वलौकिकमविगानेन प्रयोगपथमवतरत्यनुपपत्तिरुपत्तिमती। विप्रतिपद्यमाना(अपि) हि शब्दे नैनं प्रयोगं नानुमन्यन्ते। न चाप्रमाणत्वम्। अतो नूनमुपलभन्ते प्रमाणेन शब्दात्मा-नमेकम्। यत एवमपहस्तितविप्रतिपत्तयः प्रयुञ्जते पश्चात्। न च पश्चात्तनज्ञान-निवेशिभ्यो वर्णेभ्योऽर्थप्रत्ययः। तस्मान्नैकांशमात्मानमन्तरेण लौकिकवचनो-पपत्तिः' इत्याशङ्क्याह—**अनुभवाभावात्. . . वटयक्षवत्।।** कस्मात्कारणा-**दनवयवमनुभूयत** इति वचसो रिक्तत्वात् अस्य वचनस्यानुपपन्नार्थतेत्यपेक्षायां **अनुभवाभावादित्युक्तम्।।**

ननु किमनुभवाभावेन दर्शितेन? लोको हि शब्दार्थनिर्णयकारणम्। 'सिद्धे शब्दार्थसम्बन्धे लोकतः' इति, 'लोके येष्वर्थेषु' इत्यादावाश्रितम्। लोकश्चाविगानेन प्रयुङ्क्ते इत्युक्तमेव। किं साक्षादनु भवभावोपन्यासेनेत्या-**शङ्क्यानुभवाभावा**दित्येतदेव विवृतं **अनुभव एवे**'त्यादिना। अनुभवस्यापि गाव्यादिविषये भ्रान्तित्वात् '**प्रमाणमार्गागतः**' इत्युक्तम्। **लोकः**—'सिद्धे शब्दार्थसम्बन्धे लोकतः' इत्यादौ लोकशब्दवाच्य इत्यर्थः।

ननु लोकस्तु भुवने जने वा प्रसिद्धः, कथमनुभवस्य लोकतेत्पेक्षाया-

---

१. 'लोकस्वत्वावलोकनात्' इति मु० पु० पाठः। 'लोकैरविसंवादेन तत्र प्रामाण्याङ्गीकारात्' इति टिप्पणी।

२. 'न पुनः पुरुषप्रवादमात्रं मृषावादोऽपि' इति मु० पु० पाठः।

ततो वरं शब्द[१]शब्दलक्षितानां वर्णव्यक्तीनामेकस्मृतिंसमारूढा-नामेकाभिधेयप्रत्ययोपजननलबब्धसहभावानामभिन्नकारव[२]वस्थो-

---

मुक्तं–**तत्त्वावलोकनादिति।।** परमार्थदृष्टिकरणादित्यर्थः। प्रमाणमार्गागतेः फलं **तत्त्वेति**। अवलोकहेतुत्वाल्लोक इत्यनेनोक्तम्। ततश्च लोकयतीति लोक्यतेऽस्मिन्निति वा व्युत्पत्तिरनुसन्धेया।

यथोक्तं– 'लोक्येते चात्र शब्दार्थौ लोकस्तेन स उच्यते।
व्यवहारोऽथ वा वृद्धवहर्तृपरम्परा।।' इति।।

ननु अस्मिन्वार्तिके व्यवहारस्य लोकत्वमुक्तम्; कथमनुभव एवेत्युच्यते? अत उक्तं–**न पुरुषप्रवादमात्रमिति।।** अनुभवगर्भित एव पुरुषप्रवादो लोकः न व्यवहारमात्रमिति। अनेन **चानुभव** एवेत्यस्य व्यावर्त्यं दर्शितमिति वेदितव्यम्। ततश्चान्वयव्यतिरेकाभ्यामनुभव एवेत्यायातम्। अनुभवमूरीकृत्य व्यवहारतत्कर्तृपरम्परयोर्लोकत्ववचनमिति भावः। पुरुषप्रवादमात्रस्यालोकत्वे कारणं **तत्त्वावलोकना**दित्युक्तहेतुविपर्ययं दर्शितवान् **वृथे**त्यादिना। **वटवृ(यि)क्षवदिति।।** 'वटे यक्षः प्रतिवसती'ति लोके प्रवादो वृथावादतया सिद्ध इति।

यथोक्तं–'जगति बहु न तथ्यं निय(त्य)मैतिह्ययुक्तम्।' इति।।

अतोऽनुपपन्नार्थमेवेदं वचनं जरद्गवादिवत्। अबाधबुद्धिस्तु साक्षाद्बाधकानुदयात् नेदं रजतमितिवत्, अहं स्थूल इत्यादिवत्तु परीक्षकाणां यौक्तिकबाधो भवत्येव। अतो मुधैव तदुपपादनाय वर्णातिरिक्तशब्दकल्पनेति स्थितम्। लौकिकवचनसमर्थनव्यसनिता वन्ध्यापत्येतिवदुयक्तिज्ञानमेव जायते इत्युपेक्षितव्यम्। अथवा–अस्त्वेषा समर्थनेत्याह–**यदि त्ववश्योपपादनीयं. . . .गोशब्दादिति।।** इदमाकूतम्–यदुक्तं 'न तावदिदंशब्दजात्यभिप्रायम्' इति, तत्सत्यमेवोक्तमिति वेदितव्यम्। यच्च 'न चानाश्रितव्यावृत्तयो व्यक्तः' इति, तदपि सत्यमेव। यत्पुनरुक्तं, नापि शब्दव्यक्त्यभिप्रायमिति, तत्र

---

१. 'शब्दोपलक्षितानां' इति मु० पु० पाठः।
२. 'अवस्थापदिता' इति मु० पु० पाठः।

पपादिताभेदानामेकत्वादेकवचन[१] मुपपन्नार्थं [२]गोशब्दादिति। न च 'धवखदिर [३]वृक्षः' इति न दृश्यते लोक इति दृश्यमान-

---

मृष्यामहे इति दर्शितं–**वर्णव्यक्तीनामिति**।। वर्णात्मनां व्यक्तीनामिति विग्रहः। 'ते हि जातीस्तद्वतीर्वा व्यक्तीर्निमित्तरूपोपादानेनाचक्षते' इत्यप्यसिद्धमिति दर्शितम्। **शब्दशब्दलक्षितानामिति।** व्यक्तीनामेव प्रतिपादनहेतुत्वेन गङ्गयेव तीरं जात्या व्यक्तयः स्वाधारभूता लक्ष्यन्त इत्यभिप्रायः। गौरिति गकारादीनां विभक्तैरात्मभिरुपादानेऽपि कथं बहुवचनाभाव इत्यपेक्षायां–**एकत्वादेकवचनमुपपन्नार्थमिति**।। औपाधिकादेकत्वाद्भिन्नात्मनामपि 'द्व्येकयोर्द्विवचनैकवचने' इत्येकत्वविवक्षायामेकवचनोत्पत्तिरिति भावः। न चात्रोपाधिविरहोऽप्यस्तीत्युक्तम्। '**अभिन्नकारकावस्थापादिताभेदान**'मिति।। कुतः पुनः क्रमवर्ति- नामभिन्नकारकावस्थासम्भवः इत्यत्रोक्तं–**एकाभिधेयप्रत्ययोपजननलब्धसहभावानामिति**।। कथं वा तादृशैरेकाभिधेयप्रत्ययजननमपीत्यपेक्षायाम**एकस्मृतिसमारूढाना**मित्युक्तम्। एतच्च विशेषणत्रयं '**न चात्रोपाधिविरहोऽपी**'त्यादिनिरीक्षणे सुज्ञानमिति वेदितव्यम्।।

नन्वेवं चेत्, सर्वत एव किं नैवं प्रयुञ्जते। तथा सति जात्यन्त रेष्वप्येवं प्रयुञ्जीरन्। न जातु कश्चित् 'धवखदिरौवृक्षौ तिष्ठतः' इतिवत् स्थानक्रियाकारकेणैकेनापादितैकत्ववृक्षत्वजातिलक्षितधवादिरूपव्यक्तिविवक्षया 'धवखदिरवृक्षः' इति प्रयुङ्क्ते। अत उत्प्रेक्षामात्रमेतन्न प्रामाणिकमिति चेत्तत्राह–**न च धवखदिरवृक्षः . . एतदपह्नवमर्हति**।। यद्यपि वैयाकरणैः न जातु भवति 'देवदत्तयज्ञदत्तौ ब्राह्मणः' इति 'धवखदिरौ वृक्षः' इति वेति कथितं, तथापि तुल्यन्यायतयाऽत्रापि 'गोशब्दः' इतिवत् 'धवखदिरवृक्षः' इत्यपि

१. (उपन्नार्थं)–'उपन्नमिति ३ पु. पाठः' इति टिप्पणी।

२. (गोशब्दादिति)–गोशब्दादित्येकवचनमुक्तक्रमेणैकत्वव्यवहारमात्रोपपत्तेरुपपनार्थकमित्यर्थः' इति टिप्पणी।

३. 'धवखदिरपलाशा वृक्षः' इति मु० पु० पाठः। 'धवादिषु वनत्वं प्रत्येकं न पर्याप्नोति वृक्षत्वं तु पर्याप्नोतीति विशेषाद्वनमित्येकवचनमेव वृक्षा इति बहुवचनमेव यथा यथा प्रकृते शब्दत्वस्य प्रकृतपर्याप्ततया शब्दा इति बहुवचनमेव युक्तं न त्वेकवचनमित्याक्षेपाशय।' इति टिप्पणी।

मेददपह्नवमर्हति। दर्शनादर्शनयोर्लौकि[1]कत्वेन तुल्यतया बाध्य-बाधकभावेन [2]विषयव्यवस्थोपपत्तेः[3]।।

प्रयोगः स्यादित्यपि वक्तुमशक्यमेवेति कृत्वा तस्य परिहाराय प्रस्ताव इति वेदितव्यम्। **दृश्यमानमेतदिति।। गोशब्दा**दिति वचनं अभिन्नकारकावस्थापादितैकत्वगोचरं सत्प्रतिपक्षोपलभ्यमानमित्यर्थः। एवंभूतस्य सत एव दृश्यमानतेति प्रकारान्तरासम्भवात्सिद्धमेवेति।। अत एव 'शब्दादर्थं प्रतिपद्यमाहे' इति **बन्ध्यापत्ये**तिवदित्यत्रातश्शब्देन पूर्वोक्तानुभवाभावानुसन्धानमप्येतदर्थमेवेति द्रष्टव्यम्। **लोक** इति दृश्यमानमित्यत्रापि द्रष्टव्यम्। कारणमाह–**दर्शनादर्शनयोर्लौकिकत्वेन...विषयव्यवस्थोपपत्तेः।।** लौकिकत्वं हि प्रामाण्यकारणम्। तच्चादर्शनवद्दर्शनस्याप्यस्त्येवेत्युक्तम्। अतस्तुल्यवद्बाध्यत्वं बाधकत्वञ्च प्रसज्यत इति व्रीहियवशास्त्रवद्विषयव्यवस्थाऽऽपद्यते। अदर्शनं शब्दत्वजातिव्यतिरिक्तास्वेव जातिष्वसत्त्वमापादयति। दर्शनद शब्द(त्व)जातावेव सत्त्वमापादयतीति विषयव्यवस्थोपपत्तिरिति। अथ वा–दर्शनादर्शनयोरुभयोरपि लौकिकत्वेन तुल्यबलत्वाद्बाध्यबाधकभावेन रूपेण विषयव्यवस्था, परगोचर एव बाध्यत्वं स्वगोचर एव बाधकत्वमित्येवमुपपद्यत इति।।

एवं **'मीयमानपरित्यागो बाधके नासति स्फुटे'** इत्येतद्व्याख्यातम्। सम्प्रति **'दृष्टात्कार्योपपत्तौ च नादृष्टपरिकल्पना'** इत्यस्य व्याख्यानमुपक्रमते–**न चाप्रत्यक्षं. . . .शक्यानुमानमिति।।** पूर्वत्रपूर्वार्धस्य, मीयमानास्तावद्वर्णाः पदानि वाऽवयवाः; न च तत्परित्यागः सम्भवति, नेदं रजतमितिवद्बलवद्बाधकाभावात्; वर्णातिरेकि च यदि मीयमानं स्यात्तदा तस्य न परित्यागः; किन्तु तदेव प्रतिष्ठितं स्यात्; न ह्याहत्य तस्मिन्बाधकोपनिपात इति, न तु तत्पूर्वासु बुद्धिषूत्तरासु वा मीयते, वर्णानामेव मीयमानत्वात्; न

---

१. 'लोकसिद्धत्वेन' इति मु० पु० पाठः।

२. (विषयव्यवस्थोपपत्तेः)–'यथा तैलत्वस्य प्रतिबिन्दुपर्याप्तत्वेऽपि कदाचित् प्रस्थमात्रेऽपि तैलमित्येकत्वव्यवहारः कदाचित्तु तैलानि हेमन्ते मुखानीत्यादिव्यवहारः लोकसिद्धत्वेन न विरुद्धस्तथेहापीति भावः।' इति टिप्पणी।

३. 'अविषयव्यवस्थोपपत्तेरिति ३ पुं० पाठः' इति टिप्पणी।

न [1]चाप्रत्यक्षमर्थधीकार्येण शक्यानुमानम्। अन्योन्याश्रयात्। न खलु सत्तामात्रेण शब्दोऽभिधेयभियमाधातुमर्हति। [2]शाश्वततया नित्यमाधानप्रसङ्गात् इति [3]स्वज्ञानेन तद्धेतुरेषितव्य इति। स्वज्ञानं

च वर्णानां मीयमानतापरित्यागे कारणं स्फुटं बाधकमनुसंहारबुद्धिबोध्यत्वासम्भवादि विद्यते; तेषामैवौपाधिकैकत्वसम्भवेन तद्बोध्यत्वसम्भवात्, इत्येवं व्याख्यानं कृतमित्यनुसन्धेयम्। अनेन तूपात्तेन ग्रन्थेन **'अर्थधीभेदाद्वाऽन्यथानुपपद्यमानात्'** इत्ययमवशिष्टः कल्पो दूष्यते। इदमाकूतं–अर्थधीभेदाद्व्यवस्थापनं तावदनुमानतस्तावन्नास्ति। ज्ञातसम्बन्धस्यैवानुमानसम्भवात्। न च सम्बन्धग्रहणं स्फोटात्मनोऽप्रत्यक्षत्वात्स्फोटतत्कार्ययोः सम्भवति। न च प्रत्यक्षानुमानाभ्यां व्यतिरिक्तं प्रमाणान्तरं अस्मिन्विद्यतेऽङ्गीक्रियते वा। आगमोऽपि नित्यस्तावदनुपलभ्यमानो नास्मिन्प्रमाणम्। न चानित्यः, निर्मूलत्वात्। उपमानन्तु सादृश्यमात्रविषयमनाशङ्क्यमेव। अर्थापत्तिरप्यस्मिन्न प्रवर्तितुमर्हतीरति वक्ष्यते। अतोऽनुमानासम्भवः। न च लिङ्गोत्पत्तिरपि अज्ञाते शब्देऽवकल्पते। न च प्रत्यक्षं तत्र सम्भवतीत्युक्तम्। न च प्रमाणान्तरम्। अतोऽनुमानादेव शब्दं गृहीतवतामर्थप्रत्ययः तेनैव चानुमानमित्यन्योन्याश्रयमपरिहार्यं प्रसज्यत इत्याह– **अन्योन्याश्रयात्।।** इतरेतराश्रयमेव स्फुटयति–**न खलु सत्तामात्रेण.... आधातुमर्हति।।** यदि सत्तामात्रेणार्हेत् ततो नेत्रादिवद्रूपादिज्ञानेनान्योन्याश्रयमन्तरेणैनुमानोत्पत्तिरुपद्येतेति भावः। कुतः पुनर्नार्हतीत्यपेक्षायामाह–**शाश्वततया नित्यमाधानप्रसङ्गात्।।** शब्दो हि नित्यः 'नित्यस्तु स्याद्दर्शनस्य परार्थत्वात्' इति अतश्च सत्तामात्रनिबन्धनं चेत्कार्यं ततः सत्तायाः सार्वकालिकत्वात् सर्वदैवार्थप्रत्ययः प्रसज्य इत्यर्थः। अनित्यत्वेन(त्वेपि) शब्दानां वीचीतरङ्गवृत्त्या आरभ्यमाणानां अन्त्यव्यतिरिक्तानां बोधकत्वाभावात्सत्ताव्यभिचारान्न **सत्तमात्रेण शब्दोऽभिधेय(धिय)माधातुमर्हतीति।** परमार्थतस्तु नित्यत्वस्य स्थित–

---

१. 'चाप्रत्यक्षमप्यर्थ' इति मु० पु० पाठः।

२. 'सत्तया अभिधायकत्वे तस्याः शाश्वतिकतया' इति मु० पु० पाठः।

३. 'इति। अतश्च स्वज्ञानं' इति मु० पु० पाठः। 'स्वज्ञानेनेति ३ पुं० पाठः' इति टिप्पणी।

चास्यार्थप्रत्ययलक्षणलिङ्गप्रभवमिति प्राप्तमन्यान्य[1]संश्रयम्। [2]अपि च वर्णेभ्यो नाभिधेय[3]प्रत्ययो नोपपद्यते। ते हि गौरिति स्मृतिबुद्धावेकस्यां विपरिवर्तमाना अभिधेयप्रत्ययस्येशते[4]। न [5]चास्यां क्रमाक्रमविपरीतक्रमानुभूतानामविशेषो वर्णानाम्। तथा हि–प्राचीनानुभवभावितभावनानिचयलब्धजन्मा स्मृतिरनुभवानुसारिणी तद्गोचरानक्रमानपि तत्क्रमेण क्रमवदनुभवकर्मतोप-

---

त्वाच्छाश्वततयेत्युक्तमिति। अनाद्यविद्यावासनोपाधिवशात् पदतत्त्वमेकमनेकपदार्थात्मना प्रथते। न तु पदार्थास्ततो व्यतिभिद्यमानात्मानः परमार्थतः सन्तीत्यङ्गीकरणेऽपि।

'आरोपविषयारोप्ये नाजानत्रजतभ्रमी'

इति न्यायेन यथा मुखतत्त्वमवगच्छतामेव कृपाणादिषु तदध्यासः, एवं पदतत्त्वमवगम्यैव तस्यार्थात्मनाः अध्यासः इत्यवश्यमर्थप्रत्ययात्पूर्वं शब्दो ग्रहीतव्य एवेत्यभिप्रायेणाह–**इति स्वज्ञानेन तद्धेतुरेषितव्य इति।। प्रथम इति**शब्दो हेतौ। द्वितीयस्तु 'इति किल भवतोऽपि बुद्धिः' इत्येवं योजनीयः यदि दृश्यते। एवं शब्दज्ञानापेक्षिता अर्थप्रत्ययस्य दर्शिता; शब्दज्ञानस्याप्यर्थप्रत्ययापेक्षतामाकाङ्क्षाविनिवृत्तये दर्शयति–**स्वज्ञानं चास्यार्थप्रत्ययलक्षणलिङ्गप्रभवम्।। अस्य**–शब्दस्य। पूर्वोक्तेन न्यायेनेति भावः। एवमुक्तमन्योन्यापेक्षित्वमितरेतराश्रये पर्यवसाययति–**इति प्राप्तमन्योन्यसंश्रयम्।।** भवत्सकाशे प्राप्तमेव न?. . . .अथोच्येत? **(वत्स! वेत्सि तावच्छब्दादर्थधीरुदी)यत इति।।**

---

१. 'अन्योन्याश्रयं' इति मु० पु० पाठः।

२. 'अपि च वर्णेभ्यः' इत्यारभ्य 'अत्रभवन्तो वार्तिककाराः' इति पर्यन्तो ग्रन्थः यथा मुद्रितपुस्तकं दीयते, व्याख्याने ग्रन्थपातात्।

३. 'प्रत्ययो नोपपद्यते। ते हि गौरिति स्मृतिबुध्यावेकस्यां विपरिवर्तमाना अभिधेय' इत्ययं भागः २. पु० नास्तीति टिप्पणी।

४. 'ईशते' इत्यस्मात्परं २. पु० पाठे 'वर्णमात्रेणोपस्थितौ न समर्था लोका इति शेषः' इति टिप्पणी।

५. (अस्यां) 'स्मृतौ' इति टिप्पणी।

सृष्टानपर्यायमपि समाकलपन्ती अक्रमविपरीतक्रमानुभूतेभ्यो भिनत्ति। दृश्यते हि नदीदीनेतिस्मृतिधियोरभेदेऽपि वर्णरूपाणां विशदतरः पदभेदः। न चेदमनवयवपददर्शनमिति निवेदितम्। तदनुभवकर्मताक्रमः [1]परमवशिष्यते। सोऽपि न्यूनातिरेकादिवदेकपदभेदा- वधारणोपायः। यथाऽऽहुरत्रभवन्तो [2]वार्तिककाराः—

'पदावधारणोपायान्बहूनिच्छन्ति सूरयः।
क्रमन्यूनातिरिक्तत्वस्वर[3]वक्यश्रुतिस्मृतीः।।' इति।।

सेयं वर्णातिरिक्तैकपदवाक्यानुभावमन्तरेण नोदेतुमर्हति।।' वर्णानां प्रत्येकमप्रत्यायकत्वात्। साहित्याभावान्नियतक्रमवर्तिनामयौगपद्येन सम्भूयकारित्वानुपपत्तेर्नार्नाप्रयोक्तृप्रयुक्तेभ्यः प्रत्ययादर्शनात्क्रमविपर्यययौगपद्ये च। तस्माद्वर्णातिरेकि वर्णेभ्योऽसम्भवन्नर्थप्रत्ययः स्वनिमित्तमवकल्पयति। **'तस्मात्स्वसिद्धान्तव्यामोहमपहायाभ्युपेयतामनुसंहारबुद्धेरेकविषयता'** इति। तत्त्वया किं नावहितेन श्रुतम्? एतदुक्तं भवति—आवयोस्तावत्प्रत्यक्षज्ञानवेद्यः शब्दः ततश्चार्थः प्रतीयत इत्यविवादम्। स तु शब्दो वर्णात्मैव। तेषाञ्च नानात्मनामपि समुदायोऽनुसंहारबुद्धिबोध्यः तस्माच्चार्थप्रत्ययः इति भवतां दर्शनम्। अस्माकन्त्वेकमेव शब्दतत्त्वमनेकवर्णपदाकारेण विवर्तत इति। अनुभवविषयत्वन्तु शब्दस्याविवादसिद्धमेव। तत्र दृष्टेनार्थप्रत्ययेनैव वर्णेभ्योऽनुपपद्यमानेनानुभवस्य वर्णातिरिक्तै[4](कशब्दतत्त्वविषयकत्वं सिद्ध्यतीति?). . . .।।

(पदाव)धारणोपायान्बहूनिच्छन्ति सूरयः।
क्रमन्यूनातिरिक्तत्वस्वरवाक्यश्रुतिस्मृतीः।।' इति।।

---

१. (परमविशष्यते)—'परिशिष्यते इति ३. पु० पाठः' इति टिप्पणी।

२. (वार्तिककाराः)—'श्लोकवार्तिके वाक्याधिकरणे अ० १. पा० १. श्लोक १८०' इति टिप्पणी।

३. 'स्वरवर्ण' इति मु० पु० पाठः। 'स्वरवाक्ये'ति ३. पु० पाठः। मुद्रिते श्लोकवार्तिकपुस्तकेऽप्येवमेवेति टिप्पणी।

४. अत्र पुटद्वयपर्याप्तग्रन्थपातो व्याख्यानमातृकायाम्।

न च निरन्तरमतिसदृशस्वरबहुवक्तृप्रयुक्तेष्वानुपूर्व्यवत्सु समानस्मृतिबुद्धिसमारोहिष्वर्थप्रत्ययादर्शनाद्व्यभिचार इति साम्प्रदतम् [१]एकवक्तृप्रयुक्तत्वे विशेषात्।

यदप्याहुः—

"न प्रत्ययः स्यादेकत्वे प्रयोक्तुरविभाविते।
न च तस्य परिज्ञानमकस्मादवकल्पते।।"

इदञ्च वर्णवादी वक्तव्यः—किमियं (अ)नानाप्रवक्तृकताऽर्थज्ञानाङ्गं न वा। तत्रानङ्गत्वे वक्तृभेदेऽपि तत्स्यात्। न चेष्यते, दृश्यते वा।

एवं ह्युक्तं—

'तेषाञ्च गुणभूतानामर्थप्रत्यायनं प्रति।
साहित्यमेककर्त्रादि क्रमश्चापि विवक्षितः।।
तत्रै(वक्त्रे)कत्वनिमित्ते च क्रमे सति नियामकम्।
प्रयुञ्जानस्य यत्पूर्वं वृद्धेभ्यः क्रमदर्शनम्।।
यौगपद्यन्त्वशक्यत्वान्नैव तेषामिहाश्रितम्।
कर्तृभेदश्च तत्र स्यान्न चैवं दृश्यतेऽभिधा।।' (इति)।

अङ्गत्वे ज्ञापकानुप्रवेशित्वात् नानवधारितार्थ(प्रतीति)सिद्धि(द्धौ) हेतुः। दृश्यते च तिरोहितव्यवहितोदीरितेत्यो ह्यर्थज्ञानम्। न च व्यवहिततिरोहितयोरकस्मादेकत्वज्ञानं वक्त्रोः सम्भवति। सम्भवति च स्वरसादृश्ये निरन्तरोच्चारणे वक्तृभेदेऽपि कलकलशब्दश्रुतौ च अर्थज्ञानम्। कस्तत्र वक्तुरेकत्वनानात्वे विवेक्तुं क्षमः? न च ध्वनिमात्रश्रवणं तत्र, वर्णवाक्यपदपरिच्छेदानामपि केषाञ्चिद्भावात्" इति। तत्रानङ्गत्वं भवदुक्तादेव कारणान्नाद्रियत इत्याह—न **च निरन्तर. . . विशेषात्।।**

---

१. 'एकवक्तृप्रयुक्तत्वेन विशेषणात्' इति मु० पु० पाठः।। 'एकवर्गप्रयुक्तत्वेनेति ३. पु० पाठः' इति टिप्पणी।

[1]यथाहुः–

'यावन्तो यादृशा ये च यदर्थप्रतिपादने।[2]
वर्णाः प्रज्ञातसामर्थ्यास्ते तथैवावबोधकाः।।' इति।

[3]यथा वा–

'तेषां च गुणभूतानां अर्थप्रत्यायनं प्रति।
साहित्यमेकवक्त्रादि क्रमश्चापि विवक्षितः।।' इति।।

यथाहुः–

'यावन्तो यादृशा ये च यदर्थप्रतिपादने।
वर्णाः प्रज्ञातसामर्थ्यास्ते तथैवावबोधकाः।।' (इति)।

यथा वा–

'तेषां च गुणभूतानामर्थप्रत्यायनं प्रति।
साहित्यमेकवत्रादि क्रमश्चापि विवक्षितः।।' इति।

'ते हि गौरिति स्मृतिबुद्धौ [4]सामस्त्येनैकस्याम्' इत्यादिनोक्तेषु गौरितीत्यस्य प्रकारस्य व्यभिचाराय **निरन्तरमतिसदृशस्वरे**ति विशेषणम्। अनुभवकर्मताक्रमस्याविकलत्वाया**नुपूर्व्यवत्स्व**त्युक्तम्। एकस्यां स्मृतिबुद्धौ विपरिवर्तमाना इत्येतदप्रच्युतमिति दर्शितं–**समानस्मृतिबुद्धिसमारोहेष्विति।। एकवक्तृप्रयुक्तत्वे** इति। एकेन वक्त्रा प्रयुक्तत्वे सति वर्णानां बहुवक्तृ-प्रयुक्तत्वात् **विशेषात्**–अतिशयादित्यर्थः। कार्यान्यथानुपपत्तिकल्प्यत्वाद्विशेषस्य। न चानवयवदर्शनादर्शनकृतोऽयं विशेष इति दर्शितमेवेति भावः। 'यावन्तो यादृशाः' इत्यनेनैव नैरन्तर्यादिवद्वक्त्रैकत्वमपि स्वीकृतमित्यभिप्रायेण प्रथमं तदुपादानम्। अथवा साक्षादेवान्यस्मिन्वार्तिके स्वीकृतमिति दर्शयतोक्तं–**यथा**

---

१. (यथाहु)–'श्लोकवार्तिके सम्बन्धाक्षेपवार्तिके अ० १. पा० १. अ० ५. श्लोक ६९' इति टिप्पणी।

२. 'प्रतिपादकाः' इति मु० पु० पाठः।

३. (यथा वा)–'तेषां च. . .विवक्षित' अयं भागः मु० पु० न दृश्यते।

४. एतद्व्याख्यारीत्या मूले ६६ पुटे 'सामस्त्येन' इत्यपि स्यादित्यनुमीयत।

[1]**न चैतत्कलकलश्रुतावशक्यज्ञानम्। किमिव हि दुष्करमभ्यासस्य? [2]यदाहुर्बाह्या अपि–**

'[3]परेषामनुपाख्येमभ्यासादेव जायते।
मणिरूपादिषु ज्ञानं तद्विदामानुमानिकम्।।' इति।

वा-तेषामिति।। एवमङ्गं वक्त्रेकत्वमुक्तमित्युक्तम्। सम्प्रत्यङ्गत्वे ज्ञापकानुप्रवेशादित्यादि दूषणं परिहरन्नाह–**न चैतत्कलकलश्रुतावशक्यज्ञानम्।।** वैयाकरणग्रन्थे यद्यपि तिरोहितव्यवहितयोरित्याद्यप्युक्तम्। तथापि कलकलश्रुतौ चार्थज्ञानमित्यवसान (कथि?) तस्य दुष्कराभिप्रायात् तदेव निबन्धनकृतोपात्तमिति वेदितव्यम्। कारणमाह–**किमिव हि दुष्करमभ्यासस्य?** न किञ्चिदपीत्यर्थः। दुष्करत्वाभावे प्रसिद्धिं किमिवेत्यनेन सूचितामेव दर्शयन्नाह–**यदाहुर्बाह्या अपि–**

'परेषामनुपाख्येयमभ्यासादेव जायते।
मणिरूपादि ज्ञानं तद्विदामानुमानिकम्।।' इति।।

बाह्या अपीत्यनेन मानेन यथा मेयधीरेवमभ्यासस्य दुष्करत्वा(रा) भावोऽपि सर्वतन्त्रसिद्धान्त एवेति दर्शितमिति। अथवा–नास्तिका अप्यत्र न विप्रतिपद्यन्ते। तथा सति आस्तिकेषु तत्प्रतिपादनक्लेशो मुधैवेति।।

यच्चानन्तरमुक्तम्–

''सम्बन्धज्ञानसमये ज्ञायते न नियोगतः।
तिरोहितव्यवहितप्रयुक्ता वक्तुरेकता।।''

आवृतदूरवर्तिवक्तृप्रयुक्तेष्वपि वर्णेष्वविदुषे विद्वानर्थमाचष्टे। न च तत्र वक्तुरेकतामाश्रयति प्रतिपादकः। नापि तदनुपात्तं प्रतिपाद्य(:) स्वयमेव

---

१. 'यथा च तेषां गुणभूतानामर्थप्रत्यायनं प्रति साहित्यमेकक्रादिक्रमश्चापि विवक्षित इति' इत्यधिकं ३. पु० वर्तते इति टिप्पणी।

२. 'यथाहुः' इति मु० पु० पाठः।

३. वाक्यपदीये काण्डे १. श्लोक ३५. मुद्रितपुस्तके 'परेषामसमाख्येयमिति, मणिरूप्यादिविज्ञानामिति (तद्विदा नानुमानिकमिति) च पाठः' इति टिप्पणी।

न च समबन्धाख्यानसमेय वक्रेकताया [१]अनाश्रयादनङ्गत्वम्, हेन्वन्तरसिद्धः[२]। स्फुटतरतया तु तदनाख्यातम्[३]। न खलु नैरन्तर्यादयोऽप्याख्यायन्ते॥

प्रतिपद्यते; यथोपलब्धस्य सम्बन्धाख्यानाक्तुरेकतायाश्चनिमित्तमन्तरेण प्रतिपत्तुमविभवादित्युक्तम्।"

तस्मात्–

"अनङ्गे वक्तुरेकत्वे वक्तृभेदे निरुद्धवा।
संस्कारादावभिन्नेऽपि धीर्हेत्वन्तरसूचनी॥"

तदित्थं सम्बन्धकालेऽनाश्रयणात् प्रत्ययकाले चानावेदनात् अनङ्गे वक्तुरेकत्वे (वक्तृभेदेऽपि वर्णोपलब्धि)संस्काराद्यविशेषादुत्पत्तुमर्हदर्थज्ञानमनुत्पद्यमानं निमित्तान्तरजन्मानमात्मानमावेदयति" इति। एतदपि परिहरन्नाह–**न च सम्बन्धाख्यानसमये. . . .अनङ्गत्वम्॥** अनाश्रयश्च वक्त्रा चेति द्रष्टव्यम्। अथवा वक्त्रैव, श्रोत्रा अनावेदनादित्यर्थसिद्धम्। अनेन च 'सम्बन्धज्ञाने'त्यारभ्य 'तस्मादनङ्गे वक्तुरेकत्वे' इत्यन्तस्य निषेधः; हेत्वसिद्धौ 'वक्तृभेदे' इत्यादि साध्यनिषेधोऽर्थसिद्ध इत्याद्यु(त्यु)पेक्षितः। अनाश्रयानङ्गत्योर्न हेतुहेतुमद्भाव इत्युक्तं, तत्र कारणमाह–**हेत्वन्तरसिद्धेः॥** हेत्वन्तरञ्च तद्भावभावो विवक्षितः। अनाश्रयस्तु हेतुहेतुमद्भावाभावमन्तरेणाप्युपपद्यत एवेत्याह–**स्फुटतरतया तु तदनाख्यातम्॥ तत्**–वक्त्रैकत्वं, श्रोता तु प्रतिपद्यत एवेति भावः। तदेति पाठे सम्बन्धाख्यानसमय इत्यर्थः। नाख्यातं वक्त्रेकत्वमित्यर्थसिद्धम्। अनाख्यातमिति वा च्छेदः। भावे वा निष्ठा। ख्यानमिति वा पाठः भावल्युडन्तयोस्तु तथे(तदे)ति पाठे वक्त्रेकताया इति सिद्ध्यति। समासे तु तच्छब्देन वक्तेक्रतायाः परामर्श इति। एवं हेत्वन्तरसिद्धत्वादङ्गत्वस्य नानङ्गत्वं, अनाख्यानन्त्वनुक्तसुज्ञानत्वादित्युक्तम्। एतदेव स्थिरीकुर्वन्नाह–**न खलु**

---

१. (अनाश्रयात्)–'न्यूनाश्रयादिति ३. पु० पाठः' इति टिप्पणी।

२. 'हेत्वसिद्धेः' इति मु० पु० पाठः'

३. 'तदनाख्यानम्' इति मु० पु० पाठः।

[1]**तद्भावभावस्तु नैरन्तर्यादिवद्वक्त्रेकत्वेऽपि तुल्यः। न च ज्ञानकहेतुः विदितसमस्तज्ञापकाङ्गो ज्ञापयतीत्यप्यैकान्तिकम्।**

नैरन्तर्यादयोऽप्याख्यायन्ते।। अयमर्थः—न खल्वेकं वक्त्रेकत्वं लक्षीकृत्य प्रयोक्तव्यम्। वक्त्रेकत्ववदेव नैरन्तर्यादीनामपि वर्णानां पदभावेऽङ्गत्वेनाङ्गीकरणात्। न च तेऽपि वक्त्रा आश्रीयन्ते सम्बन्धज्ञानसमये, अङ्गत्वन्तु हेत्वन्तरसिद्धेरेव, स्फुटतरत्वात्तु नाख्यायन्त इति।।

ननु अनवयवदर्शनाभावादेव वक्तृभेदेऽर्थप्रत्ययादर्शनं न वक्त्रेकत्वाभावादिति न सिद्धा हेत्वन्तरसिद्धिरित्याशङ्क्याह—**तद्भावभावस्तु. . . .तुल्यः।।** इदमाकूतं—न तावदनवयवदर्शनमस्तीत्युक्तमेव। अतो 'यावन्तो यादृशाः' इति नैरन्तर्यादीनामिव वक्त्रेकत्वस्याप्यङ्गभावः स्वीकर्तव्यः। न च नैरन्तर्यादयोऽप्याख्यायन्ते। न च वक्त्रेकत्वमपि। प्रतिपत्ता तु सर्वमेव प्रमाणान्तरेणाङ्गतया प्रतिपद्यत एवेति। ननु नैरन्तर्यादयोऽनि नानवयवपदवाक्यवादिभिरङ्गीक्रियत इति किन्दृष्टान्तेन वक्त्रेकता दार्ष्टान्तिकीक्रियते, उभयोरपि सिद्धमेव दृष्टान्त इति स्थितत्वात्। न च नैरन्तर्यादयः परेषां सिद्धाः 'निरस्तभेदं पदतत्त्वमेकम्' इत्यङ्गीकरणादिति। सत्यमेवमेतत्। इह तु 'वक्तृभेदे निरुद्भवा' इत्यादिदर्शनात्तन्मात्रस्य दूषणमुपक्रान्तं, तत्र च नेरन्तर्यादिदृष्टान्तोपन्यासो नानुपपन्न इति। यदि तत्रापि विप्रतित्तिः, ततस्तत्रापि प्रतिविधानं कर्तव्यमेवेति। तच्च कृतमेव अनवयवस्य दर्शनाभावसाधनात् इति।।

एवन्तावद्वक्त्रेकत्वमनाख्यातमपि स्फुटतया प्रतिपत्ता प्रतिपद्यत इत्यभिप्रायेणोक्तम्। सम्प्रति ज्ञापकानुप्रवेशान्नानवधारितेत्यप्यसिद्धमेवेत्याह—**न च ज्ञापकेहेतुः....इत्यप्यैकान्तिकम्।।** विदितानि समस्तान्येव ज्ञापकभूतान्यङ्गानि ज्ञापकस्यैव वा हेतोस्तस्याङ्गानि यस्य सहकारितया सन्तीति विग्रहः। स्वरूपोपयोग्यङ्गेभ्यो व्यावृत्त्यर्थं ज्ञापकविशेषणम्। षष्ठीसमासेऽपि ज्ञापकावस्थापन्नस्याङ्गित्वमिति सूच्यते। विशेषणे च तात्पर्यं लोहितोष्णीषादिवत्। अतोऽङ्गानामेव वेदने नियमाभावो नाङ्गिनः। ज्ञापकहेतुरिति लिङ्गशब्दानुपपद्यमानेषु विशेषतः प्रसिद्धत्वाच्चक्षुरादौ न व्यभिचार इति। यो हि विदितो

---

१. 'तद्भावस्तु नैरन्तर्यादिष्विव वक्त्रेकत्वेऽपि समानः' इति मु० पु० पाठः।

भवति हि मनोऽनुमानाङ्गम्। न चास्य वेदनमत्रोपयुज्यते। [१]**तदिह दृश्यमानेभ्यो दृश्यमानप्रकारानुपातिभ्यः अभिधेयप्रत्यय उपपद्य-**

भूत्वा ज्ञापयति स ज्ञापकहेतुः, न ज्ञानकारणमात्रमित्यङ्गीकृत्य तदुपकरणानां ज्ञापकानामेव सतां न वेदननियमः। कानिचिद्विदितानि सन्ति सहकुर्वन्ति, कानिचिदविदितान्येवेति। कुत एवं तदधिगतमिति चेत्तत्राह—**भवति हि मनोऽनुमानाङ्गम्।।** ततः किमित्याह—**न चास्य वेदनमत्रोपयुज्यते।।** मनसो ह्यनुमानाङ्गत्वम्, सर्वज्ञानोत्पत्तिष्वेव मनसोऽङ्गत्वात्। यथाहुः—'युगपज्ज्ञानानुत्पत्तिर्मनसो लिङ्गम्' इति। विभुनैवात्मनाधिष्ठितेष्विन्द्रियेषु नानार्थसम्बन्धेष्वपि यत्संयोगक्रमवशाज्ज्ञानोत्पत्तिक्रमः प्रक्रमते तन्मन इति। एवञ्चाणुन एव मनसः सिद्धिः। अन्यथा युगपदनेकेन्द्रियाधिष्ठानाद्युगपज्ज्ञानोदयप्रसङ्गात्। तथा च विभुत्वहेतवः सर्वे सर्वदा स्पर्शरहितद्रव्यत्वादित्यादयो धर्मिग्राहकप्रमाणबाधिता भवन्तीति तार्किकाः। **न्यायकणिकायान्त्य**वेवमेवाश्रितमिति प्रतीयते। **यथोक्तं**—'इन्द्रियभावत्वणुन एव मनसः' इति। **भावनाविवेके च**—

'मनोभूतपरिस्पन्द आत्मनस्तत्प्रयत्नजः'।। इति।

अत्र भूतानामिव मनसोऽपि परिस्पन्दं ब्रुवताऽणुत्वमङ्गीकृतमिति प्रतीयते। एवमन्येषामपि वार्तिककारीयाणामणुत्वाभ्युपगमोऽस्त्येव। प्रायेण तु वार्तिककारीया विभुत्वमातिष्ठन्ते। अतो यथा शब्दस्यालौकिको व्यवहा(व्यापा)रोऽभिधा वा विधिः, इष्टसाधनता स्वरूपेण प्रवर्तनारूपेण वा विधिः, इति विधौ, यथा च तमसि द्रव्यगुणत्वयोरित्यादौ वार्तिककारीयाणामेव दर्शनभेदः तथाऽत्रापि द्रष्टव्यम्। तथा,

'सुखादेरापरोक्ष्यस्य साधानं मन इन्द्रियम्।'

इति सुखाद्यन्यतमग्रहणसाधनत्वं मनसो लक्षणं **निबन्धनकृतो**ऽभिमतमिति द्रष्टव्यम्। अणुत्वन्तु पूर्ववदेव, युगपज्ज्ञानानुत्पत्तेः। विभुत्वादिनोऽपि हि

---

१. 'तदिह दृश्यमानेभ्य एव वर्णेभ्यो दृश्यमानप्रकारभेदानुयायिभ्योऽभिधेयप्रत्यय उपपद्यमानो नैतानवज्ञायानवयवं' इति मु० पु० पाठः।

मानो [१]नैवाज्ञातावयवमत्यन्ताननुभूतं पदतत्त्वमुपकल्पयति[२]; अतिप्रसङ्गात्। न चापि समभिव्याहृतपदाभिहितपदार्थप्रत्यया-

---

सुखाद्यापरोक्ष्यसाधनतया मनोऽनुमाय, मनो विभु, स्पर्शानर्हद्रव्यत्वादित्याद्यनुमानेन विभुतामाश्रित्य सर्वज्ञानेष्वेव मनसोऽङ्गभावमातिष्ठन्त। एवं 'मानसो वेन्द्रियैर्योग' इत्यादिवार्तिकदर्शनादन्यमनस्कस्य सम्प्रयुक्तेष्वपि रूपादिषु ज्ञानानुत्पत्तेश्चेति। **अस्येत्यत्रेति** च सर्वनाम्ना यथाक्रमं मनोऽनुमानयोः परामर्शः। वेदनानुपयोगस्तु कार्यान्यथानुपपत्तिप्रमाणत्वान्मनसः, अनुमानस्य च कार्यान्तर्भावादिति द्रष्टव्यम्। एवञ्च वर्णेषूक्तस्य दोषस्यासत्वात् 'यावन्तो यादृशा' इत्येव स्थितमित्याह—**तदिह दृश्यमानेभ्यो दृश्यमानप्रकारानुपपत्तिभ्यः (नुपातिभ्यः)।** दृश्यमानं प्रकारं येऽनुपतन्ति ते तथोक्ताः। 'यादृशा' इत्यस्यानुवाद एष इति द्रष्टव्यम्। अनुपपत्तिभ्य इति पाठे अदृश्यमानप्रकारानुपपत्तिभ्य इत्यकारप्रश्लेषेण च्छेदः। अदृश्यमाना प्रकारे वक्त्रेकत्वादिके प्रयोक्त्रनुपपत्तिर्येषामेवमिति विग्रहः। किन्तेभ्यो भवतीत्यपेक्षायां आह—**अभिधेयप्रत्यय उपपद्यमानः॥** एवं 'वर्णेभ्यो नार्थप्रत्ययो नोपपद्यते' इत्यारभ्योपपाद्य, अन्यथोपपत्तेः पक्षनिष्ठत्वं दर्शितम्। सम्प्रति अन्यथोपपत्तिमर्थापत्तिदूषणे प्रकृते पर्यवसाययति—**नैवाज्ञातावयव-मत्यन्ता (न) नुभूतं पदतत्त्वमुपकल्पयति। अज्ञातावयवमिति॥** अनवयवमित्येवार्थः। तथैव वा पाठः। न चान्यत्प्रमाणमस्तीत्युक्तमेवेति दर्शितं—अत्यन्ताननुभूतमिति॥ न तु कल्पनाभावेऽत्यन्ताननुभवो दोषतया मन्तव्यो गुणत्वात्। न च प्रत्यक्षं प्रमाणमित्युक्तमित्यभिप्रायः। अथवा—अत्र शब्दोऽपरोक्षज्ञानयोग्योऽन्यथानुपपत्त्या कल्प्यते। तद्विषयत्वेन च कल्प्यते योऽयं प्रत्यक्षविषयः शब्दः स न वर्णातिरिक्त इति। न च वर्णातिरिक्तं अनवयवमनुभूयते इत्युक्तं, अतोऽनुपलब्धिनिराकृतस्य नानवयवस्य कल्पना शशविषाणवद्युक्तेति सम्भवत्येव कल्पनाभावे दोषत्वे हेतुता। कारणमाह—**अतिप्रसङ्गात्॥** अयमर्थः। अन्यथोपपत्तौ सत्यामपि कल्पने कल्पितेऽपि स्फोटे शब्दान्तरकल्पना, पुनश्च तथा। एवमन्यत्रापि, शक्त्यादौ शक्त्यन्तरादि-

---

१. 'नैवानवज्ञाये'ति ३. पु० पाठः इति टिप्पणी।
२. 'उपकल्पयितुमर्हति' इति मु० पु० पाठः।

धीनोत्पत्तिर्वाक्यार्थधीरन्यथोपपद्यमानाऽनुभूयमानपरस्परव्या[१] **वृत्तमूर्तिपदान्यपह्नुत्यात्यन्तापरिदृष्टं वाक्यमेकमनवयवमिति।**[२]

कल्पनेऽप्यतिप्रसक्तिसमभवादिति। अथवा–अनुपलब्धिबाधितस्य कल्पने शशविषाणादेरपि कल्पनाप्रसङ्गादिति। तामेवान्यथोपपत्तिं वाक्यान्यथानुपपत्तिदूषणे पर्यवसाययन्नुत्तरार्धमेव योजयति–**न चापि समभिव्याहृत. . . . अनवयवमिति।।** न चापि वाक्यार्थधीरेकं वाक्यमुपकल्पयतीति सम्बन्धः। कुतः? **अन्यथा**–वाक्यमन्तरेणोपपद्यमानत्वात्। कुतोऽन्यथोपपद्यमाना? यतः समभिव्याहृतैः पदैरभिहिताः पदार्था ये तेषां प्रत्ययेष्वधीनोत्पत्तिर्यस्या इति विग्रहः। एतच्च सिद्धान्त एव साधयिष्यत इति न प्रस्तूयते। अनुभूयमानानि, परस्परं व्यावृत्ता मूर्तयो येषां पदानामिति परस्परव्यावृत्तमूर्तीनि, पदानि इति विग्रहः। **अनुभूयमान**तेत्यस्य व्यावर्त्यं वैपरीत्यं **अत्यन्तापरिदृष्ट**मिति। **परस्परव्यावृत्तमूर्ती**त्यस्यैक**मनवयव**मिति। इह **दृष्टा**दिति पदान्यधिकृत्योक्तमिति दर्शितं **अनुभूयमानानि पदानि** इति। अदृष्टेति।। वाक्यकटाक्षेणोक्तमिति दर्शितं **अत्यन्तापरिदृष्टं वाक्य**मिति। इह च **'तदिह दृश्यमानेभ्यः'** इति वाक्यविषये तस्यैव व्याख्यानमिति विवेक्तव्यम्। उत्तरार्धव्याख्यासमाप्ता**विति**शब्दः। उत्तरार्ध-व्याख्यासम्पन्नमर्थं दर्शयति–**तत्सिद्धमेतत्. . . पदवाक्यभावसाधनीति।।** अत्र कथं तन्मात्रनिवृत्तिरभावं साधयतीत्यपेक्षानिवृत्तये 'न चाप्रत्यक्षमर्थधीकार्येण शक्यानुमानम्' इत्युपक्रममूरीकृत्य **तदेकगोचरे**त्युक्तम्। **'अर्थापत्तेरनुमानस्य वा'** इति निर्देशादेतदुन्नीयते 'येनोच्चारितेन' इत्यादि**महाभाष्ये** यदर्थप्रत्ययोन्नेयत्वं शब्दस्योक्तं तत्किमनुमेयत्वम्, उतार्थापत्तिकल्प्यत्वमिति विकल्प्य **'न चाप्रत्यक्षमर्थधीकार्येण'** इत्यादिना अनुमेयत्वं निराकृत्य **'अपि च वर्णेभ्यः'** इत्यादिना अर्थापत्तिकल्प्यत्वं दूषितम्। श्लोकार्थस्त्वर्थापत्तिविषय एवेति। कृत्स्नश्लोकसम्पन्नमर्थमुपसंहरति–**इति स्थितं. . .बोधकमिति।।**

---

१. 'परस्परव्यावृतमूर्तीनि पदानि' इति मु० पु० पाठः।

२. 'अनवयवमवगमयति' इति मु० पु० पाठः।

तत्सिद्धमेतदर्थापत्तेरनु मानस्य वा निवृत्तिस्त[१]देकगोचरापद-वाक्याभावसाधनीति स्थितं नानवयवमेकं वाक्यं वाक्यार्थस्य बोधकमिति।।

नापि द्वितीयः कल्पः। तथा हि–

नान्त्यवर्णश्रुतिः स्मृत्या नीता वाक्यार्थबोधिनी।
नस्मृतिस्तदपेक्षत्वाद्यौगपद्यं न चानयोः।।

साधनीशब्दानन्तर **इति**शब्दस्तन्त्रेणोभाभ्यां सम्बन्धनीयः। पूर्वत्र प्रकारवचनः। उत्तरत्र हेत्वर्थः। न च पौरुषेयेत्वनेकार्थत्वं दोषः।

'बह्वभिप्रायमप्येकं पुरुषास्तु प्रयुञ्जते।'

इति न्यायात्। एतत्सङ्ग्रहस्तु **न्यायसमुच्चये** द्रष्टव्यम्।।

एवान्तावत् **'अनवयवमेव वाक्यमनाद्यविद्योपदर्शितालीकवर्णपद-विभागमस्यां निमित्तमिति केचित्'** इति प्रथमः पक्षो दूषितः। वाक्यार्थस्य वाक्यं वाचकमित्यौचित्यात्। एवं च वर्णा एव पदानि तान्येव वाक्यमित्यायातम्। सम्प्रति वर्णवादिनामेव विवादे वाक्यार्थस्य किं मूलमिति निरूपणम्। तत्र च वर्णानामौपाधिकं रूपं पदमिति स्थापितम्। औपाधिकाच्च स्वाभाविकस्य रूपस्य प्राथम्यमिति वर्णस्वरूपं निमित्तमित्यापतति। वर्णस्वरूपस्यापि स्मर्य-माणावस्थायाः अनूभूयमानावस्थायाः प्राथम्यादेकस्य निमित्तत्वसम्भवे वाऽनेक-कल्पनाया अन्वाय्यत्वादन्त्वर्णपक्षमनन्तरोपन्यस्तं 'पूर्वपूर्वपदपदार्थानुभवजनित-संस्कारसहितमन्त्यवर्णविज्ञानमित्येके' इति द्वितीय पक्षं दूषयति–

नापि द्वितीयः कल्पः। तथा हि–

नान्त्यवर्णश्रुतिः स्मृत्या नीता वाक्यार्थबोधिनी।
नस्मृतिस्तदपेक्षत्वाद्यौगपद्यं न चानयोः।।

---

१. 'तदेकगोचरपदवाक्य (स्फोटाभावसाधनीति २. पु० पाठः' इति टिप्पणी) **स्फोटावभासिनीति** नानवयवमेकं वाक्यार्थावबोधकमिति' इति मु० पु० पाठः। (स्फोटावभासिनी)–'स्फोटाभावसाधनीति २. पु. पाठः' इति टिप्पणी।

[1]स खल्वयमन्त्यो वर्णः पूर्वपूर्ववर्णपदपदार्थविज्ञानजनितवासनानिचयसचिवश्रवणेन्द्रियसमधिगतजन्मग्रहणस्मरणरूपस[2]दसद्वर्णनिर्भासप्रत्यय[3]विपरिवर्ती पद[4]वाक्यार्थधी हेतुरुपेयते।

यद्यन्त्यवर्णश्रुतिर्वाक्यार्थबोधिनी तर्हीतरेषामानर्थक्यमिति न वक्तव्यमिति दर्शयन् पदार्थप्रत्ययवद्वाक्यार्थप्रत्ययेऽपि प्रकारा द्रष्टव्य इति तावदाह–**स खल्वयं. . . उपेयते।।** पूर्वपूर्वेषां वर्णानां पदानां पदार्थानां च विज्ञानैर्जनितानां वासनानां निचय एव सचिवो यस्य श्रवणेन्द्रियस्य तादृशाच्छ्रवणेन्द्रियात्समधिगतं लब्धं जन्म येन प्रत्यनेन तस्मिन्ग्रहणस्मरणरूपे तत एव तथा सदसद्वर्णनिर्भासे प्रत्यये विपरिवर्ती पदार्थधियः तथा वाक्यार्थधियश्च हेतुरभ्युपेयतेऽन्त्यवर्णवादिना। पूर्वपूर्ववर्णेत्यत्र वर्णग्रहणं पदार्थधीहेतुत्वोपयोगाय। पूर्वपूर्ववर्णविज्ञानजनितवासनानिचयसचिवश्रवणेन्द्रियलब्धजन्मतादृशप्रत्ययविपरिवर्ती यथा पदार्थप्रत्ययधीहेतुरुपेयते तथा पदपदार्थविज्ञानजनितवासनानिचयसचिवश्रवणेन्द्रियसमधिगतजन्मतादृक्प्रत्यय(विपरि)वर्ती वाक्यार्थधीहेतुरुपेयत इति योजना।।

अथवा–वाक्ये पदपदार्थवद्वर्णज्ञानमपि वाक्यार्थधीहेतुत्वोपयोग्येवास्तु, अन्वयव्यतिरेकयोस्तुल्यत्वात्। **पदवाक्यार्थधीहेतु**रित्यत्र पदग्रहणं दृष्टान्तार्थमेव। पदशब्दं विना वा पाठः। अनेन च–

'चित्ररूपाञ्च तां बुद्धिं समसद्वर्णगोचराम्।
केचिदाहुर्यया वर्णो गृह्यतेऽन्त्यः पदे पदे।।'

इति पदोक्तप्रकारेण वाक्ये चित्ररूपा बुद्धिरुपदर्शिता। उपन्यासकाले तु

---

१. 'स खल्वन्त्यो वर्णः' इति मु० पु० पाठः।

२. 'जन्मस्मरणरूपावाप्तवैचित्र्य' इति मु० पु० पाठः।

३. (पूर्वपूर्व ....विपरिवर्ती)–'पूर्वपूर्ववर्णप्रत्यक्षजन्यानां संस्काराणां समूहः सहकारी यस्य तादृशेन श्रोत्रेण जनितः पूर्ववर्णांशे स्मरणरूपतया चरमवर्णविषये चानुभवरूपतया प्राप्तरूपद्वयः सतोऽन्त्यस्यासतां च पूर्ववर्णानां प्रकाशको यः प्रत्ययस्तद्विषय इत्यर्थः' इति टिप्पणी।

४. 'वर्ती वाक्यार्थधी' इति मु० पु० पाठः।

[१]स चरमपदतदर्थसम्बन्धस्मृतिमाधाय वाक्यार्थधिया(यमा) दधीत, अनाधाय वा। आधाय चेत्तद्धेतुभावनोद्बोधसमये [२]स्वजन्यसंस्कारकारणविनाशाघ्रातश्रुतिरश्रूयमाणः सम्बन्धस्मृतिसमये कथं

'पारमार्थिकपूर्वपूर्वपदपदार्थानुभवजनितसंस्कारसहितमन्त्यवर्णविज्ञानमित्येके' इति पूर्वपूर्ववर्णजनितसंस्कारसहितोऽन्त्यो वर्णो वाचक इत्यनेन मार्गेण पूर्वजनितसंस्कारसाहित्यमात्रं दर्शितम्। तत्किमेतत्? सत्यम्; संस्कारसाहित्यमपि तत्कार्ययागित्वमेव विवक्षितमित्यनेन दर्शितं वेदितव्यम्। अथवा–अन्त्यवर्णस्य पदार्थबोधकत्वे यानि प्रकारान्तराणि तानि सर्वाणि विवक्षितानि। तेषु पूर्वमुपन्यासकाले संस्कारान्तरानुगृहीतोऽन्त्यो वर्णः प्रतिपादक इति स्मृतिहेतुसंस्कारानुगृहीतो वेत्युभयोरपि साधारण्येनोक्तम्। इदानीं **चित्रबुद्धौ** गृह्यमाणोऽन्त्यो वर्णः प्रतिपादक इत्ययं पक्ष उपन्यस्तः। क्वचिद्धि किञ्चिदुपन्यस्तं दूषणं तु सर्वसाधारणमित्यदोषः। **उपेयत इति।।** एवं वाक्यान्त्यवर्णस्य वाक्यार्थवाचकत्वमाचक्षणैरङ्गीक्रियते। अतो नात्रोपपत्तिरस्माभिर्वक्तव्येत्यभिप्रायः।। अथवा–पदेषु संस्कारान्तरानुगृहीतान्त्यवर्णवाचकत्वे स्मृतिहेतुसंस्कारानुगृहीतान्त्यवर्णवाचकत्वेऽपि विद्यमाने किमर्थं वाक्ये चित्रबुद्धिग्राह्यत्वमेवोपन्यस्यत इत्यपेक्षायामुक्तं अभ्युपेयत इत्येवं विवेकः।।

एवं **'अन्त्यवर्णश्रुतिः'** इत्ययमंशो व्याख्यातः। सम्प्रति श्लोकपूर्वोत्तरार्धयोर्विषयव्यवस्थया व्याख्यानाय विकल्पयति–**स चरमपद. . . अनाधाय वा। सो**ऽन्त्यवर्णः। चरमपदतदर्थयोर्यः परस्परं सम्बन्धः तत्स्मृतिमिति विग्रहः। अनेन श्लोकगतस्य **समृत्ये**त्यस्य व्याख्यानं कृतम्। **अनाधाय वा** चरमपदतदर्थस्मृतिं वाक्यार्थधियमादधीत इति। एवं विकल्प्य प्रथमं शिरो दूषयति–**आधाय चेत्. . . आदधीत।।** अयमर्थः–स चरमपदतदर्थसम्बन्धस्मृतिमाधाय यदि वाक्यार्थधियमादधीत, तर्हि तत्स्मृतिहेतुर्या भावना

---

१. 'स च चरम' इति मु० पु० पाठः।

२. (स्वजन्यसंस्कारकारणविनाशाघ्रातश्रुतिः)–'संस्कारस्य स्मृतिशयत्वास्त्स्मृतौ जातायां संस्कारनाशेनोत्तरज्ञानेन पूर्वज्ञाननाशाद्वर्णप्रत्यक्षनाशेन चेति भावः' इति टिप्पणी।

[1]तत्सहकारी [2]वाक्यार्थधियमादधीत। न (च) तदसहकारिणो वाक्यार्थधीहेतुभाव इति साम्प्रतम्। अस्मरणे तदनुभववैयर्थ्येन

संस्कारः तदुद्बोधोऽवश्यं पूर्वमनुत्पन्नः तदानीमेव कुतश्चित्कारणादुत्पन्न इत्यङ्गीकर्तव्यम्। कारणञ्च सम्बन्धिनोरन्यतरस्य पदस्य श्रवणं, अन्वयव्यतिरेकानुसारात्। अतः श्रवणानन्तरक्षणे तदुद्बोधः, तदैव चान्त्यवर्णानुभवेन संस्कारान्तरं स्वजन्यमुत्पादितम्। सर्वानुभवानामनन्तरक्षणे संस्कारोत्पादनियमात्। संस्काराश्च जन्यः स्वजनकस्यानुभवस्य विनाशे कारणम्। फलं हि कृत्वैव क्रिया नश्यति। फलविनाश्यं कर्मेति वदन्ति। ततश्च स्वजन्यसंस्कारणकेन विनाशेनाघ्राता स्वीकृता श्रुतिः यस्यान्त्यवर्णस्य स तथाविधः। अत एव अश्रूयमाणोऽन्त्यवर्णः चरमपदतदर्थसम्बन्धविषया या स्मृतिः तत्समये श्रवणात् श्रोत्रानुभवादुत्तरक्षणो विनाशक्षणः तस्मादप्युत्तरक्षणे कथं तत्सहकारी चरमपदतदर्थसम्बन्धस्मृतिः सहकारी उपायो यस्येति बहुव्रीहिः। अथवा–तया सह स्वकार्यं कर्तुं शीलवानिति। **वाक्यार्थधियमादधीत।** न च स्मृतिसमयं मुक्त्वा श्रवणसमय एव तदाधानमिति वक्तव्यम्, तत्सहकारित्वस्याङ्गीकृतत्वादिति भावः।।

एवं पूर्वार्धो व्याख्यातः। सम्प्रति द्वितीयं शिरो दूषयन्नुत्तरार्धं व्याचष्टे–**न (च) तदसहकारिणो. . . .साम्प्रतम्।। तदसहकारिण** इत्युक्तार्थम्। अनेन श्लोके **'नस्मृतिः'** इत्ययमंशोऽन्त्यवर्णश्रुतिश्चरमपदतदर्थसम्बन्धस्मृतिरहिता वाक्यार्थबोधिनीति न युक्तमित्येवं व्याख्यातमिति द्रष्टव्यम्। **'तदपेक्षत्वात्'** इत्येतद्व्याचष्टे–**अस्मरणे तदनुभव. . . .अर्थप्रत्ययप्रसङ्गात्।।** अयमर्थः–चरमपदतदर्थसम्बन्धस्यास्मरणे तस्य सम्बन्धस्यानुभवेन कर्तव्याभावात्, स्मरणस्य च तत्प्रयोजनत्वात्, चानपेक्षिततत्वेनानुभववैयर्थ्यात्, गृहीतसङ्गतेरपि तथा प्रथमश्राविणोऽविशेषणार्थप्रत्ययप्रसङ्गात्। गृहीतसङ्गतेरिवेति क्वचित्पाठः, स साधुः। क्वचित्त्वगृहीतसङ्गतेरपीति। तत्रैतदेव व्याचष्टे–

---

१. (तत्सहकारी)–'तत्सहकारिणमिति २. पु० पाठः' इति टिप्पणी।

२. 'वाक्यार्थप्रत्ययं' इति मु० पु० पाठः।

गृहीत [१]सङ्गतेरपि प्रथमश्राविणोऽपि 'भिन्धि प्रासेन सिन्धुरम्' इति वाक्यादर्थप्रत्यय- प्रसङ्गात्। न चान्त्यवर्णबोधितसंस्कारा स्मृतिरनुभवेन सह युगपदुत्पत्तुमर्हति। न च न्याय्यो युगपदुत्पादः प्रत्ययानाम्। [२]कारणस्य[३] प्रत्ययपर्याये सामर्थ्यात्। अन्यथा [४]समान विषयबुद्धिधारानुपपत्तेः। सहसैव यावत्कर्तव्यकरणात्,

---

प्रथमश्राविणोऽपीत्यनेनेति योजना। श्लोके **'तदपेक्षत्वात्'** इत्यस्य पद-श्रवणस्य पदार्थबोधने सम्बन्धस्मृत्यपेक्षित्वस्य स्थितत्वादित्यर्थोऽभिप्रेतः। एतदेवा**स्मरण** इत्यादि व्यतिरेकेण व्याख्यातमिति। अत्रैव दूषणान्तरपरतया चतुर्थपादं व्याचष्टे—**न चान्त्यवर्ण. . . .युगपदुत्पत्तुमर्हति।।** इदमाकूतं—ननु मा भूद्वर्णश्रवणानन्तरभाविनी स्मृतिः स्मृतेः पूर्वकालीनस्यान्त्यवर्णश्रवणस्य सहकारिणी। मा च भूत् तन्निरपेक्षमेवान्त्यवर्णश्रवणस्य वाक्यार्थबोधित्वं; किन्तु युगपत्कालीना स्मृतिरनुभवस्य सह करोतु। नैवं शक्यम्। संस्कारो हि स्मृतिकारणं, स चोद्बुद्ध एव तत्कारणं, उद्बोधश्च पदानुभवनिमित्तः, सम्बन्धिदर्शननिमित्तत्वात् सम्बन्धस्मृतिकारिसंस्कारोद्बोधस्य, पदस्य च सम्बन्धित्वात्, निमित्तान्तरस्य चानाशङ्कनीयत्वात्, पदान्वयव्यतिरेकानुविधानात्, अनङ्गीकृतत्वाच्च। न चासञ्जातोऽनुभवः संस्कारोद्बोधं कर्तुमीष्टे। अतोऽनुभवानन्तरकालीनत्वात्स्मृतेः स्वकालात्प्रागेवानुभवजन्मकाले(न) जन्मोपपत्तिरिति। एवञ्च वदता यौगपद्यं **'न चानयोः'** इत्येतद्धर्मिविरोधादेव

---

१. 'वेयर्थ्येनागृहीतसङ्गतेरपि प्रथमाश्राविणो 'भिन्धि प्रासेन भिदुरम्' इति वाक्यार्थप्रत्ययप्रसङ्गात्। न चान्त्यवर्णोद्बोधितसंस्काराधीनजन्मा स्मृतिः' इति मु० पु० पाठः।

२. (कारणस्य)(करणस्य)–'मनसः। अत एव न्यायसूत्रं–'युगपज्ज्ञानानुत्पत्तिर्मनसो लिङ्गम्' इति। गौतमसूत्रं–अ० १. आ० १. सू० १६' इति टिप्पणी।

३. 'करणस्य' इति मु० पु० पाठः।

४. (समानविषयबुद्धिधारानुपपत्तेः)–'प्रथमानुभवेन संस्कारोत्पादाद्द्वितीयादिज्ञानानां स्मृतित्वेन धारावाहिकप्रत्यक्षानुपपत्तेरित्यर्थः।' इति टिप्पणी।

(**[१]समर्थस्य) क्षेपायोगात्। न च तावन्तं कालमस्ति प्रथमोत्पन्नधीजनितसंस्कारभेदः, यतः पुनरपि चरमविषयं विज्ञानं[२] जनयेत्।। यथाहुः—**

यौगपद्यधर्मोऽशक्याभ्युपगम इत्यभिप्रेतमिति व्याख्यातम्। तत्र च विशेषरूपस्य बाधकत्वं यथा भवति, तथाऽनेन दर्शितम्। ज्ञानवत्त्वसामान्यस्यापि बाधकत्वं दर्शयन्नाह—**न च न्याय्यो. . . प्रत्ययानाम्।।** अन्याय्यत्वे हेतुमाह—**कारणस्य प्रत्ययपर्याये सामर्थ्यात्।** अर्थात्प्रत्ययानां कारणस्येति सिद्ध्यति। अथवा—काकाक्षिवदनुषङ्गेण तन्त्रेण वेत्युक्तप्रकारेण पूर्वमे(वंत्रे?)व प्रत्ययानामित्येतदत्रापि सम्बद्ध्यते। **प्रत्ययपर्याये सामर्थ्यात्।** पर्यायेणैव स्वकार्यं प्रत्यय कर्तुं सामर्थ्यं नान्यथेति यत इत्यर्थः। **कारणस्येति।।** यद्यत्प्रत्ययकारणं प्रत्येत्रा(ता?) प्रत्येतव्यं करणमिन्द्रियादि तथात्ममनोयोगादिकं, तत्सर्वंग्रहीतुं **कारणस्ये**ति सामान्यवचनमिति द्रष्टव्यम्। कुतोऽवगतमीदृशं सामर्थ्यमस्येति चेत्तत्राह—**अन्यथा समानविषयबुद्धिधारानुपपत्तेः।।** अयमर्थः—यदि प्रत्ययकारणस्य प्रत्यययौगपद्ये सामर्थ्यं स्यात्, तर्हि यद्रूपादिषु बहुषु सन्निहितेषु रूपमेकमेव प्रत्यक्षीक्रियते, तन्नोपपद्यते। अथ यच्चक्षुषा जनितं ज्ञानं तद्रूप (?). . . त्युच्यते। ततो यदेकस्मिन्नेव विषये बुद्धिधारा दृश्यते तन्नोपपद्यते। कुतो नोपपद्यते इति, (तत्राह—)**सहसैव यावत्कर्तव्यकरणात्।।** अयमर्थः—यत् ज्ञानकारणं तेन यादृशं ज्ञानं कर्तुं शक्यते तादृश(स्य सर्वस्य एक?) स्मिन्नेव कस्मिंश्चित्क्षणे कृत्वेनोत्तरकालमौदासीन्यप्रसङ्गादिति। तदपि कुतः, तत्र(हि—**समर्थस्य) क्षेपायोगात्।।** अयमर्थः—यौगपद्ये शक्तस्य प्रत्ययकारणस्य कालक्षेपो विलम्बो (न युक्तः?)। अतो यौगपद्ये शक्तावनुपपद्यमानं समानविषयबुधिधारादर्शनं पर्याये सा-(मर्थ्य) वेदयति। तथा च प्रत्ययानामुत्पत्तियौगपद्यमन्याय्यमिति न स्मृत्यनुभवयोः युगपदुत्पत्ति(सम्भवः?)। अस्तु पर्याये सामर्थ्यम्, तथापि प्रथमं चरमं पदं श्रोत्रेण गृहीत्वा पुनश्चरमपदतदर्थपद

---

१. 'समर्थस्य' इति यथामुद्रितपुस्तकं दीयते, व्याख्याने ग्रन्थलोपात्।

२. 'विज्ञानं जनयेत्' इत्यारभ्य 'वर्णमालैव वाक्यर्थधीहेतुः' इत्यन्तो ग्रन्थः यथामुद्रितपुस्तकं दीयते; व्याख्याने ग्रन्थपातात्।

'क्षणिकं साधनञ्चास्य बुद्धिरप्यनुवर्तते।
मेघान्धकारशर्वर्यां विद्युज्जनितदृष्टिवत्।।' इति।

न चाननुभूयमानस्य सत्तामात्रेण बोधकत्वमित्यसकृदवोचाम।।

(?). . . तदनन्तरं श्रौत्रेणैव गृह्यमाणोऽन्त्यो वर्णो वाक्यार्थस्य वाचकः, ततो नोक्तदोषप्र(सङ्ग इति)। तत्राह–**न च तावन्तं. . . (विज्ञानं जनयेत्।।** इदमाकूतम्–श्रोत्रं हि दिगात्मकमाकाशात्मकं वाऽभ्युपेयते। तच्च नित्यवाद्ग्रहणवस्थापूर्वावस्थमेव कथं कादाचित्कस्य ग्रहणस्य कारणं स्यात्; तस्मात्पूर्वमनुत्पन्नः तदानीमेवोत्पत्स्यमानः?) कश्चिदतिशय एषितव्यः। स च 'अभिघातेन (हि) प्रेरिता वायवः' इत्यादिना मार्गेण वायुसंयोग(विभाग?)जन्यः संस्कारः। स च क्षणिक एव, उत्तरकालमग्रहणात्, संस्कारान्तपेक्षणाच्च। अ (?) श्रोत्रसंस्कार इत्यभ्युपेयम्। तथा च यावति काले स्मृत्युपत्त्यनन्तरक्षणे भूयश्चरम(वर्णविषयं?) ग्रहणमुत्पादयितव्यं न तावन्तं कालं प्रथमोत्पन्ना चरमपदविषया या श्रोत्रधीः तस्या (?). . र्थत्वात्तदन्तरमेव(वा?) विनष्टश्रोत्रसंस्कारभेदोऽस्ति। यतः पुनरपि चरमपदविषयं विज्ञानं जनयेदिति। **प्रथमोत्पन्नधीजनितसंस्कारे**ति। धीजनकेति पाठो द्रष्टव्यः। **अथवा**– प्रथमोत्पन्नाया धियः(पुनरु?)पादनाय वक्त्रा जनितः श्रोतुः श्रोत्रसंस्कारभेद इति विग्रहो द्रष्टव्यः। 'न च तावन्तम्' इत्यस्यैव प्रसिद्धिं[१]. . . . . . स्मर्यमाणा? चेद्धेतुः कालान्तरानुभूता कालान्तरे स्मर्यमाणेऽपि हेतुः स्यादिति वाच्यम्। यतः श्रवणेन्द्रियजन्यानुभवगृहीता हेतुः स्यादिति वाच्यम्। यतः श्रवणेन्द्रियजन्यानुभवगृहीता हेतुः तस्यास्त्ववान्तर- व्यापारस्मृतिसमारोह (?) इत्यवान्तरव्यापारत्वं च कर्तृत्वोक्त्यैव सूचितमिति वेदितव्यम्। **वर्णमालेति।।** सर्ववर्णसमुदायः कारणं न त्वन्त्यस्य हेतुत्वमितरेषां सहकारित्वमिति वैषम्यमाश्रीयत इति सूचयति। एवकारेणान्यत्पदपदार्थादिकमिति दर्शयति। पदार्थहेतुत्वे शाब्दत्वाभावात्, पदहेतुत्वे पदार्थत्वप्रसङ्गात्, अन्त्यवर्णाखण्डयोश्च निराकरणात्, अन्यत्रानुपयुक्ता वर्णमालैव वाक्यं भूत्वा वाक्यार्थस्य वाचिकेति।

---

१. व्याख्याने एकपत्रपरिमितग्रन्थपातः।

अस्तु तर्हि स्मृतिदर्पणारूढा वर्णमालैव वाक्यार्थधीहेतुः। वृद्धप्रयोगाधीनावधारणो हि शब्दार्थसम्बन्धः। न च पदमात्रं व्यवहाराङ्गं प्रयुञ्जते वृद्धाः, किन्तु वाक्यमेव, तच्चानवयवं [१]न्यषेधीति स्मृतिसमारूढा वर्णमाला [२]परिशिष्यते [३]सा च नैमित्तिकं वाक्यार्थबोध

अथवा–पदार्थस्यापि पदवर्तिनी वर्णमाला वाचिकेत्यभ्युपगम्यते। एवमेव वाक्यवर्तिनी वर्णमाला वाक्यार्थस्य वाचिकेति युक्तमाश्रयितुम्, दृष्टसामर्थ्यत्वात्। मा भूदखण्डं वाक्यं वाक्यार्थस्य वाचकम्, मा च भूत्तदन्त्यवर्णः, तथापि पदान्येव वाचकानि सन्त्विति चेत्; तत्राह–**वृद्धप्रयोगाधीनावधारणो हि शब्दार्थसम्बन्धः।। हि**शब्द उपपादने। वृद्धप्रयोगेऽधीनमवधारणं वृद्धप्रयोगस्य वाधीनं अवधारणं यस्येति विग्रहः। यथोक्तं–सिद्धे शब्दार्थ(सम्बन्ध)[४]. . . . . . .। **(न च पदमात्रं व्यवहाराङ्गं प्रयुञ्जते) वृद्धाः।। व्यवहाराङ्गं**–व्यवहाराङ्गतेत्यर्थः। किन्तर्हि व्यवहाराङ्ग प्रयुञ्जत इत्याह–**किन्तु।** उत्तरमाह–**वाक्यमेव।।** इदमाकूतं–पदेभ्यस्तावद्वाक्यमर्थान्तरमास्थेयं इदं पदमिदं वाक्यमिति प्रतीतिभेदात्; तस्मात्पदार्थबोधाय पदं प्रयुञ्जते, वाक्यार्थबोधाय च वाक्यमित्यङ्गीकर्तव्यम्। तर्हि तदेवास्तु अनवयवमेव वाक्यं वाक्यार्थस्य वाचकम्' इति न वक्तव्यमित्याह–**तच्चानवयवं न्यषेधि।।** निषेधश्च **'मीयमानपरित्यागः'** इत्यादिना। ततः किमित्याह–**इति स्मृति समारूढा वर्णमाला परिशिष्यते।।** इदमाकूतम्–अनवयवं तावन्निषिमेव, अन्त्यवर्णविज्ञानञ्च। न चान्त्यवर्णे वाक्यत्वप्रतीतिः। पदार्थास्त्वशब्दत्वादेवा-नाशङ्कनीयाः। पदानां च पदत्वादेव न वाक्यत्वमित्युक्तम्। अत आदावुपन्य-स्तानां पक्षाणामेष एव पक्षो वर्तिष्यत इति।। ननु वर्णानां युगपद्ग्रहणाभावात्कथं

---

१. 'न्यषेधीदिति ३. पु० पाठः' इति टिप्पणी।

२. 'अवशिष्यते' इति मु० पु० पाठः।

३. 'सा च नैमित्तिकं' इत्यारभ्य 'वाक्यार्थधीहेतुरिति' इत्यन्तो ग्रन्थः यथामुद्रितपुस्तकं दीयते, व्याख्याने ग्रन्थपातात्।

४. अत्र व्याख्याने ग्रन्थपातः।

माधत्ते। [१]पारमार्थिकस्तु पदतदर्थबोधो निमित्तमात्रेणावतिष्ठते वर्णमालैव वाक्यार्थधीहेतुरिति। तदयुक्तम्।।[२]

गौरवाद्विषयाभावात्तद्बुद्धेरेव भावतः।
वाक्यार्थधियमाधत्ते स्मृतिस्था [३]नाक्षरावलिः।।

यहि हि वर्णमालैव [४]स्मृतिस्था वाक्यार्थं [५]बोधयेत् ततोऽर्भक! गामानय, अर्भक! गां बधान, शिशो! गामानय,

---

तत्समुदायसम्भव इत्यत्रोक्तं– **स्मृतिसमारूढेति।।** स्मृतौ च (?)[६]. . . . . .बहवोऽपि वर्णा एकं वाक्यमुच्यत इति विवेकः। दूषयति–**तदयुक्तम्।।** कारणमाह–

गौरवाद्विषयाभावात्तद्बुद्धेरेव भावता(तः)।
वाक्यार्थधियमाधत्ते स्मृतिस्था नाक्षरावलिः।।

नाधत्त इति। नाधातुमर्हतीत्यर्थः। अयुक्तत्वे हेतूपन्यासः उत्तरार्धेन। तत्र हेतूपन्यासः पूर्वार्धेन। तत्राद्यं हेतुं व्याचष्टे–**यदि हि वर्णमालैव स्मृतिस्था वाक्यार्थं बोधयेत्**, अभिदध्यात्, **ततोऽर्भक! गामानय।** द्वितीयं वाक्यमुपन्यस्यति–**अर्भक! गां वधान।** तृतीयमुपन्यस्यति–**शिशो! गामानय।** चतुर्थमुपन्यस्यति–**शिशो! गां बधान।** पञ्चममुपन्यस्यति–**बाल! गामानय।** षष्ठमुपन्यस्यति–**बाल! गां बधान।** सप्तममुपन्यस्यति–**डिम्भ! गामानय।**

---

१. (पारमार्थिकस्तु)–'वाक्यघटकस्मर्यमाणसकलवर्णमालाया एवान्यथानुपपत्त्या वाक्यार्थबोधे हेतुत्वं, पदज्ञानपदार्थोपस्थित्योस्तु तत्र सहकारितामात्रमित्यर्थः।' इति टिप्पणी।

२. 'तदप्ययुक्तम्' इति मु० पु० पाठः।

३. 'नाक्षरावली' इति मु० पु० पाठः।

४. 'स्मृतिसमारूढा' इति मु० पु० पाठः।

५. 'अवबोधयेत्' इति मु० पु० पाठः।

६. अत्र व्याख्याने ग्रन्थपातः।

शिशो! गां बधान [1]बाल! गामानय, बाल! गां बधान, डिम्भ,! गामानय, डिम्भ! गां बधाने [2]त्यष्टानां वाक्यानां अष्टौ शक्तयः कल्पनीयास्तवेति कल्पनागौरवम्। पदवादिनस्तु [3]सप्तानां सप्तैव शक्तयः इति कल्पनालाघवम्। शुक्लामिति[4] पदप्रक्षेपेण पुनः पदवादिनोऽष्टानां पदानामष्टौ शक्तयः इति। तव तु षोडशानां षोडशापराः शक्तय इति महदगौरवमापन्नम्। अपि च,

---

अष्टममुपन्यस्याति—**डिम्भ! गां बधान।। इत्यष्टानां वाक्यानां. . . कल्पनागौरवम्।।** न चैतत्पदवादिनोऽपि तुल्यमित्याह—**पदवादिनस्तु. . . कल्पनालाघवम्।।**

> डिम्भार्भक शिशो बाल गां बधानानयेति यत्।
> पदसप्तकमेतेन रचिते वचनाष्टके।।
> शक्यत्ष्टकं कल्पनीयं स्याद्वर्णावलिवादिनः।
> पदानामेव सप्तानां सप्तैव खलु शक्तयः।।
> पदवादिमते कल्प्या इति स्यात्तस्य लाघवम्।।

अत्रैव विशेषान्तरमाह—**शुक्लामिति. . . अष्टौ शक्तयः। इति।।** लाघवमिति सिद्ध्यति। **तव तु षोडशानां. . .महद्गौरवमापन्नम्।।**

अयमर्थः—

> **शुक्लमिति पदन्यासाद्वाक्ये षोडशके कृते।**
> **शक्त्यष्टकं त्वेव भवेदष्टानां पदवादिनः।।**

---

१. 'बालक! गामानय, बालक! गां बधान' इति मु० पु० पाठः।

२. (अष्टानां)—'अन्तानामिति ५. पु० पाठः' इति टिप्पणी।

३. 'सप्तैव सप्तानां पदानां शक्तयः कल्पनीया इति लाघवम्' इति मु० पु० पाठः। 'लाघवमिति ३. पु० नास्ति' इति टिप्पणी।

४. 'एवं शुक्लामिति पदप्रक्षेपे पदवादिनोऽष्टानां पदानामष्टौ शक्तयः कल्पनीया इति लाघवम्; तव तु षोडशानां वाक्यानां षोडशापराः शक्तयः कल्प्या इति' इति मु० पु० पाठः।

इयमक्षरमाला पदार्थावगमपूर्वकं वाक्यार्थविज्ञानं जनयेत्, [१]अतत्पूर्वकं वा। न तावदतत्पूर्वकम्। संसृज्यमानपदार्थ-विषया[२]धीनज्ञानो हि संसर्गो न संसृज्यमानान्पदार्थानन्तरेण

वर्णमालावादिनस्तु षोडशानां तु षोडश।
वाक्यानां शक्तयः कल्प्या इति स्याद्गौरवं महत्।।

शुक्लपरहितान्यष्टौ वाक्यानि पूर्वाण्येव। तान्येव च शुक्लपदसहितान्यष्टौ भवन्तीति षोडशवाक्यान्यष्टावेव पदानीति। द्वितीयतृतीयहेतुव्याख्यानायारभते–**अपि च।।** तत्रादौ तयोर्विषयविभागप्रदर्शनाय विकल्पं करोति–(इ)**यमक्षर-माला. . . अतत्पूर्वकं वा।।** विधिनिषेधयोर्विधेरग्रिमत्वात्पदार्थावगम-पूर्वकत्वपुरस्कारः। पश्चिमं शिरो दूषयन्पूर्वं हेतुं व्याचष्टे–**न तावदतत्पूर्वकम्।।** अत्र 'इयमक्षरमाला वाक्यार्थविज्ञानं जनयेत्' इत्यनुक्तमपि सिद्ध्यति। अनेनोत्तरार्धोक्तप्रतिज्ञार्थो दर्शितः। तत्र **'विषयभावात्'** इत्येद्व्याचष्टे–**संसृज्यमान. . . शक्यनिरूपणः।।** अनेन च संसर्गरूपे वाक्यार्थे धियं नाधत्ते, पदार्थानां संसर्गविषयाणामभावात्। न हि सम्बन्धिनावन्तरेण सम्बन्धो ज्ञायत इति व्याख्यातम्।।

सम्बन्धावगमस्तावत्सम्बन्धिज्ञानपूर्वकः।
पदार्थानाञ्च सम्बन्धो वाक्यार्थ इति निश्चितः।।
तस्मात्पदेभ्यः प्रथमं पदार्थानवगच्छताम्।
पश्चाद्वर्णावली कुर्याद्धियं संसर्गगोचराम्।।
अतत्पूर्वकपक्षे च न ते सन्ति कदाचन।
बुद्ध्यन्ते वा कथं तेषां संसर्गो बुद्धिमारुहेत्।। इति।

---

१. 'अतत्पूर्वा वा। न तावदतत्पूर्वा' इति मु० पु० पाठः।। 'अतत्पूर्वं वा। न तावदत्पूर्वमिति ३. पु० पाठः' इति टिप्पणी।

२. 'संसृज्यमानपदार्थविषयविज्ञानाधीनो हि संसर्गः संसृज्यमानपदार्थनिरूपणमन्तरेण न शक्यनिरूपणः' इति मु० पु० पाठः। 'पदार्थावगममिति ३. पु० पाठः' इति टिप्पणी।

शक्यनिरूपणः। तत्पूर्वकश्चेत्; [१]तथा हि–यथा यथा पदानि श्रूयन्ते [२]तदा(था) तदा(था) पदार्था अपि प्रतीयन्ते। तदेताः पदतदर्थप्रतीतयो [३]भावनानिचयाधानद्वारेण स्वगोचरचारिणीमेकामेव स्मृतिधियमादधति, तदारूढानि पदानि [४]प[५]दार्थाद्यानिति(द्यनति)दूरवर्तीनि वाक्यार्थबुद्धेरीशत इति। तदप्यचतुर-

---

प्रथम शिरो भाषते–**तत्पूर्वकश्चेत्।** अत्रापि स एव सम्बन्धः। एतदेव विवृणोति–**तथा हि–यथा यथा. . . .वाक्यार्थबुद्धेरीशत** इति।। इदमाकूतम्। तत्पूर्वकश्चेदित्यत्र चोद्यते–यदि वर्णमाला वाक्यार्थं बोधयेत् तर्हि पदपदार्थतत्सम्बन्धसंवित् कमिवोपकारं कुर्यात्; पदार्थज्ञानमिति चेन्न। तेनाप्युपकाराभावात्। न हि वाक्याद्वाक्यार्थावगतौ पदजनितेन पदार्थज्ञानेन कश्चिदुपकारः। कोऽपि नाम कल्प्यत इति चेत्, तस्यादृष्टस्य कल्पनैव दोषः। अत्र ब्रूमः–दृष्ट एव पदार्थज्ञानेनोपकारः। तथा हि–'संसृज्यमानपदार्थविषयाधीनज्ञानो हि संसर्गो न संसृज्यमानपदार्थानन्तरेण शक्यनिरूपणः' इत्युक्तमेव। तस्मात्पदार्थज्ञानं तावदुपकार्येव। तच्च तदैरेकैकश आधीयते। तथा हि–यथा यथा पदानि प्रतिस्वमुच्चारणेषु श्रूयन्ते तथा तथा प्रातिस्विकेषु श्रवणेषु पदार्था अपि प्रत्येकमेकैकशः प्रतीयन्त एव। तदेवं सति सर्वा एवैताः पदधियः पदार्थधियश्च यथास्वं संस्कारानुत्पादयन्त्यो भावनानिचयमादधति। तदाधारद्वारेण स्वगोचरे वर्तमानामेकमेव स्मृतिरूपामेव धियं श्रोतुरादधति। एकैकानुभवेऽपि युगपदेकस्मृतिसम्भवः उक्त एव। एवञ्च तस्यामारूढानि पूर्वं श्रवणावस्थायामेव प्रतिस्वमर्थान्प्रतपादितवन्ति पदानि; प्रातिस्विकप्रतिपादिनातां **पदार्थादी**नाम्; आदिशब्देन पदार्थसंसर्गस्यो- पादानम्; **अनतिदूरवर्तीनि** सन्ति संहत्य वाक्यार्थे पदार्थसंसर्गे बुद्धेः। कुत ईशत

---

१. 'यथा हि इति २. पु० पाठः' इति टिप्पणी।

२. 'तथा तथा' इति मु० पु० पाठः।

३. 'भावनानिचयद्वारेण' इति मु० पु० पाठः।

४. 'अपदार्थानीति ३. पु० पाठः' इति टिप्पणी।

५. '**सपदार्था**न्यदूरवर्तीनि' इति मु० पु० पाठः।

श्रम्। [१]'एवं सत्यप्रेक्षणीभेभ्यः पदार्थज्ञानेभ्य एव तत्सिद्धेरलमनया वर्णमालया। तथा तत्सामर्थ्यं निवेदयिष्यते। अपि च त्रिचतुरपञ्च-

---

इति चेत्–**तदारूढानि पदानी**ति।। पदार्थानां प्रतिपादका ये वर्णसमूहा अल्पे ते महासमूहीभूत्वा स्मृतौ भासमाना इत्यर्थः। 'निमित्तमात्रेणावतिष्ठते' इत्यत्रापि पदार्थसन्निधापनद्वारा निमित्तत्वमभिप्रेतमिति वेदितव्यम्। एतदेव 'सहंत्यार्थमभिदधति पदानि वाक्यम्' इति वदतो **भाष्यकारस्यापि** सम्मतमिति वेदितव्यम्। अभिहितान्वये तावदभिधानमेव नास्ति। दूर एवं संहत्याभिधानम्। अन्विताभिधानेऽपि न संहत्याभिधानं, पदानां प्रातिस्विकाभिधानेन संहत्याभिधानाभावादिति।।

वर्णावल्यपि वाक्यार्थं पदार्थज्ञानपूर्वकम्।
अभिधत्ते, विना तेभ्यो नासौ बुद्धिमुपाश्नुते।।
वर्णावल्यः पदाख्या या अल्पिका नियतास्थिताः।
लोके स्वेषु पदार्थेषु ताः सम्भूय परस्परम्।।
वाक्यार्थधिमादध्युस्तेषां संसर्ग एव सः।
तेनेयं भागशो भूत्वा पदार्थानभिधाय नः।।
विशिष्टार्थप्रबोधाय पश्चाद्भूत्वा महावली।
अभिधत्ते पदार्थानां संसर्गमिति बुद्ध्यताम्।।
एवं च सति शाब्दत्वं वाक्यञ्चान्यत्प्रसिद्ध्यति।
'तद्भूतानां क्रियार्थेनं'त्यत्राप्येषैव वर्णिता।। इति।।

दूषयति–**तदप्यचतुरश्रम्।।** कारणमाह–**एवं सत्यपेक्षणीयेभ्यः. . . . निवेदयिष्यते।।** एवं सत्यलमनया वर्णमालया, अपेक्षणीयेभ्यः पदार्थज्ञानेभ्य एव तत्सिद्धेरित्यन्वयः। तच्छब्देन वाक्यर्थबुद्धिं परामृशति। **तथा तत्सामर्थ्यमिति।।** तथा पदार्थज्ञानाधानप्रकारेण वाक्यार्थबुद्धिसामर्थ्यं पदानामित्यर्थः। क्वचित्तु तेषां च तत्सामर्थ्यमिति पाठः। पदार्थज्ञानानां

---

१. 'एवं च सत्वश्याश्रयणीयेभ्यः पदार्थज्ञानेभ्य एव सिद्धेः कृतमनया वर्णमालया। तेषां च सामर्थ्यं निवेदयिष्यामः' इति मु० पु० पाठः।

षपदवाक्यवर्तिनी[१] [२]पदार्थप्रत्ययव्यवहितापि क्लेशेन वर्णमाला स्मर्येतापि, तदभ्यधिकपदवति तु[३] वाक्ये सातिदुष्करा।।

वाक्यार्थबुद्धिसामर्थ्यमिति। अनेन च '**तद्बुद्धेरेव भावतः**' इत्येतत्पदार्थबुद्धेरेव कारणाद्वाक्यार्थबुद्धिकार्यस्य भावादुत्पादादिति व्याख्यातम्। '**अलमनया वर्णमालया**' इत्यनेन यो हेतुर्वाक्यार्थधियमाधत्ते स न वर्णावलिरिति निषिध्यत इति दर्शितम्। **विषयाभावा**दित्यत्र **वाक्यार्थे**त्यत्र भागे, **गौरवा**दित्यत्राधत्त इत्यत्र भागे, **स्मृतिस्थे**त्यत्रापि, निषेधान्वयादेषोऽप्यर्थो दर्शित इत्यभि-प्रायेणाहि–**अपि च त्रिचतुर. . . सातिदुष्करा।।** त्रिचतुराणि वा पदानि येषु वाक्येषु तानि त्रिचतुरपञ्चषपदानि वाक्यानि तद्वर्तिनी वर्णमालापि तावन्न स्मर्यते, पदार्थप्रत्ययव्यवहितत्वात्। न हि विलक्षणपदार्थप्रत्ययावरुद्धे चेतसि वर्णमालाया अनुभूताया अपि स्मरणसम्भवः, पदार्थप्रत्ययव्यवहितत्वात्, तदनन्तरञ्च पदार्थेष्वेवान्योन्याकाङ्क्षोत्थानात्तद्द्वारेण च वाक्यार्थे प्रतीतिसिद्धेरिति नास्त्येव तस्याः स्मृतिर्वाक्यार्थोपयोगिनी। न हि पदार्थाकाङ्क्षायां उदयमासादयन्त्यां पदस्मृतिरपि तावदुपजायते, प्रागेव पदेभ्योऽवरुह्य वर्णमालामात्रस्मृतिः। अथ तु कथञ्चित्क्लेशेन तदानीं वर्णमालामात्रस्मृतिप्यस्तीत्युच्यते तथापि त्रिचतुरपञ्च-षाभ्यधिकपदवत्सु वाक्येषुसातिदुष्करा वर्णावली स्मर्यमाणतामापादयितुं (अ)शक्येति।।

अपि च त्रीणि चत्वारि पञ्च षड्वा पदानि चेत्।
वाक्ये सन्ति तथाप्यत्र स्मर्यते नाक्षरावलिः।।
न हि वर्णावलीमात्रं पूर्वानुभवगोचरः।
पदात्मनानुभूतत्वात्तथा च तदनन्तरम्।।

---

१. (वर्तिनी)–'वर्तिनीनां पदार्थेति २. पु० पाठः। तदा पदव्यक्तीनामिति विशेष्यमध्याहार्यम्' इति टिप्पणी।

२. 'वर्तिनी नानापदार्थप्रत्ययव्यवहिता' इति मु० पु० पाठः।

३. 'तु वाक्येऽसावतिदुःस्मरा। तस्मादिदमपि मतं अविमृश्यमानसुन्दरमिति नाद्रियन्ते वृद्धाः।।' इति मु० पु० पाठः। 'दर्शनमिति ३ पु० पाठः' इति टिप्पणी।।

तस्मादिदमपि दर्शनं अदृश्यमानसुन्दरं नाद्रियन्ते बुधाः।।

अस्तु तर्हि–

पूर्वानुभूतसम्बन्धस्मृतिद्वारा पदार्थधीः।
पदार्थज्ञाननिचयस्तदनन्तरमेव तु।।

आकाङ्क्षासत्तियोग्यत्वनिरूपणपुरस्सरम्।
वाक्यार्थधियमाधत्ते ततः श्रोता प्रवर्तते।।

निवर्तते वा कुत्रापि कुतश्चिद्वा तथा यदि।
वर्णावलीमात्रगता भवेत्कथमिव स्मृतिः।।

अथ क्लेशेन तत्रापि स्मृतिस्तीति वर्ण्यते।
तथापि सप्त वाष्टौ वा नव वा दश वा पुनः।।

पदानि येषु वाक्येषु तेषु वर्णावलिस्मृतिः।
अशक्या सुतरां कर्तुं न हि तत्र पदेष्वपि।।

कार्त्स्न्येन स्मृतिरस्तीह प्रत्येकं सहितेषु वा।
वर्णसंख्यापरिज्ञानमीश्वरस्यापि दुश्शकम्।।

अतो वाक्यं पदेभ्योऽन्यन्नास्तीत्येवमस्थितम्।। इति।।

उपसंहरति–**तस्मादिदमपि दर्शनं न (अ)दृश्य . . . बुधाः।। अदृश्यमानसुन्दरमिति।।** पदार्थवाक्यार्थयोरिव पदवाक्ययोर्भेदः, पदार्थवद्वाक्यार्थस्यापि वाच्यत्वम्, यथा च पदार्थसंसर्गो वाक्यार्थः तथा पदसंसर्गो वाचकः, इति सामान्यज्ञानेन सुंदरतया गृह्यमाणम्, युक्तिनिरूपणेऽन्यथा दृश्यमानम्, पारमार्थिकरूपाज्ञाने सति सुन्दरतया गृहीतमित्यर्थः। **अपि**शब्देन पूर्वदर्शनसमुच्चयः। अथवा पूर्वस्माद्विशिष्टत्वेनावस्थापितमपीति।।

सम्प्रति **टीकाकारीय**मतमुपन्यस्यति–**अस्तु तर्हि।। यद्येवं तर्हि** अन्यत्सर्वं तिष्ठत्वित्यर्थः। किन्तर्हीत्याह–

पदान्याकाङ्क्षितासन्नयोग्यार्थान्तरसङ्गतान्।
स्वार्थानभिदधन्तीह वाक्यं वाक्यार्थगोचरम्।।

पदान्याकाङ्क्षितासन्नयोग्यार्थान्तरसङ्गतान्।
[1]स्वार्थानभिदधन्तीह[2] वाक्यं वाक्यार्थगोचरम्।।
पदार्थमेव हि (एकं) प्रधानं गुणभूतार्थान्तर[3]न्तरव्यतिषक्तं

यदिह शास्त्रे लोके वा वाक्यं वाक्यार्थगोचरमभिमतं तत्पदान्येव। कीदृशानीत्यपेक्षायां पदविशेषणम्–**आकाङ्क्षितेत्यादि।।** 'नाभ्यस्ताच्छतुः' इति नुम्प्रतिषेधस्य 'वा नपुंसकेष्वनित्यत्वादभिदधन्तीति नुमः प्रयोगः। अथवा–'अस्तु तर्हि' इत्यस्य श्लोकेन सहैकवाक्यतास्तु। श्लोकस्यानन्तरं इतिशब्दोऽध्याहार्यः। **तर्हि,** इति–एवं, **अस्तु अस्तु** इति सम्बन्धः। अथवा–इतिशब्दाध्याहारं बिना **तर्हि** तादृशान्पदार्थानभिदधन्ति पदापि नाम वाक्यमिह वाक्यार्थगोचर-मस्त्वित्यन्वयः। 'वाक्यार्थगोचरम्' इति बहुव्रीहिः।।

ननु पदार्थानां संसर्गो वाक्यार्थः; न च पदानि पदार्थेभ्योऽन्यत्र व्याप्रियन्ते; न च संसर्गः पदार्थत्वेन व्युत्पन्नः इति कथं पदानि नाम वाक्यं वाक्यार्थगोचरं स्यात् ; अत आह–**पदार्थमेव हि . . . . .आचक्षते धीराः।।** न तावद्भेदम् ; न च पदार्थसंसर्गमाचक्षते, किन्तु पदार्थमेव संसर्गिणम्। तर्हि कथमर्थैकत्वादेकवाक्यत्वम्, पदार्थानां बहुत्वात्? अत उक्तम्–**एकमिति।।** एकत्वे को नियमः? अत उक्तम्–**प्रधानमिति।।** नान्वितरपदानां येऽर्थाः ते सर्वे यदि (अर्थान्तरव्यतिषक्ता आख्यायन्ते तदा कथं न वाक्यभेद इति ; तत उक्तम्–?) **गुणभूतार्थान्तरव्यतिषक्तमिति।।** गुणभूतार्थव्यतिषक्तप्रधान-पदार्थस्य वाक्यार्थस्यैकत्वादेकवाक्यत्वम्, गुणप्रधानभेद एव वाक्यभेदः, अङ्गप्रधानवाक्यभेदयोरपि गुणान्वितप्रधानभेदोऽस्त्येव वाक्यभेदावस्थायाम्। यदा तु ग्राहकग्रहणं तदैकवाक्यमेवेति। **आचक्षते धीरो इति।।** 'तद्भूतानां

---

१. 'अर्थान्' इति मु० पु० पाठः।

२. (अभिदधन्ति)–'अभिदधन्ति पदानि वाक्यम्। वाक्यपदेन पदसमूह एव व्यवह्रियत इति यावत्।' इति टिप्पणी। 'वाक्यवाक्यार्थगोचरमिति २ पु० पाठः' इति टिप्पणी।

३. 'गुणभूतार्थान्तरेण व्यतिषक्तं वाक्यार्थमाचक्षते वृद्धाः' इति मु० पु० पाठः।

वाक्यार्थमाचक्षते धीराः। तच्च पदान्येवाकाङ्क्षाद्युपधानलब्ध-सुकरव्य[१]तिषक्तीनि प्रयोजयितुमीशत इति कृतमप्रामाणिकानुपपद्यमानानवयववाक्यादिकल्पनाभिः।।

क्रियार्थेन समाम्नाय', 'आम्नायस्य क्रियार्थत्वात्', 'चोदनेति क्रियायाः प्रवर्तकं वचनमाहुः', 'भावनैव च वाक्यार्थः' इत्यादिषु। एवं **'स्वार्थानभिदधन्ति', 'वाक्यार्थगोचरम्'** इत्यनयोः सङ्गतिर्दर्शिता। **'पदानि', 'वाक्यम्'** इत्यनयोरपि सङ्गतिसम्भवं दर्शयन्नाह–**तच्च पदान्येव. . . वाक्यादिकल्पनाभिः।। प्रयोजयितुमिति।।** प्रबोधयितुमिति पाठः। अथवा प्रयोजयितु-मनुष्ठापयितुमित्यर्थः। प्रबोधनं ह्यनुष्ठापनमिति भावः। न च पदानि केवलान्स्वार्थानभिदध्युः नान्वितानिति वाच्यम्। विशिष्टार्थ विषयव्यवहारदर्शनेन हि व्यवह्रियमाणविशिष्टविषयैव व्युत्पित्सुना संविदुन्नीयते। सा च पदश्रवणानन्तरमुपजायमाना तत्कारणिकैव निश्चीयत इति दर्शितम्। **'पदान्येव'** इत्येवकारेण न पदातिरिक्तं वाक्यमिति दर्शयति। अथवा–यानि पदार्थस्य वाचकत्वेन निर्ज्ञातानि तान्येवेति। ननु व्यतिषक्ते सिद्धै पदैस्तदभिधानम् ; न च व्यतिषङ्गमन्तरेण व्यतिषक्तसिद्धिः; अतो व्यतिषङ्गोऽपि पदैरेव बोधनीयः ; अत उक्तम्–**आकाङ्क्षाद्युपधानलब्ध- सुकरव्यतिषक्तीनीति।।** व्यतिषक्तिर्व्यतिषङ्गः, सुकरा व्यतिषक्तानां व्यतिषक्तिर्येषाम् ; व्यतिषक्ताभिधानमेव पदकार्यं व्यतिषक्तादेव व्यतिषङ्गसिद्धेः तस्याः सुकरत्वम्। कथं सुकरत्वम्? अत उक्तम्–**आकाङ्क्षाद्युपधानेति।।** आकाङ्क्षायोग्यतासत्त (त्तीनां) उपधानमुपाधिः तेन लब्धा, अत एव सुकरा, व्यतिषक्तानामन्योन्यं व्यतिषक्तिर्येषु पदेषु तानि तथोक्तानि। व्यतिषक्तेषु पदैरभिहितेषु व्यतिषक्तैरेवा-काङ्क्षायोग्यतासत्त्युपहितैरन्योन्यव्यतिषङ्गसिद्ध न पदानामन्वितेषु अन्वये च शक्तिः कल्प्येति। **अप्रामाणिकानुपपद्यानानवयववाक्यादिकल्पनाभिरिति।। आदि**शब्देनान्त्यवर्णावलीपक्षयोरुपादान्। अनुपपद्यानानां अनवयवाक्यादीनां कल्पनाभिरिति। ननु 'न (हि) दृष्टेऽनुपपन्नं नाम' इति प्रामाणिकत्वे

---

१. 'सुकरव्युत्पत्तीनि प्रत्यापयितुमीशते' इति मु० पु० पाठः।

ननु

पदान्तरस्य वैयर्थ्यमश्रुतान्वयबोधने।[१]
श्रुतान्वि[२]ताभिधाने तु व्यक्तमन्योन्यसंश्रयम्॥

अथापि स्यादनभिहितेनैवार्थान्तरेणान्वितमर्थमभिदधीत पदम्, अभिहितेन वा। [३]तत्रानभिहितस्वार्थान्तरान्वितस्वार्थाभिधाने पादानेकस्मादेवोच्चारिताद्विवक्षितार्थप्रतीतेः वैयर्थ्यमितरेषाम्। अभिहितान्विताभिधाने तु यावत्पचेदित्यनेनान्वितस्वार्थो नाभिधानीयः, तावत्तूखायामित्यनेनाधिकरणमुखा नाभिधीयते। एवमुखायामित्यनेनापि यावत्स्वार्थो नाभिधानीयः, तावत्प-

---

सत्यनुपपत्तिपरिहारोऽपि कश्चित्सिद्ध्येत् ; न तु तदप्यस्तीत्युक्तम्– **अप्रामाणिकेति॥** अप्रामाणिकत्वं चानवयवाक्यस्य स्वरूपे, अन्ययोर्वाक्यत्व इति। अथवा–**अप्रामाणिके**त्यनवयवाक्यविशेषणम्, **अनुपपद्यमाने**त्यनयोः इति भेदः। अथवा–अप्रामाणिकानां वादिनामनुपपद्यमानेषु अनवयववाक्यादिषु कल्पनाभिरिति विग्रहः॥

अभिहितान्वयवादी चोदयति–ननु

पदान्तरस्य वैयर्थ्यमश्रुतान्वयबोधने।
श्रुतान्विताभि([४]धाने तु व्यक्तमन्योन्यसंश्रयम्)॥

. . . . .श्लोकव्यावर्त्यां शङ्कां निषेधयन्नाह–**न च पदजातं.**

---

१. (बोधने)–'कल्पने इति ३ पु० पाठः' इति टिप्पणी।

२. 'श्रुतान्विताभिधाने' इत्यारभ्य 'अनुपपद्यमानमापद्येत' इत्यन्तो ग्रन्थः यथामुद्रितपुस्तकं दीयते, व्याख्याने ग्रन्थपातात्।

३. (अनभिहितस्वार्थान्तर)–'अनभिहितार्थान्तरेति ३ पु० पाठः' इति टिप्पणी। 'अनभिहितं स्वेनानुपस्थापितं स्वबोध्यत्वेनाभिमतमर्थान्तरं तदन्वितस्वार्थस्याभिधाने इत्यर्थः' इति टिप्पणी।

४. अत्र व्याख्याने मातृकायां एकपत्रपरिमितग्रन्थलोपः।

चेदित्यनेन स्वार्थो नाभिधीयत इति परस्पराश्रयप्रसङ्गः; पदार्थस्वरूपाभिधानपूर्वके तु तद्वदन्वितार्थाभिधाने द्विरभिधान-मप्रामाणिकमनुपपद्यमानमापद्येत। न च पदजातं प्रथममर्थजातं स्वरूपेणानभिदधदेव यथास्वमभिधेयानि [१]साहचर्यमात्रादर्थ-रूपाणि स्मारयति, अथैतान्यन्वितान्यभिधत्त इति साम्प्रतम्। यतः—

> पूर्वानुभवयोनित्वात्स्मृतिस्तदनुसारिणी।
> [२]स चान्विते न स्वरूपे ततोऽपेक्ष्यानपेक्षणम्।।

न खलु पदं पदार्थमात्रे क्वचिदपि [३]दृष्टचरप्रयोगम्, येन[४]

. . .अभिधत्त इति साम्प्रतम्।। नेति।। साम्प्रतमिति सम्बन्धः। मध्यमग्रन्थेनेयमाशङ्का दर्शिता—ननु नावश्यमभिधानसन्निहितेनैवार्थेनान्वितं शब्दानामभिधेयम्, यतोऽयं दोषः स्यात्, सन्निधिमात्रस्य तदुपलक्षणत्वात्। सन्निधेश्चान्तरेणाभिधानं स्मृत्यापि सम्भवात्। सर्वाणि हि पदानि प्राक्प्रतियोगिसन्निधेर्निमित्तभूतमर्थरूपं स्मारयन्ति। ततो न्यायावधारितवचन-व्यक्तिनिपाताद्वाक्यार्थमभिदधतीति न कश्चिद्दोष इति। **प्रथममिति।** श्रवणवेलाया-मित्यर्थः। **अनभिदधदेवेति।।** प्रतियोग्यसन्निधानादिति भावः। **साहचर्यमात्रा-दिति ।।** न तु शब्दशक्त्येति । **स्मारयतीति ।।** स्मरणादभिधानमर्थान्तरमेवेति भावः। कारणमाह—

> **पूर्वानुभवयोनित्वात्स्मृतिस्तदनुसारिणी।**
> **स चान्विते न स्वरूपे ततोऽनपेक्षापेक्ष्यानपेक्षणम्।।** इति।।

---

१. (साहचर्यमात्रात्)—'साहचर्यादिति ३. पु० पाठः' इति टिप्पणी।

२. 'सा चान्वितस्वरूपेण ततोऽपेक्षानपेक्षणा' इति मु० पु० पाठः।। 'सा चान्वितेन रूपेण ततोऽनपेक्षणम्' इति ३ पु० पाठः। 'अपेक्ष्यमाणस्य आकांक्ष्यमाणस्यार्थान्तरस्यापेक्षणा जिज्ञासाभाव इत्यर्थः। तथैवोपपादयिष्यति' इति टिप्पणी।

३. 'दृष्टचरं' इति मु० पु० पाठः। 'दृष्टचरप्रयोगमिति ३ पु० पाठः' इति टिप्पणी।

४. 'येन तत्साहचर्येण तन्मात्रं. . .अपि त्वन्वितस्वार्थे' इति मु० पु० पाठः।

तन्मात्रं स्मारयेत्, तन्मात्रेण व्यवहारायोगात्, तत्प्रयुक्तत्वाच्च तदुच्चारणस्य; अपि त्वन्विते स्वार्थे। तथा च गामानयेत्यत्रानयनान्वितस्वार्थो गोशब्दः तेन [१]सहचारितो गां पश्येत्यत्र[२] तदन्वितामेव गां स्मारयेन्नं तन्मात्रम्। तथा च तन्निराकाङ्क्षो गौर्न पश्येत्यनेनान्वियात्। एवं प्रासादं पश्येत्यत्र प्रासादान्वित[३]स्वार्थं पश्यपदं तन्निकाराङ्क्षं न गवा सम्बध्यते इति

कारिकां व्याचष्टे—**न खलु पदं पदार्थमात्रे क्वचिदपि दृष्टचरप्रयोगम्॥** अनेन, श्लोक **'सः'** इत्यनेनानुभवः परामृश्यते, तस्य च स्वरूपाविषयत्वे तत्कारणस्य प्रयोगस्य तदविषयत्वं कारणमिति दर्शितमित्यवगन्तव्यम्। एवं हेतुं स्वरूपेणोक्त्वा यदि क्वचिद्दृष्टचरं स्यात्, किन्ततः, अत आह—**येन तन्मात्रं स्मारयेत्।** पदार्थमात्रे प्रयोगादर्शने कारणमाह—**तन्मात्रेण व्यवहारायोगात्॥** अंशत्रयविशिष्टभावनविषयत्वात् प्रवृत्तेरिति भावः। ततः किमित्याह—**तत्प्रयुक्तत्वाच्च तदुच्चारणस्य॥** तच्छब्दाभ्यां यथाक्रमं व्यवहारः पदं च परामृश्यते। अनेन च पदोच्चारणस्य व्याप्यत्वं व्यवहारस्य च व्यापकत्वं दर्शित वेदितव्यम्। क्व तर्हि दृष्टचरप्रयोगम्? विशिष्टायां भावनायां इत्याह—**अपि त्वन्विते स्वार्थे॥** अयमर्थः—क्रियान्वितेषु कारकेषु तदन्वितायाञ्च क्रियायां यथायोगं पदं दृष्टप्रयोगमिति। अनेन च **'स चान्विते'** इत्ययमंशो व्याख्यातः। सम्प्रति चतुर्थपादं व्याचष्टे—**तथा च गामानयेत्यत्र. . . .न तन्मात्रम्॥ तथा चेति॥** अन्वित एव पदप्रयोगे सतीत्यर्थः। आद्याभ्यां तच्छब्दाभ्यां आनयनं परामृश्यते, अन्त्येन गौः। **सहचरित** इति। साहचर्यमात्रादिति ह्युक्तमिति भावः। ततः किमित्याह—**तथा च . . . . .**

---

१. 'सहोच्चरितः' इति मु० पु० पाठः।

२. 'अत्रापि' इति मु० पु० पाठः।

३. 'प्रसादान्वितं पश्येति पदं' इति मु० पु० पाठः।

[१]सर्वपदार्थप्रत्ययो दत्तजलाञ्जलिः प्रसज्येत। न चाव्यभि-चाराद्गमिति पदं स्वार्थमेव स्मारयति न तु [२]पदार्थन्तरार्थं, व्यभिचारादिति साम्प्रतम्। पट्वभ्यासा[३]हिता हि भावना प्रबोधवती [४]स्मृतिः सङ्गीयते। तस्याश्च प्रबोधः प्रणिधानादिजन्मा

नान्वियात्।। तथा चेति।। आनयनान्वितस्मरणे सतीत्यर्थः। **तच्छब्देनानयनमेव** परामृश्यते। एवं नामपदमूरीकृत्योक्तम् ; आख्यातपदमूरीकृत्याह–**एवं प्रासादं पश्येत्यत्र. . . . न गवा सम्बध्यते।। एवं**–गोपदवदित्यर्थः। **तच्छब्देन** प्रासादपरामर्शः। **न गवेति।** गां पश्येति सन्निहितेनेति। अत्र च गां पश्येति वाक्यमुदाहरणम्। गामानय प्रासादं पश्येति चान्यसाहचर्यप्रदर्शनायोपात्तमिति वेदितव्यम्। एवं चतुर्थपादं व्याख्याय तत्फलं दर्शयति–**इति सर्वपदार्थप्रत्ययो दत्तजलाञ्जलिः प्रसज्येत।। इतिशब्दः** प्रकारे। **गां पश्येतिवदन्यत्रापि** दर्शयितव्यमिति भावः। हेतौ वा। सम्प्रति प्रकारान्तरमाशङ्क्य परिहरन्नाह–**न चाव्यभिचारात्. . . . .साम्प्रतम्।।** इदमाकूतम्–अव्यभिचारादेव हि स्वार्थत्वं व्यभिचाराच्च पदान्तरार्थत्वमिति स्वार्थत्वपदान्तरार्थत्वसिद्ध्या तद्व्यापकयोरव्यभिचारव्यभिचारयोरपि सिद्धिः।। न चानैकान्तिको हेतुरर्थं प्रतिपादयतीति। कारणमाह–**पट्वभ्यासाहिता. . . .सङ्गीयते।।** अभ्यास-शब्देनानुभवपौनःपुन्यमुच्यते। अस्फुटाभ्यासस्य वस्तुविशेषविषयसंस्कार-जनकत्वासम्भवात्पटुताप्यभ्यासस्यापेक्ष्यतामित्यभिप्रायेणोक्तम्–**पट्विति।।** स्थिराया भावनायाः स्वरूपतः कादाचित्कीं स्मृतिं प्रति हेतुत्वायोगात्तदुपपत्तये तदानीन्तनप्रबोधयोगित्वमप्यपेक्षणीयमिति दर्शितम्–**प्रबोधवतीति।। सङ्गीयति इति।।** परीक्षकैरिति सिद्ध्यति। समा परीक्षकाविवादं दर्शयति। इदमाकूतम्–

---

१. 'सम्बध्येतेति सर्वत्र वाक्यार्थो दत्तं' इति मु० पु० पाठः। 'वाक्यार्थप्रत्यय इति ३ पु० पाठः' इति टिप्पणी।

२. 'पदार्थान्तरं' इति मु० पु० पाठः।

३. 'पट्वभ्यासादरप्रत्ययाहिता भावना' इति मु० पु० पाठ;।

४. 'स्मृतिहेतुः' इति मु० पु० पाठः।

[१]नाव्यभिचार [२]एवायतते। साहचर्यमात्रस्यापि[३] तु सम्बन्धरूपेण

स्मृतावव्यभिचारस्ते कथङ्कारमपेक्ष्यताम्।
न तावत्करणत्वेन भावनायास्तथाः स्थितेः।।
सहकारितया नापि प्रबोधो हि तथा स्थितः।
स्वरूपोत्पत्तये नास्या अभयासाधीनता स्थितेः।।
अभ्यासे सहकारित्वं पटुत्वस्यैव सम्मतम्।
इयती स्मृतिसामग्री सम्मता न्यायवादिनाम्।।
न चात्राव्यभिचारोऽपि कारणं व्यभिचारतः।
उपाध्यायेन शिष्यस्य स्मृतेर्याज्येन चर्त्विजाम्।। इति।।

न चाव्यभिचारस्य प्रकारान्तरेणापि स्मृत्युपत्तावपुयोग इत्यभिप्रायेणाह–**तस्याश्च प्रबोधः. . . . .एव(ह)यतते।।** अयमर्थः–नाव्यभिचारस्यैवासाधारणं प्रबोधहेतुत्वम्, किन्तु प्रणिधानादिवत्सोऽपि क्वचित् प्रबोधहेतुतामनुभवतीति। अथवा–प्रणिधानादिजन्मत्वान्नाव्यभिचार एवायतत इति योजना। इदमाकूतम्–

पटुत्वाभ्याससंस्कारप्रबोधेष्वस्य हेतुता।
नैकं प्रत्यपि वक्तव्या यतोऽभ्यासे दृगादयः।।
प्रसिद्धा हेतुभावेन तत्पौष्कल्यात्पटुश्च सः।
भावनाहेतुरभ्यासः प्रबोधोऽस्यास्ततो यदि।।
सोऽप्यस्तु क्वचिदेतस्याः प्रबोधं प्रति कारणम्।
बहवोऽन्येऽपि सन्त्येव तद्बोधं प्रति हेतवः।।
ते चोपरिष्टाद्वक्ष्यन्ते तेष्वेषोऽन्तर्गतः परम्। इति।।

---

१. 'जन्माऽव्यभिचार एव नायतते' इति मु० पु० पाठः।

२. 'अव्यभिचारे सत्येव स्मृतिजनक इति नियमो नास्तीर्थ्य' इति टिप्पणी।

३. 'साहचर्यमात्रमस्याप्यस्तीति पदार्थान्तरसहितमेव' इति मु० पु० पाठः।। 'साहचर्यमात्रस्यापि च सम्बन्धतया प्रणिधानादिगणे पाठाद्युपपत्तेश्च तदुद्बोधहेतुभावो, न विरुद्धयते। तच्च स्वार्थस्येव पदार्थान्तरस्याप्यस्तीति ३ पु० अधिकः पाठः' इति टिप्पणी।

प्रणिधानादिगणपाठादुपपत्तेश्च तद्बोधो न विरुद्ध्यते। तच्च स्वार्थस्येव पदार्थान्तरस्याप्यस्तीति पदान्तरार्थसहितमेव [१]स्वार्थमनाकाङ्क्षितं सहसैव स्मारयेदिति हता वाक्यार्थ-

---

ननु साहचर्यमात्रात्संस्कारोन्मेषः सिद्ध्यतीति त्वयेष्यते ; न च साहचर्यं प्रणिधानादिषु पठ्यते ; न च साहचर्यमात्रं विशेषविषयसंस्कारोद्बोधकारणम्, बहुसाधारणस्य विशिष्टसंस्कारोद्बोधहेतुत्वायोगात् ; अतो विशिष्टविषय-संस्कारोद्बोधः साहचर्यं च परस्परेण विरुद्ध्यते, उभयोरुभयविपर्ययव्याप्तत्वात्। तथा हि–साहचर्यं गवादीनां पश्यत्यादिसाधारणं साधारण्यामेव स्मृतावुपयुज्यते। विशिष्टसंस्कारोद्बोधश्चाव्यभिचारिणा साध्य इति विरोधः, इति आह–**साहचर्यमात्रस्यापि तु. . . . . .न विरुद्ध्यते।।** उपरिष्टात्स्वयमेव **निबन्धनकृता** प्रणिधानादिगणपाठ उदाह्रियते। तत्र यद्यपि साहचर्यमात्रस्य पाठो नास्ति तथापि सम्बन्धेति सम्बन्धस्य पाठात्साहचर्यमात्रस्य सम्बन्धत्वाविशेषात्सम्बन्धरूपेण पाठोऽस्त्येव। यदि च संस्कारोद्बोधकत्वं साहचर्यमात्रस्य नोपपद्येत, ततः सम्बन्धरूपेण गणपाठो नाश्रीयेतापि। न च तदप्यस्ति। साहचर्यमात्रेणापि शिष्योपाध्यायादौ स्मृतिदर्शनान्न हेतुसाध्ययोर्विरोध इति। **मात्र**शब्देनाव्यभिचारं व्यवच्छिनत्ति। **अपि**शब्देनाव्यभिचारं प्रणिधानादिकं कृत्स्नमेव वा समुच्चिनोति। **तु**शब्दः किन्त्वित्यपेक्षाद्योतनार्थम्। 'तद्बोधः' इति **तच्छ**ब्देन भावनां परामृशति। **'साहचर्यमात्रस्य'** इति षष्ठ्याः **'पाठात्'** इत्यादिकेन सम्बन्धः। ततस्तद्बोध इति ततश्शब्दो द्रष्टव्यः। अस्तु साहचर्यमात्रेणापि स्मृतिः, तथापि गां पश्येत्यत्र गामिति पदं स्वार्थमात्रं तावत्स्मारयति। तथा पश्येति पदमपि स्वार्थमात्रम्, ततो झटित्येव पदद्वयमन्योन्यार्थान्वितं स्वार्थमभिधत्ते इति कुतः साहचर्यमात्रस्यपि स्मारकत्वं प्रतिषिध्यते ; अत आह–**तच्च स्वार्थस्येव . . . . तपस्विनी।।** **तत्**–साहचर्यमात्रम्। एतच्च 'स चान्विते न स्वरूपे ततोऽपेक्ष्यानपेक्षणम्' इत्यस्य यद्व्याख्यानं **'तथा च'** इत्यादिक(कं, त)स्य संक्षेप इत्यवसातव्यम्।

---

१. 'स्वार्थमनाकाङ्क्षं स्मारयेदिति हता बत वाक्यार्थधीः' इति मु० पु० पाठः।

धीस्तपस्विनीति पदानामर्थस्व[१]रूपमात्रमेषितव्यम्। तथा च [२]तेऽर्थाः क्रियादयः स्वसामर्थ्येन स्वरूपमात्रेण पदैरभिहिता विना कारका[३]दिभिरपर्यवस्यन्तस्तकादाङ्क्षायोग्यता[४]सत्तिसहकारिणो वाक्य[५]बाह्यार्थ(क्यार्थ)धियमादधतीति युक्तम्।।

अनाकाङ्क्षितम्—आकाङ्क्षारहितमित्यर्थः। अनाकाङ्क्षमिति वा पाठः। अनाकाङ्क्षन्निति पाठे पदस्य शब्दताविवक्षया पुल्लिङ्गनिर्देशः। अनाकाङ्क्षदित्येव वा पाठः। अनाकाङ्क्षितमिति पाठेऽपीतरेणानाकाङ्क्षितम्, इतरस्याप्येवंधित्वादिति वा योजना। सर्वथा **'ततोऽपेक्ष्यानपेक्षणम्'** इत्यस्य सङ्क्षेपः। **सहसैवेति।।** पदान्तरप्रतीक्षणात्प्रागेवेति। **तपस्विनी**ति शोचनीयतानिर्देशेन निष्प्रतिकारतां दर्शयति। एवदान्विताभिधानात्प्रागेव पदैः पदार्थस्य स्वरूपमात्रस्य स्मृतिमुक्त्वाऽभिधानतयै(त ए)व सन्निधे(धि)रेषितव्य इत्याह—**इति पदानां. . . .एषितव्यम्।।** भवतु तथापि प्रथमं तावत्केवलाभिधानम्, पश्चादन्विताभिधानमस्तु, अत आह—**तथा च तेऽर्थाः. . . .आदधीतीति युक्तम्।। तथा**—स्वरूपमात्रस्यैषितव्यत्वे सतीत्यर्थः। **तेऽर्थाः**—व्युत्पतिप्रसिद्धाः। **स्वसामर्थ्येन**—पदानां यथास्वमस्थितेन सामर्थ्येन। **स्वरूपमात्रेण**—क्रियादिस्वरूपमात्रेण। **मात्र**शब्देनान्वितावस्थां व्यवच्छिनत्ति। **तदाकाङ्क्षेति।।** तच्छब्देन कारकादेः परामर्श इति। **युक्तमिति।।** 'अनन्यलभ्यः शब्दार्थः' इति न्यायादिति भावः। अनेन च **'ननु पदान्तरस्य वैयर्थ्यम्'** इत्यादिकं सिद्धान्तिनश्चोद्यमिति दर्शितमिति वेदितव्यम्।।

अन्विताभिधानवादी परिहरति—**अत्रोच्यते**—

---

२. 'अर्थरूपमात्राभिधानमेषितव्यम्' इति मु० पु० पाठः।

३. 'ते ते पदार्थाः' इति मु० पु० पाठः।

४. 'कारणदिभिः' इति मु० पु० पाठः।

५. 'योग्यतासन्निधिसह' इति मु० पु० पाठः।

६. 'वाक्यार्थधियं' इति मु० पु० पाठः।

अत्रोच्यते–

विधान्तरानवगमात्स्मृतिलक्षणयोगतः।
अभ्यासातिशयाद्रूपस्मृतेर्नान्योन्यसंश्रयः[1]॥

[2]इदं भवानपि निरूपयतु [3]प्रमाणसंशयविपर्ययस्मृतिषु कतमेयं पदात्पदार्थप्रतिपत्तिरिति। तत्र न तावत्प्रमाणमनधिगतार्थ- बोधनं तदुपेयते। यथाहुः–

'[4]सर्वस्यानुपलब्धेऽर्थे प्रामाण्यं स्मृतिरन्यथा।' इति।

न च पदात्पदार्थधीरनधिगतार्थगोचरा। न खलु सम्बन्ध संवेदन-समये समधिगतोऽर्थः पदैरभिधीयमानो देशकालावस्था-विशेषेणाप्यतिरिच्यते। अनतिरिच्यमानश्च न स्वरूपे विज्ञानं प्रमाणयति। अत एवाहुः–

'परोक्षश्चानुभूतश्च यस्तत्र स्मृतिरिष्यते।
प्रमितेऽ[5]नुप्रयुक्तत्वात्स्मृतेर्नास्ति प्रमाणता[6]॥' इति।

विधान्तरानवगमत्स्मृतिलक्षणयोगतः।
अभ्यासातिशयाद्रूपस्मृतिर्नान्योन्यसंशयः॥

कारिकां व्याख्यातुं पीठिकां दर्शयति–इदं भवानपि निरूपय(तु[7]). . .

---

१. 'नान्योन्यसंश्रयम्' इति मु० पु० पाठः।

२. 'इदं तावन्निरूपयतु भवान्' इति मु० पु० पाठः।

३. 'प्रमाणसंशय' इत्यारभ्य 'तुल्यो दोषः' इति पर्यन्तो ग्रन्थः यथामुद्रितपुस्तकं दीयते, व्याख्याने ग्रन्थपातात्।

४. 'श्लोकवार्तिके वृत्तिकारग्रन्थे श्लोकः ११.' इति टिप्पणी।

५. (अनुप्रयुक्तत्वात्)–'तु प्रयुक्तत्वादिति ३ पु० पाठः' इति टिप्पणी।

६. श्लोकवार्तिके शब्दवादे श्लोक १०२, १०५।

७. अत्र व्याख्याने पत्रद्वयपरिमितग्रन्थलोपः।

'पदमभ्यधिकाभावात्स्मारकान्न विशिष्यते।' इति च।

न हि पदस्य प्रणिधानादिभ्यः संस्कारोद्बोधहेतुभ्यः कश्चिद्विशेषः। संशयविपर्ययहेतुभावस्तु पदस्येति स्थवीयः। न च पञ्चमी विधा समस्तीति स्मृतिः परिशिष्यते। सा चान्वितगोचरा न स्वरूपगोचरेति तुल्यो दोषः। अभिधानतः स्मारितं वाक्यार्थान्वयि न साहचर्यमात्रादिति चेत् – कुतस्तर्हि गङ्गायां घोषः प्रतिवसतीत्यादौ तीरादीनामनभिधेयानां प्रतिवासान्वयः। अपिच, अभिधानतः स्मरितस्य[1] स्वरूपमात्रस्य साहचर्यस्मरितेनैवार्थान्तरेणाकाङ्क्षोपरतेनाकाङ्क्षस्य [2]चरमप्रतीतेनाभिधानतोऽर्थान्तरेण सङ्गमायोगात्समुत्पन्नसङ्कटो वाक्यार्थः [3]प्रतिषज्यते

. .(अभिहितान्वय)वादी अतुल्यत्वं दर्शयन्नाह–**अभिधानतः. . . . साहचर्यमात्रादिति चेत्।।** इदमाकूतम्–यदि वयं यूयमिव साहचर्यमात्रात्स्मारितैः कारकादिभिः साहचर्यमात्रात्स्मारितानां क्रियादीनामन्वयमाचक्ष्महे ततः तुल्यदोषतया पर्यनुयोज्येमहि। न त्वेवमस्माभिरुच्यते, किन्त्वभिधानतः स्मारितं वस्तु वाक्यार्थान्वयतीति ब्रूमहे इति कथं तुल्यदोषतेति। अन्विताकभिधानावादी परिहरन्नाह–**कुतस्तर्हि. . . . प्रतिवासान्वयः।। 'प्रतिवासान्वयः'** इत्यतदुपलक्षणम्, प्रतिवासाद्यन्वय इत्यर्थः। **'इत्यादौ तीरादीनाम्'** इत्यत्रादि-शब्ददर्शनात् प्रतिवासाद्यन्वय इति पाठः श्रेयान्। एवं **'अभिधानतः स्मारितम्'** इत्यस्य व्यभिचारो दर्शितः। किञ्च **'अभिधानतः स्मारितम्'** इत्येतदेव न मृष्यामहे इत्याह–**अपि चाभिधानतः . . . . प्रतिषज्यते ।।** अस्य ग्रन्थस्य **'पूर्वानुभवयोनित्वात्'** इत्यारभ्य **'दत्तजलाञ्जलिः प्रसज्येत'** इत्यवसानो ग्रन्थो व्याख्ये (यः ?)।

---

१. 'स्मारितस्वरूपमात्रस्य' इति मु० पु० पाठः।

२. (चरमप्रतीतेनाभिधानतः)–'पदान्तरसमभिव्याहारोत्तरमुद्बुद्धयाऽभिधया पश्चादुपस्थितेनेत्यर्थः' इति टिप्पणी।

३. 'प्रसज्येत' इति मु० पु० पाठः।

इति कुतस्तद्भावना, कुतस्तरां च पदैरुद्बोधः, कुतस्तमाञ्च तदन्वयस्मरणं इत्यकामेनाप्यन्वित[1]स्मरणमभ्युपेयम्।। [2]आतश्चैतदेवं

(अभिधानतः चरम)प्रतीतने' इत्यन्वय?। **समुत्पन्नसङ्कट इति।** सङ्कटशब्देन विनाशो विवक्षितः। क्वचित्तु समुच्छिन्नसङ्कथ इति पाठः। युष्माभिरेव मापादितत्वादिति भावः। एवं त्व(या) पदानामर्थस्वरूपमेषितव्यमित्यादि यदुक्तं, तदपि मुधैवेत्याह–**इति कुतस्तद्भावना।।** तच्छब्देन वाक्यार्थः परामृश्यते। वाक्यार्थस्यैवाभावे कथन्तदनुभवजन्यः संस्कार इत्यर्थः। वाक्यार्थबोधेनैव हि पदपदार्थसम्बन्धो गृह्यते, ततः पदार्थानुभवजन्यः संस्कार इति वाक्यार्थसंस्कार एव पदार्थसंस्कार इति संस्काराभावे तदुद्बोधो दूरापास्ता इत्याह–**कुतस्तराञ्चपदैरुद्बोधः।।** भावनाया इति सिद्ध्यति। तथा पदार्थानां वाक्यार्थान्वयस्य कृते स्मरणमपीत्याह–**कुतस्तमां च तदन्वयस्मरणम्।।** तदन्वयस्मरणं वाक्यार्थन्वयाय, तस्य कृते वा पदार्थानां स्मरणमिति। अथवा–एवञ्च कथमिव त्वयास्मान्प्रति **'पूर्वानुभवयोनित्वात्'** इत्यादिकमापाद्यते, त्वदुक्तेन प्रकारेण साहचर्यमात्रस्मारितेनैवार्थान्तरेणान्वये सति श्रुतयोरनन्वयाद्वाक्यार्थोच्छेदात्कुतो वाक्यार्थविषयस्संस्कारः, अनुभवस्यैव तद्विषस्याभावात्, कारणासम्भवे कार्यासम्भवात। पुनश्च, गामानयेत्यत्र वाक्यार्थानुभवाभावेन तज्जन्यसंस्काराभावे, तथा प्रासादं पश्येत्यत्र संस्काराभावे, गां पश्येत्यत्रोभयवाक्यार्थाभावेन कुतस्तरां पदैरुद्बोधः, उद्बोधविषयस्याभावात्। पूर्वं कारणाभाव एव ; सम्प्रति विषयरूपस्य कारणस्य न केवलमभावः तत्कारणस्यापीति तरप् प्रयुक्तः, पुनश्च, उभयवाक्यार्थगतस्यान्वयस्य स्मरणं, पश्येतिपदेन प्रसादान्वयस्य गामिति पदेनानयनान्वितस्य स्मरणं दूरापास्तम्, प्रपितामहस्थानीयस्य कारणस्याप्यभावात्तमप्प्रयुक्तः। एवं **'स्मृतिलक्षणयोगतः'** इत्यस्य दोषतोद्भाविता। सम्प्रति तस्य साध्यान्वयं दर्शयति–**इत्यकामेनाप्य–**

---

१. 'अन्वयिस्मरणम्' इति मु० पु० पाठः। 'अन्वितस्मरणमिति ३ पु० पाठः' इति टिप्पणी।

२. 'इतश्च' इति मु० पु० पाठः।

यदभ्यासातिशयः संस्कारातिशयमाधत्ते। स च द्रागित्येव प्रबुद्ध एकपदे स्फुटतरं स्मरणमुपजनयति। [1]दर्शनमात्रजन्मा पुनर्मन्दो [2]विलम्बितप्रबोधो मन्दमेव कार्यमाधातुमुत्सहते। अभ्यास-

---

नन्वितस्मरणमभ्युपेयम्।। अकामेनेति।। अनिच्छयेत्यर्थः। अकामेन सतापि भवता इत्यर्थः। **'अनन्वितस्मरणम्'** इति **'रूपस्मृतेः'** इत्यस्य व्याख्या। **अभ्यासातिशयात्'** इत्येतत्तत्रैव हेत्वन्तरमिति दर्शयन्नाह–**आतश्चैतदेवम्।। आतश्चेति।।** अस्मादपि कारणादित्यर्थः। यथोक्तं **वैजयन्त्याम्**–'आतो निन्दाहेतुचित्रेषु' इति। **एतदिति।।** स्मरणमित्यर्थः।। **एवामिति।।** अनन्वितविषयमित्यर्थः। क्वचित्तु **एव**मित्यस्य स्थाने एवकारो दृश्यते। तदा **'एतत्'** इत्यस्यानन्वितविषयं स्मरणमित्यर्थः। पूर्वपाठेऽपि वाऽनन्वितविषयं स्मरण**मेत**च्छब्देन परामृश्यते। **'एवम्'** इत्यनेन तु **अभ्युपेय**मित्येतदिति व्याख्या। **आतः'** इति निर्दिष्टं हेतुमेव दर्शयति–**यदभ्यासातिशयः संस्कारातिशयमाधत्ते।।** इन्धनातिशय इवाग्न्यतिशयमिति भावः। ततस्ततः, अत आह–**स च द्रागित्येव. . . .स्मरणमुपजनयति।। सः**–संस्कारातिशयः। **द्रागित्येव**–झटित्येव। **प्रबुद्धः**–उन्मिषितः। **एकपदे**–एकस्मिन्नेव स्थाने। यस्मिन्नवसरे उद्बोधकप्राप्ति तस्मिन्नेवोद्बोधः कार्यजननञ्चेति। यदेन्धनातिशयो योजितः तदैवाग्नीन्धनसंयोगः, तदैव च ज्वलनम्। यद्येवं ततस्ततः, अत आह–**दर्शनमात्रजन्मा. . . . उत्सहते।। मात्र**शब्देनाभ्यासव्यावृत्तिः। **मन्दः**–अनतिशयानः। **विलम्बितप्रबोध इति।।** विलम्बितः प्रबोधो यस्येति बहुव्रीहिः। न द्रागित्येव वा प्रबुद्ध इति। अत्र च संस्कार इति सिद्ध्यति। **मन्दमेव**–न स्फुटतरम्। **कार्यम्**–स्मरणम्; यथा–आर्द्रेन्धनसंयोजनायां विलम्बेनाग्नीन्धनसंयोगः विलम्बेन ज्वलनमिति। अस्तु संस्कारातिशयस्य स्फुटतरस्मरणजनकत्वमेकपद एव। अस्तु च मन्दस्य मन्दस्मरणहेतुत्वम्,

---

१. (दर्शनमात्रजन्मा)–'तत्सहितार्थान्तरसाहचर्यदर्शनजन्य इत्यर्थः। स्वार्थेन सङ्गतिग्रहो भूयानर्थान्तरेण तु प्रयोगभेदेनानियतत्वान्न तथेति भावः' इति टिप्पणी।

२. 'विप्रलम्बिप्रबोधो' इति मु० पु० पाठः।

वती च पदस्य स्वार्थेन साहचर्यानुभूतिर्यथा न तथाऽर्थान्तरेण। अन्वयेऽभ्यासवत्यप्यर्थान्तरेषु तेष्वनभ्यासात्तद्रूपनि[1] रूपणत्वाच्चान्वयस्यानभ्यास एव । तथा च [2]स्मृतिसन्निहिताः स्वरूपमात्रेणार्थान्तराकाङ्क्षाः पदैरन्विता अभिधीयन्ते इति न परस्पराश्रयः।[3] नाप्यनाकाङ्क्षता, आकाङ्क्षा

इह तु यथा पदस्य स्वार्थेन सह साहचर्यानुभूतिरभ्यासवती, तथार्थान्तरेणापि साहचर्यानुभूतिरभ्यासवत्येव, अन्वितविषयत्वादनुभूतेरित्याशङ्क्याह–**अभ्यासवती च . . . . अर्थान्तरेण।। यथा**–यादृशी। **तथा**–तादृशी। **अर्थान्तरेण**–साहचर्यानुभूतिरभ्यासवतीति सिद्ध्यति। **'स चान्विते न स्वरूपे'** इत्येतत्परिहरन्नाह–**अन्वय इति।। अभ्यासत्वपि. . . .अनभ्यास एव।।** इदमाकूतम्–सत्यं अन्वितावस्था अभ्यासवती, तथापि यादृशी पदस्य स्वरूपमात्रेण साहचर्यानुभूतिर्न तादृशी अर्थान्तरेणान्वितावस्था अभ्यासवती। ननु अन्वयोऽर्थान्तरैः स्वरूपमात्रस्य ; तथा च स्वरूपवदन्वयस्यार्थान्तराणाञ्चाभ्यासवत्त्वमिति चेन्न ; अतुल्यत्वात्। सत्यं स्वरूपवदेवान्वयस्यापि पदार्थान्तरेषु स्वरूपान्वयिषु तत्र तत्राभ्यासोऽस्त्येव, तथापि तेष्वर्थान्तरेष्वनभ्यासात्, पदार्थान्तराणां तत्र व्यभिचारेण तेष्वभ्यास्य तथैवानुदयात्, तद्रूपनिरूपणत्वाच्च अन्वयस्य, सम्बन्धस्य सम्बन्ध्यधीननिरूपणत्वात् फलतोऽनभ्यास एवान्वयस्यपद्यत इति।।

एवमभ्यासातिशयो व्याख्यातः। सम्प्रति श्लोकशेषं व्याचष्टे–**तथा च स्मृतिसन्निहिताः . . . . परस्पराश्रयः।।** अत्र 'स्वरूपमात्रेण' 'स्मृतिसन्निहिताः' इत्यन्वयः। **स्मृति**शब्देनाभिधानं व्यवच्छिनत्ति। अत एवार्थान्तराकाङ्क्षा इति । एतदेव साधयितुं **'ततोऽपेक्ष्यानपेक्षणम्'**

---

१. 'तद्रूपणाच्च' इति मु० पु० पाठः। 'तद्रूपनिराकरणत्वादिति ३ पु० पाठः' इति टिप्पणी।

२. 'स्मृतिसन्निहितस्वरूपमात्रेण अर्था अर्थान्तरराकाङ्क्षाः' इति मु० पु० पाठः।

३. 'परस्पराश्रयम्' इति मु० पु० पाठः।

च प्रतिपत्तुर्जिज्ञासा। सा च क्वचिदभिधानापर्यवसानाद्भवति; यथा – द्वारम्[1] इति। न ह्यत्र [2]प्रकृत्यर्थातिरिक्ते प्रत्ययार्थे प्रतीतिरस्ति, येनान्वितः प्रकृत्या स्वार्थोऽभि[3]धीयते,

---

इत्यपाकुर्वन्नाह–**पान्यनाकाङ्क्षता।।** अत्र पदानामिति सिद्ध्यति ; स्वरूपमात्रेण द्रागित्येव पदार्थन्तरेभ्यः प्रागेव श्रुतानामेवान्विताभिधानमपीषत्करमिति भावः। अनाकाङ्क्षताभावे हेत्वन्तरमाह–**आकाङ्क्षा च प्रतिपत्तुर्जिज्ञासा।।** इदमाकूतम्–यदि पदानामेव चेतनत्वेनाकाङ्क्षा स्यात्, तदा येन ये तेषां साहचर्यमासीत् तेन तेनान्विताभिधानमाशङ्क्येत वा, न वा। परमार्थतस्तु प्रतिपत्तुर्जिज्ञासैव आकाङ्क्षा ज्ञानेच्छैव, नाकाङ्क्षामात्रम्; नापि शब्दस्य ; नापि वक्तुः। तथा च प्रतिपत्तारं झटित्येव पदानि श्रुत्वा अभ्यासाति-पात्स्मारितानामर्थमात्राणामाकाङ्क्षासन्निधियोग्यतासमीक्षया तदन्वयोन्मुखं प्रति पदानामन्विताभिधानं सेत्स्यतीति। यदि 'आकाङ्क्षा हि' इति पाठः तदा साकाङ्क्षतामेव प्रतिपादयति, 'आकाङ्क्षा हि प्रतिपत्तुर्जिज्ञासा' ; सा च तदानीमुपक्रान्तैव नोपरतेति भावः। एवं प्रतिपत्तुरेव जिज्ञासा पदानामाकाङ्क्षा; श्रोतारं प्रति च पदानां तुल्यत्वात्समभिव्याहारमनतिक्रम्य तेषामेव सोऽन्योन्यस्मा(रित?)पदार्थान्तरान्वितस्वार्थाभिानमध्यवस्यति, न त्वश्रुत-पदार्थान्तरान्विताभिधानं मृष्यत इत्युक्तम्। **'अभ्यासाति(शयाद्रूप)स्मृतेः'** इति चाभिधानात्पदस्मारितार्थान्तरान्वितस्वार्थाभिधानं सार्वत्रिकमिव प्रतीयते। न चै(तद्युक्तम्, यतः?) कदाचिदन्विताभिधानमश्रुतेनाप्यर्थेन श्रुतस्य पदस्य भवति। तत्र च प्रतिपत्तुर्जिज्ञासा नामाकाङ्क्षैव निमित्त(?). . . । **(सा च) क्वचित्. . . .द्वारमिति।। क्वचिदिति।।** वाक्ये। **अभिधानापर्यवसानात्,** न त्वभिहितार्थपर्यवसानात् (इति भावः)।। ननु द्वारमित्यत्रापि संवरणेन वा विवरणेन वा यदन्विताभिधानं तदप्यभिहितार्थपर्यवसानादेव (भवति?),

---

१. 'यथा दारा इति' इति मु० पु० पाठः।।

२. 'प्रकृत्यर्थादतिरिक्ते' इति मु० पु० पाठः।

३. 'अभिधीयेत' इति मु० पु० पाठः।

प्रातिपदिकार्थमात्रे [1]प्रथमोत्पत्तेः। तदत्रा[2]भिधानपर्यवसानाय प्रतिपत्ता पदार्थान्तरं स्मारितान्वययोग्यं जिज्ञासते। क्वचिच्च अभिहितार्थापर्यवसानात्; यथा–'विश्वजिता यजेत' इति। इह हि [3]कार्यस्य विषयकरणान्वितस्याभिधानं पर्यवसितम्, न पर्यवस्यति[4] हि तत्कार्यं नियोज्यभेदमन्तरेण; न खलु कार्यमनु-

---

प्रकृत्यपात्तस्यार्थस्यार्थान्तरेण प्रत्ययार्थेनान्विताभिधानात् ; अत आह–**न ह्यत्र प्रकृत्यर्था. . . प्रतीतिरस्ति।। प्रकृत्यर्थातिरिक्त इति।।** प्रकृत्यर्थव्यतिरेको हि प्रत्ययार्थलक्षणमिति भावः। यद्यस्ति (ततः किम्? अत?) आह–**येनान्वितः प्रकृत्या स्वार्थोऽभिधीयते।। येन**–प्रत्ययार्थेन। पुनश्चाभिहितापर्यवसानं स्यात्(?). . . .**'न प्रतीतिरस्ति'** इत्यत्र कारणमाह–**प्रातिपदिकार्थमात्रे प्रथमोत्पत्तेः।।** लिङ्गसख्ययोस्तु न प्रकृत्यर्थातिरेक इति भावः। यद्यपि तयोरपि प्रकृत्यर्थातिरेको विद्यते तथापि ताभ्यामन्विताभिधानस्यासाधारणत्वेन प्रयोजना(नत्वा?)भावात्कारेणान्विताभिधानस्यैव प्रयोजनत्वान्न कारके प्रकृत्यर्थातिरिक्ते प्रतीतिरस्तीत्युक्तमिति वेदितव्यम्। तथा च नात्राभिहितापर्यवसानम्, किन्त्वभिधानापर्यवसानमेवेत्याह–**तदत्र. . . . जिज्ञासते।। स्मारितान्वययोग्यमिति।।** स्मारितेन द्वारार्थेन योऽन्वयः तद्योग्यमिति।। अथवा–द्वारमिति पदेन स्वार्थस्यार्थान्तरेण केनापि योऽन्वयो व्युत्पत्तववधृतः स्मारितस्य तस्यान्वयस्य योग्यमिति। अभिहितापर्यवसानादपि भवत्येवेत्याह–**क्वचिच्चाभिहितार्थापर्यवसानात्।।** अत्र सा भवतीत्येव सम्बद्ध्यते। क्वचिदित्युक्तमेव दर्शयति–**यथा–'विश्वजिता यजेत' इति।।** न चात्राप्यभिधानापर्यवसानादेवेति दर्शयन्नाह–इह हि. . . **नियोज्यभेदमन्तरेण।। विषयकरणान्वितस्येति।।** विषयेण करणेन वा अन्वितस्य। **'विश्वजिता**

---

१. (प्रथमोत्पत्तेः)–'प्रत्ययोत्पत्तेरिति ३ पु० पाठः' इति टिप्पणी।

२. 'तदत्रान्विताभिधान' इति मु० पु० पाठः।

३. (कार्यस्य)–'कार्यस्येति ३ पु० नास्ति' इति टिप्पणी।

४. 'पर्यवस्यत्यभिहितं कार्यं नियोज्यभेदमन्तरेण' इति मु० पु० पाठः।

ष्ठानं विना [१]अवतिष्ठते; तदेव नाकर्तुकम्; न चानधिकृतः कर्ता; न चानियोज्योऽधिकृत [२]इत्यानुपूर्वी[३] (र्वि)कसिद्धम्। तेनात्रापि तत्पर्यवसानायास्ति [४]तदन्वययोग्यनियोज्यजिज्ञासा।।

यजेत' इत्यत्र धातुना विषय उपात्तः। **विश्वजिते**ति शब्देन तस्यैव करणत्वमुपात्तम्। ताभ्याञ्चान्वितस्य कार्यस्याभिधानं कारकत्वेनानुष्ठानोपयोगित्वात्प्रथममेव निर्वहति इत्यभिधानं पर्यवसितम्। न चाभिधानपर्यवसानान्नियेज्योनान्विताभिधानासम्भवः। अभिहितविषयकरणाभ्यां अन्वितस्याभिहितस्य कार्यस्य नियोज्यविशेषण(शेष?)मन्तरेणापर्यवसानात्। एतदेव स्फोरयन्नाह–**न खलु कार्यमनुष्ठानं बिना अवतिष्ठते।।** कार्यत्वादेवेति भावः। ततः किम्? इत्याह–**तदेव नाकर्तृकम्।।** यत्तु कार्यत्वार्थं कल्पितमनुष्ठानम्, तदेवेत्यर्थः। एवकारस्थाने तुशब्दो वा। न हि कर्तारमन्तरेणानुष्ठानमेवावतिष्ठते। हेतुमन्तरेण कार्यानिष्पत्तेरिति भावः। ततस्ततः; आह–**न चानधिकृतः कर्ता।।** न हि मदभिलषितसाधनत्वान्मदर्थमिदं कर्मेत्यविज्ञाय बुद्धिपूर्वकारी कर्तृत्वमनुभवतीति भावः। ततोऽपि किम्? अत आह–**न चानियोज्योऽधिकृतः।।**

'नियोज्यः स च कार्यं यः स्वकीयत्वेन बुध्यते।'

कार्यं स्वकीयत्वेन बुद्धवतो हि तद्विषयभूते कर्मण्यधिकारबोधो भवतीति भावः। एतच्च सर्वं पौर्वापर्येण सिद्धमित्याह–**इत्यानुपूर्वी(र्वि)कसिद्धम्।। आनुपूर्वी(र्वि)कम्**–आनुपूर्वी। आनुपूर्व्यशब्दादनुपूर्वीशब्दाद्वा विनयादित्वात्स्वार्थे ठक्। यथोक्तम्–'विनयादिभ्यष्ठक्' इति, तेन **सिद्धम्;** तत्कार्यानुष्ठान–

---

१. 'व्यवतिष्ठते। न चाकर्तृकं तत्' इति मु० पु० पाठः।

२. (आनुपूर्व्या)–'क्रियायाः सकर्तृकत्वनियमादिष्टसाधानताज्ञानं बिना कर्तृत्वानुपपत्तेरनुष्ठानमन्तरेण फलासम्भवात्स्वर्गकामः कर्तृत्वेनान्वेतीति भावः' इति टिप्पणी।।

३. 'इत्यानुपूर्व्या सिद्धं' इति मु० पु० पाठः।

४. 'तदन्वययोग्ये नियोज्ये जिज्ञासा' इति मु० पु० पाठः।

[1]च चानन्वितस्वार्थस्मरण[2]मात्रावसितव्यापारेषु पदेषु तदर्था एवाकाङ्क्षादिसहकारिणः करिष्यन्ति वाक्यार्थधियमिति कृतमत्र

कार्त्रधिकारनियोज्यसमुदायात्मकं पौर्वापर्येण लोके, वेदे च 'स्वर्गकामो यजेत' इत्यादौ प्रसिद्धमित्यर्थः। सामान्यन्यायमुक्त्वा प्रकृतेऽपि योजयति– **तेनात्रापि. . . .जिज्ञासा।। अत्रापीति।।** श्रुतनियोज्यकवाक्यवदित्यर्थः। **तच्छाब्दाभ्यां** विषयकरणान्वितस्याभिहितस्य कार्यस्य परामर्शः। **अत्र श्लोकाः**–

प्रमाणं वा संशयो वा भ्रान्तिर्वा श्रु(स्मृ?)तिरेव वा।
पदार्थधीर्ज्ञानजातिर्विधास्वासु समाप्यते।।
न तावदेषा प्रमितिवर्गेऽवस्थातुमर्हति।
स्थित **ह्यनुलब्धेऽर्थ** इत्यत्राज्ञातगोचरा।।
प्रमितिर्येनमेतादृग्यतः सम्बन्धसंविदः।
समयेऽधिगतो योऽर्थः पदानां तस्य संप्रति।।
तैरेव बोध्यमानस्य देशतः कालतोऽपि वा।
अवस्थया वा पश्यामः किञ्चिदाधिक्यमाहितम्।।
अनाधिक्यवता शक्या न प्रमेयपदे स्थितिः।
प्रमेयेन बिना ज्ञानं न च प्रामाण्यमश्नुते।।
किन्तु तत्स्मृतिरेव स्यात्पदजन्यं तु तादृशम्।।
एतच्च **वार्तिककृता** स्वयमेव समाश्रितम्।।
"पदमभ्यधिकाभावात्स्मारकान्न विशिष्यते।"
पदस्य वृत्ति(प्रणि?)धानादेः संस्कारोद्बोधकारणात्।।
विमृश्यमाने यः कश्चिद्भेदो नास्माभिरीक्ष्यते।
अवधारणरूपत्वान्न चेयं संशयत्वभाक्।।

---

१. (न चानन्वित....) 'विश्वजिता यजेतेति वाक्येऽश्रुतमपि स्वर्गकाममन्वितमालोच्य सर्वत्र तथैवास्त्वित्याक्षिपति' इति टिप्पणी।

२. 'न चानन्वितस्वार्थस्मरणमात्रावसितव्यापारेषु' इत्यारभ्य 'कारणत्वं वाक्यार्थप्रत्ययं प्रत्यध्यवस्यामः' इत्यन्तो ग्रन्थः यथामुद्रितपुस्तकं दीयते, व्याख्याने ग्रन्थपातात्।

मिथ्येति प्रत्ययो नास्यां न च कारणदुष्टता।
दृढत्वात्सर्वथा बुद्धेर्भ्रान्तिस्तद्भ्रान्तिवादिनाम्॥
विधा च पञ्चमी कापि न च ज्ञाने समस्ति नः।
एवञ्चाश्रीयतामेषा स्मृतिरेवेत्यकामतः॥
सा च त्वदुक्तमार्गेण भवेदन्वितगोचरा।
स्वरूपगोचरा नेति तुल्यो दोषाः प्रसज्यते॥

यस्त्वयास्मान्प्रति पुरा **पट्वभ्यासेति** वर्णितः।
पदैः स्वरूपमात्रेण स्मारिता अभिधानतः॥
पदार्था रुचिता मह्यं वाक्यार्थान्वयशालिनः।
न साहचर्यमात्रेण स्मारितास्ते तथा मताः॥
भवतः साहचर्येण स्मारितार्थान्विताभिधा।
इति दोषस्तवैव स्यान्नास्माकमिति चेन्मतम्॥
गङ्गायां घोष इत्यादौ कुतस्तर्हि भवन्मते।
तीरादेरभिधाभावात्प्रतिवासादिनान्वयः॥
किञ्च स्वरूपमात्रस्य स्मारितस्याभिधानतः।
गवादेः सहकारित्वस्मारितानयनादिना॥
आकाङ्क्षोपरतेस्तावद्गामित्येतत्पदश्रुतौ।
पश्येति श्रवणे पश्चादनाकाङ्क्षस्य गोः सतः॥
नाभिधानप्रतीतो(ते?)ऽपि दर्शनार्थेऽन्वयं व्रजेत्।
अभिधानप्रतीतोऽर्थो वाक्यार्थान्वयमश्नुताम्॥
नेतरस्त्विति नो वेदे वचो राजनि वास्ति नः।
ततस्त्वदुक्तमार्गेण वाक्यार्थाच्छेद आपतेत्॥
ततश्चानुभवाभावादन्वितस्यैव वस्तुनः।
कुतस्तज्जन्यसंस्कारो भवेदन्वितगोचरः॥
कुतस्तरां चासतोऽस्य पदैरुद्बोधनास्तिता॥
कुतस्तमां च पूर्वानुभूतार्थान्वयसंस्मृतिः॥
पट्वभ्यासाहितेत्यादिकेनोक्तातः पदैः स्मृतिः।
कार्या स्वरूपमात्रेण स्वार्थेष्वित्यावयोः समम्॥

पदानां सामर्थ्येनेति साम्प्रतम्। [१]पदानभिहितानां तेषां मानान्तरगोचराणां [२]वाक्यार्थधीहेतुभावादर्शनात्। श्वेतमध्यक्षं पश्यतो हेषारवं च शृण्वतः खुरनिष्पेष(क्षेप)शब्दं च 'श्वेतोऽश्वो धावति' इत्यन्वितधियः पदश्रवणमन्तरेणोत्पादो दृष्ट इति चेत्—न। अनुमानादर्थापत्तेर्वा तदवगमात्। [३]अनवगमाद्वा एवंवादी हि तावत्प्रष्टव्यो[४] व्याचष्टाम्—किंस्विच्छ्वेतसमानाधिकरणौ येन हेषाध्वनिखुरनिष्पेष(क्षे)शब्दाववसितौ तस्य ज्ञानं निरूप्यते, आहोस्विद्येन सितिमा च पदनिष्पेष(क्षेप)शब्दो हेषाध्वनिश्च स्वरूपमात्रेणावसितः; तत्र पूर्वस्मिन्कल्पे लिङ्गसामर्थ्यजमेतत्, न पदार्थसामर्थ्यजम्। उत्तरस्मिन्नपि द्रव्यान्तराभावनिश्चये सत्यर्थापत्तिः, तदभावे च नावसाय एव।

अपि च पदार्थसामर्थ्यजत्वाभ्युपगमे शब्दमूलत्वाभावे नाशाब्दत्वात् मनसश्च बाह्यानपेक्षस्याप्रवृत्तेः षट्प्रमाणीव्यतिरिच्यमानसहकारिसापेक्षत्वे [५]सप्तमप्रमाणाभ्युपगमप्रसङ्गः।

अतश्चैतद्वेदितव्यमेमेव विपश्चिता।

संस्कारातिं[६]. . . . .

---

१. (पदानभिहितानां)—'यदनभिहितानामिति ३ पु० पाठः' इति टिप्पणी।

२. (वाक्यार्थधीहेतुभावादर्शनात्)—'तथा च तत्र पदाध्याहार इति भावः। अन्यत्रापि क्वचित्प्रविश पिण्डीमित्यादावध्याहारस्थले इष्टापत्तिः।' इति टिप्पणी।

३. (अनवगमाद्वा)—'व्याप्तिज्ञानाद्यभावे इति शेषः। तत्सत्वेऽपि तस्याः शाब्दत्वाभावाच्चेत्यपि वक्ष्यति' इति टिप्पणी।

४. (प्रष्टव्यो)—'पृष्ट इति ३ पु० पाठः' इति टिप्पणी।

५. (सप्तमप्रमाणाभ्युपगमप्रसङ्गः)—'अर्थसहकारिकारणकमनसोऽर्थस्य वा केवलस्य प्रमिति जनकताया अक्लृप्तत्वादिति भावः' इति टिप्पणी।

६. अत्र व्याख्यायां पत्रषट्कपरिमितग्रन्थलोपः।

तत्सिद्धमेतन्नानभिहिता अर्था वाक्यार्थधीहेतव इति पदैरभिहिता-नामयं महिमा अभ्युपेतव्यस्तेषाम्। तथा च पदार्थानां वाक्यार्थ-प्रत्ययाधानसामर्थ्यम्, पदानां च तत्सामर्थ्याधानसामर्थ्यमिति शक्तिद्वयं कल्पनीयम्। अन्विताभिधानवादिनस्तु प्रथमावगतानां पदानामभिधायकानां वाक्यार्थप्रत्ययोपजनपर्यवसिततात्पर्यवृत्ती नामेकमेवाकाङ्क्षायोग्यतासत्तिरूपोपाध्युपायगृहीतार्थान्तरान्वित स्वार्थाभिधानसामर्थ्यमिति लाघवात्(वम्?), अतोऽर्थाभिधा-यिनां पदानामेव वाक्यार्थधीहेतुभाव इति चतुरस्रम्।।

अत्राभिधीयते—एष तावदौत्सर्गिको न्यायो यदसति बलवद्बाधकोपनिपाते—

> सहकारिणि कार्ये च प्रत्यासन्नं हि कारणम्।
> सति तद्भावभावित्वे तथा चार्थस्मृतिः पदात्।।

भवति हि कुतश्चिन्मानसापराधाद्वि (दवि?)दितपदार्थो विदितपदरूपमात्रश्चेतनो न मनागपि वाक्यार्थमवगच्छति,

---

पदप्रसक्त्यासत्ति(प्रत्यासत्ति?)र्दर्शिता। तथा च पदानां सहकारित्वमिति भावः। **अत्र श्लोकाः**—

> कारणञ्चेत्पदज्ञानमङ्गमेव पदार्थधीः।
> पदार्थबुद्धेर्हेतुत्वे पदधीरुपकारिका।।
> पदस्य सन्निधिः सिद्ध्येत्स्वार्थेन सहकारिणा।
> वाक्यार्थप्रत्यये कार्ये विप्रकर्षः प्रसज्यते।।
> पदार्थबुद्धेः कार्येऽपि पदज्ञानेऽपि सन्निधिः।
> इति सैवाभ्युपेतव्या वाक्यार्थज्ञानकारणम्।।

अथवा—पदानि वाक्यार्थधीहेतव इति भवनतो मन्यन्ते, वयन्तु पदार्था इति। आकाङ्क्षादित्रयस्य तु सहकारित्वमावयोः समानम्, वाक्यार्थप्रत्ययस्य कार्यत्वं

अवगच्छति तु समभिव्याहृतपदम्बकोपजनितस्वार्थस्मृत्यनन्तरम्। तदमूषामेव ([1]मानसीनां) स्वार्थस्मृतीनामाकाङ्क्षायोग्यता-सत्तिसहकारिणीनां कारणत्वं वाक्यार्थप्रत्ययं प्रत्यध्यवस्यामः।।

च। तत्रैतत्तावदविवादसिद्धम्, यदसति विधुरप्रत्ययोपनिपाते सहकारिणः कायस्य च प्रत्यासन्नं कारणमिति यत्तद्भावभावित्वं स्यात्, ईदृशी च पदार्थस्मृतिरिति सैवान्तरङ्गत्वाद्वाक्यार्थबुद्धेः कारणमित्युक्तम्। **अत्र श्लोकाः**–

आकाङ्क्षासत्तियोग्यत्वं सहकारीति निश्चितम्।
वाक्यार्थप्रत्ययः कार्यं वाक्यस्येत्यप्यवस्थितम्।।
व्यतिषङ्गो हि वाक्यार्थः स पदार्थेष्ववस्थितः।
आकाङ्क्षादित्रयमपि पदार्थेष्वेव वर्तते।।
अतोऽन्तरङ्गता युक्तेश्च पदार्था एव कारणम्।
पदानान्तूपयोगित्वं पदार्थप्रतिपादने।।
यदि तद्भावभावित्वं पदेष्वेव प्रतिष्ठितम्।
अन्तरङ्गत्वयुक्तिश्च ततो बाधनमिष्यताम्।
न त्वेवमस्ति खल्वेतन्मानसादपराधतः।।
यदज्ञातपदाथोऽयं विज्ञातपदमात्रकः।
न मनागपि वाक्यार्थमधिगच्छति चेतनः।।
पदोपजनितस्वार्थस्मृत्यनन्तरमेव तु।
अधिगच्छति वाक्यार्थं स एव पुनरित्युत।।

ननु पदानि प्रत्येकमेव पृथक् स्वार्थस्मृतीर्भावयित्वा निवृत्तव्यापाराणि, पश्चात्तेषां सम्भूय स्मृतिजन्मनि न पदान्येव कारणम्, विरम्य व्यापारप्रसङ्गात् ; अत उक्तम्–**मानसीनामिति।।** सत्यम्, प्रत्येकस्मृत्यनन्तरं प्रणिधानात्सम्भूय प्रत्येकं च स्मृत्यो मनसैवाविर्भाव्यन्त इति। अथवा–वाक्यार्थप्रत्ययं प्रत्यन्तरङ्गत्वं दर्शितम् । मानस्यो हि स्मृतयः । मानस्यः प्रत्यासन्नतरा इत्यर्थः। अथवा–वाक्यार्थप्रत्ययपूर्वभावित्वेविव न वेदितव्यम्। मनसैव तासां गृह्यमाणत्वा-

---

१. 'तदमूषामेव मानसीनां स्वार्थस्मृतीनां' इति व्याख्यात्रभिमतः पाठः।

यदपि मतम्–स्वार्थस्वरूपस्मृत[1]योऽ(पि) हि [2]वस्तुतस्तदर्थान्तरसङ्गतार्थगोचरा न [3]स्वरूपगोचरमर्थान्तरेण घटयन्ति, विभ्रमप्रसङ्गात्। न खलु प्रासादमात्रस्य [4]स्मरन्तोऽस्मरन्त(श्च) तद्देशं पाटलिपुत्रं स्वरूपमात्र[5]स्मृतया माहिष्मत्यैनं घटयितुमीशते, ईशाना वा भवन्त्यभ्रान्ताः।।

दित्यभिप्रायः। तथा पदान्तरवर्तित्वसाधनायापीति योजना (?)। अथवा–स्मृतय एव न सन्तीति (?) वक्तव्यम्, सर्वस्वसंवेद्यत्वादिति। अथवा–स्मृतौ तु मनसो बाह्यप्रवृत्तौ न कारणान्तरापेक्षेति दर्शयितुं **'मानसीनाम्'** इत्युक्तम्। यद्यपि पदार्थस्मृतयः कारणम्, तथापि नातिप्रसङ्गः, आकाङ्क्षादित्रयसहकारित्वं प्रति सर्वेषामविवादात् इति दर्शितम्–**आकाङ्क्षेति।।** अनेन चाकाङ्क्षायोग्यतासत्तीनां पदार्थस्मृतीनां चैकालम्बनत्वेन प्रत्यासत्तिविशेषो दर्शित इति वेदितव्यम्। एतच्च सर्वं भवताप्यङ्गीकृतमेवेति दर्शित **एव**कारेण।।

सम्प्रति श्लोकात्पूर्वतनस्य **'असति बलवद्बाधकोपनिपाते'** इत्यस्य व्यावर्त्यामाशङ्कान्दर्शयति–**यदपि मतम्।।** किन्तदित्याह–**स्वार्थस्वरूपस्मृतयो. . . विभ्रमप्रसङ्गात्।।** एतदेव निदर्शनेन प्रतिपादयन्नाह–**न खलु. . . . भवन्त्यभ्रान्ताः।। वस्तुतस्तदर्थे**त्यादिविशेषणं विभ्रमप्रसङ्गे बीजतयोपन्यस्तमिति वेदितव्यम्। **स्वरूपगोचरम्'** इति कर्मधारयः। **प्रासादमात्रेति।।** 'अधीगर्थदयेशां कर्मणि' इति षष्ठी। तस्या वैकल्पिकत्वात् **'तद्देशम्'** इति द्वितीया; प्रसाददेशमित्यर्थः। **स्वरूपमात्रस्मृतयेति।।** प्रणिधानादिना संस्कारोन्मेषात्।

---

१. 'स्मृतयोऽपि हि **वस्तुततदर्थान्तर'** इति मु० पु० पाठः। 'वस्तेतस्तदर्थान्तरेति ३ पु० पाठः' इति टिप्पणी।

२. (वस्तुतदर्थान्तरसङ्गतार्थगोचरा)–'वस्तुभूतेन ततोऽर्थान्तरेण सङ्गतोऽर्थो गोचरो यासां तादृश्यः स्मृतय इत्यर्थः।' इति टिप्पणी।

३. 'स्वगोचरं' इति मु० पु० पाठः।

४. 'स्मरतोऽस्मरतश्च तादृशपाटलिपुत्रं' इति मु० पु० पाठः।

५. 'स्मृतयो' इति मु० पु० पाठः।

तदप्यसाम्प्रतम्।। मा नाम भूदीदृशं [1]स्मरणफलस्य संस्कारस्य सामर्थ्यम् यत् अनुभूताननु[2]भूतस्वरूपतदर्थान्तरसंसर्गविषयमाधत्ते स्मरणं [3]समीचीनमिति। सम्भवति तु समभिव्याहृतपदावलीलब्ध-

---

एनम्–प्रासादम्। **ईशते**–लौकिका इति सिद्ध्यति। तेषाञ्च विशेषणम्–**'स्मरन्तोऽस्मरन्तश्च'** इति। **ईशानावेति।। वा**शब्देन न खल्वेतदित्य (ल्वित्येतद)नुकृष्यते। **'अभ्रान्ता'** इत्यस्यानन्तरं इतिशब्दो द्रष्टव्यः। अतोऽसामर्थ्यं नाम बाधकं बलवदस्त्येवेति दर्शितमनेनेति।।

अत्रोत्तरत्वेन **'असति बलवद्धयाकोपनिपाते'** इत्येतद्व्याचष्टे–**तदप्यसाम्प्रतम्।।** असाम्प्रतत्वमेव दर्शयन्नाह–**मा नाम भूत्...सामर्थ्यम्।।** नामशब्दो यथायोगं 'नाम प्रकाश्यसम्भाव्यक्रोधापगमकुत्सने' इत्येषु द्रष्टव्यः। **ईदृशम्**–वक्ष्यमाणम्। **'मा नाम भूत्'** इत्यस्य बीजत्वेन **स्मरणफलस्य'** इत्युक्तम्। बहुव्रीहिश्चायम्। संस्कारत्वादेव स्मरणफ- लत्वमभिप्रेतम्। **'ईदृशम्'** इत्येतदेव व्यनक्ति–**यदनुभूत. . . समीचीनमिति।। यत्**–यस्मात्सामर्थ्या-दित्यर्थः। **आधत्ते**–संस्कार इति सिद्ध्यति। अथवा–संस्कारसामर्थ्यमाधत्त संसर्गानुभवदशायां यदनुभूतस्वरूपं प्रासादादि तच्छब्दनिर्दिष्टं तस्य, यच्चाननुभूतस्वरूपं अर्थान्तरं माहिष्मत्यादि तस्य च द्वयोः संसर्गो विषयो यस्य स्मरणस्य तत्तथोक्तम्। असमीचीनन्तु प्रत्यभिज्ञानविभ्रमे स्वप्ने चाधत्त इति समीचीनग्रहणम्। 'समीचीनम्' इत्यस्यानन्तरं यदि इतिशब्दो दृश्यते यदा 'इति यत्' इत्यन्वयः। क्वचित्पाठः–'अनुभूतस्वरूपतत्तदर्थान्तरसम्बन्ध-विषयम्' इति। अत्रानुभूतस्वरूपत्वेन स्वरूपमात्रस्मृतत्वमपि विवक्षितमिति द्रष्टव्यम्। तथा च **'स्वार्थस्वरूपस्मृतयोऽपि हि'** इत्यादेः प्रतिनिर्देशोऽयमिति

---

१. 'स्मरणफलसंस्कारस्य' इति मु० पु० पाठः।

२. 'स्वरूपतदर्थान्तरसम्बद्धद्वयविषयं' इति मु० पु० पाठः।

३. (समीचीनमिति)–'संस्कारस्य स्वगोचरागोचरविषयकस्मृतिजनकत्वाभावेऽपि स्मृतेर्वक्ष्यमाणानुपपत्त्या तादृशप्रमितिजनकत्वमङ्गीक्रियते इति यावत्। सामर्थ्यं कर्तृ, समीचीनमबाधितं स्मरणं कर्म। आधत्ते जनयतीत्यर्थः।' इति टिप्पणी।

जन्मनाम् अर्थस्वरूपस्मृतीनाम् आकाङ्क्षादिरूपसहकारिभेदोपधानाहितदशान्त[१]रोपात्तप्रमाणभावानाम् अनन्तरदृश्यमानमानान्तरानधिगतस्वार्थपरस्परसम्बन्धनिर्भासप्रकाश फलानाम्। अन्यथा प्रत्यभिज्ञानमपि नोपजायेत । तत्रापि देशकाला

स्पष्टमेव। पूर्वपाठेऽपि तस्यैव निर्देश इति द्रष्टव्यम्। कथन्तर्हि वाक्यार्थप्रतिपत्तिसिद्धिः? अत आह–**सम्भवति तु. . . प्रकाशफलानाम्।।** अत्र **'ईदृशं सामर्थ्यं यदनुभूत'** इत्यादेरनुषङ्गो द्रष्टव्यः। समभिव्याहृतानां पदानामावल्याः सकाशाल्लब्धं जन्म याभिरिति विग्रहः। **अर्थस्वरूपे**ति व्यतिषक्ततां व्यवच्छिनत्ति। आकाङ्क्षादिरूपैः सहकारिभेदैः यदुपधानं तेनाहितं यद्दशान्तरं अवस्थान्तरं तेनोपात्तः प्रमाणभावो यासां यासु वेति विग्रहः। **उपधान**शब्दो भावसाधनः। करणसाधनत्वे त्वाकाङ्क्षादिरूपैः सहकारिभेदैरेवोपधानैः उपाधिभिराहितमित्यादि। **सहकारिभेदेति।।** यथा प्रत्यक्षानुमानयोः सम्प्रयोगो व्याप्तिस्मरणं च सहकारिविशेषः एवमत्राकाङ्क्षादित्रयं विशिष्टं सहकारीति। स्वोत्पत्त्यनन्तरमेव दृश्यमानम्, मानान्तरैरनधिगतस्य स्वार्थानां परस्परसम्बन्धस्य निर्भास आकारो यस्मिन्प्रकाशे तथाविधप्रकाश एव फलं यासामिति विग्रहः। **सम्बन्धनिर्भासेति** कर्मधारयः बहुव्रीहिर्वा। अत्रापि **मानान्तरानधिगते**ति सम्बन्धविशेषणम्। **अनन्तर**शब्देनान्वयव्यतिरेकौ दर्शितौ। **दृश्यमाने**त्यनेन प्रकाशफलस्य मानसप्रत्यक्षत्वं दर्शितम्। स्वार्थपरस्परसम्बन्धस्य प्रमाविषयत्वायान**धिगत**विशेषणमिति स्पष्टम्। समभिव्याहारान्यथानुपपत्त्या पदार्थैर्वाक्यार्थबोधः क्रियत इति दर्शयितुं **समभिव्याहृते**ति **पद**विशेषणं **तदावली**विशेषणं वा दर्शितमिति वेदितव्यम्। यदेतदर्थ(स्व)रूपस्मृतीनां विशेषणत्रयमुक्तं तदन्विताभिधानवादिनामभिहितान्वयवादिनामुभयेषामपि सम्मतमेवेति न तत्प्रसाधनापेक्षेति। अन्विताभिधानवादिभिस्तावदुक्तम्–'यावन्ति पदानि वाक्ये, तावन्ति श्रुत्वा न्यायानुसारेण वचनव्यक्तिविशेषमवसायार्थोऽ–

---

१. 'दशान्तरोपपादितप्रमाणभावाना' इति मु० पु० पाठः। 'दशान्तरापादितप्रमाणाभावानामिति ३ पु० पाठः' इति टिप्पणी।

[1]दिभेदोपहितस्वरूपसंवेदनजन्मा संस्कारः तदाहिता वा स्मृतिः कथं स्वार्थं देशान्तरेण कालान्तरेण वा घटयेत्। [2]तत्

वगम्यते' इति। तथा 'न च सम्बन्धग्रहणाशक्तिः, उपाधिविशेषाश्रयणेन सुकरत्वात्। आकाङ्क्षासन्निधानोपस्थापितान्वययोग्यार्थान्तरान्वितस्वार्थाभिधायीनि पदानीति व्युत्पत्तिपरिग्रहे न किञ्चिदनुपपन्नम्' इति। तथा 'तत्प्रतिपत्तये शब्दार्थव्यवहारः' इति। व्यतिषक्तप्रतिपत्तय इत्यर्थः।।

तथा वार्तिके–

'विशिष्टार्थप्रयुक्ता हि समभिव्याहर्तिजनः।' इति।

तथा–

'तेऽपि नैवास्मृता यस्माद्वावाक्यार्थं गमयन्ति नः।
तस्मात्तत्स्मरणेष्वेव संहतेषु प्रमाणता।।' इति।।

तथा–

'अपेक्षया च सर्वोऽसौ सम्बन्धं प्रतिपद्यते।' इति।

तथा–

'यस्य येनार्थसम्बन्धो दूरस्थस्यापि तस्य तत्?।' इति।

तथा–

'आनन्तर्याद्धि वाक्यार्थस्तद्धेतुत्वं न मुञ्चति।' इति।

तच्छब्देन पदार्थपरामर्शः।

तथा–

'पदन्त्वतोऽ(दमभ्य)धिकाभावात्स्मारकान्न विशिष्यते।'
'स्तोकोऽपि व्यतिरेको यस्य (यस्स?)
वाक्यस्ये(स्यै?)व गोचरः।।' इति।।

ननु यत्पदार्थस्मरणम् तन्न प्रमाणम्, स्मरणत्वात्प्रसिद्धवदित्यनुमानबाधितं

---

१. 'देशकालोपहित' इति मु० पु० पाठः। 'देशकालभेदोपहितेति ३ पु० पाठः' इति टिप्पणी।

२. 'तत्र हि इन्द्रियादि' इति मु० पु० पाठः।

इन्द्रियादिसहकारिसमवधानप्राप्तदशान्तरयोरेतयोः पूर्वापरदेश-कालानुगतैकवस्तुगोचरप्रत्यभिज्ञा[१]प्रसवसहः कोऽपि महिमा तादृगभ्युपेतव्यः।।

पदार्थस्मृतिप्रामाण्यमिति ; अत्राह–**अन्यथा प्रत्यभिज्ञानमपि नोपजायेत।। अन्यथेति।।** स्मृतेः प्रमाजननशक्त्यसम्भव इत्यर्थः। वाक्यार्थज्ञानप्रत्यक्ष-प्रत्यभिज्ञानयोस्तुल्ययोगक्षेमत्वादिति भावः। एवं प्रत्यभिज्ञाने सम्यं दर्शयन्दोषसाम्यं तावदाह–**तत्रापि देशकालादि . . . घटयेत्।। तत्रापि**–प्रत्यभिज्ञानेऽपीत्यर्थः। **देशकालादिभेदोपहितस्वरूपसंवेदनजन्मा**–देशकालावस्थाकृतेन भेदेनोपहितमनुरक्तं यत्स्वरूपं तस्य यद्वेदनं तस्माद्यस्य जन्मोत्पत्तिः तदेव वा जन्म प्रभवो यस्येति विग्रहः। केचित्संस्कारं प्रमाणमाचक्षत इति संस्कारग्रहणम्। **तदाहितेति।।** देशकालादिभेदोपहित-स्वरूपसंवेदनजन्मना संस्कारेणाहितेत्यर्थः। **देशान्तरेण कालान्तरेण वेति।।** अनुभवगोचराभ्यां देशकालाभ्यामन्येन देशेन कालेन वेत्यर्थः। केचित्तुः वादिनः संस्कारस्य प्रत्यभिज्ञाहेतुत्वमाचक्षते, अन्ये तु स्मरणस्येति मतभेदेन स्थितिरिति वेदितव्यम्। एवमनुपपत्तिसाम्यं दर्शयित्वा परिहारसाम्यमपि दर्शयति–**तत् इन्द्रियादि. . . .तादृगभ्युपेतव्यः।। तदित्वययम्**, तस्मादित्यर्थः। अनुपपत्तिसाम्यादन्यस्य च परिहारस्यासम्भवादिति। **इन्द्रियादीति।। आदिशब्दः** प्रकारवाची। तेनान्यदपि यत् कार्यतः सहकारितया गम्यते तदपि न तथात्वम-तिवर्तते। ततश्चाकाङ्क्षादीनामपि सहकारित्वं नासम्भावितमिति भावः। अथवा–अनुमानस्यापि प्रत्यभिज्ञानत्वाङ्गीकरणाद्धेतोरादिशब्दोपादानम्। इन्द्रियादीनामेव सहकारिणां यत्समवधानं तेन कारणेन प्राप्तं दशान्तरमन्यादृशत्वं याभ्यां तयोः। **एतयोः**–संस्कारस्मरणयोरित्यर्थः। मतभेदेनेति भावः। **पूर्वेति।** पूर्वापरयोः कालयोर्देशयोर्वानुगतमेकं वस्तु गोचरो यस्यास्तस्याः प्रत्यभिज्ञायाः, प्रसवसहः प्रसवं सहत इति, प्रसवाय पर्याप्तो भवति यः, स इत्यर्थः। स्मृतिसंस्कारौ

---

१. 'प्रत्यभिज्ञानस्य प्रसवसहः' इति मु० पु० पाठः। 'प्रत्यभिज्ञानप्रसवसह इति ३ पु० समस्तः पाठः' इति टिप्पणी।

स चेहापि समानः, अन्यत्राभिनिवेशात्। न च देशकाला-

देशकालाद्यतिरेकं बोधयितुं न पर्याप्नुत इत्येतत्स्वरूपप्रयुक्तम्, दशान्तरप्राप्तौ त्वपरदेशकालानुगतत्वाधिक्यबोधजननमपि न विरुद्ध्यत इत्यर्थ। **'कोऽपि'** इत्यनेन प्रमाणान्तरविषयत्वाभावं सूचयति। **महिमा**–सामर्थ्यम्। **तादृगिति।** अनुभूताननुभूतस्वरूपतदर्थान्तरसम्बन्धविषयस्य स्मरणस्याधातेत्यर्थः। **अभ्युपेतव्यः**–केवलया कार्यान्यथानुपपत्त्येति भावः। तत्र संस्कारपक्षे प्रत्यक्षप्रत्यभिज्ञाने प्रथममालोचनज्ञानम्, तदनन्तरं संस्कारोन्मेषः, तदनन्तरं स्मरणं जायमानम्, इन्द्रियसंयुक्तत्वात्स्मर्यमाणस्य, इन्द्रियसहकृतेन संस्कारेण प्रत्यभिज्ञात्मकमुपजन्यत इति स्थितिः। स्मरणपक्षे त्वालोचनानन्तरं संस्कारोन्मेषः, ततः स्मरणम्, तदनन्तरमिन्द्रियसंयुक्ते स्मर्यमाणे वस्तुनि स्मरणमेवेन्द्रियसहकृतं प्रत्यभिज्ञानमुत्पादयतीति। एवमनुमानेऽपि द्रष्टव्यम्।।

एवं सपक्षे साधितं पक्ष उपनयन्नाह–**स चेहापि समानः।। सः**–महिमेत्यर्थः। **इद**–पदार्थस्मृतितत्संस्कारेष्वित्यर्थः। हन्त! विस्मृतमस्माभिः, नात्यन्तसाम्यं विद्यते, अभिनिवेशविषयो हि भवतां प्रत्यभिज्ञागोचरे महिमा, नेहेति महान्विशेष इत्युपहसन्नाह–**अन्यत्राभिनिवेशात्।।** अभिनिवेशविषयत्वमात्रं त्वसमानमेवेत्यर्थः। अथवा–ननु पदानामन्वितविषयैकयैव शक्त्योपपत्तौ न पदार्थानां तच्छक्तिकल्पनोपपद्यत इति, अत्राह–**अन्यत्राभिनिवेशात्।।** यद्यभिनिवेशं मुक्त्वालोच्यते तदा समानः समानः। परमार्थतस्तु न पदार्थशक्तिकल्पनामन्तरेण वाक्यार्थज्ञानस्योपपत्तिरिति भावः। एतच्च परीक्षाप्रस्तावायान्विताभिधानवादिनं सन्धुक्षयितुमुक्तमिति वेदितव्यम्।।

ननु कुड्ये सति चित्रकर्मसम्भवः। तथा हि–न तावत्प्रत्यभिज्ञा नाम पूर्वापरदेशकालानुगतैकवस्तुगोचरं ज्ञानान्तरं सम्भवति, अस्यापि क्षणिकवत्वन्तरविषयत्वात्। एकत्वावसायस्तु समारोपमात्रमिति स्थितिः। न च तद्दृष्टान्तेन पदार्थस्मृतिषु तथात्वकल्पनासम्भवः, सर्वेषामेव भावानां क्षणिकत्वेन स्मृतिगतानां पदार्थानामन्वयबोधक्षणेऽवस्थानासम्भवात्। अन्वयकालवर्तिनां च क्षणिकत्वपक्षेऽन्यत्वेन स्मर्यमाणत्वाभावात्। स्मृत्यभिमानस्तु पूर्ववद्भ्रान्तिरेव।

वस्थानानात्वेऽपि[१] वस्तुनो रूपं नानेत्युपपादितं न्यायकणिका-

वाक्यार्थबोधस्तु प्रतिभामात्रमिति न्यायविदः प्रतिपेदिरे। अतोऽनवसर एवायं विचारः–किं पदान्यवे वाक्यार्थबुद्धिनिमित्तम्, अथ पदार्थस्मृतय इति। अता मुधैवायं प्रस्ताव इत्याशङ्क्याह– **न च देशकालावस्था . . . . न्यायकणिकायाम्। न्यायकणिकायां** हि क्षणभङ्गनिराकरणे–'नन्वस्त्व-भेदप्रतिभासो न पुनरक्षिणकतामावहति भावानाम्, बाधके सति समारो-पितपगोचरत्वात्। अस्ति हि बाधकम्–यत् सत् तत् क्षणिकम्, यथा–घटादिः, संश्च विवादास्पदीभूतः शब्दादिः इति स्वभावहेतुः' इत्यादिना क्षणभङ्ग-पक्षमुपन्यस्य 'क्षणिकत्वप्रतिक्षेपात्' इति ग्रन्थमवतार्य 'इदमाकूतम्। न तावत्सत्त्वं क्षणिकत्वसाधनसमर्थम्, क्षणिकत्वेऽप्यस्यानु(त्वे व्यवस्थानु) पपत्तेरसाधारणत्वात्' इत्यादिना **न वस्तुनो रूपं नाना,** न प्रतिक्षणं भिन्नम् इत्येतदुपपादितमिति।।

नन्वेवमर्थक्रियाकारित्वेऽपीति वक्तव्यम्, न तु देशकालाद्य-वस्थानानात्वेऽपीति (इति)। सत्यमेतत्। न त्वेतत्क्षणिकत्वहत्वनुवादमात्रम्, अन्यत्त्वेनाशङ्क्यते–नन्वनवयववाक्यविवर्तो वाक्यार्थो न पारमार्थिकः, अतः पदानि वा पदार्थस्मृतयो वा तत्कारणमिति निरूपणा निरवकाशा। अनवयववाक्यविवर्तत्वेन तन्निमित्तत्वात् । न च क्रियाकारकसंसर्गादयो वस्तुभूताः सम्भवन्तीति, तत्राह–**देशकालावस्थानानात्वेऽपीति**।। न वस्तुनो रूपं नानेति सम्बन्धः। एतच्चोत्तरत्र संसर्गपरीक्षायां 'पुनः प्रकारान्तरेण प्रत्यवतिष्ठते परः–नन्वेवंजातीयकेष्वेवाभेदबुद्धेः एकं शब्दात्मानमुपागमन् (धीराः)। तथा हि–क्रियाकारकगुणगुणिप्रयोजनप्रयोजनिप्रभृतिषु संसर्गिषु, समूहिषु वा शिंशपाशोककिंशुकादिषु संसर्गः समूहश्चैको वस्तुभूतश्चकास्ति। चकासति च शशविषाणालातचक्रादयोऽवस्तुभूताः। सेयमवंविधेष्वेकबुद्धिश्च वस्तुबुद्धिश्चैमनवयवं शब्दात्मानमेवावलम्बते' इत्यादिना वैयाकरणमतमुपन्यस्य, परिहरति–'नान्यथासिद्धेः' इत्यादिना। देशकालावस्थाभेदेऽपि वस्त्वेकमेवेति

---

१. 'अपि' नास्ति मुद्रितपुस्तके।

याम्। [1]ननूक्तं न मानान्तरानुभूतानामर्थरूपाणां वाक्यार्थ-धीप्रसव सामर्थ्यमुपलब्धम्, उपलम्भे वा [2]सप्तमप्रमाणप्रसङ्गः, [3]आगमस्य वा तत्रैवान्तर्भावः। तदेव प्रत्यक्षादिभिस्सह

प्रतिपादितम् ; एतदेवानेन ग्रन्थेन कृत्स्नेन क्रियते ग्रन्थक्लशाभावाय। **'अन्यत्राभिनिवेशात्'** इत्येतदसहमान आह–**ननूक्तं न. . .प्रसङ्गः।।** उक्तिः–'स्थितिर्मानमव्यक्तम्' इत्यादिना अन्विताभिधानवादिभिश्चोक्तम्, 'यदि च श्वेतिमा मानान्तरगम्यान्वयबोधिनः(धी?) तदा तस्मिन्नन्वये शब्दमूले मानमपरमुपेयम्' इति ।। अथवा न सप्तमत्वापत्तिः, किन्तु 'शास्त्रं शब्दविज्ञानादसन्निकृष्टेऽर्थे विज्ञानम्' इति लक्षितं यच्छाब्दं प्रमाणं अभिमतम् तद्धीति। एवंवादिनां मा भूत्सप्तमं प्रमाणम्। शाब्दं खलु शास्त्रं पदार्थस्मृतेरसन्निकृष्टेऽर्थे विज्ञानमित्येव लक्षयितव्यमापद्यत इत्याह–**आगमस्य वा तत्रैवान्तर्भावः।।** तत्र–सप्तमे प्रमाणे। पदार्थः खलु तृतीयं प्रमाणम्। तत्पञ्चविधम् प्रत्यक्षादिपञ्चकजनितानुभवप्रसूतत्वात्। अतो यथा चक्षुरादेः प्रत्यक्षत्वमेव न प्रमाणान्तरत्वं प्रत्यक्षान्तर्भावात्, एवं पदानुभवजन्मनोऽपि शास्त्रस्य पदार्थाख्यप्रमाणान्तर्भाव आपद्येत। एतदेव व्याचष्टे–**तदेव प्रत्यक्षादिभिस्सह तुल्यकक्ष्यतयोपन्यसनीयम्।।** तदेव–पदार्थाख्यं प्रमाणमित्यर्थः। **उपन्यसनीयम्–वृत्तिकारादिभिः।।** एवकारव्यावर्त्यमाह–**न त्वागमः।।** उपन्यसनीय इति सिद्ध्यति। कारणमाह–**तद्भेदः।।** अस्यार्थः–यतोऽयं **तद्भेदः** पदार्थाख्यप्रमाणविशेष इति। न त्वागमस्तद्भेदः प्रत्यक्षादिभिः सह तुल्यकक्ष्यतयोपन्यसनीय इत्यत्र निदर्शनमाह–**न हि ब्राह्मण. . .इति वा लौकिकाः।** प्रयुञ्जत इति वाशब्दादनुकृष्यते। तृतीयस्थाने विशेषोपन्यासादि-

---

१. 'ननूक्तं न मानान्तरतोऽनुभूतस्मृतानामर्थरूपाणाम्' इति मु० पु० पाठः। 'ननूक्तं च मानान्तरतेऽनुभूतस्मृतमर्थरूपाणामिति २ पु० पाठः' इति टिप्पणी।

२. 'सप्तमप्रमाणाभ्युपगभप्रसङ्गः' इति मु० पु० पाठः। 'प्रत्यक्षानुमानोपमान-शब्दार्थापत्त्यनुपलब्धिव्यतिरिक्तस्यार्थस्वरूपस्यापि प्रमाणतापत्तिरित्यर्थः' इति टिप्पणी।।

३. 'आगमस्य चात्रैवान्तर्भावे प्रत्यक्षादिभिस्तुल्यकक्ष्यतया तदेवोपन्यसनीयम्' इति मु० पु० पाठः।

तुल्यकक्ष्यतयोपन्यसनीयम्, न त्वागमस्तद्भेदः[1]। न हि [2]ब्राह्मणयुधिष्ठिराविति प्रयुञ्जते, प्रयुञ्जते तु ब्राह्मणराजन्याविति, वसिष्ठयु[3]धिष्ठिराविति वा लौकिकाः। न च भेदान्तरोपन्यासेन भेदान्तरमुपन्यस्तं भवति। तदयं समस्तमानलक्षणप्रवृत्तो मानतुषस्यापि परित्यागे तेनैव सह स्वकौशलमपि

तरत्रापि सर्वत्र विशेषा एवोपन्यस्ता भवेयुरिति चेत्, तत्राह—**न च भेदान्तरोपन्यासेन. . . .उपन्यस्तं भवति।।** श्रुतहान्यश्रुतकल्पनाप्रसङ्गादिति भावः। अथवा—तदेव प्रत्यक्षादिभिः सहोपन्यसनीयं तुल्यकक्ष्यवादित्यत्रैव हेत्वन्तरमाह—**न च भेदान्तरोपन्यासेन. . . भवति।।** इदमाकूतम्—भेदानां परस्परव्यभिचारित्वान्नैपन्यासेनान्यसिद्धिः, सामान्योपन्यासे तु विशेषाः सर्व एवोपन्यस्ता भवेयुः; अतोऽपि तदेवोपन्यसनीयम् 'न त्वागमस्तद्भेदः' इति।।

ननु मा नाम भूद्विशेषान्तरमुपन्यस्य(न्यस्तम्?), लक्षितं स्वन्तत्रोपयोगिताम(गितया अ?)पेक्ष(क्ष्य?)माणं त्वागमप्रमाणं (इति तदेवोपन्यस्तमिति, तत्राह—?) **तदयं समस्तं. . . .स्वकौशलमपि त्यजेत्।। तत्**—तस्मात्। **अयम्**—परीक्ष्यमिषेणापि लक्षणानि वदन्नयं **भाष्यकार** इत्यर्थः। **समस्तमानलक्षणप्रवृत्तः,** न तु चोदनामात्रलक्षणप्रवृत्तः, प्रत्यक्षाद्यभावान्तलक्षणकथनात्। **मानतुषस्यापीति।।** किं पुनरत्र सप्तमस्य परित्यागे षट्सु वा तृतीये षष्ठांशमात्रलक्षणेन पञ्चानामप्यंशानां परित्यागे इति **अपिशब्देनैव** दर्शितम्। **तेनैवेति।।** अनुपन्यस्तेन भेदान्तरेण, सप्तमेन प्रमाणेन वा। **स्वकौशलमपीति।।** तस्य परित्यागं कुर्वन्नेव तद्वत्स्वकौशलमपि त्यजेदेवेत्यर्थः। एतच्च—

---

१. (तद्भेदः)—'अर्थस्वरूपसमारकत्वादागमस्यार्थस्यैव प्रमितिजनकत्वात्पूर्वोदाहृते श्वेतिमचाक्षुषप्रत्यक्षखुरिनिष्पेषश्रावणप्रत्यक्षदशायामश्वो धावतीति धियोऽर्थमात्रप्रभवत्वस्वीकारे आगमस्य क्वचिदर्थस्मृतावुपयोगेऽपि तस्याव्यापकत्वादिति भावः।' इति टिप्पणी।

२. 'न हि लोका ब्राह्मण' इति मु० पु० पाठः।

३. 'युधिष्ठिराविति वा। न च' इति मु० पु० पाठः।

[1]त्यजेदिति [2]पदाभिहितानुभवानां वा पदाहितस्मृतिरूपाणां वा अथ[3]रूपाणामयमीदृशः[4] सामर्थ्यातिशयः, यतोऽर्थधिय[5] उदय इत्यकामेनाप्यभ्युपेयम्। तथा च तिस्रः शक्तयः कल्प्येरन्, द्वे

'कोकिलालापसुभगाः सुगन्धिवनवायवः।

यान्ति सार्धं जनानन्दैर्वृद्धिं सुरभिवासराः।।'

इत्यादिवत्सहभावस्य कथनं सहोक्तिर्नामालङ्कार इत्यवगन्तव्यम्। उक्तमर्थं प्रकृते पर्यवसाययितुं प्रक्रमते–**इति पदाभिहिता. . . .अकामेनाप्यभ्युपेयम्।। इतिर्हेतौ । 'पदाभिहितानुभवानां वा'** इत्यन्विताभिधानवादिवत् अभिहितान्वयवादिनां केषाञ्चित्पदार्थबाधस्यानुभवत्वाङ्गीकरणमभिप्रेत्योक्तम्, **'पदाहितस्मृतिरूपाणां वा'** इत्यभिहितान्वयवादं स्थास्यन्तं आश्रित्योक्त-मिति वेदितव्यम्। पदैराहितं स्मृतिरूपं ज्ञानं येष्विति विग्रहः ; अथवा–पदैराहितास्मृतिरेव रूपो रूपणं निरूपणमनुसन्धानं येषामिति विग्रहः। **अर्थरूपाणा(मित्य?)**–न्वयं व्यवच्छिनत्ति। अर्थरूपाणामीदृशः सामर्थ्यातिशयः न स्वरूपप्रयुक्त इत्यर्थः। **अयमित्यनेन** कार्यस्य प्रत्यक्षत्वात्तत्कारणस्यापि प्रत्यक्षदेशीयतां सूचयति । **ईदृशः**– अनुभूताननुभूतेति निर्दिष्ट इति। **सामर्थ्यातिशयः,** अस्तीति शेषः। **यतः**–यस्मादतिशयादित्यर्थः। अथवा हेतौ; **अर्थधियः उदयो**ऽस्तीति यत इति। **अर्थधियः**–वाक्यार्थधिय इति। **अकामेनेति** पूर्ववत्। ततः किम्? इत्याह–**तथा च तिस्रः शक्तयः कल्प्येरन्, द्वे वा।।** अत्र शक्ती कल्प्येयातामिति विपरिणम्यानुकृष्यते पदद्वयम्। विकल्पाभिधानं संख्ययोरुपपादयन्नाह–**पदानां हि. . .अभिधानरूपा**

---

१. 'परित्यजेत्' इति मु० पु० पाठः।

२. (पदाहितानुभावानां वा)–'बौद्धपदार्थानामेव शाब्दधीविषयतापक्षे' इति टिप्पणी।

३. 'अर्थरूपाणाम्' इति मुद्रितपुस्तके नास्ति।

४. (अयमीदृशः)–'पदाभिहितानुभवानामिति यदीदृश इति च २ पु० पाठः' इति टिप्पणी।

५. 'अन्वयधियः' इति मु० पु० पाठः।

वा। पदानां हि तावदर्थरूपा[१]भिधानरूपा शक्तिः, तदर्थरूपाणामन्योन्यान्वयशक्तिः, [२]तदाधानाशक्तिश्चापरा पदानामेवेति। स्मारकत्वपक्षे तूक्तं शक्तिद्वयम्। अन्विताभिधाने तु पदानामेकैव शक्तिः, तत् कल्पनालाघवात् एतदेव न्याय्यमिति।।

अत्रोच्यते—सत्यम्;

कल्पनालाघवं यत्र तं पक्षं रोचयामहे।
तदेव कतरत्रेति निपुणं सम्प्रधार्यताम्।।

एकैव किल शक्तिरन्विताभिधानवादिभिरन्वितस्वार्थगोचरा अभिप्रेयते पदानाम्, [३]न तु विशेष, [४]तदप्यभिधीयते। सेयं न तावदन्वयमात्रविषया। तन्मात्रविषयत्वे तस्याविशेषात् सर्वशब्दानां पर्यायताप्रसङ्गः। नापि व्यतिषक्ताभिधायि पदं न व्यतिषङ्गस्य

शक्तिः।। अत्र कल्प्येतेति सिद्ध्यति। तावच्छब्देन सूचितमेव दर्शयति— **तदर्थरूपाणां अन्योन्यान्वयशक्तिः।।** अन्योन्यान्वयस्य बोधने शक्ति **अन्वयशक्ति**रभिप्रेता। क्वचित्तु शक्तिरित्यस्मात्पुरस्तात् प्रत्यायनेत्यपि दृश्यते। तच्छब्देन पदानां निर्देशः, कल्प्येतेत्येव[५]. . .

---

१. 'अर्थरूपानुभवजननशक्तिः अर्थरूपाणामन्योन्यान्वयप्रत्यायनशक्तिः' इति मु० पु० पाठः।

२. 'तदाधानशक्तिश्च' इत्यारभ्य 'तद्विषयतया अभ्युपगते भवतः' इत्यन्तो ग्रन्थः यथामुद्रितपुस्तकं दीयते, व्याख्याने ग्रन्थपातात्।

३. (विशेषे)—'अन्विते न तु विशिष्ट इति ३ पु० पाठः' इति टिप्पणी।

४. (एकैव किल. . . .लदप्यभिधीयेते)—'स्ववाच्यप्रतियोगितानुयोगिताकत्वविशिष्टे तत्त्वेन तात्पर्यविषिये वा, न तु सम्बन्धत्व्याप्यतत्तद्रूपावच्छिन्ने, नानार्थत्वप्रसङ्गात्' इति टिप्पणी।

५. अत्र व्याख्यानमातृकायां पत्रषट्कपरिमितग्रन्थपातः।

वाचकम्, जात्यभिधायकमिव व्यक्तेः, व्यतिषक्तोऽवगतेर्व्यतिषङ्गस्य, व्यतिषक्तानां च स्वरूपतो भेदात् नैकार्थ्यं पदानामिति साम्प्रतम्। व्यतिषक्त इति स्वरूपमात्रं वोपलक्ष्येत्, व्यतिषङ्गवद्वोच्येत। तत्र [१]रूपाभिधानजन्मा ख्यातिः जात्यभिधानजन्मेव व्यक्तिम् न व्यतिषङ्गमपि गोचरयितुमर्हति। न हि यथा आकारिणमन्तरेणाकारोऽशक्यनिरूपण इति शब्दसार्थ्यगोचरत्वमनापन्नोऽप्याकार्याकाराभिधायिशब्दजनितविज्ञान विषयभावं [२]नातिपतति तथा अर्थस्वरूपम् अन्वयमन्तरेण दुरधिगमम्, येन स्वगोचरशब्दसामर्थ्यजन्मनि विज्ञानेऽन्वयमपि समर्पयेत्, तद्रूपस्यान्वयमन्तरेणापि शक्यनिरूपणत्वात्। नान्वंय विना तद्रूपं क्वचिदपीति चेत्, तत्किं लिङ्गमपि न लिङ्गिनं

तथैव पदशक्तिर्या स्थितेहा(र्थनिरूपणे?)।
नागोचरं कल्पयेत् (?). . . . . . ॥
(कल्पयेत्?) पदसामर्थ्यं नाप्यपेक्ष्येत
(नानपेक्ष्य?) पृथग्धियम्।
विशेषणविशेष्यत्वादन्वितान्वययोर्द्वयोः।
विशेषणेऽन्वये पूर्वं ग्रहीतव्ये भवत्यपि॥
एतदप्यत्र वदितुं शक्यते न विपश्चिता।
न हि जातिधियो व्यक्तिर्विषयत्वेन सम्मता॥
पदशक्तिरियं यस्माज्जातिमात्रैकगोचरा।
न व्यक्तिबोधनायालं कुतो व्यक्तिः प्रतीयताम्।

---

१. (रूपाभिधानजन्मा ख्यातिः)–'स्वरूपमात्रनिरूपतिशक्तिज्ञानमित्यर्थः' इति टिप्पणी।

२. (नातिपतति)–'शुक्लादिशब्दगतशत्तयविषयोऽप्याकारी गुणाश्रयो गुणमात्रवाचकपदजन्यबोधविषयतां न मुञ्चतीत्यर्थः। आकारीति पृथक्पदम्' इति टिप्पणी॥

न च प्रतीत्युपारूढजात्यपर्यवसानतः।
व्यक्तिप्रतीतिस्तत्रैव सिद्ध्येदिति च साम्प्रतम्।।
अपर्यवसितत्वस्य सर्वथैवानिरूपणात्।
अपर्यवसितिर्नाम किं खल्वत्र विवक्ष्यते।।
व्याप्तिर्वानुपपत्तिर्वा यद्वार्थान्तरमिष्यते।
न तावदन्तिमः कल्पः तस्य क्वाप्यप्रसिद्धितः।।
प्रथमो वा द्वितीयो वा कल्पो नैवेह कल्पते।
ज्ञातावेव प्रमाणत्वमनुमापककल्पकौ।।
ऋच्छतस्तेन विज्ञेया जातिस्ते प्रथमं भवेत्।
अतश्च प्रतिपन्नैव जातिर्व्यक्तिप्रबोधिनी।।
व्याप्त्या वानुपपत्त्या वा पश्चादेव कुतोऽनयोः।
एकप्रतीतिविषयभावे दृष्टान्तता भवेत्।।
दृष्टान्तेनापि नो सिद्ध्येदन्वितान्वययोरतः।
एकप्रतीतिविषयभाव एतेन हेतुना।
न रूपिशून्या रूपेषु बुद्धिरित्यपहस्तितम्।
चक्षुरादेर्हि शक्तत्वमुभयो रूपरूपिणोः।।
रूपे तज्जनिता बुद्धिरशून्या रूपिणा ततः।
न चक्षुषो रूपमात्रे शक्तिस्तद्बोधकत्वतः।।
केवलाद्रूपिणो बुद्धिर्न शक्तेरिति साम्प्रतम्।
चक्षुषः स्पर्शसंयोगाद्धटादिद्रव्यधीस्थितेः।।
रूपिण्यपि न चेदिष्टा शक्तिः शब्दस्य रूपवत्।
विना रूपिप्रतीते(स्स्यात्?) रूपधीसम्भवस्ततः।।
अन्यथानुपपत्त्यातो जातेर्व्यक्तः प्रतीयते।
पार्थसारथिमिश्रैश्च व्यभिचारोऽत्र वर्णितः।।
'रूपिशून्या च रूपेषु धीरस्त्येव तु तद्यथा।
हिमवर्तिनि हेमन्ते शैत्यसंवित्त्वगिन्द्रियात्।।
तथा गन्धवति द्रव्ये नासामग्रमधिरोहति।
न द्रव्ये जायते संविद्गन्ध एव तु जायते।।

तस्माज्जात्यभिधायित्वाच्छब्दस्तामेव बोधयेत्।'
किञ्चास्तु वाश्वादिपदैरन्तर्भावितरूपिणः।।
रूपस्य प्रत्यये शक्तिः पृथग्रूपिणि मा स्म भूत्।
तथापि न प्रतीतिः स्यादन्विते गर्भितान्वये।।
तथा ह्यङ्ग! भवान्पृष्टो व्याचष्टमिदमादरात्।
वर्ततेऽन्वितशब्दोऽयं वस्तुन्यन्वययोगिनि।।
विशेषणं किं ब्रूषे तमुपलक्षणमेव वा।
अन्वयेन विशिष्टं यत्तन्न तावदिहा(दिमम्?)।।
(विशेषणा?)नवगतौ तथा सति विशिष्टधीः।
नोत्पेतैव नाप्यन्यत्कारणं तस्य बोधने।।
इति शक्तिः पदस्यैव विशेषणविशिष्टयोः।
तत्र शक्तिद्वयं कल्प्यमापतेदन्वितस्य हि।।
रूपमन्वयवत्तैव तेन तस्य प्रबोधने।
अन्वयोऽप्यभिधेयः स्वान्नान्या गतिरिति स्थितम्।
किञ्चान्वितेतरस्वार्थबोधकस्येतराभिधा।
नैवास्त्य(त?)सतु बह्वीनां कल्पनानां निराकृतिः।।
मधुरा शर्करेत्यादिबहुदृष्टान्तवर्णनात्।
अन्वितान्वययोः शक्तिद्वैतं केन निवार्यते।।
प्रतियोगीतरपदादेव स्मृतिपथं गतम्।
आत्मना तद्वदात्मीयं तत आत्मीयमन्वितम्।।
पदस्य ब्रुवतः शक्तिगोचरोऽन्वय एव तु।
इति चेन्नैतदप्यस्ति व्यतिषक्ताभिधानतः।।
व्यतिषक्ताभिधानं हि टीकाकारनिरूपितम्।
अवधीरितमेवं च वदतानेन वादिना।।
स्वार्थेतरार्थभेदश्च कथमेवं प्रसिद्ध्यति।
न हि कस्यचिदप्यर्थस्वरूपं शक्तिगोचरम्।।

शक्तिगोचरमेवाहुः स्वार्थं लौकिकवैदिकाः।
शक्तिश्चेदन्वयेष्वेव सर्वपर्यायतापतेत्।।
अन्वितं चेदर्थरूपमभिधाशक्तिगोचरम्।
ततोऽन्वयप्रतीतिस्ते केनोपायेन सेत्स्यति।।
न तावदभिधानेन शक्तिगौरवभीतितः।
अन्विताशांभिधानं नो विमर्शमधिरोहति।।
अन्वेयसम्मतं तस्मान्नान्वये शक्तिकल्पना।
इति चेन्नैतदप्यस्ति वृथात्वादन्विते गिराम्।।
इतरेभ्यः पदेभ्यो हि विज्ञाताः प्रतियोगिनः।
स्मारितञ्च पदार्थस्य स्वरूपं प्रथमं स्वयम्।।
अन्वयश्चान्यतः सिद्ध इति किं नावबोधितम्।
यद्बोधनायान्विताशें शक्तिराश्रीयते त्वया।।
न चान्वयादृते सिद्ध्येदन्विताशोंऽपि कश्चन।
यदि त्वन्वययोगित्वमन्वयित्वं विवक्षितम्।।
तदप्यन्वयविज्ञाने विज्ञातमिव लक्ष्यते।
अन्येनास्यान्वयो नूनमिति सोऽयं विमृश्यते।।
अथ चान्वयवत्पश्य विमृष्टोऽन्वित एव च।
न चेत्सन्देहरूपत्वाद्विमर्शस्य प्रमाणता।।
अन्वये(यो?)ऽपि कुतः सिद्ध्येन्मानत्वे तद्वदेव तु।
अन्वितोऽपि प्रसिद्ध्येत्ते वृथा स्यादन्विताभिधा।।
ज्ञापनं ह्यभिधा नाम त्वन्वितोऽप्यन्वयाश्रयः।
यथैव धातुना पूर्वं तत्रान्वयविबोधनम्।।
प्रत्ययेन च तद्योगी निष्ठया पुनरुच्यते।
विना विशेषणधिया विशिष्टे नैव धीरिति।।
तथैवान्वयवाचित्वात्सर्वेषामपि ते भवेत्।

समुदायगता शक्तिरर्थद्वितीयबोधने।।
विशिष्टवाचके शब्दे विशेषणविशेष्ययोः।
उभयोरभिधानं स्याद्गोमयादिपदेष्विव।।
सिद्धा गवादयः शब्दा न विशिष्टार्थवाचकाः।
नाप्यन्यत्पदमस्तीह विशिष्टार्थस्य वाचकम्।।
विशेषणं विना किञ्चिदशेषस्याभि(धायकम्?)।
(?). . . . . . . .ह वार्तिककृत्स्वयम्।।
'पाकं हि पचिरेवाह कर्तारं प्रत्ययोऽप्यकः।
पाकयुक्तः पुनः कर्ता वाच्यो नैकस्य कस्यचित्।।'
विशेषणत्वेऽन्वयेऽपि शक्तिः स्यादन्वितांशवत्।
नाप्यन्वितोऽर्थमात्रं स्यात् (धातुनान्वयबोधतः?)।।
अन्तर्भाव्यैवान्वयं तन्न प्रतीतिमुपाश्नुते।
न हि जातिर्यथा व्यक्तिमन्तरेणेह दुर्गमा।।
पदार्थरूप(मप्येवं दुर्गमं ह्यन्वयादृते?)।
व्यक्तिरिव जातिवित्तौ
यन पदार्थस्वरूपवित्तौ च।
प्रविशेदन्वय एषः
प्रतीयते ह्यन्वयं विना (तदपि?)।।
एवं च सत्यन्वयस्य पदान्नास्त्यन्यन्तो गतिः।
तथा च सति तत्रापि शक्तिकल्पनमापतेत्।।
ननु जातिर्यथा व्यक्तिमन्तरेण न सिद्ध्यति।
तथा पदार्था अपि न व्यतिषङ्गं विना क्वचित्।।
अस्त्यर्थेनान्वितत्वं स्यात्पदार्थानामिहान्ततः।
अतोऽपर्यवसायित्वादन्वयस्यापि सिद्धितः।।
व्यक्तिवन्नाभिधेयत्वं सत्यमन्वयमात्रधीः।
अर्थापर्यवसानात्स्यान्न त्वन्वयविशेषधीः।।

विनेति तदपि तन्निरूपणधीननिरूपणमस्तु, तथा न लिङ्गत्व-मपीति अनुमानमुत्पन्नसङ्कटं [१] आपद्येत। तस्मादन्वितं शब्दसामर्थ्य-गोचर इत्यभ्युपगच्छता अर्थस्वरूपं च तदन्वयश्च तद्विषयतया अभ्युपगते भवतः। तदिह यदि पदसामर्थ्ययस्य स्वरूपमात्र-

---

विशिष्टस्त्वन्वयशशक्तिमन्तरेण न सिद्ध्यति।
किञ्चापर्यवसानार्थो नान्योऽस्ति परमार्थतः।।
व्याप्तेर्वानुपपत्तेर्वा ततो मानान्तरात्प्रमा।
अतोऽन्वयस्य शाब्दत्वं दूरापेतं प्रसज्यते।।
वक्तृज्ञानानुवादित्वं यथा लोकगिरां तव।
अर्थापत्त्यनुवादित्वं तथा वेदगिरां भवेत्।।
व्याप्यकल्पकयोर्यद्वा प्रत्यक्षेणोपलब्धयोः।
बिना व्यापककल्प्याभ्यां बुद्ध्यपर्यवसानतः।।
तद्बुद्ध्यनुप्रवेशेन तयोः प्रत्यक्षता भवेत्।
उत्सन्नसङ्कथं तत्र तत्प्रमाणद्वयं भवेत्।। इति।।

निबन्धनकृता तु 'यथा आकारिणमन्तरेण' इत्यादिना दृष्टान्त-दार्ष्टान्तिकयोर्वैषम्यमात्रमुक्तम्, तेनैव प्रयोजनसिद्धेः। **पार्थसारथिमिश्र-चिदानन्दपण्डिताभ्यां** दृष्टान्तत्वासिद्धेरेव (बह्व्यो युक्तयः प्रदर्शिताः?), तत्प्रकारश्च किञ्चिद्द्योतित एव। **अनुमान**मित्यर्थापत्तेरुपलक्षणम्। तथा लिङ्गलिङ्गि(?). . . .प्रधारणाप्रस्तावायनिश्चितत्वमन्विताभिधानस्य निरस्तम्। **तस्मादन्वितं शब्दसामर्थ्यगोचर. . . .(भवतः)।।** (?). . . . . व्यतिषङ्गवद्वोच्येत' इत्येतत्पक्षाश्रयणमेवोपपद्यते नान्या गतिरस्तीत्यर्थः। विशेषण . . . (?) तथा च सति द्वयोरपि शब्दशक्तिकल्पना, नान्या गतिरस्ती-

---

१. (आपद्येत)–'लिङ्गस्य लिङ्गत्वस्य वा व्यापकाधीननिरूपणत्वेन तज्ज्ञानकाल एव व्यापकज्ञानाभ्युपगमे पक्षधर्मताज्ञानोत्तरजायमानप्रमितिविषयतानुपपत्तेरिति भावः' इति टिप्पणी।

गोचरतयाप्यन्वयधि उदयमुपपादयितुं शक्ष्यामः, ततस्तावतैव परितोक्ष्यामः, तदन्वयविषयत्वकल्पनायाश्च विरंस्यामो लाघवाय; अथ तु सहस्रेणाप्यनुस[1]रणप्रयत्नैः स्वार्थरूपमात्रोपक्षीण-प्रवृत्तिनि पदसामर्थ्ये वाक्यार्थबुद्ध्युदयासम्भवः ततः परावृत्त्य शब्दसामर्थ्यस्यैवोभविषयत्वं कल्पयिष्यामः। किं [2]प्राप्तम्।।

त्यनुक्तसुज्ञानमित्यभिप्रायेण(?). . . संप्रधारणाप्रकारं प्रयोजनं च सूचयन्नाह–**तदित यदि. . . .कल्पयिष्यामः।। लाघवाये**त्यन्त-मभिहितोन्वयविषयम्। **परितोष्या(क्ष्या)म इति**।। न साक्षाच्छब्दवादिलोभेन क्लिश्यामह इति भावः। **तदन्वयेति।। तच्छब्दे**न पदसामर्थ्यस्य परामर्शः। तस्य यदन्वयविषयत्वं तत्कल्पनाया इति पञ्चमी। अपादाने चेयम्। **लाघवाय**–कल्पनालाघवाय। **सहस्रेणेति, अनुसरणप्रयत्नै**रित्यनयोः सामानाधिकरण्यम्। स्वार्थरूपमात्रोपक्षीणा प्रवृत्तिर्यस्येति बहुव्रीहिः। वाक्यार्थस्य या बुद्धिः तस्याः शब्दादन्यतः उदयस्यासम्भव इति। वाक्यार्थबुद्ध्य-दया(य?)सम्भव इति नञ्रहितश्चेत्पाठः तदा पुनरपि स्वार्थरूपमात्रो-पक्षीणप्रवृत्तेरपि पदसामर्थ्यादेव वाक्यार्थबुद्धेरुदयस्य सम्भव उपपत्तिरिति योजना। **ततः परावृत्त्येति।।** स्वार्थरूपमात्रोपक्षीणप्रवृत्तेः पदसामर्थ्यात्स्वत-स्तावन्निवर्तामहे, पुनर्गत्यन्तराभावात् पदसामर्थ्यस्यैव सम्भवाद्वा **परावृत्यशब्द-सामर्थ्यस्यैवो**पक्षीणप्रवृत्तिनोऽपि पूर्वमुपेक्षितस्यै**वोभयविषयत्वं** स्वरूपान्वय-द्वयविषयत्वमपि कल्पयिष्यामः।

'प्रमाणवन्त्यदृष्टानि कल्प्यानि सुबहून्यपि।'

इति न्यायमवष्टभ्येत्यर्थः।।

सम्प्रति परीक्षापदवीमारूढो मीमांसकशैलीमनुविदधानः स्वयमालोचयति–**किं प्राप्तम्।।** किं युक्तमित्यर्थः। सम्प्रधारणा ह्येवमुक्ता–किमभिहितान्वयः

---

१. 'अनुसरणप्रकारेण प्रयत्नामर्थस्वरूपमात्रोपक्षीणवृत्तिनि' इति मु० पु० पाठः।

२. 'किन्तावत्प्राप्तम्' इति मु० पु० पाठः।

वाच्यरूपाविनाभूतव्यतिषक्तदशापराः।
समभि[1]व्याहृते(तेः?) शब्दा भवन्त्यनुपपत्तिः॥

सामर्थ्याधिगमो हि भावानां न [2]मानान्तरजन्मा, किन्तु कार्योत्पत्त्यन्थानुपप[3]त्तोवेवायतते। [4]तदियमपि व्यतिषङ्ग-प्रतीतिः कथमपि दृष्टदृष्टप्रकारभेदसहायादुपपद्यमानोत्पत्तिर्न पदसामर्थ्य-मात्मनि प्रमाणयितुमर्हति। 'अनन्यलभ्यः शब्दार्थः' इति हि त्रैविद्यवृद्धाः। अत एवाख्यातादौ कर्त्राद्यभिधायितां नाद्रियन्ते। लभ्यते च समभिव्याहारान्यथानुपपत्त्या पदाना- मन्वितार्थपराणां स्वाभिधेयार्थरूपसमवेतान्वितावस्थाप्रत्यायनं लक्षणया। न हि पदान्यसमभिव्याहृतानि स्वाभिधेयप्रत्ययमात्रेण पर्यवसातुमीशते।

सम्भवी, सम्भवेऽन्विताभिधानपरित्यागः, उतासम्भवी, तदा अन्विताभिधान-स्वीकारः इति। तत्र. पूर्वपक्षस्य पूर्वमेवोपन्यस्तत्वात्तन्निराकरणेन सिद्धान्त-वर्णनमेवात्रापेक्षितमिति कृत्वा सिद्धान्तमाह–

वाच्यरूपाविनाभूतव्यतिषक्तदशापराः।
समभिव्याहृते(तेः?) शब्दा भवन्त्युपपतिः॥

कारिकां व्याचष्टे। अत्र **अनुपपत्तिः** इति पञ्चमं प्रमाणमुपन्यस्तम्। तत्र चतुर्णां परित्यागे पञ्चमस्य चोपन्यासे कारणं तावद्दर्शयति–**सामर्थ्याधिगमो हि. . . आयतते॥ हिशब्दः** श्लोकार्थोपपादनद्योतनार्थः। अथवा–मानान्तरजन्म-त्वाभावस्य कार्योत्पत्त्यन्यथानुपपत्त्या[5] . . . . . समधिगते पदोच्चारण

---

१. 'समभिव्याहृतेः' इति मु० पु० पाठः।
२. 'मानान्तराधीनजन्मा' इति मु० पु० पाठः।
३. 'अनुपपत्तावायतते' इति मु० पु० पाठः।
४. 'तदियमपि व्यतिषङ्गप्रतीतिः' इत्यारभ्य 'पदार्थमात्रं बुभुत्सन्ते' इत्यन्तो ग्रन्थः यथामुद्रितपुस्तकं दीयते, व्याख्याने ग्रन्थपातात्।
५. अत्र मातृकाग्रन्थे पत्रद्वयपरिमितग्रन्थपातः।

न हि लौकिकाः पदार्थमात्रप्रत्यायनाय प्रवर्तन्ते। प्रति पित्सतं खल्वेतदिति प्रतिपादयिष्यन्तः पदान्युच्चारयन्ति। अबुभुत्सिताव-बोधने त्वनवधेयवचनतया नामी लौकिका नापि परीक्षका इत्युन्मत्तवदुपेक्ष्येरन्। न च भूयो भूयः समधिगतं परं पदार्थमात्रं बुभुत्सन्ते। तदनधिगतमर्थमवगमयितुमनसः समभिव्याहरन्ति वृद्धाः पदानि । तदयं समभिव्याहारः पदानामनधिगतार्थ-प्रत्यायनप्रयुक्तः [१]तमन्तरेणानुपपद्यमानः स्वाभिधेयसमवेता-मन्वितावस्थां लक्षयत्यन[२]धिगतचराम्।। तदुक्तम्–

'विशिष्टार्थप्रयुक्त हि समभिर्व्याहृतिर्जनः(ने?)।' इति।।

(णा?)सम्भवादित्यर्थः। **अनधिगतमर्थमवगमयितुमनस इति।।** अनधि-गतार्थावगमोद्देशेनेति यावत्। **समभिव्याहरन्ति**–एकवाक्यतया रचयन्ति। एकवाक्यतानिर्माणमेव हि शब्दरचना, पदानां नित्यत्वादिति भावः। उत्तर-विवक्षया 'समभिव्याहरन्ति' इति निर्देशः। अत एवाह–**तदयं समभिव्याहारः .. . . . लक्षयत्यनधिगतचराम्।।** अनधिगतार्थस्य प्रत्यायनेनाङ्गिना प्रयुक्तः प्रेरित इति; अथवा–अनधिगतार्थप्रत्यायनस्य कृते वक्त्रा प्रयुक्तः अनुष्टितः; अथवा–शब्दप्रयोग एव तद्धर्मे समभिव्याहारे उपचरित इति। **तमन्तरेणानुप-पद्यमानः**–अनधिगतमर्थमन्तरेणासम्भवन्नित्यर्थः। मुख्यार्थासम्भवात् गङ्गायां घोष इत्यादिष्विव तदविनाभूतमर्थं लक्षयति। अतः प्रसिद्धलक्षणायोगक्षेमत्वमस्या इति भावः। **अनधिगतचरामिति।।** अन्वितावस्थायास्तत्र तत्रान्यत्वादिति भावः। एतच्च नोत्प्रेक्षामात्रम्, **वार्तिककारमिश्रै**रेवाङ्गीकृतत्वादितिभावः। (दित्याह?)–**तदुक्तम्**–

'विशिष्टार्थप्रयुक्ता हि समभिर्व्याहृतिर्जनः(ने?)।' इति।।

---

१. 'तदन्तरेण' इति मु० पु० पाठः।

२. 'अनधिगतचरीमन्वितावस्थां लक्षयति' इति मु० पु० पाठः।

तदेवमनुपपद्यमानसमभिव्याहारपदजाता[१]हितस्मरण[२]प्रत्यासत्त्या दृश्यमानया[३] अर्थगताकाङ्क्षासत्तियोग्यतासध्रीचीनया लक्ष्यमाणा अन्विताववस्था नात्मनि पदसामर्थ्यं प्रमाणयति, [४]अन्यलभ्यत्वात्।।

एतत्तु **निबन्धन** एव व्याख्यातमर्थत इति वेदितव्यम्। उक्तमेवार्थं संक्षिप्य दर्शयन्नुपसंहरति–**तदेवमनुपपद्यमान. . . .अन्यलभ्यत्वात्।। तत्**– तस्मात्प्रकारान्तरस्यासम्भवादित्यर्थः । **एवम्**– उक्तुन प्रकारेण। **अनुपपद्यमानसमभिव्याहारेति।।** विशेषणं बहुव्रीहिः, पदजातं चान्यपदार्थः। **पदजातेति** षष्ठीसमासः। **जाते**त्यन्तस्य **आहित**पदेन तृतीयासमासः। **आहित**शब्दस्य **स्मरण**शब्देन कर्मधारयः। **स्मरण**शब्दस्य **प्रत्यासत्ति**शब्देन षष्ठीसमासः। **लक्ष्यमाणे**त्यन्वयः। न चैवंभूतं स्मरणमेव नास्ति, कुतः तत्प्रत्यासत्तिरिति वक्तव्यम्, प्रमाणसिद्धत्वादित्युक्तं **दृश्यमानयेति**। एतच्च **'तदमूषामेव स्वार्थस्मृतीनां मानसीनाम्'** इत्यादेः संङ्ग्रह इति वेदितव्यम्। ननु जरद्गवादिवाक्येऽपि समभिव्याहारपदजाताहितप्रत्यासत्तिर्विद्यत एव। न च तत्र वाक्यार्थावबोधस्य सत्यत्वम्, अत उक्तम्–**अर्थगताकाङ्क्षेति।।** जरद्वादिवाक्ये तु स्मरणप्रत्यासत्तिरेव केवला नाकाङ्क्षादित्रयसहकारिसाहित्यमिति भावः। शेषं सुगमम्।।

अत्र **नयविवेककृतोक्तम्**–

"वाचस्पत्युक्ता(क्तम्–अ?)न्विताभिधानपक्षेऽनेकत्र शब्दः (क्तिः?) अन्वये स्वार्थ च। अभिहितान्वये त्वकत्र स्वार्थे। अन्विताववस्था तु लक्ष्यताम्,

---

१. 'पदजातजातस्मरणस्वार्थप्रत्यासत्त्या' इति मु० पु० पाठः।

२. (तदेव. . . प्रत्यासत्त्या)–'अनुपपद्यमानः संसृवृतात्पर्यकत्वाभावेऽनुपपन्नः पदान्तरसमभिव्याहारो यस्य तादृशेन पदजातेन पदसमूहेन जातं स्मरणं यस्य तादृशस्यार्थस्य प्रत्यासत्त्या सम्बन्धेनेत्यर्थः।' इति टिप्पणी।

३. 'दृश्यमानया दृश्यमानार्थगताकङ्क्षायोग्यता सन्निधि' इति मु० पु० पाठः।

४. (अन्यलभ्यत्वात्)–'अनन्यलम्भत्वादिति २ पु० पाठः' इति टिप्पणी।

सम्बन्धात्, तत्परपदप्रयोगव्युत्पत्त्यनुपत्त्या च। यथा मानान्तरदृष्टोऽर्थो लिङ्गम् अनुपपन्नो वा अन्वितधीहेतुस्तथा पदोक्तोऽपि व्युत्पत्त्यनुपपत्त्या अस्तु। वाच्येऽन्वयायोग्ये योग्यसम्बन्ध्यन्वयो लक्षणावृत्त्यां निरूढः, नेह तथेति चेत्–न। अनन्यलभ्ये शब्दशक्तिरिति वरं वाच्यानुपपत्तिमात्रात्सम्बन्धिस्वीकार-मात्रं व्यापि लक्षणालक्षणमस्तु। अन्वितभेदावस्था सम्बन्धिनी न पूर्वदृष्टेति चेत्–न। सन्निध्याद्युपाधेः सामान्यतोऽन्वितभेदस्य धीस्थता अस्तु। सम्बन्धस्मृतावेव स्मृते स्वार्थमात्रे नाभिधातृतेति चेत्–न। शब्दार्थदर्थ-धीरेवाभिधोच्यते लोके। अतः स्मृतिरप्यभिधा, व्युत्पत्तितः। स्मार्यस्मारकत्वा-दसत्यपि सम्बन्धान्तरे स्मृतिरस्तु, तन्न। अस्त्वेवमिति(स्त्वेवम्?)। एवं चेल्लक्षणा विधान्तरेण कल्प्या, कल्पनाद्वयं दुर्वारम्। स्मारकत्वे लक्षणाविधापदस्मारिते चेत्सेति(चेति?) सूक्तम् स्मारकत्वे कल्पनाद्वयम् अन्वयविशिष्टे चार्थे एकस्यैवैकत्र शक्तिः। उपेत्यैवेदमुक्तम् वृत्त्यन्तरेऽपि कल्प्यं(ल्प्ये) जघन्य(न्यं)धीहेतुत्वम्, वरं शक्तिः कल्प्या इति दिक्'' इति।।

एतद्व्याख्यायते। ''मतान्तरमुपन्यस्यति–वाचस्पत्युक्तमिति। ननु प्रसिद्धलक्षणाप्रयोजकरूपाभावान्नेयं लक्षणेति कथं तदपेक्षया शब्दतोऽभ्युपगम इति शङ्कते–वाच्येऽन्वयायोग्य इति। परिहरति–नानन्यलभ्य इति। यद्यपि प्रसिद्धलक्षणायां स्वार्थस्यान्वयायोग्यत्वं अन्यस्य तदर्हत्वं चास्ति तथापि व्यापि अ(वाच्या?)नुपपत्तिमात्रात् तत्सम्बन्धिमेयग्रहमात्रं तल्लक्षणमुपेयम्, न सम्बन्धिनोऽन्यान्वयोऽपि । शब्दस्य तद्धीजननशक्तिकल्पनापत्तेः, कल्पनायाश्चान्यथोपपत्तावयोगात्, इति लक्षणैवेत्यर्थः। ननु गङ्गाघोषादौ वाच्यसम्बन्धितया स्मर्यमाणस्य वाच्यानुपपत्त्यामेव तया ग्रहस्तत्र प्रसिद्धः। अन्वितरूपि(वि)शेषरूपवाक्यार्थस्य त्वननुभूतत्वादस्मर्यमाणस्य मेयत्वग्रहस्तुल्यो नेति नेयं लक्षणेति शङ्कते–अन्वितभेदावस्थेति। परिहरति–न, सन्निध्याद्युपा-धेरिति। पूर्वदृष्टोपाधिसामान्यस्यापूर्वविशेषवृत्त्यवगमे तदुपाधिसम्बन्ध्यनु-भूतान्वितावस्था स्मृतिरननुभूतविशेषनिष्ठानुषङ्गः स्यात् इति स्मर्यमाणस्यैवानुप-पत्त्या मेयत्वमत्रापीति प्रसिद्ध(द्धि)साम्याल्लक्षणैवेत्यर्थः। नन्वेमप्यभिहितान्वयो न सिद्ध्येत्, स्वार्थमात्रस्याधिगतत्वाभावात् स्मृतिमात्राङ्गत्वादिति शङ्कते–

[१]स्यादेतत्। अस्तु लौकिकानां पदसङ्घातानां प्रेक्षावत्पुरुष-सन्दृब्धानां सन्दर्भितुरभिप्रायमनुरुध्यमानानामनुपपत्त्या अनधिगतार्थलक्षणापरत्वम्, वैदिकानान्तु पुरुषासन्दृब्धानामबुद्धिपूर्वाणां नानुपपत्तिः, [२]ययाऽन्वितावस्थां लक्षयेयुः। य एव लौकिकाः

सम्बन्धस्मृतावेव स्मृते स्वार्थमात्रादि(त्र इ?)ति। परिहरति–न, शब्दादर्थधीरेवेति। न स्मृतिव्यतिरेकाभिप्राया अभिधोक्तिः, स्मृतिविशेषार्थतया वृद्धप्रसिद्धेरित्यर्थः। ननु स्मृत्यनतिरेके स्मृतिहेतुसम्बन्धासिद्धिर्दोष इत्यत्राह–स्मार्यस्मारकत्वादिति।। संस्कारोद्बोधमात्रं हि तदपेक्षितम्, न सम्बन्ध एव, पुरुषान्तरस्मृति-करत्वावगतिमात्रेणापि तदुद्बोधसम्भवात्स्मृत्युपपत्तेः सम्बन्धान्तराभावेऽपि न हानिरित्यर्थः। एवं शक्तिलाघवमुखेनापि तत्समर्थनमयुक्तमिति(त्याह–तन्न।?) . . . .अस्त्वेवमिति। विशिष्टार्थपरपदप्रयोगव्युत्पत्तिः पदार्थस्य तत्प्रमिति-करत्वापादिका लक्षणायामित्येतदेव तावदसिद्धम्, तदभ्युपगमोऽस्ती(स्त्व?)ति दर्शितः। तथापि प्रसिद्धलक्षणातो विधान्तरकल्पनयैवं लक्षणां गतिरिहोपेयेति कल्पनागौरवं **प्र(भा?)करोक्त** (प्रकरणोक्त?)मलङ्घ्यमेवेत्यर्थः। ननु पदार्थमात्रे स्मारकत्वोपगमान्न गौरवमित्यत्राह–स्मारकत्वमि(त्व इ?)ति . . . . . व्यवहितलक्षणाया अपि दृष्टत्वादर्थस्मारितस्यापि क्लृप्त-प्रमितिकरत्वाविशेषादव्यवस्थाप्रसङ्गे सर्ववाक्यसाधारणं प्रमितिकरत्वं पदस्मारितमात्रस्यैवेत्युपेयमिति कल्पनाद्वयमुक्तमलङ्घ्यमेव। अन्विताभिधाने तु एकैव शक्तिरिति स्थितमेवेत्यर्थः। ग्रन्थोक्तानुसारादियं गौरवोक्तिः, वस्तुतस्तु शब्दप्रयोगानुपपत्तिगम्यं प्रमितिकरत्वं शब्दस्यैवोपेयम्, स्वतः प्राप्तस्य साक्षात्त्वस्य बाधापत्तेरित्याह– उपेत्यैवेदमुक्तमिति। ननु क्लृप्तशक्त्युपजीवनसम्भवे

---

१. 'स्यादेतत्' इत्यारभ्य 'वैदिका अपीति चेत्' इत्यन्तो ग्रन्थः यथामुद्रितपुस्तकं दीयते, व्याख्यायां ग्रन्थपातात्।

२. (यया)–'तात्पर्यानुपपत्त्येत्यर्थः' इति टिप्पणी।

शब्दास्त एव वैदिका अपीति चेत्, तत्किं गङ्गायां घोष इति गङ्गाशब्दो लाक्षणिक इति गङ्गायां पयांसि यादांसि गङ्गायामित्यत्रापि स एव लाक्षणिकोऽस्तु। अनुपपत्तिविरहान्नैवमिति चेत्–समानमेतबुद्धिपूर्वकेषु वैदिकेष्वपि। [1]**अथ परस्यापि**

साक्षात्त्वहानिर्न दोषः। क्लृप्ता च शक्तिः लक्षणायां ; स्मर्यमाणस्यार्थस्यान्वयप्रमितौ तदस्मृतौ तदभावात्। तदस्य चामुख्ये धीशक्त्यनुपगमात्तदन्वयपरपदोक्त्यनुपपत्तिसहायवत्तया चेति शङ्कानिवर्तकहेत्वर्था दिगुक्तिः। नान्वयप्रमितिशक्तिस्मर्यमाणस्यार्थस्य न क्लृप्ता पदैः स्वार्थान्वयोक्तौ तदनुषङ्गसिद्धं स्मरणप्रतियोगिनः तदुक्तप्रमितिविषयत्वं[2] (?). . . . तज्जननशक्ति(?). . . . . .न लक्षणापेक्ष इत्यभिप्रायेणाह–**तत्किं गङ्गायां घोषः . . . . लाक्षणिकोऽस्तु।।** क्वचित्तु 'पयांसि गङ्गायामितीहापि' इति पाठः। सिद्धान्तिन एवभिप्रायमाशङ्कते–**अनुपपत्तिविरहान्नैवमिति चेत्।।** यथा जात्यादिशब्दानां व्यक्तिलक्षणा लोकवेदयोरविशिष्टा। एवमन्वितावस्थालक्षणापि समभिव्याहारान्यथापपत्त्येति भावः। परिहरति–**समानमेतदबुद्धिपूर्वकषु वैदिकेष्वपि।। एतदिति।।** अनुपपत्ति(राहित्यमित्यर्थः ?)। अनुपपत्तिराहित्ये हेतुः अबुद्धिपूर्वकत्वम्। अबुद्धिपूर्वकत्वात्अपौरुषेयत्वात्। ततश्च न हि लौकिका(र्थपरेष्विवात्र समभिव्याहारान्यथा?) नुपपत्तिप्रकारसम्भवः। अनुपपत्त्यभावे च न लक्षणा। अभिधानं त्वबुद्धिपूर्वकत्वेऽपि शब्द(?) . . . . व्यापारोऽपि सम्भवत्येव, न लक्षणा कारणाभावादिति भावः । अतोऽत्राव्यापकत्वान्न लाक्षणिकत्वं वाक्या (र्थस्य), किन्त्वाभिधानिकत्वमेवेति सिद्धम्। सम्प्रति सिद्धान्ती परिहारमाह–**अथ**

---

१. (अथ परस्यापि)–'अन्विताभिधानवादं दूषयति–अथेति। लोकेऽर्थान्तरान्वितस्वार्थे पदानां सामर्थ्यग्रहादगृहीतसङ्गतिकस्य स्वर्गापूर्वादिर्वैदिकबोधविषयत्वासम्भवादिति भावः।' इति टिप्पणी।

२. मातृकायां एकपत्रपरिमितग्रन्थातः।

वैदिकेषु पदसन्दर्भेषु कुतोऽनधिगतार्थबोधनम्। अर्थान्तरान्विते स्वार्थे पदसामर्थ्यावगमाल्लोके वैदिकानां[1] पदानां लौकिकेभ्योऽनन्यत्वादिति चेत्—तन्न। [2]लौकिकानि वचनानि पुरुषाधीनरचनतया तदभिप्रायानुरोधीनि नान्वितार्थपरतया तमवगमयितुमीशते [3]इति वृथा अर्थान्तरान्वितस्वार्थकल्पना तेषाम्।।

परस्यापि. . . .बोधनम्।। परस्यापीति।। अन्विताभिधानवादिनोऽपि। **कुत इति।** निष्कारणन्तदिति भावः। न लक्षणावन्निष्कारणत्मभिधानस्य, शब्दव्यव(हाराधीनसमयज्ञा?)नपेक्षितत्वा(नापेक्षत्वा?)दित्यभिप्रायेणान्विताभिधानवादी चोदयति—**अर्थान्तरान्विते स्वार्थे. . . .अनन्यत्वादिति चेत्।।** एतच्च **'कुतः'** इति प्रश्नस्योत्तरम्। **लोक** इत्यन्त एको हेतुः। यथोक्तम्—('व्यवहारे च) यथाव्यतिषङ्गमेवावापोद्धारौ। 'अस्यार्थः—वृद्धव्यवहारे च यथा-व्यतिषङ्गम्—व्यतिषङ्गमनतिक्रम्य—(आवापोद्धारौ)। तथा हि—'गामानय' इत्यानयत्यन्वितस्यैव गोरावापः 'महिषमानय' इति तदन्वितस्यैवो(द्धारः,) तेनान्वित एव शब्दस्य सामर्थ्यमवसीयते। तच्च द्विधा सम्भवति। साक्षाद्वाभिधाने(न), पदार्थप्रतिपत्त्यवा(न्तरव्यव)धानेन वेति सम्प्रधारणीयम्। न तत्र साक्षात्सम्भवे प्रणाडीसमाश्रयणमुचितमित्यन्विता(भिधानमेव) निश्चीयते' इति। लौकिकेभ्योऽनन्यत्वं लोकवेदाधिकरणे स्थिममिति। परिहरति—**तन्न। लौकिकानि . . . . तमवगमयितुमीशते।। तदभिप्रायानुरोधीनीति।।**

---

१. 'वैदिकानां च लौकिकेभ्यः' इति मु० पु० पाठः।

२. 'लौकिकपदानि हि पुरुषाधीनरचनया तदभियानुरोधेनान्वितार्थपरतया' इति मु० पु० पाठः।

३. 'इति किमर्थान्तरान्वितस्वार्थाभिधानकल्पनया' इति मु० पु० पाठः। 'पदैरर्थस्वरूपमात्रोपस्थितौ वक्तृतात्पर्यज्ञानवशात् तत्संसर्गबोध इति भावः।' इति टिप्पणी।।

'पौ(रुषेयाद्वचना)त्–एवमयं पुरुषो वेदेति प्रत्ययः, नैव(मय)मर्थः' इति न्यायादिति भावः। **तमिति**–अन्वितार्थमिति। ततः किमित्याह–**इति वृथा अर्थान्तरान्वितस्वार्थकल्पना तेषाम्।। वृथेति।।** असत्या निर्विषयेति यावत्। **तेषाम्**–लौकिकानां वचनानामिति। इदमाकूतम्। एवं हि वदतो(न्तो) भवन्ति भवन्तो–वाक्यं तावन्न चक्षुरादिवदपरामृश्य ज्ञापकं भवति। तत्र पदपदार्थ-सम्बन्धसंवेदनतत्स्मरणाकाङ्क्षासन्निधियोग्यत्वपरामर्शतात्पर्यानानामभावेऽभिधानमेव न भवति। यत्रापि 'नद्यास्तीरे फलानि सन्ति' इत्यादौ पश्चाद्व्यभिचारः तत्रापि कस्य वैकल्यात्प्रमाणज्ञानं नोत्पद्यत इति विचार्यम्। वक्तृ-दोषाच्छक्तिप्रतिबन्ध इति चेन्न। तर्हि प्राचीनं विज्ञानमभिधानं न स्यात्, शब्दशक्त्यजन्यत्वात्। शब्दशक्तिजन्यं प्रमाणमभिधानमित्युच्यते। तत्र धूमादिष्विव परामृश्य ज्ञापकानां परामृश्यमानवैकल्याज्ज्ञानानुदय इति वाच्यम्। तत्र तात्पर्यनिश्चयेऽभिधानं भवति तात्पर्यानिश्चये न भवतीत्याश्रयणीयम्। तदनिश्चयश्चविविधाभिप्रायाधीनत्वाद्वाक्यस्य। ननु भ्रमाद्यभावे यथार्थतात्पर्यनिश्चय इति चेन्न। तन्निरासान्तर्गतं सम्यग्ज्ञानम्, न (ज्ञेयमवशिष्यते?)। तथा हि–ज्ञानचिकीर्षाप्रयत्ना वाक्यप्रयोगकारणम्। तद्दोषेषु भ्रमादिषु निराकृतेषु अन्तर्गतं सम्यग्ज्ञानमिति, न तु ज्ञेयमवशिष्यते। ननु केन तर्हि ज्ञानानुमानम्? उच्यते। यो वाक्यप्रयोगेष्वाशयादिदोषरहितोऽयमिति निरूपितस्वभावः तस्य वचनश्रवणानन्तरमस्मिन्नपि प्रयोगे आशयादिदोषरहितोऽयम्, तत्पुरुषत्वादिति यावदेव नानुमीयते तावद्यथार्थतात्पर्यनिश्चयो नास्ति, अयोग्यपदसन्निधानाशङ्कापि नापैति, विस्मृततत्स्वभावस्य शङ्कोदयदर्शनात्। यस्तु निरूपितविपरीतस्वभावः तस्य वचनाद्भ्रमादिरेवानुमीयते। अनिरूपितोभयस्वभाववाक्ये प्रथमं शङ्कैव, पश्चाद्देशकालादिना तत्स्वभावमवगम्य भ्रमाद्यभावे सम्यग्ज्ञानमनुमीयते। एवं ज्ञानानुमाने ज्ञेयभूतवाक्यार्थस्यापि नान्तरीयकसिद्धत्वाद्वाक्यं पश्चादनुवादकं भवतीत्यादि। तदेतदयु(दु?)क्तम्। **लौकिकानि वचनानि पुरुषाधीन-रचनतया तदभिप्रयानुरोधीनीति।।**

अत्र ब्रूमः। यत्तावदुक्तम्–वाक्यन्तावन्न चक्षुरादिवदित्यादि, तदयुक्तम्, असिद्धत्वात्। यथाहुः–

'अत्यन्तासत्यपि ज्ञानमर्थे शक्तिः(ब्दः)करोति हि।' इति।

वाक्यार्थस्यापि नान्तरीयकसिद्धत्वाद्वाक्यं पश्चादनुवादकं भवतीति। मैवम्। शङ्कायामपि वक्तुर्मनश्चक्षुरादिशङ्कैव जायताम्। तन्निरासे निर्दोषाद्वाक्याद्वेदवदभिधानमेवास्तु न तत्र सम्यग्ज्ञानान्तर्ग(नावग?)तिरस्ति। यद्यपि वाक्यप्रयोगस्य ज्ञानादिरेव साक्षात्कारणम्, न चक्षुरादि, तथापि हेतुनिषेधेन ज्ञानदोषनिषेध एव सेत्स्यति। अतो ज्ञानहेतुदोषाभावात्तत्कार्यज्ञानदोषाभावसिद्धेरभिधानमनुमानात्प्रागेवास्तु। एवं च विदितसङ्गतेस्तात्पर्यज्ञानात्पूर्वमेव वाक्यं स्वार्थबोधकमित्युक्तम्। एवञ्च ज्ञानविशेषमनवगम्य सामान्येन ज्ञानस्य निर्दोषतामवधारयतोऽभिधानं सिद्ध्येत्। यद्याप्त्वं ज्ञानस्य निर्दोषत्वम्। अथ यथार्थदर्शित्वम् यथादृष्टार्थवादित्वम् च पुरुषधर्म आप्तत्वम्, तथापि प्रथमप्रयोगमारभ्य तस्य सकृदेव निश्चितत्वात्तद्वाक्यादभिधानं प्रागेवानुमानात्सिद्ध्यति। यद्यपि प्रथमप्रयोगोपाधित्वमाप्तत्वस्यास्ति, तथापि तदीयप्रयोगसामान्यस्योपाधित्वात्सकृदेव ग्रहणसम्भवः। यद्यप्यदुष्टोऽयमिति सामान्येनावगतम्, तथापीदानीमयमदुष्ट इति ज्ञानं तात्पर्योपयोगीति चेत्—न। सामान्यावगतस्मृतेरेवापेक्षितत्वात्। येन हेतुना सकृदाप्तत्वप्तमवधारितम्, तेनैव ज्ञानमप्यवगंस्यते इति चेत्—न। सामान्येनावगतत्वात्। एतदीयं ज्ञानमदुष्टमिति विशेषज्ञानस्यादृष्टत्वात्। कथञ्चानवगते वाक्यार्थे तद्विषयं ज्ञानमनुमीयते। पदैः पदार्थेषु स्मारितेषु आकाङ्क्षादिवशेन तदन्वयप्रतिपादनयोग्यत्वपरामर्शो भवति। तद्विषयं वक्तुर्ज्ञानमनुमीयत इति चेत्—न। उक्तोत्तरत्वात्। न ह्यभिधानादन्यत्पदैः पदार्थानां स्मरणमस्ति। अभिधानमेव चेत्—अभिहितान्वयस्वीकार एव भवेत्। अपि च यदि स्मृतानां पदार्थानां आकाङ्क्षादिवशेन स्वान्वयप्रतिपादनयोग्यत्वमस्ति किमर्थन्तर्हि पदेन तेषामन्विताभिधानमङ्गीक्रियते। शाब्दत्वायेति चेत्—तत्त्वन्यथापि सेत्स्यतीति वक्ष्यते। किञ्च परामृष्टे त्वन्वययोग्यत्वे नान्तरीयकसिद्धत्वादन्वितान्वययोरप्राप्ते च शास्त्रार्थवत्त्वादन्विताभिधानभङ्गः। परामर्शश्च तर्कपरपर्यायः। प्रमाणेतिकर्तव्यताकोटिरिति चेत्—सत्यम्, तथापि 'प्रमाणं स्मृतिश्च प्रत्ययः' इति **गुरु**वचनात्प्रमाणत्वं वा

स्मृतित्वं वा परामर्शस्य स्यात्। सर्वथा यथार्थज्ञानत्वात्प्राप्तत्वेनाभिधान-भञ्जकत्वमिति।।

अपि च

'स्मरणव्यतिरिक्तत्वान्मानपक्षं विगाहते'

इति वदतां प्रामाण्यमेवाभिमतमिति। अपि चाभिधानात्प्रागनुमानमिच्छतां पश्चादनुवादत्वेनाभिधानमपि न सिद्ध्यति। तथा हि–पदस्मारितानां पदार्थाना-माकाङ्क्षादित्रयशालिनामन्वयस्य सिद्धत्वात् न पुनरन्विताभिधानावकाशः। एतच्च **न्यायरत्नमालायां पार्थसारथिमिश्रै**रभिहितान्वयनिर्णये प्रपञ्चितमनुसन्धेयम्।।

तथा हि–

अभिधानत एवेष्टा यद्घोषान्वयधीस्तव।
कथं घोषद्य(न्वयः स्या)त्तीरादेरभिधानतः।।
तीरस्वरूपमपि न गङ्गाशब्दोऽभिधास्यति।
प्रागेवान्वितमत्राह गङ्गाशब्देन केवलम्।।
स्मारिते स्वनिमित्तार्थे सति तत्समवायतः।
स्मारितं तीररूपं यत्तेन स्वार्थं समन्वितम्।।
घोषशब्दोऽभिधत्ते नो गङ्गाशब्दस्तु केवलम्।
तीरस्मृत्युपयोगीति यत्र तर्हि श्रुतं पदम्।।
सर्वं लाक्षणिकार्थं न किञ्चिन्मुख्यार्थभाग्भवेत्।
अन्वितार्थप्रतीतिस्ते कथन्तत्र भविष्यति।।
'अस्ति वा तादृशं वाक्यं यत्र मुख्यो न विद्यते।
कार्यं तदन्वितं वापि' पदानां विषयो मतः।।
कार्यं वाच्यं लिङादीनामन्येषान्तु तदन्वितम्।
प्रश्नप्रत्युक्तिरूपस्तु प्रयोगः शब्दगोचरः।।
दृश्यते कार्यशून्यो य कुतूहलवतां नृणाम्।

'कोऽयं गच्छति भूपालो गच्छती'त्यादिकं बहु॥
कवीनाञ्च विशिष्टार्थवर्णनारूप ईक्ष्यते।
'नीलोत्पलवनेष्वद्य चरन्तश्चारुसंरवाः॥
राम(माः)कौशेयसंवीताः प्रदृश्यन्ति कदम्बकाः
(कादम्बा इव शोभनाः)।'
स लाक्षणिक एवेति भवतां समयः स्थितः॥
तत्रापि चान्वये संविदुदेत्येव न चाप्यसौ।
पदे(द ?)हेतुरुदेतीति शक्यमत्रोपवर्णनम्॥
गच्छतेः कार्यवाचित्वाद्भूमिपालपदस्य च।
कार्यन्विताभिधायित्वान्नाकाङ्क्षादिविशेषणैः॥
त्रिभिरेवाभिधानन्ते सिद्ध्येदन्वितगोचरम्।
वाच्यकोटौ निविष्टत्वात्कार्यकार्यान्वितत्वयोः॥
भूमिपालपदेनातो नाभिधेयो भवन्मते।
गच्छत्यर्थान्वितः स्वार्थो वाच्यो गच्छतिना न च॥
भूमिपालान्वितस्वार्थो भवत्यन्वयधीस्ततः।
पदकारणिका नैवेत्यतो वाच्यमिदन्त्वया॥
अभिधानं पदार्थानां पदैर्नैवेह सम्मतम्।
अन्वयस्य निमित्तं यदर्थरूपमवस्थितम्॥
तत्तावत्स्मर्यते पश्चात्स्मृतैः स्वार्थैर्मिथोऽन्वयः।
आकाङ्क्षायोग्यतासत्तिसध्रीचीनैः करिष्यते॥
इत्यवश्यमकामेनाप्यनुज्ञातव्यमापतेत्।
ततश्च सर्वदैवास्तु तथैवाभिधया विना॥
किमन्विताभिधानेन बहूपद्रवकारिणा।
'अथ तत्रानुमानेन संविदन्वितगोचरा॥

जायते न पदैर्नापि पदार्थैरिति मन्यसे।'
न हि सिद्धार्थवाक्येषु पदेभ्योऽन्वयधीर्मता।।
न पदार्थनिमित्ता वा भवेत्किन्त्वनुमानतः।
निर्मितिः पौरुषेयी हि वाक्यानामुपलक्षिता।
विशिष्टार्थविवक्षायाः समनन्तरभाविनी।
ततश्च सा हेतुभूतां विवक्षामनुमापयेत्।।
स्वकारणञ्च विज्ञानं सानुमापयति स्थितम्।
ज्ञानेन च स्वविषयः पदार्थानां समन्वयः।।
अनुमीयत एवं च सिद्धे सत्यनुमानतः।
पदार्थानाञ्च हेतुत्वं नैवान्वितधियं प्रति।।
आद्रियामह एवं च न विरोधः प्रसज्यते।
यद्येवमिष्यते दोषस्तवैषोऽपि प्रसज्यते।।
'यत्रापि कार्यसंवित्तिस्तत्राप्येवं भविष्यति।
पदानामपि सामर्थ्यं अन्वितेऽर्थे न सिद्ध्यति।'
सिद्धार्थवाक्यविषया या त्वयोक्तानुमाततिः।
प्रवर्तकेष्वपि तथैवास्तु वाक्यार्थधीस्तव।।
पदानामन्विते शक्तिरिष्यते केन हेतुना।
ततश्च सर्वसिद्धान्तभङ्ग इत्यत्र चोद्यते।।
'यदर्थविषयं वाक्यं तेनासावनुमीयते।
नान्यस्तेनान्विते सिद्ध्येत्पदानां शक्तिनिर्णयः।।'
विशिष्टार्थव्यवहृतौ विशिष्टार्थैकगोचरम्।
विज्ञानं कारणमिति नात्र कश्चिद्विचारभाक्।।
तदेतद्वाक्यमात्रेण न प्रसिद्ध्यति कुत्रचित्।
विशिष्टवाक्यार्थमतिर्विशिष्टादेव वाक्यतः।।

वाक्यार्थभेदाभिधानाद्वाक्यस्य च विशिष्टता।
तथा चोत्तमवृद्धोक्तवाक्यस्य समनन्तरम्।।
प्रयोज्यवृद्धचेष्टातो विशिष्टार्थधियोऽनुमा।
तस्याश्च कारणत्वेन वाक्यमेवेह कल्प्यते।।
वाक्येन च विशिष्टार्थसंविदुत्पत्तिहेतुना।
स्वकारणतया वक्तुर्विवक्षापि प्रकल्प्यते।।
विवक्षया विशिष्टार्थे वक्तुर्ज्ञानं प्रकल्प्यते।
एवं प्रयोज्यवृद्धस्य विशिष्टव्यवहर्तृता।।
नान्यथातोऽभ्युपेतव्या विशिष्टार्थाभिधायिता।
वाक्यस्य सा चावयवैः पदैरेवेत्यवस्थितम्।।
अतोऽन्विताभिधायित्वं पदानां सिद्धमुच्यते।
'पार्थिवो गच्छती'त्यादेः सिद्धार्थादपि वाक्यतः।।
राजगत्यादिको व्यक्तं विशिष्टोऽवगम्यते।
विशिष्टविषयं ज्ञानमेतद्वाक्यकृतं स्फुटम्।।
विशिष्टविषया वक्तुर्विवक्षा च प्रकल्प्यते।
तत्कारणतया वक्तुर्विशिष्टज्ञानमेव च।।
एतत्सर्वं तदेवं(तदैव ?) स्याद्वाक्यं चेत्प्रतिपादकम्।
नान्यथा तेन सिद्धार्थे वाक्ये कार्याभिधायिनाम्।।
तदन्विताभिधातृणामभिधाया असम्भवात्।
पदार्थैः स्मारितैरेव पदार्थप्रतिपादनम्।।
भवद्भिरभ्युपेतव्यं नान्या तत्रास्ति ते गतिः।
यद्युच्येतेह नावश्यमन्वितप्रतिपादकम्(कात् ?)।।
वाक्यादेवानुमीयेत धीर्विशिष्टार्थगोचरा।
विशिष्टार्थस्मारिका या पदपङ्क्तिस्तयैव हि।।

सिद्ध्यद्विशिष्टज्ञानं नो विनाप्यभिधया यतः।
तथा हीदृग्व्यापि(प्ति)संविद्येषामाप्तः पदान्यसौ।
इतरेतरयोग्यानां पदार्थानां विवक्षया।
उच्चारयति तेषां स विजानीते समन्वयम्।।
एवं सति पदार्थानामन्वयं प्रति हेतुता।
नाङ्गीकार्या पदैरेव विशिष्टरचनान्वितैः।।
ज्ञानानुमानद्वारेण वाक्ये सिद्धार्थगोचरे।
विशिष्टवाक्यार्थधियोऽप्यनुमानस्य सम्भवात्।।
न पदार्थनिमित्तत्वं वाक्यार्थस्य प्रसिद्ध्यति।
एवं तर्हि विधा यैषा सिद्धवाक्यार्थगोचरा।।
तयैव कार्यवाक्यार्थविज्ञानमपि सेत्स्यति।
'गामनये'त्यादिषु ते पदार्थैः पदबोधितैः।।
विशिष्टवाक्यार्थधियः सिद्धत्वादन्विताभिधा।
कुतः सिद्ध्येदतो येऽमी पदार्थाः पदबोधिताः।।
तैरेव वाक्यार्थधियः सिद्धत्वान्नान्विताभिधा।।
एवं स्वरूपाभिहितैः पदार्थैः
वाक्यार्थसंविद्भवतोऽपि सिद्ध्येत्।
स्वरूपमात्रं च न वाभिधेयं
पदैस्तु वाक्यार्थधियोऽनुमानात्।।
यथा पदविशेषाणां व्याप्तिर्वाचकशक्तिभिः।
तथा विशिष्टज्ञाने च व्याप्तिग्रहणसम्भवः।।
पदार्थजनितेनैव धूमधूमध्वजादिवत्।
सास्नादिभिर्विशिष्टस्य गोशब्दोऽयन्तु वाचकः।।
अश्वशब्दो वाजिनोऽयमिति वाचकशक्तिता।

यथा य(त)था तत्तदन्वितार्थगोचरसंविदा।।
तस्य तस्य पदस्ये(स्यै)व ग्रहीतुं शक्यते स्फुटम्।
आप्तस्य गोपदादीनां रचनेयं प्रतीयताम्।।
आकाङ्क्षायोग्यतासत्तिसध्रीचीनान्यवस्तुना।
अन्वितार्थज्ञानपूर्वेत्येवं व्याप्तिग्रहे सति।।
'अर्थस्वरूपवाचित्वमपि नैव प्रसिद्ध्यति।
प्रागेवान्वितवाचित्वमतो वेदाप्रमाणता।।'
वक्तृज्ञानानुमाद्वारं वाक्यार्थप्रतिपादनम्।
अपौरुषेयवेदस्य न हि सम्भवमर्हति।।
अप्रमाणत्वमेव स्याद्वेदस्य भवतां मते।
ननु व्युत्पत्तिवेलायां वाक्यानन्तरभाविनीम्।।
प्रयोज्यचेष्टामालक्ष्य धीर्विशिष्टार्थगोचरम्।
कल्प्यते तस्य बालेन हेतुरात्मनिदर्शनात्।।
सा च शब्दानन्तरत्वात्तत्कार्येति ततः परम्।
शब्दस्य तत्र शब्द(क्त)त्वं कल्प्यतेऽनुपपत्तिः।।
पश्चाच्च कस्यचिद्वक्तुरयथार्थपदाश्रयाम्।
रचनामुपलभ्यासौ कथं नु व्यभिचारिणः।।
वाक्यात्प्रयोज्यवृद्धस्य धीर्विशिष्टार्थगोचरा।
जातेति विचिकित्सै(त्स्यै)वमवधारयति स्फुटम्।।
अनेन नूनं वक्तायमित्यभूदवधारितः।
न युज्यतेऽस्यान्वि(नास्य युक्तानन्वि ?)तार्थपदसन्दर्भकारिता।।
तेप नूनमनेनैषामन्वयोऽप्यवधारितः।
इति ज्ञानानुमाद्वारमर्थं निश्चितवानसौ।।

इति कल्पयति ज्ञाता शक्तिर्वा(क्तिं वा ?)शब्दगोचरा(राम ?)।

न तां मिथ्येति मनुते तस्माद्वाचकता स्थिता।।
नैतत्सारतया ग्राह्यं यदनेनेह वर्णितम्।
'न हि कार्यादि(द)तज्जन्या श(न्याच्छ)क्तिः शब्दस्य कल्प्यते।।
स्यात्तु तज्जन्यतामात्रे(ताभ्रन्तेः)भ्रान्ति सा च निवर्त्स्यति।'
न हि प्रयोज्यवृद्धस्य शब्दानन्तरभाविनी।
प्रतीतिः शब्दजन्या यत्तस्य शक्तिं प्रकल्पयेत्।
शब्दानुमितवक्तृस्थकार्यलिङ्गप्रसूर्हि सा।।
न चान्यतोऽस्य निष्पन्नं कार्यमन्यस्य शक्तताम्।
कल्पयत्यव्यवस्था स्यात् कार्यकारणयोस्तथा।।
यद्यप्यभूदवस्थायां तादृश्यामन्यजन्यता।
न स्फुटावधृतेत्येवं शब्दानन्तरजन्यता(म् ?)।।
भ्रान्त्यावगम्य शब्दस्य शक्त्या भ्रान्त्या निरूपणम्।
तथापि पूर्ववत्पश्चादज्जन्यत्वनिश्चयात्।।
तज्जन्यत्वभ्रमे नष्टे तत्कार्यः शक्तिविभ्रमः।
निवर्तते पुनर्बाष्पकृतवह्न्यनुमानवत्।।
तद्धि साक्षादबाध्यं सल्लिङ्गबाधां नि(धात्रि ?)वर्तते।
तथा शब्दे वाचकत्वकल्पनापि निवर्तते।।
कार्यस्यातज्जन्यतेति कृत्वा पूर्वोक्तया दिशा।
नन्वस्त्वनुमितोऽप्यर्थः पश्चादस्यानुवादकृत्।।
वाक्य(क्यं ?)वाचकशक्तं स्यान्न मानाभावनिश्चयात्।
अन्तरेणानुमान(वाद ?)त्वं किं वेहानुपपत्तिमत्।।
यतः कल्प्येत शक्तत्वादनुवादकतेति चेत्।
अन्योन्याश्रयमापन्नं दुरुत्तरमिदं तव।।
शक्तिसिद्ध्य(द्ध्या ?)नुवादत्वं तस्माच्छक्तत्वमेव च।
तस्मान्न वाचकत्वस्य सिद्धिरस्ति कदाचन।।

तैरेवं तत्र कथितमास्तां तावदियं कथा।।

एतत्सर्वं हृदि निधायोक्तम्–**तन्नेथ्यादि।।** अयमर्थः। यानि **लौकिकानि** प्रत्ययितप्रणीतान्यप्रत्ययितप्रणीतानि च **वचनानि** तानि पुरुषेष्वधीना रचना येषां तानि **पुरुषाधीनरचनानि,** तत्तया कारणेन पुरुषाभिप्रायानुरोधीनि। त(य ?)था हि, आशयादिदोषवतोऽनाप्तस्य वाक्याद्भ्रमादिरेवानुमीयते, अनिरूपितोभयस्वभावस्य वाक्यात्प्रमाणान्तरेण सम्यग्ज्ञानं वा भ्रमादिर्वानुमीयते, एवमाप्तवाक्यादपि ज्ञानमेवानुमीयते, वक्तृज्ञानाधीनत्वात्पुरुषवचसाम् ; अतोऽनाप्तवाक्यवदाप्तवचसामपि नाभिधायकत्वम्।।

ननु तात्पर्यनिश्चयोऽपि सम्बन्धसंवेदनादिवदभिधानकारणतया व्युत्पत्तिसिद्ध एवेत्युक्तम्। तत्र तात्पर्यानिश्चयादभिधानं मा भूदनाप्तवाक्येषु, आप्तवाक्येषु त्वभिधानं तात्पर्यनिश्चयानन्तरं भवत्येव, अन्यथा व्यवहारावसितशक्तिबाध-प्रसङ्गात्। एवं हि शक्तिविषय एवार्थसन्देहात्तदज्ञा(त्तज्ज्ञा ?)नानुमानात्तात्पर्यानि (र्यनि ?)श्चये नैवास्ति शक्तिभङ्गः। किन्तु पुरुषसम्बन्धोपाधिनानुभूता शक्तिरुपाधिविगमे निरुपद्रवमवतिष्ठते, अतो न कश्चिद्दोषः ; अत उक्तम्–**नान्वितार्थपरतया तमवगमयितुमीशत इति।।** यद्यन्वितार्थे तात्पर्यं निश्चितं अभिधानात्पूर्वं तत्सिद्धये, तर्ह्यन्वितस्य पूर्वमेव ज्ञातत्वान्न वचसां तद्बोधने शक्तत्वम्, 'अनन्यलभ्यः शब्दार्थः' इति न्यायात्। एवं च व्यवहारेऽपि शक्तिः भ्रान्त्यैवावसिता न पारमार्थ(र्थि)क्येवेत्युक्तमिति वृथा अर्थान्तरान्वितस्वार्थाभिधानशक्तिकल्पना तेषामिति। चोदयति–**तथा सति . . . अनुपपन्नेति चेत्।।** इदमाकूतम्–अभिहितान्वये तावन्न वेदप्रामाण्यं सिद्ध्यतीत्युक्तम्। यद्यन्विताभिधानमपि न स्वीक्रियते लौकिकानां वाक्यानाम्, तर्हि कुतो वेदवाक्याद्वाक्यार्थावगतिः सिद्ध्येत्।। यथोक्तम्–

"व्यतिषक्ताभिधानं पदम्। किमेवं (वं) भविष्यति।"

"नानन्विताभिधायी शब्द उक्तो भवति"। "(न)भवत्य(वत्वन) न्विताभि-धायिता(धायी), तथापि किमित्याह–"ततश्च कार्यान्विताभिधायिता लोके नियोगस्यावगता"। अस्यार्थः–आचार्यादिवाक्येषु देवदत्त! 'समिधमाहर' इत्यादिषु प्रवर्तमाने देवदत्ते पार्श्वस्थ (एव)मवधारयति–बुद्धिपूर्विकेयमस्य

तथा सति वैदिकार्थप्रतीतिरनुपपन्नेति चेत्–

[१]मोपपादि। किं नश्छिन्नं नैयायिकानाम्। मानानुसारि हि

प्रवृत्तिः; यच्चाहं बुध्वा प्रवृत्तः तदयमपि, मदविशेषात्; अहं च न क्रियामात्रावगमात् प्रवृत्तः, नापि फलमात्रावगमात्, नापि फलसाधनत्वावगमात् प्रवृत्तः, नापि फलमात्रवगमात्, नापि फलसाधनत्वावगमात्, किन्तु कार्यावगमात् ; स्तनपानादिकापि क्रिया यावन्मया कार्यतया अनवगता तावदहं न प्रवृत्तः। न च या श्रेयस्साधनता सैव कार्यता। श्रेयः प्रति साधनत्वमन्यत्, अन्यच्च कृतिं पुरुषप्रयत्नं प्रति प्राधान्यं साध्यत्वलक्षणं कार्यत्वम् ; क्लेशात्मनस्तु कर्मणः फलसाधनत्वानुविधायिनी कार्यतेति मन्दा अभेदं प्रतिपन्नवन्तः। तथा सुखस्य फलसाधनतां विना कार्यावगतिरस्ति। अतः फलसाधन-तातिरिक्तकार्यबोधात् प्रवृत्तिर्ममेति देवदत्तोऽपि तदवगमादेव प्रवर्तत इति कल्पयति। तदवगमश्चास्य शब्दानन्तरं भवच्छ(ज्छ)ब्द निबन्धन एवेति कार्याभिधायितां लिङ्शब्दस्य कल्पयति। तच्च कार्यमन्वितमभिधेयमिति स्थिते 'अग्निहोत्रं जुहुयात्स्वर्गकामः' इत्यादिषु वाक्येषु षष्ठाद्यराद्धान्तानुसारेण स्वर्गकामपदेन नियोज्यतया स्वर्गकामः समर्पणीय इति। यश्च कार्यमवबुद्ध्यते स नियोज्यः। स्वर्गकामस्य च तस्मिन्नेव कार्ये नियोज्यतया अन्वयः, यदेव तस्य काम्यमानसाधनतामनुभवितुं क्षमते। न च क्रिया क्षणभङ्गिनी कालान्तरभाविफले हेतुर्भवति। तेन सा कार्यतया नियोज्येन सहा(ह ना)न्वीयते। यत्तु कालान्तरस्थायि कार्यम्, तदेव तेन सहान्वयं गन्तुमर्हतीति क्रियातिरेकि मानान्तरावेद्यमेव लिङादयः कार्यमभिदधति। तच्च मानान्तरापूर्वत्वादपूर्व (मित्युच्यते। ननु तस्यापि कार्यस्य कुतः सिद्धिः ? यागादेरिति चेत्,) अनन्तरभाविता तर्हि फलस्य प्रसक्ता, क्रियानन्तरभाविनस्तस्य फलहेतुत्वात्। उच्यते (–अनन्तरभावित्वेऽपि तस्य न फलमनन्तरं) भविष्यति, सहकारिव्यपेक्षया विलम्बनोपपत्तेः। स च (न च) सहकारिव्यपेक्षायां

---

१. इतः परं यथामुद्रितपुस्तकं मूले पाठो दीयते व्याख्यायां ग्रन्थपातात्।

प्रयोजनम् न तु तदनुसारि मानम्। तस्मात्स्वदृष्टिपक्षपातं परित्यज्यास्थायास्तिकपथमृजुमनुसरावो निमित्तमप्रत्यूहमस्या वैदिकार्थप्रतीतेः। तत्रानादिवृद्धव्यवहारपरम्परायां तदतदर्थसम्बन्ध-बोधोपाये सति असत्यपि सम्बन्धरि शब्दादर्थप्रतीतेरुपपत्तेः अर्थभेदनिरूपणस्य च ज्ञानभेदनिबन्धनत्वात् ज्ञानभेदस्यार्थभेदा-त्तदभिधानेऽभिधानाभावात् अर्थ भेदाभिधाने वा तत एव सिद्धस्तदभिधानानुपपत्तेः तद्धेतुतया तु तत्कल्पने ताल्वादिव्या-

---

कारणभाव(हानिः। किं तत्सहकारीति चेत्, देशकालादिकमिति)ब्रूमः। न (च) तस्य विशेषज्ञानमन्तरेण कश्चिदुपा (?)(किञ्चिद्दुष्यति। न च) फलजनकतया गुणभावादपूर्व(स्य वाक्यार्थत्वहानिः ; स्वानुगुणनि)योज्यलाभाय फलानुकूलतावलम्बनात् स्वामिवत्। यथा यथात्मन एव संविदा(दधा)नः स्वामी (गर्भदासस्योपकरोति, तद्वदेतदपि। ततश्चान्वित)ताभिधाने स्थिते कार्याभिधायिता लोके नियोगस्य लिङादेरवगता(तेति। "अतो नियोगाभिधानाम्" इति वक्ष्य)माणेन सम्बन्धः। नियोगशब्देन क्रियाव्यतिरिक्तमपूर्वं कार्यतया आत्मनि पुरुष नियुङ्क्ते(?) (नियुञ्जानमुच्यते। न चैवं वदत एव) व्युत्पत्तिः, लोकव्युत्पत्ति(त्ते)रव वेदवाक्यानुसारेणापूर्वपर्यन्ततावगमात्। (ननु न लोके कार्याभिधायिता लिङादेरस्तीत्यत्राह–) "आचार्यचोदितः करोमि इति हि दर्शितम्"। चोदितः–प्रवर्तयितुः। क(?) (कार्यमवबोधित) इत्युच्यते ; नान्यथा चेतनः प्रवर्तयितुं शक्यते यतः। "ननु च प्रेषणादयोऽप्यवगम्यन्ते लोके"। तत्कथं कार्याभिधायित्वमेव लिङादेरित्यर्थः। परिहरति–"उपाधो हि त, न शब्दार्थाः"। एतदेव विपरीतं(विवरीतुं) पृच्छति–"के पुनरमी उपा(धयो नाम)[१]"। . . . . .

---

१. अत्र ग्रन्थपातः मातृकायाम्। इतः परं व्याख्याग्रन्थो नोपलभ्यते।

पारस्यापि वाच्यत्वप्रसङ्गात् स्वाभाविकः शब्दार्थयोः [१]सम्बन्ध इति स्थितिः। [२]स तु किमर्थान्तरान्वितस्यार्थस्य, अर्थरूपमात्रस्य वा; यदापि रूपमात्रमुयते पदैः तदापि [३]किं तन्मात्रपरैः, आहोस्विदन्वितावस्थाप्रत्यायनपरैः। तत्र रूपमात्र- प्रत्यायनपरत्वे पदानां वाक्यार्थप्रत्ययानुपपत्तेः अप्रयोजनस्य [४]प्रयोजना-सम्भवादत्यन्तान्धमूकं जगत्प्रसज्येत । [५]तदुभयं परिशिष्यते लौकिकपदसन्दर्भस्य विशिष्टार्थप्रत्यायनप्रयोजनपरस्य। तत्रार्थान्तरान्वयपरस्य स्वार्थमात्राभिधानेऽप्यन्वितप्रतिपत्तेरुप-पत्तेरर्थापत्तिपरीक्षया अत्रान्वयं (परिक्षयान्नान्वयं?) यावत्पदस्य

---

१. (सम्बन्ध इति स्थितिः)–'वृद्धव्यवहारपरम्परारूपे शब्दार्थसम्बन्धज्ञानकारणे सति 'अनेन शब्देनायं बोध्यः' इत्युपेष्टर्यसत्यपि बोधदर्शनात्ततदर्थगतभेदप्रतिपादनस्य तत्तद्विषयकज्ञानाकारभेदप्रयुक्त्वाज्ज्ञानगतवैलक्षण्यस्य विषयतासम्बन्धेन ततदर्थरूपतया अर्थाभेदात् ज्ञानगतवैलक्षण्यस्य वस्तुतः सत्त्वेऽपि तस्य बोधविषयत्वाभावेन पदेषु तत्तज्ज्ञानगतवैलक्षण्यनिरूपितशक्तेर्वक्तुमशक्यतया अर्थानामिव तत्तदर्थगत-वैलक्षण्यस्यापि वाच्यत्वाङ्गीकारे तावन्मात्रेण शत्यैवेतरव्यावृत्ततत्दर्थविषयकशाब्दधिय उपपादियतुं शक्ततया अन्वयांशे पदवाच्यताभ्युपगमवैयर्थ्यादर्थगतवैलक्षण्यबोधस्य त्वन्वयप्रयोज्यत्वमात्रेण स्वरूपतोऽर्थाभेदातद्वैलक्षणनिर्वाहाकन्वयांशस्यापि वाच्यत्वाभ्युपगमे भिन्नभिन्नार्थबोधकारणीभूतपदप्रत्यक्षकारणपदोच्चारण-कुक्षिप्रविष्टतात्वादिव्यापारस्यापि परम्परयेतरव्यावृत्तार्थबोधं प्रत्युपयोगित्वेनानिष्टस्य वाच्यत्वस्यापत्तेः शब्दार्थसम्बन्ध स्वाभाविक एवेति सिद्धान्त इत्यर्थः।' इति टिप्पणी।

२. (सः)–'सम्बन्धः' इति टिप्पणी।

३. (किं)–'किमिति २ पु. नास्ति' इति टिप्पणी।

४. (प्रयोजनासम्भवात्)–'स्वरूपमात्रतात्पर्यकैः पदैः तात्पर्यविषयस्य संसर्गस्य बोधनीयत्वासम्भवादित्यर्थः।' इति टिप्पणी।

५. (उभयम्)–'अर्थान्तरान्वितस्वार्थाभिधायकत्वं अन्वितावस्थाप्रत्यायनतात्पर्यकत्वं च' इति टिप्पणी।

सामर्थ्यमनुवर्तनीयम्[१]। तथा हि– वृद्धप्रयुक्तवाक्यश्रवण-समनन्तरं प्रवृत्तिनिवृत्तिहर्षशोकभयसम्प्रतिपत्तेः व्युत्पन्नस्य व्युत्पित्सुस्तद्धेतुप्रत्ययमुमिमीते। तस्य सत्स्वप्यन्येष्वनुपजातस्य पदजातश्रवणसमनन्तरं सम्भवतः [२]तद्धेतुभावमवधारयति। न चैष प्रत्ययः पदार्थमात्रगोचरः [३]प्रवृत्त्यादिभ्यः कल्प्यत इति विशिष्टार्थगोचरोऽभ्युपेयते, तद्विशिष्टार्थपरता अवसिता वृद्धव्यवहारे पदानाम्। न चेयमविशिष्टार्थस्मरण-मन्तरेणेत्य-विशिष्टार्थस्मारकत्वं[४] [५]तदुत्पत्त्यैव प्रत्युप्तम्। न चैतदेषां विशिष्टार्थतामुपहन्तुमर्हति। न जातु भावाः स्वनिमित्तमुपघ्नन्ति, मोपघानिषत स्वमपीति । न चैतावता विशिष्टाभिधानम्। अविशिष्टविषयेभ्योऽपि [६]तत्परेभ्यस्तदुपपद्यते। तस्माल्लोका-नुसारेण वैदिकव्यापि पदसन्दर्भस्य विशिष्टार्थप्रत्ययप्रयुक्त-

---

१. (सामर्थ्यनुवर्तनीयम्)–'स्वार्थमात्रनिरूपपितशक्तिस्वीकारेऽपि पदसमूहस्य विशिष्टाथबोधतात्पर्यकत्वेऽन्वयप्रतीतेः पदविशेष्यकतात्पर्यज्ञानेनैवोपपत्तेः 'यजेत स्वर्गकामः' इत्यादावपूर्वेऽर्थापत्तिलभ्ये पदानामशक्यार्थान्तर इवान्वयांशेऽपि (न?) सामर्थ्यसङ्गीकार्यमित्यर्थः' इति टिप्पणी।

२. (तद्धेतुभावम्)–'तत्कारणकत्वम्। वाक्यकारणकत्वमिति यावत्' इति टिप्पणी।

३. (प्रवृत्त्यादिभ्यः कल्पते)–'प्रवृत्त्यादीनां पदार्थमात्रप्रतीत्या अनुपपत्तेः प्रवृत्त्यादय एव विशिष्टार्थप्रतीत्यनुमापका इति भावः।' इति टिप्पणी।

४. (अविशिष्यर्थस्मारकत्वम्)–'विशिष्टबुद्धि प्रति विशेषणज्ञानस्य विशिष्टवैशिष्टयावगाहिबुद्धिं प्रति विशेषणतावच्छेकविशेष्यतावच्छेदकधर्मप्रकारकनिश्चयस्य च हेतुत्वात्' इति टिप्पणी।

५. (तदुत्पत्त्यैव प्रत्युप्तम्)–'विशिष्टविषयकबोधो[illegible]त्त्यैव पदानामविशिष्टार्थस्मारक-त्वमाक्षिप्तमित्यर्थः।' इति टिप्पणी।

६. (तत्परेभ्यस्तदुपपद्यते)–'असंसृष्टस्वार्थमात्रन्यिपिताभिधाख्यवृत्तिविशिष्टेभ्यः पदेभ्यो विशिष्टार्थतात्पर्यकेभ्यस्तात्पर्येणैव संसृष्टार्थपतीतत्युपपत्तेः संसृष्टानिरूपिता अभिधा न स्वीक्रियत इत्यर्थः।' इति टिप्पणी।

स्याविशिष्टार्थाभिधानमात्रेण [१]लक्षणया विशिष्टार्थगमकत्वम्। स्वार्थमात्रपरत्वे तु प्रयोजनाभावेन [२]तस्याप्यनुपपत्तेः। यथाहुरत्रभवन्तो [३]वार्तिककारमिश्राः–

'साक्षाद्यद्यपि कुर्वन्ति पदार्थप्रतिपादनम्।
वर्णास्तथापि नैतस्मिन्पर्यवस्यन्ति निष्फले।।
वाक्यार्थमितये तेषा [४]प्रवृत्तौ नान्तरीयकम्।
पाके ज्वालेव काष्ठानां पदार्थप्रतिपादनम्।।'

तथा च

'वाक्यार्थो लक्ष्यमाणो हि सर्वत्रैवेति नः स्थितिः'।।

इति [५]अन्वितेऽर्थे तात्पर्याभ्युपगमात् तदभिधायित्वं पदानामिति चेत्, तत्किं 'गङ्गायां घोषः' इत्यत्र गङ्गापदं तीराभिधायि भवत्,

---

१. (लक्षणया)–'लोके वक्रभिप्रायरूपतात्पर्यसम्भवेऽप्यपौरुषेयेषु वैदिकवाक्येषु तदसम्भवाच्छतया पदार्थमात्रेपस्थितावपि लक्षणया संसृष्टार्थबोधजनकत्वमित्यर्थः।' इति टिप्पणी।

२. (तस्याप्यनुपपत्तेः)–'तदन्यप्रतीतीच्छयानुच्चरितत्वे सति तत्प्रतीतिजननयोग्यत्वरूपेण तात्पर्येण युक्तस्य वैदिकपदजातस्य स्वार्थमात्रे प्रदर्शितात्पर्यस्वीकारे प्रयोजनभूतस्य प्रवृत्त्यादेः स्वरूपमात्रज्ञानेनासम्भवात्प्राक् प्रदर्शितरीत्यानुमिति कारणभूतप्रवृत्त्याद्यभावेन स्वार्थमात्रबोधस्याप्यनुपपत्तेरिति भावः। एवं च स्वरूपमात्राभिधानेन प्रयोजनशून्येषु वैदिकपदेषु लक्षणाश्रयणेन संसृष्टबोधाङ्गीकारेऽपि निर्विशेषात्मतत्त्वबोधनेन निखिलप्रपञ्चबाधरूपपरमप्रयोजनसंपादकेषु महावाक्येषु तत्त्वमस्यादिषु नान्वयांशे लक्षणेति भावः। अत्र भूमिकानुसन्धेया' इति टिप्पणी।

३. (वार्तिककारमिश्राः)–श्लोकवार्तिके वाक्याधिकरणे श्लोक ३३९? (३४२, ३४३) इति टिप्पणी।

४. (प्रवृत्तौ नानतरीयकम्)–'प्रवृत्ताविति फले निमित्ते सप्तमी। प्रवृत्त्यर्थम्—आश्रितवाक्यार्थबोधार्थम्। नान्तरीयकम्–प्रदर्शितदिशा आवश्यकम्' इति टिप्पणी।

५. (अन्वितेऽर्थे)–'शत्तयविषयस्यापि तात्पर्यविषयत्वमात्रेण बोधाभ्युपगमेऽतिप्रसङ्गं मन्यमानः शङ्कते' इति टिप्पणी।

तत्र तात्पर्यात्। न[१]; स्मारितस्वार्थप्रत्या- सत्त्यापि तदवगतेर्न तत्परस्यापि तदभिधानमिति यद्युच्येत तदितरत्रापि समानमुक्तेन क्रमेण।[२] तस्मादनेकान्तं तात्पर्यं न बीजं [३]सामर्थ्यसाधने। न जातु ज्वलन्ति काष्ठानि [४]पाकपराण्यपि पाके साक्षात्समर्थानि, किन्तु ज्वलन एव, तया द्वारा तत्सिद्धेः। तेषामतुल्यकक्ष्याणां प्राथम्यं न विशेषयोपयुज्यते, येन पदानां तदर्थेभ्यः प्राथम्ये-नान्विताअर्थधियं प्रति [५]सामर्थ्यं कल्प्येत। दर्शिता त्वतुल्यकक्ष्यता, रूपमात्राभिधानात्, अन्विताभिधाने गौरवात्। न च पदार्था-नामुपलभ्यमानाकाङ्क्षादिसहकारिणां विशिष्टार्थधीजन्मनि सामर्थ्यमपरं कल्पनीयम्,[६] [७]तेभ्य एव तादृग्भ्यस्तदुत्पत्तेरुप-पत्तेः। न चैते मानान्तरदृष्टा अर्था न [८]विशिष्टार्थबुद्धे-रीशते। तथा हि– यत एवानुमानभावमर्थापत्तिभावं वा समापन्ना दृष्टा विशिष्टार्थधियमादधाना यथा तथा आधा-स्यन्ति तामेव [९]तत्परैः स्मारिताः सन्तः [१०]शब्दत्वमापन्नाः।

---

१. (न)–'न। अभिधायकत्वं तस्येष्टमिति शेषः।' इति टिप्पणी।

२. (उक्तेन क्रमेण)–'लक्षणयापि विशिष्टधीसम्भवादिति भावः' इति टिप्पणी।

३. (सामर्थ्यसाधने)–'शक्तिसाधने' इति टिप्पणी।

४. (पाकरपराण्यपि)–'पाकसम्पादकान्यपि। पाकेच्छयोपात्तान्यपीति यावत्।' इति टिप्पणी।

५. (सामर्थ्ये कल्प्येत)–'अन्यथाप्युपपद्यमानानां विशिष्टज्ञानानां प्रवृत्त्यादिहेतुकानु-मितिप्रथमिकविषयत्वं शत्तयनुमापने न पर्याप्तमित्यर्थः।' इति टिप्पणी।

६. (अपरं कल्पत्तीयम्)–'प्रत्यक्षादिनावगतानां श्वैत्यखुरनिष्पेषशब्दश्रवणादीनां विशिष्टार्थ-बोधजनकत्वस्य प्रागुपपादितत्वात्तथैव पदैरुपस्थितानां अप्यर्थानां विशिष्टानुभवजन-कत्वाभ्युपगमे कारणत्वकल्पनाधिक्यं नेति भावः।' इति टिप्पणी।

७. (तेभ्य एव)–'येभ्य एवेति २ पु० पाठः' इति टिप्पणी।

८. (विशिष्टार्थबुद्धेः(–'मानान्तरदृष्टानर्थानविशिष्टार्थबुद्धेरिति २ पु० पाठः' इति टिप्पणी।

९. (तत्परैः)–'तत्पदैरिति २ पु० पाठः' इति टिप्पणी।

१०. (शब्दत्वम्)–'शब्दोपस्थिततत्प्रकारकानुसन्धानविषयत्वम्' इति टिप्पणी।

[१]अनुपपत्तिसम्बन्धमात्रप्रभावितं च तात्पर्यमुपपादके न शक्तिमपेक्षते, गङ्गादिपदानां च काष्ठादीनां च तीरादौ पाकादौ च कल्पनाप्रसङ्गादित्युक्तम्। [२]न च सर्वत्र स्वार्थपरित्यागेनैव लक्षणेत्यैकान्तिकम्। लक्षणीयानुरोधेनैव हि सर्वत्र परिग्रह-परित्यागौ। तद्यथा 'गङ्गायां घोषः' इत्यत्र गङ्गापदेन घोष-प्रतिवासार्हतीरलक्षणया स्वार्थस्य गङ्गायास्त्यागः, 'दण्डिनो गच्छन्ति' इत्यत्र तु दण्ड्यदण्डिषु समूहिषु लक्ष्यमाणेषु तदन्तर्गतस्याविशेषाद्दण्डिशब्दार्थस्य परिग्रहः, त(य?)था वेदे 'सृष्टीरुपदधाति' इत्यत्र [३]गणिकानां लक्ष्यमाणत्वे तदन्तर्गतस्यापि सृष्ट्यर्थस्य परिग्रहः, एवमिहापि व्यतिषक्तावस्थायां लक्ष्य-माणायां तदन्तर्गतस्यापि परिग्रहः, तदग्रहे [४]लक्ष्यमाण-परित्यागप्रसङ्गात्। [५]लक्षणालक्षणायोगादलक्षणेति चेत्—न; [६]अलक्षणत्वात्। तत्रैतत्स्यात्—नेयं लक्षणा, सा किलाभि-धेयस्यार्थस्यायोग्यतया अनुपपद्यमाने वाक्यार्थसम्बन्धे सति

---

१. (अनुपपत्तिसम्बन्ध. . . .शक्तिमपेक्षते)—'पदार्थस्वरूपमात्रेऽनुपपत्त्या सम्बन्धेन प्रतियोगित्वादिना च केवलमुपपादितं वाक्यांसंसर्गनिरूपितं तात्पर्यं पद शक्तेर्गमकं न, तामन्तराप्युपपत्तेरित्यर्थः।' इति टिप्पणी।

२. (न च सर्वत्र)—'अन्वयांशे लक्षणामसहमानः शङ्कते' इति टिप्पणी।

३. (गणिकानाम्)—'तद्गपठितानां सृष्टिशब्दरहितानामपि। शाबदभाष्ये अ० १. पा० ४. सू० २७' इति टिप्पणी।

४. (लक्ष्यमाण-परित्यागप्रसङ्गात्)—'ससंर्गिणः पदार्थस्य परित्यागे संसर्गमात्रप्रतीते-र्निष्प्रयोजनत्वेन संसर्गस्यापि परित्यागप्रसङ्गादित्यर्थः।' इति टिप्पणी।

५. (लक्षणालक्षणायोगात्)—'वक्ष्यमाणस्वार्थान्यपदार्थबोधकत्वघटितलक्षणालक्षणस्य स्वार्थसम्बन्धेऽभावादित्यर्थः।' इति टिप्पणी।

६. (अलक्षणत्वात्)—'वक्ष्यमाणस्य लक्षणालक्षणस्य प्रदर्शयिष्यमाणदूषणेनाव्यापक-त्वादिति भावः।' इति टिप्पणी।

तत्सम्बन्धलब्धबुद्धिसन्निधौ वाक्यार्थसम्बन्धार्हे भवत्यर्थान्तरे; तथा आह कश्चित्—

'वाच्यस्यार्थस्य वाक्यार्थे सम्बन्धानुपपत्तिः।
तत्सम्बन्धवशप्राप्तस्यान्वयाल्लक्षणेष्यते॥'

न च 'ओदनं पचति चैत्रः पिठरे' इत्यादौ चैत्रपिठरादीनामर्थानां वाक्यार्थे सम्बन्धानर्हत्वम्; न च तल्लक्षिताया अन्वितावस्थया अन्वयान्तरशालिता; न चैव लक्षणा, [१]तल्लक्षणविरहात्—इति। तत्किमिदानीं न लक्षणेयमित्यनन्यलभ्यस्यापि शब्दार्थत्वमस्तु। न हि 'मासमग्निहोत्रं जुहोति' इत्यत्राग्निहोत्रपदं अलाक्षणिकमिति मुख्यं भवति। कर्मान्तरसादृश्येन गौण्या वृत्त्या तत्र प्रवृत्त्युपपत्तेर्न तदभिधानशक्तिकल्पनेति चेत्, इहाप्युन्नीतया नीत्या अन्तरेणाप्यभिधानसामर्थ्यमन्वितावस्थाप्रतीत्युपपत्तेः कृतमभिधानशक्तिः। एव च न चेदियं पदप्रवृत्तिर्लक्षणालक्षणमन्वेति, भवतु तर्हि चतुर्थी, दृष्टत्वात्। अस्तु वा लक्षणैव। नो खल्वेतल्लक्षणम्; अप्रसिद्धवृत्त्यन्तरावतारप्रसङ्गात्। तस्मादेतद्वक्तव्यम्। तदिदमुच्यते—मृष्यामहे 'वाच्यानुपपत्तिः' इति, 'सम्बन्धवशप्राप्तस्य' इति च, न पुनः 'वाक्यार्थे सम्बन्धे'ति च 'अन्वयात्' इति च। [२]अस्ति चेहापि लोकानुसारतो विशिष्टार्थप्रत्यायनप्रयुक्तसमभिव्याहृतीनामर्थ-

---

१. (ताल्लक्षणविरहादिति)—'लक्षणयोपस्थिततीरादेः पश्चाद्बोधविषयत्वमिव प्रकृते लक्षितेन संसृष्टस्वार्थरूपेण प्रयोजनसिद्धेः पुनरन्वयान्तरस्यानुपयोगादनवस्थाप्रसङ्गच्चेति भावः।' इति टिप्पणी।

२. (प्राप्तस्येति)—'इतिशब्दः २ पुस्तके नास्ति' इति टिप्पणी।

रूपमात्रपरत्वे पदानामनुपपत्तिः [१]अर्थरूपसम्बन्धवशप्राप्ता चान्विता- वस्थायाः। व्यापकं चैतलक्षणं लक्षणानामनवयवेन[२] वैदिकानां च लौकिकीनां चेति चतुरस्रम्। अभिधावृत्तित्वं च पदानां रूपमात्रप्रज्ञापनेऽपि [३]न तेनोपपद्यते। अपि नाम पदानि साक्षाव्द्यापारेण बोधयन्त्यर्थान् वाक्यार्थमितये तद्बोधनमिति वाक्यार्थं लक्षयिष्यन्ति। तदवस्थाभेदस्य तैः सहादृष्टचरत्वेन बुद्धावसन्निधानादलक्षोति चेत्–न। [४]सामान्यतो दर्शनात्, पदार्थानां च तद्विशेषकत्वात्। नो खल्वन्वितेभ्यः पदार्थे- भ्योऽन्यो[५]ऽन्वितावस्थाविशेषः। तथा चार्थस्वरूपबोधन- सामर्थ्यान्नाधिकं [६]सार्थ्यद्वयं कल्पयिष्यते। नाप्यभिधान- शक्तेरेवान्वयविषयत्वम्; अर्थस्वरूपमात्रगोरत्वेऽपि तत्प्रतीत्युपत्तेः। यदि पुनः प्रमाणसंशयविपर्ययेभ्यो [७]विधान्तरानुपगमान्न पदार्थबोधः [८]शब्दव्यापारजन्मोपेयते तर्हि स्मृतिरस्तु, न त्वेषां

---

१. (अर्थरूपसम्बन्धवशप्राप्तता)–'अर्थसम्बन्धवत्प्राप्तेति २ पु० पाठः' इति टिप्पणी।

२. (अनवयवेन)–'साकल्येन' इति टिप्पणी।

३. (न तेनोपपद्यते)–'स्वरूपमात्रोपस्थापनेन न परिसमाप्यते, प्रयोजनवैकल्यादिति भावः।' इति टिप्पणी।

४. (सामान्यतः)–'अलक्षणनिवेशनसामान्यत इति २ पु० पाठः' इति टिप्पणी।

५. (अन्वितावस्थाविशेषः)–'तथा चेतरपदार्थान्वयेन विशेषरूपतामान्नः संसृष्टोऽर्थः सामान्यविशेषभावसम्बन्धे स्वरूपसम्बन्धीति तत्र लक्षणा युज्यते इति भावः।' 'नो खल्वनन्वितेभ्यः पदार्थेभ्योऽन्यान्वितावस्थाविशेषेभ्यः इति २ पु० पाठः' इति टिप्पणी।

६. (सामर्थ्यद्वयम्)–'प्रागुक्तं पदानामन्वयानुभवसामर्थ्यम्–अर्थस्वरूपाणां अन्वयानुभवसामर्थ्ये च। आद्यस्यान्यथाप्युपपद्यमानत्वादन्त्यस्य क्लप्तत्वाच्चेति भावः' इति टिप्पणी।

७. (विधान्तर)–'विधानान्तरेति २ पु० पाठः' इति टिप्पणी।

८. (पदार्थबोधः)–'पदार्थानुभवः' इति टिप्पणी।

संस्कारोन्मेषमात्रप्रभवेति कृतमभिधातृभावेन [१]पदानाम्। तदुन्मेषे तदुपयोग इति चेत् हन्त! अर्थोऽप्यालोचितः स्वपदगोचर-संस्कारोद्बोधहेतुरिति सोऽपि पदस्याभिधाता स्यात्। तदिदमन-भिधातृत्वमनधिगतान्वयबोध एव कल्प्यते पदानाम् [२]नान्यथा। अथैवंवादी पृष्टो व्याचष्टाम्—को नु खल्वयमभिधाव्यापारः शब्दानाम्, येनामी तद्वन्तोऽन्वस्याभिधातारः। न तावत्परिस्पन्दः; तस्य मूर्तानुविधायिनो द्रव्ये विभुनि विभुगुणे वा शब्दे मूर्त्यभावेनासम्भवात्। 'असर्वगतद्रव्यपरिमाणं मूर्तिः' इति हि [३]पदार्थविदः। नाप्यस्पन्दात्मा प्रयत्नादिरिवादृश्यमानः, प्रमाणा-भावात्। अन्वयधियश्च कार्यस्य सति सङ्गतिसंवेदने [४]शब्दनिश्चय-ज्ञानादेवोत्पत्तेः। तस्मात्स्वगोचरं विज्ञानमेव शब्दानां व्यापारः स्वार्थबोधे। यथा आह भगवान्भाष्यकारः—[५]

'शास्त्रं शब्दविज्ञानादसन्निकृष्टेऽर्थे विज्ञानम्' इति।।

[६]स एव स्वाभाविकशक्तिशालिनः शब्दस्य स्वशक्त्या अर्थधीहेतुतया अभिधेति गीयते। शब्दाभासस्यैन्द्रियकत्वेऽपि रूपतः सामर्थ्योपधानेनाभिधात्वात्तस्य चातीन्द्रियत्वादतीन्द्रिय-

---

१. (पदानाम्)—'पदानामभिधातृत्वेन पर्याप्तम्, तावन्मात्रेण प्रयोजनसिद्धेरिति भावः। 'युगपर्याप्तयोः कृतम्' इत्यमरः।' इति टिप्पणी।

२. (नान्यथा)—' अर्थवादादिवाक्येषु प्राशस्त्यादेरशक्यत्वेऽपि संसर्गस्य प्राथमिकशक्ति-ग्रहकालेऽवगतत्वात्संसर्गत्वेन संसर्गस्य शक्यतेति भावः।' इति टिप्पणी।

३. (पदार्थविदः)—'वैशेषिकदर्शनप्रशस्तपादभाष्यटीकायां उदयनाचार्यकृतायां किरणावल्यां साधर्म्यप्रकरणे' इति टिप्पणी।

४. (शब्दनिश्चयज्ञानादेवोत्पत्तेः)—'शब्दजन्यस्वार्थनिश्चयेनैवान्वयधिय उपपन्नत्वाद्व्या-परान्तरकल्पना अनुचितेति भावः' इति टिप्पणी।

५. (भाष्यकारः)—'शाबरभाष्ये अ० १. पा० १. अ० ५.' इति टिप्पणी।

६. (स एव)—'स्वविषयज्ञानरूपव्यापार एव' इति टिप्पणी।

त्वमास्थिषताभिधायाः।[१] न चेयं साक्षादर्थधियमाधत्ते, येन न तत्साधिका स्यात्, अपि तु संस्कारोद्बोधनक्रमेण। तथा च नार्थविषयविज्ञानं स्वपदगोचरसंस्कारोद्बोधनक्रमेण पदस्मरणमपि विदधदभिधाशब्दगोचरः, अपि तु शब्दविषयं विज्ञानम्, तस्य च [२]तद्भावनियमात् लौकिकपरीक्षकाणां प्रयोगसंप्रतिपत्तेः। प्रणिधानादिष्वपाठाच्छब्दस्य[३] न स्मारकत्वमिति चेत्—न; तत्सम्बन्धात्। अथापि स्यात्, परिगणिता हि स्मृतिहेतवः—'[४]प्रणिधाननिबन्धनाभ्यासलिङ्गलक्षणसादृश्यपरिग्रहाश्रयाश्रितसम्बन्धानन्तर्यवियोगैककार्यविरोधातिशयप्राप्तिव्यवधानसुखदुःखेच्छाद्वेषभयार्थित्वक्रियारागधर्माधर्माः'— प्रामाणिकैः। न चैतेषु किञ्चित्पदं तत्रार्थस्य स्मारकमिति चेत्—तन्न, अर्थसम्बन्धेन तदुपपत्तेः। सम्बन्धो हि स्मृतिहेतुषु पठितः, यतोऽन्तेवासिनो गुरुम् ऋत्विजो याज्यं [५]स्मरन्ति। (स चास्ति शब्दार्थयोरौत्पत्तिको) वाच्यवाचकभाव इति तदनुभवाहितभावनासहितं शब्दविज्ञानमन्वितार्थप्रत्यायनप्रयुक्तं स्वार्थे स्मारयिष्यति। वाच्यवाचकत्वं च प्रत्याय्यप्रत्यायकत्वम्, तच्च विचार्यमाणं स्मार्य-

---

१. (अभिधायाः)—'शब्दगताभिधाया अर्थबोधानुकूलसामर्थ्यरूपायाः कुक्षौ प्रविष्टस्यार्थस्यातीन्द्रियत्वेन तद्विशेषितसामर्थ्यस्यप्यतीन्द्रियत्वमाश्रीयत इत्यर्थः।' इति टिप्पणी।

२. (तद्भावनियमात्)—'शब्दविषयकज्ञानेन नियमतोऽर्थप्रत्ययस्येवार्थज्ञानेन पदस्मरणनियमाभावादर्थगतक्वाचित्कपदोपस्थापकव्यापारस्य नाभिधात्वम्, नियमेनोपस्थापकव्यापारस्यैवाभिधात्वादिति भावः।' इति टिप्पणी।

३. (शब्दस्य . . . . अथापि स्यात्)—'शब्दस्य तत्स्मारकत्वमिति चेन्न। तत्सङ्घात्' इति पु० पाठः'। 'अथापि' इत्यत्र 'तथापीति च' इति टिप्पणी।

४. (प्रणिधानः . . . .)—'गौतसमत्रे अ० २. आ० २. सू० ४४. (३-२-४१)' इति टिप्पणी।

५. (स्मरन्ति)—'स्मारयिष्यन्तीति ३ पु० पाठः ( ) एतदभ्यन्तरश्च पाठः ३ पु. नास्ति' इति टिप्पणी।

स्मारकत्वमे। ननु सम्बन्धान्तरेणाध्यापका- ध्यापनीयभावादिना अन्तेवासीस्मरति गुरुम्, न [१]स्मारकत्वेनैव, तथैवेहापि सम्बन्धान्तरमनुसर्तव्यम्; न च तदस्ति, तत्कथमस्य स्मारकत्वम्; अन्विताभिधाने त्वभिधेयसाहचर्यमेवास्यास्ति सम्बन्धान्तरमिति युज्यते स्मारकत्वं पदानाम्। अथान्विताभिधाने[२]ऽप्यन्वितप्रत्यायनाय किमस्ति सम्बन्धातरं पदानाम्। दृष्टा हि चक्षुरादयो धूमादयश्चार्थसन्निकर्षलक्षणनियतसाहित्यादिलक्षणेन सम्बन्धान्तरेण प्रत्याययन्तो यथायथमर्थान्। यद्युच्येत विनापि सम्बन्धान्तरमौत्पत्तिकार्थप्रत्यायनशक्त्या वृद्धव्यवहारोन्नीतया प्रत्यायनमिति, पदत्रापि समानम्। इहापि तादृशस्यैव स्मृतिजननशक्त्या वृद्धव्यवहारोन्नीतया स्मारकत्वमस्तु पदानामर्थरूपे, तच्च स्वज्ञानमेव, तस्य चाभिधात्वमुपपादितमधस्तात्। तस्मादभिधातृत्वमपि [३]नान्विताभिधान इति कल्पनालाघवादाकाङ्क्षादिलक्षणसहकारिप्रत्यासन्नैश्च समभिव्याहृतपदस्मारितैः पदार्थैः प्रत्यासत्त्या गम्यमानो [४]वाक्यार्थो लाक्षणिकः शाब्दश्चेति रमणीयम्। तस्मात् [५]सुष्ठूक्तम्—'पदानि स्वं स्वमर्थमभिधाय निवृत्तव्यापाराणि अथेदानीं पदार्था अवगताः सन्तो वाक्यार्थमवगमयन्ति' इति।।

---

१. (स्मारकत्वेनैव)—'स्मार्यस्मारकत्वेनैवेति २ पु० पाठः' इति टिप्पणी।

२. (अन्वितप्रत्यायनाय)—'अन्वितानुभवनिष्पत्तये। सामान्यतोऽन्वितस्योपस्थितत्वेनानुभवविषयताया असम्भवाद्विशेषस्य च सामान्याभिन्नत्वेन सम्बन्धान्तरानुपपत्तेरिति भावः' इति टिप्पणी।

३. (नान्विताभिधान इति)—'अन्विताभिधानवादे प्रदर्शितदिशा पदानामन्विताभिधातृत्वं न सिध्यतीत्यर्थः।' इति टिप्पणी।

४. (वाक्यार्थो लाक्षणिकः शाब्दश्चेति)—'संसर्गो लक्षणागम्यः स्वज्ञानादिपरम्परया पदजनितत्वेन शाब्दश्चेत्यर्थः।' इति टिप्पणी।

५. (सुष्ठूक्तम्)—'शाबरभाष्ये अ० १. पा० १. सू० २५' इति टिप्पणी।

तत्त्वबिन्दुपरामर्शपुष्टानां बुद्धिवीरुधः।
वाक्यार्थधीसुमनसः पुरुषार्थफलप्रदाः।।
वाक्यार्थमितये पुंसां भ्रमसन्तमसच्छिदा।
इन्दुनेवामुना मार्गो दर्शितस्तत्त्वबिन्दुना।।

इति आचार्यश्रीवाचस्पतिमिश्रविरचितः
तत्त्वबिन्दुः समाप्तः।।

APPENDIX I

[An Alphabetical Table of the Authors and their Works in the Pūrva-Mīmāṁsā-Śāstra, whose Dates may be fixed between A.D. 1600 and 1850.]

	AUTHORS	WORKS	REMARKS
1.	*Aṇṇuśāstri*, son of *Rāmabudha* of *Prayāga gotra*—a member of the *Kaṇḍarmāṇikka Bṛhaccaraṇa* Brahmin Communityan inhabitant of the *Peralam* village in the Tanjore District.	*Tantradarpaṇa*—a Commentary on the P.M. Sūtras, beginning with the second chapter. It belongs to the Bhāṭṭa school.	A Ms. preserved in the Madras Govt. Oriental Mss. Library, Madras. [R. Nos. 3879 (b) & 3886]
2.	*Anantācārya.*	*Vidhisudhākara*—an independent treatise on the nature and scope of *Vidhi*, *niṣedha* and *arthavādas*. It belongs to the Bhāṭṭa school.	Do. [No. 4477]
3.	*Appayya Dīkṣita*, son of *Appā Dīkṣita* and a descendant of the famous Appayya Dīkṣita—patronised by one *Cinnabommabhūpāla*, Minister of Cokkanātha (son of Cinnamāmbā) of Nalla Bomma family.	*Durūkhsaśikṣā*—containing seven main sections beginning with *udāharanoddhārabhaṅya*,—a rejoinder against the refutations of the views of Appayya Dīkṣita as embodied in his Vidhirasāyana. It also belongs to the Bhāṭṭa school.	Do. [R. No. 3934 (a)] Whether this author is identical with the author of two works— (1) *Tantrasiddhāntadīpikā* and (2) *Pūrvamīmāṁsāviṣayasaṅgrahadīpik* (both described in the Introduction, p. 136) is not known.
4.	*Ahobila* (or Aubhala or Aubala), son of one Mārayārya (?) of	*Vākyārtharatnamālā*—with his own gloss—*Tātparyaprakāśikā* or *Suvarṇamudrā*	Preserved in the Madras Govt. Oriental Mss. Library.

	AUTHORS	WORKS	REMARKS
	Srīvasta gotra.	—an independent treatise dealing with the nature and scope of the *adhyayana-vidhi*, refuting the view of *Kriyāsthāyitva* and elucidating the true import of *liṅpratyaya* viz., *apūrva* or *niyoga*, according to the Prābhākara school.	
5.	*Udayapūjyapāda* (probably a Malabarian).	Adhikaraṇaślokārthadīpikā—in 48 verses with explanatory prose for the Tarkapāda, according to the Prābhākara school.	Do. [R. No. 2901]
6.	*Uttamaślokatīrtha.*	*Laghuvārttikaṭīkā* or *Laghunyāyasudhā*, a good commentary on the Citrapaṭa, otherwise known as Laghuvārttika.	Do. The author of this work is known by the name Uttamaślokatīrtha. cf.— *"Viśveśvarapreritena śritaviśveśamūrtinā; Uttamaślokatīthena tatprītyai grathitam shuṭam."*
7.	*Keśava*, son of Viśvanātha.	*Mīmāṁsābālaprakāśavyākhyā*—(Bhāṭṭa school.)	*Vide* Dr. A. B. Keith's Karmamīmāṁsā, p. 13.
8.	*Garuḍadhvaja*, son of Śrīnivāsa (by Alamelumaṅgā), and grandson of Sūryanārāyaṇa (the author of a Commentary on the Śāstradīpikā).	Tantrasiddhāntasaṅgraha—a commentary on the P.M. Sūtras. (Bhāṭṭa school.) (It contains chapters VII & VIII complete and IX incomplete).	Preserved in the Madras Govt. Mss. Library. [R. No. 1803 (a)]
9.	*Gopālabhaṭṭa.*	*Vidhirasāyanabhūṣaṇa.*	Mentioned by Dr. A. B. Keith in his Karmamīmāṁsā, p. 12.
10.	*Govindabhaṭṭa.*	Mīmāṁsānyāyasaṅgraha—a commentary of the P.M. Sūtras according to the Prābhākara school. (It contains from the second pāda of the first adhyāya to the fifth pāda of the third adhyāya.)	Do. [R. No. 2768] It is mostly in verses except in Viṣayavākyas and saṁśayas.
11.	*Govindāmṛtamuni*	*Vivaraṇa*—a commentary	A portion of it is preserved

AUTHORS	WORKS	REMARKS
alias *Devendrasarasvatī*, a disciple of Nārāyaṇāmṛtapūjyapāda.	on th Śābarabhāṣya from the second pāda of the first adhyāya, according to the Bhāṭṭa school.	in the Madras Govt. Mss. Libraries. [R.No. 2767]. A transcript of the same is available in the Ann. Univ. Library.
12. *Lakṣmaṇārya*, the son of Timmārya by Giryambā, the brother of one Śrīnivāsa, and the disciple of Śrīnivāsa, and the disciple of Śrīnvāsa, and the disciple of Śrīnivāsopādhyāya (probably his brother) who was well-versed in the Madhva System of Philosophy.	*Tantravilāsa*—containing refutations of the siddhāntas of some well-known adhikaraṇas like *guṇakāmādhikaraṇa*. It has six main sections.	He is later than Khaṇḍadeva and Gopīnātha (the author of the Maṇisāra); so he might be placed between A.D. 1700-1800. Preserved in the Madras Govt. Mss. Library. [No. 4416 & R. No. 1344]
13. *Mahādevavedāntin*.	*Pūrvamīmāṁsāsūtravyākhyā* (?)	Mentioned by A. B. Keith in his K.M., p.12.
14. *Mukundānandayati* —probably a Keralīya.	Nītitattvāvirbhāvavyākhyā.	A part of it is preserved in the Madras Govt. Ms. Libraries. [R. No. 2939]
15. *Murārimiśra*.	15. *Aṅgatvanirukti*.	Later than Khaṇḍadeva. Printed in the Anandasrama Press, Poona.
16. **Nārāyaṇa** (Probably a Keralīya), son of Viṣṇu.	*Viṣamagranthabhedikā*— an excellent commentary on the Bhāvanāviveka of Maṇḍanamiśra.	16. Preserved in the Madras Govt. Mss. Libraries. [R. No. 3065 (b)] Whether the author's father Viṣṇu is identical with Bhāṭṭa viṣnu the author of the *Nayatattvasaṅgraha*, is yet to be known.
17. *Nārāyaṇa*, son of Śrīnivāsa.	*Vidhicamatkāracandrikā*— dealing with the nature and authority of vedic injunctions. It refutes the views of Appayya Dīkṣita as set forth in his Vidhirsāyana.	Do. No. 4469.
18. *Nārāyaṇasudhī*.	*Bhāṭṭanayodyota*—a summary of Khaṇḍadeva's Bhāṭṭadīpikā.	Preserved in the Madras Govt. Mss. Library.

	AUTHORS	WORKS	REMARKS
19.	*Nārāyaṇatīrtha-muni.*	*Bhāṭṭabhāṣāparīkṣā*—'an exposition of the terminology of the Mīmāṁsā.'	Vide A. B. Keith's Karmamīmāṁsā, p. 13. It has been published at Benares (1900).
20.	*Nīlakaṇṭha*, (probably a Keralīya Brahmin belonging to Payyoor family of Bhaṭṭatiris).	*Nītitattvāvirbhāvavyākhyā.*	A part of it is preserved in the Madras Mss. Libraries, Madras. [R. No. 3588]
21.	*Peddadīkṣita.*	Bhāṭṭaparibhāṣā—dealing with the six pramāṇas of the Bhāṭṭa Mīmāṁsakas.	Do. [No. 4439] Whether this author is identical with the commentator on the *Vedānta Paribhāṣā* is not known.
22.	*Ravi.*	*Mīmāṁsā(nyāya)prameyasaṅgraha*—a summary of the contents of the P.M. Śāstra, belonging to the Bhāṭṭa Mīmāṁsakas.	A part of this work is preserved in the Madras Govt. Ms. Library. [R. No. 4456]
23.	*Rāghavānda Sarasvati* —pupil of one Advaya (pupil of viśveśvara).	*Mīmāṁsāsūtradīdhiti* or *Nyāyāvalidīdhiti*—a commentary on the sūtras.	Mentioned by Dr. A. B. Keith in his Karmamīmāṁsā, p. 12.
24.	*Rāmacandrārya*, son of Veṅkateśvara Sūri of Kolhapur.	*Adhikaraṇamālā*—an elaborate discussion of certain adhikaraṇas beginning with the Saṅkhyāmuṣṭyadhikaraṇa.	Preserved in the Madras Govt. Mss. Library.
25.	*Rāmānujadāsa*, son of Raghunāthadeśikādhvarin and younger brother of Vedāntacārya of Śiivatsa gotra, and pupil of both his father and brother.	*Tantranītilaharī*—a commentary on the sūtras following the Śāstradīpikā and the Nayaviveka of both the schools of Mīmāṁsā.	Preserved in the Madras Govt. Mss. Library. [R. No. 2337]
26.	*Rāmeśvara*, son of Subrahmaṇya Sūri.	*Vidhiviveka*—on the nature and classification of Vidhi.	Do.
27.	*Rāmeśvarasūrin.*	*Subodhinī*—a gloss on the P.M. Sūtras.	A Reprint from 'the Pandit.'

	AUTHORS	WORKS	REMARKS
28.	*Rāmakṛṣṇa-Udīcya-bhaṭṭācārya.*	*Mīmāṁsādhikaraṇakaumudī.*	Mentioned by Dr. A.B. Keith in his Karmamīmāṁsā, p. 13.
29.	*Śrīvāsadāsa*, son of one Nṛsiṁhārya of Vādhūla gotra of Thirumaligai village and pupil of his own paternal uncle, Lakṣmaṇārya.	Vidhiratnāvali—a rejoinder of the Vidhidarpaṇa of Kollūr Nārāyaṇa Śāstri.	Preserved in Ms. in the Madras Govt. Ms. Library. [R. No. 1376]
30.	*Subrahmaṇya*, pupil of another Subrahmaṇya.	*Śāstropanyāsamālikā*—an exposition of the first sūtra of the P.M. Śāstra on the line of Cidānanda and his commentators.	Do. [R. No. 3069]
31.	*Vallabhācārya.*	(1) *P.M. Kārikās* in 42 verses. (2) *Jaiminīyasūtra-bhāṣya.*	Mentioned by Dr. A.B. Keith in his Karmamīmāṁsā, pp. 13 and 14.
32.	*Vāñcheśvaraśīṣya.*	*Tantrasiddhāntasaṅgraha*—dealing the metaphysics of the Mīmāṁsā Śāstra.	Preserved in the Mss. Libraries in Madras. [R. No. 1802 (b)]
33.	*Veṅkaṭanārāyaṇa*, son of Rāmacandra and grandson of Mīnākṣīvallabha of Bhāradvājagotra-a native of Madura (in south India) where his family was patronised by the Pāṇḍya kings. His teacher was Lakṣmaṇa.	*Vidhibhūṣaṇa*—on the nature and kinds of Vidhi.	Do. [R. No. 8121 (b)]
34.	*Vaidyanātha*, son of Tatsadāmabhaṭṭa.	*Prabhā*—a commentary on the Śāstradīpikā.	Do.
35.	*Vaidyanātha.*	A commentary on the Sūtras.	Mentioned by Dr. A.B. Keith in his Karmamīmāṁsā, p. 12.
36.	Yallubhaṭṭa, son of Darbhavelubhaṭṭa (the-disciple of Annambhaṭṭa).	Mīmāṁsāsūtradīpikā-a commentary on the Sūtras, following the Bhāṭṭa school.	Preserved in the Madras Govt. Mss. Library. [R. No. 1564]. He might have belonged to the 18th century.

APPENDIX II

[An Alphabetical Table of Works, the Authors and Dates of which are not known]

WORKS	REMARKS
1. *Adhvaramīmāṁsāsūtrārthadīpikā*—(probably written by a Keralīya)-a commentary on the Jaiminīya-sūtravṛtti (see below).	1. Preserved in the Madras Govt. Mss. Library. (R. No. 3038). This work refers to Mādhavācārya and Somanātha's Mayūkhamālikā.
2. *Aṁśatrayavicāraḥ*	2. ....
3. *Granthayojanā*—a commentary on the Takapāda of the Śābarabhāṣya.	3. Preserved in the Madras Govt. Mss. Library. A transcript is available in the Annamalai University Library. It abruptly breaks off in the middle of I.1. 5.
4. *Jaiminīyasūtravṛtti*— (Keralīyā)—a commentary on the Sūtras of Jaimini.	4. Preserved in part only to the end of 4th adhyāya in the Madras Govt. Mss. Library. [R. No. 2973].
5. *Prakaraṇapañcikāvyākhyā*	5. Do. [R. No. 3237]. It breaks off in the Nayavīthī.
6. Do. *Nyāyasiddhi*— (probably written by a Keralīya)	6. Do. [R. No. 3647]. It breaks off in the anumāna of the Pramāṇapārāyaṇa. It quotes a Kārikā from the Bṛhaṭṭīkā:

WORKS	REMARKS
	'Yathā lokaprasiddham calakṣaṇairanugamyate; Lakṣyam na lakṣaṇaireva tadapūrvam prasādhyate.'
7. *Bālabhāskara* with the commentary *Prabhā*.	7. Preserved in the Madras Govt. Mss. Library. [R. No. 2179]. It extends to the sixth pāda of the Third Adhyāya.
8. *Mānaratnāvali*—(by a Keralīya)—dealing with metaphysical problem of the Bhāṭṭa Mīmāṁsā System as against the Bauddhas, the Prābhākaras, the Naiyāyikas and the Māyāvādins (Advaitavedāntins).	8. Preserved in the Madras Govt. Mss. Library. [R. No. 3747]
9. *Mīmāṁsādhikaraṇanyāyavicāra.*	9. Do. [No. 4456]
10. *Mīmāṁsābhāṣyavivarana-vyākhyānam*—a commentary on the Vivaraṇa (already described, Serial No. 11 of the Śābarabhāṣya.	10. Do. [R. No. 3948]. A fragment only.
11. *Mīmāṁsāviṣyaḥ*—a *prakaraṇa* work based on Cidānanda's Nītitattvāvirbhāva	11. Preserved in the Madras Govt. Mss. Library. [Nos. 3593, 4463 & 4464] A fragment only.
12. *Vādakutūhalam*—a controversial tract on Mīnāṁsā.	12. Do. [No. 4468 & R. No. 1375]
13. *Ṣoḍaśādhyāyī*—a good commentary on the 16 Chapters of the Pūrva and Uttara Mīmāṁsā Sūtras—by a Keralīya.	13. Do. [R. No. 3400]

WORKS	REMARKS
14. Do. *Ṭippaṇam*	14. Do. [R. No. 4387]
15. *Siddhāntamuṣṭi* (by one Mādhava (?) or a disciple of Mādhava)-a summary in verse of the topics of each adhikaraṇa.	15. Do. [R. No. 2967]

APPENDIX III

अनुबन्धस्तृतीयः।

।। तत्त्वबिन्दुकारिकार्धानां वर्णानुक्रमसूची।।

APPENDIX IV

अनुबन्धश्चतुर्थः।

तत्त्वबिन्दु-तत्त्वविभावनयोरुदाहृतानां कारिकार्धानां वाक्यानां च वर्णानुक्रमसूची।

पुटसंख्या	ग्रन्थादिः		आकरनाम
160	अजैकपादहिर्बुध्न्यः	...	विष्णुपुराणम्
162	... अतोऽस्ति वाक्यधी	....	श्लोकवार्त्तिकम् 1. 1. 7. श्लो. 108 Ben. Ed. पु. 876
166	अत्यन्तादृष्टवाक्यार्थ	....	....
166	अत्यन्तासत्यपि ज्ञानम्	....	श्लोकवार्त्तिकम् 1. 1. 2. श्लो. 6, पु. 46.
192	अथ कस्मादेषः....निरवद्यम्		स्फोटसिद्धिः पु. 169–171.
297	अथ तत्रानुमानेन	...	न्यायरत्नमाला Madras Edn., पु. 88.
162	अथ यदसन्दिग्धमप्रयोजनं करटदन्ता वा		... ... भामती N. S. Edn., पु. 5.
183	अथवा वासनैवास्तु	....	श्लोकवार्त्तिकम् 1.1.5. श्लो. 99, पु. 535.
269	अधीगर्थदयेशां कर्मणि	...	अष्टाध्यायी, सू. 2. 3. 52.
225	अनङ्गे वक्तुरेकत्वे	....	स्फोटसिद्धिकारिका, पु. 122.
255, 303	अनन्यलभ्यः शब्दार्थः	...	...
162	अनादिमध्यनिधना	....	...

पुटसंख्या	ग्रन्थादिः		आकरनाम
160	गङ्गाधरो महादेवः	...	लोकविदः (?)
210	गत्यर्थाश्च नानार्थाः	...	...
181	गौरित्येकमतित्वन्तु	...	श्लो. वा. स्फोट. पु. 540, श्लो. 120
179	ग्लाज्याम्लाहाभ्यो णिनिः	...	उणादिसूत्रम्
186, 231	चित्ररूपां च तां बुद्धिम्	...	श्लो. वा. 1. 1. 5, स्पोट. श्लो. 111, पु. 538
248	चोदनेति क्रियायाः...वचनमाहुः	...	शाबरभाष्यम्,1.1.2
216	जगति बहुन तथ्यं		
214	जातिमाचक्षते ते हि	...	स्फोटसिद्धिकारिका 9, पु. 73
298	जायते न पदैर्वापि	...	न्यायरत्नमाला, पु. 88 Benares Edition
259	ज्ञानं महेश्वरादिच्छेत्	...	स्मृतिः (?)
179	ज्या वयोहानौ	...	धातुपाठः, क्रयादिः, 1035
163	ज्योतिष्टोमाऽङ्गसापेक्षः	...	...
179	टुओश्वि गतिवृद्ध्योः	...	धतुपाठः, भ्वादिः, 1035
303	ततश्च कार्यान्विताभिधायिता...		बृहती, पु. 386-87,
305	के पुनरमी उपाधयो नाम...		Madras Edition
162	ततश्चार्थाद्भवेल्लोके	...	श्लो. वा. 1.1.7, श्लो. 108, 876
271	तत्प्रतिपत्तये शब्दार्थव्यवहारः...		बृहती. पु. 383, Mad. Ed.
311	तत्सम्बन्धवशप्राप्त	...	(प्रकरणपञ्चिकायां वाक्यार्थमातृकायामुद्धृतम्)
148	तत्र जातिरुपेता स्यात्	...	...
186	तत्र ज्ञाने च वर्णानाम्	...	श्लोकवार्त्तिकम्, स्फोट. श्लो. 110
174	तथाहि सर्वत्र...प्रकाशन्ते	...	स्फोटसिद्धिः, पु. 126-27

पुटसंख्या	ग्रन्थादिः		आकरनाम
281	तथा गन्धवति द्रव्ये	...	न्यायरत्नमाला, पु. 100, Benares Edition
225	तदित्थं सम्बन्धकाले आत्मानमावेदयति	...	स्फोटसिद्धिः, पु. 122--23
184	तद्भावभाविता हेतुः	...	श्लोकवार्त्तिकम् 1.1.5, स्फोट. श्लो. 100, पु. 535
181	तद्ग्राह्यैकार्थताभ्यां च	...	" स्फोट. श्लो. 120
165, 248	तद्भूतानां क्रियार्थेन.... तन्निमित्तत्वात्	....	पूर्वमीमांसासूत्रम् 1.1.7 (2)
186	तदारूढास्तदावर्णाः	...	श्लोकवार्त्तिकम् स्फोट. श्लो. 116
184	तदिदमसमञ्जसमिव लक्ष्यते...		स्फोटसिद्धिः, पु. 52
182	तस्माज्जात्यभिधायित्वात्...		न्यायरत्नमाला, पु. 100 Benares Edition
227	तत्यमात्तत्स्मरणेष्वेव	...	वार्त्तिकम् (?) बृहट्टीकेति भाति (प्रकरणपञ्चिकायामुद्धृतम्)
183	तस्यार्थबुद्धिहेतुत्वे	...	श्लोकवार्त्तिकम् 1.1.5, स्फोट. श्लो. 100, पु. 535
161	तस्याहं सकलां बाधाम्	...	...
224	तिरोहितव्यवहित	...	स्फोटसिद्धिकारिका 16, पु. 120
203	तेन जन्मैव विषयम् (?)...		...
186	तेन श्रोत्रनमनोभ्यां स्यात् ...		श्लोकवार्त्तिकम् स्फोट. श्लो. 115
227	तेऽपि नैवास्मृता यस्मात् ...		वार्त्तिकम् (बृहट्टीकेति भाति) (प्रकरणपञ्चिकायामुद्धृतम्)
223, 222	तेषां च गुणभूतानाम्	...	श्लोकवार्त्तिकम् स्फोट. श्लो. 70, पु. 528
161	तेषां हि प्रार्थितं सर्वम्	...	...
217	ते हि जातीस्तद्वतीर्वा...आचक्षते...		स्फोटसिद्धिः, पु. 77

पुटसंख्या	ग्रन्थादिः		आकरनाम
173	नन्वर्थाभिव्यक्ताविव...		
	तुल्यः प्रसङ्गः,	...	स्फोटसिद्धिः, पु. 124
180	नन्वस्तीदं पश्चात्...		
	स्फुटो भेदः प्रतीयते	...	"
275	नन्वस्तु अभेदप्रतिभासः	...	न्यायकणिका, पु. 127
	स्वभाव हेतुः		Benares Edition
222	न प्रत्ययः स्यादेकत्वे	...	स्फोटसिद्धिकारिका 15, पु. 115
303	न भवत्वन्विताभिधायी	...	ऋजुविमला, पु. 386–87
	विवरीतुं		
305	पृच्छति		Madras Edition
302	न हि कार्यादतज्जन्यात्	...	...
171	न हि तत्क्षणमप्यास्ते	...	न्यायरत्नमाला, पु. 91
248	न हि दृष्टेऽनुपपन्नं नाम	...	बृहती 1.1.5, पु. 216
162	न हि पालनसामर्थ्यम्	...	वायुसंहिता
172	नानेकावयवं वाक्यम्	...	स्फोटसिद्धिकारिका 29, पु. 238
298	नान्यस्ते नान्विते सिद्ध्येत्...		न्यायरत्नमाला, पु. 89, Benares Edition
175	नापि प्रत्येकमवद्योतनात् ...		
	स्फोटमभिव्यञ्जयन्ति	...	स्फोटसिद्धिः, पु. 128–29
216	नापि शब्दव्यक्त्यभिप्रायम्...		" पु. 75
247	नाभ्यस्ताच्छतुः	...	अष्टाध्यायी, सू. 7.1.78
270	नाम प्रकाश्यसम्भाव्य	...	...
186	नावश्यं यौगपद्येन	...	श्लोकवार्त्तिकम् स्फोट. श्लो. 110
163	नावाचकस्तथाशक्ति	...	....
179	नासावर्थमितिं प्रति	...	...
219	नित्यस्तु स्याद्दर्शनस्य		
	परार्थत्वात्	...	पूर्वमीमांसासूत्रम्, 1.1.6
263	नियोज्यः स च कार्यं यः...		प्रकरणपञ्चिका, वाक्यार्थमातृका, Benaras Edn., पु. 182
212,226	निरस्तभेदं पदतत्त्वमेकम्...		स्फोटसिद्धिकारिका 37, पु. 261

पुटसंख्या	ग्रन्थादिः		आकरनाम
297	नीलोत्पलवनेष्वद्य	...	शाबरभाष्ये 1.1.6, न्यायरत्नमालायां वाक्यार्थनिर्णये चोद्धृतम् 88
214	नेक्षिता जातिशब्दानाम्	...	स्फोटसिद्धिकारिका 9, पु. 73
166	नैव वेदप्रमाणत्वम्	...	वार्त्तिकम् (?)
264	पदमभ्यधिकाभावात्	...	श्लोकवार्त्तिकम् 1.1.5, शब्द-श्लो. 107, पु. 432
264	पदमभ्यधिकाभावात्	...	" "
272	पदमभ्यधिकाभावात्	...	" "
	पदानि स्वं स्वमभिधाय... वाक्यार्थमवगमयन्ति	...	शाबरभाष्यम्, 1.1.7
298	पदानामपि सामर्थ्यम्	...	न्यायरत्नमाला, पु. 89, Benares Edition
166	पदार्थपदसम्बन्ध	...	श्लोकवार्तिकम्, 1.1.7, श्लो. 1, पु. 845
221	पदावधारणोपायान्	...	" 1.1.7, श्लो. 1, पु. 180
275	परिहरति-न अन्यथासिद्धेः...		न्यायकणिका, पु. 288, Benares Edition
224	परेषामसमाख्येयम्	...	वाक्यपदीयम्, काण्डः1, श्लो. 35
256	परोक्षश्चानुभूतश्च	...	श्लोकवार्त्तिकम 1.1.5, पु. 431, श्लो. 103
284	पाकयुक्तः पुनः कर्ता	...	वार्त्तिकम् (?) (प्रकरणपञ्चिकायां वाक्यार्थमातृकायामुद्धृतम्)
284	पाकं हि पचिरेवाह	...	" "
308	पाके ज्वालेव काष्ठानाम्	...	श्लोकवार्त्तिकम् 1.1.7, श्लो. 343, पु. 943
275	पुनः प्रकारान्तरेण... अवलम्बते	...	न्यायकणिका, पु. 286, Benaras Edition

पुटसंख्या	ग्रन्थादिः		आकरनाम
168	पुराणमानवादेश्च	...	...
186	पूर्वज्ञानं परस्तात्तु	...	श्लोकवार्त्तिकम् स्फोट. श्लो. 115
190,174	पूर्वोपलब्धिभेदेऽपि	...	स्फोटसिद्धिकारिका 8, पु. 65
174,190	पूर्वोपलब्धयो हि... भिन्दन्ति	...	स्फोटसिद्धिः, पु. 65–70
164	पूर्वपूर्ववर्णजनित... इत्यदोषः	...	शाबरभाष्यम्,1.1.5
294	पौरुषेयाद्वचना... नैवमयमर्थ इति	...	" 1.1.2
314	प्रणिधाननिबन्धन... धर्माधर्माः	...	न्यायसूत्रम्, 3.2.41
192	प्रत्यक्षज्ञाननियता	...	स्फोटसिद्धिकारिका 23, पु. 169
174	प्रत्येकमनुपाख्येय	...	" "
163	प्रथमश्रवणेऽप्यर्थः	...	...
179	प्रमाणमविसंवादि... अविसंवादनम्	...	बाह्यः (?)
286	प्रमाणवन्त्यदृतानि	...	...
295	प्रमाणं स्मृतिश्च प्रत्ययः	...	गुरुवचनम् (बृहती ?)
256	प्रमितेऽनुपयुक्तत्वात्	...	श्लोकवार्त्तिकम् 1.1.5, पु. 431, श्लो. 104
174	प्रयत्नभेदतो भिन्ना	...	स्फोटसिद्धिकारिका 18, पु. 125
222	प्रयुज्यमानस्य यत्पूर्वम्	...	वार्त्तिकम् (?)
301	प्रागेवान्वितवाचित्वम्	...	न्यायरत्नमाला, पु. 61, Benaras Edition
184	प्राचीनानुभव...सामर्थ्य	...	...
161	प्रातश्चैवापराह्ने च	...	...
230	बह्वभिप्रायमप्येकम्	...	...

पुटसंख्या	ग्रन्थादिः		आकरनाम
177	यथा रत्नपरीक्षिणः	...	विशेषाभावात्. स्फोटसिद्धिः, पु. 131–32
163	यथैव श्रवणापेक्षः	...	...
213	यदप्युक्तं सतोपि वर्णातिरेकिणः आचष्ट इति	...	स्फोटसिद्धिः, पु. 21–2
298	यदर्थविषयं वाक्यम्	...	न्यायरत्नमाला, पु. 89 Benaras Edition.
276	यदि च श्वेतिमा... मानमपरमुपमेयम्	...	अन्विताभिधानवादिनः
180	यदि चार्थान्तरत्वं स्यात्	...	श्लोकवार्त्तिकम् स्फोट. श्लो. 119
199	यदि वा नैव गृह्णाति	...	वार्त्तिकम् (?)
176	यद्यपि वर्णपद... शब्दान्तरग्रहणाभिमानः	...	...
174,165	यद्वा प्रत्यक्षतः पूर्वम्	...	...
186	"	....	" "
224	यद्वैककार्यहेतुत्वात्	...	श्लोकवार्त्तिकम् 1.1.5, स्फोट. पु. 538, श्लो. 109
160	यमृषयस्त्रैविदा विदुः	...	तैत्तिरीयब्राह्मणम्, 1.2.26.2
272	यस्य येनार्थसम्बन्धः	...	वार्त्तिकम् (?)
173	यस्यानवयवः स्फोटः	...	श्लोकवार्त्तिकम्, 1.1.5, पु. 533, श्लो. 91
178	यादृशा पूर्वदृष्टोऽसौ	...	श्लोकवार्त्तिकम्, स्फोट. पु. 522, श्लो. 53
278	यान्ति सार्धं जनानन्दैः	...	काव्यादर्शः, परि. 2, श्लो. 354
271	यावन्ति पदानि... अर्थोऽवगम्यते	...	ऋजुविमला, पु. 385, Madras Edition

पुटसंख्या	ग्रन्थादिः		आकरनाम
213	वस्त्वन्तरं प्रसिद्धं स्यात्	...	"
308	वाक्यार्थमितये तेषाम्	...	श्लो. वा. 1.1.7, श्लो. 343, पु. 943
308	वाक्यार्थो लक्ष्यमाणो हि	...	वार्त्तिकम् (?) (प्रकरणपञ्चिकायां वाक्यार्थमातृकायामुद्धृतम्)
289	वाचस्पत्युक्तम्-अन्विताभिधान...		
290	कल्प्य इति दिक्	...	नयविवेकः, 1.1.7
163	वाच्यवाचकशक्त्योश्च	...	...
311	वाच्यस्यार्थस्य वाक्यार्थे	...	(प्रकरणपञ्चिकायां वाक्यार्थ-मातृकायामुद्धृतम्)
247	वा नपुंसकस्य	...	अष्टाध्यायी स. 7.1.79
213	विधूतभेदग्रहमेतयैव	...	स्फोटसिद्धिकारिका 36, पु. 261
263	विनयादिभ्यष्ठक्	...	अष्टाध्यायी सू. 5.4.34
177	विनिविष्टस्फोटबिम्बप्रति बिम्बिप्रत्ययं	...	वैयाकरणग्रन्थः (?)
196	विप्रतिषिद्धधर्मसमवाये भूयसां स्यात्सधर्मत्वम्	...	पूर्वमीमांसासूत्रम् 12.2.7
288		...	वार्त्तिकम् (?)
272	विशिष्टार्थप्रयुक्ता हि	...	"
159	विशुद्धज्ञानदेहाय	...	श्लोकवार्त्तिकम् 1.1.1, श्लो. 1
262	विश्वजिता यजेत	...	...
160	वृषा कपिश्च शङ्कुश्च	...	विष्णुपुराणम्
172, 180	वैलक्षण्यं च तस्येष्टम्	...	श्लोकवार्त्तिकम् स्फोट. पु. 539, श्लो. 118
303	व्यतिषक्ताभिधानं किं... शब्द उक्तो भवति	...	बृहती पु. 385-86
293	व्यवहारे च... आवापोद्धारौ	...	" "
197	व्यक्तयः शब्दशब्दस्य	...	...

पुटसंख्या	ग्रन्थादिः		आकरनाम
161	व्यत्यासोऽपि भवेत्सद्यः	...	वायुसंहिता
216	व्यवहारोऽथवा वृद्ध	...	वार्त्तिकम् (?)
183	शक्त्यन्तरकल्पना... अर्थापत्तिक्षयात्	...	स्फोटसिद्धिः, पु. 48
166	शब्दप्रामाण्यनिर्णीत्यै	...	श्लोकवार्त्तिकम् 1.1.7, पु. 914, श्लो. 247
186	शतादिरूपं जायेत	...	" 1.1.5, स्फोट. श्लो. 114
186	शब्दार्थमतिस्तेन	...	"' "' "' 116
185	शक्तेः शक्त्यन्तरायोगः	...	स्फोटसिद्धिकारिजा 7, पु. 52
276	शास्त्रं शब्दविज्ञानात्... विज्ञानम्	...	शाबरभाष्यम् 1.1.5
181	शैघ्र्यादल्पाक्ष(च्त) रत्वाद्वा	...	श्लोकवार्त्तिकम् स्फोट. श्लो. 121
197	श्रोत्रग्रहणे...प्रसिद्धः	...	शाबरभाष्यम् 1.1.5
199–200	श्रोत्रग्राह्यतापि च... प्रख्यानात्	...	स्फोटसिद्धिः, पु. 22–24
197	श्रोत्रधीलक्षिता वर्णाः	...	...
256	सर्वस्यानुपलब्धेऽर्थे	...	श्लोकवार्त्तिकम् 1.1.5, पु. 211, श्लो. 11
186	सर्वेषु च तदर्थेषु	...	" स्फोट. श्लो. 113
174, 165	समस्तरूप (वर्ण) विज्ञानम्	...	" " 109
186	समस्तरूप (वर्ण) विज्ञानम्	...	" " 109
162	समस्तलोकयात्रार्थम्	...	वायुसंहिता
222, 223	साहित्यमेकवक्त्रादि	...	...

पुटसंख्या	ग्रन्थादिः		आकरनाम
308	साक्षाद्यद्यपि कुर्वन्ति	...	श्लोकवार्त्तिकम् 1.1.7, श्लो. 342, पु. 943
161	सिद्धिकामो विनायकम्	...	...
215	सिद्धे शब्दार्थसम्बन्धे	...	कात्यायनवार्त्तिकम् (पस्पशाह्निकभाष्यम्)
161	सुकृतं दुष्कृतं वापि	...	वायुसंहिता
228	सुखादेरापरोक्ष्यस्य	...	..
310	सृष्टीरुपदधाति	...	...
173	सोऽपि पर्यनुयोगेन	...	श्लोकवार्त्तिकम् 1.1.5, स्फोट. श्लो. 91
163	सम्बन्धज्ञानसापेक्षः	...	...
224	सम्बन्धज्ञानसमये	...	स्फोटसिद्धिकारिका 16, पु. 120
179	संयोगादेरातो धातोर्यण्वतः	...	अष्टाध्यायी, सू. 8. 2. 43
225	संस्कारादावभिन्नेऽपि	...	स्फोटसिद्धिकारिका 17, पु. 122
272	स्तोकोऽपि व्यतिरेको यः	...	वार्त्तिकम् (?)
276	स्थितिर्मानमव्यक्तम्	...	अन्विताभिधानवादिनः (?)
296	स्मरणव्यतिरिक्तत्वात्	...	...
186	स्मरणं यौगपद्येन	...	श्लोकवार्त्तिकम् स्फोट. श्लो. 112
302	स्यात्तु तज्जन्यता भ्रान्तेः	...	न्यायरत्नमाला, पु. 91
264	स्वर्गकामो यजेत	...	...
179	हन हिंसागत्योः	...	धातुपाठः, अदादिः 2
160	हरश्च बहुरूपश्च	...	विष्णुपुराणम्
281	हिमवर्तिनि हेमन्ते	...	न्यायरत्नमाला, पु. 99 Benaras Edition
178	हिमाचलो नाम नगाधिराजः	...	कुमारसम्भवः, सर्गः 1, श्लो. 1

APPENDIX V

अनुबन्धः पञ्चमः

SUGGESTED READINGS

Page	Line	Original		Suggested
159	19	(स्त्रयि) विदा	...	स्त्रैविदा
160	6	स्त्रै (स्त्रयि) विदा	...	"
162	7	स्त्वदधीना	...	स्तदधीना
162	14	तथा	....	कथा
162	25	सिद्धमेषां	...	सिद्धं समेषां
163	14	इत्येवं	...	इत्येव
163	23	चारार्थं	...	चरितार्थं
167	16	गोशब्दावयवी	...	गोशब्दोऽवयवी
169	13	षङ्गस्तुल्य	...	षङ्गोऽतुल्य
169	18	अवयविनं बिभ्रति	...	अवयवि (नोऽसमवायिकारणं) बिभ्रति।
171	10,11	वृत्तिकार्या	...	वृत्तिः कार्या
187	19	चक्षुरादयो वा रूपानु-	...	चक्षुरादयो वा (श्रोत्रापेक्षाः)।
187	19	विद्धम्		रूपानुविद्धं (प्रत्ययम्)।
189	5	इति	...	Delete
193	7	प्रकाशते	...	Delete
197	7	गोत्वेऽप्येका	...	गोत्वादिष्वेका

Page.	Line.	Original.		Suggested.
197	11	योग्यतात एवेत्यस्तु etc.	...	योग्यतात एवेति। अस्तु। योग्यता
197	13	„ „		विवक्षितेत्यदोषः।
198	8	पूर्वककारा	...	पूर्वकारा
198	14	तस्मात्ककार	...	यदयुक्तं— ककार
198	17	यद्येका	...	यत्रैका
199	24	च शब्दत्व	...	च सत्त्वशब्दत्व
200	5	शब्दत्वसम	...	शब्दसम
202	1	असन्तो वा सतोऽसतो	...	असन्तः (सन्तो) वा सतोऽसतो
203	5	विषयं (?)	...	विषये
203	6	प्राक्कलीने	...	प्राक्कालीलेन
203	9	ज्ञापकत्वमपि..विरोधादिति।	...	अयं ग्रन्थः 18 पङ्क्तौ 'ननु पृथगेव'
203	10			इत्यतः पूर्वं पठितव्य मिति भाति।
204	8	सन्धानापेक्षेति	...	सन्धानापेक्षा इति।
204	10	(क्त्या)	...	Delete
206	2,4	संबन्धाख्याम्	...	संबन्धाख्या
207	6	व्यपदेशभेद इति	...	व्यपदेश इति
210	210	धेयि हि पदं	...	धायि हि पदपदं
210	3	पदं	...	पदपदं
211	90	संबन्धिनां संबन्धा	...	संबन्धिनां संबद्धा
214	19	समूह	...	Delete
215	14	नैकांशमात्मान	...	नैकं शब्दात्मान
218	5	सत्प्रतिपक्षो	...	सत्प्रपक्षो
220	18	प्राप्तमेव न?............	...	प्राप्तमेव न (पुनः सुपरिहरमिति
		अथोच्येत? वत्स	...	भावः। य (त्पुनरुक्तं)— वत्स!
221	18	सिद्ध्यतीति?	...	सिद्ध्यतीति, (तत्परिहारा- योक्तं— अपि चेति)।
222	17	ह्यर्थज्ञानम्	...	प्यर्थज्ञानम्।

Page	Line	Original		Suggested
223	13	व्यभिचाराय	...	अव्यभिचाराय
228	18	दोषतया मन्तव्यः	...	दोषतया हेतुर्मन्तव्यः।
228	23	दोषत्वे	...	दोषत्वेन
231	11	प्रत्यय (before धी)	...	Delete
233	11	भवादुत्तरक्षणो विनाश	...	भवादुत्तरः (संस्कारक्षणः तदुत्तरो) यो विनाश
235	15	भवादुत्तरक्षणो विनाश	...	तद्रूप (विषयमि)त्युच्यते
235	24	तदर्थपद?	...	तदर्थ (संबन्धस्मरणे सति)
236	10	अ? श्रोत्र	...	अ(यमेव शब्दग्रहणहेतुः) श्रोत्र
236	11	" "		" " "
"	13	तस्या?.....र्थत्वात्	...	तस्या (जनकः, तदुत्पादना) र्थत्वात्।
"	17	प्रसिद्धि......	...	प्रसिद्धिं (दर्शयति— यथाहुः — क्षणिकं...दृष्टिवत्)।
"	23	कारेणान्यत्पद	...	कमारेण नान्यत्पद
250	5	स्मृतिः	...	स्मृति (हेतु):
268	5	यत्तद्भाव	...	यदि तद्भाव
268	24	मानस्यः प्रत्या	...	मानसप्रत्या
269	6	पदान्तर	...	पदानन्तर
270	24	स्वगोचरागोचर	...	स्वागोचरगोचर
274	3	गतत्वाधिक्य	...	गतत्वाद्यधिक
276	6	'स्थितिर्मानमव्यक्तम्'	...	'सितिमानमव्यक्तम्'
276	7	मानान्तरगम्यान्वयबोधी etc.		मानान्तरगम्योऽन्वयबोधी तदा तस्मिन्नन्वयेऽशब्दमूले
277	15	परीक्ष्य	...	परीक्षा
279	25	सम्बन्धत्व	...	सम्बन्धित्व
287	19	नुपपत्त्या	...	नुपपत्त्या (यत्ततायाश्च प्रसिद्धि-द्योतनार्थः।)

Page	Line	Original		Suggested
290	10,11	स्मारकत्वे लक्षणाविधापद...		स्मारकत्वम्, लक्षणाविधा पद
290	13	(लप्ये) after लप्यम्	...	Delete
291	17	(त्व इ) after मि	...	Delete
292	19	शब्द?	...	शब्दनिष्ठः
296	12	घोषाद्य(न्वयः स्या)त्......		घोषाद्य(न्वितस्य)तीरादेरभिधा-
296	12	धानतः		यतः
300	21	ज्ञाने च	...	ज्ञानेन
301	24	शक्तिर्वा(क्तिं वा)	....	शर्त्तिर्या शब्दगोचरा
301	24	शब्दगोचरा (राम्?)		
304	10	कार्यावगति	...	कार्यतावगति

BIBLIOGRAPHY

I. Original Texts in Sanskrit

(a) Printed

Anantadeva:— *Bhāṭṭālaṅkāra* (Benares Edition). Smṛtikaustubha (Nirnayasagara Edition).

Āpadeva:— *Mīmāṁsānyāyaprakāśa* (N.S. Edn.) with F. Edgerton's English Translation.

Appayya Dīkṣita:—*Vidhirasāyanadūṣaṇa* with his gloss. Upakramaparākram (Benares Edition). Citrapaṭa (J. O. R.) Kalpataruparimala (N. S. Edn.)

Bādarāyaṇa:— *Vedānta Sūtra* (Nirnaya Sagara Edition).

Bhartṛhari:— *Vākyapadīya* (Benares Edition).

Bhāskararāya:— *Candrikā* (on the Saṅkarṣakāṇḍa, Reprint from the *'Pandit'*).

Bhaṭṭasomeśvara: —Nyayasvedhā (Bonares Etm)—Bhavabhūtī *Mālatīmādhava* (N.S. Edn.)

Brahmānandasarasvatī:—*Nyāyaratnāvali* (Advaitamañjarī Series).

Citsukhācārya:— *Tattvapradīpikā* (with Commentary—N.S. Edition).

Diṅnāga:— *Nyāyapraveśa* (Gaekwad Series, Baroda).

Gāgābhaṭṭa:— *Bhāṭṭacintāmaṇi* (Benares Edition).

Gaṅgādevī:— *Madhurāvijaya* (Trivandram Edition).

Jaimini:— *Pūrvamīmāṁsā Sūtra* (Benares Edition).

Jayantabhaṭṭa:— *Nyāyamañjarī* (Vijayanagaram Sanskrit Series).

Kṛṣṇamiśra:— *Prabodhacandrodaya* with Candrikā (N.S. Edn.)

Kṛṣṅayajvan:— *Paribhāṣā* (N.S. Edn.)

Kumārilabhaṭṭa:— *Ślokavārttika* with the Nyāyaratnākara (Ben. Edn.) do. with Kāśikā (T. S. S.)
Tantravārttika (Ānandāśrama Edition, Poona). Ṭupṭīkā (Benares Edition).

Khaṇḍadevamiśra:—(1) *Bhāṭṭadīpikā* (Mysore Edition).
(2) *Bhāṭṭakaustubha* (Benares Edition).
(3) *Bhāṭṭarahasya* (Benares Edition)

Laugākṣibhāskara:—*Arthasaṅgraha* (with the Kaumudī—N.S. Edn.)

Mādhavācārya:—*Nyāyamālāvistara* (Ānandāśrama Edition).
Parāśaramādhavīya (Bombay Sanskrit Series).
Śaṅkaradigvijaya (Ānandāśrama Edition).
Sarvadarśanasaṅgraha (Bhandarkar Research Institute Edition).
Do. Cowell's Translation.

Maṇḍanamiśra:— (1) *Vidhiviveka* (Benares Edition.)
(2) *Bhāvanāviveka* (Saraswati Bhavana Series).
(3) *Vibhramaviveka* (J.O.R., Madras).
(4) *Sphoṭasiddhi* (Madras University Sanskrit Series).

Mukulabhaṭṭa:— *Abhidhāvṛttimātṛkā* (N. S. Edn.)

Murārimiśra:— *Tripādīnītinayana* (J.O.R., Madras).
" *Aṅgatavanirukti* (Ānandāśrama Edition).

Nandīśvara:— *Prabhākaravijaya* (Saṁskṛta Sāhitya Pariṣad Series).

Nārāyaṇabhaṭṭa:—*Mānameyodaya* (T.S.S. & T.P.H.)
Nārāyaṇīya (T.S.S.)
Prakriyāsarvasva (Do.)

Parameśvara II:— Gopālikā (Madras University Series).
Pārthasārathimiśra:—(1) *Śāstradīpikā* with Mayūkhamālikā (N.S. Edn.)
(2) *Tantraratna* (Saraswati Bhavana Series).
(3) *Nyāyaratnamālā* (Benares Edition).
Prabhākaramiśra:—Bṛhatī (Madras Edition).
? *Prapañcahṛdaya* (T.S.S.)
Rājacūḍāmaṇi Dīkṣita:—*Rukmiṇīkalyāṇam* (Adyar Edition).
Rāmakṛṣṇabhaṭṭa:—*Yuktisnehaprapūranī*. (N.S. Edition).
Rāmānujacārya:—*Tantrahasya* (Gaekwad Series).
Śabarasvāmin:— *Pūrvamīmāṁsāsūtrabhāṣya* (Benares Edn).
Śālīkanātha:— (1) *Ṛjuvimalā* (Madras Edition).
(2) *Prakaraṇapañcikā* (Benares Edition).
Śambhubhaṭṭa:— *Prabhāvali* (N.S. Edition).
Śaṅkarabhaṭṭa:— *Mīmāṁsābālaprakāśa*.
Sureśvarācārya:— Naiṣkarmyasiddhi (Bombay Skt. Series).
Tatachari, D.T.:—*Mīmāṇsābhyudaya*.
Umvekabhaṭṭa:— *Bhāvanāvivekavyākhyā* (Saraswati Bhavana Series).
Vācaspatimiśra:— (1) *Bhāmatī* (N. S. Edition).
(2) *Nyāyakaṇikā* (Benares Edition).
(3) *Tattvabindu* (Reprint from the '*Pandit*').
(4) *Nyāyavārttikatātparyaṭīkā* (Benares Edi tion).
Vāñcheśvarayajvan:—Bhāṭṭacintāmaṇi (Madras Edition).
Vāsudeva Dīkṣita:—Adhvaramīmāṁsākutūhalavṛtti (Vani Vilas Edition).
Vedāntadēsika:— (1) *Seśvaramīmāṁsā* (Conjeevaram Edition).
(2) *Mīmāṁsāpādukā* (Do.).
(3) *Yādavābhyudaya* with Appayya Dīkṣita's Vyākhyā (Vani Vilas Edition, Srirangam).

***(b)* Manuscripts (available in the Madras Govt. and Adyar Oriental Mss. Libraries).**

Annambhaṭṭa:— (1) *Rāṇakojjīvinī*.
(2) *Subodhinī*.

Bhāskararāya:— *Candrodaya*.

Bhaṭṭaviṣṇu:— *Nayatattvasaṅgraha*.

Bhavanāthabhaṭṭa:—*Nayaviveka* with Varadarāja's Dīpikā.

Cidānandapaṇḍita:—*Nititattvāvirbhāva* with three commentaries.

Devasvāmin:— *Saṅkarṣakāṇḍabhāṣya*.

Govindāmṛtamuni:—*Vivaraṇa* on the Śābarabhāṣya.

Parameśvara II:— *Tattvavibhāvanā*.

Parameśvara III:—*Mīmāṁsāsūtrārthasaṅgraha*.

Paritoṣamiśra:— *Agitā* (with Vijayā).

Rājacūḍāmaṇi Dīkṣita:—*Tantraśikhāmaṇi*.

Rāmānujācārya:—*Nāyakaratna*.

Ravideva:— *Vivekatattva*.

Śālīkanātha:— *Mīmāṁsābhāṣyapariśiṣṭa*.

Udayapūjyapāda:—*Adhikaraṇārthamālā*.

Veṇkaṭeśvara Dīkṣita:—*Vārttikābharaṇa*.

Yajñanārāyaṇa Dīkṣita:—*Prabhāmaṇḍala*.

? Granthayojanā

? Ṣoḍaśādhyāyī with its gloss.

II. CRITICAL WORKS AND LECTURES IN ENGLISH

Belvalker, Dr., S. K.:—Sree Gopal Basu Mallik Lectures.

Das Gupta, Dr.:—*A History of Indian Philosophy*, Vols, I & II

Ganganatha Jha, Dr., MM.:—
(1) *Prabhākara School of Mīmāṁsā*.
(2) *Translations of Ślokavārttika*, Trantravārttika and Śābarabhāṣya.

Heras:— *The Aravidu Dynasty of Vijayanagar*.

Hirayanna, M.:— Outlines of Indian Philosophy.

Kane, P. V.:— (1) *A History of the P.M. System*.
(2) *The History of the Dharmaśāstra*.

Keith, Dr., A.B.:— (1) *Karmamīmāṁsā*.
(2) *Sanskrit Drama*.
(3) *A History of Sanskrit Literature*.
(4) *Indian Logic and Atomism*.

Krishnaswami Iyengar, Dr., S.:—Maṇimekhalai in its historical setting.

Kuppuswami Sastrigal, MM., S.:—*A Primer of Indian Logic*.

Max Müller:— (1) *Six Systems of Indian Philosophy*.
(2) *Indian, what can it teach us?*

Paśupatinātha Śāstri, Dr.:—Introduction to the P. M. Śāstra.

III. PERIODICALS, REPORTS, ETE

Annals of Bhandarkar Research Institute, Vol. X.

Annamalai University Journal, Vols. I & II.

Annual Report of Arch. Survey of India for 1907-8.

Descriptive Catalogues of Sanskrit Mss. Library, the Adyar Library and T. M. S. M. Library, Tanjore.

Epigraphica Indica, Vols. III, XII, XV.

Indian Antiquary, Vols. XLV, L.

Indian Historical Quarterly, (1932, 1933, 1934).

Journal of American Oriental Society.

Journal of Bombay Branch of Royal Asiatic Society, Vol. XXIV.

Journal of Oriental Research, Vols. II, III, IV.

Proceedings of the Second and Thirsd All-India Oriental Conference (1922 & 1924).

Report of the Mysore Arch. Dept., 1917.

INDEX

✡✡✡